Edinburgh

The Savage Brood: Book One

Emyll O'Bryan

Cover design by Emyll O'Bryan, featuring a detail from *A View of Edinburgh from the West* by Alexander Nasmyth, 1822-6.

This book is a work of fiction. Names, characters, places and incidents either are a product of the author's imagination or are used fictitiously. Any resemblance to actual persons, living or dead, events, or locales is entirely coincidental.

This edition produced by Jade Publishing Company, P.O. Box 223, Austin, AR 72007.

NOTICE: This work may contain descriptions of adult situations including language, nudity, sex, and violence that some readers may find objectionable. It is intended for mature audiences only, and reader discretion is advised.

ISBN:
978-1-944040-01-7

Acknowledgements

Ann, this one certainly took a long time. It didn't quite make it to 666 pages, but I tried, I really did. Maybe next time…or maybe not. This has been a convoluted journey, but the end is finally in sight. Yay!

I want to thank all of the researchers and authors who have researched the era I use for this novel. Without your input, this book would not have been possible. There is no one person in particular that I went to for guidance on this, so if you've ever written anything on the Regency era or the 19th Century United Kingdom in general, thank you.

Last, but most certainly not least, thank you, reader, for taking a trip with me.

Emyll O'Bryan
September 15, 2015

Okay, this one's gotta be for Phil...wherever you are...just because....

Chapter One

The leaves on the trees in Hyde Park were just beginning to bud and bloom for the spring, giving everything a hazy green aura. The only sounds to be heard were those of the birds in the trees and the squirrels chittering competitively over the fallen nuts from the previous autumn below them.

Then came the thud of horses' hooves racing across the turf of the park as if the beasts were careening out of control, and above the sound of hooves came shrill giggles and laughter. An exuberant shout would burst, and then more shrieks of enjoyment would trill, breaking the once peaceful, early morning silence with a rude and decidedly unrepentant cheer.

Of course, to the man in the phaeton trotting along sedately, it sounded as if the woman (or women) was screaming for dear life. Accustomed to not being concerned for the welfare of anyone but himself on his morning drives, he glanced over his shoulder and around the park to see if there were anyone else to attend to the matter. A scowl marred his previously impassive face when he saw that he and the unseen party in danger were the only ones present. He didn't know why he had expected anyone else to be there; he came to the park at this hour specifically to *avoid* anyone else. Disgusted that his meditative morning drive was to come to an abrupt end, he clicked to his pair of blood bays and urged them to move at a faster gait down the trail.

He searched to both sides for the women (for now he was convinced the unholy sound of deranged harpies couldn't possibly be coming from just one throat), but he could still only hear their cries. To his displeasure, they didn't seem to be getting any closer. He rounded the turn near the Corner and caught a brief glimpse of burgundy flitting through the trees. It certainly wasn't a bird, and he was more convinced than ever that the women had lost control of their horses to be traveling at such an ungodly speed without a trail to follow this early in the morning.

《 》

"I'll win, Psyche! You know I'll win! Bellerophon is much too fast for Achilles to catch him! You shouldn't have fed him that extra apple!" shouted one of the girls gleefully, her black stallion a full length ahead of her sister's white gelding.

"Oh, pooh!" cried Psyche with a confident smile as she steered Achilles past a tree. "Achilles' stride is longer than Bellerophon's! The only reason you're ahead is that you cheated at the start!"

"I did not!" shrieked Pandora in only mock consternation as she glanced back over her shoulder with an impudent smile because she knew her sister was telling the truth.

The two girls sped along through the small stand of trees without any concern for passersby or danger. They had specifically come to race in the park in the early morning hours to avoid such worry. Their parents knew where they were and exactly (well, not really) what they were doing and had given their consent last night before retiring to bed. Their twin daughters could manage well for themselves, and what mischief could they cause in Hyde Park?

The early morning sun didn't streak through the trees to shine on their blonde hair and make it glow like haloes of spun gold around their heads, but that would have been the treacly, poetic description had anyone seen them. They both had their hair done in the same style, the same length (which some would say was unfashionably long), and with the same naturally bouncing waves. Their skin was a delicate golden peach, tinted rose on their high cheekbones from good health and their brisk morning excursion. Their eyes were almond-shaped, slightly tipped upward at the outer corners; the irises were tinted the purest grass green, giving them an almost feline appearance. Their lips were full, the bottom in a permanent pout, giving them an innocently—though decidedly—sensual shape. Their noses were short and pert, pointed at the tip to give them a naturally impish expression. They were startlingly beautiful, tall and fine-boned, with skin tinted a shade darker than what was considered the fashionable lily white, but their gaze was usually far too keen, their bearing far too determined, for them to be mistaken for the typical simpering female of the *ton*.

The reason for this, of course, was that neither should have been born female as far as personal pursuits were concerned. Like the rest of their sisters, they disliked sewing, cooking, needlepoint and housekeeping (even though they had been unwillingly instructed in all of them by the duchess in order to know how to properly run their own households one day); they'd rather leave the overseeing of those things to their mother, who seemed content to give the girls time to pursue fields of interest that were usually left to boys. Their mother and father had refused them nothing within reason, so they had grown up quite wild, unrestricted by the staid norms of the *ton* on their country estate in Glamorgan.

The girls were mirror images of each other, almost in a literal sense. Unless one was well acquainted with them, they looked exactly alike. The only physical differences were things that would not be apparent to the casual observer: Pandora was left-handed; Psyche was right-handed. Psyche occasionally had to wear spectacles to correct her nearsightedness; Pandora had perfect vision. The only other difference was that Psyche had a small strawberry birthmark on her back just above her right buttock, shaped (rather appropriately) like a reclining sphinx; Pandora had no birthmark at all.

For most people, the only way to distinguish between the two was by the color of clothes they wore and by how each presented herself when she spoke. Although they were born only twenty minutes apart, the difference between their attitudes was marked—not necessarily by maturity and demeanor but by the way in which each managed to control her temper and mischievousness.

While Pandora, true to her name, loved looking into things that were best left unlooked at and sometimes exaggerated things until they took on enormous, outrageous proportions that were nothing near the truth, Psyche was content to leave well-enough alone and always, no matter how painful to her or others, told the truth, with no embellishment to lessen or worsen the result of that honesty. Of course, that didn't necessarily mean she would tell the *entire* truth if it could be managed.

Then there was how they dressed. Psyche usually chose pastels and muted colors that matched her light coloring and kept her from drawing unwanted attention; Pandora, on the other hand, was wont to wear bold colors that made her look like a vibrant butterfly. Neither dressed in a way that would make them appear to be anything other than the daughters of aristocracy they were, but their clothes seemed to match their personalities perfectly.

Psyche was wearing an olive green velvet habit trimmed in black ribbon that accentuated the vibrant green in her eyes. Pandora was wearing one of a burgundy velvet cut in the same pattern and using the same trim that also brought out the green in her eyes. If anyone had been about to see them, which they believed no one was, the twins would have attracted many admirable stares from the gentlemen and some envious stares from the ladies.

"I'll get the garnets you promised me!" shouted Psyche, trying to spur Achilles past her twin's horse.

"Oh, no you won't!" shouted Pandora jovially. "I'm going to get your emeralds!" She leaned closer to Bellerophon's neck, urging the beautiful horse to the faster speed she knew he could provide.

They rounded a huge oak and jumped a recently fallen trunk as large as the one still standing as if there were nothing in their way. Both girls had dispensed with riding aside, confident no one would see them and more comfortable riding astride as they did at home in Wales. They startled a rabbit from some nearby bushes, and it ran away in a frightened scurry before the thunderous hooves that threatened to trample it.

Pandora still remained in the lead as they rounded yet another tree. They would be crossing one of the normal riding paths soon, and she was grateful there would be no one about to prevent her winning. Oh, she did like to win. Losing wasn't so bad either, as long as the sport was entertaining, and with Psyche, it usually was. Still, winning was so much better. She smiled excitedly as she glanced back and saw that Psyche was at least two lengths behind her. Pandora decided she would have to give Bellerophon extra sugar when they got home as a reward for his outstanding performance. Victory was to be hers, and so were her sister's emerald earrings.

That was before she turned back to face where she was going as she rounded another tree and saw the phaeton situated in front of her, completely blocking her course. There was really no way to avoid it. If she didn't rein in Bellerophon now, he would collide with the vehicle and injure himself and her in the process without drastic measures. As it was, he was going so fast there was no guarantee she wouldn't be thrown if she tried to stop him, a humiliation she didn't want to consider. Maybe if she caught the driver's attention and asked him to move?

"You in the buggy! Move out of the way!" she shouted, standing in her stirrups to wave her hand in a shooing gesture.

The gentleman in the driver's seat was looking directly at her, but he didn't seem to notice she was trying to get him to move. In fact, it appeared as if he had purposely set the phaeton in her path. *Had Psyche...?* It *was* the first of April. Her twin wasn't prone to practical jokes (unlike Pandora), but it wasn't impossible. No, Pandora quickly dismissed the suspicion Psyche would have a hand in this. He was a stranger to them, that much Pandora could tell from even this far away. She decided to try again.

"Would you, please, move out of the way!" she shouted once more in exasperation.

≪ ≫

Islington stared at the girl in the burgundy habit and decided she had lost her mind if he understood her hand gestures correctly. She wanted him to move out of her way, to let her horse continue racing across the park like a wild thing. He noted she was riding astride and assumed she was a common guttersnipe. Women of quality did *not* ride astride, not any that readily came to mind. He was tempted to let her and her companion fend for themselves; then he just as quickly brushed aside the idea. After all, he was a gentleman (even if at times it seemed only by birth).

When he arrived at the intersection, he had caught a glimpse of another rider behind the first. He logically determined the only way to stop the horses from their mad dash was to place his buggy in their way so they had nowhere to go, but the blond in burgundy didn't seem to care the buggy was there. It appeared she was going to run into it.

"Pull on the reins, and try to slow him down!" he shouted in irritation, his lips forming into a grim line.

"Get out of the way!" Pandora yelled.

4

"I beg your pardon?" called Islington.

"Get out of the way, you big oaf!" repeated Pandora, now perturbed the man appeared to be deaf as well as ignorant.

"I will not!" returned Islington, deeply insulted the girl would call him an oaf. It confirmed his suspicions that if she was not someone of low station just recently endowed with new money, she was most definitely an inhabitant of Bedlam who had somehow managed to escape.

Pandora was ready to use every bad word her older brothers had ever uttered in her presence. It wasn't as if she were asking the man to perform some complicated task; she simply wanted him to move, and it caused her no end of annoyance that he wouldn't. She decided if the man wouldn't move his rig, then she and Bellerophon would go *over* it.

She was confident her stallion could make it; he had once (much to her consternation) jumped a hay-wain at home, even though he couldn't see the other side of it, just because he loved to jump. It had not been full, but it had been high enough Pandora had expected to land in it...with Bellerophon on top of her. He had easily sailed over it with her still in the saddle. She was sure this obstacle would be far easier to scale, and the path curved at just the right angle before the phaeton to provide even more probability of a jump being successful. She just needed her horse to build up a little more speed....

"*Yala*, Bellerophon!" she urged near his ear. As if the speed he already maintained were not unbelievable, the stallion began to charge even faster toward the phaeton. "You know you can do it, fella! Come on! Let's show that gudgeon!"

Meanwhile, Psyche realized what her sister planned and began to slow Achilles before she, too, had no choice but to jump. She was not so confident her gelding would make it. She crossed her kid-gloved fingers and began to pray her twin wouldn't break her neck, although Pandora and Bellerophon were probably quite capable of doing it.

"Be careful, Pandora!" she shouted concernedly as she finally slowed her mount to a brisk canter. She was sure her sister couldn't hear her.

Islington watched with a jaundiced eye as he too realized what the girl planned. It was foolhardy, idiotic, and insane. He had every confidence she was going to kill herself, that she had been attempting to do so since he had first heard what he thought were her terrified shrieks. He was glad the other hoyden had slowed her horse and was approaching sedately.

Pandora saw that the man still sat upright in his seat, his body poised stubbornly, his chin tilted at an arrogant angle. It seemed as if he thought he could make her stop by sheer will. *Fool! Does he not realize that if he doesn't get out of his carriage, Bellerophon is liable to knock his head off?* She supposed she owed him the courtesy of a warning.

"If you value your head, you'll at least duck!" she shouted disgustedly.

The phaeton came closer and closer still, Bellerophon gaining more speed with each stride. Pandora could almost see the exact pattern of the filigree scrollwork decorating the brass trim of the carriage. Had she not been bent on another purpose, she may have paused to admire his bays and may have even complimented him on his taste. She could only assume he was a gentleman of some means, but it mattered not the slightest as far as his manners were concerned. Gentleman or not, he was being downright rude by parking in her path and refusing to move when she asked.

As the moment arrived for the leap, Pandora felt Bellerophon's muscles bunch with energy. He was enjoying this as much as she, his first chance at a free rein since they had arrived in London. Pandora leaned close to his neck and raised herself for balance as his forelegs left the ground in a graceful leap. He sailed over the phaeton as if he had grown wings. They landed on the soft turf on the other side, divots flying in every direction, and continued speeding along as if the obstacle had been no more than a child's toy.

Islington ducked as she suggested, but only at the last minute, not quite believing the girl had the nerve to carry it through. As soon as the horse sailed over, he quickly righted himself to see her continue on, unperturbed. His jaw went slack in amazement that she hadn't killed herself or him in the process.

"I must apologize for my sister," said the girl in green, trotting up to the side of his phaeton and coming to a stop.

He turned to glance at her, prepared to see some ill-bred wench. What he *actually* saw took him by surprise. Sitting on a piece of horseflesh that was better than some in his own stables was one of the most beautiful women he'd ever seen. Her hair was a gold-kissed blonde, surrounding a beautiful face with stunning green eyes. For a moment, he could think of nothing to say that would even remotely sound intelligent. Then, as he began to get his reasoning back from the set of shocks he had received in the past few minutes, he remembered how he had come to meet this vision. His lip began to curl in a sneer as his outrage overrode any other emotion he may have had.

"Yes, I'm sure you must as she didn't see fit to do so herself," he stated arrogantly.

Psyche sat back in her saddle and glanced at him with some irritation. She almost wished she had taken suit after Pandora. She gave him a polite smile that held no warmth.

"May I point out, sir, that if you hadn't been in her way, she wouldn't have jumped you," said Psyche coolly.

Islington detected the stiffness in her tone but ignored it.

"Perhaps," he said tightly, providing Psyche with a smile no less arctic than her own. "Yet if she hadn't led me to believe her horse was out of control, I would not have placed my phaeton here at all and would have been *enjoying* my morning drive."

Psyche blinked in astonishment and then began to giggle uncontrollably, quite forgetting her manners. She leaned over in her saddle and wound her arms around Achilles' neck while the horse patiently withstood the assault with a slight shift of his feet and a blowing out through his nose.

Islington glanced at her as if she had grown horns. Had she just escaped from Bedlam like her sister? What had he said that was so funny?

"Pardon me, Miss—" he paused, not knowing her name.

He caught Psyche in the middle of taking a breath, long enough for her to look at him straight for one moment and give him a direct answer.

"Savage," she said, and then she began to giggle again.

"I'll say you are," he muttered to himself darkly. "Pardon me, Miss Savage, but—"

"That would be Lady Psyche Savage," she interrupted on a chortle.

"Indeed?" he said in a shocked tone. Then the name dawned on him, and it made him all the more disbelieving of the situation. "Yes, of course. Beg pardon. However, Lady Psyche, what have I said that you find so amusing? Are you going into the vapors?"

"*Vapors*?" she shrieked hilariously, almost ready to renew her laughing fit. Then, finally seeing the effect her demeanor was having on him, she calmed somewhat. "My apologies, sir. It's simply that Pandora would never lose control of Bellerophon. Of course, you not knowing her, you couldn't possibly know that."

"Pandora?" he voiced in a dull tone, somehow unsurprised that was the nuisance-on-horseback's name.

"Yes, my sister." Then a thought occurred to Psyche, and her lips formed into a pout. "And she's probably won our race by now, no thanks to you," she sniffed petulantly, gathering up her reins and preparing to find her sister.

"Just a moment," said Islington, raising a hand to stay her. She tilted her head questioningly. "I wish to come with you and receive a direct apology from your sister; you doing it for her shouldn't be necessary."

"But the reason I did is because she won't."

He gave her a disdainful look, although his initial resentment had lessened somewhat.

"Well, you see, she won't see it that she owes you an apology," said Psyche calmly.

Islington gave her a look that indicated he found that attitude incredibly lowborn. Psyche shook her head exasperatedly but patiently began to explain.

"She did ask you to move...*repeatedly;* she didn't ask for a rescue; she did tell you to duck; and no one was injured," said Psyche, listing reasons on her gloved fingers. It made sense to her; she couldn't understand why he couldn't see it as well.

"Hmm, I see," said Islington, not really seeing at all.

These sisters were a strange sort. He could think of one person in particular that he was going to have a talking to...today, if he could arrange it; coincidence didn't begin to cover it.

"Of course, you may accompany me if you wish and try to get an apology from her, but I'm sure it won't do you any good."

"Hmm," said Islington again, flicking his reins to follow Psyche down the trail to her sister.

《《《 》》》

Pandora arrived at the Serpentine with no more difficulty after the phaeton incident, and as soon as she realized Psyche hadn't followed suit and jumped also, Pandora let out a whoop of victory. Psyche's emerald earrings were hers! And her twin couldn't say she had cheated by jumping the phaeton because Pandora knew she hadn't...at least, not really. The matter of how she *began* the race could not be disputed: she had cheated.

She scowled as she recalled the oaf in the rig. He was so overbearing. She was being polite when she asked him to move...until she called him an oaf. *How rude!*

She dismounted from Bellerophon and walked him back and forth from one tree to the next to cool him down from their jaunt as much as to ice her simmering temper. Distractedly, she led the stallion to the edge of the lake to get a drink of water she probably shouldn't be letting him have and stood there staring into space.

Oh, the nerve of *that* man! She couldn't stop thinking of him as *that* man, and she would probably never think of him as anything but such, even if she did one day learn his name. She patted Bellerophon's neck affectionately and began to lead him back and forth between the trees again, her mind distant. She hadn't taken a good look at the stranger (there really hadn't been much time as she went sailing by), but she was sure from the anger she felt that she would recognize him in an instant.

At the jingle of harness and Psyche's whistle of greeting, Pandora lifted her head from absently examining the toes of her boots and looked at her sister. Then her gaze went to her sister's companion. She had to resist the temptation to throw something. Seated in his phaeton, trotting comfortably beside Psyche, was *that* man! Pandora gripped her hands into tight little balls at her sides, trying to control her irritation. She put on an engaging smile tinged with a malice only Psyche would recognize.

"Oh, twin dear," called Pandora sweetly.

Psyche glanced at her sister and knew she meant business. Pandora didn't use that phrase unless she was highly perturbed. Although the twins cherished the bond they shared with each other, both had decided long ago that calling each other by the term *twin* was not very nice because it implied a certain subordination and lack of individuality. Psyche trotted over to Pandora and looked down at her from her saddle. She could see the thin line of white beginning to form around her sister's compressed lips and knew Pandora was more than just a little angry.

"What's he doing here?" Pandora hissed through clenched teeth, still keeping her polite smile.

"He wants you to apologize," said Psyche, calmly adjusting her gloves.

"He *what?*" shrieked Pandora in outrage, her fists clenching and unclenching.

"Pandora, wait before you do something foolish," said Psyche with a long-suffering sigh.

Why did she always seem to be cooling her sister's temper? It was true her anger was generally short-lived, but she could become annoyed easily at times. Pandora looked up at Psyche, her face in a dark scowl.

"He was trying to rescue you when he parked his phaeton in our way." Pandora didn't care. "He wanted to *rescue* you," reiterated Psyche slowly. Pandora crossed her arms and set her chin stubbornly. "He didn't know we were racing. You can't be angry with him for trying to be chivalrous."

Pandora looked a little less sullen, but Psyche knew an apology was something too ridiculous to expect. It was true that he should have realized Pandora wasn't in distress when she told him to move, and Pandora would see it that his refusal absolved her of any guilt for her following actions.

Islington waited patiently while the girls hissed quietly at each other. He couldn't see Pandora's face as the two talked, and he began to imagine what it looked like. *She probably has a wart on the end of her nose and green teeth,* he thought in dark amusement. *Her eyes are probably crossed and nearsighted.* Even darker imaginings began to fill his mind about this unseen *Pandora* until he had himself convinced her parents should have named her *Medusa.* He should have known from the example of other members of her family that his imaginings had no possibility of being accurate.

But Pandora could clearly see him. When she glanced at him, she almost yelped in surprise. To her, he was unbelievably handsome. Rather unusually, he wasn't wearing a hat, providing her with a clear view of his features. His hair was a blond that called to Pandora's mind the color of sun-aged straw, with the varying shades from the brightest gold to darkest brown that composed it. He wore it swept back from his high forehead, but its wavy length did not stay that way willingly as one lock of it curled across his brow. His skin was golden brown and stretched tautly over the angular bone structure of his face. His nose was aristocratically straight; his cheekbones were high; and his chin was firm and set with arrogance. She couldn't tell from this distance *exactly* what shade his eyes were, but from where she stood, Pandora could tell they were blue…an incredibly deep blue.

He was dressed in a gray wool morning coat with a white satin waistcoat shot through with silver. His breeches were black, and he wore fine leather Hessians that glimmered with a fresh polishing. Although the colors were more subdued than what would be worn by the typical man of fashion, they suited him well. All of this finery encased a well-formed male physique, if he didn't pad and corset himself as some men of the *ton* did to make themselves look perfect when in fact they had paunches and hunched shoulders. Pandora felt sure it was all-natural. Her mouth began to dry unfamiliarly as she looked at him, and she licked her lips to control the strange flutter of her heart.

At the moment, his face was set in a fierce scowl that made him appear dangerous. She looked away from him reluctantly and back to her sister.

"What's his name?" she asked Psyche resignedly, deciding the only way she'd ever get to meet him was if she apologized prettily, and she did want to meet him for some odd reason.

"His name is Theodore Marshall, the *Marquess* of Bardsey," said Psyche. "Or so *he* says, but his *manners* want to say countrified idiot," she muttered.

"Theodore!" gasped Pandora dreamily, as if the rest of his name went past her. It was such a strong-sounding name to her—fearless and masculine.

"Pandora! What's the matter with you?" asked Psyche, looking at her sister curiously.

Pandora snapped her eyes open and looked at her twin guiltily. After the way she had abused Lord Bardsey, Psyche would never believe her if Pandora told her sister that she thought he was the most handsome man she had ever seen. It would be strange enough for her to say that about *any* man.

"Well, are you going to apologize or not?" asked Psyche exasperatedly, expecting her sister to refuse vehemently.

"Of course I'm going to apologize!" said Pandora atypically, making Psyche's eyes widen in astonishment.

"Well, make sure you call him Lord Islington. He insists on being called Lord Islington. Some lesser title or other, I suppose," said Psyche, adding a few choice phrases under her breath about politesse and contrariness. She had no doubt from his behavior that he was at least the fifth or sixth marquess. He was too arrogant for it to be otherwise, and she wouldn't be surprised to discover the Islington title was just another in a very long string.

Pandora brushed out her skirts and calmly walked toward the phaeton. Lord Islington didn't notice her coming. She reached the side of the buggy, and still he sat with the dreadful scowl on his face, staring off absently. She waited patiently for him to see her standing there, but after a few minutes more of his inattentiveness, she decided to get his attention. She cleared her throat softly without result.

"Lord Islington?" she called calmly. He shook his head to clear it and looked down at her with a polite smile. Now that she had his attention, Pandora continued before he drifted off again. "I must apologize—" she began but didn't have time to finish because he cut her off mid-sentence.

"So the harpy won't apologize?" he sneered.

"I beg your pardon?" she asked uncomprehendingly.

"Your sister will not apologize?"

"But I—"

He cut her off again. "You don't need to apologize for your sister yet again; if she's not graceful enough to do it on her own, then I need no apology," he said disdainfully.

Pandora tried to begin again, now realizing he mistook her for Psyche.

"But, Lord Islington, I am Lady *Pandora*," she said as calmly as she could. She wasn't angry; she was trying not to laugh because his mistake was so common.

Islington looked down at her with antipathy to cover his momentary surprise. When he took a closer inspection, he realized she was indeed a different girl from the one he had spoken to previously. The clothes were different (he noticed that once he managed to tear his gaze away from her eyes). The voice was just slightly deeper and its inflection a little more sultry (but only to his ears). They looked exactly the same! Here, he had assumed he would meet Medusa, and he was meeting another Aphrodite. It was incredible.

"But...you look so much alike," he said bemusedly.

"Yes, well, we are identical twins," said Pandora evenly, folding her arms calmly across her chest.

"Lady Psyche neglected to tell me," said Islington dully.

"Is that why you looked that way? Did you think I'd be more like Medusa after ruining your peaceful morning?" teased Pandora with an impish smile, intuitively hitting the nail on the head. It was so much fun when she guessed correctly.

For the first time in fifteen years, Islington felt himself blushing like a schoolboy. He couldn't understand why this girl could provoke such a reaction when women of far more experience and grace could not. Pandora effortlessly pretended not to notice his discomfiture.

"Actually...," he trailed off.

"It's not important," said Pandora calmly, gracefully waving a hand through the air in dismissal. "I quite imagined you as having the manners of a yahoo myself." She smiled pleasantly.

"Me?" Islington pointed at himself disbelievingly and compressed his lips at the insult. Pandora didn't notice as she proceeded into a typically meandering explanation.

"Why, yes. Of course, Psyche explained to me why you had blocked my path, and I truly do thank you for your intervention, but it was unnecessary. You see, my sister and I had a wager regarding who could beat whom to the lake, and we had a set of earrings agreed upon as the prize. Usually Psyche comes out the victor when we race in Hyde Park, but this morning, Bellerophon—that's my horse—was in excellent form, and we were winning until you got in our way. I do like to win, as I'm sure most anyone else does; therefore, I had no choice but to jump you. Do you understand?" asked Pandora plaintively.

Islington clenched his jaw, his anger forming all over again.

"No, as a matter of fact, I don't," he said disdainfully.

Pandora blinked her eyes in surprise. She understood; he was trying to make her feel repentant for what she had done. Of course, she could act and make him think she was devoutly sorry for ruining his morning, that she was heartbroken he was so inconvenienced, but she wouldn't plead on her knees for forgiveness for something she truly didn't feel deserved an apology in the first instance. He was lucky he was getting this!

"Lord Bardsey, I am truly sorry you had your morning ride ruined by my excursion, but if only you had moved out of my way when I asked you to, this whole situation could have been avoided. Don't you think so?" she asked cajolingly.

Pandora purposely used his other title because Psyche had told her not to, and Pandora felt it was something that would annoy him. For some reason, as if she couldn't stop herself, she really wanted to annoy him.

"No, I *don't* think so," he said stiffly, looking down at her haughtily. Then, before she had a chance to reply, he picked up the reins and motioned for his horses to move on.

Pandora stared after him in disbelief, her hands resting on her hips. She thought they were on their way to settling this disagreement amicably before he got his nose out of joint. She dismissed the part *she* might have played in that by purposely trying to rile him. Psyche was right: countrified idiot.

Psyche walked over to her and stared after him as well with some bewilderment.

"Did you apologize?" she asked mildly.

"Of course I did! I told you that I would!" huffed Pandora hotly, still staring after his retreating phaeton.

"Then why did he leave in such a bluster?" asked Psyche, her forehead wrinkled in puzzlement.

"I apologized to him, and then he left."

"Why was he in high dudgeon if you apologized?" persisted Psyche.

"Maybe it was because I told him that I thought he acted like a yahoo," said Pandora evenly.

"Pandora, you didn't?" gasped Psyche, a hand flying to her throat in dismay.

"Well, what did you expect me to say after he said I looked like Medusa?"

"He *said* that?" asked Psyche, shocked.

"Of course he did! And if he said *I* looked like Medusa, then that means he meant *you*, too."

"Ooh, the nerve of *that* man," said Psyche, clenching her fists in outrage and stomping her foot.

"Exactly," said Pandora calmly, adjusting her gloves.

Chapter Two

Psyche and Pandora reached home just as the sun was beginning to rise over the tops of the trees, amazingly managing to shoot through the early morning mist to limn the outdoors with a delicate cast. The two of them took their mounts back to the mews behind their family's home on Bruton Street off Berkeley Square and gave their care over to Tajik, the family's long-serving stable master. They then glumly made their way to the rear entrance through the garden, neither taking any notice of the way their mother's roses were beginning to bloom with brilliant color.

The silence of the awakening city was pierced by the mellisonant tones of a violin playing a Mozart sonata wafting through an open upstairs window of their home. That would be their younger sister, Eurydice, the musician of the family. The twins trudged up the stairs in a slough of despond over the events of the morning, both of them for different reasons.

Psyche was depressed over the loss of her emeralds. She *really* liked her emeralds, and she couldn't believe she had wagered them. She tried to tell her twin the bet was off because of what had loosely become termed the Phaeton Incident, but Pandora told her the race wasn't forfeited and would not be so because of a silly jump over the rig of a yahoo.

That comment brought a rise of anger from Psyche. She was beginning to believe Pandora had hatched another one of her farfetched tales over who had called whom what and told her so. After some delicate prodding, Pandora admitted he hadn't *said* she looked like Medusa, but he also hadn't refuted the prospect when she presented it to him, so he had just as good as.

That wasn't good enough for Psyche, who felt her sister had been doing one injustice to the unknown man after another. It was one thing to embroil her family in her machinations but quite another to tow in a complete stranger. For that, Psyche refused to give over her earrings, which prompted Pandora to state smugly that she already had them in her jewel box from the last time she had borrowed them, and they would stay there because there would be no crawfishing out of the bet.

Pandora was bothered for another reason entirely. If the truth be known, she didn't want her sister's earrings. She'd put them back in Psyche's things after she finished changing clothes. She was magnanimous enough to agree it had not been a fair race because she had started before Psyche was ready. Although she loved winning, she wouldn't do so by cheating…ever. She did not, however, think jumping the phaeton was unfair. No, she was piqued because Lord Islington hadn't accepted her apology.

She admitted to herself in a detached manner as the two of them went up the back stairs to their bedrooms that she didn't often offer regrets for her actions, and she was probably, in all likelihood, out of practice, but surely even the most ignorant dolt could have recognized her apology for what it was! He had treated it as an insult to his person, as if it would be beneath him to disclose whether he accepted or not. Pandora didn't know why it bothered her so much that he had ridden away as he did; she usually blew it off and went on without such bemusement.

"Psyche? Pandora? Is that you two hellions I hear skulking up the stairs?" called a masculine voice from the top of the stairwell.

The two girls came around a turn in the stairs to see their older brother, Dorian, standing at the landing with his arms folded across his chest irefully. The affect was lost on the two girls, who dissolved into giggles over his appearance. He was in his pajamas and slippers, and he was also covered in a sticky substance well-coated with chicken feathers. He looked like a man only partially metamorphosed to a fowl. Psyche and Pandora wrapped their arms about each other's waist to keep themselves from falling over with mirth.

Dorian began to tap his foot with growing anger and reached up to pull free a feather that had become attached to his upper lip.

"I do *not* find this amusing," he said darkly. "I'm going to tell Mum and Dad what you did, and then you'll never get to go riding again."

"Oh, Dorian, don't be such a goose!" cried Psyche hilariously. "Or should I say chicken?" The two girls went into louder guffaws.

"I mean it, you two!" he ground out between clenched teeth.

"Dorian, you git, where's your sense of humor? Surely, you're not too old to keep *that*?" asked Pandora jovially of her twenty-two-year-old brother, helping Psyche up the stairs. "It's only honey and chicken feathers."

"Only honey and chicken feathers!" mimicked Dorian sarcastically.

"Well, Dorian, if you can't look at the humorous side of it, try to consider it an experiment for the furtherance of science," said Psyche, wiping tears from the corners of her eyes.

"Hardly likely," scoffed Dorian.

"It is," swore Pandora, catching the thread that Psyche had cast and knowing she excelled much better at weaving tales than her sister. "We truly didn't know you would walk through the doorway. We were expecting to come back and continue our experiment after breakfast."

"I certainly *did* intend to come out my bedroom door," said Dorian flatly.

"We only wanted to test gravity," said Pandora quickly.

"Poppycock," said Dorian contemptuously, but he had to keep back a smile over his sister's inventiveness. It was, after all, the first of April. He would have felt slighted if she hadn't tried *something.*

"We wanted to see which bucket would fall first," continued Pandora. "We filled them equally with light and heavy substances to see which would topple first." She looked her brother up and down and rubbed a hand over her mouth to hide her smile of amusement. "Apparently, the honey did."

"Wrong, sister," said Dorian calmly. "They fell at the same time, and if you think I believe any of this taradiddle about scientific experiments, you are truly daft."

Psyche brought a hand to her mouth in feigned surprise and grabbed her twin's arm to lead her away.

"They fell at the same time?" cried Pandora with mock excitement, her eyes rounding in pretended astonishment, quickly following her sister's cue. "Come on, Psyche, I've got to write that down in my notebook. Thanks, Brother Dorian," she said with a huge grin.

Dorian watched his sisters hurry down the hall chattering gaily to each other and reached up to scratch the back of his head confusedly. He brought the hand down and saw the honey and chicken feathers stuck to it. He had the distinct feeling that he had been had once again by his mischievous twin sisters. Dorian didn't know how they always seemed to manage wrapping him around their finger with little trouble. The even more baffling matter was that he and no one else in the family seemed to mind it. Still shaking his head, he turned to go back to his room. It was a good thing his valet, Hiroshi, had already drawn him a bath.

<<< >>>

"Pan, I told you we shouldn't have done that," chided Psyche after they made it to Pandora's bedroom without further outbursts from their brother.

"Oh, pooh," said Pandora blithely, going to her closet to look for something to wear. She turned back to her sister with a pensive look on her face, becoming belatedly misgiving. "You don't think he minded overly much, do you?"

Psyche looked thoughtful for a moment, chewing on the side of her thumb. She finally shook her head.

"No, I don't think he was too terribly upset, but you can be sure he'll tell Mamà and Papà."

Pandora dismissed that with a wave of her hand and turned back to her closet. She wasn't concerned with punishment from her parents; they would get a chuckle out of it, as would the rest of the family. She reached for one of her favorite new dresses, a lavender- and violet-striped morning gown, and went to lay it on her bed.

"I wonder who that oaf was in the park this morning," she mused aloud, almost to herself.

"Pan, he was not an oaf! After his initial anger over *your* escapade, I found him to be pleasant," said Psyche, refraining from comment about certain of his mannerisms that she found uncouth.

"To *you* maybe!" said Pandora in vexation, turning to look at her sister. "He was positively horrid to me! Before he knew I was me, he called me a *harpy*! If he wasn't an oaf, he sure had the manners of one!"

"Well, I must say you deserved it," said Psyche in gentle reproach, although she silently agreed with her sister.

"Whose side are you on?"

Psyche rose from her perch on the bed with an exasperated sigh. "There are no sides to be on! I would say he was within his rights to be mad at you." She shrugged her shoulders diffidently and shook her head. "Anyhow, it doesn't matter because we'll probably never see him again."

"Thank God for small blessings," muttered Pandora tartly, fetching her undergarments. She flopped down in a nearby chair dejectedly and put her face in her palms. "I wish we didn't have to go through this London farce."

"You have my wholehearted agreement," said Psyche feelingly. "But Mamà and Papà said it was one of those coming of age things…like the vision quest those Indians in America do. It doesn't seem quite so terrible when you look at it that way."

"No, I suppose not, but I'd much rather be at home in the solar right now, or with the Indians doing a vision quest." Psyche made a face that suggested she was agreeable to the first wish but not the second.

The solarium at their family home, Wilderland Castle, was the twins' private domain. Their mother had actually used it for her flowers once upon a time, as had previous ladies of the manor for hundreds of years, but after finding so many of Psyche's books and Pandora's experiments nestled between her rare orchids and potted palms, she had graciously relinquished its use to them and moved her love for botany to the greenhouse her husband had built for her in the garden near the castle. No one (not even the servants) entered the solarium at the top of the castle unless they came with one of the twins; none of them wished to chance losing a finger or blowing up the entire estate. The entrance wasn't trapped purposely, but one never knew exactly what kind of projects the twins were involved in at any given time.

Pandora had a great love for mathematics, chemistry and engineering, along with a smattering of mechanics and dynamics. The only dire results of her hobbies were that she often tried her experiments on the rest of the family or her proposed tests were no more than practical jokes. She once concocted a chemical compound made from natural ingredients filched from her mother's prized plant specimens and had guaranteed it would curl the hair. The outcome had been that her oldest brother, Myron, had his beautiful blond hair turned an even prettier shade of jade green without the promised curls. The cook absolutely forbade her to enter the kitchen after one of her experiments with electricity charred the family's Christmas dinner to an unrecognizable ruin. Her accuracy and skill with her inventions had improved astonishingly over the years, but because of her prankish bent, one was never sure if her latest failed attempts were not purposely so.

Psyche's pursuits, while not as dangerous as her sister's, were not the sorts of things a properly-reared young lady of quality was expected to pursue, either. She shared her father's affection for things ancient and foreign. One interior wall of the solar was lined with great bookcases loaded to overflowing with decaying scrolls and parchments and tomes so thick that when once their unwary brother, Gregory, had opened the door to the room, one fell on his head with such force it sprawled him across the floor senseless for some time. Psyche had chosen an area on that side of the room for the artifacts her father had given her from his travels, and she would often sit at her worktable with a glazed expression, dreaming of the places to which she one day hoped to travel. Her parents had so far flatly refused to allow her that freedom, having the presence of mind not to let one of their daughters roam about the countryside like a vagabond. So, Psyche continued to study and dream.

The two of them had grown up in Glamorgan with the rest of their large family unrestricted by the tethers normally placed on girls of aristocratic lineage. None of the children had outside education except for the three older boys, who had gone to Harrow then on to Oxford or Cambridge. Two of the three younger boys were still tutored by their father and mother in preparation for going away (the youngest, Damon, would be unable to go but was tutored nonetheless), but the five girls were allowed their own pursuits intellectually, their parents unwilling to go along with the common belief that women were, like children, better to be seen and not heard.

Their mother had seen to their etiquette and deportment, but only because she knew her daughters wouldn't be with her forever. Even if they happened to find a man who admired a woman with intelligence (and, amazingly, there *were* a few), their chances of attracting one were better if they didn't behave like heathens. After their parents' somewhat contemptuous view of society, it was little wonder Psyche and Pandora, like the rest of their sisters, viewed the London social season and debut with arched skepticism.

When the duke and duchess told the girls of their plans to take them to London for the Season and that this time they would be presented, Psyche and Pandora had thought to avoid it, but their mother, Julia, held firm to her decision. She told them that they were nearly nineteen years old, and it was time they joined the "hallowed ranks" like their older sister, Arachne, had done the year before.

During Arachne's Season, she filled her younger sisters' heads full of tales about balls and dinner parties and soirées geared toward displaying females and males for the purpose of obtaining a *suitable* marriage and *breeding*. Psyche and Pandora blinked disconcertedly and tried from that point on to persuade their parents to excuse them from such barbaric practices, but their parents pooh-poohed and cajoled until the twins relented and agreed to at least one season. The twins also decided it must not have been too much of a debilitating and degrading experience if stubborn, stuffy Arachne agreed to another one—she who had vowed from the age of five that she would never marry and had she been Catholic would have become a nun.

The girls didn't regret they were female; they actually, genuinely, liked being women. Besides, the only sister who seemed to strongly pursue more obviously masculine occupations was the youngest, Persephone. All five of them knew they would eventually marry; they only hoped it was to a man as intelligent and gentle as their father.

"Maybe we can get something out of this Season debacle," said Psyche, her face brightening.

"Such as?" asked Pandora absently. Her mind was on her latest chemical composition, temporarily abandoned to go to London.

"We can consider placing a wager between us."

"What do you have in mind, Psy?" Pandora's eyes held a gleam that suggested she already guessed what her sister meant to be the prize, but what the wager would be piqued her curiosity.

"Mamà has reared us to be proper young ladies, and—while we would never do anything to embarrass our family or give anyone undue misconceptions—we both do love a good joke. You know how Arachne went on and on about how stiff-necked some of the *ton* could be, how the men seemed to have this sense of superiority." Psyche was pacing the floor with a keenly avid expression.

"I believe we met an example this morning," said Pandora darkly.

Psyche waved her hand dismissively and continued. "Why don't we take a little starch out of their collars?"

"We can't break into people's houses!" said Pandora, scandalized.

"No, no, I didn't mean it literally. Pandora, sometimes you are such a cake." Psyche ignored her sister's outraged gasp. She tugged at her bottom lip thoughtfully then snapped her fingers. "I have it! Cravats!" She looked at her sister enthusiastically…only to see Pandora's completely lost expression.

"Psyche, is there a cog loose in your machinery?" asked Pandora casually.

"No, there is not!" said Psyche in an affronted tone.

"Then *what* are you talking about?"

"Why don't we have a little contest to see how many of them we can get?" Pandora still looked bumfuzzled. "We both know the cravat is a necessity to a man's attire, and heaven forbid they should be even caught *dead* without one. That's what we'll do."

"What? Kill them and steal their cravats?" asked Pandora, becoming more convinced her sister had lost her mind as things progressed.

Psyche sighed in vexation. For all her brilliant intelligence, her sister sometimes took things too literally, and often, with her fertile imagination to add impetus, got things completely wrong.

"No, you widget! We're going to have a contest to see how many men we can get to give us their cravats, by hook or by crook."

"Oh, Psyche, I like that one," said Pandora admiringly, leaning back in the chair with a devilish look on her face. "Can we just take them?"

"It's highly improbable they will give them to us without a fight, so just asking isn't going to do it. Whatever you can use to convince them is fair, but you can't just conk them on the head and steal it while they're unconscious. They must willingly and knowingly give it to you. You can't take more than one from any one man. And for the *pièce de resistance*: they must be seen in public without it."

Pandora clapped her hands gleefully. It was such a perfect idea; she was amazed she hadn't thought of it herself.

"Oh, Psy, your scheming mind is only surpassed by my own. This sounds so fun I'm tempted to do it without a wager."

"Fine, you don't have to wager, but if I end up with the most cravats by the end of the Season, I get my emerald earrings back."

"What if I win?"

"Then you get to keep them fair and square."

"Shall we shake on it, then?" asked Pandora, holding out her hand.

Psyche returned her sister's conspiratorial smile and clasped her hand tightly, giving it a good shake.

"When do we begin?"

"Tomorrow night."

"At our come-out ball?" gasped Pandora, surprised by Psyche's eagerness. Did she want the earrings back so much?

"Why not? The sooner we begin our revenge, the sooner our fun starts."

Pandora nodded agreeably, making plans for her first acquisition.

The Savage family sat around the table for breakfast chattering and eating with a total lack of formality some of their contemporaries would have found appalling. His grace, Alexander Savage, the ninth Duke of Aberdare, sat at the head of the table. His wife and love of his life, Julia, sat at its foot, both smiling fondly at their eleven beautiful children. They realized long ago that they had an inordinately large number of children, but it was a matter of luck. They had been blessed with five beautiful daughters and six handsome sons imbued with their parents' love of learning and fondness for adventure.

Alexander and Julia met and fell in love in Venice. He had found the green-eyed, raven-haired beauty to be too quick-witted and practical to be without, and she had decided the sometimes absentminded yet intelligent and equally handsome blue-eyed, blond-haired then Earl of Neath was just what she needed after her father's restrictive control. Once they discovered how well they complemented each other, their current bliss of nearly twenty-five years' standing began.

Even after the birth of their first child, the elder Savages had traveled extensively to places some people would have raised eyebrows about. They had seen the great pyramids of Egypt, the Acropolis of Athens, the mysterious wonders of China and India. They had reluctantly returned to the bonds of

British society upon the death of Alexander's father determined to see their children raised with opportunities for growth...all of their children. Alexander and Julia couldn't refuse any of them the chance to discover the wide and varied wonders they had seen.

They had also decided they wouldn't force their children into marriage. They would not arrange matches for their daughters. They wanted them to marry for love. Although the age of consent was twenty-one, the duke and duchess had told their girls once they reached eighteen years, should they find someone to their liking, his grace would wholeheartedly give his consent. If they did not, Wilderland was a large castle that would be empty without them. That was their legacy.

Their contemporaries viewed the Aberdares' unorthodox upbringing of their children with equanimity. The *ton* had dubbed their offspring the Savage Brood. The duke found the sobriquet amusing. The duchess thought it utterly fitting at times. The children didn't care, their sense of self-worth and disdain for the norm already deeply instilled. Society was pleasantly surprised to find the children well-behaved, attentive of their station, and entirely exquisite in appearance. If they sometimes did things unusual, it was excusable.

Aside from that, Aberdare was a powerful man. His sometimes vague appearance was deceptive. Behind that still-handsome-at-fifty face with the unassuming look was a quick mind. Although he had acquired a few enemies over the years, there were none who dared cross him because he had the power and the shrewdness to return the favor as required. This unsavory task seldom arose, and the Duke of Aberdare was glad of that, being gentle and easygoing by nature. He only exerted his force when that was the only option left to him, but when necessary, he used it very swiftly and efficiently.

Her grace was the perfect accompaniment to Aberdare. She matched him in all ways, although some of her talents were more prominent than others. Her gentleness was most often at the fore, but hidden behind that soft trait was a core of steel. She attended the functions of society and accepted all it entailed gracefully, but she would not tolerate injustice or deception. She turned away from those fawning over her station for favors, but should she find a situation intolerable, her iron will and determination were unquenchable in pursuit of a better condition...whether the unfortunate party willed it or not.

Their children now seated around the table laughing and talking possessed the same traits to a greater or lesser degree. They were all very much in self-possession. The family shared a very close bond. There were no secrets, no restrictions...within reason. Because of their rearing, they shared a relaxed, informal relationship with their parents that often did not exist among the aristocracy. But, they came out the better for it; they were confident, intelligent and shrewd, just like the parents they so admired and respected.

Myron, the oldest son and first born, styled Earl of Neath, sat at his father's right, his blond hair and blue eyes so much like his sire's. He was nearing twenty-four years of age, but at the present time he was acting very much the juvenile by making faces at his sister across from him. He was strongly built and cut a fine figure in his riding clothes, which the young misses of the *ton* were all sighing over. He had almost been married the previous Season, but his offer had been refused. He didn't anticipate it would happen again, but he was content to remain a bachelor for the time being. He was so like his father in both appearance and temperament, the younger Savages had nicknamed him Sham.

To his father's left sat Dorian, the next-eldest son and bestowed as the first (sometimes fourth, depending on who was asked) Viscount Glamorgan after his Grandfather Sanders' demise. Having no males to inherit (not even a distant cousin), the viscountcy had become extinct on his death. The king had offered to recreate the letters patent for either the duke or Myron to receive the title. His parents, seeing no reason why Myron should be the future duke, be styled an earl *and* also be entitled to a viscountcy, had managed to have letters patent created that transferred the right of inheritance for the title to their second son rather than the first; it was unusual, but the king had agreed to it.

Dorian's coloring was his mother's, the same startling blue-black hair and emerald green eyes. Of the older boys, he was the most handsome, his lithe build and already chiseled-at-twenty-two features causing many of the mamas on the marriage mart to seek him out even at his youthful age. For that, he received occasional teasing from the females of the family. He was also the most serious boy, so their teasing about his social appeal was usually met with an indifferent shrug. Privately, the constant pursuit by the females of the *ton* bothered him, but he wasn't going to let a desire to have them leave off prompt him to marry just anyone.

Seated beside Myron was Gregory. At twenty-one, he was a combination of his mother and father. His hair was an unruly mass of dark brown curls that became blond-streaked when he stayed too long in the sun, which he often did because of his love of sailing. If not out on the lake in a small skiff, then on the ocean in the Bermuda sloop he had recently purchased with his inheritance from Grandfather Sanders. His eyes were a fascinating shade of blue-green, easily compared to the color of the sea he loved. He possessed his mother's gentle nature and his father's sense of democracy, which made him a popular third party in disputes between his siblings.

Across from Gregory sat Arachne, the oldest daughter. She had her mother's raven tresses and eyes so gray they glowed like silver when her emotions ebbed high. She possessed an unaffected beauty that was the trait of her younger sisters, and she was so like them by not realizing it, making it all the more precious. She had made her debut the Season before, and many suitors had called; some had even spoken to her father, but she had refused them all. She would not marry until she found someone she loved, and she had her parents' wholehearted agreement.

Next came the mischievous twins, Psyche and Pandora. After they had determined what profit they were going to enjoy from the Season, they were able to join in their family's banter, the incident in the park (mostly) forgotten. They were in a debate over the benefits of using stone in architecture as opposed to wood. Their parents were also joined in the discussion, which was dissolving into outlandish theories and amusing statements of fact.

Seated beside Psyche was Eurydice, a serious seventeen-year-old. She had the most unusually-colored hair of the family, so different from that of her siblings and parents. It was an extraordinary shade of dark red-gold, more red than gold, which had come from her father's Russian mother, Alexa. Her eyes were also of an unusual color, a shade not quite brown, more yellow, like those of their cat, Archimedes. Unlike that of most red-haired people, her skin was smooth and even, no ruddiness, no freckles. She dreaded the day her debut would come because she feared it would signal the end of her affair with music. Her love of the violin was her greatest passion, something else she shared in common with the late duchess. She was extremely talented, and her only heartbreak was that music was still considered a man's world by most.

The rambunctious, impetuous, sixteen-year-old girl seated beside Pandora was Persephone, the youngest daughter. She had the most masculine pursuits of the girls, which included fencing, archery, pistols, racing and cards. Despite her tomboy ways, she was no less beautiful than her sisters. Her hair was a rich, blonde-streaked, mahogany brown that haloed a face possessed of the same amber-colored eyes as Eurydice's. She could usually be found at the heels of Myron, who indulged her in her atypical pastimes. She also shared Gregory's love of the sea, and when not following Myron, she could be found with Gregory.

Below the girls, near their mother, sat the three younger boys: the nearly ten-year-old twins, Cosmo and Christopher; and the angelic, seven-year-old Damon. Cosmo and Christopher were identical twins like Psyche and Pandora, possessing the same gold locks and green eyes. Their faces were wreathed in gleeful smiles as they told their mother what they planned to do for the day, which among other things included making a papier mâché kite shaped like a dragon that Kwan, one of the nursemaids who assisted Nanny Bixley, was going to help them with. They were joined in their enthusiasm by Damon, who signaled his inclusion with hand gestures and nodding his head.

Damon had been the victim of scarlet fever when he was three years old, leaving him afflicted with deafness. He communicated with his family by reading lips and a system of hand signs Arachne had developed for him based on the French system of sign language. The deafness now was no more than a nuisance and did not hinder his sweet, mischievous disposition or his astounding intelligence. He adored Arachne and followed her everywhere she went. His coloring was the same as hers, even the color of his eyes, and his chubby pink cheeks gave him the appearance of a Botticelli cherub.

"Dorian, would you care for some honey?" asked Pandora, her eyes glinting amusedly.

Dorian nearly choked on the egg he had just put in his mouth and gave his sister a quelling glare. Psyche's added giggle behind her hand caused his face to redden even more.

"No, thank you," he grated after he managed to swallow his food.

Aberdare watched them curiously and turned to look at Psyche. "Did you do something to your brother this morning?" he asked mildly.

"Why, Papà, what makes you ask that?" she returned innocently.

"Perhaps it is this aversion to honey that he's suddenly developed."

"It was only an experiment in gravity," said Pandora calmly.

Dorian scoffed, and she looked at him guilelessly.

The duke looked to Dorian for enlightenment. Dorian told his father what had happened with the buckets, and after he finished, his father sat back in his seat and wiped his mouth with his napkin to hide his amused smile. Not so for the rest of the family, who had turned from their own conversations to listen to Dorian's story. They were all chortling amusedly. Persephone, irrepressible as ever, went so far as to rib Pandora and say, "Good show!" Dorian tried to keep a serious expression, but their ingenuity was brilliant. The duke looked at the two girls with a barely-controlled stern expression.

"Is this so?" he asked them.

"Yes, Papà," said the two of them with downcast faces.

"And what did you learn from this?" asked Aberdare, bending his head to stop them from seeing his lips twitching with amusement.

"That things of different masses falling from the same height are not affected by gravity concerning weight if they fall at the same time and have the same configuration dimensionally," said Psyche after chewing on her lower lip for a thoughtful moment, her brow furrowing as she tried to make sure she didn't confuse mass and gravity. Pandora was so much better with physics than she was.

Looking equally as thoughtful and serious, Pandora made her own statement regarding the matter.

"I learned Dorian looks quite dashing when doused in honey and chicken feathers." She looked at her brother devilishly and gave him a playful wink.

Dorian and Aberdare couldn't repress themselves any longer and joined the rest of the family in laughter. Pandora was never doleful over her practical jokes for long.

"You brazen minx!" chortled Dorian. "I believe you would tamper with the Devil himself without a twinge of conscience."

Pandora waxed thoughtful. "I suppose you're right. Although, if ever I play a joke on Lucifer, you can be sure it will be one he finds amusing enough to let me go."

"Fear not, sister," chortled Dorian. "If he doesn't find it amusing, he'll let you go no matter because you can charm the stripes off a tiger."

"Oh, really, Dorian," said Pandora, blushing profusely. Then she looked up at him and grinned mischievously. "Well, maybe I could."

Chapter Three

Pandora awoke the next morning feeling a strange sense of excitement over the evening to come. She didn't know why she was so looking forward to something she didn't want, but there it was, causing her heart to flutter with eagerness. She tried to put it down to her expectation for her contest with Psyche, but it wasn't so easy to excuse. She sighed and rose from bed, heading for her closet to get a riding habit and dress quickly.

She didn't know how many times she had dressed without the help of her maid, Maiyin, a curious little Mandarin woman her father had brought home with him from one of his trips to China when Pandora was young, along with Maiyin's husband, Keung, who worked for the family as a gardener...among other things. Maiyin often chastised Pandora for dressing alone, completely forgetting who was the servant, but Pandora adored her to distraction and wouldn't trade her for anything. Maiyin had brought Pandora tea and toast, but Pandora shooed her back to the servants' quarters after that and told her to go back to bed for a few more hours.

Pandora knew it was considered odd they had so many foreign servants: a Syrian stable master, her Chinese maid, Psyche's Greek maid, and many others foreign and closer to home ranging from an Indian butler to an Irish cook. But, aside from all being trustworthy and honest, it allowed the family to learn of other cultures and languages firsthand. Most of the children could speak with the servants equally well in their native languages or English, whichever suited, and they held a respect for those views and ways of life not the same as their own. It gave them an understanding for the ranges of human nature, an intuition and empathy for others that were not normally found.

After inspecting her appearance in the mirror, Pandora went to the door of the adjoining sitting room between her and Psyche's bedrooms and went to the other side of it to Psyche's room just as her sister was completing the task of lacing up her boot.

"Are you ready yet?" asked Pandora, adjusting her wrist-length kid gloves uncomfortably, wishing she didn't have to wear them.

"Let me grab my gloves," answered Psyche, going to a drawer.

The two of them tromped down the back stairs toward the stables, giggling with each other over the outrageous statements they quipped. Tajik, accustomed to the unusual habits of his employers, had Bellerophon and Achilles saddled and waiting for them when they reached it. They greeted him cheerfully and mounted their horses, telling him as they departed to expect them back within two hours.

Their jaunt in the park was uneventful, with no sign of their nemesis in the phaeton, which made Pandora sigh in relief. She didn't think she could face him again without spewing more insults on his head. She didn't know what it was about him that turned her into such a termagant. Pandora believed she was usually good-natured, but there was something about him that rubbed her the wrong way. She wasn't sure she disliked him because she had found him physically compelling in an odd sort of way; she seemed aggravated by him more than anything.

The ride in the park cleared her head and set her heart to pounding with anticipation as it had that morning when she thought of the ball she was to attend that night. By the time she and Psyche returned to the stables, Pandora's bluedevils had been chased away and her usual frolicsome disposition was back. The ball was going to be sensational, whether she actually wanted to be debuted into society or not.

"Missy Pandora, you sit still and let me finish your hair!" commanded Maiyin in her singsong voice. "Your dress fine, but you get no gentleman to look at you with your hair in big mess!"

"Then, please, hurry. The ball will be over before you're done."

The Chinese woman harrumphed but continued her task without saying another word. After she finished, she stood back to let Pandora rise and look in the full length mirror, her face beaming proudly.

"Missy Pandora, you will be prettiest girl there," said Maiyin, her hands clasped to her breast. "You find a nice man for husband in no time."

Pandora gazed at her reflection and had to admit Maiyin had outdone herself. For the first time in her life, Pandora began to wonder if men *would* find her attractive. It was an odd question but appropriate, considering what the ball signified.

She turned to look at Maiyin. "Do you think so?" she asked pensively.

"I know so," beamed Maiyin. "No one as beautiful as you."

Maiyin put her arms into the sleeves of the loose silk jacket she wore contemplatively, and it reminded Pandora of a porcelain doll her father had brought her when she was five. Maiyin was still beautiful and without wrinkles, even after sixty years. And she was tiny. Pandora was taller by eight inches, and Maiyin's slender frame made her seem as if a breeze could knock her over. Pandora knew that look was deceptive, however. She studied herself in the mirror with Maiyin looking on proudly behind her, as pleased as a mother would be for her own child.

Pandora's dress was emerald green velvet, with short, puffed sleeves and a tight bodice gathered beneath her breasts to a skirt that fell in graceful lines to the floor, accentuating the gentle swell of her hips.   There was an underskirt of pale green silk that peeked through at the front, trimmed in tiny seed pearls sewn on in the shapes of flowers and leaves.   The bodice's scooped neckline dipped low enough to allow the soft rise of her breasts to be exposed temptingly, the single baguette emerald trimmed with tiny diamonds she wore around her neck drawing attention to them.   Her hair was piled on her head in artless curls, a few allowed to escape the coiffure's confines to spiral softly at her ears and nape.   For most women, white was *de rigueur*, but Pandora and white clothing did not do well together, and emerald green was one of her favorite colors.

As Psyche sauntered into the room after Chrissoula's ministrations, Pandora's lips quirked in an amused smile.

"There's at least *one* other person in this world as beautiful as I," Pandora chuckled. Maiyin looked at Psyche and giggled behind her hand.

Psyche was dressed in a lavender velvet gown styled much like Pandora's. The cutaway was filled with deep purple silk trimmed in a swirling pattern of purple glass beads. Around her neck was a cabochon amethyst. The sleeves of her gown were a puff of lavender velvet at the shoulders that tapered in the middle of her upper arm to a fitted lower sleeve of the same silk as the underskirt. She wore white satin gloves and held an oriental fan. Her hair was left loose in the front where its natural ringlets framed her face while the long length in the back had been braided and twisted into a golden coronet. Pandora felt a twinge of sisterly pride as she looked at her.

"Do you think the *ton* can sustain both of us at one time?" asked Psyche in amused, pretended conceit.

"If they can't, then we shall have to attend all their funerals. I *do* look good in black," returned Pandora airily, a mischievous glint in her eyes.

"Shall we go down?" asked Psyche, reaching out her hand to take her sister's and head for the door.

"Missy Pandora, *dài shàng nǐ de shǒutào!*" said Maiyin, holding out a pair of long white gloves to Pandora.

Pandora wrinkled her nose but went to take the gloves and put them on.

"*Wǒ bù xǐhuān de shǒutào,*" said Pandora sulkily as she slid one of the gloves over her arm. "*Tāmen ràng wǒ yǎng.*"

"Itch they may, but you wear gloves like proper missy!" said Maiyin with a determined nod of her head. After Pandora had on both gloves, Maiyin smiled with satisfaction. "Now you ready to go."

Pandora and Psyche went down the front stairs arm-in-arm, their excitement making them giggle. The ball was to be held in their home, saving them the trouble of rushing to a carriage to go to an assembly hall. The guests had already started to arrive, the ones who didn't bother with the rude custom of being *fashionably* late…or just plain late. Pandora and Psyche were familiar with some of the names that had been on the guest list, but there had been many more that they were not. Their father and Myron were at the foot of the stairs waiting for them when they arrived.

"My dears you are looking quite the thing this evening," said their father, his eyes twinkling mischievously.

"Thank you, Papà," said Psyche and Pandora, ducking their heads and blushing profusely.

"Dad, I don't believe it, the two imps are blushing," said Myron, his eyes wide with pretended shock. "Is there a mending of their ways?"

"Not likely, Sham," said Pandora saccharinely, sticking out her tongue.

"Ah, there's the brat I know and love," chuckled Myron amusedly.

"Where's Mamà?" asked Psyche, looking around the empty hallway.

"She is greeting the guests, and I should be with her," said his grace. "If there's one thing I would love to avoid in this lifetime, it's having to be polite to people I loathe."

"If you don't like them, why invite them? Psyche and I don't know them, so it would be no slight to us if you hadn't," said Pandora, thinking the fewer strange people she had to see, the better she would feel.

"Because it would be a slight to *them,*" sighed Aberdare. "I don't care whose toes I step on, but there's a certain way some things have to be done if you want to have other things run smoothly." Pandora nodded her head in resigned understanding, sympathizing with her father's position. "Now, I best be getting back to your mother before she pounds me over the head for deserting her," he said with a chuckle. "Myron, perform your brotherly duty and escort these two devilkins to the ballroom."

"But, Papà, we don't need an escort," pouted Psyche.

"You will this evening," said Aberdare. He smiled cajolingly and pinched her cheek. "I know you don't want to do this whole Season thing, but at least for tonight, try to use those manners your mother taught you."

"Papà, you take all the fun out of a thing," said Pandora, smiling pertly and folding her arms across her chest obstinately.

"And you, my dear, little brat, are incorrigible," said Aberdare, bending to kiss his daughter on the cheek. "I shall see you later."

His grace made his way to the front hall, a pleased smile on his face. He was proud of his daughters, all of them graced with beauty and intelligence beyond worth. His only hope was that they would be happy no matter what. He joined his wife, and upon seeing no one standing nearby, he swept her into his arms to place an affectionate kiss on her lips.

"My dear, we have beautiful children."

"Yes, we do, love. Now, what brought on this pleasant display of affection?" asked her grace, resting her head on his shoulder.

"Psyche and Pandora." Julia looked up at him skeptically. The twins did not often cause happy thoughts; they were usually creating fits of exasperation and amusement. "They look very beautiful tonight."

Julia nodded in understanding. "How else could they look?"

"Do you think we're doing right to allow them so much freedom?" asked the duke, his face thoughtful.

"Xan, you know better than to ask me *that*," said Julia in gentle reproach. She kissed his cheek. "You've no need to worry. We've not gone wrong so far."

≪ ≫

"Myron, do you know all the people Papà has invited?" asked Psyche as she walked beside him down the hall, her arm linked through his.

"Most of them, yes," said Myron. He looked at her with deviltry. "Are you planning to find some man to sweep you off your feet?"

"Absolutely not," said Psyche firmly, her chin tilted.

"She was only asking because you would look much the ninny if you had to introduce us to someone and had not been introduced yourself," said Pandora, her arm linked through his on the other side. "Imagine: my lord whoever-you-are or whatever-you-are, let me present to you my lovely young sisters and myself." She giggled.

Myron chuckled also. "We've no need to worry about that because I know everyone who has arrived so far." He steered the two girls down the hall that would lead them to the ballroom. "Most are associates of Dad's, but some are friends of mine and Dorian's and Gregory's."

They were almost to the door when they saw Dorian, who had a hunted expression on his face. He looked dashing in his sapphire blue velvet evening coat pulled over a silver brocade vest and white linen shirt. The white breeches and stockings he wore displayed the fine musculature of his legs. The gold buckles on his shoes glinted brightly from the healthy polishing his valet had provided. When he saw them, he rushed toward them, bunching his bicorn in his hands.

"Myron, thank God you're here," he panted, rubbing an arm over his forehead in relief.

"Good heavens, what's hounding you?" asked Psyche, looking at her usually calm and controlled brother curiously.

"*Hounding* is right," groaned Dorian. "It's Lady Ramsey and her simpering niece who trailed me all last Season. They will not leave me alone!"

"You didn't leave the guests in there unattended did you?" asked Myron concernedly.

"No, Arachne is in there. She tried to pull those two harpies away from me, but they're like bad debts!" Dorian looked at Myron with uncharacteristic desperation. "Myron, you've got to get them off my back, or I swear I'll lose my mind!"

"Wish I could help you, but I'm performing my brotherly duty," said Myron, having no wish to be chased by the women any more than his brother;

28

once they latched on, they were most likely there for the duration. "If you can just suffer through until more guests arrive."

Dorian grabbed Pandora's arm and tucked it into his elbow, deciding he would use the same excuse as Myron. She began to giggle hilariously at the picture of long-suffering desperation he made. He looked down at her with a dark scowl that made her laugh all the more.

"Oh, Dorian, if you could only see your face!" she chortled. "Are they really so bad?"

"Wait until you meet them," he groaned, shaking his head. "They're like leeches in muslin. Lady Ramsey is approaching sixty if she's a day, and her niece, Lucy Cranston, is just awful. She doesn't have a thought in her head except for the desire to marry someone titled. It would take something as subtle as cannon shot for them to take a hint to leave off."

Pandora patted his arm in patronizing consolation. She didn't know why women chased after Dorian. She supposed they found him attractive with his good looks and muscular figure, but her being his sister, she couldn't see the point of it. To her, he was just Brother Dorian. She would act as his shield if it would be of any help, but she didn't intend to perform that service all night. After all, she had a contest to win.

"Fear not, beleaguered knight!" she cried, placing a hand to her breast dramatically and holding an imaginary weapon in the air. "I shall save you from the dragons! Rally to my standard, woebegone warrior, and the enemy shall taste the wrath of my sword!"

"Your tongue can be rather sharp-edged, can't it?" teased Myron, smiling over his sister's theatrics.

"Shall I hone it on your hide, infidel?" questioned Pandora in pretended anger, taking a half-step around Dorian toward him.

Myron scuttered behind Psyche as if to use her as a shield from his sister's purported wroth. He knew at his age that he shouldn't behave so immaturely, but with Pandora, it was difficult to act anything else.

"Pandora, you promised to mind your manners," reminded Myron.

"Mind your manners, mind your manners!" copied Pandora like a parrot. She made a face. "Makes me feel like a raffish two-year-old, I tell you it does," she pouted, reverting back to the normal Pandora. She raised her nose in the air arrogantly. "Well, Brother Dorian, lead me into battle," she sighed, waving her hand with condescending grace.

The four of them walked through the doorway abreast of each other, and many heads in the room turned at the dazzling sight they made as Tannaz, one of their footmen and the son of their Indian butler, Rajeesh, held open the door. The girls' cheeks were glowing from their playful banter, and the boys, being firmly reminded they were never too old for make-believe, had their chins tilted at a daring angle, causing Lady Ramsey and Miss Cranston to sigh. The four of them had no knowledge of the stir they caused, but Arachne recognized it and smiled amusedly. They walked over to her, and Myron took her hand to place a gallant kiss upon it. She quickly took it back and said something to the extent he was making a scene but returned his mischievous smile.

The small orchestra their mother had hired for the evening was seated unobtrusively near the back of the room in the musicians' box already playing a waltz. No one was dancing yet, waiting for the rest of the guests and their host and hostess to join them.

The ballroom was large, well-able to accommodate the number of guests they had invited. The sets of French doors onto the terrace had been opened to allow the night air to drift in, steeped sweetly in the scent of the duchess's roses from the garden beyond. The walls of the room were decorated in a soft pink and white floral print with cherry wainscoting. The ceiling rose twenty feet, its surface painted with the seasons and winds in a sylvan setting, trimmed with ornate gilt-work. There were comfortably-padded chairs lining the walls upon which the old who wouldn't dance or the young who needed to rest from dancing could sit and socialize. Tables were placed in a gallery, reached through doors near the orchestra, laden with bowls of champagne punch and trays of all manner of food. The duchess had decided against a sit-down meal after the people who replied as attending reached over one hundred. She had been planning the ball for several months, even before they left Wilderland (although the invitations had only been sent out two weeks beforehand), and everything was perfect.

The siblings stood chatting with each other for several minutes until they could continue no longer without seeming rude. More guests were arriving by the minute, and the ballroom was fast filling. Gregory soon joined them and took Arachne's hand. Matched off as they were, the six of them began to mingle with their guests.

Dorian and Myron introduced Psyche and Pandora to the strangers, and the twins found several of their brothers' friends quite fascinating. It came as no surprise the men found the twins equally so. 'Where have you been hiding them?' cried a red-haired bear of a young man, introduced as Lord Georgie Beckinsale, Earl of Plimpton. '*Two* women of such magnificent beauty?' had sighed another introduced as Sir James Klein, of Whissendine. As Psyche and Pandora were led from one to another, their heads began to swell with so many names and compliments they thought they would burst from it all. When Pandora voiced that to Dorian, he laughed and told her that would be the day.

Pandora's dance card quickly filled, and she dreaded the thought she would have to be on her feet for so long. There would be more dances than what were on the card, but she didn't know when one would be played that wasn't spoken for to allow her to rest. She was sure her mother would have planned them well. At least, Pandora hoped she had.

She was glad her mother had thought to use the dance cards. They weren't common in London but were used all the time on the continent, particularly in Vienna. Her mother was not using them in the strictest fashion, thankfully. Otherwise, every dance would be accounted for, and Pandora would be exhausted by the end of the night. They were pretty little things, and

Pandora appreciated her mother's artful tendencies. The card resembled a small book, the covers made of thin mother-of-pearl with filigreed silver at the corners. The pencil fit into the spine out of sight, and it fit over the wrist by a thin white satin ribbon. It reminded Pandora of the books her twin loved to read—only on a much smaller scale.

Alexander and Julia soon left the front of the house near the door and joined their guests in the ballroom, signaling the event was truly ready to commence. As the orchestra struck up the music for the opening minuet, the guests strolled onto the dance floor.

Pandora and Psyche were led out by Lord Georgie and Sir James. The twins, although they knew they had to dance at their own ball, would rather have avoided the first one of the evening. It wasn't that they didn't enjoy dancing, for they did and were quite accomplished at it. They wanted to compare notes over the men they thought likely candidates for cravat-snatching. As it was, they plotted how they could get their present dancing partners to give them the sought-after article of clothing. It didn't take long to discover they had set themselves a challenging task. As Psyche had said, the men wouldn't even be caught dead without one. Without making themselves seem too forward, the goal was near to impossible.

After the dance, Lord Georgie escorted Pandora back to the edge of the floor. She only had time to thank him before being whisked out by another eager partner. When he led her back to her seat, she was accosted by the next. Psyche was suffering the same fate. They exchanged helpless glances and were once more taken to the floor. After three more such occurrences, Pandora was put out. Her throat was dry, and the closeness of the bodies on the floor was making it difficult to breathe. If the men didn't cease, she would be hard-pressed not to scream bloody murder. She heaved a sigh of relief when the quadrille ended, and her current partner, Lord Fielding, led her back to her seat. The next dance starting up was *not* on her card, and she wasn't going to let anyone convince her to dance it.

"Lord Fielding, you are an excellent partner," said Pandora when she slumped down in her seat bonelessly.

He raised her hand to his lips. "Thank you, Lady Pandora. Dancing with you is a dream."

"Oh, my lord, you're too kind," said Pandora dully, wishing her thirst and exhaustion *were* a dream. She gave him an engaging smile. "I would find you even kinder if you would fetch me something to drink."

Lord Fielding bowed and left. Several men approached as she sat waiting for his return, but she politely refused. She would *not* dance again until she drank something, and she was sure some of them had their names on her card already. She looked up with a start from examining the toes of her slippers when she heard Dorian's teasing voice.

"Poor little brat, have your partners all deserted you so soon?"

"Indeed, blackhearted twit!" said Pandora, lifting her chin, her eyes flashing emerald. "And a pox on 'em if they come back!" she hissed in disgust. Dorian whooped amusedly. "Don't laugh at me, you addlepated whelp, or I'll see what I can do about setting two certain ladies onto you like bloodhounds!"

Her brother put a hand to his chest and raised his eyes heavenward for salvation. "You wound me to the quick. How abruptly you betray me." He chuckled mischievously. "Had I known you were a wolf in sheep's clothing, I wouldn't have brought my best mate to meet you."

At that moment, Lord Fielding chose to return, and Pandora ignored her brother temporarily. She drained the glass in one unladylike draught and smacked her lips satisfactorily. Dorian laughed hilariously, and Lord Fielding gasped in shock. She looked at him and saw his astounded expression. Pandora thought it best to pretend she had done nothing wrong.

"Thank you, Lord Fielding, you are a true life saver," she said, giving him a radiant smile. She then gave him a beseeching look that seemed to work well on her family when she wanted to wheedle something out of them. "Would you be a dear and fetch me another?"

He held out his own glass. "Here, Lady Pandora, have mine."

She turned to her brother and gave him a wink, her annoyance over his teasing forgotten for the moment.

"I say, Dorian, your friend, Lord Fielding, is such a charming gentleman." She raised the glass daintily and took a small sip, deciding not to astonish Lord Fielding any more than she already had.

"What was that about a pox?" asked a mocking voice from behind Dorian, causing Pandora to choke on her small sip in shock.

The speaker gracefully moved from behind her brother to pat her on the back, and she nearly flew from her seat as if stung when his hand made contact with her skin.

I should have known! It had to be *that* man. Her nemesis, and she was giving him the satisfaction of seeing her nearly choke to death on less than a teaspoon of punch! She couldn't believe she was meeting him again. She chanced a look at him through teary eyes and choked again, this time on rage. *The oaf is laughing at me! Not fair.*

"There, there dear," he soothed condescendingly, still patting her back. "One should be careful not to swallow too much at one time."

Pandora was livid. She withstood his patronizing pats as well as Lord Fielding's genuinely concerned ones while Dorian looked on with barely contained mirth. If it wouldn't cause a scene, she would call Lord Islington every name floating through her mind. He had no right to throw her words back at her like that then laugh at her distress, revealing charming dimples that made her heart beat with a curious anticipation.

Lord Islington looked at Pandora, enjoying his moment of revenge. Her eyes sparkled with ill-concealed outrage, reminding him of an angry feline. He didn't know why she couldn't be more like her sisters, Arachne and Psyche, with whom he had already danced. They were so pleasant. She was high-strung.

Dorian had told Islington that his family was large. He had met Myron while briefly attending Oxford before deciding Cambridge was a better fit (where he met Dorian) and Arachne last Season. The other siblings…Dorian had mentioned them in passing, including the youngest, who was deaf, but Islington couldn't recall Dorian ever mentioning any of them by name or that two of his sisters were identical twins.

After the incident in the park yesterday, Islington had been tempted to tell Dorian what he thought of the two heathens but changed his mind. Islington couldn't blame his friend (or their parents, he was sure) for their shortcomings, especially those of the one he was looking at right now.

He hadn't wanted Dorian to bring him over to Pandora. He would have been far more pleased if he hadn't come within ten feet of her, but his friend had insisted, saying Pandora was such an incorrigible chit that one couldn't help but be charmed by her. The marquess had thought it a mild definition for her and believed she had about as much charm as a pit viper, but given that it came from a friend who was often too serious for someone so young, Islington had decided to give her another chance.

When they had approached her chair, Pandora had looked limp, and Islington had almost felt sympathy for her. He was surprised how quickly that changed, how quickly her sharp tongue had struck. No wonder Dorian was always so quiet and serious; a sister like that was enough to make anyone lose his sense of humor. Yes, he was enjoying her discomfort.

Islington had no trouble discerning which twin was which when he arrived, something people other than those related to them found almost impossible. He watched the way they danced with their partners, their demeanor, their expressions. While both were equally beautiful and vivacious, Pandora seemed to exude a wild, volatile air that reminded him of her stunt in the park, thus helping him know which twin to dodge.

He had taken every opportunity to avoid her until Dorian had left him no choice. Other than his disapproval over her actions in the park and certain of her remarks during their conversation afterward, he didn't know why he felt such a strong urgency to keep as much distance between himself and Pandora as could be managed, but something in the back of his mind warned him that she was trouble. What kind of trouble…he didn't know; he wasn't sure he wanted to know. He still remembered the way she had seemed to read his mind and how it had left him feeling defenseless. He didn't like that feeling. For now, he had the upper hand, and he was enjoying it.

Pandora regained control of her breathing and took a deep inhale and let it out through her nose to restrain her temper. Her parents had asked her to mind her manners, and because she didn't want to embarrass or shame them, she would not slap the grin from Lord Islington's face. Instead, she rose from her seat and graced him with a pleasant smile that didn't melt the ice in her eyes.

"All right now, Lady Pandora?" asked Lord Fielding with polite concern.

"Yes, I'm fine now, Lord Fielding, thank you," said Pandora absently, her eyes attempting to burn holes through Lord Islington.

"Pandora, may I present Theodore Marshall, the Marquess of Bardsey, also Viscount Islington?" said Dorian. "Lord Islington, this is my sister, Lady Pandora Savage."

"My lord," said Pandora evenly, holding out her hand as expected.

She was tempted to jerk it back when she felt his warm touch but kept her poise as his lips brushed her knuckles. Pandora compressed her lips angrily when she saw his eyes were still mocking her. Then her eyes glinted wickedly as a thought occurred to her.

"For someone so small of mind, you certainly have a big title."

Dorian's mouth dropped open in surprise, and Lord Fielding looked as if he had turned into a beet. Islington threw his head back and laughed amusedly while Pandora grew all the more agitated. She had wanted to rile him but had instead amused him.

"Have you two already met?" asked Dorian uncertainly.

"Not really, Brother Dorian," said Pandora coolly. Her expression softened with amusement when she turned to look at him. "I jumped Lord Islington's phaeton in the park yesterday morning."

"You jumped his…," Dorian trailed off in amazement. He turned to look at Islington. "Did she really?"

"Oh, yes," said Islington, wiping the corner of his eye. "As I seem to recall, she and Lady Psyche had some earrings wagered on who could beat whom to the lake."

Dorian rounded on Pandora. "Dodo, you know how Mum and Dad feel about you racing off the estate." A hand flew to his mouth as he realized what he said.

Dodo was the affectionate nickname Pandora's family had bestowed on her when she was still too little to walk. 'Pandora is too big a name for someone so small' had been the reason. The only one who never used it was Psyche, who called her Pan. As Pandora grew and matured, the nickname had become something of a burden. While she didn't mind her family using it when they were at home, she didn't want society to know it. People like Lord Islington might think it stemmed from some aspersion on her mentality, which the look on his face confirmed. She wasn't angry with her brother because she knew it was an accident, but she was embarrassed nonetheless. Her back grew stiff with discomfiture and anger as she looked at him, her cheeks coloring hotly.

"Yes, Dorian," she said tightly, "I know Mamà and Papà don't like us racing in the City, but because it was quite early and no one was about, except for Lord Islington—"she cast him a hateful glance—"we saw no reason not to indulge ourselves."

"Who won, by the way?" asked Islington quizzically, certain Pandora was the victor through sheer idiocy.

"No one won because you got in our way. We forfeited until it can be settled in another manner." She turned to Dorian and gave him a pleading smile. "I'm going for some air. It's suddenly feeling quite stuffy in here."

She turned to Lord Fielding and Lord Islington. "My lords." She tilted her head in adieu then turned to go outside through one of the open doors.

Pandora walked onto the terrace and went to lean against the stone balustrade overlooking her mother's garden. She pulled off the gloves Maiyin had made her wear and scratched her arms with satisfaction. She took a deep breath of the cool, rose-scented air and looked up at the stars in the clear night sky. She wished more than ever that she was at home in the solar. She didn't want to be in London. She didn't want to be one of the *ton*. All she wanted was to stay in the high tower room and do her tests and experiments and create her new inventions. She hadn't been in society very long, but she was discovering it held no interest for her; then again, she never thought it would.

Pandora listened to the strains of a waltz being played by the orchestra and sighed fitfully. Psyche seemed to be enjoying the ball somewhat better than she, but of course, Psyche didn't have *Lord Islington* to make her feel miserable. *Lord Islington* liked her. Pandora made a face and went to the stairs leading down to the garden. Psyche was welcome to him. He was arrogant and uncouth and…. Pandora stopped herself before she became angry again. It wouldn't do any good. He'd already spoiled the evening for her; there was no sense in making it worse for herself. She was going to get some air; then she would go back to the ball. There was no reason to *let* him ruin her night.

The garden was silent except for the sound of music floating through the open doors, and the farther Pandora walked into the lamp-lit haven the softer the notes became until it seemed she was listening to only the memory of the waltz. She went to the farthest wall near the gate to the mews and sat down on a bench inside the gazebo nestled among some tall rhododendrons. None of the other guests had made it out to the garden yet, and Pandora was glad of the solitude. She always did her best thinking when she was alone. What she was thinking about, she didn't know; it seemed to be everything and nothing.

She absentmindedly began to pull leaves from a nearby shrub and tear them into tiny pieces with distracted wistfulness. Oh, but Lord Islington was handsome. When he had laughed over her failed insult, he had looked even more so, with his dimples and twinkling blue eyes. She sensed there was something more there, more than animosity, and that left her with a peculiar breathlessness. Even with his taunting and mockery, she had still felt drawn to him in an indescribably, uncommonly sensual manner. She was able to recognize that. He was awakening feelings she was sure she shouldn't be feeling for anyone at all, let alone for him.

She leaned her head back against the side of the gazebo and sighed fitfully. It was no use for her to attempt thinking this situation through in one night. The things she was feeling were too new for her to sort them out so easily. She thought even if she tried, she would still not be able to brush them aside, to dissect and theorize them like one of her experiments, until she could dismiss them into obscurity. She wasn't dealing with science; she was dealing with emotion, something that was not always well-defined.

She heard the sound of footsteps on the other side of the wall and decided it must be Tajik or one of the other stable hands seeing to the horses before retiring for the night. With a fond smile, Pandora thought it was so like the pleasant but aloof Syrian to make sure the animals were comfortable and safe before he took care of himself. He treated horses better than he treated most people, but it was only because his friendship and respect were not given easily and had to be earned. Tajik's standards were not easy to meet for some people. Pandora deliberated about going to tell him good night when she heard voices. Neither of them belonged to the family's stable master.

"What took you so long?" asked one voice that sounded so deep and dark Pandora felt a chill race up her spine.

She shook her head and dismissed the notion. It was impossible and wrong for her to assume someone was evil just by the sound of his voice. After all, Lord Islington had a very pleasant voice, but he was obnoxious. These men could be simply passing on their way to somewhere else and doing nothing amiss, although it was downright odd for them to be passing through the mews at this hour, unless they worked there. If it were guests from the ball, there was a livery hand available at the house to fetch their carriage for them. To her knowledge, the vehicles of the people attending the ball—at least this time—were not in her family's part of the mews.

"It was difficult for me to get away without attracting attention. There were a couple of antidotes there that I could not seem to elude," said the other voice.

It was cultured and pleasant…aristocratic, but Pandora could detect a subtle malice in it that made her feel more uneasy than on hearing the first, blatantly malignant speaker. That appeared to answer the rather unimportant question of what had become of Lady Ramsey and Lucy Cranston, if he had indeed been attending the ball.

"Never mind that. Did you get the information we needed?" asked the other impatiently.

"Yes, I got it."

"Well, what is it? We haven't got all night."

"He'll be coming in another four-and-a-half months, at the close of the Season. He's waiting until the first of September to give the stragglers time to leave for the country. He'll be returning to Edinburgh a fortnight later. As far as I know, he'll be traveling alone—no outriders. He plans this to be a hugger-mugger excursion. No one is supposed to know he's been to London. He must be trying to hide from his creditors again."

The other remained silent for a moment, a seemingly pleased silence. "Good. Very good," he said thoughtfully. "That will make our task easier. No witnesses that way. It will be stated that he disappeared from his home when in actuality we will meet him somewhere on the road between here and Edinburgh on his return trip. They'll be looking for clues where there aren't any. And when the time is right, we'll send our missive to the appropriate people. We'll be sitting in the nines then."

"What are we to do with the man once we get what we're after?" asked the one with the softer voice.

"That's simple. He will have a fatal mishap that was unavoidable."

"I can accept that," said the other agreeably and laughed malevolently, providing proof to Pandora that voices could be deceptive.

They spoke sibilantly with each other for a while longer, but Pandora was only able to catch bits and pieces of the conversation, and not enough of it for her to understand what was being said, just occasional words like *employ* and *travel*, which made no sense to her. They then went their separate ways, one returning to the ball, the other to some place called the Dog. Pandora sat back on the bench and drew an anxious breath. She really should tell her father what she had heard. He would want to know one of his guests was involved in a nefarious plot to kidnap someone from Edinburgh.

The question was who? She couldn't believe something like that was in the planning, let alone that it would actually be carried out. It sounded so gothic. Why would anyone want to kidnap someone? Who were those men? Perhaps if she went back to the ball she could discover the one who had returned. She didn't recognize his voice from those of the men she had met that evening, but he could have arrived late, or he could not have been introduced to her by her family. She was sure, however, that she would know who he was if she heard him speak again.

"Are you here to pout?" asked a voice so close to her ear that Pandora jumped in alarm and yelped.

She hadn't heard him come into the gazebo and sit down, so deep in thought had she been. She didn't think he was capable of being that quiet; there were few people she knew who could.

"Do you always sneak up on people and try to scare them to death?" she asked tartly, moving away from him on the bench, yet privately— unwillingly—relieved it had not been the criminals behind the wall. "Go away, Lord Islington. I came here to be alone."

"So you *did* come here to pout," said Islington, smiling amusedly with a soft chuckle.

"I did *not* come here to pout! That would imply I have something to pout about, and I do not. Aside from that, I *don't* pout. I came here to think!" defended Pandora angrily, made all the more irritated because she was trying to justify herself to this…boil on the backside of humanity.

His eyes widened in pretended astonishment. "Dodo came to think?"

"Don't call me that! Only my family calls me that, and you do not qualify," said Pandora coldly, rising from her seat to move away from him, folding her arms in front of herself protectively. "Leave me alone, Lord Islington. You're beginning to annoy me."

"Glamorgan sent me to make sure you were all right," said Islington, ignoring her request.

"You can go back and tell him that I'm fine, and I'll return to the ball when I'm ready," said Pandora stiffly, turning her back on him dismissively.

Islington walked behind her and spun her around angrily. *No one* dismissed him as if he were a servant, least of all this she-demon.

"Someone should tan your backside," he ground out. "You're spoiled and selfish and borné!"

"Petit trouduc!" spat Pandora.

She was trying to keep some form of ladylike propriety by not uttering the insult in English, but she really wanted to call him a lot worse than just an arsehole. That word did not even begin to cover her opinion of him. She *really* wanted him to leave her alone. She tried to twist free of his grasp and looked down at his hand with suppressed fury.

"If you want to keep your hand, you'll let me go," she warned softly, her gaze steady.

He grabbed her other arm in the same tight grip and smiled wickedly.

"You should be careful what insults you toss. As for letting you go, I don't think you're in a position to threaten anyone."

"You think not?" quizzed Pandora, raising her eyebrow with skeptical amusement. Lord Islington had no idea what he was letting himself in for when he made her angry; her family knew better.

"Who is holding whom?"

Pandora reacted to the taunt instinctively, unable to resist the challenge. She brought her arms up to grab the front of his coat and placed her foot on his midsection. Luckily, the skirt of her dress was full enough she could complete the movement, but the silk made her foot slip tenuously. She fell backwards as she ducked into a ball, exerting pressure with her foot on his stomach to flip Islington over her head and force him to release her as the air whooshed out of his lungs when he landed on his back. She scuttered into the far corner of the gazebo and stood up, straightening her gown and looking at him warily.

After a moment, once he managed to start breathing normally again, he stood and stalked toward her menacingly. That was when Pandora knew she had made a mistake. She looked around desperately for some way to escape without having to resort to more violence, but she had literally backed herself into a corner. He grabbed her arms again and towered over her wrathfully. She could break free and escape him, but there was something about his expression that told her if she tried, it wouldn't have pleasant results.

She shouldn't have flipped him. She should have remained calm and bided her time, but he had been purposely trying to rile her. Her family accused her of being short-tempered. Pandora had to agree with them, but they didn't accuse her of acting rashly. Yet this man had provoked her to do just that. She raised her eyes to look at him defiantly, ridiculously hoping all he wanted to do was *talk* about what she had just done. If her parents found out she had beaten one of their guests, she would be in for it.

"Apologize," he demanded in a quiet, barely pleasant tone.

"I will not!" croaked Pandora querulously.

He released one of her arms and grabbed a handful of her hair in a move that sent pins flying in several directions and surprised her with its swiftness.

Pandora sucked in her breath and bit down on her lip to keep from crying out. While she was quite sturdy, her one weakness was a tender scalp, something she and Maiyin got into no end of *discussions* about. She was tempted to acquiesce but decided not to give him the satisfaction. Pandora continued to look up at him spitefully, her eyes glittering from unshed tears. He brought his face closer to hers.

"I said apologize!" he hissed.

"Go swiftly and directly to hell!" she hissed back.

There was nothing he could do to drag an apology out of her now. Pandora might have considered it if he had been more polite, but his assault on her person completely ruined his chances. Besides, did he really think an apology *beaten* out of her would be sincere?

Islington jerked her head again, and as Pandora opened her mouth to cry out in pain he covered it with his own. It was not a pleasant kiss, this first kiss she ever experienced. It was brutal and punishing, as he had intended it to be. Pandora would have been surprised if she'd known it was just as punishing to him. He felt no pleasure in hurting her. He could taste the salt of her blood on his lips from the pressure of his mouth pushing the tender inside of her lips against her teeth, and he regretted it. He could feel her shaking, feel her struggling to break free, and he knew what he was doing was unforgivable. He had not intended to do it, but when she stood there pressed close to him, her chest heaving with anger, his mind ceased to work logically.

Pandora tried to get away, tried to make him let her go without having to cause him bodily harm, but the grip he had on her hair and arm held her immobile beneath the pressure of his kiss. She had expected him to retaliate but not in this way. She was too unsure of her feelings for him, and this brutal assault did nothing to settle the matter. Then to confound her even more, she felt his lips soften on hers, and his hold on her hair loosened. The once severe grip on her arm became a caress that slowly moved up to the side of her neck.

As the manner of his kiss changed so did Pandora's reaction to it. She felt a strange heat begin to curl in her stomach that made her quiver with anticipation. It was odd, but it was so pleasant. She knew that now, once his grip had relaxed, would be the time for her to get away from him, but she found she didn't want to go anywhere at the moment.

She could feel the coaxing touch of his tongue on her lips and parted them for its tantalizing examination of her mouth. Her hands' anxious clutching of his lapels relaxed, and her arms wound around his neck slowly, as if of their own accord. She swayed closer to him, the peaks of her breasts hardening as they brushed against his chest. She wanted more than she was getting, instinctively knowing there was much more.

Islington left off his exploration of her mouth and trailed his lips across her cheek to gently nip on one sensitive earlobe. Pandora gasped with pleasure and clutched his shoulders weakly. She could feel her knees beginning to weaken and knew his strength was the only thing holding her up. She knew she shouldn't be kissing him, shouldn't be letting him do this, but it was hard to resist. She felt alive and warm and indescribably content. She wondered why society thought it was such an awful thing, that it was something a woman was expected to suffer through; she found it to be quite exhilarating and pleasant and not in the least bit degrading.

He lifted her in his arms to carry her to one of the benches and sit down, nestling her onto his lap. She could feel his need for her pressed against her thigh, and she sighed with a sense of power over him, believing he couldn't dislike her if she could provoke him like that. She couldn't logically think of a reason why she wanted him to like her, why it mattered so much. All she could think was that she wanted his touch, wanted it like she'd never wanted anything before.

His lips burned a path down the smoothness of her throat to the edge of one breast exposed by the low bodice of her gown. She arched toward his touch, her hands clutching in his hair convulsively. She felt his hand lift the edge of her skirt and push it to her thighs, his fingertips lightly brushing against the silk of her stocking to sear her skin as if with a hot iron. She at first thought to push his hand away, but she couldn't resist the sensations his touch aroused.

His lips came back to hers with an ardent hunger she responded to with her own newly awakening passion. She felt him loosen the fastenings at the back of her gown, and the bodice dropped lower, exposing the soft fullness of her breasts beneath the filmy gauze of her chemise. He pulled the straps to that garment and her dress off her arms, and Pandora felt a gentle wind blow across the heated flesh of her exposed breasts. He cupped their fullness in his palms, and Pandora leaned toward his touch, a soft moan of pleasure escaping from the back of her throat as his thumbs brushed against her aroused nipples.

She smoothed her hands down the powerful wall of his chest, her pulse skipping a beat as she felt the racing thunder of his own heart beneath her palm. Oh, yes, he wanted her. The insistent pressure of his arousal against her thigh and his quickened heartbeat told her things women recognized instinctively—even the inexperienced ones like Pandora, things that made words superfluous. She unfastened the buttons of his coat and waistcoat and undid the complicated knot of his cravat, recognizing beneath all the folds that it was just a simple square. She released the ties at the neck of his shirt and pulled the front of it loose from his breeches, sighing from the purely tactile pleasure of running her fingers over the smooth, well-muscled expanse of flesh it allowed her to access.

He eased her back onto the cushion and bent over her, drawing the peak of one breast into his mouth. Pandora gasped breathlessly and arched toward him, the heat in her stomach tightening almost painfully. She felt as if she would explode from the tension, the feeling of unquenched need. She wasn't exactly sure what it was she needed but felt certain it was something only he could give her, and she didn't think she could wait much longer for it.

He shifted until the length of his body was stretched out above her, settled between her thighs, his weight resting on his powerful arms. Pandora was made even more aware of his erection, the only barrier separating them being the material of his trousers. She finished pulling his shirt loose from his waistband and ran her hands over the muscles of his back, lightly raking her nails over it and causing him to moan in pleasure. Pandora lifted one of her legs to smooth it against his and moved herself against him with impatience.

Islington raised his head from her breast to look at her features outlined by the dim gaslight of the lamps on the mews wall sifting through the bushes and latticework of the gazebo. He should remember she wasn't one of the common doxies found in a brothel, not even one of the slightly more respectable courtesans, that she was the innocent daughter of a duke and practically a stranger.

He should stop before he couldn't, before he compromised her further, but she felt so good beneath him. He couldn't remember a time in all his nearly twenty-seven years when he had felt such an uncontrollable longing to possess something. The soft, exotic scent of her perfume and the satiny smoothness of her skin made him ache for her with a consuming need. Her kiss-swollen lips called out to him, the blatant desire in her eyes like the song of a siren before she lured a sailor to his death on the rocks. And Islington could so easily, willingly, drown there.

Pandora pulled his head to hers hungrily, her lips joining to his with an intensity that made them both moan, staving off the hesitation Islington felt for just a little longer. He ran his hand up her thigh slowly, caressing its inner softness just beneath its juncture. He moved higher until his hand cupped her, and Pandora quivered liquidly. He ran his fingers through the springy curls, gently teasing her until she arched toward him mindlessly, the breath catching in her throat.

"Lord Islington, please," she gasped almost inarticulately.

"Please what?" asked Islington as he bent his head to tease the tip of one breast, his tongue outlining its aroused hardness until Pandora whimpered in ecstasy.

"I hurt," she whispered hoarsely.

"Do you want me?" he asked with an almost condescending pleasure. Pandora nodded her head pleadingly. "Say it." She looked at him hesitantly, not sure she should admit it aloud. He nipped gently on her neck, biting on one ear sensually.

"I want you, Theo," she whispered longingly, raising her head to meet his passionate kiss with an equal ardor.

There was something inside him that stirred excitedly at the way she said his name, and Islington could no longer resist the temptation she so innocently yet willingly offered.

As they continued their feverish kiss, Islington became aware of an insistent calling from somewhere in the garden. It was Dorian, and he was looking for them. That voice was like a splash of cold water to Islington, and real awareness of what he was doing dawned on him. *What had he almost done?*

Pandora felt an alarmed surprise when he broke their embrace and moved away from her. She opened her eyes in confusion and raised herself up on her elbows to see him straightening his clothes with efficient swiftness. She could hear her brother's voice, but it didn't register in her mind with any importance. Islington saw that she still lay there half-naked, her expression one of utter bemusement, and he couldn't believe he had lost so much control of himself.

"God forgive me for what I almost did," he muttered darkly.

Pandora jerked as if she had been slapped and sat up on the bench to move as far away from him as she possibly could. She began straightening her dress with trembling hands, trying to smooth the creases in the skirt. It was hopeless. Her hands shook so violently she couldn't fasten the back of her bodice. Islington saw she was still not finished. Dorian would be to the gazebo any moment. Islington walked over to her.

"Here, let me," he said. He reached out a hand to turn her back to him, but she flinched away from his touch.

"Don't *touch* me!" she hissed.

"Don't be a fool!" he sighed impatiently. "Your brother will be here soon, and I don't want him to see you like this."

Pandora wanted to refuse, was tempted to refuse, but she realized she couldn't do it on her own, and she didn't want Dorian to see her like this either. She sighed resignedly and turned to let Islington begin to do the fastenings.

"What's the matter, Lord Islington, are you afraid my brother will see me like this and call you out? Or are you worried my father will force you to marry me?" she asked coldly.

"Don't be foolish. In the first instance, my friendship with your brother is too valuable to me for it to be ruined because of *you*. In the second, I wouldn't marry you if the Prince Regent commanded it."

Pandora felt tears sting her eyes and was glad her back was turned. She would never let him know how much those words hurt her. How could she be so foolish to think she meant anything to him? He was a complete stranger, and it was rather simpleminded and naïve to believe something like that could happen so soon. *Oh, stupid, stupid,* stupid! she berated herself. *You were just a warm body, and at the last minute he decided he wanted anyone but you after all. He was using you, punishing you for what you did! But he wanted me,* she tried to reason with herself. *No, he didn't; he just wanted* someone! *You happened to be handy!*

Pandora rubbed the back of a hand over her face to wipe away the tears that escaped from her eyes. She wouldn't let him see how much he had wounded her. If he could treat what had almost happened as nothing, she would do the same, and she would try to make sure it never happened again.

She tried to straighten her hair as Islington finished fastening her dress, but it was useless. Maiyin's handiwork was a ruin. Pandora brought a hand to her lips worriedly and flinched when her fingers touched her tender bottom lip, cut by Islington's first bruising kiss. She could see a small amount of blood on her fingers in the dim lamplight. Funny, she hadn't really felt it. No matter, it gave her an idea for covering her disheveled appearance.

"Give me your cravat, please," she said calmly, turning to look at Islington and holding out her hand.

"Why?" he asked suspiciously, his hands stilling as he was reaching up to retie it after fastening her dress.

"There is no possible way for me to fix my hair back the way it was, and my lip is bleeding. If you intend to fully protect your worthless hide, you'll give me your cravat and go along with whatever I say happened," said Pandora coldly, still holding out her hand to him.

He looked as if he were about to refuse, but Islington removed the starched piece of linen and gave it to Pandora. She promptly folded it into a neat little square and placed it against her bleeding lip. Islington was about to protest, but her cold look silenced him…almost.

"If I had known that's what you were going to use it for, I would have given you my handkerchief."

Pandora scoffed unbecomingly and glared at him.

"Stow it, Lord Bardsey. One piece of linen is as good as another. Besides, I don't think you could have gotten it back to its perfect form without the help of your valet anyhow. You can consider this payment for making me lose the race in the park yesterday."

Islington took her arm in a tight grip that Pandora knew would leave marks. Although it hurt, it was so much the better he became so disgusted with her he wouldn't want to come near her because she wasn't sure she could keep her vow to herself that she would never let him touch her again.

"So I'm just part of another wager?" he asked coldly.

Pandora gave him a sidelong glance she hoped was slightly amused and disdainful. She wouldn't let him know he had astonishingly somehow managed to become part of something more than that.

"Perhaps," she said calmly. His grip tightened, and Pandora tilted her head regally. "Go ahead," she said tauntingly, "leave a quite unattractive bruise. It will make what I tell Dorian all the more believable."

Islington snarled angrily and released her. He stalked away and then turned back to face her with an arctic glare. He felt like strangling her but knew he wouldn't have enough time to do it and hide the body before her brother arrived. He also still felt like kissing her, and he had to clench his hands at his sides to resist reaching out for her.

"And what, exactly, do you plan to tell him?" he asked darkly, convinced it was something hopelessly doomed to fail.

"I fell," said Pandora simply, putting on her gloves again and adjusting them with fingers that still shook slightly. "After I came outside to get some fresh air, I decided to take a stroll through the garden. Clumsy fool that I am, I tripped on the hem of my dress here in the gazebo, fell, and busted my lip on the edge of the bench. *Trustworthy* friend that you are, you came at the behest of my brother to see how I fared and found me here, in the gazebo, bleeding like a stuck pig and bawling my eyes out because my hair was ruined, making it impossible for me to return to my ball." She gave him a cool stare that dared him to argue. "I think it sounds truthful, don't you?"

Chapter Four

Pandora was miserable. For the first time in her life she was keeping a secret from everyone in her family. She was afraid to trust even Psyche with what had happened almost two weeks past. Although her family loved her and would forgive her almost anything, Pandora knew they would view her lovemaking with Lord Islington as an unpardonable sin. It was one thing to dye all her father's new linen shirts blue when she was fourteen years old, but it was quite another to be dallying with a complete stranger she thought she couldn't stand the sight of. She couldn't tell anyone, and it was eating her up.

They had all believed her story of falling and busting her lip, making her feel all the more wretched for them being so trusting of her, even after all her farfetched tales.

Dorian had found her in the gazebo with Islington bent over her attentively, his consoling pats on her back as false as the ones had been when she had choked on the punch. But the tears she cried had been all too real. It hadn't taken much dramatic ability on her part to let the scalding tears flow down her cheeks. When Dorian had hugged her, trying to comfort her, Islington had given her a disgusted sneer over her brother's shoulder, never guessing he had been the cause of what he thought were crocodile tears. He had taken his leave soon after that, unable to bear the sight of her. Islington had no reason to remain anyhow; after all, he'd only been seeing to his friend's sister and had no part in her mishap. If Pandora hadn't ached so much inside, she would have laughed over the Grecian comedy of it.

Her family had been supportive and sympathetic. She had missed most of her debut. That was remedied a week later when she and Psyche went to Almack's. No one was considered properly introduced unless seen there and given acceptance from Lady Jersey. Pandora went farther than that by making the matron and her cronies giggle like schoolgirls. Invitations had been steadily arriving since then. Pandora and Psyche both attended the functions, but Pandora's heart wasn't into enjoying a London season she'd never wanted and wanted even less since her interlude with Islington.

She'd seen him twice since then. At the first, he was formally polite, a beautiful brunette on his arm for most of the night. Pandora had felt a peculiar stab of jealousy. He wouldn't have said anything to Pandora had her companion been someone other than Dorian. She managed to muddle through the conversation with a semblance of dignity and grace, owning up to her promise that she would forget what had happened, that she would be civil. She thought there was a questioning light in his eyes when he noticed her withdrawn quietness, but she dismissed it to the illumination in the alcove where she and Dorian had met him. She had been stupid once to believe he felt something for her; she would not be so again. At least, she tried to tell herself that…repeatedly.

The second occasion was tonight. Her family was attending a ball held by the Earl of Lundey to celebrate the upcoming marriage between his son, Viscount Drake, and Miss Lilane (known to friends as Lilly) Manson. Pandora was suffering from a migraine earlier and was tempted to stay home, but it cleared an hour before they were to leave. She decided to attend because the Lundeys were very close friends. Drake was one of Myron's best friends, and Lilly was Arachne's best friend. Pandora was there only an hour before the headache returned much worse than before.

The affianced pair looked very attractive and happy together. Lilly was petite and pretty with wheat blonde hair and dark blue eyes. She looked very much like society's epitome of genteel womanhood. Lord Drake was equally handsome with black hair and hazel eyes that were more green than brown, and he towered over his prospective bride by at least a foot. They spent much of the time standing near each other at one end of the ball room receiving congratulations from their guests. When Pandora offered hers, she managed to speak without her headache making it sound too illogical.

As usual, Pandora's dance card was full. Dorian had penciled in a slot for a waltz, and as she finished a set with one partner, she went to sit in one of the available chairs while waiting for him. She sat massaging her temple, wishing she had stayed in bed. When Dorian finally came, Pandora would tell him to take her home without delay. She was miserable.

Someone's slight cough made her raise her head, and her look of polite expectance slowly chilled. It was Lord Islington.

Pandora knew he was attending the ball. She had seen him arrive with the same brunette, but there had been no reason to speak to him. They had nodded to each other stiffly and went about their business. Pandora had been relieved that would be the extent of it. And now here he stood.

"Lord Islington," she stated neutrally.

"Lady Pandora."

"Is there something you want?"

"I believe this dance is mine."

Pandora blinked in surprise. Her headache was dulling her senses, and for a moment she was at a loss for words.

"No, I don't think so," she finally stated woodenly. "This dance belongs to my brother. Besides, in order for this dance or any other dance to be yours, your name has to be on my card, and it is not."

"Yes, it is. Would you care to look?" he asked dourly.

Pandora lifted her wrist and looked at the card, trying with some difficulty to focus her eyes. On the line for the waltz, Dorian had written *Vis. Islington.* She was going to kill him, plain and simple. She was going to slow roast him over an open fire…if she ever managed to get rid of her accursed headache.

"But—" she began dully.

"I don't like this any more than you do, so let's just get it over with," said Islington flatly.

He held out his hand to her, and Pandora reluctantly took it to let him lead her onto the floor as the waltz began.

Pandora kept her gaze averted from him, looking at anything—the ceiling, the wall, other couples—except his face. She didn't want to see his expression of distaste. She should have refused to dance with him and could not understand why she hadn't. The dull throbbing at the base of her neck gave her a hint, and the turns of the dance were making her overly dizzy. She wanted to go home and lie down.

She could feel the warmth of his hand on her back, and her face colored as she remembered his caresses. His embrace was loose but close, and Pandora could feel his breath on her forehead, teasing the wispy curls that rested there. She didn't want to look up at him, but something told her that she should. Her breath caught in her throat on that glance because she surprised him and saw his unguarded expression. It quickly changed to one of neutrality, but there was something there when she first raised her head. She wanted to say tenderness, but that was impossible. It had to be the light.

"You dance well," he said conversationally, feeling her eye contact required it of him.

"Thank you, so do you," she replied in the same tone.

"Have you been enjoying the Season?"

"Yes, thank you," she replied shortly.

Why wouldn't he be quiet? She would much rather they finish the dance in silence, but the tune was only half over.

"Why did Dorian put your name on my card?"

The question seemed to surprise him, and he refrained from answering until they had completed a difficult turn.

"He seems to be under the impression that we dislike each other."

Pandora scoffed. "I wonder what gave him such a preposterous idea," she said sarcastically.

"He believes we got off on the wrong foot," continued Islington, ignoring her sarcasm, although his grip did tighten somewhat.

"So he thought making us dance a *waltz* together would change that?" asked Pandora disbelievingly.

"Apparently," stated Islington flatly, not any more convinced of it doing that than Pandora.

"Well, we do seem to be behaving civilly for the moment, but I don't believe we'll be bosom chums…ever," said Pandora airily.

"No, I don't think we shall."

They came near a set of chairs near one wall and Pandora saw Lord Islington's companion watching them curiously.

"Will your friend not be upset for you not dancing with her?"

"My *friend* could care less with whom I dance." Pandora raised a skeptical eyebrow. The girl seemed *quite* interested. "She's my sister."

"Oh," said Pandora dully.

"You wouldn't be jealous, would you?"

"Whyever would I be jealous, Lord Islington?"

He pulled her even closer, and Pandora felt the tips of her breasts brush his chest. She colored hotly at his silent reminder, and she struggled to put more space between them again. He held her firmly, and Pandora knew she couldn't break free without causing a scene.

"That was a mistake, and you should be ashamed of yourself for bringing it up. You, my lord, are no gentleman," she said coldly.

Islington chuckled lowly and smoothed his hand across her back in a caress. He leaned close to speak quietly in her ear, and Pandora felt a familiar tingle at his nearness.

"Then I suppose we are even because you, m'dear, are no lady."

Pandora compressed her lips angrily and stomped on his instep, making it seem as if it were a misstep in her dancing.

"Oh, pardon me," she said tartly.

"You little minx!" he grated.

"Please, let's not resort to name-calling, Lord Islington," she said dryly. "I could insult you in twenty different languages or more, but I have a headache. I put that out of my mind some time ago, and you'd be wise to do the same. It must have meant more to you than it did to me since you seem intent on bringing it up. While I found it titillating, I don't think anyone else would, so let's just not have another word on the subject, shall we?"

"Fine," he bit out between clenched teeth.

They looked away from each other then with tight expressions and finished the dance in silence. When it was over, Islington promptly released her and turned his back with a curt nod. Pandora sighed with relief and put a hand to her throbbing head. It was time to go home.

She tried to locate one of her brothers or her father to arrange her return home, but she was unable to find them in the crush of well-wishers. In the end, she went to the garden and sat down by a beautiful Rococo fountain decorated with nymphs and charging stallions.

The fresh air helped her head somewhat. The little lace and linen square Maiyin had shoved into her reticule dipped in the cold water of the fountain and ran across her forehead also seemed to help ease the throbbing pain she felt behind her eyes and at the back of her neck. She still wanted to go home. The best thing was to have Keung stick needles in her skin at certain points in a process called *zhēnjiŭ* to alleviate the pain.

The next best thing was a series of exercises Keung had taught her to help concentrate her mind and diminish the pain by focusing on something else—basically nothing. Usually, they only worked if she did them before her headache got to the point it now was, but she was willing to try anything. The problem was that they were undignified to perform in a dress and certainly not in public. After several more minutes of the continuous throbbing pain, Pandora decided to solve the public problem by finding a more secluded spot in the garden. She hoped if the exercises didn't completely alleviate the pain, perhaps they would at least lessen it enough to let her find her family.

It wasn't difficult to find a private place in the garden. After following a path for several yards, she found a small courtyard with a bench enclosed by tall hedges. It was perfect. There was only one entrance, which could be easily missed unless searched for in the dark. It was just large enough, and the full moon provided the only light she needed. With just a little hesitation, she removed her dress and carefully laid it on the bench.

Standing only in her undergarments, she took several deep breaths and began the slow, fluid movements. She often did them at other times besides for the remedial properties for her migraines because the exercises required balance and endurance, toning the muscles and improving coordination. Keung had taught everyone in the family, and Pandora, Psyche and their brothers and sisters often did them together, looking like a troupe of ballet dancers performing to no music.

Her mind floated in a void of silence, yet she was aware of her surroundings with increased clarity. She could hear small creatures scampering in the bushes and across the gravel of the path. She heard the cry of a nighthawk as it captured its prey, the hooting of an owl on a distant tree branch. The sounds did not distract her but blended to soothe her and ease the tension in her head.

At the sound of gravel being crushed by human feet, she stopped mid-motion, her arms raised, her leg lifted in front of her and bent at the knee. Someone was coming down the path. She scampered to the bench and slid into her dress, doing the fastenings swiftly. She was tempted to leave but decided to stay, hoping whoever it was would miss the entrance. She had no such luck. A darker shadow separated from the entrance and moved toward where she was seated on the bench.

"Do you often wander off to secluded spots in gardens by yourself?" asked a mocking, familiar voice.

"Why should it matter to you?" asked Pandora coldly, wishing it were anyone but Islington. She didn't want to see him anymore.

"Because it isn't safe for unprotected females to be strolling around in the dark," said Islington, taking a seat beside her on the bench.

"I can take care of myself, thank you," said Pandora stiffly.

"If you're alluding to the flip you gave me in the gazebo, that was only luck."

"You think so?" quizzed Pandora dully, her head beginning to throb again. Had it not ached so terribly, she might have been tempted to prove to him conclusively that luck had nothing to do with it.

She had thought they weren't going to discuss that night anymore, but it seemed to be stuck in his craw. She didn't want to argue with him; she didn't want to argue with anyone. All she wanted to do was go home. And now here he sat, determined to start a quarrel her brain wasn't going to let her keep up with. She couldn't understand why he seemed to be continuously dwelling on what had happened in the gazebo. She still hadn't forgotten about it either and doubted she ever would, but at least she had the decency to keep her thoughts about the incident to herself. She tried to concentrate on his words.

"Of course it was. If not, why didn't you break free when I grabbed you the second time?" He waved his hand in the air to stop her from replying (not that she was going to). "Oh, yes, that was a prelude to helping you settle a wager with Lady Psyche. How could I forget?" he asked himself cynically. "By the way, I must commend you on your acting ability. You had me *quite* convinced, and those tears for Glamorgan at the end of all of it...." He kissed his fingers to the air. "*Magnifique.* I almost thought they were real."

Pandora massaged her throbbing temple and tried to sort the muddled thoughts her headache was causing to jumble in her head. He thought it had *all* been an act? The need? The passion? He thought she would have given herself to him just to win a wager? He thought she would purposely provoke his anger on a bet? To what end? And even if she had, why would she have done so without witnesses? She closed her eyes and tried to clear her head, but the pounding seemed to have increased, the good done by her exercises already gone.

"So silent, Dodo? Not going to compliment yourself on a job well done?" he asked mockingly.

Pandora stood up and began backing toward the exit, shaking her head and massaging her temples in confusion. She couldn't think. Her head was in agony. Had she felt better, she would have already slapped the smug expression from his face. She didn't know what was wrong with her. Inside she was livid, something urged her to violence, but her body refused to act.

"I told you not to call me that," she said haltingly, her tone neither forceful nor even slightly argumentative.

Her vision blurred when she tried to focus on anything specific, and a white shaft of pain shot through her skull with swift regularity. She had the feeling she was going to be violently ill if she didn't escape from this man and his cruel jibes.

"I do what I please," said Islington flatly. He watched her actions and laughed mockingly. "Come now, *Lady* Pandora, surely you're not going to escape without thrusting at least one little barb. No cursing? No insults? You surprise me," he said in feigned reproach.

Pandora held up a wavering hand toward him to try and silence him. Where was that blasted exit? She had to get away from him.

"You know, I believe I'll have to see if Lady Psyche performs as well as you do. They say identical twins are so very much alike."

Pandora managed to glare at him violently. "Don't you *dare* touch her!" she hissed venomously.

He laughed amusedly. "Not jealous by any chance, are you?"

"You *bloody* bastard!" she spat.

He rose from the bench with the fluid-like grace of a cat and grabbed her upper arms tightly.

"*Déjà vu*, m'dear?" he asked silkily.

He had seen her leaving her seat by the fountain through one of the open doors and had been unable to resist following her. He couldn't understand why he had wanted to. Their waltz had been a minor debacle that should not be having a second act, but here they were. This scene was quite unpleasant. Islington looked at her coldly. She seemed pale, but he dismissed it to the light. She was quite stunning in the deep rose velvet gown trimmed in burgundy satin rosettes, but then she was always so very beautiful. He was still curious why she hadn't reacted to his taunts until he mentioned Psyche.

"Are you going to apologize?" he asked harshly, giving her a rough shake that snapped her head on her neck. She cried out in pain and tried to break free of his grasp.

"I'm sorry!" she choked. Her head hurt. "Please, leave me alone," she begged in a cracked whisper, tears beginning to roll down her cheeks.

She felt all the more frustrated and miserable because she couldn't seem to control anything about her body. She couldn't understand why she couldn't make herself slap him or maim him somehow. She didn't want to be crying, and she didn't want to be here arguing with him. Yet here she stood, and she could not make herself *leave.*

"An apology and a please," he said mildly. "There may be hope for you yet, but the tears are unnecessary."

"*What?*" she asked disjointedly. Why wouldn't he leave her alone?

"Don't waste your talent," he said savagely, giving her yet another harsh shake.

Pandora whimpered in pain, her knees weakening. She couldn't stand up anymore. She wanted this cruel man to go away and leave her alone. She wanted her papa. She wanted to go home. She wanted more than anything to make this feeling in her skull as if it were being ripped apart to go away. She sagged in Islington's grip and almost fell.

"Fainting won't help you either," he said coldly. "I accepted your apology without all these frills. Now, get up."

Pandora raised her head weakly and tried to focus on his face. "Please, help me," she whispered imploringly.

"You certainly need help," said Islington darkly.

"My head," she entreated.

"You're definitely not right there," he continued cruelly, unmindful of her pallor and the boneless way she strained in his arms, her weight so slight he didn't even notice.

"Please, I'm not acting," she whimpered. "Get my father, please," she choked. *"Please!"*

The appeal in her voice finally reached him, and he really looked at her. What he saw made his heart go into his throat in alarm. Her face had turned so pale it could have easily matched the color of his shirt. The skin beneath his hands felt clammy and cold to his touch. She was literally hanging in his arms, the cruel grip he maintained on her the only thing preventing her from collapsing in a heap at his feet.

He lifted her in his arms to carry her to the bench and raised a limp wrist to feel for her pulse. He caught a thready, rapid flutter beneath his fingers and swore softly under his breath. Why hadn't he listened to her? He had been too bent on punishing her for something that was not her fault. He hugged her tightly and pressed a gentle kiss on her forehead.

"Oh, God, I'm so sorry, Pandora," he sighed.

"Please. Help me," she whispered weakly, trying to clutch his lapel. "Please, help me. My head," she whimpered.

He cradled her limp form against his chest and went to the exit of the courtyard, surprising a young couple strolling down the path.

"Terribly sorry. Excuse me," he muttered, completely ignoring their astonished gazes and heading toward the house purposefully.

Pandora raised her head to look at his face, but it was a blur. She tried not to think about anything, and it made her head hurt worse when she did, but she couldn't help feeling a little desolate that he thought so little of her. She had never meant him to believe what had happened between them had been part of a wager; she would never have done anything so low for any kind of stakes. Had she behaved so hatefully toward him on the few occasions they had met for him to believe she would be so despicable?

She knew she often exaggerated the truth and frequently indulged in practical jokes, but she never purposely set out to harm anyone; she had never played with someone's emotions. Most often her tales were told and pranks played to make someone happy. Even the prank with the honey and feathers for Dorian served a purpose. He had been upset over the death of his favorite mount after it had irreparably broken its leg and had to be put down. He had been in the doldrums for weeks.

She'd never lied to save herself from punishment...until the night in the gazebo. She couldn't even use the excuse of trying to save Lord Islington for that. She could have and should have at least told Psyche the truth of it, and the longer she waited the worse she felt. She wouldn't have lied if it had not been for Islington. Now he thought every word she spoke was false, every action for another, hidden purpose.

She raised a weak hand and placed it on his shoulder, hoping it would help focus her gaze in that direction. She was tired of fighting. All she wanted to do was lie down somewhere and let someone shoot her. She wanted to be put out of her misery.

"I'm sorry you didn't believe me," she whispered.

Islington looked at her ashen features and compressed his lips grimly. She definitely wasn't feeling well. She was apologizing for everything when usually she was sorry for nothing. He couldn't help wondering with a shudder what would have happened to her had she not finally convinced him she was truly ill, had he left her in the courtyard as he had intended to do.

Could he really place all the blame on Pandora for his being so distrustful of her? Aside from the untruth she had told to protect both of them, he had never caught her in a lie, even though Dorian had said she was capable. And what exactly had been the wager between her and Psyche that he had been a part of? Had he been so quick to misjudge her because she didn't flutter and simper like most females, because she was strong-willed and independent and had definite thoughts of her own that didn't include doing what he wanted?

"You don't like me very much," stated Pandora sadly with a sniffle.

She felt so dizzy; the pain in her head was a constant throbbing. She closed her eyes and leaned her head against his chest, wishing this wasn't happening. She could hear the soft thud of his heart beneath her ear, and it began to echo in her head like a cannon.

"I don't like *you* very much either," she muttered. "You're always laughing at me and making me feel like a baby. You're always bothering me and insulting me. You treat me as if I'm one step away from being gutter trash, and you don't even *know* me."

"Shush," whispered Islington, brushing his lips against her forehead.

"You're as bad as those two men I heard talking about kidnapping someone from Edinburgh."

Islington skipped a step then looked down at her sweat-beaded face and decided she was delirious. She could not be serious.

They were nearing the back of the house, already skirting the fountain, coming into the shadows cast by the lights from inside. He didn't want to take her into the ballroom and cause a scene, so he scanned the back wall until he found a set of doors leading to another room and went for them.

"I think you should go to sleep, Pandora."

"How can I when there're these little armies of men running 'round in my head shooting guns at my eardrums and firing cannons against my skull? Why should I listen to you anyhow?" she complained peevishly. "Lord Islington?"

"Hmm?" he said absentmindedly, going up the steps to the set of doors he had spotted.

"I think I'm going to throw up," she said feebly, and then she did.

She managed to turn her head and avoid spilling her stomach onto herself and Islington, but it left an unsightly puddle on the terrace of Lord Lundey's home. Islington would attend to that after he found Pandora's parents or one of her brothers.

He carried her through the doors and laid her down on a dark leather couch facing them. It appeared to be the earl's study. Islington removed his coat to use as a pillow for her head and removed his cravat and wet it with some water from a nearby pitcher as a compress for her forehead. He then prepared to leave the room.

"Lord Islington?" whispered Pandora. He came around the back of the couch to sit beside her and brushed some wisps of hair from the wet cloth on her forehead. "Can you turn down the lamps? The light hurts my eyes."

He reached over her head and dimmed the already weak lamp situated on the table, the only light on in the room. Pandora closed her eyes and looked as if she were resting, and Islington once again prepared to leave. He reached the door and had his hand on the knob when she spoke again.

"Lord Islington?"

"Yes, Lady Pandora?" he sighed. He would never be able to get her family and their physician to tend to her if she didn't let him go.

"Why can't you be nice?" she asked wistfully. Islington looked at her thoughtfully for a moment then left the room.

Pandora lay on the couch with her eyes closed, willing the pain to stop. She had never had a headache this bad develop so quickly. It felt like someone was tightening her skull in a vice. Even the slightest sound was amplified to a painful pitch. She hoped her father sent for Keung before he even tried to move her.

She must have dozed off because she was awakened by the sound of two voices arguing in heated, sibilant tones not far from where she lay. Her head still pounded, and she was tempted to tell the two men not to whisper so loudly when it occurred to her that they didn't even know she was in the room. She decided to lie still and pretend she wasn't there. Maybe if she did they wouldn't find her on the couch and think she was eavesdropping. They would leave when her family arrived, hopefully before, and would be none the wiser.

She felt a chill work its way up her spine when she realized who it was. She didn't want to believe it was actually the same men, but there was no mistaking the evil accents of the voices. She prayed more than ever that they didn't find out she was there. It was the two men from behind the wall.

Pandora tried to tell her father what she had overheard, but he tut-tutted and said she must have been mistaken. No matter how much railing Pandora did, how many family members she told, no one believed her. Persephone had rolled on the floor in a fit of giggles, thinking it the grandest tale she had ever heard.

Pandora began to doubt her own sanity. Surely they could recognize when she was serious, that she wouldn't make up a story about something as horrible as kidnapping. But then Pandora began to reason that she often told her fabrications with a straight face; her ability to make people believe the fiction was one of her personal prides. She had never invented a story about kidnapping, though, and never about someone other than a relative.

Her head was in agony. She couldn't think straight. Like Islington, she thought she was becoming delirious. It wasn't possible that she was hearing another conversation between the same two men about the same crime. If her head wasn't hurting, she would have risked looking over the top of the couch to see who they were. Maybe if she could put names to at least one of the voices, people would begin to believe she wasn't lying. But her head hurt so much she couldn't see straight, and whenever she tried to move, the throbbing in her skull increased. She wouldn't be able to unmask the criminals. She would have to be satisfied with stagging another of their conversations.

"I don't think we should do it," said the aristocrat.

"And I tell you we have no choice!" spat the other. "He has become a liability. If he should tell everything he knows to the authorities as he threatens, our schedule—our whole plan—could be put in jeopardy. He must be eliminated...quickly," he said with finality.

"But he doesn't know that much!" protested the aristocrat.

"He knows who we are," reasoned the other.

"I tell you I don't like it!" hissed the aristocrat worriedly. "We can't do it right now; it could arouse suspicion."

"I don't like it either, but it must be done. If he hadn't fallen into his inheritance, he would have been with us to the end. Now that he's got his nest egg, he doesn't need us. A desperate man has no conscience, but a secure man is a principled man."

Pandora thought for a moment in confusion. Were they talking about the man they intended to kidnap, or was there another party involved in the conspiracy? *Curse this blasted headache! I can't think practically with a war going on in my skull.* She heard the aristocrat sigh resignedly.

"Very well, Castleton, we'll do it your way. Let us just be thankful no one can link us with Bertram Batts."

Who the deuce was that? Is it the one they plan to eliminate (which probably means kill*)* or is it the one they intend to kidnap? Or to confound Pandora even more, were they the same? She had to quit listening to these two before she went crackbrained. She consoled herself with the thought that she now knew one of their names.

The two continued to hiss at each other, but Pandora was in too much pain to listen or to care, no matter if it might have helped identify them or not. She wished her parents would come. She was nauseous again. If the two men didn't leave soon, they would discover her presence in an unpleasant manner. Pandora took deep breaths to control her stomach, but her body had been rebelling all evening, and she didn't think she would be able to contain herself much longer.

She almost released a sigh of relief when the two men parted ways but quickly stifled it when she heard one of them coming toward the couch. Pandora scrunched her eyes closed and held her breath, waiting for a violent outburst that never came. She heard the latch on the double doors click and opened her eyes to see a tall, dark figure moving through them to go outside to the terrace. It would have been a perfect exit after the doors whispered closed had the malefactor seen Pandora's pool of vomit on the flagstones. But he did not, so he lost his footing and fell with a loud grunt. Pandora heard several muttered expletives, but all was soon silent again.

Pandora had been unable to see his face, but he was tall, rail thin, and had a pronounced stoop. Unfortunately, that could match the description of half the male population. From the smell of him (a strong base of garlic, plenty of stale liquor and cigar smoke, and a hint of wood smoke) Pandora determined he was Castleton. She knew of no man of high society who would smell like that in public if he could help it.

Pandora began to massage her temples, knowing it wouldn't help but needing to think. If she told her father what she heard, would he now believe her? She had the hopeless feeling he wouldn't. She found herself uselessly wishing she had never played a practical joke, never told a fib. Until now, she'd never had cause to regret her actions. This self-doubt would do her no good, but she couldn't seem to break free of it.

She put a hand over her eyes and shook her head. She needed her family here—anyone—to stop her from thinking. She thought too much when she was alone, and the thoughts she was having were leading nowhere. The more she used her brain, the more it hurt, and it already hurt too much for what she was thinking to make any sense.

The pain in her head was radiating down her neck to her back. She could barely move, and when she did it put her in acute agony. As time progressed, she had the feeling this was much worse than a migraine. She dozed off hoping she would soon begin to feel better.

"Pandora, darling," called a voice that seemed far away.

Pandora tried to turn her head toward the sound, but she whimpered as a sharp pain traveled down her neck to make the action impossible.

"Papà?" she whispered, "I can't move my neck. It hurts." She tried to focus her eyes on the fuzzy blur of her father's face. "I feel so dreadful."

After that, Pandora lost recognition of reality. She didn't know when her father lifted her in his arms with her worried mother and siblings gathered around him and carried her to the family's carriage. She wasn't aware the doctor came to visit and told her distraught parents that she had meningitis. She didn't hear Maiyin's piteous weeping. She would regain consciousness for a few minutes to see a family member or her maid bent over her applying a soothing ice pack to her head and neck, but she didn't understand why. They would wake her to pour a tasteless broth or foul-tasting medicine down her throat, but she didn't know why. At one moment of lucid thought, she wondered why they were making such a fuss over a migraine, why they didn't have Keung apply *zhēnjiŭ*.

She once awoke to see Dorian standing over her bed looking down at her with an expression more serious than usual.

"Brother Dorian, you shouldn't frown like that. I've heard of people's faces freezing. I'd much prefer to see yours frozen into a smile." She swallowed a dry lump in her throat and gave him a weak grin. Her forehead creased, and she tried to focus on his face again. "I haven't done anything bad, have I?" she asked worriedly. She couldn't remember.

He sat on the edge of the bed and kissed her cheek. "No, you haven't done anything wrong."

"Then you are being much too serious," chided Pandora in a cracked whisper. "Can I have some water please?" She knew she should get it herself, but she couldn't seem to move.

Dorian reached for a glass on her night table and lifted her head for her to drink. After she finished, she lay back against the pillows and closed her eyes tiredly, her forehead wrinkled with pain and confusion.

"Dorian, why do I feel so terrible? I feel as if I've gone ten rounds with a boxer and tried to swim the Channel after losing."

"You're sick, Dodo," said Dorian softly, brushing hair off her forehead.

"I'll be over this headache in no time. I'll be fine," she assured him. "But you should smile more. It's so much more fun than frowning, and you'll see the more you do it, the easier it is." Pandora drifted back to sleep.

Dorian sat watching her for a few minutes and swallowed an emotional lump in his throat, wiping a hand over his eyes. He rose and took a seat across from the other man in the room. Neither spoke for some time, both looking at the pathetic figure in the bed. Pandora had been ill for three days. The words she said to Dorian were the only lucid ones she'd uttered in all that time. She was losing weight from the lack of solid food, and there were dark circles under her eyes from lack of restful sleep. Keung *had* applied *zhēnjiŭ* to ease her discomfort without the use of addictive narcotics, but even now her forehead was creased with pain. The family's physician had given them the fairly definite assessment that she wasn't going to live, and the best they could do was make her comfortable for the remaining time she had.

"She doesn't even realize how unwell she is," said Dorian dully.

"Perhaps that's for the best," replied Islington gravely.

"If she dies, I don't know what I'll do," groaned Dorian, running a shaking hand over his face and looking at his sister.

Islington looked from his friend to the figure on the bed. He didn't like seeing her that way any more than Dorian did. He preferred her yelling and violent to the way she was now. He also didn't know what he'd do if she died. He wasn't sure if he felt that way because of guilt over being so cruel to her in the courtyard or for some other reason. He only believed the world would lose some of its sparkle if Pandora were no longer in it.

Islington was surprised when Dorian invited him to visit Pandora. He agreed to go because he didn't think Dorian could bear to go alone to see his sister so ill. Either that or perhaps the Aberdares had allowed it because of his training and wanted a second opinion on their physician's prognosis. As much as Islington would like to disagree with what the man had said, Islington, unfortunately, could not, and there wasn't anything he could find to say of true encouragement to Dorian.

He didn't discover until he saw Pandora how wrong Dorian was in choosing him as company. It was difficult for Islington to see her lying there so silent, so inanimate. His first reaction had been to leave the room, but he stayed for Dorian. Islington didn't go near the bed; he didn't think he could bear to be close to her without reaching out to touch her. Instead, he sat in his chair in the corner and watched Pandora try to cheer her brother, not even realizing she might die.

"She'll live, Glamorgan," said Islington with more confidence than he felt. "Lady Pandora likes living too much."

"I asked Mum and Dad to let you come see her because if you hadn't found her in the garden, she might not be here."

Islington blinked in surprise. He hadn't been invited on Dorian's behalf after all. Why would her parents let him see her? Surely, they must have known the way he and Pandora acted toward one another only marginally bordered on civilized.

"Mum thought it would be all right, seein' as how you seem to be playing Pandora's knight errant." Dorian looked at his friend seriously. "Although, from the times I've seen you two together, I'd lay odds you play the part unwillingly."

Islington shifted in his seat uncomfortably, scratching at his temple contemplatively. He didn't know what to say. While he didn't exactly *like* Pandora, he didn't *dislike* her either. The times he had saved her, he had been saving her from himself. No wonder Pandora was always so hateful toward him. As he thought about it, it seemed he initiated their arguments. Pandora was only defending herself. Perhaps it was because she was able to account for herself so well that made it seem she was the one who started it. He was always seeking her out, not the other way around. The question that kept going through his mind was why? If he professed to dislike her so much, if he knew she was *Trouble*, then why did he always track her down and fight with her? He looked at Dorian uncertainly for a moment.

"I don't know how to answer that," he finally replied honestly. "I suppose it's because Pandora is so different, even from her twin."

"You can tell the difference between the two of them?" asked Dorian, mildly surprised.

"Certainly. Psyche is quiet and well-behaved. Pandora is wild and hot-tempered."

Dorian chuckled and shook his head. "I don't know about *hot*-tempered, but wild most definitely. I suppose you've not seen Psyche at her worst then, either." He ran a hand through his already mussed hair. "You're the first person outside my family that I can ever recall being able to tell them apart after knowing them so little."

"Perhaps it is because Pandora has left a very distinct impression on me," said Islington dryly. "Did she tell you that the day she jumped my phaeton she called me a big oaf?"

Dorian grinned amusedly. "She does have a sharp tongue, but I suppose if she let it loose on the complete stranger you were, you must have perturbed her exceedingly." Dorian rose from his seat. "Why don't we continue our conversation in the study? My dad has the best whisky, and I am feeling the need for a drink."

Islington nodded and followed Dorian to the bed, where his friend looked down at Pandora's restless figure. If Islington were granted one wish, it would be to see her well, if only to have someone to argue with. Dorian turned for the door, but Islington stayed by the bed for a few seconds. He brushed his forefinger against her cheek tenderly.

"Get well, Pan," he said softly and then turned to follow his friend out of the room.

Pandora remained in her half-dead state for two more weeks after her visit from Dorian and Islington. She didn't speak another lucid word or regain full consciousness. At one point her breathing became so shallow and slow, her family feared she wouldn't survive another minute. But Pandora began to improve. It seemed the worst of the ordeal was over. The duke and duchess were relieved; Pandora had become so emaciated and weak, they were certain she wouldn't come through if the symptoms had not begun to disappear.

She suffered fits of delirium in which she muttered about Castleton and Batts and Edinburgh, but her parents couldn't place the importance of any of it. She once cried out for Theo, but only Maiyin was there to hear. Maiyin couldn't place the name and shrugged dismissively when she heard it. The room smelled of the ether used to control the convulsions she began to have the night of her brother's visit.

The pain eventually became too much, and because of the gravity of her condition, the doctor didn't recommend laudanum if they wanted her to have any chance to live. Keung was able to find an herb that helped to lessen the pain without the deeply sedative qualities of the opiate, but it was obvious to all who saw her that she was still suffering. The doctor drained away excess fluid pressing against her brain near the end of the fortnight, and that was when the improvement in her health began to be noted. Her sleep became more relaxed and peaceful, healing instead of harmful.

Pandora awoke one fine spring morning at the end of the two weeks to see her mother and father sitting in the matching chairs by the window in her room. Both looked older than she had ever seen them, their faces worn by worry. Why were they in her room, and why did they look that way?

"Mamà, Papà? What's wrong?" she asked weakly.

What was wrong with her voice? Her parents looked at her in surprise.

"Pandora!" cried Julia, going to wrap her daughter in a tight hug.

"Why are you crying?" she asked bemusedly. "What's happened?" Pandora tried to raise herself off the bed only to flop back down weakly. She couldn't feel her left arm. Her head began to spin crazily and make four of her father appear over her mother's shoulder.

"What happened to me?" she asked anxiously.

Aberdare squeezed his wife's shoulder comfortingly and looked down at his daughter, his face still set in a wondering expression.

"You've had meningitis," he replied.

"Meningitis?" squeaked Pandora.

"We carried you home from the ball as soon as Lord Islington took us to you in Lundey's study. We've been so worried about you."

"How long has it been?" asked Pandora, plucking at her counterpane.

"Almost three weeks," said the duchess, brushing the hair off Pandora's forehead.

"Oh, my," said Pandora in surprise. She looked from one parent to the other. "Have I worried everyone overly much?"

"Yes, Pandora, you have worried us to distraction," said her mother, chucking her under the chin affectionately and giving her a fond smile, "but we wouldn't love you if we hadn't been."

"Mamà, I can't feel my left arm," said Pandora quietly, her concern over the matter beginning to outweigh any other thought. She tried to move her legs, and she began to feel a rising panic. "I can't move my left leg either."

"Dr. Hinton said it was possible, but it may not be permanent," soothed Aberdare. "Now you're getting well, perhaps the feeling will return."

Pandora's forehead creased, and she began to chew her lower lip worriedly. A knotting sensation began in the pit of her stomach, and she thought she might scream. She didn't want the feeling to be gone at all. How was she going to ride, or walk, or dance? She didn't want to be paralyzed, but at the moment she was too drowsy to do anything about it.

"Tell everyone I'm fine," said Pandora, yawning fiercely.

Her parents kissed her on the cheek then left the room. She was still sleeping soundly when Maiyin brought her food two hours later. Maiyin smiled happily over the peaceful way she slept. It was good to have Missy Pandora back again.

Chapter Five

The doctor wouldn't allow Pandora to leave her bed for a week after she became sensible. Although the inactivity bothered her, it was for the best. The hair that was shaved from her head was in an inconspicuous spot behind her ear and was growing back, although the stitches still remained where the doctor had made the incision to put the small hole in her skull. She was regaining the weight she had lost, but she was still too weak to stay awake for long periods of time. Sensation was slowly returning to the left side of her body, but she still had no control of her limbs. She would try to tell her arm to move, make her fingers pick up the glass by the bed, but it lay useless on the counterpane. She could wiggle her toes, but her leg wouldn't move.

She felt like a baby. She was never left alone for more than five minutes during her waking hours. She suspicioned they watched her when she slept also, only she was never awake to catch them.

Once she began to recuperate, she was not the model patient. She detested her medicine. She disliked the gruel and porridge they made her eat; it quickly got to the point that she refused to eat anything unless they brought her *real* food. Her parents didn't want to go against the doctor's orders, but Maiyin brought her a tray with some of her favorite foods: breaded fried oysters, asparagus, chicken stew with dumplings, and coffee ice cream. Once her parents saw that she was able to eat it, they let her have regular food from then on, which relieved Pandora of some of her frustration. She didn't like staying in bed, and she was growing restless.

Her room resembled a flower garden. Admirers and friends had been sending bouquets of various sizes and varieties. Lord Georgie sent her an urn full of mums she promptly had taken out because of her disagreeable reaction to them. (She got itchy eyes and a runny nose if within ten feet of them.) She received a dozen red roses from Lady Jersey. Lord Lundey sent a small nosegay of shy violets and primroses. Even her family brought her flowers, including a bunch of yellow-throated, red gladiolus (her favorite) from Psyche. So many had been sent, Maiyin had run out of space for them on top of the desk and dressers and began to place them on the floor.

The one Pandora treasured most was the bouquet set on one of her night tables. Compared to the others, it wasn't as commanding of attention or admiration, except to Pandora. It consisted of four roses, each of a different color, nestled in maidenhair fern. One rose was a deep red, its petals like velvet, its color deepening to almost black at their base. Another was a pure, sparkling white, its scent so strong it overpowered that of all the other flowers in the room. The third was an exquisite shade of shell pink that faded to soft yellow at the tips of the petals, reminding Pandora of a summer sunset over the lake at home. The fourth was a wondrous shade of deep yellow, the veins of the petals tinged with a color like gold until the flower looked as if it had been dipped in the precious metal and was not at all real.

The bouquet arrived the day after Pandora awoke to her parents' worried faces, before any of the others, before she was even fully aware of what had happened to her. But her interest in it came from its sender. There was a small card attached to the crystal vase, the missive signed with a simple '*Yours, T.*' It took Pandora a moment to realize who sent it, and when she did, her mouth dropped open in surprise. She never pictured Lord Islington as the type to send flowers to someone, not even to her in her ill state, especially not to her in any state. The message on the card was mysterious to her: *Ce n'est que le premier pas qui coûte*—it is only the first step that costs. What did he mean by *that?*

Pandora was sitting up against the pillows on her bed, a sour expression on her face, when Dorian strolled into her room with a pleased smile to find her awake and alert.

"Good morning, Dodo. How are we today?" he asked, coming to flop beside her on the bed in a sprawl.

"*We* feel like a useless puddle of mud. Maiyin comes in to see that I eat, helps me into my dressing gown, and brushes my hair, but all I do is sit here and do nothing." She gave Dorian a self-deprecating smile. "I can't even twiddle my thumbs because I can't use my left hand."

"Cheer up, m'dear, that's about to change," said Dorian, bursting with an uncharacteristic excitement.

"Not unless a miracle's going to happen within the next ten seconds," said Pandora with a dour grimace.

Her eyes widened in surprise when Dorian rose from the bed and lifted her in his arms.

"Brother Dorian, what are you doing?" she squeaked, nervously clutching his shoulder and looking longingly back at the bed.

"Nothing," replied Dorian blithely, carrying her to the door. "Dad talked to the doctor, and he said you were well enough to go downstairs. Would you like to see downstairs again, Dodo?"

"You're funning me, Dorian," said Pandora, her face hopeful.

"No, I'm not," replied Dorian in a wounded tone. "Why did you give me the nickname Brother Dorian?"

Pandora sighed and clutched his shoulder even tighter as they went down the stairs. "Because you've always been too serious for your own good. You won't even go swimming in a *fundoshi* in the lake at home because you're worried some unsuspecting damsel may happen upon you and lose her view of the world as all things bright and wonderful."

"I believe that's sensible," defended Dorian calmly.

Pandora gave him a teasing smirk. "Dorian, we're the only ones to be found for miles in any direction, far from any roads, and I've seen you in *less* than a *fundoshi*. We all go swimming in less…except you. You see, it doesn't matter what you wear."

Dorian looked down at her with disbelief.

"You did not, have not, nor ever will see me in less, Dodo."

"I did," averred Pandora. "Psyche, Persephone and I climbed the ivy outside your window while you were bathing. We didn't do it for that purpose—we were going to give you a hedgepig in your boot—but we didn't see anything extraordinary. And you can't deny that I've seen you without your shirt."

"Pandora, you're shameless," sighed Dorian as he went through the paneled doors of the family's private sitting room, continuing on to the French doors that led to the garden.

"What shame is there in the human form?" defended Pandora simply. "Did not Adam and Eve live together in unashamed nakedness before they were cast out of Eden?"

"Yes, but that was before they got—" Dorian halted mid-sentence, beginning to believe this conversation was getting out of hand.

"Urges," finished Pandora flatly. "All I'm saying is if there ain't no urge, there ain't no shame."

"Pandora, you're being ridiculous, simplifying it way too much," said Dorian, setting her on a chaise near the fountain in the garden.

Pandora pointed over his shoulder where he sat on the edge of the fountain to draw his attention to the unclad nymph at its center that held a pitcher from which water poured into the basin. Dorian tightened his lips, beginning to wish he hadn't encouraged Pandora by taking an opposing viewpoint.

"Are you ashamed to look at that statue?" she quizzed.

"No, but—"

"It's a naked woman, is it not?"

"Ye-es, but it's a statue."

"Art is the imitation of life," replied Pandora. "If you can look at that statue without getting urges, can't you control them when looking at people?"

Dorian shifted uncomfortably, knowing it was useless to argue with her because she would continue to find things to prove her point that seemed perfectly logical but came nowhere near reality.

"How did we get stuck on this accursed subject?" he groaned.

"You asked me how you got your nickname to divert my attention from you carrying me downstairs, which you know makes me a wee bit anxious." Pandora gave him a sour look. "I would much rather have walked down them on my own or slid down the banister."

"And you know you're incapable of doing either one right now. Would you rather I had let you stay imprisoned in your room?"

Pandora sniffed and leaned back against the cushions, closing her eyes and letting the sun wash over her face. It felt heavenly to be outside again. She could hear birds chirping and bees humming over her mother's flowers. Fluffy white clouds drifted across the blue of the sky with relaxing laziness. She sighed contentedly and wriggled her toes. She squinted an eye open and looked at her brother affectionately.

"Thank you, Dorian. This was just what I needed."

"Now I've done this for you, I want you to promise when you have to go back to bed that you'll behave like the proper invalid."

"I am not an invalid." She wrinkled her nose. "Just temporarily out of commission is all."

"If you don't start behaving like one, I will be forced to make you one."

Pandora feigned surprise. "A joke from the stone-faced one?"

"I mean every word," threatened Dorian.

Pandora sighed and flopped back into the pillows, pretending more weakness than she felt.

"Oh, Dorian, I feel so thirsty," she simpered, raising a limp hand to her forehead. "Would you be a dear and fetch me some lemonade?"

Dorian smiled amusedly and began to leave, but she called him back.

"Brother Dorian? I'm *so* hungry. Could you fetch me some of those divine watercress sandwiches that Mrs. O'Flaherty makes?"

"Of course," replied Dorian, bowing obeisantly with an amused smile.

"And a novel from the library, something lurid," continued Pandora with a pretended shudder. "I'd also like one of my notebooks in case an equation comes to mind while I'm out here enjoying this solar energy."

Dorian turned to leave again, but Pandora stopped him before he got a few feet. Dorian shook his head and raised a hand, believing if he didn't, she would request he bring her everything in the house.

"Enough, Dodo," he chuckled. "If you want anything else, you'll have to get it yourself."

With that, he turned to leave. Pandora let him go, an expression of ecstatic inspiration forming on her face.

"Get it myself, you say?" she muttered as she swung her legs over the side of the chaise. "I'll have to see if I can attend to that."

She grabbed the back of the couch with her right hand and took several deep breaths to prepare herself. She reasoned that if she could move her toes, she could move her legs—both of them. She slowly stood and promptly collapsed to the ground. Sighing, she grabbed the edge of the chaise and pulled herself back up, realizing what she had done wrong. She sat on the edge of the chaise, gripping the back. This time when she rose, she placed most of her weight on her right side, and she didn't fall. She wobbled and weaved, but she stood.

Pandora restrained herself from whooping but allowed a giddy, victorious grin. She stood holding onto the chaise and tested putting some of her weight on her left side. She chanced a look toward the door of the house for Dorian, but there was no one in sight. If Dorian or anyone else saw her trying to stand up, she'd be taken back to bed and never be allowed to move from it again. She had some time before Dorian returned with the items on her list. She hadn't sent him off for all those things for this purpose, but now it presented the perfect chance.

After some time, she was ready to begin phase two: walking. She slowly began to loosen her hold on the back of the chaise. The bottom of her left foot had some feeling in it. All she had to do was adjust to the lack of sensation and compensate for it. She soon had only the palm of her hand on the back of the couch and decided it was time to move on to something more difficult. She lifted her hand from the back of the chaise, holding her arm up slightly away from her side for balance. A film of perspiration beaded her upper lip, and she felt the urge to reach her hand up and wipe it away. But if she made any sudden movement, she would end up on her bottom on the ground. She felt like a baby learning to walk for the first time. Well, she was standing again, and she would be walking again.

Pandora stood near the chaise, its back within easy reach of her hand, building up her courage. She tried lifting her leg, and with concentration and exertion, she could do it. She could lift her foot about an inch from the ground and bend her knee slightly—all that was necessary for walking. *But can you do it, Pandora? What are you going to do if you fall in a heap again?* Pandora took a deep breath and steadied herself.

"If I fall, I'll just get back up again," she said to herself determinedly. "God knows how many times I fell when I learned to walk as a babe. If I could do it then, I can do it now."

So saying, Pandora began to take her first step. She was surprised by how tired and hot she was becoming. Her shift was sticking between her shoulder blades beneath her dressing gown, and she resisted the urge to wriggle it loose. She moved her left foot forward slowly, using all her concentration, keeping her right arm extended from her side. It was starting to quake from just hanging in the air. She realized with detachment that while her mind wanted to keep going, her body wasn't going to comply for very much longer. She moved her foot far enough to qualify as a step and placed it down with the same care she had used in lifting it. Then the big test: letting her left foot support her weight.

She looked to her extended arm, making sure her hand still hovered over the back of the couch. She hesitated for a moment, screwing up her courage. Then, with her breath held in anticipation, she lifted her right foot, calculating how fast to move by how long she thought her left side could support her. The timing was perfect. Her right foot landed just as she felt the left beginning to give. She wavered a little and almost fell but soon regained her balance. She released a small, nervous giggle.

"Can you do one more?" she asked herself.

She looked to her extended arm then back at the house. The couch was right beside her, and Dorian was still occupied. She calculated she had time for one more step before he came back. Then again, perhaps she wouldn't be in so much trouble if he saw that she could do it. She would soon find out unless she moved.

Pandora picked up her left foot and moved it forward again. It landed awkwardly. She tried to move its crooked position back to straight ahead, but her body wouldn't cooperate. Pandora felt herself losing her balance, and in her panic to keep herself from toppling over, she began to pinwheel her right arm in the air and forgot about reaching for the chaise. Because her feet weren't in the right place, she began to fall backward instead of forward, and without the use of her left arm, she wouldn't be able to soften the landing effectively.

She felt herself going backwards as if time had slowed and she tensed, waiting for her body to land on the hardness of the pavers. She began to wish she had tried this while someone was there to catch her when she felt two strong arms come around her and hold her up, pulling her back against a well-muscled chest. Her first reaction was a startled 'oh'; her second, elation that she had walked without anyone's help. She managed to twist around in the arms that held her, burying her face in the shirtfront joyfully and giving the man she thought was her brother a tight hug with her good arm around his neck.

"Dorian, isn't it wonderful? I was walking! Did you see me, Do—"

Her words cut off as she looked up at Lord Islington's furious face. Her forehead wrinkled in confusion as she wondered what he was doing there. Where was Dorian? She didn't wonder for long before the marquess hefted her in his arms and carried her toward the house.

Pandora had no choice but to grip his neck, but she tried to struggle out of his arms, even if it meant landing on her bottom. She didn't like being carried, not because it made her feel helpless, but because she had a fear of being dropped. It was ridiculous, she knew, but there it was. And here was this man, this *monster*, carrying her around like baggage.

She remembered the way he had treated her in the Lundeys' garden in bits and pieces (as everything from that time was somewhat cloudy), but she couldn't forget his cruelty or his taunts, and the flowers he had sent her—while beautiful—did nothing to ease her hurt. His face at the moment was a frigid mask, his gaze straight ahead toward the stairs. Pandora tried to fight down her panic and began to struggle all the more desperately. His response was to hold her even tighter.

"Lord Islington, let me go! Put me down!" she gasped, continuing to struggle.

He didn't say anything as he walked up the stairs. Pandora couldn't watch what she was certain would be her last journey up or down the stairs and buried her face in his shirt, clutching his neck even tighter because she just knew her life depended on it. *Just don't drop me. I'll never slide down the banister again as long as he doesn't drop me.*

She didn't dare to look where they were going. She wanted to be put down, but she was too scared to do or say anything. Pandora didn't notice him carrying her into her room. She didn't even realize they had stopped moving and that he had sat on the edge of her bed with her on his lap. Pandora kept her death grip on his neck, her face buried in his chest as if she wanted to crawl inside him.

Islington looked down at her in puzzlement and disbelief. Tannaz had answered the door and informed him that Dorian was in the garden with his sister. So Islington had gone to the garden and found Pandora alone and ready to fall backward. He had reached her just before anything happened. He was angered by her carelessness, by what he thought was foolishness. He also had a good mind to speak to his friend about leaving someone so irresponsible unattended. He decided if she wasn't going to behave, then she needed to be put back in bed.

And now here he sat with her holding on to him as if she intended to remain there forever. While it was pleasant, it wasn't proper, and it certainly wasn't normal. He thought it was unusual that after her initial struggles she had ceased to move at all and hid her face. After several more minutes of her inaction, he realized something was wrong.

"Pandora, we seem to be making a habit of this," he said calmly, his anger put aside for the moment by her strange behavior. No response. "Pandora, you're crushing my cravat." Silence. "Pandora, will you let go of me now, please?" He felt her begin to tremble in his arms like a leaf. "What the deuce—?"

He was at a loss. He didn't think she was having a relapse. She had seemed quite healthy (all things considered) until he picked her up and carried her. Then he began to see the reason. At first it didn't make any sense because she hadn't reacted this way at the ball, but then she also hadn't been quite herself. He smiled in gentle amusement as he felt her continue to quiver in his arms. He wasn't amused by the fear itself, only that it was Pandora—the intrepid virago—who felt it. Because of his knowledge of her thus far, Islington would have thought her incapable of feeling fear.

He found this unexpected weakness endearing, even if he'd never admit it to her.

Islington smoothed his hands over her back soothingly, resting his chin on top of her head. Pandora slowly relaxed her grip on his neck, and her trembling began to subside as he continued to caress her back softly through the thin silk of her dressing gown. He realized he did this as much for her as for himself. Without thinking, he let his hands smooth her hair, her thigh. She was quite enjoyable to soothe, and the way her body was positioned against his was very intimate if he forgot about who she was, who he was, where they were, and why he shouldn't be forgetting any of the above.

Pandora was enjoying herself a great deal, although for the life of her she couldn't understand why. It seemed that as long as she and Lord Islington didn't touch each other, she was able to remember all the horrible things he had done and said to her. But when he touched her, everything dimmed except for their closeness and the fluttery feeling it brought about in her stomach. She found his continued caresses making her forget that she should be angry with him for everything he had done.

He smelled intoxicating. He wore no cologne, but the sandalwood scent of his shaving lotion blended with that of pipe tobacco and leather to make a combination that was profoundly masculine. Pandora couldn't imagine Lord Islington smelling any other way, and she inhaled deeply to immerse herself in the scent of him.

Pandora began to regain her common sense (with a bit of a struggle). As content as she would be to continue this initially innocent embrace, someone would eventually come to her room. She also knew that this man who held her so tenderly at the moment felt nothing for her, even though she was beginning to wish otherwise. As pranks were her forte, it seemed emotional artifice was his (at least where she was concerned). She was unable to hold it against him, recognizing just as she couldn't be anything other than herself, neither could he. Her upbringing helped her accept that, even though it saddened her.

She lifted her face to look at him, and her breath caught in her throat as she saw the passion in his eyes. Even though she knew it wasn't really for her, she found it very hard to resist, and she wasn't sure she wanted to.

"Ah, Lord Islington," she said hesitantly. "I don't really…."

Her words trailed off as he lowered his lips to hers. Pandora felt a tingle at the contact that worked its way down her body to curl her toes. He coaxed her lips apart, and she could taste angelica and mint as his tongue began to explore her mouth teasingly. She felt herself melting, loving the taste of him, the smell of him, the restrained power she felt in him. She didn't doubt he was passionate; it was his emotional honesty she questioned. She found it quite pleasant to pretend he wanted her. He moved his lips down her neck, and Pandora thought it would be the appropriate time to insert the voice of sanity.

"Uh, Lord Islington?"

"Hmm?"

Pandora felt a thrill race up her spine as he gently bit on her earlobe. She almost lost her train of thought.

"Lord Islington, I think you should stop now," sighed Pandora, breathing in sharply as his hand moved up her side to cup her breast.

"Don't you like this, Pandora?" he whispered in her ear, his breath making goose bumps rise all over her body.

"Oh, ye-es, I do," Pandora practically purred. "But Dorian…Maiyin…. We shouldn't be doing this."

Islington nuzzled her exposed skin leisurely, as if he hadn't heard her, and Pandora tilted her head to allow him access. He brought his lips back to hers, and she opened them to let his tongue tease hers, a soft moan escaping from the back of her throat as she felt that newly-familiar tension beginning in the pit of her stomach. Islington was exciting her to the point she didn't care who walked in. He laid her back against the pillows, his lips never losing contact with hers, and Pandora ran her hand through the hair at the nape of his neck, thrilling at the way it feathered over her fingers.

She was attempting to undo his complicated cravat with one hand when he broke the kiss with little nibbles to her lower lip and sat up to look down at her. Pandora was about to protest when she saw his face. Her breath caught in her throat when she saw hunger and something gentler mingled there. She reached up to wonderingly trace the line of his jaw to his chin then up to his lips. *Why can't he be like this all the time?* Was it any more difficult for him to be nice than to be cruel?

"Maybe I should carry you around more often," said Islington with a teasing nip at her finger as he adjusted the blankets over her.

Pandora snatched her hand away and looked at him defensively.

"What is that supposed to mean?"

"Only that fear seems to calm you down immensely. I find this acquiescent you much more pleasing."

Pandora looked away from him and closed her eyes for a moment, her cheeks turning pink. *It isn't fair. He only has to say a few words, and I feel like a two-year-old again.* She turned to look at him, her chin lifted determinedly. She would try to remain polite. She didn't want this niceness to be over, and it would be if she tried to defend herself.

"Lord Islington, you'll not carry me anywhere," she said pleasantly. "I won't let you."

"You can't stop me," said Islington with a superior smile, "because as soon as your feet leave the ground you are like a babe."

Pandora scoffed. "I'd let Castleton carry me sooner than I'd let you."

"Who is Castleton?"

"I don't know, but I do know he's positively evil."

"And how would you know that if you don't know who he is?"

"Because I've heard him talk."

Islington smiled amusedly and brushed at an imaginary piece of lint on his sleeve in an effort to hide it from her.

"You're laughing at me!" gasped Pandora in outrage.

"No, I'm not," denied Islington with a patronizing pat on her arm, his features barely controlled.

Pandora jerked away from him angrily.

"You are! You don't believe me. No one will." She shook her head in vexation. "I keep trying to tell people that he's going to kidnap someone from Edinburgh—I think his name is Bertram Batts—and he's going to kill him…or it could be someone else, but I know he's going to do it. I've heard him talking about it twice with another man whose name I don't know. Castleton is evil, absolutely evil. I get chills just thinking about his voice, it's so—" Pandora cut off mid-prattle when Islington let out a loud hoot.

"Oh, my dear, that is too rich," he laughed. "You really should do something with that imagination of yours."

Pandora forgot about her decision to be civil. She grabbed one of her pillows and threw it at him angrily. It wasn't a very forceful lob, but it was well-aimed, hitting him squarely in the face. Islington looked at her in surprise, not sure what he had done to raise her wrath.

"Get out of my room!" she hissed. "I never want to see you again, you big oaf! I'm tired of you treating me like a child."

"Perhaps if you didn't behave like one, you wouldn't be treated as such," said Islington, tight-lipped and rising from the bed. He calmly adjusted his coat sleeves and waistcoat.

"I don't know why Dorian likes you. You are such a pig!"

"The same goes for you, you fire-breathing shrew!"

"What is going on in here?" cried Dorian from the doorway, his face set in a comical expression of shock.

Pandora yelped and began to turn a bright shade of red. Islington did not seem so affected.

"I was told by the footman that you were in the garden with your sister, and when I got there I found her trying to kill herself."

"I did not, was not, nor ever will try to kill myself. It would be more probable if I tried to kill you, you arrogant clod!" spat Pandora.

"Enough!" shouted Dorian, looking between them in exasperation.

"Dorian, I was walking," said Pandora with a proud smile.

"You were not; you were falling," said Islington flatly.

Dorian held up his hand and looked at his friend impatiently for a moment then turned back to Pandora, who wanted to grab another pillow.

"I had already taken a step before you got there, Lord Islington," said Pandora tartly, giving him a brief, dark look. She looked at Dorian happily. "In any event, I was at least standing on my own." She threw the covers aside and sat up. "I'll show you, Dorian."

"No, you won't," stated Islington flatly, moving toward the bed with the determination that she wasn't going to rise from it ever again.

"Don't touch me, you dolt!" crowed Pandora furiously. "You lay a hand on me, and I swear I'll break it."

"Not in the shape you're in, honey," said Islington patronizingly.

"Islington, let her be," said Dorian with a long-suffering sigh, knowing Pandora could follow through even with one arm incapacitated.

Pandora was too excited over showing her brother her progress to smirk at Lord Islington for being put in his place.

"I know I shouldn't have been trying, Dorian, but I can't stand being carried around or staying inside all the time. I want to ride Bell. I want to take Cosmo and Topher to the zoo. I would be happy just being able to walk again. I was *walking,* Dorian!"

Pandora scooted to the end of the bed where she grabbed the post at the corner. She looked at Dorian and gave him a radiant smile. Islington tightened his lips and went to sit in a chair by the window, seeming only half-interested in this great leap Pandora was about to make in her recovery.

"I know I need more time to get better, to get my strength back, but watch how well I'm doing."

Dorian crossed his arms expectantly, his heart beginning to pound hopefully. The doctor had told his parents that Pandora would be lucky if she regained even partial use of her arm. He had been almost positive Pandora had suffered too much damage to walk again. Her parents hadn't wanted to tell her for fear she might have a setback. They had decided to wait until she was stronger before telling her the bad news. And now, here she was, preparing to stand up and walk.

Pandora grinned at Dorian cheekily, giving him a playful wink as she slowly lifted herself with the help of the bedpost and stood. Dorian watched in amazement as she stood hanging on, wobbling erratically as she again accustomed herself to the loss of sensation on her left side. His throat began to tighten as she gradually pushed herself away from the support until only the tip of her index finger touched the wood. She soon removed that, too, and there she was, standing on her own.

"Will you catch me if I start to fall?" she asked with a tremulous smile. Dorian nodded silently, holding his arms out for her.

Pandora judged he was about three steps away. She began to worry it might be too far but brushed the anxiety aside. She would do it, even if it were only to spite Islington. It was a simple equation of mechanics. *Remember that, Pandora. All you have to do is remember that your machinery isn't running at full capacity and compensate for it. Think of this as a scientific competition in which the prize is regaining your freedom and failure means being laughed at by the big oaf.*

She looked up once from her feet to give Dorian a wink. She slowly lifted her left leg and moved it until it was just in front of her right one. *Tiny steps. Easy does it.* She then lifted her right foot and moved it quickly to take her weight. One step. She'd gotten this far before, and now she had an audience. She lifted her left foot again and daringly moved it a little farther forward than before. She completed the movement with her right foot and spared a glance to her brother.

"I know this looks ridiculous, and it will take me until dinnertime to get down the stairs to breakfast at this rate, but *better late than never* is going to be my motto from now on."

"Breakfast is vastly overrated," said Dorian with a proud grin.

She was almost there…just one more step, and she wanted to make it impressive. She lifted her left foot without looking, the rest of her becoming accustomed to the numbness, taking an almost normal-sized step. She moved her right foot, then her left, and she was taken up in her brother's arms to be swung in a circle, both of them laughing jubilantly.

"Wait until I tell Mum and Dad! They will be *so* happy! The doctor said you would never be able to walk again."

"Then you had better tell them they might need another doctor."

Dorian placed her on her feet, and Pandora stood quite easily with his support. She smiled up at him cheekily.

"You're not tired, are you?"

"Somewhat. I just have to remember everything is a little numb, but it works."

"What about your arm?"

Pandora tried to lift it from where it rested on top of Dorian's but found it still wouldn't move on its own. She was peeved by that, but she would more than likely regain its use, too. She looked up at Dorian's disappointed face and reached up to pinch him on the cheek to coax a pained smile from him.

"You've no need to be upset, Brother Dorian. I'm the one who'll be known as 'all right'." Dorian rolled his eyes at the pun and groaned with a pained expression.

Pandora looked over her shoulder at Islington and saw him sitting in the same position with an unreadable expression. She felt like sticking out her tongue and making a rude face but instead chose to keep herself contained. Still, she didn't like seeing him in the corner.

"Well, Lord Islington, aren't you going to at least congratulate me for not falling on my face?"

It seemed as if her words called him out of a trance, and he shook his head and rose to walk over to Pandora and her brother. He took her right hand and placed a kiss on it, the contact lingering for just a little longer than necessary. Pandora felt a tingle at his lips, and a blush began to rise as memories of previous times of his touch came into her thoughts.

"Yes, m'dear, congratulations. I must say it would have served you right, though."

Pandora shrieked in outrage and boxed his ear without thinking.

"Arrogant, pompous, egotistical, rude, lowborn, oafish, cowbrained, pig-poking, toad-eating—"

"Pandora!" interjected Dorian.

"Selfish, simple-minded, scum-sucking, backward, bottom-dwelling, louse-infested, self-effacing, beady-eyed, rat-toothed—"

"Pandora!" shouted Dorian again, but she was not to be deterred.

"Pigeon-toed, blackhearted, knuckle-dragging throwback!" And she nodded her head for good measure. "Maybe that'll teach you some manners, you peaheaded, loutish, despicable...*ooh!*...idiot!"

"Pandora, that's enough!" shouted Dorian, giving her a good shake.

She clamped her mouth shut and continued to look daggers at Islington, who was gingerly massaging his ear and looking at her dazedly. Her assault came as completely unexpected...to both of them. She couldn't recall anyone ever making her so angry.

"Pandora, apologize to Islington this instant!" grated Dorian, suggesting dire consequences if she didn't comply. She opened her mouth to argue, and Dorian gave her another shake. "*Now!*" he roared.

"I apologize, Lord Islington. I don't know what came over me. I'm feeling much better now," she said brightly.

"Yes, I'm sure you are," muttered Islington as he tried to relieve the ringing in his ear.

"Islington, quit provoking her," said Dorian firmly. He sighed in vexation. "Nanny Bixley would be much better suited for this. I feel as if I'm dealing with two infants."

Islington and Pandora both turned to look at him indignantly. Then they looked at each other accusingly.

Chapter Six

Pandora's recuperation progressed steadily, if not speedily, and she was soon able to walk at a fairly spry gait with the use of an ivory-handled cane pilfered from her father's wardrobe. Her left arm was still weak, although she was regaining more of its use. She was glad it was recovering so she could write with it again. She had taught herself to write with her right hand long ago, but her left was her favored hand for nearly everything. She became frustrated when she discovered there were still things she was unable to do on her own, but Dorian was always there to remind her of the doctor's inaccurate prediction.

After a few weeks of walking again, she felt ready to resume her social duties. Although she still despised the purpose of the functions she attended, she wanted to see the friends she had made and surprisingly missed. She hadn't realized that, for the most part, she had no friends other than her family. She had acquaintances she had known since childhood, but there weren't many she would actually consider friends. As an added bonus, Pandora's infirmity excused her from dancing with her clamorous beaux, many of them her brothers' friends, which pleased her to no end.

One day while Dorian (who seemed to have designated himself both her supporter and tormentor) was sitting with her in the garden, she dared to ask him how he had become friends with the oafish prig. After a brief admonition for her name-calling, Dorian told her they had met while he was attending Cambridge. Lord Islington was already into his final session when Dorian had just arrived. Dorian had gone with several of his friends to a house the type of which he didn't want to mention. Pandora supplied the word *brothel* and grinned cheekily at her brother's discomfiture. Dorian tried to say he had gone simply to play cards, but Pandora was willing to bet otherwise. There was an argument over one hand at the table that Dorian had won, and the other players tried to attack him. Dorian blushed when he admitted he was deep in his cups, but Islington helped him escape with only a few bruises. Since then, they had been good friends. Pandora thought better of asking what Islington had pursued as his course of study but viewed him in a less harsh light after hearing the tale; it appeared he wasn't completely self-interested.

Pandora had gotten nowhere in her pursuit of the kidnappers. She could gain no support for her story...when she could get someone to hear her say more than *Edinburgh*. There was no one she could turn to for aid. Even if it did sound improbable, it was going to happen. What frustrated her more than anything was that she knew about it and could stop it if someone would just listen to her. She had the names of two conspirators (she had firmly come to believe Bertram Batts was an *abductor* rather than the *abductee*); she could give them the Dog as the place from which they could begin their search. However, it was useless because it seemed she had become the village idiot.

Pandora decided if anything were going to be done, she would have to do it herself. If she were able to get more proof, then someone better suited could take over. Time was running out for the man in Edinburgh and Bertram Batts (if it hadn't already). It would be so much easier if she had the abductee's name; then she could warn him. He wouldn't find her tale so amusing. He would believe her because he would know why someone would want him killed.

How Pandora intended to get more information was a sticking point. She couldn't just hide in some dark, secluded spot and hope for the two men to have a conversation again. She couldn't very well go to the Dog in search of Castleton either. She got the impression it wasn't an establishment a lady could frequent. Although she suspected it was a place her sister Persephone might attempt to visit—at least once, Pandora doubted the imp would do it as a favor to her. Without a male supporter, Pandora would have to find the Aristocrat. It became capitalized in her mind because she didn't have a real name to attach yet.

He had to be someone of high station, if not nobility; otherwise, he and Castleton wouldn't have had their conversations where they did. The best way to begin would be to peruse her mother's guest list for the come-out ball. Pandora wasn't sure she could remember the names of all the people she had met, but she could cross off the ones she did and narrow it down from there. When Pandora asked her mother for the list, she told Pandora it would take her some time to remember if she had kept it and where she had put it. That tried Pandora's short store of patience, but at least the process was begun. She didn't know what she would do if the duchess had discarded it. She had to hope her grace had kept it out of sentimentality.

Something else Pandora might try was asking Lady Ramsey and Miss Cranston who it was they had found so captivating that night. That quest would probably not yield much information; the two women seemed to be entranced by any man of means who still had a pulse. Yet if he had been attractive enough to dissuade the two from following her brother, chances were they would remember the man. The visit wasn't something Pandora looked forward to. Ramsey and Cranston would fawn over anyone with money, male or female. Still, Pandora believed it might be worth an hour or two of vexation (hopefully even less) if they could give her the answer she sought.

Psyche refused to go. She would not subject herself to those women to find out something that meant nothing to her. Besides, Myron had promised to take her to the Museum. Gregory had gone to Glamorgan for the week. Arachne refused to entangle herself in any of Pandora's schemes. Period. Her parents were taking her younger siblings to Greenwich for the day.

That left Dorian. It would take no small amount of wheedling to convince him to go with her. Aside from that, the two women might be so besotted by him that they wouldn't pay Pandora the slightest attention. However, she needed someone to go with her.

Pandora finally found him in the library, reading Shakespeare. *Typical.* Dorian was often too busy looking for the ideal to enjoy the real. He was lounging in one of the chairs, his legs sprawled casually over one of the arms, his head propped up on his hand while his elbow rested on the other arm. He glanced up from the pages when he heard the clicking of her cane on the parquet floor of the room.

"Whatever it is, no," said Dorian flatly before she opened her mouth.

"Rude," said Pandora tartly, flopping down in the chair across from him.

"No, Pandora," said Dorian again.

"I only need you for an hour. That's all. I need you to go with me to visit someone. Just an hour of polite conversation with pleasant people."

"Who might this someone be that you can't go visit alone?"

"Dorian, you know I'm still not comfortable going about by myself yet. Besides, you know them."

"Who is it?" he asked again, his forehead wrinkling with trepidation.

"Lady Ramsey and Miss—"

"No way! Absolutely not, Pandora! Have you lost your *mind*? You know how those women are. Dodo, you're my sister, and I love you, but I will *not* go into the lion's den for you. You'll have to find someone other than me to take with you for a torture session."

"Please, Dorian. There's no one else to go with me."

"No."

"Please?"

"No." Dorian's mouth set in a firm line. "Why do you want to go see them? I thought you didn't like them."

"I need to ask them something about the night of my come-out ball."

"Such as?"

"Why another man enticed them more than my charming brother."

"Why should that matter?"

"Because whoever he is, he's going to kidnap someone from Edinburgh and kill Bertram Batts."

Dorian groaned exasperatedly. "Not that again."

"Why will no one believe me?" asked Pandora, pounding her fist on the arm of the cushioned chair in frustration. "Bertram Batts may already be dead, and in less than three months another man, from Edinburgh, is going to suffer the same fate. I don't know what I can do to convince you that I'm not imagining this. Maybe after they're both dead?"

"Oh, Pandora, please. Quit being so melodramatic. I can't go with you because I've an appointment of my own."

"You're making that up so you won't have to go with me. I know you don't like those women," she pouted.

"No, I don't like them, but I'm not making up an excuse. There's a man coming to town from Cumberland who's getting rid of some of his stable." Dorian observed her distraught countenance and felt the least bit ashamed. "I will *find* someone to go with you. Does that suit?" he asked resignedly.

Pandora's face brightened and she stood up, straightening the folds in her lilac-sprigged morning gown.

"Thank you, Dorian. You don't know how important this is."

"Mm-hmm, if only to you," he muttered.

"You just wait. I'm going to prove to everyone that I'm not trying to put one over on them. I know what I heard, Dorian. There is no way I can have completely lost my mind," she said seriously.

"Mm-hmm," was the only response she could get once he turned his attention back to Shakespeare's sonnets.

Once it was settled she would go see the two women, Pandora decided to go outside and enjoy the sun. The weather had been uncharacteristically mild lately, and she didn't want to miss the opportunity to be outdoors. She still didn't feel ready to ride Bellerophon, and she missed their excursions to the park terribly. Her horse was also becoming impatient. Although Tajik exercised him every day, the stable master told Pandora that Bellerophon missed her. She would soon be able to ride him again, although not at the same breakneck speed for a while longer.

Pandora made her way to the gazebo at a leisurely pace, pausing to smell a rose or watch an insect scurry along. The sun felt wonderful. When she reached the gazebo, she sat on a bench, propping her back into one corner and raising her feet onto the cushion after removing her slippers. As she wiggled her toes, Pandora decided to take a nap. She didn't know how long it would be before Dorian found someone to go with her on her visit, but a servant would find her when the time came. Besides, she wasn't expecting any visitors herself, and the sun was making her feel sinfully lazy. She had a while yet before it was even the proper hour to go calling.

She wondered what she was going to do when she discovered the Aristocrat's identity. It wasn't as if she could accuse him with no proof; it would be her word against his. That would not suit. Those who knew her mischievous ways would believe him if he denied it. Aside from that, it would make him all the more careful to cover any evidence of his involvement. As her eyelids started to droop, Pandora began to see the reason why Persephone sometimes wished she were a man; their sex seemed to automatically give them more credibility.

Pandora was startled awake by a loud clap of thunder. She wasn't sure what time it was because the sky had grown dark with roiling clouds. She'd forgotten to bring a watch. Rain was pouring down. She was not going to attempt an escape to the house. The path was probably too slick for her to walk safely in her condition, and the soaking she got would give her a cold she didn't want. Maiyin would give her no end of berating.

"Oh, drat," she muttered.

She wouldn't be going to visit Lady Ramsey and Miss Cranston that day, she realized disappointedly. She couldn't subject one of her family's drivers to riding around in this unnecessarily. She wouldn't be seeing the two women that night, either, because she was staying home.

Pandora pulled her knees up to her chest and rested her head on them, staring out the doorway at the rain, which was falling in heavy gray sheets. She had seen it rain like this before. It wasn't going to stop for hours. She wished she had told someone where she was going, but she hadn't foreseen a rainstorm. The sky wasn't cloudy at all when she went outside that morning. She hoped no one was concerned about where she was. She could just imagine her family forming a search party to look for her. Then again, depending on the time, they would all still be out and completely unaware she had "gone missing." The only one who might still be home was Dorian.

She looked around herself in the gazebo, hoping to find something to occupy her time. There wasn't anything. She hadn't thought to bring any of her notebooks or even a novel with her. She couldn't read anyhow; the dark sky had made the already gloomy interior of the gazebo unsuitable. She would have to content herself with watching the storm, which had become even more ferocious.

She felt a chill when a particularly strong gust broke through the surrounding bushes and latticework. The mews wall protected her from the worst of it. She rubbed her bare arms to smooth down her chill bumps and clenched her teeth on a shiver. This was impossible.

"Bollocks," she groaned and hugged her knees even closer.

The thin muslin of her dress did little to stop the wind or provide warmth. She was thankful for the well-sealed shingles of the gazebo's roof; at least she wasn't getting wet. The wind was probably going to give her a chill anyhow. Pandora sighed fitfully and rested her forehead on her knees, her chin tucked into her chest. Curled up in a ball as she was, the wind didn't seem quite as bad.

She was pondering her situation when a thought occurred to her. There might be a blanket or two in the benches; there were storage compartments for such things beneath the cushions—an ingenious idea on her father's part. Pandora remembered sharing one with Psyche the year before. She stood up and lifted the cushion and panel she had been sitting on. Empty. She slowly worked her way around, looking in every compartment. She found one of Cosmo's magnifying glasses in one; a book of prose and poetry by John Donne in another (Dorian's); and a discarded pair of kid gloves (hers). She disliked it, but she put the gloves on her hands and continued her search.

She was almost to the last panel when she found what she sought—two heavy, woolen blankets knitted by her mother. They smelled musty from being in the gazebo for a year, but they were warm. Pandora went back to her favored bench and wrapped one of the blankets around herself. She set the other one aside, deciding she would take both of them in for cleaning when the rain finally stopped. Before she fully resituated herself, Pandora gleefully removed the gloves and tossed them onto another bench.

She sat that way for a time, her breath warming her legs and nose beneath the blanket. She was almost comfortable…almost. Boredom was the worst part. Pandora wished she had brought something—anything—to break the monotony. She didn't have a candle or she might have attempted to read John Donne. An umbrella or parasol would have been good, too.

A particularly loud drum roll of thunder made her head snap up in surprise to look out the doorway. She stifled a scream when her view was blocked by a man standing there.

It was Lord Islington, Pandora realized…a very soaked, very irate Lord Islington. Once her initial shock over finding someone in the doorway faded, Pandora began to laugh amusedly. He was soaked from head to toe. His hair was plastered to his head. His cravat hung in a limp mess at his throat. One knee of his fawn-colored riding breeches was coated with mud and small pieces of gravel where it seemed he had slipped on the path to the gazebo. He was glowering at Pandora as if he intended to strangle her, which made it all the more comical. She lowered her bare feet to the floor and stood to walk toward him, a hand over her mouth as she tried to control her hilarity, the other holding the blanket around her shoulders for warmth.

"Dear Lord Islington! You look positively drowned!" she managed to get out between giggles.

Islington clenched his teeth on a violent retort. He would maintain his calm. He would not yell at her, he vowed. However, that promise would soon be broken if she didn't quit laughing at him behind her hand.

Pandora's humor died as she realized he had to be freezing. The hairs on her arms were standing up from the cold wind and the chill that had come into the air. When she reached him, Pandora tugged at one of his hands to coax him from the doorway. It felt like ice, even though the walk from the rear of the house was not even two hundred yards.

"Oh, my heavens! You're going to catch your death of cold."

"I'm fine," he bit out. Pandora suspected he clenched his jaw as much from anger as to keep it from chattering.

"No, you aren't," stated Pandora firmly. She wasn't trying to argue; he would become ill if he didn't dry out.

Pandora tossed the blanket onto the bench then reached up for his cravat. A dribble of water ran down her arm to her elbow when she touched it. She clicked her tongue and shook her head. This would not do. Before Islington had time to react, Pandora deftly untied the material and dropped it to one of the side benches. She then grabbed the lapels of his coat and began to remove it as well, unfastening the cuffs and working the soaked woolen material off his arms. It joined the cravat on the bench. She unbuttoned his waistcoat...and tossed it onto the pile. She grabbed the bottom of his shirtfront where it went into his breeches and pulled it loose; then she carefully reached around him to avoid getting wet to free the back and began to unfasten the buttons at the top of it after she unfastened the cuffs.

"Lady Pandora, what are you doing?"

Pandora looked up for a minute and shook her head as she noticed the bluish tinge around his lips. She went back to unfastening buttons.

"You're going to catch your death in these wet clothes. I'm not going to be responsible for that, even if there has been many a time it might have appealed to me. The storm isn't going to let up for a few hours, and these things need to dry out. I'm not going back to the house in this weather, and judging from your condition, you shouldn't either."

She loosened the last button and removed his shirt, exposing his chest. Pandora ignored the thrill the sight gave her and tossed the shirt on the growing pile of clothes. She thought his breeches also needed to come off, but there had to be some kind of decency left to the situation. Besides, she didn't want to give him thoughts. Then she remembered the blankets.

"Now take off those boots and breeches while I try to wring these out," she said, pointing first at the bench then at his clothes.

"I will not!" said Islington in a firm, shocked tone. The chatter of his teeth spoiled the effect.

"Oh, please, Lord Islington. I won't peek. There's a warm blanket there to wrap yourself in. Now quit being infantile."

Without waiting for a response, Pandora turned her back. She took the shirt in her hands, watching in amazement as at least a pint or two of water dripped to the floor as she twisted it. She was unable to do a good job of it because of the weakness still in her left hand, but any wringing was better than none. She tossed the shirt over her head across one of the exposed rafters. She did the same with the other articles then clenched and unclenched her fingers several times to thaw them out. The clothes would be wrinkled, but hopefully they would be mostly dry by the time the rain stopped.

She turned to see Lord Islington had done as she asked and removed his boots and britches. He had to be freezing to be that compliant. The boots were ruined. He could wear them home but only to toss them in the trash heap. He sat with his shoulders hunched, his hands clasped between his thighs, his feet one on top of the other to warm himself. He looked forlorn. Pandora walked over to the bench and sat beside him, draping the other blanket around her own shoulders to ease the chill she felt returning.

"Turn your back to me," she requested gently. He looked at her questioningly for a moment but did as she asked. "Now put your feet up on the cushion."

Pandora moved into the same position, her back resting against the corner. She grabbed his waist and pulled him backward so that when she spread her thighs his back rested against her chest, his head lying on her shoulder. She then reached her arms around his shoulders and placed her hands on his chest, cocooning him and herself in her blanket. He was so cold, the smoothly-muscled expanse felt like marble beneath her palms.

"My God! You didn't get so cold and wet walking from the house!"

"Actually, no. I spent awhile looking for you in the garden. I should have remembered your liking for secluded places," said Islington wryly.

"Dorian asked you to go with me to see Lady Ramsey and Miss Cranston, didn't he?" she asked, realizing it only a moment before.

"Ye-es. Is that who you wanted to call on?"

Pandora nodded then realized he couldn't see her.

"Yes. I wanted to ask them about the Aristocrat."

"The Aristocrat?"

"Dorian didn't tell you?" Islington shook his head negatively. "I see now why you agreed to go with me; as you'd found it so amusing before, you probably wouldn't have wasted the effort had you known."

"And what is that?"

"I told you about Castleton and Bertram Batts."

"Oh, that," he said dismissively. Islington didn't seem to find it as comedic now. "What do those two antidotes have to do with it?"

"Well...," she hesitated.

Pandora wasn't sure she wanted to bring up that night or discuss the matter with him. She didn't want Islington to laugh at her again, but she decided to plough ahead.

"The night of my ball, Lady Ramsey and Miss Cranston literally chased Dorian out of the ballroom; they were harassing him so badly. Then later, when I came out here, I heard the Aristocrat and Castleton talking behind the stable wall. The Aristocrat told Castleton that it was difficult for him to get away because two women were chasing him."

"And you think it was those two?"

"As far as I know, there wasn't anyone else there to fit the 'antidote-in-twos' description. Seraphina Halsey and Lady Asterwick weren't there, nor were Baroness Fribourg and Sarah Mitchell-Langworthy. I want to know who it was that made them forget about my wonderful, handsome brother. Once I discover that, the intrigue is halfway cleared."

There was silence after that statement. Pandora wasn't sure if Lord Islington held his tongue in an effort to be polite (not likely) or because he was beginning to believe her (also, not likely). She felt him shudder every so often and realized he was still quite cold. There was nothing she could else do for him. There was nothing in the gazebo that could be used to warm him, other than Pandora and the blankets. Pandora looked out the doorway at the rain, which seemed to be even worse.

"Lord Islington?"

"Hmm?"

"Do you believe me?"

Islington wasn't truly concentrating on the question. Pandora had absently begun to smooth her hands over his chest in an effort to warm him. She didn't realize the effect it was having; he was becoming warm in more ways than one. It wasn't her intention, he was sure, but he could feel himself becoming aroused.

"Lord Islington, are you all right?" quizzed Pandora worriedly, her mouth close to his ear, when he didn't respond.

"Yes, I'm feeling much better."

"Then do you believe me?"

"Lady Pandora, I honestly don't know."

"But I heard them talking about it twice. It's not possible that I was hearing things wrongly."

"Twice?"

"Yes, I heard them talking behind the wall here and then again in Lord Lundey's study when you left to find my family. That's when they talked about killing Bertram Batts."

"Pandora, you were very ill; are you sure you weren't delirious?"

"No, I was *not* delirious!" she stated vehemently.

What was the use? If her family didn't believe her, why would Lord Islington, a man who thought every word she spoke was a lie? Pandora felt the sting of tears and blinked to hold them back. It didn't work. One slipped out and ran down her cheek. She was so frustrated by all this doubt. No one would believe her, and people were going to die because of it. Another tear escaped to follow the first, causing it to drip onto Islington's chest. He looked up at the ceiling.

"The demmed roof is leaking," he muttered.

"No, it isn't" said Pandora, her voice made husky from her crying.

Islington heard the change and looked at her face. He saw the tears and pursed his lips to hide his discomfort. He did not deal well with weepy females.

"Why are you crying?" he demanded.

"Because no one believes me. You'd believe me if I were a man!"

"Not if he had your history," muttered Islington.

"They're going to kill people! Why won't anyone believe me?" Pandora hiccupped as she held back a sob. "If I could get just one person to believe me and look into it, then people would see I'm telling the truth." Pandora sniffled and reached up a hand to wipe one of her cheeks. "What am I telling *you* for? You think I'm always lying anyhow."

Islington had nothing to say because he knew *that* wasn't a lie. He didn't know why it was so hard for him to believe Pandora. He had truly never caught her lying, except to save him. Although Dorian had stated Pandora was capable of weaving incredible tales that seemed to be nothing but the truth, Islington was yet to witness it. She had always been painfully straightforward with him.

"Crying isn't likely to make me believe you either," he stated in an effort to make her desist.

"I don't care if you believe me, and I'm not crying to convince you of anything!" she huffed.

"Then will you, please, stop?"

Pandora wiped at her cheeks and hiccupped, biting her lower lip in a manner Islington found enticing yet so very innocent. She honestly didn't realize the effect she had on him. She did stop crying then. He decided to investigate her tale, although he wouldn't tell her that…at least not until he discovered for certain if there was any truth to it. He did not want to be the fool in one of her pranks.

Once she calmed down, he returned to his previously comfortable position. He could feel the steady rise and fall of her breasts against his back with every breath she took. She didn't seem bothered by his weight bearing against her. Her hands soon resumed their movements across his chest, and he closed his eyes contentedly. He was no longer chilled, but he didn't plan to tell Pandora that. Islington was enjoying her caresses immensely, innocent though they were. The whole situation was wrong, but he couldn't let it end. Besides, the rain looked as if it wouldn't be stopping anytime in the immediate future.

Pandora at first resumed her ministrations in an effort to remove his chill, but it soon became a sensual experience. It was so tantalizing to smooth her hands over his chest, to feel the hard muscle beneath the velvety surface. She took great pleasure in running her hands across his smoothly rippled stomach, and she began to fantasize he was hers, that she was free to do to him whatever she wanted because they belonged to each other. Her curiosity lent to her touching a keen sensitivity that made her want to caress every inch, to explore and memorize every ridge and ripple she could feel with her fingertips.

Pandora felt her heart begin to beat erratically in her chest and hoped Islington wouldn't notice. She closed her eyes and leaned her head back against the corner, licking lips that had become dry. She was thankful he couldn't see her face because she was sure it was flushed with excitement the likes of which he would easily understand.

She slowly moved her hands back up his chest, letting her palms brush against his nipples lightly. She barely suppressed a gasp when she felt them harden beneath her touch. *Most interesting.* Islington had turned his face into her neck, and she felt his sharp intake and release of breath at the caress. *Yes, most interesting, indeed.* She worked her way back down his stomach, daring to go lower than before, and she felt the material of the other blanket brush her hands. Islington's arms rested slightly away from his sides, and at Pandora's touch, his hands came up to stop her movements.

Pandora raised her head and gasped in surprise when she felt him turn in her arms, bringing his face just inches from hers.

"Lady Pandora?"

"Yes, Lord Islington?" she said breathlessly, her heart pounding in her throat.

Islington looked at her features and knew that, innocent though her caresses may have been, she had become excited. He saw the flush on her cheeks, the way her pupils had dilated, the way the green of her eyes sparkled. He had thought to stop her, but the way she was looking at him with nervous expectation was hard to resist.

"Say my name," he demanded softly.

"Lord Islington?" she asked uncertainly.

"Say my name," he repeated, moving closer.

"Theo," she sighed.

He brought his lips to hers gently, waiting to gauge her reaction. Pandora accepted his advance without protest, her lips slowly opening beneath his, beckoning him to continue. He deepened the kiss, darting his tongue across her lower lip before claiming her mouth hungrily, moving his tongue past her teeth to tease the roof of her mouth and tongue. At first she passively withstood his kiss, but then her arms wrapped around his neck, and she returned his touch by playing her tongue against his.

Islington raised himself until they were both on their knees, their lips never losing contact. He smoothed his hands down Pandora's back, moving lower until they rested on her hips. He pulled her against him, and Pandora gasped when she felt his erection through the layers of material. She felt a tingle work its way up her spine as he caressed her buttocks, keeping himself placed firmly against her.

"Pandora, how can you do this to me? How can you drive me insane with your crazy notions one minute and make me like this the next?"

Pandora chose not to answer him. She felt they were rhetorical questions he asked only of himself. Instead, she trailed her hands down his back then slowly raked her nails back up, making gooseflesh form on his exposed skin. She tilted her head sideways to allow him access to her neck and sighed silkily as his lips trailed lower to the edge of her gown. Pandora became aware of his hands working at the fastenings down the back and a slight smile formed on her lips.

For the moment, she had won. Whatever else he might feel for her, Pandora felt sure that he wanted her. She knew this was wrong in society's eyes, wrong in the eyes of the Church—wrong in most any light placed on it, but she didn't want him to stop. No other man had ever touched her, had ever *dared* touch her, but this one did despite himself. Pandora didn't believe for an instant that he could actually love her, but when they were together like this, he was hers.

Islington reclaimed her lips, and Pandora felt him raise his hands to her shoulders, slowly lowering her dress and chemise in one movement. She released him for a moment to remove the garments from her arms and let them pool around her waist then brought her arms up around his neck. She moaned softly as her nipples brushed against him and moved closer. When he lowered his head to take the tip of one breast hungrily in his mouth, Pandora's hands clutched involuntarily in his hair. She couldn't decide if it were to pull him away or closer. The sensation made her dizzy and breathless.

"Stand up," he whispered, loosening his hold on her.

When she did, her clothing fell into a pool around her feet on the floor of the gazebo, and she was left clad in nothing but her white silk stockings, a look he found utterly appealing. His gaze slowly traveled up her body, and Pandora could imagine his hands touching her. She withstood his perusal unashamedly, and without any hesitation, she reached out and loosed the blanket from around his waist so that he, too, was bare for her viewing.

Pandora's eyes widened with awe. Of course, she had seen statues and paintings, anatomy books and other medical texts, but she quickly realized it wasn't the same thing. Seeing Dorian in his dress-downs had also not prepared her. Islington was beautiful. The taut skin covering the well-formed muscle, the fine soft hair that covered his legs. Although his chest was bare, Pandora saw that a trail started just below his navel, ending in a springy mass around his erection. As for that part of his anatomy, she could see why it had been easy for her to feel through layers of clothing. She wasn't sure how he compared with other men, but Pandora thought he looked perfect.

Her gaze finally rose to meet his, and Pandora could see he was pleased she wasn't embarrassed by their nudity. He grabbed her waist and pulled her close, nuzzling the valley between her breasts before reclaiming a nipple with his mouth. Pandora sighed and leaned closer still, her knees weakening with desire.

She could feel his erection pressing against her abdomen, and Pandora reached down to gently grasp its thickness, marveling at its hard silkiness. Islington groaned at her touch as his hips thrust involuntarily toward her caress. Pandora thrilled at the knowledge of this newfound power over him. She slowly moved her hand back and forth on its hardness, and Islington stilled in his attention to her breasts, his breathing ragged.

"Pandora," he sighed.

She looked at his face, a slow smile beginning to form. His eyes were closed in pleasure, his hands resting on her hips as she continued to stroke him. She leaned forward and began kissing down his neck to his chest, pausing to place tiny teasing bites on one of his nipples.

"Pandora, you're a wanton," he groaned as she went lower, toward his navel, never releasing her grasp on his erection.

Islington soon tired of her teasing and grabbed her wrists, pulling her onto the cushions and guiding her onto her back. He held her still and looked at her features. Her eyes were half-closed as she returned his gaze, her lips parted in a slight smile of anticipation and pleasure. They shouldn't be doing this, but it was too late for him to stop. He had to have her now, no matter the consequences.

"Pandora, we shouldn't be doing this," he whispered, brushing a hand down the side of her neck to place it on her chest.

She reached up to place gentle fingers against his lips to silence him, a tender smile raising the corners of her mouth.

"But we're going to do it anyhow," she whispered back.

Whatever restraint he may have retained vanished at her words. In that moment, he knew she was right. From the day they had met in the park this had been building between them, and he slowly realized his harshness toward her had been a feeble attempt at fighting it. He didn't want to fight it anymore.

He parted her legs and positioned himself to enter her. He pressed slowly into her until he felt the barrier of her virginity. This would hurt her, he knew, but there was no way to avoid it.

"Kiss me, Pandora," he whispered.

As their lips met, he gave one deep thrust and filled her completely. Pandora's cry of pain and surprise was muffled by his mouth over hers, and he stayed unmoving within her. Islington raised his head to look at her and saw that a single tear had escaped from the corner of her eye. He reached up a hand and tenderly brushed it away with his thumb.

"I'm sorry for that," he said gently. "The pain will pass."

Pandora hadn't known what to expect. At the sharp stab of pain, she had been frightened, but as Islington remained still inside her, gently kissing her face to calm her, it had already begun to subside and be replaced by a sense of fullness and completeness. The passion she felt was only momentarily banked by the shock. She moved her hips against his and heard him gasp. He looked down at her with a knowing smile.

He began then slowly, giving her time for her body to adjust to his, watching her face for any sign of discomfort. There was none. Her eyes were closed, her lips parted with a sigh of pleasure, and he began to increase his pace. She whispered his name as the ecstasy began to build, convulsively clutching at his arms. Islington lowered his head to kiss her hungrily, drawing his lips down her throat to a taut nipple, continuing to thrust in and out of her with a steadily increasing pace she matched.

Pandora felt something inside her drawing as tight as a bowstring until she knew it must surely break. She felt almost frantic as she moved against him, her thoughts becoming less coherent as the world shrank to contain just the two of them. As she felt the first wave of release wash over her, Pandora felt her mind begin to shatter into a million tiny shards as her body seemed to be floating in a sea of ecstasy.

As the expression of rapture spread across Pandora's features, Islington felt his control slip away. With one final deep thrust he reached his own climax, his body shuddering. He slowly lowered himself to rest his head against her breast, her heartbeat and breathing as erratic and ragged as his own. She gently cradled him against her, smoothing a hand across his hair.

They remained entwined like that for a while, recovering from the tide that had swept over them, listening to the steady thrum of the rain on the roof. Neither of them wanted to speak because of the knowledge that once they did, the dream would end. They wanted to hold back the consequences of what they had done because neither of them wanted it to be over.

"Do you...," Pandora began slowly, her fingernails trailing across his shoulder blade in a pretended motion of casualness. "Do you regret that we did this?"

Islington lifted his head to look at her, his expression unreadable yet telling Pandora everything she needed to know. A lump began to rise in her throat, and she tried to push him away. She succeeded in sliding backwards into the corner, still trapped but not quite imprisoned.

"Which part did you find so distasteful?" she asked bitterly. "That it was *me* or that it was *you*?"

"Pandora—" he began.

She raised her hand imperiously.

"*Don't!* Don't try to humor me."

She managed to scrabble past him off the bench and grab her clothes from the floor. She began to put them on quickly, as quickly as her arm would let her. Rain or not, she had to get away from him before her courage failed her and she burst into tears, further humiliating herself.

"I'll do the honorable thing. I'll speak to your father," he said calmly.

She looked up at him sharply.

"No, you won't. What was it you said? I wouldn't marry you if the Prince Regent commanded it! You haven't displayed a smidgen of honor before, so why start now?"

She finished fastening the back of her dress and began to look for her slippers. She was sure they couldn't have gone far.

Islington stood up and grabbed her by her arms.

"It's not that simple anymore, Pandora."

"Isn't it?" she sneered at him. "I'll not be a salve to what little conscience you have! You didn't force me."

"I'm afraid the world isn't going to see it that way."

"The *world* doesn't know about it! I'm certainly not going to enlighten them either!" She spied her shoes and twisted free of him to grab them and put them on her feet. "This never happened."

"Yes, it did," said Islington, pulling her toward him for a brutal kiss. She struggled for a moment then relaxed submissively. He released her harshly and glared at her. "Would marrying me be so unbearable?"

"Knowing you did it out of some sense of duty would be. Making a mistake to atone for another is downright criminal."

"This wasn't a mistake," denied Islington flatly.

"Wasn't it? Isn't that what this argument is about? You don't *love me!*"

"What does that have to do with it?"

"If you don't know that, then this whole conversation is pointless."

With that, Pandora grabbed her cane and walked into the rain just as the tears began to burn her eyes.

Chapter Seven

Pandora knew going to see Lady Ramsey and Lucy Cranston would be a bad idea. Not only did she have to tolerate *their* fawning, but it seemed all the other kowtowing socialites of London were gathered there, too. She had hoped for a little privacy, but that was not to be.

She arrived to find a tea party in full swing. At first she thought she could endure it to get the information she needed, but now, not so much. The drawing room was full of women who had nothing better to do than spread gossip and try to scrabble up the social ladder whatever way possible.

"Tell me, Lady Pandora, have you been to Brighton?" asked Lucy as she poured Pandora more tea.

"Whatever for?" asked Pandora in puzzlement.

"Why, my dear, it is *the* place to be when one is not in London," retorted Lady Ramsey in a shocked tone. Everyone within hearing range gaggled agreement. "The Prince's pavilion is marvelous, and the sea air is quite bracing, excellent for the constitution."

"Really?" responded Pandora politely.

"Most certainly," affirmed Lucy, placing a small cake on her plate. "I must tell you how pleased we are you came to call, Lady Pandora."

Pandora smiled amiably and took a sip of the weak tea in her cup. She was looking for an opening to make her enquiries but had thus far not found one. Also, while most of the women in the room were social-climbing tabbies, there was one other besides herself who was not.

"Lady Selena, you must try the Battenberg. Cook went over the top today," said Lady Ramsey, eating another piece of the buttery, sweet cake.

"Perhaps in a moment," responded the young woman, smiling politely with a slight shake of her head.

Pandora was surprised to find when she arrived, by herself in the end, that the women had another visitor besides herself. That anyone besides other gossips would willingly subject themselves to Lady Ramsey and Lucy Cranston was cause enough to give her hesitation, but who the victim was gave her even greater concern. Seated across from Pandora, looking almost as uncomfortable as Pandora felt, was Lady Selena Marshall, Islington's sister. Even before they had been introduced by their hosts, Pandora recognized her from the few times she had seen her. Selena seemed nice from what Pandora could tell, but the discomfiture she felt over the secrets that she kept was hard to move beyond.

Selena was beautiful. Impassibly perfect. Her features were finely sculpted and proportioned. They gave her an almost unapproachable air. Her eyes were the same pure, startling blue as those of her brother. She and Pandora were almost of the same height and figure, yet she carried herself regally, adding to her distant quality. Her hair was a rich chestnut that glinted gold in places. Although she seemed distant and haughty, Pandora felt more than saw that wasn't the case. She sensed a shyness hidden behind the cold façade. Pandora was curious why, haughty or shy, Selena would willingly subject herself to these two women who made no pretense of hiding their desire to climb socially.

"Now, Lady Pandora, you must tell us how you are feeling these days. We were all horrified to learn of your illness."

Pandora nearly choked on her tea.

"I'm quite fine, thank you," she said calmly, absently rubbing on the spot behind her ear where she still had a hole in her skull beneath the healed layer of skin. "It wasn't nearly so bad as you make it."

"Oh, but you're still barely able to get about! To think that you could have *died!*"

Pandora set her tea-cup down, seriously contemplating an immediate exit. Only her need for answers held her tongue in check.

"Well, I suppose God wasn't ready for me yet," said Pandora calmly.

"I trow that's so," concurred Lady Ramsey with an affirming nod, oblivious to Pandora's coldness.

Selena hid an amused smile by drinking from her cup.

Pandora decided enough was enough. Whether Islington's sister or the other women were there or not, she was going to get what she came for and leave as quickly as possible. She didn't know how much more of this she could suffer without becoming downright rude.

"Well, yes," said Pandora. "Actually, I came to call for an indirect purpose, I'm ashamed to admit." That got everyone's attention. "I'm not sure you can help, but you see, the night of the ball at my parents' home—"

"Oh, that was a most *unfortunate* evening for you, wasn't it?" said Lucy with gushing sympathy.

"Yes, quite," said Pandora dully. She could feel the beginnings of a headache, but fortunately, it was a normal one rather than a migraine.

"Do continue, Lady Pandora," prompted Selena helpfully.

"Well, I met so many people that night, and circumstance since then being what it was, I'm afraid I can't remember them all."

"Oh, you poor dear," tutted Lady Ramsey.

"It wouldn't be so terrible, you see, but there was one particular man I met that I would like to remember, but I can't recall his name. I don't think I've seen him again since. I thought I might enlist your help."

"My dear, we would be honored to be of assistance," gushed Lucy.

"Oh, yes, we would be more than happy to help a blossoming romance," cooed Lady Ramsey. "Now, what did he look like?"

"Well," began Pandora, chewing on her lower lip thoughtfully. "He was tall, but not too tall, and sturdy. He was handsome, of course. What truly fascinated me was his voice."

"Come again?" quizzed Lady Ramsey blankly.

"He spoke with such decorum, and he had a very nice baritone."

"What color was his hair? His eyes?" asked Lucy vexedly.

Pandora achieved a believably crestfallen expression.

"Ah, that, you see, is another difficulty. I can't remember. I have only a clear memory of his voice and a hazy recollection of the rest."

"Oh, la, you poor thing!" cried Lucy, horrified.

"But, surely you can help," said Pandora hopefully. "I'm positive he was handsome and of good quality. He must have been striking, else I would remember nothing about him. My brother, Lord Glamorgan, told me that you had abandoned him in your affections for someone more fair that evening. He seemed most upset by it." Dorian would kill her for that, but the wretch deserved it for making her come alone. "Maybe *he* is my handsome dream prince."

The two ladies grew thoughtful. Selena was watching calmly, but Pandora detected an amused twinkle in her eyes. Everyone else had resumed their idle chit-chat. Lady Ramsey snapped her fingers.

"I have it! It must have been that charming Lord Hendon!" she cried excitedly.

"Lord Hendon?" asked Pandora blankly. She didn't recall that name from the list her mother had given her.

"Of course!" agreed Lucy. "Ector Marsh, the Earl of Hendon. Oh, he is dashing," she sighed dreamily. Her expression became dismayed. "Oh, dear, I'm afraid I've some upsetting news."

"What is that?" asked Pandora absently, still trying to find the name in her mental list.

"If Lord Hendon is your dashing *amor*, I'm sorry to say it can be nothing more than a flirtation. For he's married, you see. Yes, for not too many months past he was wed to Georgiana Jeffries, the Marchioness of Morecambe. In November, I believe, yes," said Lucy thoughtfully.

"Oh," said Pandora, managing a look of desolation. "Yes, that does put a damper on things."

"Well, we mustn't dwell," said Lady Ramsey cheerily, reaching across to pat Pandora on the knee. "Perhaps we can find someone better suited." She sat for a moment, eating another piece of cake, and then she gained a look of inspiration. "My dear, I know just the one for you!"

"Indeed?" quizzed Pandora absently, storing away the name *Ector Marsh, the Earl of Hendon.* She would look over her mother's list again the moment she got home.

"Why, none other than Lord Islington, Lady Selena's brother!"

"Lord Islington?" said Pandora weakly.

"My brother?" said Selena in the same tone.

"Oh, he would be perfect for you, I trow," continued Lady Ramsey definitely. "He is handsome and well-connected, and I'm sure he's quite capable of attending to your *every* need." She gave Pandora a meaningful wink.

It wasn't difficult for Pandora to blush a glaring shade of pink. This was not where she wanted the conversation to head. From Selena's uncomfortable expression, Pandora could see she'd rather not have it go there either. Pandora was beginning to wonder if the little bit of information she had gathered was worth this. Luckily, none of the other women in the room seemed aware of what was being said, all of them content to converse about their own idle gossip.

"You know, Aunt, I believe you may be right. They would make a dashing pair, don't you think?" asked Lucy, shaking her hands in the air excitedly and bouncing up and down on the settee.

"Indeed," agreed Lady Ramsey with a satisfied smile. "What do you think, Lady Selena?"

The young woman across from Pandora shifted uncomfortably when the two turned to look at her expectantly. Pandora couldn't help but give Selena an inquiring look as well, although her gaze was not disconcertingly avid like theirs. Selena's opinion about the notion would be enlightening.

Selena sat for a moment as if she wouldn't say anything.

"Well, I never really thought about it," said Selena calmly. "These days, my brother says he will never get married."

"You cannot mean it!" gasped Lady Ramsey in shock.

"But he must marry, if only to carry on the family name, now your brother William is gone!" continued Lucy in an equally scandalized tone.

"He has said many times that women are a nuisance." Pandora didn't doubt that. "He says they have no common sense, courage, congeniality, or intelligence. He says they are capricious and cruel, and that they like nothing better than to vex mankind and make their lives miserable." Selena shrugged her shoulders diffidently.

That sounds like Islington, thought Pandora.

"Obviously, he's neglected to see you, his own sister, as proof that his idea is unfounded," said Lady Ramsey sagely. She took a sip of her tea.

"Well, it's no wonder he thinks that way after what that awful Miss Jessica Wainwright did to him. Leaving him at the altar like that," added Lucy sadly.

Pandora had an honestly lost expression, and Lady Ramsey leaned over to pat her hand.

"Lord Islington was betrothed to a Miss Jessica Wainwright, oh, I guess nigh on five or six years ago," said Lady Ramsey with a thoughtful expression. "She was well beneath him socially and financially, but he was besotted. The late Lord Bardsey, Lady Selena's father, agreed to the match—if he couldn't prevent it because of his son's age—on the condition the current Lord Bardsey not take the marquessate but that his firstborn son would inherit. He agreed to it—he loved her that much.

"Well, the day came for the wedding and everyone was gathered at the church, but Miss Wainwright never showed. She literally jilted him at the altar, m'dear. Not to anyone's knowledge did she ever explain her reasons. The only thing to be assumed was that she was after him for his inheritance. Word came back that she had gone to the continent and wed to some German count or other, who—while definitely not as striking a catch as Lord Islington—was most certainly wealthy."

Pandora tried to keep her features calm. She was shocked, shocked by the tale and by Lady Ramsey's audacity and indecency of telling it in front of Lord Islington's sister. Pandora's mother had taught her things of that nature were not spoken of this way. However, Lady Ramsey was not finished, to both Pandora and Selena's dismay.

"The late Lord Bardsey tried to mend the parting of ways between him and his son, but there was no success. Some say when he died not too long after, it was from a broken heart. In his will, he rescinded his condition, and the present Lord Bardsey inherited after all. It's apparent the hard feelings still exist, though. Lord Islington wouldn't even attend his father's funeral. That's why he uses the lesser viscountcy as his address…it was one he inherited from his mother's father, not *his* father."

Pandora was speechless with shock. What could she say after hearing a tale like that? Selena was mortified, her cheeks pale, her eyes rounded in alarm. It was past time for Pandora's departure.

"My goodness, look at the time! I told Mamà that I wouldn't be gone long," said Pandora, rising from the sofa. "Perhaps I can drop you somewhere?" she asked Selena kindly.

"Yes, I do believe it's time for me to be going also," agreed the young woman dully, rising as well.

"Must you go?" asked Lady Ramsey.

"Yes, I'm afraid so," said Pandora hurriedly.

"I really must," said Selena at the same time.

"Let me accompany you to the door," said Lady Ramsey cheerily, oblivious to how bothered the young women were by her story.

Pandora and Selena nodded their goodbyes to the rest of the women in the room and hastily made their way out. The family carriage was in front of the door, and Pandora was glad she had told Jim to wait.

"Take us to the Marshall residence on Upper Grosvenor, Jim," said Pandora as he held the door open for them.

"Yes, my lady," he replied, touching the brim of his cap.

After they were seated and the carriage was under way, Pandora leaned back against the cushions and heaved a tired sigh. She wasn't feeling strong enough yet to go through scenes like that.

"I'm sorry you had to endure that," said Pandora softly.

Selena waved a hand through the air and sighed.

"Oh, I was asking for it," she said wryly.

"If you don't mind me saying so, you don't seem like one who would intentionally be in their company."

"Well, you don't seem so either."

"Not under ordinary circumstances. Not on your life! But they had some information I needed."

"Ah, yes, Lord Hendon," said Selena with a slight smile.

"Yes, well, the reason I needed his identity had nothing to do with what I told them."

"Indeed?"

Pandora hesitated a moment but decided to plough ahead. She instantly liked Selena and wanted to befriend her. The only reason she hesitated was the past results she had received on her recounting the story. She hoped maybe this time she would be believed unreservedly.

"Well, right off, let me say that those who know me best also know I am prone to exaggerate the truth and make up stories. I don't know if you'll believe me either, but this is the honest truth or, so help me, my name is not Lady Pandora Aphrodite Oriel Savage."

"Go on."

"It all started the night of my come-out ball when I heard two men talking in the mews behind my family's home. They were—are—planning to kidnap a man—a man that I think may be of some importance—from Edinburgh. He will soon be coming to London to tend to some business, and they intend to nab him on his way back to Scotland. Then they plan on killing him!"

Selena's eyes widened in shock.

"One of the men was at the ball. Lady Ramsey and Miss Cranston were chasing him most of the night when they weren't after my brother, Dorian, so I thought they could tell me who he was. Hence, Lord Hendon. I have learned since then that the other man I heard is named Castleton. There is a third conspirator named Bertram Batts, but they plan to kill him also because he doesn't want to help them anymore."

Selena leaned back in the cushions of her seat and inhaled deeply. Pandora, meanwhile, was holding her breath, waiting for Selena to laugh as everyone else had. After a moment, the slightly older girl spoke.

"I can see why no one believes you; it is an incredible tale." She looked at Pandora with a wry half-smile. "Still, I've come to believe that the things so unlike the truth usually are." Pandora smiled with relief at Selena's acceptance of what she said. "Perhaps we can get my brother to help you."

"Oh, no!" said Pandora quickly.

Selena's eyebrow shot up quizzically in a move so like her brother that Pandora blinked in bemusement. She groaned and shook her head.

"He knows. I told him, and he doesn't believe me any more than my family does. He's the only one outside of them that I've talked to about the whole sordid thing...and you...now."

"Might I ask why?"

Pandora chewed her lip. "I don't know. I guess because he's Dorian's best mate, and he's always around these days. Aside from that, he just...I don't know. When he's around, I can't think straight."

"Indeed?"

"Truly! He makes me so mad sometimes I'm sure I could strangle him and not think twice about it!"

The corners of Selena's mouth quirked up in amusement because he often provoked the same emotions from her.

"And what about the rest of the time?"

Pandora blushed profusely. Selena waved her hand through the air dismissively and gave a slight shake of her head.

"Forget I asked that." She reached across the carriage to take Pandora's hands reassuringly. "You leave my brother to me. He'll help you get this sorted out, or *my* name's not Lady Selena Maureen Marshall."

Just then the carriage came to a sudden halt, so sudden that Pandora was flung across it to land on the seat beside Selena. They heard a loud curse from Jim on the driver's seat, and then the door was opened to reveal him standing outside it, his hat askew on his head.

"I'm sorry, my lady. All right?"

"Yes, Jim, I think we're fine. What's happened?"

"Road's blocked, mum. There's a crowd o' folks an' other carriages in the way," he said in his strong Cockney accents.

"What?" gasped Pandora in surprise. She stood to exit the carriage.

Jim was right. There was no way to move forward. Twenty or thirty people were scattered around carriages of various sizes with more joining them from carriages stopped behind her own.

"You want that I should go see what's 'appening?"

"Yes, please, if you would, Jim," said Pandora, turning to look up at Selena perplexedly in the doorway of the carriage. "Well, if this isn't an odd state of affairs."

She was tempted to go see what was causing the obstruction herself but decided she would wait. She was still using her cane, and her arm—while vastly improved—was still not working properly. Besides, she didn't know what Selena might think of her if she did. It would be somewhat uncouth. Selena, meanwhile, was standing on tiptoe in the doorframe trying to see for herself. After seeing that, Pandora shrugged and climbed into the driver's seat, standing on the seat itself for a better vantage point. Selena soon joined her.

"Can you see anything?" asked Selena, shielding the sun from her eyes with her fan.

"No. You?"

"It seems traffic is blocked both ways, so I don't think it's a carriage that's lost a wheel. Something like that wouldn't be attracting this much attention."

"I think I see a constable or two up there."

"Oh, I hope it's not anything serious," said Selena worriedly.

About that time, Jim staggered to a stop by the carriage, trying to catch his breath from running.

"We'll not be getting through anytime soon, Lady Pandora," he panted, leaning on a wheel.

Pandora and Selena climbed down from the seat to the ground.

"What's happened, Jim?" asked Pandora concernedly.

"Someone's been killed, mum."

"What?" gasped both Selena and Pandora.

"Yes, my lady. From what I got, seems a gentleman was walking along an' a piece of masonry fell down from one of the buildings an' kilt 'im dead."

"My heavens!" gasped Selena in dismay.

"Did you get a name, Jim?" asked Pandora stilly.

She had a very bad feeling, a sense of premonition that raised the hair on the back of her neck and caused goose bumps to rise on her arms.

"No, my lady. I think he was a lord or something though."

Pandora grabbed the sleeve of a well-dressed man walking by, leaving the front of the commotion.

"Excuse me, sir, but do they know who it was?"

"The new, young Marquess of Tarlborough, Bertram Batts," he replied. "Hasn't been titled more than two months now. It's an awful tragedy. Did you know him? Miss, are you all right?"

Pandora staggered backward, looking for a place to sit down. She felt dizzy, her breath catching in her throat. Her vision was narrowing, and she thought she was going to faint. Jim and Selena guided her to the step of the coach. After an apologetic glance to the gentleman Pandora had accosted, they turned their full attention to her. She was bent forward, her head resting on her knees and shaking from side to side in disbelief.

"Oh, please, tell me I'm dreaming this, Lady Selena," she moaned. "Please, tell me he didn't say Bertram Batts."

Selena placed a hand on Pandora's shoulder, her brow etched with concern. She needed to get Pandora away from this place; they were beginning to attract attention. She spied an alleyway across from them that led to a street where traffic was moving easily.

"Jim, can you get the carriage through that space?" she asked.

"It'll be tight, my lady, but I'll give it a go," he replied gamely.

Selena raised Pandora to an upright position. She was very pale and seemed to be on the verge of panic.

"Come on, Lady Pandora. We're going to get you home," she said, helping Pandora stand and get into the carriage.

"Oh, I'll be all right," dismissed Pandora with a weak smile. "Jim, let's get Lady Selena seen home first, please."

"Yes, mum," said Jim, closing the door after seeing them seated.

They felt the carriage rock slightly as Jim climbed up to the driver's seat and a lurch as he got the horses to turn for the alley. Selena sighed audibly once they were moving again. She glanced concernedly at Pandora, who sat on the seat across from her with her eyes closed.

"Lady Pandora?"

Pandora's eyes shot open with surprise.

"Hmm? What's the matter?"

"I was just making sure you were all right."

Pandora smiled apologetically.

"I'm sorry for that display back there. I really am not one for fainting and histrionics, truly. It's just that it came as a bit of a shock, especially as we were talking about it."

"Maybe it was just a coincidence," dismissed Selena hopefully.

"Oh, I'm sure that's what everyone will say. The constables will never find anything to prove it was more than an accident caused by shoddy workmanship. Meanwhile, Castleton and his cohort, Hendon or otherwise, will continue with their plot to kidnap and murder the man from Edinburgh." She shook her head. "I can't believe this. No wonder no one else can."

"Well, I believe you, and if I needed any convincing, I would say that did a pretty fine job of it. Maybe it will convince my brother as well," said Selena hopefully.

"You'll forgive me if I don't hold my breath," said Pandora dryly, but she smiled to soften the sarcasm. "And it's just Pandora, by the way," she added with another smile. "I think we've been through enough together over the past hour or so that formality is something we can put aside."

"And you may call me Selena," said the other girl with a happy smile of her own. "Will you come in for dinner?"

Pandora was about to refuse but changed her mind at Selena's hopeful expression. *She must be as friendless as I am,* thought Pandora sadly.

"Well, I can't say I'm hungry, but I'd be delighted to join you."

They remained silent for the rest of the ride. Pandora's mind raced at the day's turn of events. While she had possibly discovered the identity of the second conspirator, one of their victims was now dead. Pandora wondered if he might still be alive if she had sent him a warning. She might have done, if she had known there would be so little time to save him. She was unconscious for the better part of three weeks after learning his name, but it had been almost three months. She couldn't help feeling a little guilt over his death because of her hesitation. Would he even have believed her, though? She tried to dismiss all these might-have's and should-have's because it was too late to save Bertram Batts now, but there was still one man left to deliver from the criminals. Pandora didn't even know his name. She didn't like feeling this helpless.

There had to be some way to discover the intended victim's identity. She had been racking her brain for days trying to determine who from Edinburgh would be important enough for someone to want his demise. Who would be wealthy enough to pay a ransom to set up two felons for life? He was possibly a peer, but he could just as easily be a merchant or someone in the military or government. They were at war with America and with France (well, Napoleon), but was there anyone in Scotland intrinsically involved in either that would make these men want his death? If that were the case, then these men were not only immoral murderers, they were possible traitors to their country as well.

For a few stray moments, Pandora let her mind wander to Islington. While she had been shocked by the tale of Lady Ramsey and Miss Cranston, she had to wonder how much was idle gossip and how much was truth. Selena had said or done nothing to refute the story, and Pandora wasn't lowborn enough to come right out and ask her. Pandora knew well enough for herself that the part about his not inheriting the title had been an outright falsehood. Anyone with sense knew entitlement didn't work that way; it had taken a recreation of the letters patent for Dorian to inherit his viscountcy from their grandfather. Yet, even if only the other half of it were true, it was easy enough for Pandora to see where his high-handed attitude toward women had come from. It did rouse a little sympathy for him, but she still couldn't quite forgive him for everything he'd done—real or imagined. Some of her wounds were still a little too fresh for that.

And what of this new development in the intrigue? Would Islington help her now? She believed he would say Bertram Batts's death was an accident and a coincidence, no matter what Selena said to the contrary. Pandora had given him names and locations already, and it had done nothing. He was content to disbelieve her. Pandora was beginning to think it was pointless to convince him that it was the truth.

She had panicked for a moment when she wondered what was going to happen if he was at home when she arrived with Selena. Pandora had told him she was going to forget what happened in the gazebo, but she hadn't yet. She didn't think she ever would, and she had been lying to herself and him when she said it.

It didn't take much reasoning on Pandora's part to realize she was in love with him. Which was why she couldn't marry him. Could she see him again and pretend nothing had happened? She would have to. She didn't want Islington to fall on his knees and profess undying love and eternal devotion, but for him to admit he felt *something* would be a good start. She didn't foresee that happening. She would try her best to put it out of her mind and avoid him as much as possible.

The coach stopped, and Jim opened the door for them.

"I'll be staying for dinner, Jim," said Pandora as she stepped down.

"Yes, my lady," said Jim, touching the edge of his hat respectfully.

"Oh, don't look at me like that," Pandora scolded fondly. "I'm fine, really." She pinched his cheek and winked at him, and he smiled with relief.

Pandora followed Selena up the short walkway to the door, her cane making a soft click as she moved. She was almost to the point she might be comfortable without it, but her leg still felt a little wobbly sometimes.

"Do you always do that?" asked Selena.

"Do what?" asked Pandora blankly, completely at a loss.

"Tease your driver like that?"

Pandora stopped for a moment to look at Selena contemplatively.

"I've never thought about it, actually. I'm sure it might seem odd to most people that my family is so familiar with our servants, but we just like them all so much. *They're* like family." She shrugged and followed Selena through the door.

They were met by the butler: traditional, formal, and very British.

"Waldon, this is Lady Pandora Savage. Pandora, this is Waldon, our butler," said Selena as she handed him her belongings.

The butler bowed slightly to Pandora and reached out to take her things. He started to take her cane, but she held onto it.

"This is for more than just appearances," said Pandora with a wink.

His mouth opened in surprise, and Selena looked at him apologetically.

"Is my mother home?" she asked quickly.

"Yes, Lady Selena. She and his lordship are presently in the private sitting room having dinner."

"Excellent, Waldon."

Selena led Pandora down the hall to a doorway on the right. Pandora was walking a little slower than necessary. She was in no hurry to see Islington again. It had been a little over a month since they had made love in the gazebo, but it felt as if it were yesterday to Pandora. And what response would he have to seeing her? She couldn't imagine he would feel the same anxiety she felt; after all, he didn't have any emotions involved, except for his pride.

Selena opened the door to a room flooded with late afternoon sunlight from a bank of windows overlooking the garden. It was decorated in shades of blue and white, making it cheery and welcoming. It was obvious from its appearance that it wasn't the sitting room where the Marshalls normally entertained guests. There was a small dining table by the windows and a writing desk in one corner littered with writing apparatus and opened letters. It was also decorated with personal mementos like needlework and art done by family members. Pandora thought it was charming.

When the girls walked in, Islington and his mother were seated at the table conversing quietly. They stopped as the door opened, and Islington stood. His expression was impassive, but he was looking at Pandora and ignoring his sister. Their mother, on the other hand, looking at her also, was openly curious.

"Why, Selena, we were hoping you would be back in time for dinner. And who is this you've brought with you?"

Pandora looked at the marchioness with equal curiosity, trying to ignore Islington and the way he seemed intent on burning holes through her with his eyes. Lady Bardsey was several inches shorter than her son and daughter (easily a foot shorter in her son's case). Her hair was already white, but her features were still fairly free of wrinkles. Her eyes were those of her children, and they had inherited her bone structure, too. Pandora detected a slight Scottish lilt in her voice

Selena went to her mother and kissed her on the cheek affectionately.

"Mama, this is my newfound friend, Lady Pandora Savage," said Selena with a pleased smile. "We met at Ramsey's. I've invited her for dinner."

Lady Bardsey turned to look at her son in surprise.

"Teddy, this is the one? Glamorgan's sister and Aberdare's daughter?"

Pandora was momentarily nonplussed. First, she had to accustom herself to other people addressing Dorian by his formal title, something she was not quite used to. She only ever heard him addressed by his given name or nickname by family; it was only rarely that she heard someone call him by his title, and she sometimes forgot what it was. Second, she discovered she wasn't the only one who had been cursed with a diminutive nickname by her family. She almost laughed because Islington's didn't sound any more dignified than hers.

"Yes, Mother," he replied blandly, drawing Pandora's attention back to the matter at hand.

Lady Bardsey looked at her with a warmhearted smile.

"I am so pleased to finally meet you. Your brother and my son have told me so much about you."

Pandora raised a quizzical eyebrow and looked at Islington. His face remained unreadable, and he would provide her no information, either by word or expression. Just what, exactly, had they been telling this poor woman? Certainly not the truth…at least, Pandora hoped not.

"It's a pleasure to meet you as well," replied Pandora, reaching out a hand to the woman.

"Mama, you'll never guess what just happened while we were on our way home!" said Selena excitedly.

"First, you and Lady Pandora will sit down and join your brother and me for dinner. Then you can tell me your news," said Lady Bardsey firmly but with a smile.

Pandora trailed behind them, as much from her infirmity as from her nervousness about the situation. She watched as Selena chattered happily with her mother about the things she had found in the shops. Islington turned slightly and paused to reach out a hand to Pandora.

"Do you require assistance, Lady Pandora?" he asked politely.

"No, thank you, Lord Islington. I can manage quite well these days," she returned in the same impersonal tone.

Pandora felt relatively safe with him in the company of the other two women. It wasn't as if he would be able to bring up anything as private as what had happened in the gazebo while in their presence, and Pandora didn't intend to be left alone with him at any time for him to mention it to her either. Their family shared an informal relationship much like that of Pandora's own, but it would only go so far.

Lady Bardsey rang a small bell sitting on the table and was answered by a footman in finely-pressed livery. She requested settings for her daughter and Pandora. He soon returned and had the plates and utensils placed neatly before them and removed the covers from the dishes. Tea was poured and the meal was served without a word. Pandora looked down at the food, but she wasn't sure she could eat. The poached salmon with new potatoes and fresh peas looked appetizing, but she felt a peculiar nausea settle into her stomach at the smell of the fish. It was peculiar because she adored salmon.

"Now, what was it that had you in such a dither when you came in?" asked Lady Bardsey, looking at her daughter with a smile.

"A man was killed!" said Selena excitedly.

"Oh, really? How awful!" said Lady Bardsey in a breathless voice, a hand going to her throat.

"And what's more, Pandora knew it was going to happen!" said Selena with a telling nod.

Pandora grew uncomfortable when three pairs of blue eyes came to rest on her. She set down her fork. Now she *really* didn't want to eat.

"Is that so?" enquired Lady Bardsey.

"It wasn't due to any premonition on my part," said Pandora calmly. "It's simply that I knew someone was plotting to kill this particular man."

"Who was it?" asked Islington, his brow furrowing.

"Bertram Batts, the young, newly-titled Marquess of Tarlborough," said Pandora evenly.

"How did it happen?"

"We were unable to get specifics, but from what my driver was able to discover, it seems he was crushed by a piece of falling masonry."

"What a terrible accident!" said Lady Bardsey, her forehead wrinkling concernedly.

Islington continued to look at Pandora speculatively.

"You don't think it *was* an accident, do you?" he asked her calmly.

"You'll forgive me if I can't dismiss it as such, not when I know two men were plotting to kill him more than two months ago. I'm sure to most people it seems nothing more than a tragic coincidence, but if they were trying to kill him without arousing suspicion, I couldn't think of a more perfect way to accomplish it."

Islington looked at her seriously as he took a sip from his tea. He wasn't expecting her to arrive with his sister. He had sent Selena on the errand to Lady Ramsey and Lucy Cranston. Chances were likely, however, that she had been unable to find out what he wanted to know, considering the object of the foray was present at the time. That would have to wait until after Pandora left.

He had been making enquiries into the plot that Pandora was convinced was happening, but he hadn't been able to find anything. There *was* a place called the Dog. He had even gone there, but it was the type of establishment where even if anyone knew anything, they thought wiser of saying so without a generous incentive. Now there was this new development, and Islington wasn't so sure he could pretend Pandora was imagining or creating things any longer.

"I was able to get what may be the name of the Aristocrat from Lady Ramsey and Lucy Cranston. I'm not familiar with him, but perhaps you've heard of him?" continued Pandora.

"Who?" asked Islington calmly.

"Ector Marsh, the Earl of Hendon?"

Islington wiped his mouth with his napkin and set it by his plate, his expression impassive. He was now finding it difficult to believe she was making this up. He finally nodded his head, his lips set in a firm line.

"I know him, in a manner of speaking. He is a man who has the classification of gentleman only by birth. He has a very dark reputation that has never been substantiated by proof, and he is personally not pleasant."

"Do you think he might be the Aristocrat?" asked Pandora hopefully.

Islington shrugged and tilted his head slightly to indicate it bore probability. "Had you been given any other suspect, I might have said no, but this is the sort of thing I certainly wouldn't put past him."

"So what do we do now?"

"*We* aren't going to do anything."

"But—" began Pandora.

"No." Islington held up a hand imperiously to silence her, and Pandora blinked. "I think this is something you need to leave to me and your brother going forward. If Ector Marsh is the other conspirator, he is extremely dangerous. It would be best if you forgot about this business."

"Nǐ xiǎng fàn yīqǐ qù ma?" muttered Pandora to herself under her breath, shaking her head. She looked at him disdainfully, her chin raised determinedly. "Pardon me, but have you gone mental?" asked Pandora coldly. Selena and Lady Bardsey looked at her with shocked expressions. "I have been trying for months to get someone—*anyone*—to listen to me and do something, and now you want me to *forget* about it?" Pandora snorted unbecomingly. "No one would even know about it if it hadn't been for *me*. You wouldn't have the names of the conspirators if it weren't for *me*. You cannot mean to ask me to forget it simply because I am a woman and Hendon is an 'extremely dangerous' man?"

"That's exactly why you should. Any other woman would see the sense in it and leave off."

Pandora compressed her lips coldly and decided she had enough for one day. *People!* She looked at Lady Bardsey and Selena apologetically for her outburst, and then she looked at Islington disgustedly and stood up.

"I am *not* any other woman," she said plainly and calmly. "Lady Bardsey, it was a pleasure to meet you. Selena, I would love for you to please come by anytime. Lord Islington," she finished shortly.

She nodded her head and walked to the door. She could have started an argument and ranted until she was blue in the face, but she was exhausted and starting to feel unwell. It would have been useless anyhow. More than ever, she wished she was at home in the solar…just so she would be able to scream out her frustration at the top of her lungs without anyone being the wiser.

Chapter Eight

Pandora made it to the coach without any further *orders* from Islington and asked Jim to take her to the house the long way around. She rested her head against the cushions and heaved a tired sigh. She wanted a nap, and her stomach hurt. Although she had thought she would attend Almack's that night, today's melodrama had deflated her enough that she would like to just stay home. She would be unpleasant company.

So she was to be delegated to the position of simple female, waiting at home while the *he-man* faced danger. She had hoped someone better equipped would take up the cause, but she didn't expect once someone had that she would be dismissed like…like a woman. She was feeling misused, but she couldn't say Islington surprised her. After everything she had seen and heard, it wasn't a shock that he thought this was "man's work."

She thought back to her brief meeting with his mother. Lady Bardsey seemed to be well informed about Pandora by Islington and Dorian, and she could only guess what had been discussed. It was unlikely Islington had spoken of their indiscretions. But what had Lady Bardsey been told, and why would he have mentioned Pandora to his mother? The marchioness seemed to be a very pleasant, no-nonsense individual, who Pandora was sure she would get on well with and would like to become better-acquainted with at some future time. She didn't see that as a likelihood.

Pandora was infinitely glad to have met Islington's sister. Pandora was surprised they hadn't met before, but it may have been delayed due to her illness, among other things. Selena seemed to be very sweet and easygoing, with an exuberance that had not been obvious on their first meeting. Pandora could easily see her becoming a fast friend. She would have to make sure they kept in touch once the Season was over.

What Pandora couldn't understand after meeting the women was where Islington's sometimes insufferable demeanor had come from. Perhaps it was from the late marquess, his father. Having never met the man, Pandora could not say so definitely, and it would be unfair of her to assume it. He wasn't *always* unpleasant. At times he could be tender and gentle, and he did have a healthy sense of humor. It made her wonder.

The carriage came to a halt as it reached Oxford Street when Jim was obliged to wait for oncoming traffic to clear before he could make the right-hand turn to take them onto it. It would be another half-hour or so before they were to Aberdare House. The day was over half done, the sun beyond its zenith and beginning to set, but the temperature was unseasonably warm. Pandora reached over to drop one of the windows of the enclosed carriage to allow any possible fresh breeze to blow through. The carriage continued on its way then with a gentle lurch, and its rocking motion began to lull Pandora to sleep.

She needed to find the man in Edinburgh. Islington had told her not to get involved with Castleton or Hendon, but—if she chose to obey his command—he had said nothing of their victim. Pandora needed to focus her attention to that end. Time was running out for that man, whoever he was, and even if Dorian and Islington were taking up the banner for stopping their plan, there was still no *evidence* of a plan—just Pandora's word. Everything was circumstantial, even Bertram Batts's death. There was no proof any of the men involved even knew each other. It wasn't as if her brother and Islington could set someone to watch Castleton and Hendon day and night, waiting for them to take action. It also wasn't as if they could straightforwardly accuse the two men of planning the deed.

And what of the two criminals? Castleton had been called by name, but could Pandora be sure that was his *real* name? She only knew him by name and voice, not by appearance. If he were devious enough to be planning someone's kidnapping and death, providing a false name would be of little consequence. As for Hendon, Pandora had no proof that *he* was the Aristocrat. Islington said he was a likely suspect, but Pandora only had his name to go by. They would have to be caught with their hands around the victim's throat to be apprehended.

Her drowsy mind began to review the conversations she had heard between Castleton and Hendon. She was searching for any little detail that might have been mentioned that could provide the identity of the Edinburgh victim. The only things she had been able to determine were that he was someone of importance and apparently no small amount of wealth. He was also someone who didn't appear to travel with a large retinue. That ruled out someone of the royal family, but it didn't exclude the aristocracy, military, or government. The possibilities were endless, and that was not a good thing.

Edinburgh was the capital of Scotland, but not the capital of Great Britain. All political decisions were made in London. Most government and military leaders were also in London. There was nobility in Scotland, but most were in London for the Season. Even most of the wealthy merchant class came to town for the Season. Who would still be in Edinburgh then? Someone to whom the London season meant little, thought Pandora logically, but who would that be?

The carriage came to a halt at a crossroads again, and Pandora looked out to see where they were. It appeared to still be the shopping district. The storefront she saw was a jeweler's. The window display was dripping with diamonds and other precious gems, which would shortly be locked away when the store closed for the night. One necklace in particular, Pandora noticed, was so gaudily encrusted that she could scarcely believe one person would want to wear it. The carriage was close enough to the walkway, and the walkway was narrow enough that Pandora was able to read the print on the card placed beside it.

Three hundred fifty carats of Yellow & White Peruzzi-cut Diamonds set in Gold. Formerly in the Royal Crown Jewels of France, created for Marie Antoinette. Enquire within for pricing.

There you have it. Anyone who would sport that much wealth was begging to have their head cut off to have it liberated, and the Republic had obliged. Pandora spared the necklace one more glance as Jim started the carriage moving and relaxed into the cushions. She shouldn't be so uncharitable, but someone would have to be unbelievably naïve not to realize if one's country is starving, one doesn't wear something that would feed a good deal of its population for a month around one's neck.

The ride home seemed short to Pandora, but perhaps the nap she had taken made it that way. She dozed off not long after the carriage started moving again, and she jerked awake with surprise when Jim opened the door to let her step down. She had hoped a nap would make her feel better, but Pandora felt more drained than before. She firmly decided she wouldn't be going to Almack's, and she would be perfectly happy to stay home working on the equation she had been fiddling with for the past week.

She started to go to the house but went to visit Bellerophon in the stables first. As she reached the end of the row where her stallion was kept, she released a low whistle. It was promptly answered by a loud whinny and a thump to the wood of Bellerophon's door near the middle of the row as he tried to get out. That was not going to happen, so he had to be satisfied with stretching his neck over the top and straining against it, trying to see her.

"Hey, fella," said Pandora as she neared him, reaching out her hand to smooth it across his muzzle.

"Oh, my, you are looking lovely today, my big, handsome boy," she soothed. Bellerophon nickered softly and placed his nose between her arm and her side, nearly knocking her off balance.

"I know. You're looking for sugar, aren't you?" Pandora sighed and rubbed his forehead with her knuckles, giving him a good scratch. "I'm afraid I don't have any today, pet."

Pandora looked around to see if any of the hands were about, but she was alone with her horse.

"Give me two minutes, sweetie," said Pandora with a pat to his neck, and she turned to go back down the aisle to the stable master's quarters.

Bellerophon whinnied loudly and kicked the door again, making Pandora pause to look back over her shoulder.

"I'll be back with something, boy," she called and quickened her pace a little.

Visiting her horse made Pandora smile with pleasure, but it also saddened her. She had seen him very rarely since her illness, and she was yet to ride him again. She very much wanted to, but she was smart enough to realize he was a powerful and spirited animal, one that required someone with a firm hand to control him. Unfortunately, she wasn't confident hers was up to the challenge yet. She was afraid she might never be able to ride him again.

Bellerophon had been her horse since he was a yearling. Her father had let her pick him out of the year's foals as a present for her thirteenth birthday, when his grace had felt she was old enough to graduate from riding ponies. Psyche had chosen Achilles the same year. Tajik had worked with both animals and had the two girls spend as much time as possible with them. When the horses were finally old enough to be broken, they weren't really *broken*; their spirits remained intact, and they submitted to being ridden because there was a complete trust between them and the girls. That was why they disliked being ridden by anyone other than their mistresses. Even Tajik, who had no peer for expertise with horses, sometimes found Bellerophon difficult to control when he was exercised.

Pandora entered the stable master's office and found it empty. She was able to locate a sack with lumps of sugar without much difficulty and grabbed a handful. She ambled back down the aisle to Bellerophon's stall, where he still strained against the door. Pandora gave him some sugar on her outstretched palm, and after Bellerophon had eaten it, he lifted his head to rest it on her shoulder, his cheek against Pandora's. Pandora wrapped her arms around his neck and felt tears sting her eyes.

"I know, fella. We'll go out on a jaunt again soon. I promise. I just need a little more time."

"That's not a horse. That's an overgrown spaniel," said a cheeky voice beside her.

Pandora jumped in surprise and turned to see Dorian standing at her elbow with a teasing grin.

"Maybe so," said Pandora softly, blinking her eyes to clear away her tears. "But there's not a horse we own that's faster or can jump higher."

"Hunh," grunted Dorian, but he didn't argue the point.

"So are you just returning from somewhere?"

"Yes, the house. I think I'll go out for a while."

"Oh?"

"Yes. Myron is a bit noisily inconsolable at the moment. Mum and Dad and everyone else have been talking to him, trying to smooth him out, but it seems someone's twisted his screws a bit too tight today."

"Whatever has happened?" asked Pandora in dismay.

Myron was even-tempered just like their father. Something terrible must have happened for him to be out of sorts...or to at least let it show.

"Well, it would seem he received some disturbing news a short while ago. A good friend of his from his Oxford days was killed in a terrible accident just a few hours ago."

"I think I know, but who was it?"

"Bertram Batts, the new Marquess of Tarlborough." Dorian's brow furrowed bemusedly. "How did you know about it?"

"I ran into the hub-bub after it happened. Jim had to take us through a tight squeeze to get out of it."

Bellerophon bumped his head against Pandora's arm, and she absently gave him more sugar. She could feel the skin tightening on the back of her neck again, and she thought she might be sick. This was too much. She wasn't going to tell Dorian the full extent of her knowledge about Bertram Batts. He would find out soon enough.

She couldn't believe she had never mentioned to Myron that the two men were plotting to kill Bertram. If she had, Myron would have recognized the name, and he might not have been killed today. Then again, Myron might have thought she knew the name of his friend beforehand and simply wove it into the story, and he still would have done nothing.

"Why is Sham so upset though?"

"Apparently, he was killed by a bit of falling masonry. The owner of the building maintains he bears no responsibility. He says the building's not more than ten years old, and the rock wouldn't have just fallen."

"Who's the owner?"

"Dad."

"*What?*" shrieked Pandora in surprise. Bellerophon's head came up at the loud noise, and he snorted in Pandora's face.

"Exactly."

"So either he has to accuse Papà of making a dodgy building, or he has to believe his friend was murdered."

Pandora could offer him some consolation on one of those concerns, but Myron was still going to have the upset of knowing his friend was murdered by his co-conspirators in a criminal plot. Pandora was thinking she should— again—not mention her extent of knowledge on the matter. Her family still thought her story about someone being kidnapped from Edinburgh was imaginary. If she were to tell them Bertram Batts had been murdered by his co-conspirators, her family would think it in bad taste to use the tragedy as part of a joke.

"It's definitely a sticky wicket. You might want to avoid the mess yourself. I'd take the back stairs straight to my room if I were you. Either that, or you're welcome to join me."

"Where are you going?"

"I thought I'd go see Islington."

"No, thank you. I just came from there." Pandora's lips tightened.

Dorian's eyebrows shot up quizzically.

"I met Selena at Lady Ramsey's and gave her a ride home. I stayed for dinner...somewhat...," Pandora trailed off lamely.

"What was *she* doing at Ramsey's?" Dorian's brow furrowed.

"No earthly. Must have been some fool's errand like the one I had."

"Must have," mused Dorian.

Pandora saw an odd expression on his face, and she smiled thoughtfully.

"You *like* her, don't you?" teased Pandora.

Dorian looked guilty.

"No, I don't," he huffed.

Pandora punched him in the arm.

"Go on, admit it! You do. I can tell," she teased.

"No, I don't!" he fumed.

"She's very pretty, isn't she? And she seems very nice."

"I don't know," Dorian bit out.

Pandora's face grew serious.

"Well, I think it's wonderful," she said calmly.

Dorian looked surprised and opened his mouth to speak.

"But—" he stopped himself. "Oh, never mind." He reached over to pat Bellerophon on the neck. "You sure you don't want to come with me? It would give you a chance to ride this big puppy dog."

"Again, no, thank you. I've seen enough of the big oaf for one day," said Pandora shortly.

"Don't tell me you two have had words again," groaned Dorian, shaking his head exasperatedly.

"A few, but they weren't too awful. I asked him if he'd gone mental, and he told me I needed to be more like a woman." Pandora shrugged self-deprecatingly. "Actually, I think we've made progress."

"Why can't you two get along? You are both wonderful people!"

"Perhaps we are, but chocolate and pickles are both wonderful as well, and you wouldn't want to put them together, would you?"

Dorian shook his head bemusedly, and Pandora hugged him.

"Don't worry, Dorian. It isn't your job to mend our ways. They're our own, and if there's anyone to fix them, it will be him and me. Neither he nor I are sad about our inability to co-exist, so neither should you be."

She pecked him on the cheek, and he grimaced and wiped his hand at it as he had always done since he was a boy.

"Ugh! Don't do that!"

Pandora giggled and fed the rest of the sugar to Bellerophon. He turned from his door and went to the hayrack in the corner of his stall, realizing there would be no more.

"And, if there was any other reason I needed to not see him again today, Lord Islington wants to have a word with you about something he doesn't want *me* talking about."

"Oh?"

"I'll let him explain it to you." Pandora wiggled her eyebrows and gave a fair imitation of Islington at his most dour. "I don't want to be accused of being unwomanly again."

Dorian watched Pandora go, his forehead wrinkled with thought. He couldn't believe she was doing what Islington told her to. She was up to something. In fact, it would be more surprising if she weren't. He started to whistle the tune from the latest sonata Eurydice was practicing as he went to retrieve the tack for his horse with a spring in his step. Pandora was right about one thing—he did like Selena.

Pandora took Dorian's advice and went up the back stairs. She could hear an occasional raised voice, and while it was possible it was raised for some reason other than anger, she would rather not find out. She was tired. She would have Maiyin draw a bath and bring a tray. Pandora wasn't even going to read or work on her equation. She just wanted to sleep.

She paused with her hand on the railing for a moment and gripped it tightly. She wanted to find out how things were with Myron, but he wouldn't welcome what she had to say. There was still no proof for any of it, and her family would think it a sick joke. She could go see what was happening and not say anything, but she knew herself well enough she didn't think she would be able to keep quiet. In the end, she resumed her climb up the stairs to her room.

When she reached her room, she glanced at the clock on the nearby stand and realized Maiyin was still having her dinner. Pandora sighed tiredly and flopped onto her stomach on the bed, closing her eyes. She would take a nap for a few minutes until Maiyin came to check on her.

Pandora awoke as the bed was jostled vigorously. Her eyes felt sticky, and she had to blink several times to make them stay open. The stomachache she had earlier was still there, and she wondered if she had managed to pull a muscle when she was thrown to the other seat in the coach that afternoon. Her room was dark, and a lamp had been lit on her night table. Apparently, Maiyin had come in to find Pandora asleep and lit the lamp against the oncoming gloom and left Pandora to her rest. Maiyin had even placed a knitted shawl over her legs against the chill. Pandora craned her neck to see her own face looking back at her.

"Ugh, Psyche, I was sleeping," she groaned.

Psyche grinned cheekily and lay on her back on the bed beside Pandora, her head resting on the pillow.

"Yes, but there's the ball at Almack's to consider. We'll be late if you don't start getting ready now."

"I'm not going. I've had a trying day, and I'm too tired to move."

"What do you mean you've had a *trying* day? Myron's the one who lost a friend, or don't you know about that?"

"I know. I was almost there when it happened."

"*What?*" shrieked Psyche.

Pandora scrunched her eyes closed at the shrill sound near her ear.

"Ow." She rolled onto her back and looked at Psyche. "I was on my way home from Ramsey's and got caught in the traffic after it happened. I would have avoided it if I hadn't been taking Selena Marshall home."

"Selena Marshall?" said Psyche blankly. Her face cleared. "Oh, Islington's sister. Dorian likes her, you know," Psyche stated drolly.

"I know, and he wants to pretend he doesn't. So, how is Myron? When I came in, I could hear the shouts all the way from the back stairs."

"He is better. At least he's come to accept it wasn't Papá's building that was at fault."

"I could have told him that, but since no one seems to believe what I say these days, he would have thought I was being really naughty."

"What do you mean?"

"Myron's friend was one of the conspirators. The others, Castleton and the Aristocrat, killed him because he was going to the authorities."

"You're not still on about that, are you?" groaned Psyche, shaking her head in disbelief.

Pandora sat up on the bed and felt lightheaded for a moment. She glared at Psyche once she could focus on her again.

"It is the truth," Pandora said simply. "I'm beyond understanding why no one believes me. What's the longest I've carried on a joke?"

"Does this include our wager we have going now?"

"No, it does not. That is not a joke."

"Then I'm not really sure…a week, two maybe."

"Exactly. And why would I want to pull a deception involving things like kidnapping, murder, and treason?"

"Treason? When did *treason* enter into it?"

"When I tried to determine who might be the intended victim, depending on who it is, the conspirators might also be traitors."

Psyche looked at her sister assessingly. It was true. Pandora had never been prone to telling stories about anyone she didn't know, and she (generally) did not involve anything criminal in her tales. Horse thievery, maybe, had been used once, but certainly not murder, kidnapping, or anything else that dastardly had ever been used. Pandora seemed to be very sincere, and to Psyche, if to no one else, it was beginning to have the disturbing ring of truth.

"So what do you intend to do about apprehending the wrongdoers?" she asked seriously.

Pandora blinked. It seemed Psyche was finally going to give her the benefit of doubt. She felt her eyes sting with tears and flung herself at her twin for a grateful hug.

"Aagh! Pandora!"

"Thank you! I'm just so happy you believe me!"

"Well, someone has to," muttered Psyche, overwhelmed by her sister's display.

Pandora released Psyche and sat back to look at her seriously. There was one secret she was keeping that Pandora really had to tell someone, and Psyche was the only one she felt she could trust with it. And yet, Pandora wasn't sure she *could* tell her. She needed someone to give her consolation…more likely, absolution, but Psyche would probably consider her actions shameful. Psyche wouldn't tell their parents or anyone else, but she would expect Pandora to do so herself.

"Well, actually, Lord Islington believes me," said Pandora slowly.

Psyche's jaw dropped in surprise.

"Lord *Islington* believes you? The man you're always abusing *believes* you?" Pandora nodded. "If that's so, then you have been doing him a terrible disservice by constantly insulting him the way you do."

"Oh, Psyche, you have no idea what I've gone through to make him believe me! I only had him convinced today when I returned Selena home." She sighed gustily. "Dorian was on his way to see him just as I returned home this afternoon, and Lord Islington said he would have Dorian help him look into it."

"Do you think he will?"

"I don't know. I feel he is a man of his word, at least this time."

"What do you mean 'at least this time'?"

In the end, Pandora couldn't bring herself to confess all to Psyche. At the time she had been with Islington, Pandora had felt no shame or remorse. Now she was filled with a bereft guilt, knowing the things she felt for him, that she had thought were reciprocated, had been nothing more than a mirage. She was left with *nothing* to justify what they had done. It was true, he had never said anything to indicate he returned her feelings, but Pandora was heartbroken to realize she had misunderstood his actions for more than what they were.

"Let's just say he is more deceptive than you think he is."

Psyche scoffed and rolled her eyes in a manner that suggested she thought Pandora was just being unfair.

"So that's it, then? You're not going to do anymore with it?"

"We-ell," said Pandora slowly. "He has asked that I not involve myself with catching the conspirators, but he didn't say anything about me looking into who their victim might be. If I can find him and warn him, then any machinations on their part will be for naught, regardless of whether Lord Islington does anything to find them."

"And you're actually going to do what he says? I find that doubtful," said Psyche with an arched eyebrow.

Pandora looked affronted.

"I think I will, but not because he *asked* me to. It's just I've decided my energy will be better-focused in that direction."

Psyche saw the clock and jumped up from Pandora's bed in alarm.

"My goodness, speaking of time! We've been chatting so long I've forgotten I need to dress. Are you sure you don't want to come with?"

"Yes, I'm sure. I want to bathe, read, and then I want to go to bed."

"You're already in bed."

"Yes, but I'm also hungry."

"You know, you will never win our wager if you never go anywhere to acquire cravats."

Pandora honestly hadn't thought about their wager for weeks. She had, as a matter of fact, already put Psyche's earrings back in her jewel box and was surprised her sister hadn't noticed their return. Pandora had *attempted* to participate. She would ignore the fact that her participation had been based more on luck than skill, however.

"I have one—two—cravats, actually, but they're both from the same man. I guess that means one. How many have you managed so far?"

"How have you gotten two cravats?" asked Psyche in surprise, completely ignoring the question.

"I am accident prone, remember?"

"We are both accident prone, but that hasn't helped me any." Psyche looked at Pandora suspiciously. "So whose cravat have you lifted?"

"Lord Islington's, of course."

"He gave you his cravat? I thought we decided we couldn't remove them while the man was unconscious."

"He was definitely conscious. I'm surprised his being cravat-less didn't cause gossip. Although, I suppose my condition on both occasions overshadowed his state of dress a bit."

"When did you get them?"

"The first one was when I tripped and fell in the gazebo, and he gave it to me for my lip. The second was when I was ill at Lord Lundey's ball, and he gave it to me as a compress."

"Hunh," grunted Psyche. She couldn't argue they had been gained unfairly, but it certainly didn't seem Pandora had *connived* for them either, which had partially been the point.

"Well, how about you? Have you managed to get any?"

Pandora felt guilty she hadn't talked to Psyche about the wager. Regardless, she had put the earrings back, and even if her twin didn't manage to get a single cravat, Pandora didn't want the earrings.

"I've not managed any so far," said Psyche glumly. "Can I have one of yours?" she asked brightly.

"No, you cannot!"

"Humph," retorted Psyche. "Oh, well, the Season's not over for another month-and-a-half. I'm going to get ready for Almack's."

She started to leave the room but paused and turned back as she reached the door to the sitting room.

"I almost forgot. Mamà wanted me to let you know she's having a dinner party in about two weeks."

"Ugh," was Pandora's unenthusiastic response.

"Don't worry. It's only going to be family and close friends." Pandora didn't appear to be listening; she had rolled over and put a pillow over her head. "It's to celebrate their wedding anniversary and her birthday." Psyche thought she heard snoring. "You're requested to invite someone, and you need to let Mamà know who it is as soon as possible because she's already late sending invitations."

There was no immediate response from the bed, and Psyche started to continue on to her room when she received a mumbled reply.

"I'll invite Selena and Lady Bardsey. Dorian will like that."

"What *you* won't like is that he's inviting Lord Islington."

"Aagh. I surrender. Go get ready for Almack's."

Psyche giggled as she left the room.

Chapter Nine

Pandora was not looking forward to the coming evening. As Psyche had told her (or warned her), their mother had planned a dinner party to celebrate her twenty-five years with the duke...and her birthday. While Pandora was overjoyed her parents' marriage had been successful and contented for so long, she would rather not have to attend a social function in her own home...again. The twins' come-out ball had been, as a social event, successful and enjoyed by all who attended, but the personal side that Pandora was still suffering was something she didn't want compounded.

The guest list was large for a dinner party. Including members of the family, there would be twenty-four. Julia had requested that Eurydice attend so she could play her violin after dinner. Unfortunately, for their sister to feel less anxious about performing in front of strangers, their mother had drafted the twins and Arachne for singing at some point. Dorian would play the piano, if necessary.

Pandora's interest in the event was nonexistent. She tried to beg off having to sing, claiming she was just getting over a cold and her voice was still hoarse, but her mother would have none of it. Pandora would have to sing with her sisters, and that was all there would be on that.

Pandora hadn't been lying about a cold, which inconveniently decided to clear off a few days before the party arrived. At least, she *thought* it was a cold. She had felt under the weather, but she never had a runny nose or even a cough. She came down with whatever it was the day Bertram Batts was killed, and at first, no amount of herbal teas Maiyin plied her with seemed to help. Unfortunately, it eventually did. The hoarseness had been a fib, but she had truthfully been ill.

Singing wasn't one of Pandora's strong suits. Give her an equation or chemical formula to solve, and she would astound with how easily the answer came to her. Singing fell into the category of *womanly* arts, which her mother had educated her on but was not something at which she could be considered more than passable. And she would have to sing in front of *Islington.* She detested that part of it the most.

Pandora had tried to convince Dorian to invite someone else, but he would have none of it. She had suggested Sir James Klein or Lord Georgie. Dorian said he was inviting Islington, and Pandora would have to be civil. She managed to catch a hedgehog in the garden and put it in his boot the next morning. He limped for a day after that, and Pandora smiled pleasantly every time she saw him. She was tempted to beg off inviting Selena and her mother and invite Lucy Cranston and Lady Ramsey instead for revenge, but her mother wouldn't let her go that far. In the end, she decided she could tolerate Islington for one evening.

She had been trying to determine who the intended victim might be. Every route she took wound up being a dead end, however. She had been able to rule out the royal family. She was satisfied it wasn't a member of Parliament (her father was able to verify for her that all were present and accounted for...not idling time away north of the border). The only other group left was the military, and she had not been able to arrive at a likely victim within that body after dwelling on it for almost a week. So she was stuck without a possible direction to go.

Dorian was of no help. He grudgingly let her know that he was helping Islington, but he wouldn't tell her anything more. He wouldn't let her know if they had made any progress in finding Castleton, and he would also not tell her if they had been able to find any proof that Hendon was the Aristocrat. Apparently, Dorian had been threatened with bodily harm by Islington should he tell her anything. He was more concerned about whatever Islington had threatened because Pandora threatening to break his thumbs didn't cause him to relent.

She had seen Islington only once since their row at his home, at a ball given by the Earl of Lochardale four days before the anniversary party. When she tried to ask Islington about the plot, attempting to move beyond the usual banal pleasantries, he developed a sudden case of deafness. Pandora wanted to believe it was deafness, but it was just plain stubbornness. She had wanted to box his ears, but there were too many people watching. She was pleased with her behavior that night; she was civil and affable, which was an amazing feat considering their recent past. Islington had also been pleasant, until she asked about the conspirators. Then his demeanor brought to Pandora's mind the way he behaved the first day she met him, and she gave up questioning him in aggravation.

Pandora sat calmly in front of the mirror while Maiyin styled her hair. Maiyin hummed a pleasant tune as she worked, pinning and twirling the mass of curls into submission. Occasionally, she would flip a lock forward so that it would flop into Pandora's face, obscuring her view. Pandora would blow at it until it moved, and she could see again. Maiyin was about half-finished.

Pandora sat waiting, already in her dress for the evening, a low-cut, emerald green velvet gown edged in black and green glass beads. The bodice was gathered under her breasts with a black satin ribbon bowed at the front. Pandora had wanted to wear her burgundy silk gown, but Maiyin insisted she wear the green one. When Pandora protested, Maiyin explained some trim had worked loose on the red one, and she hadn't had time to mend it. Pandora relented. She knew she was hard on her clothes.

"You are feeling much better, yes, Missy Pandora?" asked Maiyin as she continued her work.

"Yes. Unfortunately, I'm fit as a fiddle," said Pandora glumly.

"Why unfortunately? It was over quickly enough."

"Too quickly. I would much rather stay in my room tonight."

"You mother and father been married for very long time. It is happy. And there will be others for you. Be glad it was not worse than it was. It could have been much worse," said Maiyin in her sing-song tone.

Pandora's brow wrinkled thoughtfully at Maiyin's words. She rubbed the spot behind her ear nervously as she watched Maiyin in the mirror.

"I suppose it could have been the influenza or pneumonia," she said neutrally.

Maiyin paused in her work to look at Pandora's reflection in the mirror disbelievingly.

"Influenza or pneumonia? You no catch those from *huáiyùn*."

Pandora went pale, and the breath caught in her throat, which felt suddenly constricted.

"But I'm not. I haven't missed my courses. You know that. It was a little late coming and a little heavier than usual, but I had it."

Maiyin put down the brush she held and gently placed her hands on Pandora's shoulders. She knew Pandora wouldn't have even realized what had happened, but Maiyin knew from her own unfortunate experiences. She wondered if she should not have told Pandora; she could see the news had upset her charge a great deal.

"Missy Pandora, you not pregnant *anymore*," said Maiyin sadly. "I have been with you since you eight years old, and I know you almost as well as I know myself. I can tell what day of the month it is by your time. I suspected after one week; after two weeks, I was sure." Maiyin gave Pandora's shoulders a comforting squeeze. "I not ask you what you been doing, or with whom; I am sure you thought well."

Pandora felt her eyes stinging. She was going to be sick any moment.

"Maiyin, you didn't tell my parents, did you?" she asked worriedly.

Maiyin gave her a shocked look.

"Missy Pandora, I am old woman, but I am not *foolish* old woman! What you mother and father think if they knew? If it had come to that, I am sure you would have known what to do. Is over now, no matter. The tea I give you will make it all better for next time. It is just not time yet."

She nodded finally and resumed her work.

Pandora sat stilly while Maiyin worked. She was struggling not to cry, and her stomach had turned into a tight little ball. Her cheeks were flushed over skin that had become pale, and her eyes sparkled with the tears she fought. To outward appearances, she was calm and composed, and the intense emotions she felt only made her look more radiant. Her mind was rushing with thoughts that threatened to overwhelm her, and she clenched her hands into fists so tight her nails bit into her palms.

Now, more than ever, she didn't want to attend the dinner party. She didn't want to see anyone. How was she to make polite conversation, let alone eat, when she felt like her head might explode? She especially did not want to face Islington. How *could* she face him? She couldn't avoid the party, but she wasn't sure she could maintain her composure for an entire evening of pleasantries. And singing! The thought of singing made her throat constrict until she was sure not a sound would come out.

"There! All finished! And nice thing about this dinner party is that you mama said you can go with no gloves!" beamed Maiyin, either unaware of the tension in her mistress or choosing to ignore it.

Pandora looked at her reflection in the mirror. Maiyin's handiwork, as usual, was perfect. She reached out a shaking hand to pick up the simple pearl earrings she had chosen to wear with her dress. She managed to get them into her ears without dropping them, and Maiyin helped put on the matching necklace. She looked at herself one more time and managed to calmly rise from her seat. She couldn't delay going downstairs any longer.

She walked to the door of the sitting room and went through. Once she closed it and was out of Maiyin's view, she leaned her back against the door weakly, her chest heaving emotionally. She thought she might scream and bit her lip to keep it contained. She closed her eyes and tried to slow her breathing, trying to compose herself before she went to Psyche's room.

It wouldn't be long before guests began to arrive, and Pandora couldn't lose herself to her misery, as badly as wanted to. No one could know. Her indiscretions with Islington were bad enough; a pregnancy outside of marriage would have been ghastly. Yet Pandora was heartbroken she no longer was with child…his child. Her parents would be dishonored if it came to light. Her family would never trust her again. Psyche would feel betrayed worse than anyone because Pandora could have—should have— told her about the events that had caused it.

After a few minutes more of breathing deeply, she felt the ball of tension in her stomach ease to the point that she could continue to Psyche's room. Pandora would have to give the performance of her life because her family could not know. She was able to put her dramatic skills to use at other times; tonight would be their truest test.

She walked across the sitting room and raised her hand to knock on Psyche's door. She hesitated for a moment just before her knuckles touched the wood, took one last calming breath, and then knocked softly.

"Come in," called Psyche.

Pandora walked into the room evenly, with no sign of her inner turmoil. Psyche was putting on a pair of tan slippers to match the soft sea green velvet dress she had decided to wear. It was cut in a style almost exact to the one Pandora wore. She, too, had chosen pearls for her jewelry.

"My, don't we look lovely this evening?" quizzed Psyche cheekily as she rose from her task.

"We do indeed," returned Pandora with a bright smile of her own.

Psyche walked closer to her sister, tilted her head sideways thoughtfully with a slight smile, then leaned even closer and inhaled deeply.

"What is that scent you're wearing?"

Pandora blinked, momentarily at a loss.

"Uh, ginger and orange, mostly. Is it too strong? Does it smell vile?"

She lifted a wrist to her nose and sniffed, a worried look on her face.

"No, it smells divine," giggled Psyche, noting Pandora's reaction.

Pandora sighed with relief. In addition to everything else, she didn't want to smell foul.

"Come on," said Psyche. "I'm sure Mamà is wondering what's taking us so long."

They linked their arms together and went to the front stairs. Their mother was waiting with Arachne and Eurydice at the bottom.

"There you are," called the duchess in a relieved tone.

"Whatever is the matter?" quizzed Psyche blithely as they walked down the stairs. "It is not yet seven. I would be surprised if anyone in this town is punctual enough to actually be *early.*"

"Heaven forbid!" laughed Pandora.

The duchess pursed her lips to hide a smile and inspected them from head to foot when they reached her. She smiled with satisfaction. There had never been a doubt in her mind that the twins would look perfect. Pandora, in particular, was especially radiant. The shades of green they wore complimented their blond looks well. The five of them went to the front hall where Tannaz also waited to open the door and take coats and wraps from arriving guests.

Pandora was surrounded by her sisters, who continued to lean close to her and breathe in her perfume after Psyche told them they should. Now Pandora had a feeling she knew what a flower surrounded by honeybees went through.

"Mamà! Please, make them stop!" she giggled.

The duchess's response was to move closer to her daughter and inhale as well with a reminiscent smile.

"*Mamà!*" gasped Pandora in disbelief.

"They are right. You smell heavenly. It makes me think of the time your father and I went to Spain. We stayed in a villa next to an orange grove. The smell would come in through the windows and fill the entire house. Wherever did you get it?"

"Maiyin made it for me, but Keung helped, I think."

"It suits you perfectly," said the duchess with a smile. She cleared her throat. "The guests should arrive soon. Since they're all friends, we'll not be concerned about precedence; I've tried to arrange you so the conversation will be pleasant. Psyche, you'll go in with Baron de Barneville."

"The who?" asked Psyche blankly.

"He's a friend of Myron's, and his parents are the Sheernesses," said her mother calmly. Psyche shook her head with an uncomprehending look. "Regardless, he will be your escort for the evening. Arachne, you will go in with Drake. Eurydice—"

"Is Lilly not coming then?" interrupted Arachne.

"No, she's not. She sent her regrets only this morning."

Arachne had a puzzled expression. "That's odd. I saw her only yesterday, and she said she was looking forward to coming."

"She had to leave town suddenly on a personal matter, according to her note. You *will* go in with Nicodemus."

"Yes, Mama, of course," said Arachne agreeably, her expression still one of confusion.

The duchess sighed.

"Now, Eurydice, you will go in with Mr. Ellsworth. I think you'll get on; he is musical as well."

"Yes, Mother," replied Eurydice softly, her expression impassive.

"All right now, you," said her grace with a smile, giving Eurydice an affectionate chuck under the chin. "You can suffer through this *one* night. You'll get to play your violin…in front of people besides family!"

Eurydice smiled then, and it brightened her whole face. Her amber-colored eyes sparkled with gaiety at the thought of her music. She was old enough to have been presented, but her mother wanted to wait until she was eighteen. Eurydice had no interest in coming out…not any more than her three older sisters had. She looked very becoming in a russet-colored velvet gown that made her skin look golden and brought out the highlights in her auburn hair. She would have no shortage of attentions when she was finally presented. If tonight's occasion had been intended for anyone other than family and close friends, her mother would not have let her attend.

"That's better," smiled her mother.

Finally, the duchess turned to Pandora, and she knew what her mother was going to say.

"As for you, Pandora, you'll go in with Lord Islington."

"Honestly, Mamà, is it necessary for everyone to constantly be lobbing us together?" she asked exasperatedly.

"Pandora, I don't want you to argue with me. You and Islington get on well together when you don't squabble about who is in charge of whom, when—in fact—neither of you is the boss. Why don't you try being a little less *forceful* with each other this evening, hmm? I think you'll be surprised to find that you actually have a lot in common."

Pandora opened and closed her mouth speechlessly, completely at a loss for words at her mother's comments. Perhaps the duchess was right, but Pandora couldn't bear to be near him tonight, and if she had been able to find a reasonable excuse for not attending at all, she would have. She could tell, however, from the expression on her mother's face that she was not going to let Pandora talk her way out of it.

"Very well, Mamà," she answered calmly. "But if he says *one* cross thing to me, I will not be held accountable."

"Yes, dearest," said the duchess, her lips twitching amusedly. "Now, your father and brothers should already be in the drawing room. When I last checked with Mrs. O'Flaherty, she had everything prepared or nearly prepared. All we have to do now is wait."

The four girls stood with their mother discussing what they would perform for their guests. Much to Pandora's relief, the duchess told her she would only have to sing one song. It did not have to be long or intricate, and she could sing it together with Psyche and Arachne. Anything she could do to lessen the amount of time she had to endure the evening or performing was utmost in her thoughts.

It was shortly after seven when the first knock came at the door. Tannaz opened it, and two men and a woman walked in. The duchess greeted them warmly while Tannaz took their coats and wraps. The elder gentleman and lady were Hiram and Josephine Nichols, the Earl and Countess of Sheerness, with whom the girls were well-acquainted from their visits to Wilderland. The younger man, who was to go into dinner with Psyche, was Sebastian Nichols, styled Baron de Barneville. When Psyche saw his face, she recognized him, and the once relaxed smile she wore froze. She managed to greet him cordially, and the duchess asked her to direct the three to the drawing room. She reluctantly did as she was asked.

Pandora watched the exchange interestedly. It was apparent to her, if to no one else, that Psyche had more than casual feelings for the baron. Whether they were cordial or not needed some examination, but it was plain she wasn't indifferent. He seemed to be affable and immensely attractive. His dark brown hair wasn't cut to a fashionably short length but was rather pulled back and tied with a ribbon in a queue at the nape of his neck. His eyes had at first appeared to be blue, but on closer inspection, Pandora decided they were a shade of green. She could see why her twin might find him interesting.

The next three to arrive were Cora Ellsworth and her son, Gareth, and Leilah Mahone. Mrs. Ellsworth and Ms. Mahone had been friends of the duchess for many years. Gareth was older than Pandora had expected, strikingly handsome, and extremely tall. He had wavy black hair and crystalline blue eyes, and a guarded expression. He seemed pleasant when he was introduced to the sisters by their mother but reticent. Pandora suspected there wouldn't be much conversation between her sister and that gentleman because both were rather introverted. Her grace had Eurydice escort them to the drawing room to join the others.

The duchess, Arachne and Pandora had barely waited for the next guests arriving when Tannaz answered a knock on the door for six people to enter. This group included Warner and Althea Mordecai, the Earl and Countess of Lundey; their son, Nicodemus, Viscount Drake; Ephraim and Winifred Radcliffe, the Earl and Countess of Stranraer; and their eldest son, Lachlan, Baron Lambeth. They were all longtime friends of the duke and duchess, and their daughters were also familiar with them. The Stranraers had a daughter and two younger twin sons, but none had been able to attend. Their daughter, Judith, was expecting her fifth child to arrive any time. The twins, Jordan and Odoric, who had attended Oxford with Myron, were both ship's captains serving in the war in America.

Baron Lambeth was the one with which Pandora was least familiar. He, too, was a ship's captain, but his attentions were focused along the coast of Africa and that region assisting with enforcing the end of slave trading. He greeted her pleasantly, taking her hand for a kiss when they were introduced, and had the cheek to wink at her over her knuckles when he did so. He was handsome, with dark blond hair and gray eyes, but Pandora found his devil-may-care attitude unappealing.

Viscount Drake barely had time to give his coat to Tannaz before Arachne began quizzing him on where his fiancée had gone.

"Pandora, your sister and I will escort these fine people to the drawing room. If you'll just wait for the stragglers…. I believe most everyone has arrived."

Pandora started to open her mouth to speak but closed it again as she helplessly watched their retreating backs. She could hear Arachne speaking intently with Lord Drake as they went down the hall to the drawing room. Pandora groaned frustratedly and rolled her eyes. Her mother was supposed to be doing this! Of course, the only people left to arrive were Lady Bardsey, Selena, and Islington. Still, Pandora did not look forward to seeing Islington, especially not in front of his family. She put a hand to her cheek, feeling its warmth. Unfortunately, Pandora knew it wasn't a fever but only her nerves causing the heated flush.

She paced back and forth between two of the columns in the entry hall, clenching and unclenching her hands nervously. Tannaz stood near the door watching impassively. He was too well-trained to ask what was troubling her. She paused to brush at imagined specks of dust on her gown then resumed her pacing. She glanced at the clock placed into a bend in the stairs and saw it was nearing half-past seven. They would be arriving soon. *Or maybe they won't come*, thought Pandora hopefully.

A knock at the door startled her mid-pace, and she released a squeak. She composed herself and managed to stand calmly while Tannaz opened the door. There were only two people: Islington and Selena.

"Selena and Islington," said Pandora with what she hoped was a welcoming smile that didn't seem too affected. "I'm glad you could make it. I thought your mother would be coming as well?"

Selena turned from handing her shawl to Tannaz and went to Pandora to take her hands with a smile.

"Sorry, no. I'm afraid she won't be coming. She became ill shortly before we were to leave the house; otherwise, we would have sent word to the duchess earlier. I hope it won't be an inconvenience."

"I hope it's nothing serious," said Pandora with genuine concern. "As for inconvenience, Mamà will not mind, I'm sure."

Selena squeezed her hands and smiled.

"It's only a slight cold. She'll be well in no time at all, but she wasn't feeling up to leaving the house."

Pandora smiled back at her friend then turned to look at Selena's brother. Islington stood near them with an unreadable expression while he watched their exchange. At Pandora's attention in his direction, he seemed to become even more guarded.

"Don't worry. I'm not going to pester you about Castleton and the Aristocrat," teased Pandora with a tart smile.

His expression changed to one of surprise, and Pandora guessed she had discovered the reason for his reticence. He gave her a wry grin and took one of her hands from his sister's grasp to place a gallant kiss on it.

"You wound me, madam," he said mildly as he released it.

Pandora blinked, but she wasn't going to question his pleasant demeanor. That would be like looking a gift horse in the mouth.

"I've decided trying to ask you questions on that is about as useless as trying to ask my horse what is the square root of pi," she said airily. "Although, he does at least try to give me an answer."

Islington laughed. Selena had a lost expression, not being familiar with mathematics and thinking her friend was talking about food. Pandora cleared her throat and maintained an innocent expression.

"Everyone is in the drawing room. If you would like to accompany me there, it won't be long before we go in to dinner."

Selena linked elbows on Pandora's left side and started to walk with her, but she paused to look Pandora up and down with a discerning expression.

"Something's different about you," Selena said as she continued to look.

"It's the perfume. My maid gave it to me."

"No, it's not that…although it does smell exquisite," said Selena with a grin. "Something *looks* different about you."

Pandora blushed from the intense gaze of her friend. Selena's interest also drew the interest of her brother, and they both stood examining Pandora closely. Selena's gaze was curious and pondering, while Islington's was appreciative and infinitely more intense. Pandora was uncomfortable under his gaze, nervous that he would just *know* what had happened.

Selena put a finger to her lips in thought and walked around Pandora once and came to stand in front of her again. She smiled hugely and snapped her fingers when she realized what it was.

"Aha! I know! You don't have your cane anymore!"

Pandora sighed inwardly with relief that the appraisal would stop.

"Yes, it is true. I'm no longer dependent on my walking stick." She shrugged and grinned cheekily. "Pity, really. I was thinking of trying to make it *the* next necessary item of attire for ladies."

Selena giggled and re-linked arms with her.

"I'm so happy you're well enough to go without it."

"Well, truthfully, I was ready to get rid of it weeks ago, but I wanted to be sure I didn't have any residual wobbliness. The best part is that when I disposed of it, I felt I was able to ride Bellerophon again."

"Bellerophon?"

"My horse...the male I love above all others," said Pandora with a grin and a squeeze to Selena's arm. "I haven't been able to ride him since I became ill...until yesterday. Psyche and I went riding in the Park yesterday, and it was heavenly," said Pandora with a contented smile.

Islington drew his pace to match theirs and linked his arm on the other side as they ambled slowly to the drawing room.

"Did you happen to jump anyone's phaeton?" he teased softly.

Pandora turned to look at him in shock, both from his teasing tone and also from the frisson of heat the warmth of his breath on her ear created somewhere along the base of her spine.

"Egads, no!" she uttered in surprise, trying to ignore the sensation. "I was just able to remain seated with Bellerophon at a sedate canter, and I am happy with that for now."

The three of them continued to chatter pleasantly linked arm-in-arm until they reached the drawing room, and Pandora was surprised she and Islington didn't erupt into an argument of one kind or another before they made it. His sister's calming inclusion helped matters; Pandora couldn't imagine he would remain this pleasant were there no one else present.

When they entered the drawing room through its open doors, Pandora beheld an awkward sight.

The duke and the Earls of Sheerness, Stranraer, and Lundey were in a mass near one side of the fireplace involved in serious conversation about the direction of the war in America. The duchess and accompanying countesses of the earls as well as the madams Ellsworth and Mahone were standing on the opposite side discussing events of the near-ending Season.

Arachne had Viscount Drake backed into a corner, still interrogating him on Lilly's whereabouts. He looked as if he were being questioned by the Inquisition. Baron Lambeth sat on the settee, his hands linked behind his head, his eyes closed, one booted heel resting on the edge of the low table in front of it. He was sound asleep. Lord Barneville and Psyche were in an isolated corner on the far side of the room near the piano, involved in a heated argument about something Pandora couldn't determine. She hoped her twin was winning. Eurydice and Mr. Ellsworth were sitting on the settee opposite the one occupied by Lord Lambeth, and Pandora doubted they had said two words to each other since leaving the front hall. As for her brothers, they stood in a group behind the settee where Lord Lambeth dozed, discussing the next breeding season for their horses.

Pandora put a hand over her mouth to muffle the snort and giggle that escaped from her.

Pandora spared a glance to Islington beside her and saw that he, too, was struggling to contain his mirth. He hadn't needed to cover his mouth, but he did rub a hand over it to wipe away a smirk. Selena stood with her eyes wide, her jaw dropped in disbelief. She would not soon forget this evening if the rest of it were going to be anything like its beginning. Pandora cleared her throat to control her urge to laugh. For the moment, she felt almost normal.

"I'll just let my mother know Lady Bardsey will not be attending," she said evenly, gesturing in the direction of the gaggle of older women.

"By all means," returned Islington with a grin.

Pandora walked over to the women with some trepidation. Their discussion was almost as heated as that of their gentlemen discussing the war. She stood at her mother's elbow for several minutes waiting for a point in the conversation where she could interrupt. Pandora finally had to touch her mother's elbow to gain her attention. The duchess turned her gaze from the information Lady Sheerness was relating to look at Pandora, who took her slightly aside.

"Mamà, Lord Islington and Lady Selena are here. Their mother will not be attending; she is ill."

"Oh, dear. Nothing serious?" she asked worriedly.

"No, just a cold," said Pandora mildly.

Once Pandora gained her mother's interest away from talk of balls and fêtes, the duchess took an appraising look around the room. Her eyes went wide in alarm.

"Oh, mercy!" she gasped.

"Just so, Mamà," said Pandora neutrally, her lips twitching.

The duchess squeezed Pandora's arm gratefully and excused herself momentarily from the presence of her guests. Pandora slowly walked back to where Islington and Selena stood, her arms folded in front of her speculatively as she watched her mother leave the room. Though the duchess walked sedately to the doorway, once she was through to the hall out of the sight of her guests, her pace quickened dramatically.

"Is she trying to escape?" asked Islington mildly.

Pandora's lips pursed as she hid a smile.

"I believe she's going to do three things. First, she's going to find my sister, Persephone, and make her go in to dinner with Lord Lambeth," said Pandora as she watched the man continue to sleep, peacefully oblivious to the goings-on around him.

"And then?" prompted Selena.

"Then my mother will put a pillow over my sister's face so no one will hear when she screams bloody murder." Islington's shoulders began to shake with silent laughter. "After she forces my sister into a presentable dress and into the drawing room, she'll reorganize the company present so it doesn't resemble the chamber for the House of Lords."

Islington laughed out loud then. Pandora blinked in surprise. She was only partially exaggerating. Selena looked at her uncertainly and gave her a weak smile.

Pandora was content to leave her sisters to their own devices, but her brothers needed to move on to other topics. She walked over to the three of them with Islington and Selena, and they were able to find a before-dinner subject more acceptable for female company. Their conversation managed to awaken Lord Lambeth from his repose, and he turned in his position on the settee to join in as well. Eventually, Psyche moved out of the corner with Lord Barneville, and they were able to engage Mr. Ellsworth and Eurydice in some animated conversation (although Pandora didn't think she actually saw either one of them speak to *each other*). Lord Drake eventually managed to escape from Arachne's incessant questioning and joined that conversation as well. The men and women to either side of the fireplace merged into one group and began speaking together amiably. By the time the duchess literally *shoved* Persephone into the room, she was able to give a pleased smile the situation had sorted out itself.

The duchess performed a brief round of introductions for Persephone, who wore a sullen expression bordering on mutinous. The sixteen year old looked presentable...even if she would rather be wearing britches. Her hair had been quickly done up into a twist, and she wore one of Arachne's dresses, a soft, rose-colored silk with a lighter pink tulle overskirt that complimented the beige tones of her skin. After the duchess introduced her to Baron Lambeth, he attempted to engage Persephone in pleasant conversation, but she pouted unhappily.

Rajeesh came to announce dinner was served shortly after their arrival. Matched up with their pre-determined partners, everyone made the short journey to the dining room for their meal.

Pandora wasn't hungry, but she continued to hold her own in polite conversation with Islington and Lord Lambeth, who had been seated to her left. She found Lambeth to be charming once she began talking to him, and she felt she *had* to talk to him because Persephone would only give him monosyllabic or sarcastic responses to anything he said to her. Pandora felt sorry for him. Islington's expression seemed to grow more strained as the meal progressed, but he maintained his amiability. Pandora would occasionally give him a questioning glance but thought better of asking if something was wrong. She had enough things to worry about.

Mrs. O'Flaherty outdid herself on preparing the meal—it looked and smelled delicious, but Pandora could only push the food from one side of her plate to the other, taking an occasional bite, until the next course was served. She didn't hesitate to drink from her glass, and she could feel the beginnings of a slight buzzing in her ears from the wine and champagne that were being poured frequently throughout the evening. She switched to drinking only water about halfway through the meal, but she had already imbibed more than she should. The cloth was finally cleared away, and Pandora was able to eat dessert—a strawberry sorbet with slices of melon and orange—as well as drink a final glass of champagne.

When it came time for the women to go to the drawing room for tea and coffee while the men had their port and tobacco, Pandora thanked Islington and Lambeth for their pleasant conversation and rose from her seat on legs that felt unsteady. Yes, she had too much champagne, but it helped numb her to the strain that was finally beginning to catch up with her. She followed her mother and sisters and their female company back to the drawing room slowly. Persephone kissed her mother gratefully on the cheek at the bottom of the stairs as she was allowed to return to her room, and Pandora sighed enviously. She wished she could be allowed to go back to her room. She was tired; she was boozy; and she *really* wanted to cry. She quickened her pace a little and managed to come up beside her mother.

"Mamà, may I please be excused?" she pleaded in a soft voice so their guests would not overhear.

"Now, Pandora, we've already discussed this. I'll not have you begging off this way."

"No, Mamà, I am really feeling unwell. I will stay to sing, but may I please go to my room after that?"

The duchess looked at her daughter with a critical eye. Pandora was slightly pale and her cheeks a little flushed. Her eyes were feverish and strained. It appeared she was being honest. The duchess smiled and took Pandora's hand.

"Very well. If you can manage to survive for one more hour, you may be excused." Her expression turned serious. "But I expect you to put forth your best effort for the song."

"Yes, Mamà," said Pandora with a relieved smile. "Thank you."

"Hmm," was the duchess's reply. "At this rate, Eurydice will be left with no audience."

"Eurydice doesn't *need* an audience, Mamà," said Pandora mildly. "She would play in her room from dawn until dusk."

"*Does* play from dawn until dusk," chuckled the duchess.

They went to the drawing room with the rest of the women, and Pandora joined her sisters for a final discussion on what they would sing. Psyche gasped when Pandora told them she would be leaving for her room after the song was over. Arachne accused her of being a coward. Pandora stuck out her tongue after she made sure their guests weren't looking. She apologized to Eurydice for not being able to stay, but the younger girl didn't seem bothered, as Pandora suspected she wouldn't. She had a cup of coffee with cream rather than tea, and it seemed to soften the ringing that had developed in her ears, but her hands started to shake slightly from being nervous about singing in front of *people.*

It wasn't long before the male company rejoined the women in the drawing room. Pandora drew Dorian aside and told him the song they would be singing for him to provide their accompaniment. After all the gentlemen were seated and had coffee or tea, they and the women sat talking, some resuming the conversations they had begun during the meal. Pandora happened into one that her brother Myron was having with Lord Sheerness, Lord Barneville, and Psyche.

"Well, what are they going to do when Boney finally gets run to ground? They can't very well bring the monarchy back," said Myron.

"I imagine they would rather not go back to the way things were. It would be like admitting they had made a mistake," said Psyche logically. "Making that admission by itself isn't so bad, but to think of everything that's been lost because of it.... For nothing?"

"They could bring the monarchy back, if they could convince one of the successors to come back to the country," countered Barneville.

"I'm sure the king is full-well tired of their company," said Myron.

"Oh, pooh," said Psyche. "I imagine they're tired of ours. That one must be dreadfully unhappy at Holyrood."

"I don't think he's overly miserable," said Sheerness with a knowing smile. "Artois is rumored to have been entrusted with much of the crown jewels before he fled the Terror, and he's become fairly monkish since the death of his wife *and* his mistress. I imagine he's very comfortable where he is, with plenty of funds to ensure he wants for nothing, rent-free in a royal residence, not to mention he gets a very nice stipend courtesy of the British government." Sheerness shook his head. "I agree with Barneville...can they convince him he *should* come back?"

Pandora touched Psyche on the elbow to let her know it was time for them to sing, and they excused themselves from the group. Dorian seated himself at the piano in the corner and the three girls stood beside it waiting for him to start. He began the slow melody for *Black is the Color of My True Love's Hair.*

The three girls had decided this would be the perfect song for them to sing in honor of their mother and the twenty-five blessed years she had shared with the duke. The lyrics were perfect, and as an added recommendation, it was short. They hadn't rehearsed, but they were able to harmonize remarkably well, and the song didn't sound as ghastly as Pandora thought it would. The fact that, of the three, Arachne could actually sing helped.

Pandora didn't make eye contact with anyone during the song. She just wanted to finish and leave as soon as possible. The strain of maintaining her pretense was beginning to give her a headache in addition to being mildly inebriated. The evening for her only steadily grew worse, and she wanted it to be over. Her mother would make the proper excuses for her. Their guests wouldn't stay much beyond Eurydice playing her violin, but depending on what she decided to play, that could be a while. Pandora stood beside her sisters with her hands clasped in front of her to keep herself from fidgeting.

The song finally ended, blessedly, after only a few short minutes. Their guests applauded, and the three girls smiled graciously. There was banter around the room as Dorian was ribbed by his friends and brothers for his piano playing. Pandora walked over to her mother, who was seated on one of the settees, to give her a hug before exiting.

"I hope you will feel better in the morning," she whispered as Pandora leaned near.

"I'm sure I will, Mamà. I've just developed a ghastly headache."

"Not one of your migraines?" asked the duchess with sympathy.

"No, I don't think so," demurred Pandora.

"Perhaps you should go for some air before going upstairs, hmm?" asked the duchess with a smile before giving Pandora's arm a squeeze.

"Yes, Mamà, I think I shall."

She hadn't intended to go outside. She had planned to go straight to her room, but at her mother's suggestion, it seemed an excellent idea. The weather was mild, and a stroll to the gazebo and back before retiring to her room would help to clear her head.

Pandora was able to leave without attracting attention from most of the company. After retrieving a lightweight shawl from the closet in the hall, she made her way to the back of the house. She didn't encounter anyone on her way; most of the servants had either retired to their rooms for the night or were attending to their final duties before doing the same. She walked through the darkened, empty ballroom, her footsteps making lonely echoes against the high ceiling. She exited through one of the sets of French doors onto the terrace where she paused, closing her eyes and inhaling the peaceful silence. After standing that way for a moment, she made her way down the stairs to the path that would lead her through the garden to the gazebo.

She took her time walking. She didn't feel the need to rush; her mother had given her permission to be out, and other than to bed, there was nowhere she needed to go. Once she reached the gazebo, she sat down and adjusted her shawl on her shoulders. The air wasn't cold, but she felt a sudden chill that had nothing to do with the weather.

Pandora let her hand rest on her abdomen for a brief, fluttering moment, and then the tears came. She put a hand to her mouth to muffle the heaving sobs that came from the core of her being. How could she not have known? The miscarriage had been for the best, but how could she not have realized she was with child? She was familiar with human anatomy; she had cringingly read medical texts and, even though it was not one of her most stellar subjects, she knew about the reproductive cycle as it was understood. How was it that she hadn't recognized it within herself, that Maiyin had needed to enlighten her?

She had briefly thought Maiyin was mistaken, but Pandora could in hindsight recognize the effects the ended pregnancy had caused: her tiredness, her appetite by turns being overwhelming to non-existent, her tendency to become dizzy or faint for no reason. It all made sense now that she knew. Then there was the miscarriage itself. To her, it had been no more than what seemed to be a menstrual period slightly heavier than usual and painful, which had never happened before. The teas Maiyin had been giving her had nothing to do with treating a cold.

Pandora put her other hand to the cushions to brace herself as her shoulders shook from the tears. Maybe it was for the best she had come to the gazebo where she was alone, where no one could hear her. She had needed to do this all night, and now that it had started, she wasn't sure when she would be able to get it to stop.

Pandora started in surprise when she felt a hand on her shoulder, and the hand over her mouth to quiet her sobs muffled her startled scream. She looked up to see Islington seated beside her, and, not knowing what else to do, Pandora wrapped her arms around his neck and buried her face in his collar, her scalding tears soaking the material.

Surprisingly, Islington embraced her and pulled her onto his lap to cradle her against him like a child, rubbing a comforting hand on her back and resting his head against hers. He whispered soft, soothing noises and rocked her because he couldn't bear to see her so distressed. He couldn't tolerate a woman crying for no reason; this was obviously not that.

Islington left shortly after Eurydice began to play. He told Selena he had a matter to attend to and that if he hadn't come back by the end of the night, she was to go home in the carriage without him. Selena had given him a puzzled glance, but she wasn't going to question her brother.

He had seen Pandora leaving the drawing room after speaking with the duchess, and he could tell she wouldn't be returning. He needed to speak with her privately regarding the conspiracy, and he didn't feel he could wait because he wasn't sure when he would see her again. Once he left the room, it took him some time to decide where she might have gone. He hoped she hadn't gone to bed. Remembering her penchant for secluded places, he thought to check the gazebo before deciding that she *had* gone to her room. If she had gone upstairs, he would have waited for another time.

Now, here he sat trying to comfort Pandora when it seemed for all the world there had never been a more miserable soul. Islington had never expected when he found Pandora here that she would be in this condition. She was in good spirits all evening. She laughed and teased and conversed as if she hadn't a care. He wasn't aware of anything untoward that might have happened to provoke this, and he had been at her elbow for most of the night. He felt she had been a bit too friendly with Lord Lambeth, but it had all been in his imagination. In the end, he knew he was only jealous that he didn't have her undivided attention. Nothing came to mind that would account for her despair.

After a time, Islington felt her begin to calm. Pandora turned her face away from his collar and rested her head on his shoulder. The tears were still falling, but the sobs had ceased for the time being. He reached into his pocket to give her his handkerchief, which she took gratefully.

After clearing the lump from her throat, Pandora raised her head and was able to speak.

"Did you come looking for me?" she asked neutrally.

Islington hesitated for a moment with a slight frown. He wasn't sure if now was the right time to ask, but he sensed she would rather not talk about what had just happened. He would let her have her way...for the time being.

"Yes, I wanted to ask if you remembered any further details about Castleton and the Aristocrat, any element of their appearance you may recall. Your brother and I are having difficulty finding either of them, and I am willing to admit that we need your help."

Pandora looked thoughtful for a moment then shook her head.

"No, I never saw either of them. Well, I saw Castleton's *shadow*. He was tall, taller than either you or Dorian, perhaps as tall as Mr. Ellsworth, and extremely thin. He had a fairly pronounced stoop, as if his height were too much for his frame to bear. Then there was the smell."

"Smell?"

"Yes, he smelled ghastly. He was unwashed and vile-smelling—garlic, stale liquor, cigar tobacco, wood smoke. Even from across the room, the smell was unbelievably strong."

It was Islington's turn to look thoughtful then as he stored away the information she had given him.

When it seemed Islington wasn't going to ask anything further, Pandora rested her head back against his shoulder. Islington didn't let her keep it there for long. He raised her face to his with a gentle finger under her chin and kissed her tenderly. Pandora returned his kiss with a fervor that startled him. He didn't stop her and let her deepen the kiss of her own accord, and he was amazed by the yearning her actions provoked. Yet he couldn't forget the way he had found her when he came to the gazebo, and with reluctance he ended the kiss by placing a hand to either side of her face to look into her eyes.

"Pandora, what is wrong?" he asked gently.

Silent tears began to flow as she looked at him, and he brushed at her cheeks with his thumbs to clear them away. Her eyes were filled with grief and also with what Islington thought might be fear. She closed them for a moment and took a deep breath to calm herself. When she opened them again, he also saw resoluteness. Pandora surprised him then when she gently but firmly put her hands to either side of his face much the same as he held hers.

"I lost it," she said in a cracked, subdued voice.

For only a brief moment his forehead wrinkled in confusion, but Pandora's continued stark gaze left him no question of what she meant. He felt a knot build in the pit of his stomach, and he clenched his jaw to control his emotions. He could feel an unexpected and unwelcome burning in his eyes that he blinked several times to control. He tried to look away from Pandora's gaze and weakly dropped his hands from her face to her sides. She, however, continued to hold his face immobile.

"You were—with—my child?" he managed to get out brokenly. She simply nodded. "What...? Why?" He couldn't believe he was incapable of putting together a coherent sentence.

Pandora changed her position on his lap so that she now straddled him on her knees. She cradled his head against her breast comfortingly, smoothing her hand over his hair. Islington tightly wound his arms around her waist as a surfeit of emotions flowed through him. She could feel him shuddering in her arms, and Pandora closed her eyes as she rested her cheek against the top of his head. Tears she thought must surely have run dry continued to fall from the corners of her eyes as she held him, but she couldn't make them stop.

After a time, Islington lifted his head to kiss Pandora constrainedly. She could sense the dampness on his cheeks. He quickly ended the embrace and gently raised her from his lap to place her on the bench and stood.

"I have to go," he said huskily, not looking at her.

With that, he left the gazebo, and Pandora watched him leave with a furrow of confusion in her brow.

That's it? Although she knew there was nothing to say, wasn't there something that *should* be said? Pandora rubbed the spot behind her ear contemplatively for a moment as she thought, but she could arrive at nothing that seemed even remotely logical.

Sighing resignedly, she picked up the handkerchief and wiped it at her cheeks in preparation to return to the house. Pandora had told Maiyin that she wouldn't need her help, so she wouldn't have to face the questioning glance of her maid, but she didn't want to have anyone else ask questions either. She didn't know how much time had passed since she had gone, but either the guests had already left or would be leaving shortly. She left the gazebo and went to the rear of the house where she entered and went up the back stairs to her room. She glanced at the clock on the stand in her room and saw it was just nearing one.

Maiyin had left a lamp lit low and had turned down the covers on Pandora's bed before retiring. Pandora went to a drawer to pull out a soft, white silk shift and laid it on the bed. She kicked off her shoes and unfastened her gown, which she removed and draped carefully over the back of a chair for Maiyin to take care of in the morning. Thankfully, she didn't need to wear a corset; otherwise, she would have needed Maiyin's help. As it was, she removed her chemise and put on her shift.

She went to the basin and pitcher on their stand and poured a little water into it. She happened to glance in the mirror above the stand, and even by the lamp's dim light, she could see that her face was puffy and her eyes were red. She looked a fright. She splashed some of the cold water on her face and dried it with a towel. She then spent the better part of ten minutes finding and removing all the pins Maiyin had put in her hair. She quickly ran a brush through it and plaited it into a long braid, which she tied with a ribbon and was ready for bed.

Pandora placed the lamp onto the night table and put it out. She settled her head against the softness of the down pillows and snuggled under the warmth of her covers, but for all the alertness she felt they could have been made of stone and wool.

Her mind raced with thoughts. The tears seemed to have stopped, and she was able to control them now...whatever comfort that gave her. She remained puzzled by Islington's abrupt departure. She was relieved he had at least had *some* reaction to what had happened, but she wasn't sure what his reaction meant. Pandora hoped he might tell her eventually, but she wasn't anticipating that he ever would.

She was gratified Islington had asked for her help. She knew he didn't intend for his question to be an invitation to full inclusion in the search; he would still view it as dangerous for her to be looking for criminals. Still, it had been something. By what he had said, she wasn't able to determine if he had been able to find any proof that Hendon was the Aristocrat or not.

After fluffing her pillows a few times, Pandora's exhaustion caught up with her, and she drifted off to sleep.

Around 4:30, Pandora sat upright in bed, her eyes wide with surprise.
"Oh, my giddy aunt! The comte d'Artois!" she gasped.
Just as quickly, her head dropped back to her pillows, and she was sound asleep.

Chapter Ten

A week later, Pandora had not forgotten her discovery. While she had no confirmation Charles-Philippe de Bourbon, comte d'Artois, was the intended victim, now that she suspected it, it seemed logical and probable. The morning following her revelation, she tried to get her father to send a letter to the man warning him, not wanting to make the same mistake she had with Bertram Batts. Her father, as usual, tut-tutted and refused. She next went to Dorian. She told him her suspicions, but he laughed and said he thought it unlikely. She groaned in aggravation but requested he relay the information to Islington. He assured her that he would.

Pandora couldn't believe the man had not come to mind from the beginning. As the younger brother of the last king of France, should the monarchy be restored, after his elder surviving brother, the comte de Lille, he stood to become the new king. The discussion between her siblings and the Nichols men the previous night made her see him as a conceivable victim. She had no notion of whether or not their mention of his having a portion of the French crown jewels was accurate, but only the rumor of it would be enough to tempt someone. It would also behoove the current regime to dispose of him, and Pandora wondered if the conspiracy between Castleton and the Aristocrat might not have even more contributors in France. Of course, the actual number was irrelevant; the most important thing was that Artois was in danger.

In addition to his apartments at Holyrood (and Pandora couldn't believe she had forgotten), the comte d'Artois had a residence on South Audley. That would probably be his destination within London once he arrived, but Pandora wasn't sure it would be safe for him to even attempt coming to town. The criminals weren't planning to kidnap him until he returned to Scotland, but might they not attempt to abduct him earlier if necessary? Pandora had firmly come to believe the safest course would be to warn him before he left; then, perhaps, he would be sure to have other riders in attendance to protect him, as he was usually known to do, if he even made the journey at all.

The only difficulty Pandora had was finding someone in a position of authority (like her father) to send him a message. Pandora could send a letter herself, but being female would not be a point in her favor. She didn't believe he would take anything she had to say seriously…if she sent it in a letter. She was sure a man of Artois's position was accustomed to receiving warnings of threats both real and imagined, but a warning from a woman would probably be considered one of the latter. No, she would have to find someone (a man) to warn him…or she would have to go in person to make him see reason. That did not seem likely.

Yet Pandora wasn't certain that he *was* the intended victim. Artois was the only logical victim she had found, but what if she was wrong? What if he wasn't, and she warned the wrong man? To make sure that didn't happen, Pandora's brother and Islington would have to find the conspirators and stop them or find some proof of the true identity of their victim…or she would have to do it herself. That also didn't seem likely.

That night, she was going to Almack's with Psyche and Arachne. It was almost the last ball of the Season for the organization, and while Pandora didn't care for the Season—she was happy it was almost over—she had been invited by Selena to attend.

Her friend was much more interested in social functions than Pandora, but Pandora liked spending time with Selena. Attending a ball, while not Pandora's favorite occupation, gave her the opportunity. Selena didn't ride well, so they couldn't meet in the park in the mornings to ride together. Since they had met at Lady Ramsey's, Selena had come to visit Pandora at Aberdare House two or three times a week. Pandora couldn't bring herself to go to Bardsey House because of Islington; she felt she owed it to Selena to go to a ball occasionally in return. They had already made plans to visit each other in the country once the Season ended. Pandora was excited about showing Selena Wilderland and the solarium, although she wasn't sure how enthusiastic Selena's response would be to the room.

Occasionally, Pandora suspected she was being used as an excuse by Selena to visit the Savage home on the chance she might see Dorian, but Pandora didn't mind even if she were; the two of them were well-suited, and it was obvious they were both too shy to court. It was also obvious they liked each other immensely, and Pandora wouldn't be surprised when their engagement was announced.

Aside from his shyness, Dorian was worried about Islington's reaction. As far as Pandora could tell, the man was oblivious. She couldn't see why he would have any objection to the match; Dorian was undeniably of good quality in breeding, wealth, looks, and character. If Islington made any disapproval, Pandora would box his ears…again.

Pandora and her sisters made arrangements to pick up Selena at her home; then they would go to Almack's from there. Their coach stopped in front of Bardsey House, and Pandora felt it shift as Jim alighted from the driver's seat to open the door of the coach. He helped Pandora down, and she went to the door to fetch Selena. After she knocked, it was opened by Waldon, who looked down his nose with stodgy disapproval...just like a good British butler should.

"Evening, Waldon," she grinned. "I'm here for Lady Selena."

"Of course, Lady Pandora. If you will follow me to the sitting room, I will let her know of your arrival," he said dryly without a change of expression.

He turned to lead the way, and Pandora stuck out her tongue and made a face at his retreating back. He would never last with *her* family. She quickened her pace to move up beside him, and Pandora caught his sidelong look of surprise.

"So, tell me, Waldon, how long have you worked for the Marshalls?"

"I have been in service to the family for thirty-five years, Lady Pandora," he replied after a brief purse of his lips to denote his disapproval of the impertinent question.

"That's a very long time," said Pandora in surprise.

"Indeed, ma'am," he said blandly.

"So, you would know all their dark secrets, wouldn't you?" asked Pandora with a teasing smile.

"Yes, Lady Pandora," he replied dryly as he stopped to open the door to the sitting room. Before he opened the door, he turned to look at her. "I should, however, wish to inform you that I'll not tell you any of them."

"Thank you, Waldon," returned Pandora with a cheeky grin. "Besides, I don't think we have the time."

She sauntered into the sitting room, ignoring his shocked look. She was satisfied that she was able to get a personal comment out of him; there was hope for Waldon yet.

"I will inform Lady Selena of your arrival," he repeated mildly.

Pandora waved a hand in dismissal, and he left the room after a slight bow.

Once he was gone, Pandora thought about sitting but found herself walking around slowly, examining the objects she saw. Waldon hadn't taken her to the family's private sitting room, where Pandora had met the marchioness, but to the formal sitting room where they normally received visitors. The furniture looked comfortable, but Pandora found much to keep her on her feet, regardless of how rude it was.

One object in particular that drew her attention was a large painting. It was a family portrait with the mother and father and four children. It was recent enough that it had to be a portrait of Islington and Selena and the rest of their family.

The man stood near the back holding the reins of a magnificent bay hunter. He looked to be in his mid-forties, his dark brown hair just starting to gray at the temples. He was handsome and well-built and appeared to be tall, but Pandora didn't think Islington resembled him much—even had they shared the same hair color. He wore riding clothes and held a crop in the hand that wasn't holding the reins. His expression was one of indulgent pride, a slight smile on his mouth as he looked at his family spread before him. That would be the late marquess.

His wife, the marchioness, sat a little to the right on a large stump. She was fairly young as well, not quite as old as her husband, slender and beautiful with light blonde hair and blue eyes. She was dressed in a fashion that was popular toward the end of the previous century, with the fuller skirt and fitted, waist-length bodice, and a fichu of pure white lace draped at the neckline for modesty. She watched the children at play in front of her with a loving smile. A baby with light brown hair, no more than a year old, sat on her knee, a hand reaching up to grab one of her mother's curls playfully. Pandora suspected the baby was Selena.

There were two boys and another girl at play in the foreground. The older boy, who appeared to be about twelve, held a stick he was using to play with a spaniel, frozen on its hind legs as it tried to grab the object in his hand. The boy had his father's dark brown hair and his mother's blue eyes. Judging from the clothing, he was too old to be Islington. Pandora thought this might be the William that Lucy Cranston had mentioned.

The girl, who Pandora estimated to be about age ten, was a younger version of her mother, with silvery blonde hair and a slender frame. The fabric of her gown was in a matching, but smaller, pattern like the one used for her mother's. She had a delighted smile as she played with a kitten and a ball of string where she sat on the ground, her skirts artfully arranged. Her identity was a mystery to Pandora; neither Selena nor Islington had ever mentioned having an older sister.

The second boy, who looked to be six or seven, sat closer to his mother than the other children. Pandora smiled amusedly as she recognized the *very* young Islington. His hair, too, was blond but of a slightly darker shade, and his cheeks were a chubby, rosy pink. Pandora was unable to determine the color of his eyes because of the angle at which his face had been painted, but she knew from seeing them personally that they would be a pure shade of blue. Instead of being engaged in some form of play, however, he was reading a book, a rather thick, rather large book. Pandora moved closer to the portrait to look at the spine. The portraitist had a very detailed style, and she was able to read the title of the volume without any difficulty.

"Oh, surely not," she said out loud to herself in disbelief, deciding the painter had taken a bit of artistic license.

"That's a very good book," said Islington softly at her elbow.

Pandora yelped in surprise and turned to look at him.

"Do you always have to sneak up on me?" she said in consternation.

He chuckled at her discomfiture and clasped his hands behind his back, rocking back and forth on his heels.

"Perhaps if you weren't always off in your own little world, you might actually be able to hear me coming," he returned with a grin. "It's not as if I have to *try* to catch you unawares."

Pandora pursed her lips to hold in an unbecoming retort and turned her attention back to the painting, still looking at the book disbelievingly. She pointed to the picture and looked at him as he stood at her side.

"The man is your father?" she asked.

"Yes, indeed. The woman is, of course, my mother."

"The baby, I believe, is Selena, and you're the little boy sitting next to your mother with the book I can't believe you're reading at that age."

"Yes, that is me and Selena. I *was* reading *Domestic Medicine* when I was six years old...mostly," said Islington with a sheepish grin.

"Aha!"

"It wasn't that I didn't *want* to read it. I was truly making an effort, but it was a bit long." Pandora smiled. "Actually, I wanted to read some of Pringle's works, but my dad wouldn't let me. He thought it would give me nightmares."

"You're serious?" asked Pandora, her eyes wide.

"Absolutely."

Pandora finally worked up the courage to ask something she had wondered about for some time.

"Dorian said you met at Cambridge, so what did you study?"

"Medicine, of course."

Pandora looked at him with dumbstruck amazement. She never would have guessed in a million years.

"*You* are a trained physician?"

"I am." He turned to look at her with a sardonic grin. "You seem so surprised, m'dear."

"Well, I...ah," stuttered Pandora, but she decided to try a bit of Psyche's truth. "Yes, I suppose I am. It's simply you don't strike me as a body who would find it that interesting."

"I suppose not," he stated dryly with a wry grin.

She returned her attention to the painting. She pointed to the older boy.

"That would be your brother, William?"

Islington looked at the painting and nodded agreeably, but his expression held a hint of something that closely resembled dislike.

"He died when he was twenty. I was almost fifteen at the time."

"I'm sorry to hear that."

Islington shrugged negligibly. "It was a long time ago, and it was a foolish accident." Pandora lifted an inquisitive eyebrow. "He went to the local tavern, got boozy, and went for a swim. Unfortunately, it had been a particularly dry season, and the river was low. When he dove into the water from the bridge, it broke his neck. He died instantly."

"That's terrible!" said Pandora in shock.

"True," said Islington neutrally.

Pandora looked at him uncertainly, her forehead wrinkled.

"You don't seem to be too terribly upset at his passing."

Islington clenched his jaw for a moment as if he were going to change the subject, but he felt oddly comfortable talking to her.

"My brother, William—or Billy, as we called him—was a bully. He would terrorize my sisters and me when we were children because he could, and I mean terrorize, not *tease*. When Billy got older, it didn't improve, and he associated with the ruffians in the town near our country home. He let his station in life get the better of him, and he paid for it."

Pandora was almost afraid to ask, but her curiosity about his older sister stayed with her.

"And what of your older sister, there, who looks remarkably like your mother?"

As much as his expression had been one of dislike for William, the one for his sister was sad.

"That was Louise. She died in childbirth when she was seventeen."

"Oh," said Pandora quietly, as if the air had left her.

She started to reach over to take his hand in comfort, but at that moment Selena rushed into the room in a flurry of light blue silk and tulle.

"Here I am!" she called. "I'm sorry you two had to wait for me, but I had to change gowns at the last minute."

Selena seemed to be unaware of the scene she had interrupted.

"The two of us?" asked Pandora blankly.

It was then that she realized Islington was dressed in evening clothes.

"Yes, I thought I would accompany you to Almack's, as it is the next-to-last ball of the season," he said calmly.

"Well, no. I mean…that will be fine. There's plenty of room in the coach," said Pandora weakly, her cheeks flushing in embarrassment.

"Teddy, you didn't make her angry, did you?" scolded Selena as she walked toward them.

"What?" he asked with a confused frown.

"Pandora said you sometimes make her so mad she can't think straight, so I assumed it was one of those times," said Selena, setting her hands on her hips threateningly.

Pandora blushed an even darker shade of red. Islington looked at her with a raised eyebrow, his lips quirked in amusement at her discomfort. He would have to ask his sister what else Pandora had been saying about him that might become useful information.

"Unless it's one of the *other* times," said Selena teasingly, her posture relaxing as she also noted Pandora's crimson cheeks.

Pandora wanted to disappear.

"And here all this time I thought Islington was an oddity in a family of *nice* people," she grumbled.

The brother and sister laughed heartily, and Selena reached over to take her arm affectionately.

"Oh, pooh," said Selena. "You'll not get me to feel guilty for teasing you, not when you blush so well."

Pandora decided to let it go by. She wasn't used to being the object of teasing…except by Psyche and her other family members. She was sure Selena's ribbing was just as harmless.

"Shall we go to the coach then?" asked Pandora with a good-natured smile. "I'm sure my sisters are wondering what's become of us by now."

The three of them left the house with Selena chattering gaily and went to the coach, where Jim stood waiting to open the door. After a bit of rearranging, Pandora found herself seated on the forward-facing side between the two Marshalls while Arachne and Psyche had a much more comfortable seat on the opposite side. Islington had offered to take that seat, but they would have none of it. Pandora would rather she sat on the seat with her sisters, but they wouldn't have that either.

Although the coach was large, Pandora found herself seated close enough to Islington that their shoulders touched, while there was nearly a foot of space between her and Selena. Without drawing attention to the situation, she couldn't easily adjust her position. It wasn't that she found it offensive; it was that she did not which affected her. Her hand rested at her side on the seat beneath the folds of her gown, and her little finger occasionally came into contact with the material of his trousers when the coach jostled over a bump and her glove slid on the leather cushions.

To add to her agitation, not long after the trip began, he surreptitiously placed his hand over hers where it was hidden and twined their fingers together. He continued in his conversation with Psyche without the slightest change of expression or tone. Her dress and the darkness within the coach hid it perfectly, and neither of her sisters noticed. Pandora at first thought to break the contact, if only to quell any questions it might create from her sisters, but after a minute or two of their apparent incognizance, she let her hand relax into the grip and caressed her thumb against the knuckle of his little finger as a gesture of reciprocation. It wasn't long before Pandora found the hold to be perfectly natural and did not let it affect her own participation in the idle chatter in the coach.

Throughout the trip, Pandora wondered what it meant. It was a sign of affection she didn't expect from Islington because she wasn't sure he *had* any affection for her. That he felt desire for her, occasionally, Pandora did not question, and it was true her brief time of carrying his child bound them in a way that normally didn't exist between an unmarried man and woman, but his holding her hand was a spontaneous, unaffected act of tenderness that in no way sat well with her previous opinion of him. In the end, she decided not to question his motivation and accepted it for what it seemed.

After a brief wait, they were able to leave the coach and go up the steps into the building. Pandora was sure it would have been longer if they hadn't been late. She disliked being tardy and could not for the life of her understand why people were beginning to see it as a fashionable, acceptable act. She would rather *not* make a grand entrance; the less attention she received, the better.

Almack's didn't use dance cards, and Pandora could refuse partners at her pleasure. The only reason her mother and other friends of their circle seemed to use them with frequency was that most of the wives had attended finishing school in Austria, where the cards were fairly common. They did serve a practical purpose, but Pandora found them vexing at times.

As they entered the room, the late-July heat combined with the number of people made it almost difficult for Pandora to breathe. Arachne, who was affected by close spaces more than most, looked pale. She would try to avoid spending a great deal of time in the main room because of it. Pandora moved close to her sister to give her arm a comforting squeeze and leaned near to speak to her over the noise of countless conversations and the sound of music for a country dance.

"I will not mind leaving early," Pandora said with a smile.

"Nor I," said Arachne with a hearty agreement.

"Oh, no, if I can tolerate it, so can the two of you," said Psyche firmly. "Although I think I shall not wish to stay much past two hours," she said with a cheeky grin.

"Two hours?" gasped Selena. "That's only four or five dances!"

Pandora looked at Arachne's face to gauge how well she was coping with the crowd around her. She had calmed somewhat, but it wouldn't be long before she went to one of the side rooms where there were fewer people. Pandora was sure when it was time to go home that Arachne would be found, of all places, in the cloak room.

"Very well, Selena, you decide when we're able to leave," said Pandora with an agreeable smile. "Although, we should determine where we will meet when that happens."

Selena looked thoughtful for a moment. It wasn't the people and conversation she liked at the balls; she enjoyed dancing. Yet she also knew the three girls (and her brother) didn't like it nearly as much.

"We'll leave at midnight," said Selena once she determined how much time would be needed for eight dances. Unfortunately, Almack's did not let dancers waltz, else Selena would have wanted more. "We can meet in front of the cloak room."

"Fair enough," said Arachne quickly.

Pandora almost thought she would go directly there and not move for the three or so hours they would stay.

"Indeed," said Pandora and Psyche in unison. They looked at each other and grinned.

For a time, the five of them stood together conversing at the edge of the room, but Lord Georgie soon came to ask Selena to dance. She, of course, gladly accepted. Arachne gave an excuse of needing refreshment and made an exit to parts unknown. That left the twins and Islington, and conversation was waning among them.

"If you'll excuse me, I see someone with whom I wish to speak," he said with a slight bow.

After he left, the two girls followed his retreating back until he disappeared within the crowd then looked at each other.

"Do you think that means he didn't want to speak to us?" asked Psyche conversationally.

"Psy, I have long since given up trying to decide what he means when he says something. More often than not, I find, what he *says* and what he *means* are two entirely different things."

"Oh, surely not!" gasped Psyche.

"Indubitably."

"I've always found him to be rather honest myself, if a bit arrogant at times." She looked at her sister and gave her a playful nudge in the arm with her elbow. "Perhaps you have finally met your match."

"No!" said Pandora with a note of exasperation and also a little embarrassment. "I don't believe there are two people less well-suited in the world...unless it is you and Lord Barneville," she said, returning Psyche's playful nudge.

Psyche turned a shade of red, and her jaw dropped in surprise.

"Whatever do you mean?"

She tried to make the question seem unconcerned, but Pandora knew her twin too well.

"I saw the way you two were arguing at Mamá's dinner party."

"But...but...."

"Exactly," quipped Pandora.

They remained fairly silent after that and were content to find two chairs along the wall to watch the other attendees ebb and flow around them. They occasionally saw someone they knew, and they would nod and smile genially. For a time, no one seemed to feel a need to speak to them, which suited them perfectly. It wasn't long, however, before Lord Drake stood before them and asked Psyche to dance. She accepted, and Pandora could hear him asking about Arachne as they left for the floor.

Pandora sighed and relaxed into the slight cushion of her seat. She thought she might find an adjoining room with more comfortable chairs, as she didn't want to dance unless it was unavoidable. She was sure Arachne had found somewhere very comfortable to relax, and Pandora would have to let her sister know Lord Drake was asking after her.

Pandora was asked to dance a couple of times, but she begged off, claiming a lingering weakness from her illness. She almost wished she had brought her cane. She couldn't continue using her *recovering health* as an excuse to avoid dancing, especially now that she no longer limped or required her walking stick. Now that she had nothing to make it seem believable, she was going to be considered rude. She shifted slightly as she felt one side of her posterior going numb and thought she might have to dance just to keep her extremities from going to sleep.

She thought back over the past week since her mother's dinner party. The day before the party she had finally been able to ride Bellerophon again, and as the week progressed, she had ridden him every day. By that morning, she had regained enough confidence that she had guided him to a full gallop. She was still not confident enough to try jumping anything, but she would be able to by the time they returned home to Wilderland.

Home. Pandora very much looked forward to returning home. Her foray into the social arena had been more disastrous than she had dreamt it would be. There were very few things that had happened that could not be considered reputation-tarnishing. The only fortunate thing for her was that no one had been there to witness her ill-behavior and pass it along to the gossip mongers. Pandora was glad her mother had only insisted they come for the one Season. She had no intention of returning to London for society. She would come back, of course, simply to be with her family and friends, but not to go to a ball, or a dinner, or anything else that required her to be polite to strangers.

Her parents wouldn't be returning to the country for at least a fortnight after the close of Parliament because of some business dealings her father needed to attend to, but the duke and duchess had already given Pandora and her siblings permission to return home at their leisure. Pandora would be ready to leave the day after the Season ended. She wondered if her mother would find it uncouth if she abandoned the city in the middle of the night. After some consideration, Pandora was sure she would.

Then Pandora realized she wouldn't be able to immediately leave. Until this business with the conspiracy was settled, she couldn't return to Wilderland. She couldn't go home until Artois was safe. That deflated her spirits. Although Islington said he and Dorian would take care of things, she couldn't possibly leave until the criminals were stopped, with or without her help. She had invested so much of herself into seeing the matter resolved she could not, in good conscience, go home until it was.

Pandora continued to sit in her chair and semi-gracefully decline requests to dance until Sir James Klein came to ask her for a turn at a cotillion. She started to demur but agreed when he looked crestfallen. He had always been very kind to her, and she didn't want to seem harsh when there was no reason for it. They joined the bottom of the set, and Pandora smiled graciously at him as he stood across from her.

She glanced up the line at the rest of the dancers and saw Arachne had been rooted from whatever hiding place she had found by Lord Drake. She appeared calm, and there were fewer people on the floor for the dance than there were around its edges. Pandora saw her twin dancing with Lord Georgie, and Selena was dancing with an attractive if foppish gentleman that Pandora didn't recognize.

Islington wasn't participating. Pandora scanned the faces of the people around the room, but she couldn't see him. He was probably in one of the other rooms, or he might have even gone from the building. It didn't really give Pandora any cause for concern, as long as he was back by midnight for a ride home.

Pandora was glad when the cotillion ended. She found the standing and waiting tiresome. She much preferred to waltz if given a choice; at least then she didn't have to wait her turn. But the matrons of Almack's had so far not allowed the waltz at their establishment because they considered it unseemly for a man and woman to dance that close. Her parents and their social circle, however, wouldn't dream of not having it. Almack's would not stop it from arriving for much longer.

Sir James asked Pandora if she needed refreshment, and she thankfully accepted. She wasn't sure how much longer it would be until midnight, but she had sat for at least an hour or more before she accepted Sir James's request. She took his arm and let him escort her to the room where tables with beverages and food had been placed.

She was able to find a seat while Sir James went to get her a glass of lemonade. She opened her fan and fluttered it in front of her slowly to produce the maximum amount of wind she could from the small, feathery creation. It wasn't able to provide her with much relief from the heat generated by the mass of bodies surrounding her, but it was better than nothing. Selena was walking toward her with her dancing partner, and Pandora stood from her chair and smiled amiably at her friend.

"I see you didn't manage to remain sedentary for long," said Selena with a teasing grin.

"No, I didn't, but Sir James is a very dear man. I couldn't refuse; he looked positively crushed," said Pandora with a grin of her own.

Pandora got a better look at Selena's companion now that he was near. Although attractive by most standards, Pandora found him soft-looking on closer inspection. He had black hair and brown eyes that reminded her of the still pools of water in the peat marshes at home, depthless and dark. He was shorter than her brothers, standing only two or three inches above her own height of five feet, eight inches. His skin was pale, almost waxy in color, as if most of his time was spent inside far away from sunlight. He wore the latest fashion, and his cravat was tied in a particularly difficult configuration. There was nothing to truly fault with his appearance, but something about him seemed not quite right.

Pandora thought it would be good to give him a once-over, just on the chance he was competition to Dorian. Pandora thought it unlikely, but lately her instincts were wrong. Still, he wasn't nearly as attractive as her brother, and Selena didn't think so either. It showed in the way she gingerly had her arm through his, as if what she was touching might not be safe. It didn't take long for Pandora to find out her uneasiness was dead-on.

"Lady Pandora Savage, I would like to introduce Ector Marsh, the Earl of Hendon," said Selena in a pleasant but subdued tone.

Pandora tried to remain poised, and from Selena's expression, this was something she did unwillingly. Pandora wasn't aware Selena knew him. All the time they had known each other, she had never mentioned their acquaintance despite knowing of Pandora's interest in him. Judging by Selena's expression, he wasn't a *close* acquaintance, which made Pandora wonder—other than Hendon being with her when she came to speak with her friend—why Selena had introduced him. Pandora didn't believe Hendon had requested the introduction, but after Selena presented him, his expression became one of obvious sexual appraisal. Pandora felt like she was being coated with pond scum.

"Lady Pandora, it is an honor," he said with a charming smile as he took her gloved hand to place a kiss on it.

Pandora fought the urge to pull her hand away. When he spoke, she knew the truth. The voice was his. She had heard that silky yet malevolent baritone in too many nightmares. With Castleton, there was no mistaking the evil; with Hendon, it was insidious and all the more deadly.

"Lord Hendon," she said with a gracious smile.

"Your father is the Duke of Aberdare, isn't he?" he asked pleasantly.

"Yes, he is," said Pandora. She continued to keep an affable smile, but her face was beginning to hurt from the effort.

"That's a large brood he's got, ain't it?" quizzed Hendon dubiously.

"Why, Lord Hendon, that is a rather impertinent question to ask," simpered Pandora.

Sir James was returning with her lemonade, and she hoped a male presence would ease the tension that seemed to be developing in the air between Hendon and herself. To her dismay, Sir James was stopped by a young woman dressed in an unseasonable, long-sleeved gown. Selena remained at hand, and Pandora was grateful she had not been completely abandoned, but it would be up to her to disengage them from Hendon.

"Is your wife here this evening, Lord Hendon?" asked Pandora mildly.

"Yes, the mouse is about somewhere," he sneered. Pandora found that to be an uncharitable description to place on one's recent bride.

"Lord Hendon, as I understand it, you have estates up north; is that correct?" asked Selena in an effort to keep the conversation genial.

"I have several, in fact. One each in Northumberland, Cumberland, and Westmorland, and two in Scotland."

"Ooh, Scotland!" squealed Pandora with affected delight. "Have you ever been to Edinburgh?" she asked avidly.

"No, I daresay not," he said with a frozen smile.

"I've been wanting to go to Edinburgh on the chance I might meet the comte d'Artois. He's not much in London these days, and with me just coming out this year, I've not had the opportunity. Now, with three weeks left, it appears I may have to wait until next go 'round. Perhaps with the Season over, I can convince my parents to let me go for a jaunt," she said with a believable amount of rambling gaiety.

Pandora could detect a slight change in his expression, a hardening of the eyes that hinted at his growing suspicion.

"Why would you want to meet that pompous, Catholic windbag?" he asked in a tone that almost sounded like a snarl.

Selena paled slightly at the change in his demeanor. Before, he had been slyly charming. At the mention of Artois, his face twisted into that of someone unbalanced. Pandora gave him a wide-eyed, innocent smile, seemingly oblivious to his distaste.

"Well, it's not every day one has the chance to meet a future king. Of course, we have our own royal family with the Prince Regent and all, but they're not French," she said with a pleasant smile.

"I should say not, Lady Pandora," he said coldly.

"Well, everyone says the comte d'Artois is a very nice man, and he doesn't put on airs. I find airs to be so vexing, don't you?"

"Indeed, Lady Pandora," said Lord Hendon neutrally.

His expression calmed as she chattered, but he wasn't happy with the topic and found her fawning over the French repugnant. To Pandora, it was almost as good as a written confirmation that Artois was the intended victim, but a lot of her countrymen found the French obnoxious.

"Of course, I suppose we really should dislike the French, shouldn't we? After all, there was all the help they gave the Colonies—pardon, I mean the United States—during that little war. Then there was the one before *that*, and now there's this *new* one." She sighed and shook her head, waving her fan fretfully. "I daresay, I think I've just convinced myself I should *not* like to meet the comte d'Artois. What a *naughty* man." Her expression changed to one of petulant disgust.

Pandora's performance seemed to allay Hendon's suspicions. He seemed to believe she was a simple-headed debutante, and Pandora was glad. She didn't want to give Hendon cause to move forward with his plan early; she needed time to warn Artois. She also needed to be sure he *was* the man they intended to kidnap and murder; from Hendon's demeanor, her confidence on that did not seem to be misplaced.

For now, however, she wanted to extricate herself and Selena from his company. The predatory expression returned after her brainless chatter, and she found neither the insanity nor the depravity charming. Selena relaxed now that his manner had calmed, but a strain was beginning to show around her eyes. While Hendon didn't have them trapped in a corner, they did stand to the back of the room in a position between tables and chairs that would make it easy for him to keep them from leaving gracefully.

"Lady Pandora, I'm sorry I was delayed in bringing this to you," said Sir James, who finally arrived with her lemonade.

"Thank you, Sir James. As always, you are a true life saver. I was becoming quite parched." Pandora took the glass from him and swallowed a small, ladylike sip.

"Hendon," said Sir James mildly.

"Sir James," returned Hendon in the same tone.

"Your wife was looking for you not a moment ago," said Sir James.

"I'm not surprised," said Hendon with a scornful sneer. "She's probably ready to go home, poor mouse."

Sir James looked at him expectantly, and Hendon was at least sensible enough to take Sir James's unspoken hint that it would do him well to find his wife and that his company was no longer welcome.

"Lady Selena, a pleasure as always," he said as he took her hand to kiss her knuckles.

He then took Pandora's hand to do the same, and she had to fight the urge she had previously felt to snatch it back.

"Lady Pandora, it was an honor to meet you," he said with a leer.

"Thank you, Lord Hendon," she returned with an amiable smile.

Pandora watched him depart with a relieved sigh and felt at last that she could take a full breath. Looking around herself, she found a nearby chair and sank onto it gratefully. She began to fan herself again with agitation, a furrow of concern creasing her brow. If she never had to meet the earl again, she would be perfectly content.

He was able to comport himself reasonably well, and Pandora could see why Lady Ramsey and Lucy Cranston had gaggled after him. Had Pandora not been aware of his plotting, she might have just thought him to be another arrogant, self-important aristocrat. Knowing what she did, Pandora had been expecting him to do her bodily harm in some way throughout the entire conversation. She was curious about his wife and why he continued to call her a *mouse*. Pandora could only speculate it had been an arranged marriage, but why any self-respecting woman would willingly bind herself to Hendon in matrimony was beyond Pandora.

Her pretended empty-headedness had been a spontaneous attempt to find more information. Selena had presented a perfect opportunity; it seemed almost intentionally. Pandora didn't think her prattling had given him cause to become suspicious; it would most likely not even occur to him that a *woman* would have any inkling of his goings-on. Still, there had been a brief time during the conversation when he had been contemplating it, Pandora was sure.

She looked over to see that Selena had taken a seat as well. Sir James continued to stand nearby attentively, almost as if standing guard. Pandora smiled slightly. He seemed to be playing her knight in shining armor, and she was thankful he had returned when he did. She had been unable to think of a polite way to abandon the company of the earl, and doing it rudely would have caused undue attention.

"Lady Pandora, that was nicely done," said Selena.

"I could say the same to you," said Pandora with a weak smile. "That must have come from divine inspiration."

Selena's expression became guilty, and she took Pandora's hand.

"I must confess to you that this was none of my doing."

"Whatever do you mean?"

"My brother steered me in Hendon's direction and requested that I arrange for you to meet and to make sure I mentioned Scotland. He said you would be able to handle the rest."

Pandora gasped and felt her throat catch.

"Islington arranged this?" she asked dully.

"Yes, of course." She looked at Pandora's dismayed expression. "He didn't tell you?"

"No, he did not," said Pandora starkly.

Pandora wanted to find somewhere to think. She didn't blame Selena, but she felt the need to be out of company to collect her thoughts. She finished her lemonade and stood. Selena looked at her in surprise.

"If you'll forgive me, I think I'll go to the powder room to freshen up," she said neutrally.

"I'll come with you," offered Selena, hurriedly standing as well.

Pandora held up a hand.

"No, that's unnecessary, Lady Selena," she said with a smile. "You get back to your dancing." She turned to Sir James and smiled graciously. "Thank you, Sir James, for all your assistance."

He took her hand and kissed it gallantly.

"If ever you need me, just ask," he murmured with a kind smile.

Pandora left the supper room and went down the hall toward the powder room. She weaved her way through the people without much difficulty. Her thoughts were focused elsewhere, which was why when someone reached out of a side door and pulled her into a small, dark room, he had the sense to put a hand over Pandora's mouth to muffle her scream.

"Shh! Pandora, it's Islington," he said quietly.

Pandora forcefully removed his hand from her mouth and struggled out of his grasp. She nearly tripped over a piece of furniture of some type behind her in the dark once she had accomplished it and glared in his general direction.

"Would you *stop* scaring me like that?" she hissed.

"Was it him?" Islington asked without any pre-emption or apology.

"What?" she asked blankly.

"Was Hendon the Aristocrat?" he asked impatiently.

"He was," she answered dully, a knot forming in her stomach.

"Excellent. Now I know the identity of one of the conspirators."

"You used me," said Pandora mootly.

"It was necessary," he stated calmly. Pandora couldn't see his face, but she could imagine his lips pressing together in irritation.

"And you used your sister."

"I did *not* use Selena. She knew what I wanted her to do and why I wanted her to do it. It was, in fact, the reason behind her inviting you this evening. Having you meet Hendon was the simplest way for me to find out if he was one of the men that you heard."

Pandora shook her head in disbelief, her mouth forming into an angry smile, her eyes glittering.

"If you wanted me to meet him, you should have asked me directly. It wasn't necessary for you to trick me like that. At least then I wouldn't have been caught on my blind side by the whole affair. How could you even have the *audacity* to put me in harm's way like that? And Selena? You said yourself the man was dangerous, even before you knew for sure he was the Aristocrat, and yet you felt no compunction about doing what you did!" she said heatedly.

"Nothing would have happened!" he stated angrily. "I watched the whole time, aside from the fact this is a public gathering. It isn't as if he could have slit your throat!"

"No, I suppose not, but you *played* me. This whole evening, all your kindness toward me has simply been a ruse to lull me into doing what you wanted. It would have been less insulting if you had just asked. You know I want to catch these men as badly as you and that there is nothing I wouldn't do to see that happen, but you can't have it both ways."

"What do you mean?"

"Islington, either let me help, or leave me alone. I am *not* going to let you use me. I am *not* going to let you tell me this is something for a man to do and then have you use me as bait. I am *not* your dog!"

As she said these words, Pandora managed to find him in the dark and poke him forcefully in the chest with her finger with each statement. She was infuriated he had yet again managed to use her for his own ends. She was angry with him, and she was also angry with herself for having been foolish enough not to see it.

"The next time you decide you need my help, ask me," she finished simply, and with that she exited the room.

She was through talking to him. If the truth be told, he didn't want to hear anything further she had to say, and she was so incensed by the treatment he had given her that she would probably not be able to say another word. It would be more likely if she maimed him in some fashion.

As she went down the hall to the powder room where she had originally intended to go, she pulled her watch from her reticule. She still had about thirty minutes before it would be time to go. She sighed with relief. By the time she finished freshening up and collecting her thoughts, it would be time to leave.

There were still plenty of people milling around—if anything, more than before, but Pandora reached the room after being stopped a few times by acquaintances in the hall. The powder room was blessedly not well-occupied. When she first entered, there were five or six women, standing at the mirrors adjusting their hair and gowns, trying to remove wax that had dripped from the chandeliers and the stains from profusive sweating in the heat. Not long after she arrived, they departed, leaving Pandora alone with the woman she had seen speaking to Sir James.

She was young. Pandora thought she couldn't be above eighteen. Her hair was a golden blond that was done into a simple knot on top of her head with a few waves escaping at her neck and temples, but the color that should have been a shining, honeyed yellow was dull and lifeless. She moved gracefully, but her figure was very thin, as if she were underfed. Her gown sat loosely on her frame, as if it were made for someone else or for her at a time when she had more meat on her bones. Her face was heart-shaped, with a small chin and high cheekbones defining the points of the shape, but her cheeks were sunken and her features—which even still were beautiful—were drawn and pinched.

She sat at one of the mirrors, applying a dusting of white powder to her neck and hands, making her skin even paler. She didn't see Pandora watching her, and she took special care in applying the powder on her neck, attempting to conceal bruises that looked like handprints. One forearm was slightly larger than the other, and Pandora surmised the long sleeves of her gown were to conceal a bandage. Pandora compressed her lips in anger as she realized the girl had been badly beaten.

Pandora nonchalantly took the seat next to the young woman at the mirror and smiled amiably when she turned to look at Pandora in fright upon discovering she wasn't alone in the room. To Pandora's surprise, her expression changed to one of disdain. *That's uncalled for*, thought Pandora as she relocated a few wisps of hair that had managed to move from where Maiyin had placed them. She couldn't recall ever meeting the young woman, so her apparent dislike puzzled Pandora.

"He's not for you," the woman said flatly, surprising Pandora as she adjusted the puff of one of her sleeves.

"I beg your pardon?" asked Pandora confusedly.

"Lord Hendon is not for you."

Pandora chuckled in nervous relief, but she wondered why it mattered to the woman at all.

"Oh, I should say not," said Pandora with a friendly smile.

The young woman blinked in surprise at Pandora's demeanor and turned in her seat to face Pandora and look at her directly.

"You seemed taken with him; I thought I should warn you that he is not one to become enamored of," said the woman stonily, her gaze direct.

"*You* are Lady Morecambe?" asked Pandora in a stunned tone, the realization just dawning.

Pandora wasn't familiar with the marchioness. Her family was from the northern part of the country, while Pandora's was from Wales. Her father had never mentioned anything of the late marquis or his relatives, and because this was Pandora's first Season, she had never met the marchioness socially.

"Yes, I'm his wife, Georgiana Jeffries-Marsh," she said calmly.

"But you're so *young*!" said Pandora amazedly. "You poor thing!"

Pandora instinctively wanted to give her a sympathetic hug. Lady Morecambe was puzzled by Pandora's outpouring of empathy. Pandora felt an instant liking and camaraderie for the marchioness. Perhaps it was her mother's influence of being a champion for the victimized.

"Let me introduce myself. I am Lady Pandora Savage," said Pandora, reaching out her hand. The marchioness looked at it as if it were a snake. "Well, go on, take it; it's just a hand!" said Pandora with an encouraging smile. Lady Morecambe did not.

"I'm well aware of who you are, Lady Pandora," said the younger woman coldly. "You'd be wise to stay away from my husband."

Pandora turned her body in her chair to completely face the girl, her eyes round in dismay.

"I would never *dream* of becoming involved with Lord Hendon! You *cannot* mean you are jealous."

Pandora gingerly took Georgiana's hand to avoid hurting her arm where it was bandaged beneath the sleeve. Even still, the girl winced in pain, and she also tried to get Pandora to release it.

"I do not want to seem forward and presumptuous, but I can see well enough that he is very unkind to you." Georgiana started to shake her head in denial but simply sighed with relief at having someone offer her consolation. "I have absolutely no interest in your husband romantically and never would. Aside from him being married, I *know* he's not a very nice man." Pandora gave Georgiana's hand a gentle squeeze. "I think you're simply trying to warn me off to protect me, and I thank you for that. I only wish there was something I could do for you."

Georgiana waved her hand in the air dismissively.

"Oh, there's nothing you can do. It's not so bad, really. It's just occasionally I do things that make him angry."

Pandora compressed her lips firmly and shook her head.

"It is *never* fine for a man to hit you or mistreat you in any way, physically or otherwise. It doesn't matter what you've done. It's *never* something you have done that makes it happen. If a man is going to beat you, it's because he already had it in him to do it. *Do not* ever blame yourself. It's silly that in this day and age a man is still allowed to do that with impunity." Pandora squeezed her hand again. "Believe me when I say if there is ever *anything* you need of me, let me know."

The marchioness' expression grew pensive for a moment before she finally shook her head negatively.

"No, there is nothing for now. My husband is going to be out of pocket for what I hope will be several weeks, if I can manage to get through the fortnight to the end of the Season."

"He's going for grouse season, then?" asked Pandora conversationally.

"Heavens, no!" said Georgiana with a small chuckle of amusement. "He much prefers shooting deer, which are pretty hard to find—fortunately for them. He hasn't said anything about where he is going, and I would never ask him or suffer the consequences, but I think he may be going to the continent."

"That would be most excellent, to have that much distance between you," said Pandora with a comforting smile, still wondering what she might do to help her newfound friend.

"I don't know for certain that he's going, but he's been studying laboriously over a French grammar for several months. I almost hope he's going to seek a commission, but I don't see that as likely."

"A *French* grammar?" asked Pandora with wonder, her brow furrowing. "I should think he'd like to know German for the continent."

Georgiana shrugged. "I can only speculate on his itinerary. All Lord Hendon has said is that he expects me to find my own way home once the Season is over, and that I had better be there when he makes his own arrival." She shook her head. "I can only assume that he intends to travel *somewhere*, but where and for how long isn't something I would dare ask."

It was time for Pandora to meet her sisters. She regretted having to leave Georgiana so soon after becoming acquainted with her, but Pandora couldn't make her sisters (and to a lesser extent, Islington) wait for her. She recognized with disappointment that she couldn't help Georgiana unless it was requested. As a woman, Pandora wasn't sure there was much she *could* do; although, if she put a flea in the ear of the right gentleman, perhaps something could be done to ease the young woman's situation.

"I'm afraid I must go meet my sisters, but if you're able, please come to call or write to me as you will. My family will be leaving for home at the close of the Season, but if you address it to me at Wilderland Castle in Glamorgan, I'll be sure to get it."

She gave Georgiana's hand a final squeeze before rising from her seat. The marchioness stood as well.

"It was nice to make your acquaintance, Lady Pandora."

"Oh, please, just Pandora."

"Then, by all means, you may call me Georgiana," said the marchioness with a smile that brightened her whole countenance. With that smile, Pandora could see she must have been startlingly beautiful before her victimization by Hendon.

They left the room at the same time. Pandora made her way down the hall to the cloak room. The marchioness stood for a moment outside the door to the powder room, rubbing her forehead tiredly. She was preparing to make her way back to the dance room when her husband appeared beside her and took her injured arm in a vise-like grip. She bit her lip to keep from crying out in pain and looked at him with fearful, sparkling eyes.

"Hallo, little mouse," he said with a silky, dangerous smile. "Just what have we been up to, hmm?"

Chapter Eleven

Pandora reached the cloak room just as Arachne was exiting. She gave her older sister an amused grin as she came within arm's reach.

"I knew that was where you'd be found," chortled Pandora.

"Oh, pooh. I wasn't in there all night. I just went in to get our wraps."

So saying, she handed Pandora the rose silk shawl she had worn to match the burgundy silk gown Maiyin had finally mended. Arachne held Psyche and Selena's wraps in her hands and had already put on her own.

"I do recall seeing you dance with Drake earlier."

"For a cotillion, yes," said Arachne calmly. She looked at her sister with a twinkle. "As far as that goes, I think that was the *only* dance I saw you take all night. However did you arrange it?"

"I somehow managed to spend most of the evening either in the supper room or the powder room."

"And now who was hiding?" chuckled Arachne.

Pandora looked affronted.

"It wasn't as if I *intentionally* tried to avoid dancing...mostly." She smiled cheekily. "I did until I danced the cotillion, but everyone wanted to speak with me tonight, and I never made it back to the dance room."

"Hmm, a likely story," said Arachne with an arched eyebrow, nodding her head knowingly.

"It is the truth, I swear," said Pandora, holding up her hand in oath, her expression solemn.

Arachne put her hands on her hips. "Pandora, you know that will not work with me because you have fooled me with it before."

Pandora shrugged. "I don't know why I even bother telling the truth anymore. Nobody believes me when I do."

The two sisters chatted for a few minutes when Psyche joined them. Arachne handed her sister her sapphire blue velvet shawl, but Psyche didn't put it on. She was flushed, having just finished a galop. An equally-winded Selena arrived, waving a hand in front of her face to cool it. Pandora offered the girl her fan, which she accepted gratefully.

The four continued to talk as they waited for Islington. It was several minutes past midnight, and they had to move to a spot to the side of the door to let other attendees enter the cloak room and retrieve their belongings.

Pandora mentioned to Selena that she had made the acquaintance of the Marchioness of Morecambe, after which the girl explained that the marriage had been arranged by the late marquis shortly before he died. She also said the marchioness and her husband had been made the guardians of Georgiana's younger sister. Pandora hoped Hendon's mistreatment of his wife hadn't extended to her sister. It sickened Pandora's heart to know there was little she could do about it.

She did have one small victory in knowing Artois would be Hendon and Castleton's victim. Hendon's attitude during their conversation had made her fairly confident, but Pandora's discussion with his wife had clinched it. She had no doubt her reasoning was correct. She would still, however, have to find someone to send a letter to Artois to warn him.

Pandora began to grow impatient for Islington to join them so they could leave. She hadn't seen him dance once. Other than in the closet, she had not even seen him since their arrival. She could think of nothing that would account for his tardiness…unless he had decided to take a nap in the room where he had accosted her.

She was still indignant he had felt it necessary to trick her into meeting Hendon. Now Pandora had to wonder if his holding her hand on their ride to Almack's had been part of his plan to lull her into complacency. She didn't want to believe it was, but he had managed to gull her into believing he had feelings when he did not in the past. She still had not learned he was a consummate manipulator when it came to her emotions. She had hoped things that had happened between them might have changed that, but apparently they had not.

Psyche just offered to go in search of Islington when he finally could be seen striding toward them. He offered no apology for his tardiness, even though it was obvious he had made them wait for some time.

"Shall we go?" he asked tersely, holding out his arm for his sister.

He barely even acknowledged the presence of Pandora and her sisters, and Arachne gave her a puzzled look. Pandora shrugged her shoulders uncertainly and followed Islington and Selena through the hall down the stairs outside. They waited a few minutes for Jim to come with the coach. Islington conversed when asked a direct question, but he didn't offer to talk on his own. Pandora wanted to clod him with something. He was being typically arrogant, and Pandora disliked it. Of course, she wasn't surprised. He had gotten the information he wanted, so he saw no further need to retain his manners.

Once the door of the carriage was closed, Pandora removed her gloves and put them in her reticule. Psyche laughed when she saw it, but Pandora ignored her. She badly wanted to scratch her arms but decided to restrain herself. She hated wearing gloves, and she hadn't been able to discover in all the time she had been required to wear them, regardless of the material they were made of—either satin or leather, why they always made her itch. The only ones that didn't seem to bother her were crocheted. She sighed with relief once the sensation began to pass.

The same seating arrangement they had made on the trip to Almack's was kept on the way home. Again, for some reason, Pandora found herself in close proximity to Islington. It was then, once she was near him, that she could smell alcohol. He didn't seem to be drunk, but it was obvious by the smell that he had been drinking. It hadn't been served at Almack's, so he had probably left the building after their meeting in the dark room and gone to one of the clubs nearby.

She idly wondered to which of the clubs he would be a member. He wasn't overtly political, and he didn't seem to be one to gamble. Pandora couldn't really say, though. There really wasn't a lot that she knew about him. She had known him for several months and had only learned that evening that he was a trained physician and that he had a dead older sister. The only way she had to judge him was by his actions, and they were a puzzle to her, by turns endearing and infuriating. Of course, none of it altered that she loved him.

Pandora's brow furrowed in thought, and she gave Islington a sidelong glance. He didn't seem as relaxed as he had been on the way to Almack's, but that could have just as easily been part of the act to set her up for meeting Hendon. He could also be intoxicated and was making an attempt to hide it. Pandora wasn't trying to decipher his mood, and it suited her rather well that he was feeling reticent.

It was then that he once again reached over to hold her hand, the action hidden by the folds of her skirt. The contact of her hand in his without her glove felt much more intimate. As surprised as she had been before, she was even more so this time. She was even just a little angry he would presume to do it after the way he had treated her. She turned to look at him and saw he wasn't even looking at her—or anyone else for that matter. He was gazing out the window into the night, and the action seemed to be just as unconscious as before.

Pandora tightened her jaw angrily and used her thumbnail to bite into the side of his little finger sharply, just at the knuckle. It was a childish act of petulance, she knew, and she couldn't claim to be surprised when his fingers tightened harshly around her own in retaliation. She bit her lip to keep from yelping in pain and gave him a sidelong glance to find him still looking out the window. The crushing didn't last long, and his grip soon relaxed to the comfortable, yet possessive, pressure it had before. Pandora sighed resignedly and tolerated it. She would like it more if she understood *why* he was doing it.

Neither of them participated much in the conversation, but their sisters managed to keep up a running dialogue that did not miss their input. At one point, Pandora yawned and raised her free hand to cover it. She hadn't realized she was tired, but it had been an eventful evening.

Pandora couldn't say she once saw Islington take his gaze from the window. He would occasionally offer a laconic comment on something that was said, and at one point he changed the position of the way his hand held hers so their palms were together, but he seemed to be heavily preoccupied. At first, she didn't care what he was thinking or what was troubling him (if anything), but she was concerned despite herself. She was curious to know; if they had been alone, she might have asked.

They shortly arrived at Bardsey House. Before leaving the coach, Islington in turn kissed Psyche and Arachne's hands, and then he kissed Pandora's. Instead of brushing her knuckles as he had done her sisters, he kissed her palm and gently closed her hand over it. Pandora blinked in surprise. No one else had noticed what he did. She sat back against the cushions with a bemused expression. Selena gave all the sisters embraces and promised Pandora she would call at some point during the week. Pandora managed to smile and offer a reply that sounded logical.

The trip from the Marshall home was the shortest part of the journey. Pandora was grateful for that, because her thoughts were a muddle after Islington's parting kiss, and she didn't think she would have been able to provide intelligible conversation for any longer distance. Jim let them out at the front door and left to take the carriage to the mews.

"What time do you want to go riding tomorrow?" asked Psyche as they made their way up the stairs to their rooms.

"I don't know. Whatever time you wake up will suffice," answered Pandora dully, still in her own thoughts.

"Don't you think we should wait until the sun comes up?" asked Psyche blandly.

"What? Oh, sorry, woolgathering. I think 7:00, then."

"Are you feeling all right?" asked Psyche, her forehead wrinkling in concern.

"Yes, I'm fine. Just a little tired is all," grinned Pandora cheerily.

"Yes, that one dance you had to suffer through just wore you out, didn't it?" teased Arachne sarcastically.

"And just how many dances did *you* have?" asked Pandora cheekily over her shoulder as they reached the top of the stairs.

"More than one," said Arachne flatly. She kissed her sisters on the cheek and turned in the opposite direction to go to her room in the other wing. "Good night," she called.

"Good night," returned the twins.

Psyche followed Pandora into her room. Maiyin and Chrissoula had long since retired for the evening. It was unnecessary for their maids to wait for them. They weren't needed for anything; both girls had worn simple hairstyles, and they were capable of dressing themselves. After Psyche said good night to her twin, she went to her own bedroom.

Pandora went through her nightly ritual of changing into her sleeping shift and braiding her hair and flopped onto her bed on top of the covers, her face buried in her pillow. After a time, she rolled over, turned out the lamp on her night table, and snuggled under her covers. Within minutes, she was sound asleep.

Psyche came to Pandora's room a little after eight the next morning. Maiyin had already brought Pandora a pot of tea and some toast, which she had devoured hungrily before dressing for her ride. She would eat a full breakfast with her family once they returned in about an hour.

"Ooh, I like that color of green on you," said Psyche as she came in.

Pandora looked down at herself and shrugged negligibly. Her habit was made from an emerald green velvet (like most of her clothing) that draped well and was lightweight. Pandora would have preferred to wear the burgundy, but (as was often the case) Maiyin needed to attach two of the buttons on her redingote. Pandora grabbed her hat and gloves from the foot of her bed and left with Psyche for the stables.

When they got there, Tajik had their horses saddled and waiting. Pandora was sure Psyche had already made one trip to the stables to let the man know when they would be leaving. She had a tendency to rise with the sun that Pandora had never been able to appreciate. She was still a little tired this morning, even though she had at least six hours of sleep. Knowing what time Psyche usually rose, she had far less sleep than Pandora and yet seemed to bound with energy.

After Pandora retrieved a pocketful of sugar lumps, the girls mounted their horses and left the mews at a sedate walk. They took their usual route, going down Mount Street to Park Lane, crossing through Audley and Park Streets, which were both blessedly absent of traffic at that time of the morning. Once they were to the park, the girls gave their horses free rein and soon accelerated to a full gallop when they reached the riding path. It was nice to run their horses on the track without other riders getting in the way. Most people who came to the park only intended to be seen and weren't actually interested in letting their horses run...which was why Psyche and Pandora came so early.

Once they reached the Serpentine, they slowed their horses and let them walk and cool down as they made the turn that would take them past the Keeper's Lodge on their circular route back to the gate. Bellerophon shook his head and skittered sideways down the track, impatient to run again. Pandora reached down to pat his neck soothingly, but he wasn't pleased to be ambling. It was as if he were attempting to make up for the time she had not been able to ride him.

"Do you feel up to a race?" she asked Psyche.

"Do you?" asked her sister with a grin.

"I may not, but Bellerophon does. What say, the first to the corner at the turnpike?"

"Are we wagering anything?"

"No, just racing."

Psyche looked around herself for a likely starting point.

"From that tree there?" she asked, pointing to a walnut tree just to the side of the path several yards ahead.

"Perfect," said Pandora with a grin.

Bellerophon pulled at the reins as if he understood the conversation, but she held him steady. Pandora had no doubt he was going to win, but she wanted to give Psyche and Achilles every opportunity. They came even with the tree, and Pandora loosened her hold on Bellerophon and gave him a slight nudge with her heels. He bounded forward powerfully, and Pandora laughed as he sped along the trail. She looked to her left and saw Psyche steadily moving up behind her but still at least a length back. They crossed the intersection with the foot path to Kensington Gardens, and Psyche was able to push Achilles to come up even with Pandora and Bellerophon. Pandora leaned forward slightly in her saddle and whispered in his ear.

"I've got some sugar for you if you win."

At the word sugar, he incredibly managed to go faster than before, and any hope Psyche had of winning the race disappeared. Pandora whooped with exhilaration as they came to the corner, and she once again slowed Bellerophon to a walk. This time, he didn't chomp at the bit and seemed to be well-satisfied with his run. She patted his neck and waited for her sister to come up even with them.

"What did you say to him?" Psyche asked as she reached them.

"I just told him that I would give him some extra lumps if he won."

"I have never seen an animal with a sweet tooth like his," Psyche chortled. "He'd be quite rotund if he didn't run so often."

"I suppose," said Pandora with an affectionate grin for Bellerophon, ruffling her fingers through his mane.

"You want to go around one more time?" asked Psyche.

Pandora thought about it for a moment before she nodded. It was heavenly to be out of the house and riding again. She was looking forward even more to being home to ride through the fields at Wilderland. Hyde Park was pleasant enough, but the views from the hills at home were spectacular. Even better, she didn't have to worry about flibbertigibbets getting in the way at any time of the day.

They rode around the track at a leisurely pace, sometimes at a slow trot, but both were satisfied to go slowly, allowing them to have a conversation.

Once they reached the Serpentine, they dismounted. Psyche made sure to tether Achilles to a branch, but Pandora didn't worry about Bellerophon. He wouldn't wander like Achilles. Both animals began to graze as the twins walked to the edge to sit down, looking at the ducks skimming over the water in search of their morning's meal.

"You know Mamà is going to have another ball before the end of the Season," said Psyche conversationally.

"No! When?" asked Pandora with some alarm.

"I think the last Tuesday before the end of the Season, which would make it the tenth," said Psyche, after she did some mental calculations.

"Has she already sent out invitations?" asked Pandora, wondering if she might be able to convince her mother not to do it.

"She sent them out day before yesterday." Psyche saw Pandora's concerned expression. "Why don't you want a ball at the house? I don't like the Season any more than you, but it could be worse; she could make us sing again."

"Thank God for small favors," chuckled Pandora. "As for why I don't want a ball, I guess it is having all those people we don't know in our house. You cannot trust people nearly so much these days."

"You wouldn't be referring to Lord Islington, would you?" asked Psyche with a teasing grin.

"No, actually, I wasn't—for a change," she grinned back. "It's only that Papà and Mamà have to invite so many people just because they're in the same social set. How much do we really know about them?"

"Pandora, are you suffering from paranoia? You know Mamà and Papà would never invite someone criminal into their home."

"I don't think they would *intentionally* invite one into their home."

"Do you have someone particular in mind?" asked Psyche curiously.

"Yes, actually, I was thinking of the Earl of Hendon."

"Oh, that," said Psyche dismissively with a wave of her hand. "Mamà and Papà didn't invite him specifically, but they did invite his wife. Judging by the way she's all bunged up lately, I don't think she's in a position to have told him that he couldn't come as well."

"You noticed that, too?"

"It was hard not to notice at Almack's last night."

"It's unfortunate and abominable that he can get away with it. To think something like that can happen makes me happy *I* am not married." Psyche nodded her head in agreement.

They sat for a while longer watching the ducks, and the sun started to rise higher in the sky.

"I suppose we should leave now," said Pandora regretfully. "It won't be long before the *ton* decides to poke their noses out the door and see who else is doing the same. I'm also rather famished."

"Too right," said Psyche heartily.

The sisters stood up to go, dusting off their skirts. When they turned to retrieve their horses, Bellerophon was just where Pandora had left him, munching on the grass at the base of a tree, untethered; Achilles was nowhere to be found.

"Bollocks!" cried Psyche in disbelief.

"I concur."

They looked for any sign of the white gelding. He was completely gone from view.

"Where could he have gotten off to?" asked Psyche, turning in a circle in search of him. "I tied him up. I know I did."

"I know; I saw you do it. We better find him soon. We don't want him to manage his way into Kensington Gardens. If he grazes his way through the landscape, there'll be hell to pay."

Psyche looked at her sister with her eyes wide in alarm at the thought of her horse grazing on the vegetation in the public garden. Some of the plants were rare specimens, not to mention that some were also highly poisonous.

Pandora walked over to Bellerophon and grabbed his reins to secure them up from the ground in a metal ring on the saddle. She clicked at him to get his attention, and he raised his head from the grass to look at her calmly. She brushed the end of his nose with her knuckles and gave him a sugar lump.

"Go find the horse, Bell," she said resignedly.

After blowing at her, Bellerophon turned and went in the direction of the Keeper's Lodge and the foot path at a slight trot. Pandora came up to Psyche and watched him go, her hands on her hips as she saw him go in the direction she had hoped he wouldn't take; it wasn't a good sign.

"I guess we better head that way as well," said Pandora, walking back to the riding path with Psyche. "Hopefully, he did not actually make it into the Gardens."

"You know, your horse isn't a horse at all," said Psyche casually as they walked.

"Yes, he is!" said Pandora, affronted.

"He's a puppy dog," said Psyche succinctly. She shrugged. "Mind you, he's an *enormous* one, but horses don't fetch."

"He doesn't fetch everything," said Pandora, "just other horses...and people...other animals...," Pandora finished lamely.

"And another thing: I've had Achilles as long as you've had Bellerophon, and I can *never* get him to come when I whistle. I bet if you told Bellerophon to roll over, he would do it."

"I've not been able to get him to do that yet," said Pandora with a chuckle. "But I bet all I would need is more sugar."

They were almost to the footpath when they saw Bellerophon coming toward them up the path from the Gardens, Achilles' reins in his teeth. The white gelding was coming along reluctantly, but Bellerophon would shake his head and pull at the reins, causing the bit attached to them to pull at Achilles' mouth until he continued on.

"See, I told you—puppy dog," said Psyche with a giggle.

The two horses trotted up to them, and Psyche took the reins from Bellerophon and proceeded to scold Achilles, who just looked at her indifferently. Pandora walked over to her horse and gave him another sugar lump and a kiss on his nose.

"Good boy!" she crooned, scratching his forehead. "You're my good boy!"

After Psyche checked Achilles to make sure he had not managed to injure himself somehow during his brief escapade, the two girls mounted and headed for the front of the park. They reached the gate to leave and turned onto Park Lane. There were still not any people about yet, and Pandora didn't expect to see anyone out for still another hour or more. She didn't plan to call on anyone that day, and she wasn't expecting anyone to come visit her. Selena was the only one who called regularly, but to Pandora's knowledge, she wasn't coming today. She thought she might go shopping after she had breakfast.

That would be the one thing she would miss about not being in town— the ability to just walk around the corner to shop for books and scientific instruments. She also bought clothes and shoes and whatnot, but she wasn't nearly so much of a clothes-horse as her brother, Myron. She liked her frillies, but those could be ordered from the dressmaker near home, and her quality was better than that provided in London. For Pandora, the thing she appreciated being able to purchase was books.

There was a particular book she wanted to buy for Damon for his birthday, and she had yet to find it. There was a pair of earrings she wanted to buy for Eurydice for her birthday, which was also fast approaching. Pandora thought she should purchase everyone's Christmas presents while she was in town as well. The stores near home, while items could be ordered, did not have as large a selection as what was available in Town. The closest place to where she lived that offered a respectable selection was Cardiff, and even that was almost a day's ride away and required her to stay overnight.

They soon turned onto Mount Street and crossed over Park. When they reached South Audley, Pandora glanced south toward the comte d'Artois's town residence. A figure was standing across from it on the walk, lounging casually against the stone wall surrounding the front yard of the house there. The distance was too far for her to be certain, but unless Pandora was going terribly blind, it looked like Lord Hendon!

Pandora almost jerked on her reins to turn and see if it was him for sure, but she restrained herself. She didn't want to meet him face-to-face again, and she didn't think Psyche would be willing to go. She couldn't be sure it was him, but the man was dark-haired and trim. While his clothes were inconspicuous, they looked like something Pandora would expect Lord Hendon to wear. Aside from that, it would be too much of a coincidence for someone else to be watching the count's residence.

Her brow furrowed with thought as she and Psyche continued on their way home. Why would Hendon be watching the house? He knew the count wouldn't be in town until the beginning of next month. There wasn't anyone there right now, not even servants, especially since his return to the city—if what Castleton and Hendon had said were correct—was to be clandestine. It was true he was royalty, and if the French were anything like the British (and Pandora suspected it was probably worse) even a covert journey would not be without preparation of some sort for his arrival.

Pandora wondered if she should let her brother or Islington know she had seen Hendon standing there. It would probably not matter to them. Dorian didn't even believe the count was the intended victim. She wasn't sure if he had told Islington of her suspicions. He said he would, but he didn't sound sincere. In the end, there was no point in making a special effort of telling anyone, but she would keep it in mind. If it should prove helpful later, then she would tell.

Pandora did go shopping, but not until the following afternoon. She had still not found the book for Damon. She went, first thing, to Patenaude's and bought Eurydice's earrings, a lovely set of small amber drops set in silver. Eurydice would like them, as she wasn't fond of overdone jewelry. While at the store, Pandora also found a nice emerald pendant for Psyche for her birthday in October. It was tricky buying that, as her twin was with her at the time. She had needed to wait until Psyche's attention was elsewhere and have the clerk quickly wrap it up for her. Pandora thought it would beautifully match Psyche's contested earrings. She found a nice cashmere shawl for Arachne at one store, and a pair of leather riding boots (men's) for Persephone at another. The man in the shop thought it odd when Pandora held the boot up to her own foot to compare the size, but he didn't ask.

"Are you about done in?" asked Psyche as they left the store.

"I am," replied Pandora with a tired sigh. "Actually, I think I'm more hungry than tired."

"Too right," agreed Psyche. "Shall we go home then?"

"I still need to find that book for Damon."

"What is it again that you're needing?"

"*Conversations on Cymistry*," said Pandora dully.

"Are you sure he'll want to read that?" asked Psyche doubtfully.

Pandora laughed. "It could certainly be no worse than you giving him *The Odyssey*." She saw her twin's affronted look. "It's just that he is always interested in my experiments. I thought this would give him a chance to learn to do experiments of his own."

"Have you looked here?" asked Psyche as they walked past a storefront.

Pandora looked up at the front of the building, which appeared to be a bookseller's, among other things. Through the window, she could see shelves full of books, but there were also pieces of furniture and other items. She looked at the name.

"Beacham and Bagley?" she said skeptically. "No, I don't believe I've been in here, but I've tried just about everywhere else. It couldn't hurt."

The sisters went in, and both inhaled deeply the odor of parchment, dust, and old things. They thought they had died and gone to heaven, for they were sure paradise had to be such a place. After they found somewhere to leave their packages, they wandered among the stacks, weaving their way through furniture and cases containing small items such as jewelry, coins, and firearms. The store at least had a sorting system for their books, much like a library, but Pandora wasn't able to determine where in their system that she would be able to find the book she wanted. She didn't have long to wait before a clerk appeared.

"How do you do, miss? I'm Mr. Trotter. May I be of assistance?" he said deferentially.

"Oh, I do hope so. I'm looking for a book called *Conversations on Cymistry*. Do you know if you have that one?"

"I'm not sure, miss. Do you have any other information on it?"

"I believe it was printed seven or eight years ago. The author was a Mrs. Marcet?"

The salesman's expression grew thoughtful behind his spectacles, and he put a finger to his lips. His brow would wrinkle and relax as he thought, and he would occasionally lift his finger as a new idea came, only to shake his head slightly and place it back again. After a time, his expression brightened, and he raised his finger in the air in victory.

"Aha! This way, if you please, miss," he said, sweeping his hand in the direction of the back of the store.

He led Pandora to a small, dark corner and paused.

"If we have it, it will be in this area. I don't guarantee it is here, but this is the most likely location, and the name does seem familiar."

"Thank you."

Pandora looked at the spines of the volumes in front of her. Several were books she already owned or were in her family's libraries. There were books on mathematics, chemistry, botany, and mechanics…her favorite subjects. There were also books on medicine, anatomy, biology, astronomy, and other fields of science. She believed the clerk had sent her to the right location, but with every shelf her hopes began to dwindle.

While looking for Damon's book, she found a nice edition of John Pringle's *Observations on Diseases of the Army in Camp and Garrison,* and she instantly thought of Islington. She pulled the book from the shelf to look through it and just as quickly closed it. She didn't want to know. Medicine wasn't an area of science she found interesting. The sight of blood other than her own made her nauseous. She did, however, decide to buy the book. She didn't know why she should, but she impulsively held onto it.

Pandora was almost ready to give up hope of finding the chemistry book when she reached the bottom shelf. She grinned victoriously as she lifted the small book and flipped through its pages. She felt sure Damon would like it. There were several pictures of experiments and equipment related to chemistry that she easily recognized. The book was written by a woman, and the characters within it were also female, but Mrs. Marcet had written it in a manner that would make it easy for Damon to understand at his age. Pandora couldn't believe her luck at finally finding it.

In addition to the books for Damon and Islington, Pandora found a copy of Linnaeus's *Systema Naturae* for her mother. It was the enormous thirteenth edition in three volumes. Her grace had a copy, but it was a smaller, earlier edition. Pandora found another calculus book for herself. She hefted the pile of books in her arms and went to look for the clerk.

Unsurprisingly, he was standing on the other side of the stacks, giving her privacy to look but also being near at hand when she was ready to make her purchase. Thankfully, he offered to take the books from her. Pandora would still have to carry them home, but if she could get Psyche to carry the rest of her packages, she would manage. When she got to the sales desk, her plans for seeking her sister's aid were dashed.

"I see you were able to find something of interest as well," said Pandora with a laugh as she looked at the pile of books her sister had. It was the same size, if not bigger, than her own. "I suppose we'll have to take a hack home because I *cannot* carry these all the way on foot, even if it is just two blocks or so away."

"We can have these delivered, if you'd like," said Mr. Trotter helpfully.

"Could you? That would be lovely," said Pandora with a grateful smile. "If you can have them taken to Aberdare House at 11 Bruton Street, I would sincerely appreciate it."

"That *is* just around the corner, isn't it?" enquired Mr. Trotter pleasantly.

"Yes, not so very far, but we've been shopping all day, and I still have these packages to manage as well," said Pandora, pointing to the items she had placed on a nearby chaise.

"I understand, miss," said Mr. Trotter with a smile.

"If you could wrap them in paper for me; some of them are gifts, and I would rather not have their intended recipients know I have them."

"Yes, miss," said Mr. Trotter.

He pulled a large sheet of brown paper from under the counter and wrapped the books into a bundle tied with twine. He then looked at Psyche.

"Shall I do the same for yours, miss?"

"Yes, please," said Psyche with a smile.

Before he wrapped hers, he took up a quill and looked at Pandora.

"Very well, the address is 11 Bruton Street, you said?" Pandora nodded. "And who shall I put as the recipient?"

"Lady Pandora Savage," she said casually.

Mr. Trotter's eyes grew wide in alarm.

"Oh, please forgive me, Lady Pandora. I did not realize—"

Pandora held up a hand to stop the profusive apology and giggled.

"There is nothing to forgive, Mr. Trotter. It wasn't as if I had a footman to announce me when I walked in the door, and I found your service to be impeccable."

"Thank you, my lady," said Mr. Trotter, blushing.

"Now, what is the total for my books?" she smiled.

"Um, ten pounds should do it, if you please."

Pandora dropped her jaw in surprise. Ten pounds? That was a fairly large amount just for books...or anything else for that matter. Still, they were great books. She reached into her reticule and retrieved a note for him from her quickly-shrinking allowance. She also grabbed two one pound notes and handed him the lot.

Mr. Trotter looked at her in confusion.

"Lady Pandora, I'm afraid you've overpaid."

"No, Mr. Trotter. The tenner is for the books, obviously, but the two pounds over is for you and your kind assistance. I have been looking for one of those books for months now and had just about given up hope of ever finding a copy. Then there is the matter of the books being delivered. As I said, I am most appreciative," she said with a charming smile.

"Thank you, Lady Pandora," said Mr. Trotter, bobbing his head.

He then wrapped Psyche's books and wrote her name and address on. They both bid Mr. Trotter good day and retrieved their packages from where they had placed them, and then they left the shop. They were finished shopping. Any interest Pandora may have had disappeared as her stomach rumbled disagreeably. She looked up at the sky and saw it was well past mid-day. It was no wonder she felt so hungry. She'd not had anything to eat since breakfast.

Surprisingly, she wasn't attending a ball or dinner party that evening. She planned to stay home and work on her calculus equation she had been fiddling with for the past few weeks. She felt sure she almost had it resolved, but she desperately wanted some uninterrupted time to devote to it. Once her new book arrived, she thought she might be able to find some assistance there.

They made it home without finding any further temptation in the store windows...almost. There was an apothecary not far from the bookseller's, and Pandora went in quickly to purchase a few chemicals she would need once she returned home. Not far beyond that was a confectioner's where Psyche went in to buy some lemon drops for their younger brothers and a small box of chocolate-cherry bon-bons for Arachne. After that, they were truly finished, and they were happy to have Tannaz open the door for them when they reached the house.

For the next three days, Pandora and Psyche didn't get to ride early because it was pouring rain for most of the daylight hours every day. Pandora sat at her bedroom window much of the time, glumly watching the drops spit against the panes. She had her new calculus book to occupy her for a time, but even that eventually lost her interest. Now that she was able to ride Bellerophon, she wanted to ride him every day.

The first day, Pandora had hoped the rain wouldn't continue, but it would only just stop at a time when it would be too late to go riding, as the park would be full of members of the *ton* intent on seeing and being seen. That meant there would be no riding as fast as they liked...unless they wanted to risk running over several pedestrians and nabobs in carriages. Pandora would just as soon not ride at all. There would be no ride that day...or the next...or the next.

She spared a thought to Lord Hendon and if he was standing outside the comte d'Artois's house again. She felt sure it had been him, even though he hadn't been close enough for her to be certain. He was the only one who made sense.

After she was able to think about it a little more over the days that followed the sighting, she realized he was waiting for the first stirrings of activity that would prove the count was indeed traveling down from Edinburgh. He had told Castleton that Artois would be leaving the first of September, but anyone's plans could change. Perhaps Hendon wanted to be sure he was going to keep that schedule or if he was going to change it and come earlier or later. If they were waiting to abduct him until after he started back, they would have to make sure of when he was arriving. Then it would be a minor issue to find out when he left.

Pandora didn't believe Hendon had been standing outside the house during those soggy days. The rain that prevented her and Psyche from riding would also not be pleasant for him to stand in for even a short time. And while the house of the Frenchman wasn't occupied, the other houses on the street were. He was intelligent enough to realize someone would notice if he stood there every day, no matter how inconspicuously he might dress, especially in the rain. He wouldn't go by to check at a later time in the day because there would be more risk of being seen by people who were awake.

Something Pandora wondered about his spying was what he did *after* he left. Did he go home and act like nothing was out of the ordinary, or did he meet someone and impart the information he had gathered? She believed Castleton might be the senior of the two conspirators, and she was almost willing to bet Hendon would go to meet him. Where they would meet was the question. At the tavern he had mentioned called the Dog? Pandora had no idea where it was located. She didn't even know if Islington and Dorian knew where it was.

Pandora and Psyche were pleased to no end when they were finally able to go riding again. They didn't enjoy being stuck in the house all day, and three days in a row had been almost unbearable. They had gone to a dinner party at Lord Lundey's the previous evening with impromptu dancing that followed, but attending social functions was never overly enjoyable for them. They were leaving a little later than they usually did, but it was still early enough they wouldn't have to worry about other people in the park.

When they left the house for their ride, Pandora convinced her sister to take a different route, taking them across Berkeley Square to Hill Street and then up to South Street, which would have them cross South Audley within easy sight of the comte d'Artois's, almost at the corner of the intersection. Pandora looked at the point where she had seen the earl five days previously, but he wasn't there. He may not have had time to arrive yet; he was after all, even if a criminal, a member of an echelon of society that didn't tend to rise nearly so early as her own family.

On their return home, Pandora convinced Psyche to take the same route (with some grumbling from her sister). When they reached the intersection, she looked down Audley and felt some excitement at seeing Hendon standing where she had seen him before. It confirmed her suspicion he was watching the house. The only question that remained was what he did after he left. She wasn't sure what she would do to discover that, but she was beginning to think he would have to be followed.

Chapter Twelve

Pandora was in her room reading her new calculus book when Tannaz informed her that Selena was there. She marked her page and left the book in her chair then happily bounced down the front stairs to go to the drawing room where Selena waited. She was looking forward to visiting with her friend.

Pandora thought she should, as a teasing gesture, let Dorian know Selena was there. He would give her a look of indifference, as if her friend's arrival was irrelevant, but at some point, he would find an excuse to come to the drawing room. Pandora had tested it before and knew it would work.

Pandora's demeanor was somewhat nervous because she was going to do something tomorrow that she really shouldn't: she was going to follow Hendon. She had gone over the idea for some time over the past few days after realizing what he was doing. To follow him herself wasn't the first thing that occurred to her. She had thought to let her brother know, or Islington, but she had a twinge of rebellion over Islington's treatment of her on the matter that finally urged her to do it on her own.

Hendon and Castleton were dangerous men, but this would be a safe activity because she wouldn't actually be coming into direct contact with either of them. All she wanted to do was find out where Hendon went after his spying and hopefully get a physical description of Castleton. It would only provide further help for her brother and Islington. The justifications she had created for doing it seemed perfectly logical.

The only snag she had found to pursuing her plan was how she would get out of the house without someone going with her. Although she often thumbed her nose at society, for her to be out unescorted could cause scandal for her mother and father...unless she was going to call on someone. Neither her twin nor anyone else in her family would agree to go with her...except possibly Persephone (had she believed there was an actual conspiracy afoot), so Pandora would *have* to do it alone.

That was why she was glad Selena had come to visit her. Pandora was going to "visit" Selena tomorrow, but she didn't want her friend to come over and ruin the whole deception. Pandora wasn't happy she would have to use her friend, but Selena would have no guilt in the matter. If Pandora were caught (which she didn't intend to have happen), Selena wouldn't be in trouble because she wouldn't even know about it.

"Hallo, Selena," she smiled as she walked into the room.

Selena was sitting on the settee while she waited but rose with a grin at Pandora's ebullient arrival.

"You're very cheery today. Did you have good news about something?" asked Selena hopefully.

"No, no good news. I'm just glad the rain has ended. Staying in the house all day is *so* boring, and three days of it almost made me go mad."

She sat on the settee and invited Selena to retake her seat.

"Shall I send for tea?" asked Pandora graciously.

"Oh, no, thank you," said Selena, shaking her head. "How is everyone?"

"Dorian is fine," said Pandora with a cheeky grin. Selena blushed. "You two should take a drive in the park or something."

"Pandora!" said Selena exasperatedly.

"It's true!" giggled Pandora. "Why have you not become engaged yet?"

"Oh, it's not that easy," said Selena. Her brow furrowed unhappily.

"Why is it not easy? It's so obvious to everyone, except perhaps your brother, that you two are besotted with one another."

"I think if he knew, it would make the matter even more complicated," said Selena with a look of discouragement.

"And why would that be? You cannot mean he would object to my brother!" said Pandora in an outraged tone.

"Oh, no!" said Selena, her eyes round with alarm. "He would *never!*"

"Then what is there to be of concern?" asked Pandora, her brow furrowed in puzzlement. "You do care for each other, do you not?"

"Well, I do care for him," said Selena softly with misty eyes.

"And I can say beyond doubt that—whether he has said so to you—my brother cares for you as well."

"But there is you and Teddy."

Pandora blinked and tilted her head sideways, her brow furrowed in complete confusion.

"What about *me* and *Teddy?"* asked Pandora calmly.

"Well, isn't there...? What I mean to say is, aren't you...?" Selena trailed off weakly at Pandora's look of shock. She was all the more dismayed when Pandora burst into laughter. "Pandora, are you well?"

Pandora, after some struggle, managed to control her amusement and wiped at the tears of laughter caused by Selena's words.

"Oh, Selena!" said Pandora, taking her friend's hands. "What have you confused and worried yourself over?"

"But…what…why?" stuttered Selena disconcertedly.

"Selena, there are several things about this that I find utterly ridiculous, but there are only two about which you need to be concerned."

"And what would they be?" asked Selena bemusedly. "Please, tell me, for I'm afraid I don't see the humor in this at all."

"The first is that—and I can't believe you didn't know this—there is nothing to stop you from being married to Dorian, even if I were married to your brother and had an entire *dozen* of children."

"There isn't?" asked Selena hopefully.

"Not one thing. I know the affinity tables are confusing, and I can honestly tell you my mother and father made it even worse when I asked them a long time ago, but there is *nothing* irreligious about your feelings. I can think of four couples back home that are siblings all around."

"Wonderful!" sighed Selena, clasping her hands together in relief. She looked at Pandora. "And what is the second thing?"

"The second thing would be that I am *not* married to your brother, so it makes the first concern entirely immaterial."

"But aren't you going to be? Haven't you come to an understanding?"

"No, we most certainly have not," said Pandora flatly.

"Oh, dear," said Selena, raising a hand to her lips in dismay. "But I thought he…."

Pandora took both of Selena's hands and shook her head negatively.

"Selena, my acquaintance with your brother isn't that way. We have not come to an understanding. It's my impression and my feeling there will not be one…ever."

"But Dorian and I thought that…." Pandora started shaking her head again in the middle of Selena's statement.

"Does my brother think the same thing you do? That you cannot marry because of me and Islington having an *understanding*?" Selena nodded. "Then I'll be sure to go upstairs and box his ears the minute you leave," said Pandora with a grin. She finally managed to get a laugh from Selena. "He should know better. I thought he *did* know better." Pandora shrugged and sighed gustily. "I, however, cannot figure where the two of you would have come to the conclusion something like that was happening between your brother and me."

Selena's brow furrowed contemplatively for a moment, and then she decided to confess something to Pandora.

"Do you remember the day we met at Ramsey's?" Pandora nodded. "While you had been there to discover Lord Hendon's identity, my brother had sent me to find out if there were any gossip concerning him in connection with any women but particularly *you*."

"And was there?" asked Pandora with mild curiosity, although she knew full well there wasn't; her mother and sisters would have made her aware of it long ago if there had been.

"Not really, no. There wasn't any mention of impropriety or disreputable activity, only that he had an odd tendency to lose his cravat in your presence." Pandora chortled. "But there has always been a perfectly justifiable and respectable reason for it happening."

"But that doesn't explain why you think what you do."

"Well, my brother is a fine catch, if I do say so myself—"Pandora hid an amused grin—"but he's never been concerned about what the tabbies might be saying about him and a girl. I thought his interest must mean he has feelings for you."

"He may have feelings for me, but I wouldn't say they are of the tender persuasion," said Pandora mildly with a smile that must surely seem brittle.

"Oh, but I'm sure he does," averred Selena solemnly. "I can tell because he won't let me tease him about you."

"You tease your brother about me?" quizzed Pandora with a skeptically arched eyebrow.

"Well, no, I can't because he gets very irritated. In the past, with other girls, I could tease him incessantly, and he would just blow it off. I've never seen him behave the way he does about you, not even with Jessica Wainwright, that evil shrew." Selena's eyes hardened with anger.

Pandora felt she was familiar enough with Selena now she could ask the question and not seem too forward.

"Selena, how much of what Lady Ramsey said that day was true?"

Selena waved a hand through the air dismissively.

"Oh, not even half of it." She saw Pandora's concerned expression. "Well, they got the part about her being awful and after my brother for his inheritance dead-on, but they got the part about my da writing him out of his will *completely* wrong."

"I suspected as much," said Pandora with relief.

"Well, they got it wrong because my *brother* told my *da* he didn't want to inherit, not the other way 'round."

"What?" asked Pandora in surprise.

"Teddy suspected Jessica was after him for money. He didn't want to believe it because she was beautiful and excellent at pretending to be the perfect girl, at least to him. She behaved like a *nightmare* to everyone else. My da never would actually remove him from the will; Teddy just had the *rumor* spread that it had been done. He thought if she would still go through with the marriage when she thought he had nothing, it would prove she really loved him. Obviously, she didn't. He wasn't happy about it, but he wasn't so traumatized as those two biddies made it out to seem."

"Did she really leave him standing at the altar?"

Selena laughed. "No. They called the banns twice, and then she left in the middle of the night to parts unknown. She probably did go to the continent, but I've no idea what she did once she got there, and—quite frankly—I could care less."

"And what about his title?"

Selena giggled. "Oh, that. Pish! He goes by Islington because that's what he went by before my da died. Most everyone knows him that way, and to him, our father was the Marquess of Bardsey. The viscountcy has always been a lesser title my father held; it had nothing to do with my mama's family. It isn't that he didn't like our da that makes Teddy not use the title; it is that he *loved* him."

Pandora smiled thoughtfully after Selena gave her the truth. She had suspected Lady Ramsey and Lucy Cranston were wrong, but it had been something she hadn't felt she could ask Selena and would not ask Islington.

"Teddy was upset she jilted him, obviously, and it did cause him some anguish, but his reaction wasn't to the extent they made it out. He is rather mistrustful of women, as I said that day as well, but you can't blame him."

"No, I suppose not," said Pandora mildly. It would explain why he found it so easy to believe the worst of her.

"But he *must* have feelings for you," said Selena, giving Pandora's arm a comforting squeeze.

"Maybe, or perhaps he doesn't like you teasing him because he dislikes me so much."

Selena scoffed amusedly. "I seriously doubt that." She grinned. "You just wait and see. My brother will make you an offer."

Pandora went for her ride with Psyche the next morning. When they crossed Audley on their way home an hour later, she again saw Lord Hendon standing there. Today would be the day. She would follow him, and she was going to find out where he went.

As soon as they reached the house, she went to her room to change into a walking dress of pale blue muslin that would be indistinguishable from the dress any other woman might wear. She grabbed a lightweight shawl and the horrendous poke bonnet with the long brim she had so far managed to avoid wearing. Her intention was to blend into the rest of the people who might be out and about. The dress was nondescript, and the hat would hide her face. She took one of her work aprons and a dark blue reticule into which she placed a few pound notes and coins and her watch.

If there was no one else around, she would hide if necessary, but she somehow didn't think it would be. The hour was approaching when other people would be going out to call or shop; some had already started to come out when she and Psyche were returning home. Pandora would have to catch him before he left his spot or lose him in the crowd, and once more people started milling about, he wouldn't stay on South Audley because it would obviously be suspicious.

She hoped he wouldn't take a hackney but would walk wherever it was that he would go. It would be too difficult—if not impossible—for her to follow him if that happened. She would follow him as far as she could. If he did get a hack, then that would be the end of it. Pandora somehow didn't think he would.

She had taken her tea and toast, as she usually did, before going to ride in the park with Psyche, but she wouldn't be able to have breakfast with her family. Hendon would soon be leaving, and Pandora didn't want to miss him. It was late enough her going to visit someone wouldn't seem out of the ordinary, especially if it was to visit Selena.

After giving herself the once-over in the mirror, she went to Psyche's room to let her know she would be going. Her sister was still in the middle of picking out a dress to wear and was strolling around her room in her chemise. She turned to look at Pandora from examining two morning gowns, one in lilac, the other white.

"You're going out?" asked Psyche in mild surprise.

"Yes, I'm going to visit Selena. She wants to go to Kensington Gardens," said Pandora casually. "I like the lilac."

Psyche looked from one gown to the other and held them up to herself in turn, shaking her head indecisively.

"Do you think it's too frilly?"

"No, it's fine. Besides, you wore the white one day before yesterday."

"Did I?" asked Psyche perplexedly.

"Yes, wear the lilac," said Pandora firmly with a grin. "Give my regrets to Mamà and Papà for breakfast. I'm certainly going to miss having it, but I think Selena's intending to take a basket with us to the Gardens."

"Sounds wonderful," said Psyche as she slid the lilac dress over her head. "I'm almost tempted to join you, but I've gotten to a really interesting part of my book."

"I'll give Selena your regards," said Pandora with a grin, sighing inwardly with relief that her twin didn't want to come along.

"Ta," her sister called after her as Pandora left the room.

She went down the back stairs, as she usually did, and left through one of the back doors. She walked through the garden down the path to the mews gate at a fairly quick pace but not to the point of running. She didn't want someone looking out a window of the house to wonder why she was rushing. Psyche would let her family know where she was going, or at least where she had told her twin that she was going, and they would not expect her back for a few hours. Another convenience of her pretended visit to Selena was that her friend's house was within easy walking distance, and Pandora's not taking a carriage wouldn't be unusual.

She left the mews and crossed Berkeley Square, heading for South Street. She crossed over to the opposite side of the road, which would bring her up to the corner of South Audley where she could peek around to see when Hendon left. At least, that was what she had intended. Unfortunately, before she even reached the corner, she saw Hendon amble across the intersection heading north. *At least I know which way he's leaving*, she consoled herself. She waited for a carriage passing on the street to go by before she crossed back over and quickened her step.

Once she reached the corner, she slowed momentarily to peek around the edge to see where Hendon had gone. He was still moving at his casual pace, which to Pandora's agitation seemed to be much quicker than it looked. He had already crossed Mount and was heading for Grosvenor Square. He didn't seem concerned about being followed, and he didn't look left or right at the buildings and people around him.

There were carriages parked at the front of some of the houses as people were going out to tend to business before going to call on acquaintances, but he didn't even bother to politely tip his hat to any of them. Pandora felt obliged to nod her head and smile as she encountered each group, so by the time she had passed this first wave of people, Hendon had already crossed the square and was headed for Oxford Street.

Pandora had always thought herself to be in excellent physical condition, but she discovered it was no longer the case. She couldn't use the excuse that his stride was longer because the few inches difference in their heights would not account for it. Short of running, she wouldn't be able to keep him in sight. She couldn't run, however, because it would attract the attention of people she passed, and by doing that she might also call the attention of the earl. She groaned inwardly as he continued to get farther ahead of her.

When she reached Grosvenor Square, she made the decision to cut across it diagonally, heading for Duke Street. If she continued to follow Hendon in a straight line, she would lose him, and it was unlikely he would be heading for Paddington. Pandora placed odds that he would turn right once he reached Oxford; cutting over to Duke Street would allow her to close some of the distance between them without having to develop her pace into a full run. The only reason he was remaining as far ahead was that he had basically cheated at the start.

Pandora was becoming winded, and a film of perspiration was forming on her upper lip and at the small of her back. She had the shawl and work apron draped over an arm with that hand holding her reticule. Her bonnet, while it kept the sun from beating down on her face and head, didn't block the heat of it, and she could feel her scalp beginning to tingle. Pandora had forgotten to take into consideration how her past illness might be affecting her. She might have recovered the ability walk and ride Bellerophon again, but she wasn't completely back to herself. Close, but not quite.

This whole following business wasn't going according to plan, and she was beginning to wonder if it might be a mistake. She firmly put that from her mind. If there was nothing else about her that was certain, that she was determined (some would argue stubborn) was guaranteed. Besides, it had only just begun. She couldn't give in so quickly. She steeled herself for what was shaping up to be a very exhausting adventure and quickened her pace. She felt this just *had* to work.

When Pandora reached the corner of Duke and Oxford, she first looked right to determine if he had yet again managed to get out of reach. She didn't see him cross the intersection before she got there, so he would have either crossed before she arrived or was yet to make it. She didn't see him, which gave her some hope and relief. She then turned to her left and saw Hendon entering Hambledon's, a tobacconist's shop, only a few stores from the corner. She sighed thankfully and walked in that direction.

Pandora risked a casual glance into the window as she passed and saw Hendon talking with the clerk at the counter, who was showing him several different tobacco selections. Pandora continued a few storefronts further on, selecting the window of Patenaude's, the jeweler's, where she decided she would wait until Hendon resumed his journey. It wouldn't be long; how much tobacco would one man need?

The jeweler's was the one her family most frequently used, the same one where she had seen the necklace of Marie Antoinette, and it was still displayed in the window. Pandora looked at it closer. It was beautiful, dripping with diamonds of yellow and white, but it looked heavy and ostentatious. Pandora suspected the jeweler would have a hard time selling it; most women were satisfied with something much simpler—like *one* diamond on a chain. Pandora occasionally did wear something more elaborate, but the necklace in the window was something she would *never* think of wearing. Still, it did have a bit of cachet because of its previous owner, and Pandora was sure if it was sold, the buyer would only be interested in it for that reason.

After only a few minutes, Hendon left Hambledon's and resumed his walk up Oxford carrying two small packages. Thankfully, Pandora was now within an easy distance yet far enough behind him that he wouldn't find it obvious he was being followed. She hoped now that she was closer she would be able to keep up. There were enough people out that should he chance a look behind him, it would be unlikely he would suspect Pandora was following him, especially since they were in the shopping district. Any difficulty would come after they left the district, and it appeared they would be.

Hendon kept to his casual pace as he crossed Bond, and Pandora stayed within distance of him much easier than before he stopped. She was becoming tired, though. It had to do with her previous illness, not to mention that all she had to eat was tea and toast several hours earlier.

She thought about what her family would be having for breakfast: eggs, bacon, ham; fresh fruit with rolls slathered in lots of butter and jam. Then there would be porridge with honey, blueberry scones, and pancakes. Her mouth watered and her stomach rumbled unhappily as she thought about it, and Pandora quickly tried to erase the thoughts of it from her mind. She would have to wait until she got home; then she would have Maiyin bring a tray of something (anything) to her room.

She began to grow moderately curious about their destination when they crossed Swallow Street, going further into town and heading for the city proper. She had taken this route before several times on the way to the British Museum, although she had never been on foot. Usually, when she and her family went, her younger siblings were in tow, and it was too far for them to walk. Foot traffic was still good, and carriage traffic on the road had picked up. Pandora felt fairly secure in her anonymity and began to look around as she walked, looking at the different businesses and houses she passed, yet never losing sight of her quarry. She also, unlike the man she followed, took the time to smile and nod as she passed other people who made eye contact, but she didn't stop to socialize. She was having a hard enough time staying apace of the earl as it was.

They passed Dean, which would have taken them to Soho Square, and Hendon continued on. Pandora thought she should put on her work apron but changed her mind, as there were still other respectably-dressed people, although the pedestrians were now starting to become dressed more in the manner of tradesmen and working individuals. Aside from that, Pandora didn't think she could take the time to stop and put it on without losing sight of Hendon. She had chosen her dress well because it was rather plain and didn't make it obvious she was a long way from where she should be.

The earl still seemed to be unaware of her trailing after him. He did, after a time, begin to turn his head from side to side occasionally and even go so far as to nod to someone, which Pandora found odd after his rudeness in Westminster. She could only guess he wasn't a stranger in these parts, and although one of the aristocracy, he wasn't on the same level in the other district because of his reputation.

When they reached the intersection where Oxford met Tottenham, High, and Hog Lane, Pandora wondered which direction Hendon would take. If he went left, it would lead them into a more rural area that was less densely populated. Hog Lane would take them back to Westminster, and Pandora felt sure he would have gone a different route from Audley if that had been his intended destination. High Street would take them to St. Giles and Lincoln's Inn, and places that were less than savory, but Pandora bravely soldiered on when that was the direction he chose.

Pandora raised a hand to wipe away the film of perspiration that had grown on her chin and upper lip as she continued to follow Hendon into a district that—provided she had others with her and a carriage—would be safe. She began to grow apprehensive as their journey continued, and she began to make fewer gestures of friendliness toward the passersby on the street and they her. She was sure there were decent people among them and living where they did was not proof of criminality, but the reputation of the area was not one that would leave her predisposed to think them innocent. With their turn into the district, her dress *was* going to look out of place, regardless of how plain it was, but there was little she could do about it. She still believed as long as Hendon didn't look back to see her there, the other people around her were of little concern.

Her eyes rounded in dismay when he turned onto Drury. This should have been the point when she called a halt to the affair and returned from whence she came, but now that she knew where he was going, she felt she was too close to discovering what Castleton looked like to turn back. She adjusted her shawl and apron over her arm to hide her purse and tread slowly after him.

There were plenty of things that were respectable about Drury Lane. There were stores and theaters she had gone to with her sisters. Places like Lincoln's Inn and Covent Garden were almost a stone's throw away, but there were also things about it that were dangerous. This was where thieves and prostitutes were thick, not to mention the gin houses frequented by both. Pandora squared her shoulders and took a deep breath as she, too, made the turn.

There were lots of people out tending to business, but there were several others who were lounging in doorways, many of them obviously prostitutes, with part of their skirts tucked up as a means of advertising their trade. Pandora swallowed nervously.

"Hallo, sweetheart," one of them called to her with a leering smile as she passed. "Are you lost? Ginger will 'elp you out."

Pandora smiled uncomfortably and shook her head, continuing on, the sound of the old prostitute's raucous laughter ringing in her ears. Ginger's attention drew that of several others, and they teased Pandora as she passed. Fortunately for her, none of them physically approached her, and she felt some relief that they didn't.

She spied Hendon ahead of her, but he slowed and stopped to talk to one of the storekeepers at his doorway only a short distance away. The man was short and stout, and Pandora knew it wasn't Castleton. She felt a moment of panic when Hendon started to turn his head in her direction, but she was able to step into a side alley quickly and hoped he didn't notice. She chanced a peek around the corner after a few minutes and saw he had resumed his walk. Pandora stepped out and followed him, but her heart was pounding in her chest anxiously as she did so. She passed the point where Hendon had stopped, but the storekeeper had gone back inside and paid her no mind.

Pandora had only followed him twenty yards or so further when he paused again to speak to someone. This time, there was no side alley conveniently nearby for her to duck into—the nearest was still several yards ahead of her, and she felt a rising panic in her stomach at the risk of being spotted. She sighed with relief when he continued on without looking back, apparently taking no notice. She had the chance to turn around then, but she still refused to do so.

She squeaked in surprise when someone came behind her and grabbed her elbow. Pandora was prepared to fight them off, thinking the doxies had finally come for her, and she felt marginally relieved to see Islington standing over her, his face grim. He looked up the street in the direction of Hendon, and then with a tight smile he forcefully guided her into the nearby alley.

It was very narrow and dark, and it was obviously not meant for a vehicle to use but was more likely used as a footpath from Drury to the adjoining street. There was a sliver of light at the far end, but it looked barely wide enough for a person to pass through. Pandora doubted it was rarely, if ever, used for its original purpose. The buildings to either side leaned toward each other to the point the sun couldn't penetrate, and there were no doors or windows in the facing walls. It was damp, and the stones beneath her feet were slick in places with things Pandora didn't even want to contemplate. The smell in the close air was one of rotting refuse and human waste, and Pandora almost gagged when she breathed.

Islington led her some distance from the entrance and roughly stopped with her, Pandora's elbow still in a tight grip.

"I must say I am—" Pandora started calmly but was cut short when he shoved her back into the wall and pinned her there with his own body pressed firmly against hers.

He began an assault then that frightened her. He ground his lips against hers, forcing them further apart from their initial gasp of surprise to explore her mouth plunderingly. Then, to her horror, he raised the hem of her dress above her thighs and lifted her so her feet were up from the ground. He placed a bracing hand under her buttocks and put her legs around his waist so his pelvis could grind suggestively into hers, causing her spine to rub sharply against the stone wall through the thin material of her dress. Pandora was able to tell from past experience that he didn't have an erection, despite the actions he performed, but it didn't make the movement of her back being rubbed into the wall any less painful or what he was doing any less disconcerting. It was absolutely unlike anything she would expect from him.

Pandora tried shoving at his chest to push him away, but his weight kept her immobile, and her feet having no contact with the ground kept her from effectively being able to fend him off. With his free hand, he reached down to her bodice and grabbed one of her breasts through the material, squeezing it firmly until she released a muffled cry against his lips, which he would not remove from hers. He kept his hand at her breasts, kneading them almost impersonally through her dress, and Pandora couldn't get him to stop.

Pandora was shocked and afraid. She tried pounding her fists against his chest, but he didn't seem to notice. Her strength was no match for Islington's, and he effectively had her at his mercy for the moment. She was completely at a loss to understand what had provoked this, and she wasn't sure there was any excuse that would be worthy.

Even as he was punishing and obviously not intent on causing it, Pandora felt herself unwillingly growing excited at his touch. She wouldn't let him know that, and she would continue to fight him because she was sure it was wrong to feel that way. Her eyes burned with tears of mortification, and she began to feel the futility of any attempt to break free. Whatever its cause, it appeared she would have to suffer through the assault for however long he decided it should last, and she was ashamed to admit to herself that she didn't want to try harder to get away. She knew there were things she *could* do to get away, and yet she wouldn't.

Pandora uselessly tried to shake her head when she felt Islington move his hand to cup her, inserting his finger inside her as he massaged the heel of his palm against her button. To her shame, it kindled a heat in her that she couldn't dampen, and she groaned at the conflicting emotions she felt. She didn't want to feel excited by his actions, but she found it too hard to resist. Islington continued to stroke her, and Pandora weakly tried to pull at his arm to break the contact, but there was no room between them for her actions to do any good. When she had an orgasm, she cried out as much from anguish as she did from the pleasure it produced.

At Pandora's climax, Islington momentarily stilled against her, astonished by her reaction, but he didn't release her. He did attempt to soften the character of his embrace, but he couldn't completely desist. He didn't want to free her mouth because he couldn't risk having her call out or speak. Islington couldn't have her say his name, or the entire thing would be a catastrophe.

There was a third party to their assignation, and Islington wasn't satisfied that he had finished as well...so to speak.

What Pandora didn't know was that Hendon had realized at some point that he was being followed. She also didn't know Islington had been following them since they had crossed Grosvenor Square. When he saw them turn into Drury, Islington realized Hendon was leading her into a trap. He suspected Pandora was following the earl with the intention of discovering where he went to meet Castleton. Yes, the Dog was located in the district, but it was *not* on Drury, Islington knew personally. Islington quickly determined the only way he could save her from Hendon was to make it seem that he had taken care of the matter for the earl.

Despite the unrestrained nature of his assault, he tried not to do anything to truly cause her physical harm. He didn't know what had prompted him to stimulate her; brutally assaulting women in an alley was—mercifully—not something he could claim being experienced at. In hindsight, it wasn't something he should have done, especially considering what happened, and he knew it was unfair.

There was no pleasure in this for him, and he couldn't bring himself to an arousal even if he needed to. He felt no small amount of remorse at having to do any of it, and he knew it was something unpardonable. When he was faced with the choice of having Pandora killed by Hendon or earning her hatred, Islington knew what the only logical answer could be. He hoped that if he was able to explain, she might forgive him eventually.

He continued to kiss her and moved his hands so they both supported her buttocks to reduce the friction of her back against the wall while he moved against her in a suggestion of intercourse for their captive audience. Islington had never felt so much relief in his life as he did when he heard a low, evil, self-satisfied laugh from the entrance to the alley and the sound of retreating footsteps. For now, it seemed, they were safe.

Chapter Thirteen

Pandora had given up fighting Islington. There was, she felt, no further shame he could inflict on her. He had depravedly assaulted her in a public (almost) place and somehow managed to make her enjoy it. She hadn't missed the laughter from the alley entrance, and knowing someone had *seen* it only added to her distress. All that remained was for her to start sobbing hysterically, and that wasn't impossible.

Not long after the laughter faded, Islington stopped. He ended their kiss and gently released her to let her feet touch the pavers. Without his support, Pandora sank to the ground, numb with shock and exhaustion. Islington knelt beside her and removed her bonnet. Her face was ashen and streaked with tears. Her expression was listless almost to the point of being stupor. He reached up a hand to gently wipe her cheeks, but she pushed at it weakly.

"Go away," she said dully.

He didn't follow her order, but he didn't attempt to touch her again.

"We can't stay here," he said after she seemed intent to do just that.

"Go away," she repeated.

Islington's brow furrowed with concern. She was in shock, but they couldn't stay in the alley. If Hendon came back, it wouldn't be good. Islington reached into the pocket of his riding coat and retrieved a small silver flask. He opened it and held it out to her.

"Drink this," he commanded.

Pandora looked at him then, and her eyes were full of a seething rage that almost seemed to touch him with a physical intensity. Islington looked away from her and closed his eyes, trying to restrain the emotions her expression brought out in him. He then turned to look at her resolutely.

"I cannot begin to imagine what you're feeling," he said softly, "but I'm sure whatever it is, you are justified." Her expression didn't change. "Hendon *will* be coming back, and we *cannot* stay here." At the earl's name, Pandora's eyes grew wide in panic. Islington held the flask out to her again. "Please, drink this."

Pandora grudgingly took the flask from his hand and put it to her lips. Her familiarity with liquor wasn't great. She knew how to distill it, but drinking it wasn't something she could claim. She took a very large swallow, and then another, and another. She only reached that point—and probably would have gone farther—before Islington took the flask away from her. The whisky burned a trail to her stomach and radiated out toward her limbs with a warmth that numbed her. Her eyes watered, and her jaw clenched at the taste of it.

"Good girl," said Islington soothingly. "Can you walk?"

He handed her back her bonnet, and Pandora reluctantly redid the ties under her chin. She was able to find her shawl, apron and reticule on the ground where she had dropped them. Islington stood and reached down to offer his hand, but Pandora refused to take it and instead braced herself against the wall to come to a standing position.

She felt wobbly. She was unsure how much was caused by the trauma she had endured for the past fifteen minutes and how much was due to the large amount of whisky she had just consumed on an empty stomach. She weaved on her feet, and Islington reached out a hand to steady her.

"Don't *touch* me!" she bit out savagely.

"Pandora, please, let me help you," Islington said gently.

Pandora looked at his expression of worry and guilt. She wasn't inclined to be moved by it, but she also realized she could not, at that moment, manage to walk without help. She warily took the arm he offered and gingerly leaned against him for support. The dizziness soon began to lessen, but she still felt weak, as if she could faint any minute.

Instead of taking her back to Drury, Islington led her toward the narrower exit at the opposite end. Pandora was relieved they wouldn't be going the other way. Facing the knowing stares of the prostitutes wasn't something she felt capable of doing. She didn't think there had been any telltale noises coming from the alley, but their profession would give them the imagined detail their senses could not. The exit was wider than it had first appeared, and they were able to pass through easily.

Coming into the sunlight from the deep gloom of the alley made Pandora momentarily blind, and she blinked several times to get her eyes adjusted. She looked around herself, but she did not, for the moment, recognize where she was. Islington turned them left, and Pandora allowed him to lead her. She wasn't sure where they were going, but she believed he would take her home. At least, she hoped he would.

They came to a wider, busy cross street, and Pandora realized it was Long Acre. Islington crossed the street with her, and then they went right; however, instead of remaining on that street, which would have started them in the general direction of Westminster, he turned onto Bow Street. Pandora's forehead wrinkled with concern.

"Where are we going?" she asked distrustfully.

"I thought it would be easier for you if we take a boat to Whitehall and then catch a hack to your house," he said calmly after looking at her.

"It will take longer," said Pandora argumentatively.

"Perhaps, but you cannot manage to walk all the way home, and you shouldn't try."

Pandora bit back an angry retort because she knew he was right.

As they got to the entrance of Covent Garden, the smell of food from the market floated through the air to make Pandora's stomach rumble rebelliously. She didn't know how she could be hungry. She mentally didn't feel as if she could eat a thing, but her body seemed to think otherwise. Islington heard the sound and turned to look at her.

"You're hungry?" he asked with mild surprise.

"No," denied Pandora.

He turned with her into the market.

"I told you I'm not hungry," said Pandora hotly.

He stopped with her then grabbed her by the shoulders and turned her to face him.

"Pandora, you *are* hungry, and you *will* eat something."

Islington took her arm and began to guide her through the stalls. He found some small, freshly made meat pies, some cheese, apples (one of which he handed to her), and pears, all of which he placed into a basket that he also purchased. The entire excursion took less than ten minutes, and he was soon guiding her again toward the Strand down Southampton Street. Pandora began to eat the apple before they left the market, and she was finished with it before they reached the Strand. Islington silently handed her a pear, which she also began to eat with gusto.

After they crossed the Strand, they walked along the waterfront until they located a boat for hire. The older man who owned it was friendly and assisted Pandora into the boat with a smile. The craft was small and propelled by an oar at the aft end for both steering and propulsion. There was a canopy for fares to sit under, and the seat had a soft red velvet cushion with a back. Pandora gratefully sank onto it as Islington told the man to take them to the Whitehall Stairs. Islington sat down beside her and rested the basket between them by placing it on both their laps.

Pandora began to devour the food greedily. She couldn't understand how she could be so hungry. She had at first thought she wouldn't be able to eat a bite. Islington calmly ate one pear as he watched her ravenously consume a meat pie followed by a piece of the creamy yellow, mild cheddar. She had another apple then made her way through another pie and more cheese. At that point, she felt full and dusted the crumbs from the meal off her face and lap. They were still only halfway to the stairs.

"Better?" asked Islington mildly.

"I'm not hungry anymore," said Pandora obliquely. "Thank you."

"Not a problem."

They rode in silence for a time, and Pandora looked around as the small boat floated downstream. The owner was content to let the current set their pace, and he would occasionally put his paddle into the water to correct its course. She watched as larger ships sailed past on their way out to sea and the men at the docks unloading the berths of those that had just arrived. There were local tradesmen working on nets and other water trade paraphernalia along the shore, and she would hear the occasional shout as they called to one another in their work. The water was very peaceful, and it helped to relax Pandora.

"How did you—?" Islington started, stopped, and then decided to press on. "How did you manage to get out of the house?" he asked her gently.

Pandora turned to him in surprise at the question. She shrugged.

"I told Psyche that I was going to Kensington Gardens with Selena," she said calmly. "She would have told the rest of my family, should any of them have asked."

"Why did you decide to follow Hendon? *Where* did you follow him from?" he asked in puzzlement.

Pandora brushed out the folds in her skirt contemplatively.

"I decided to follow him because I wanted to know what Castleton looked like. I followed him from South Audley."

"South Audley?"

"Yes, he's been watching his victim's house for signs that he's coming to town. I was sure he would be going to meet with Castleton, so I decided to follow him and see what I could."

"You know who his victim will be?" asked Islington in a startled tone.

"Well, yes," said Pandora practically. "The comte d'Artois."

"You're sure?"

"As sure as I can be without having written proof or a confession."

"How did you find out?" asked Islington, his brow furrowed perplexedly.

"It all started when I saw Marie Antoinette's necklace in a jewelry store window, and I thought to myself having that much wealth just begs someone to kill you for it. Then, Lord Sheerness and Lord Barneville were talking at Mamá's dinner party about how rich Artois supposedly was and that he lived alone in Edinburgh." Pandora shrugged. "He just seemed to be the logical choice.

"At Almack's last week when you tricked me into meeting Hendon—"she gave him a sidelong glare—"I discovered he doesn't care for the French much, especially not Artois. Then I met Hendon's wife in the powder room, and she mentioned that he had been studying a French grammar, which doesn't make a terrible amount of sense if you don't like them...unless you're planning to kidnap and murder one of them."

Islington's expression grew thoughtful. He couldn't argue with her logic about Artois. It made perfect sense. He had to wonder what would have made

Hendon decide to kidnap the count. Although Hendon was an unpleasant man and a criminal, his illegal activities tended toward rape and murder by poison (according to rumor). Islington hadn't heard of any financial difficulties that would prompt him to kidnap for ransom.

Islington knew Hendon had married his wife for money, but that hadn't gone according to plan because her father had left her inheritance in a trust, and her real property had been entailed to her title. Other than her dowry, Hendon had received nothing, but as far as Islington knew, Hendon didn't *need* her money. It was more likely he had married the marchioness for the access she could give him to places in society that shunned him. If Hendon was committing this crime for the same reasons as his previous activities, the money was only an added incentive—most likely decided on by Castleton—and Hendon only had it in mind that Artois should be killed.

"Hendon knew you were following him," said Islington softly.

Pandora turned to look at him, her eyes round in disbelief.

"How could he have known?" asked Pandora contentiously.

"I don't know, but you don't get to the position Hendon is and not go to the gallows without being smarter than you look," said Islington firmly. "The things he is rumored to have done would have been punishable by death even for a peer." Pandora still looked doubtful. "You thought he was going to the Dog, didn't you?" he asked with some exasperation. Pandora grudgingly nodded. "It's not on Drury; it's on Little Queen, and he wouldn't have gone down Drury to get to it."

Pandora clamped her jaw tightly and crossed her arms in front of her. She didn't want to believe Islington was right about Hendon knowing she was there. She had been so careful. He had given no indication that he was aware. She remembered, however, that after they reached a certain point he had seemed to change, becoming more pleasant to the people he passed and aware of his surroundings. She had thought at the time it was just that he felt more comfortable in familiar territory. She now had to face that he had done it to lull her into complacency.

"How did you know who I was?" asked Pandora bemusedly after a time. "I thought this hat hid my face."

"It does hide your face," said Islington softly, "but I don't need to see your face to recognize you."

Pandora's cheeks reddened at what he implied, and she was glad the bonnet did hide her face because she didn't want him to see her reaction.

Their boatman pulled up to the bottom of Whitehall Stairs. Islington paid him and stepped out, and then he helped Pandora to the platform. The man tipped his hat to them as he rowed away, going back up to The Strand, as there was no one at the stairs waiting for a boat. Pandora waved as he left.

Islington escorted her up the stairs to the busyness of Whitehall. Pandora knew this was an area Islington was familiar with, as Parliament and other government buildings were there. She sighed with relief that she was almost home. They were able to hail a hack without difficulty, and Islington helped her in. After Islington spoke to the driver about their destination, he stepped in as well and closed the door. It had the curtains drawn for privacy, and the window to the driver's box was also closed. The carriage started with a jolt, and it was in no way as well-sprung as her family's coach, making Pandora wince as her back was pushed against the cushions. She took off her bonnet and set it beside her on the seat. She never wanted to wear it again.

"Pandora, I am truly sorry," said Islington quietly after a time.

Pandora gave him an angry glare.

"Are you? Do you have any idea what you did? How could you?"

Pandora's eyes sparkled with rage, and she flew at him on the seat, her fists pounding at him in wild fury. She started crying and sobbing softly as she struck him, but Islington gently took her wrists and pinned them to his chest to stop the attack before she managed to hurt herself. Pandora dropped her head defeatedly, and her shoulders shook as she cried.

"Would you rather that Hendon had done it?" he asked simply.

Pandora's head raised in surprise.

"What do you mean?" she asked huskily.

Islington took out his handkerchief and began to wipe at her face. He couldn't look her in the eye.

"Hendon knew you were following him. What do you think would have happened when he had gotten you where he wanted you? Keep in mind that he is *not* a gentleman." Islington tried to keep dismissed from his mind that Pandora didn't think *him* much of a gentleman either.

Pandora thought back to the bruises and bandages she had seen on Georgiana, and those had just been the obvious injuries. No, Hendon wouldn't have been gentle; he would mostly likely have killed her (or tried to) before it was finished. Islington had been rough, but other than the tenderness on her back where he had pinned her against the wall, she was physically unharmed. Still, there were the emotional wounds.

"So you *raped* me to stop Hendon from doing it?" she asked coldly. Islington couldn't look at her. "And what about the...you...I...."

She couldn't finish and looked at him accusingly, her chest heaving emotionally as her cheeks colored. Islington looked at her then.

"I never intended for that to happen," he said softly, his expression sincere. "I should not have done that, and I'm sorry."

"Why didn't you tell me what you were doing? You used me again, you bloody bastard!" she shouted angrily.

"I saved your life!" he shouted back in exasperation, raising his hands from his sides in surrender.

"You could have told me," said Pandora simply. "You didn't have to treat me like that, and you didn't have to scare me like that."

"It had to look convincing. Hendon would never have believed it if you knew what was happening."

Pandora closed her mouth and looked away from him. She was through arguing with him, and she wasn't ready to forgive him. He had used her again, and this time had been even more humiliating than all the other times combined. She couldn't understand why she had not learned her lesson.

Pandora wanted to believe there could have been another way to deceive Hendon, but in the end she knew there wasn't. They could have gone out the back side of the alley, but Hendon would have tried to pursue her somehow—maybe not today, but he would have felt she would still be a liability and would have at some point found some way to silence her. Now, it was likely that he believed Pandora wouldn't follow the matter any further and was no longer a threat.

The two of them remained silent for the rest of the time it took for the carriage to arrive in front of her house. Islington started to get out and help her down, but Pandora turned to look at him dully and put a staying hand on his chest.

"No, you stay here. I don't want my family to know anything about this," she said finally.

The driver had gotten down from his seat and opened the door for her. Islington started to say something but tightened his jaw and remained silent. He just nodded his head curtly and sat back against the cushion. Pandora accepted the driver's hand and stepped down. She watched from the sidewalk as Islington gave directions to his house and closed the door. She sighed tiredly and turned for the gate to her family's small front yard as the carriage pulled away from the curb.

She walked up the stairs to the front door and opened it silently. She didn't hear or see anyone, and she made it up the front stairs to her bedroom without anyone seeing her. She was relieved everyone was out because she didn't think she could be sociable. She glanced to the clock and saw it was barely past three in the afternoon. She felt as if she had been up for hours longer than that.

After dropping her shawl, apron and purse on the foot of her bed, she temporarily tossed the bonnet there as well. She went to the floor-length mirror and looked at herself. Other than appearing a bit windblown and fatigued, the day's events had left very little outward mark. Her dress was dirty around the hem, and when she turned to look at the back, she could see the grime from the wall of the alley. Maiyin would be able to wash it clean, but Pandora didn't want her to.

She calmly unfastened the gown and removed it, dropping it in a heap on the floor. Then she went to the corner and pulled the rope that would ring in the servants' quarters to let Maiyin know she was needed. Pandora removed her garters and rolled down her stockings and placed them with the gown. She added her chemise to the pile, and then she went to the bed to grab the bonnet and put it on the heap as well. She was pulling on a dressing gown as Maiyin came into the room.

"Missy Pandora, you back already?" asked Maiyin with surprise as she entered.

"Yes, Maiyin, I'm home. Could you run a bath for me, please?" she asked, rubbing a hand across her forehead tiredly.

Maiyin's face wrinkled with concern.

"Missy Pandora, what is wrong?" Maiyin walked over to look closely at her face and rubbed her arm soothingly. "You not feeling well?"

"No...yes...oh, Maiyin, I don't know," said Pandora with a bit of a hysterical laugh. "I think a nice, hot bath will do me some good."

Maiyin noted the pile of clothes.

"What are these?" she asked as she went over to pick them up, preparing to scold Pandora for carelessly leaving them on the floor.

"Burn them, please," said Pandora firmly.

Maiyin's eyebrows shot up in surprise, but she nodded her head. Pandora was troubled by something. Maiyin agreed a hot bath would be in order...and some of Keung's special tea as well.

"I'll take care of it as soon as I get water running for bath," she said softly. "I will let you know when it is ready and bring you some tea."

"Thank you, Maiyin," said Pandora with a grateful smile.

She went to her bed and curled up in a ball, rubbing the spot behind her ear. She only stayed that way a few minutes before getting up to find the chamber pot and vomit. She clutched the sides for several minutes as dry heaves continued long after her stomach was empty. She closed her eyes and sat back from it, curling her knees up to her chest and resting her forehead on them. She eventually stood up and went to sit on the edge of her bed, her eyes unfocused. Maiyin soon returned to let Pandora know her bath was ready.

Pandora went down the hall to the bathing room. She and Psyche had assisted their father in designing a system that provided the family with running water. They had created a boiler that produced hot water, which could be generated using either coal gas or regular coal when the gas ran out. All told, they had six of the rooms: one for the girls, one for the boys, and one for the duke and duchess, while the remaining three were in the servants' wing. The system was revolutionary, and it wasn't without occasional mishaps, but it had made bathing much more enjoyable for everyone. They had created a similar system at Wilderland where the water supply was much more plentiful.

Pandora entered the room and found the air steamy and scented with the oils Maiyin had used in her water. She took off her dressing gown and stepped into the tub, sinking into the hot water to let her neck and head rest against the back of it, the water line coming to just beneath her collarbone. She closed her eyes and sighed peacefully as the heat and the scented oil began to relax her and soothe away her discomfort.

Maiyin set a tray on a small table and poured Pandora a cup of the tea she had made. She roused Pandora and handed it to her, and the girl took a sip of it after breathing in its blend of chamomile, lavender, and ginger with lemon and honey. After she saw Pandora was drinking her tea, Maiyin went to the stool at the back of the tub to sit down and begin kneading Pandora's shoulders and neck, working out the knots of tension.

"Maiyin, you are a treasure beyond worth," sighed Pandora languidly. "How would I ever survive without you?"

Maiyin smiled at Pandora fondly as she continued. She had seen the bruising on Pandora's back as the girl stepped into the tub, but she would wait to see if Pandora would tell her what had happened. She wouldn't ask out of respect for Pandora's privacy, but Maiyin felt a maternal protectiveness for Pandora gained from their many years together. She knew from all the things that had happened to Pandora throughout the Season, whatever had caused it was no trivial accident.

Maiyin thought back to the day when she first came home with the duke to become Pandora's maid. She had understood almost no English and spoken even less. When they were introduced, Pandora had shyly walked up to her and put her little hands to either side of Maiyin's face and smiled beatifically. In that moment, the Mandarin woman had completely lost her heart to the girl. Pandora taught her English, Maiyin taught her Mandarin, and there was no question of their devotion to each other.

Maiyin was sold by her father to the local magistrate as a concubine when she was sixteen years old. For fifteen years, she tolerated sexual abuse from her master and other physical and verbal abuse from his wife. Several abortions and miscarriages early on had left her unable to bear further children. Her situation became only worse as she grew older and lost the bloom of youth, until Maiyin had begun to contemplate suicide. Then she had met Keung, who had been appointed the magistrate's new apothecary. They had fallen instantly in love and ran away together.

Their escape had branded them criminals because, even though she was unwanted and mistreated, Maiyin was still the property of the magistrate. If they had been caught, they would have both been killed, so they had fled the province. Being outlaws had limited their ability to find work, and they had traveled from place to place, working in the fields as laborers during the harvest season, helping to plough the fields in the planting season, and starving through the winter until the growing time returned. But they loved each other and never regretted their choice.

It was during one of their starving times that they had met the Duke of Aberdare. They had traveled to Shanghai to try their luck getting work as day laborers, but their plight was not unique among their countrymen, and the city was inundated with others seeking employment. In desperation, Keung had tried to pick the duke's pocket to buy food for himself and Maiyin. He had been caught, but instead of the duke reporting it to the authorities, his grace had taken pity on them and offered them employment in his household. Neither of them had ever been away from China, but the duke's offer would give them the freedom they had not felt in fifteen years. They had gratefully accepted, and they couldn't imagine going back to China.

After Maiyin could feel the tension had been worked out of Pandora's shoulders, she removed the pins from her hair to wash it. Pandora hadn't said she wanted her hair shampooed, and she didn't appear to be dirty, but Maiyin felt that she wanted to be washed from head to toe. Pandora dipped her head beneath the water, and Maiyin grabbed the bottle of soap she had brought in before getting Pandora for her bath. She poured some of the mixture into the palm of her hand and worked it through the long length of Pandora's hair. The scent of it matched the perfume Maiyin had made for Pandora, and the room was soon filled with the odor of oranges and ginger. Pandora then put her head back under the water to rinse it and came back up, wiping the water from her face.

"Maiyin, have you and Keung always gotten along?" asked Pandora as she moved her hands back and forth under the water.

"Gotten along?" asked Maiyin mildly.

"Do you argue?"

Maiyin chuckled as she dipped a cloth into the water and poured some of the soap onto it to begin washing Pandora's limbs.

"I would say we have *discussions*. Keung would say we have *arguments*. I think even you mother and father wouldn't be happy if they didn't argue sometimes. It doesn't mean there is no harmony; it just keeps things from getting stale."

"Have you ever gotten so mad at each other you didn't speak?"

Maiyin laughed again, and she looked into Pandora's eyes as she knelt by the edge of the tub, washing her arm.

"Yes, it has happened, but it not last long. One or the other of us will miss the other one too much. It is yin and yang, *dŏng*? We complete each other, which is why we cannot stay apart."

Pandora smiled and raised her leg for Maiyin to wash it. She braced her arms against the sides of the tub to keep her head above water.

"Has Keung ever...has Keung ever hurt you?" asked Pandora gravely.

Maiyin looked up from her task, her face solemn.

"In China, like here, women are chattel. You husband think you do something wrong, he beat you, and nobody say anything. It is no worse than beating a dog. You father want to sell you, no worse than selling his grain in the market. Keung has never raised a hand to me in anger; that was one of the reasons I love him. There are other things to feel besides anger, though, and sometimes they come out whether you want them to or not; it doesn't mean that love is not still there." Maiyin shook her head. "I have been very lucky."

Pandora relaxed and closed her eyes. For Maiyin, it was simple; she knew Keung loved her and that he would never do anything to hurt her. Pandora couldn't be so secure with Islington. He had never said he loved her. He was by turns gentle and rough. Often, she only saw the tenderness just before he dealt her an emotional blow of some type. She wanted to trust him, but he didn't trust her enough to be honest. She didn't know if she could endure it any longer without losing something within herself.

Today had been frightening, but she hadn't been able to keep herself from thrilling at his touch; there was apparently a part of her that trusted him implicitly even when the rest of her could not. He had said it was a ruse to save her from Hendon. She had heard the earl's laughter, so she believed Islington, but she still felt he should have warned her. He said it wouldn't have looked real if she had known, but he didn't understand how good an actress she was. Still, she wasn't sure she could have pretended to be frightened if she had known there was no reason to be; her fear had been all too real, and yet she had managed to become excited. Perhaps in that respect, Islington understood her all too well.

The temperature of the water grew tepid, and Pandora stood to let Maiyin towel her off before putting on her dressing gown. She went back to her room, and in the hallway she could hear the sounds of her family's return: Eurydice's violin, children's laughter, and the muted buzz of many conversations. The sounds further helped to soothe her, and that was when Pandora knew she was safe and the final strands of uneasiness floated away. She smiled peacefully as she walked into her room.

She looked at the clock and saw she had managed to spend almost two hours bathing. She didn't feel guilty; the time in her bath had done much to heal her physically and mentally, something she thought would take much longer. She was sure it had as much to do with the hot water and tea as it did with Maiyin's soothing presence.

Pandora went to sit at her dressing table and absently started to run a comb through her hair, working through the snarls that had formed there during its washing. She could wait for Maiyin to do it for her, but it was less painful when she did it herself because she could actually *feel* when she was pulling too hard and save her tender scalp. Her hair was rather fine, and by the time she had finished brushing, it was already half dry. Maiyin soon came to her room carrying a tray with more tea and small sandwiches. Pandora smiled gratefully and began to eat as Maiyin began to put her hair back up.

Pandora and Psyche had been invited to a ball at the Earl of Sheerness's, so Maiyin put Pandora's hair into a more elaborate style than it had been before her bath, placing one section into a knot while the rest was put into small braids twisted around it. It was a very elegant style, and Pandora admired Maiyin's handiwork as she finished. It was after seven by the time she was done.

Pandora chose a beautiful gown she had yet to wear. It was white, which was one of the reasons she hesitated to wear it, embroidered with silver in the shapes of flowers and vines. The neckline was low, plunging to a vee in the front and back with little puffed sleeves high on her arm. It meant, of course, that she would have to wear elbow-length gloves, but she felt what she needed that night was to feel pretty. This dress made her feel like Titania come to life, and she was willing to risk only wearing the dress once for that.

After what had happened that afternoon, she had been tempted to send her regrets, but the earl was a close friend to their father, and Pandora felt that staying at home alone was not what she needed. The best thing to do was go to the ball and try to put the whole thing from her mind.

Besides, she had to help Psyche get a cravat before the end of the Season, which was only nine days away. Her twin hadn't said so, but Pandora believed Psyche was disappointed she hadn't been able to get a single cravat. Pandora had already put the earrings back, but her twin would feel better about things if they at least *tied* for their ownership.

After Maiyin helped her put on her gloves, Pandora went to look at herself in the mirror. It was perfect. Her brow furrowed with concern when she looked at her back, but she sighed with relief that the low bodice didn't expose the bruises; they started at the small of her back to about midway, so there wouldn't be any questioning glances.

She quickly gave Maiyin a hug of gratitude after she grabbed her fan and shawl and went to the sitting room between bedrooms. After a brief knock on Psyche's door, she walked in to see herself…almost. Pandora started to laugh, and when Psyche turned from looking in the mirror, she began to giggle, too.

It wasn't a common occurrence because of the difference in their tastes, but somehow they had chosen the same dress and had also both chosen to wear it at the same time. There were differences, like the pattern of embroidery, but they were the exact same dresses in white. The only other difference that kept the two from looking like mirror images was their hairstyles, and even those were similar.

"Oh, my!" said Psyche through her giggles. "Do you think one of us should change?"

"No, let's stay this way. It will be a lark," said Pandora with a cheeky grin as she walked further into the room. "The Season is almost over, and it is high time we had a little fun."

"I agree," said Psyche as she grabbed her own fan, shawl, and bag.

They left the room and went down the front stairs to find their brothers, Myron and Dorian, waiting for them. They would be going to the ball also as escorts for their sisters. When the two looked up at the twins descending, Dorian scoffed amusedly and Myron guffawed.

"Please, tell me you didn't do this intentionally," chortled Myron.

"No, we didn't, but we've decided it was a lovely idea," said Psyche.

"Lovely idea?" hooted Dorian with a chuckle. "You do realize no one will be able to tell you apart?"

"Exactly," said Pandora with a cheeky grin. "The ones who know us best will have no difficulty, and these things are always *so* boring."

"Yes, well, just you make sure you mind yourselves," said Myron with a grin to soften the sternness of his words. "There is still enough of the Season left that *scandalous behavior will not be tolerated,"* he said, adapting the tone of a society matron.

"Oh, pooh!" said Pandora. "Our looking alike won't cause a scandal."

"No, it's not the looking alike that would be scandalous; it's what you might decide to do while being that way," said Myron.

"Oh, Sham," said Psyche, "we would *never* do anything shocking."

Myron raised his eyebrow dubiously and started to laugh.

"You had *better* behave," he said firmly.

"We will," said Psyche and Pandora in unison.

"And so it begins," chuckled Dorian, taking Pandora's arm as they went out to the carriage waiting for them.

The ride to the earl's residence on Curzon Street, Barneville Court, was brief, but several guests were already there, and dancing had already begun. Lady Sheerness greeted them warmly, kissing them affectionately on both cheeks, and she chuckled with amusement when she saw the girls. She had no trouble telling them apart because of her long association with their parents. Other guests, however, were nonplussed, and heads were constantly turning as they walked by. Psyche and Pandora winked at each other conspiratorially and settled in for what looked to be an entertaining evening.

The girls may have resembled each other to a disconcerting degree, but that didn't detract from partners asking to dance. The men would approach and greet them in a questioning tone, and the girls would usually have to correct them. If they didn't call the wrong name, it was just luck.

Blessedly for Pandora, Islington wasn't there. She wasn't ready to see him again. She wasn't sure she ever wanted to see him again. That would change after time, but she was still too angry and hurt. The Earl of Hendon was also not present, but Pandora hadn't expected he would be; this was a private ball given by people who certainly would *not* invite him. Pandora had realized long ago that the reason his name had not sounded familiar when Lady Ramsey had given it to her was because he had gone to her come-out ball riding his wife's coattails, so to speak. Without anyone there usually responsible for causing her emotional distress, Pandora was able to enjoy the evening with a carefree joy she hadn't felt for quite some time.

Pandora was sitting on the edge of the floor, having a moment without a partner, when she saw Lord Barneville approaching. She had just seen Psyche leaving the room with Lord Georgie, going into the room the countess had set out with food. There was a waltz beginning, and Pandora liked the waltz better than any of the other dances.

"Lady Psyche," he said as he reached her, bowing slightly.

Pandora started to deny it, but she was feeling raffish. She wasn't well-acquainted with Barneville, but there was something about him that affected Psyche. Pandora wanted to find out if it was dislike…or something else.

"Yes, Lord Barneville?" said Pandora with a pleasant smile, holding out her hand for him to kiss her knuckles.

"Might I have this dance?" he asked politely.

Pandora nodded and allowed him to keep his grip on her hand to escort her out. They easily found a place among the other dancers and began to glide across the floor. He was an excellent dancer, which Pandora hadn't expected from his masculine bearing. Still, Islington was also a very good dancer, and she had no doubt of his virility.

"Lord Barneville, you dance very well," said Pandora with a smile.

Lord Barneville arched an eyebrow and looked at her skeptically.

"Really? You don't think I dance like a backwater bumpkin that booze would only improve?"

Pandora's eyes grew round in surprise, and she bit back a chortle.

"Did I *say* that?" she gasped.

"Yes," he said shortly, his lips compressing.

"You must have had lessons then, or have you had some booze?" enquired Pandora, still trying to keep her amusement in check.

"No," said Lord Barneville flatly. He looked at her questioningly for a moment. "You seem to be of surprisingly good cheer this evening. Did you find another *rock*?" he asked disparagingly.

"Rock?" asked Pandora confusedly. Obviously he was referring to a past conversation with Psyche. "No, no more rocks, but all my rocks are lovely," she said blithely. "It's just the Season is ending, and I am so looking forward to returning home to the solarium."

"The solarium?" he asked disbelievingly.

"Yes, you see, that's where all my things are: rocks, books, papyri."

"You have papyri?"

"Oh, yes, lots," said Pandora drolly. Luckily, she was familiar enough with Psyche's possessions in the solarium that this was not a stretch.

"And just what kind of papyri do you have?" asked Lord Barneville, his grip tightening slightly.

Pandora almost winced as he put pressure on the bruises on her back, but she managed to stop herself. There was something he didn't seem to like about Psyche having papyrus scrolls. Pandora found that odd.

"Oh, I don't know…lots," said Pandora noncommittally.

"Indeed," he stated coldly.

"Well, my father has been to Egypt and Greece a few times, and he always manages to bring me something back." She giggled. "One time, he brought me back a maid."

"Hmm," said Lord Barneville. "Lady Psyche, have you been drinking this evening?" he asked casually.

Pandora's eyes opened wide with pretended innocence.

"Oh, no, Lord Barneville," said Pandora with a shake of her head.

"Hmm," he said again, still looking at her suspiciously.

"Of course, I one day hope to go to Egypt and Greece myself," stated Pandora calmly, deciding she should be more of herself if she was going to be convincing as Psyche, which meant she couldn't continue pretending to be empty-headed.

Lord Barneville chuckled.

"I find it unlikely that you will ever go," he said arrogantly.

"And why is that?" asked Pandora archly, finding his attitude toward her sister's dream to be insulting.

"For several reasons."

"Which are?" prodded Pandora, her opinion becoming less favorable.

"First, you don't know anything about either country."

"I do. I speak Greek, Turkish, and Arabic fluently. I know what they eat and what they wear. I even know how they dance."

He looked at her doubtfully.

"What other reasons?"

"You are a woman, and you cannot take care of yourself," said Lord Barneville finally, implying if there were any reasons beyond that, this one was the most important and made all others irrelevant.

Pandora laughed amusedly.

"My dear, Lord Barneville," she chuckled, "you are sadly mistaken."

"Indeed?" he quizzed, insulted by her reaction.

At that moment, the song ended. They were near the back of the room, where the doors were open to the terrace on the rear of the house.

"Would you care to join me on the terrace?" he asked.

Pandora almost declined, but she was enjoying this. She would have to let Psyche know all about it.

"Of course," she said amiably, allowing him to place her hand into the crook of his elbow and lead her through one of the sets of doors.

When they reached the balustrade, he turned to look at her, his expression challenging.

"Now, Lady Psyche, explain to me why I'm mistaken in thinking you couldn't defend yourself against marauding bandits."

"Marauding bandits?" asked Pandora with a blink. "I hadn't thought of marauding bandits, but having a gun would be very clever for that."

"Oh, yes, very clever," he bit out.

Then to Pandora's surprise, he pulled her close to him in an embrace, pinioning her arms at her sides. Her eyes opened wide as she looked at him, and Pandora couldn't help but thinking on closer inspection that he really did have beautiful eyes, almost the color of evergreens.

"What if they get past your gun?" he asked rakishly. "What then?"

Pandora looked up at him, but instead of feeling threatened, she giggled. He was trying to be forward with her sister!

"Oh, Lord Barneville, you're not so frightening as a bandit," she chortled.

He looked askance at her.

"Perhaps not, but it doesn't alter the fact that you can't get away from me," he ground out.

"I could," countered Pandora calmly.

"No, you couldn't," he said coldly.

"Would you like to bet on that?" asked Pandora with a challenging smile.

"Fine. What is your wager?"

"If I can get you to let me go and leave you incapacitated, you'll give me your cravat," said Pandora softly.

He tilted his head back and laughed with deep amusement.

"Oh, that's rich," he chuckled with a wicked smile. "Fine. I accept, but if I win, you will give me a kiss."

"Lord Barneville, how presumptuous of you," said Pandora impudently, "but I accept," she almost purred.

Without a moment of warning to him, Pandora stomped on the toes of one of his feet with her heel, which made him loosen his grip enough for her to bring her arms up between them and break his hold on her. She then gave him a blow to his midsection with the heel of her hand, landing just at the diaphragm and completely taking his breath away. He was bent forward gasping for air, and Pandora pushed at his forehead with her fingertip, knocking him to the ground as he struggled to get his breath back. Pandora dusted her hands together satisfactorily.

"There you have it," she said calmly as she looked at him. "I am free, and you are incapacitated. I'll be waiting inside for my cravat. Ta," she said blithely over her shoulder, strolling back inside.

Psyche was in a chair by the wall, watching the other dancers in a cotillion, when Pandora casually walked over and sat down. Pandora leaned close to speak in her sister's ear.

"Lord Barneville was being brazen with you," teased Pandora.

Psyche turned to look at her twin in alarm.

"Pandora, what did you do?" she asked, raising a hand to her throat.

"*I* didn't do anything, but it will be awhile before Lord Barneville decides to play marauding bandits with *you* again," said Pandora drolly.

Psyche started to chew the side of her thumb worriedly, and Pandora patiently kept her eye to the back of the room to see when Lord Barneville came inside. It took about ten minutes, but he did finally come in. He searched the room with his eyes, and on seeing the two sisters, he stormily stalked toward them. When he reached them, he looked at Psyche furiously, completely ignoring Pandora, which was just as well because her shoulders were shaking with silent laughter. His mouth opened and closed soundlessly before he clenched his jaw and removed his cravat to toss it at Psyche. He raised a finger in the air and started to say something, but he closed his hand into a fist and shook his head before he strode away angrily, leaving the room.

Psyche looked at the cravat in her lap, and her cheeks turned pink at the stares of people nearby who had witnessed the interaction. After a time, she shrugged and nonchalantly folded up the piece of material and placed it in her drawstring bag.

"You cheated," she said mildly to Pandora.

"What? I *never!*" said Pandora in pretended shock. "He gave it to you, not me. What did you do to him, Psyche?"

Pandora and Psyche didn't return home until well after one in the morning, and the ball was still in full swing when they left. Psyche tried to get Pandora to tell her what she had done to make Lord Barneville so angry, but her twin remained mum. All she would tell her sister was that he had insulted Psyche's rocks and papyri, and Pandora had felt it could not go unpunished.

Then Psyche tried to say the cravat should belong to Pandora since she had been the one to make Barneville give it over, but Pandora said she had pretended to be Psyche, and when it had come time to relinquish his cravat, he had given it to the right sister. Pandora also said she had done nothing Psyche wouldn't have done herself. Pandora insisted their wager was tied.

When Pandora got to her room, Maiyin was waiting for her to help take all of the braids out of her hair. Once she had gotten into her shift, Pandora went to sit in front of the mirror, and Maiyin yawned once tiredly before she began to take down Pandora's hair. Pandora was lighthearted after her chicanery with Lord Barneville, and she felt a renewal of the way she had felt at the beginning of the Season; she felt more like herself than she had in a long time.

Because she had gotten some of her old spirit back, Pandora came to a decision she had been putting off for a while. She had hoped it would be one that she wouldn't have to make, but she was left with little choice.

After the day's events, she had been made all too aware of how dangerous Hendon and Castleton were, but she was also reminded she was not the typical helpless female. Dorian hadn't told Islington that Artois was going to be their victim, even though he had assured her that he would. He hadn't done it intentionally; he had simply not taken her seriously, and it had slipped from his mind. Today, when she told Islington what she knew, he believed her, but he didn't appear to have any concern about letting the man know he was threatened. It would have been so much easier if he had.

After today, when Hendon had attempted to lead her into a trap, she knew they wouldn't wait for Artois to go back to Edinburgh before abducting him. She felt guilty her actions had probably caused this acceleration of their plan. Of course, she had no way to verify this, and she hoped she was wrong, but she couldn't wait in London for Artois to arrive to warn him.

Because she wouldn't be coming into contact with Hendon or Castleton, her life would be less threatened, but the task would be no less dangerous. She would be going somewhere she had never been, and she would be going alone. It was perilous—and foolhardy—for her to do this for a man she didn't know, but Pandora couldn't bear the thought of not acting on what she knew, not when there was still time to stop it.

She tried to decide if she was being stubborn and arrogant, thinking *she* was the only one who could do this, but in the end she knew she wasn't.

Dorian and Islington were trying to take care of it, but they weren't thinking about the victim. Forewarned was fore-armed. Warning Artois would be the easiest way to put an end to the whole matter.

Pandora would have to make the journey alone, but she couldn't make herself ready for it without help. There were things she immediately knew she would have to take with her, but having never taken on something like this, there were things about which she was totally ignorant. There were three people she would need to assist her: Maiyin (and, by extension, Keung), Persephone, and Tajik. It would require her to deceive her family, but Pandora made a vow to herself that if she was able to survive it, she would try to never lie to them again. It would take deception to get out of the house, but she would let them know where she was going.

"Maiyin, what would you say if I told you that I need to go to Scotland?" asked Pandora calmly.

"*Scotland?* Why you want to go to Scotland?" asked Maiyin with a chuckle, shaking her head at the very idea.

"Because there is an important man there whose life is in danger," said Pandora solemnly. "It would appear I'm the only one who can save him."

Maiyin looked at Pandora and realized she was being serious.

"You sure no one else can do this?" asked Maiyin searchingly, putting her hands on the girl's shoulders and looking at her reflection in the mirror.

"No, I don't think there is," said Pandora resignedly.

Maiyin sighed and gave her shoulders a squeeze.

"When you planning to go?"

"In ten days," said Pandora. Maiyin raised an eyebrow.

"You going by coach, horse, or foot?"

"Horse," said Pandora, relieved Maiyin was going to help.

"You going to sleep outside or inside?"

"Outside, I think, is going to be the only choice I have."

Maiyin nodded and resumed removing the braids and pins.

"You no worry," stated Maiyin. "I make sure you have everything you need to eat, sleep, and stay healthy just like you at home."

"Thank you, Maiyin."

"*Ayah*, let you just make sure you mother and father know it was all your doing. I want to still have *job* when you come back."

"I'm not going to tell them I'm going until I'm already gone, Maiyin, and I'll make sure they know it was all my fault."

"Hunh," said Maiyin, shaking her head and raising her eyebrows.

Pandora's skin started to tingle with excitement at the thought of going to Edinburgh. She wasn't sure which direction it was from London, other than north, but she had ten days to find out, and Maiyin would make sure she was prepared. And there were still ten days in which Dorian and Islington could find a way to make it unnecessary.

Chapter Fourteen

The close of the Season was very near...only two days away, in fact. Pandora had been steadily and secretively making preparations for going to Edinburgh once she decided she would go. She kept hoping something would happen to make it unnecessary, but as the day drew closer, she had resigned herself to the inevitable. There wasn't much more she needed, and those things would have to wait until the last minute because their absence would be noted: her father's ducal seal and a pistol.

Pandora needed her father's seal if she was going to have any chance of convincing Artois that her message was sincere. Her father's name was well-known and respected, and she would be surprised if the count hadn't heard of him, if not even met him. The count would listen to a message from the duke's daughter, but Pandora would need the seal to prove that she was. She couldn't pack it with her things yet because her father used it on his official papers, which he attended to every day. If it went missing before she left, there would be uproar, and Pandora's chances of going to Edinburgh would disappear. It would cause enough difficulty after she was gone, but by then she would have it with her.

She had decided to take a pistol for several reasons, not the least of which being that she would be a woman traveling alone. She wouldn't encounter Castleton or Hendon; they would be waiting in London for the count to arrive. However, they weren't the only criminals on English or Scottish soil, and Pandora felt safer having a gun should she chance to meet any of them.

Her brothers and father had taught all the girls how to clean, load, and fire a pistol. Persephone was an excellent shot, and no one (not even her brothers) could load a gun faster. Pandora was better at throwing knives and shooting a bow (and she would have one of those, too), but she was *capable* with a gun; she was usually able to hit what she aimed for, but the closer the target, the better. In her opinion, that was all that mattered. She hoped she would never have to use it, but it would be better to have it and not need it than to need it and have felt too squeamish to carry it with her.

Her father kept the pistols and other firearms in a cabinet in his study (where his seal was kept as well). The cabinet was always locked, but Pandora was criminally good at picking locks. Her family had long ago made her promise that if something had a lock, she wouldn't open it even if she could. This would be the only time she had ever broken that promise; she *had* to have the gun and the seal.

Pandora wasn't entirely sure what Maiyin was putting into a bag for her, but Pandora stressed it couldn't be anything too heavy. Cast iron cookware, china, and a tea set were right out—aside from the fact Pandora wouldn't know what to do with them anyhow. Maiyin had only laughed and smiled confidently, telling Pandora not to worry—everything would be taken care of. Pandora was relieved. Maiyin was keeping the bag (or possibly even bags) in her and Keung's room in the servants' quarters, and she would see that it made its way to the stables when the time arrived.

Pandora had thought about trying to travel by mail coach, but there was no guarantee an older woman would already be riding to provide her a chaperone. Even if there were another woman riding, she might not be traveling all the way to Edinburgh. To ride unchaperoned in the coach would not only be unthinkable, it would also not be allowed. Pandora couldn't take anyone with her—not that any of her sisters would go. Aside from that, her family couldn't know because they would try to stop her.

Because Pandora wouldn't have anyone with her, she couldn't enjoy the comfort of staying at an inn, either. She would have to sleep in the elements, and hopefully it wouldn't rain. Luckily, the weather was warm enough she wouldn't have to worry about getting cold, at least not until she got further north, but she didn't relish getting wet. Maiyin would give her something for that. She had said, after all, that Pandora would be able to sleep like she did at home. Pandora was sure that was an exaggeration, but she was also sure Maiyin would try her best to accomplish it.

Pandora had already borrowed some of Persephone's clothes...men's clothes. Her sister had looked at her oddly, and Pandora hadn't elaborated on why she needed them, but she had requested two changes of clothes, boots, a hat, and a riding coat. Persephone had only shaken her head and given them to her sister. They were neither fancy nor shabby; they were serviceable and inconspicuous, which suited Pandora perfectly. If Pandora wore men's clothes, at least from a distance, she wouldn't look suspicious. The clothes wouldn't disguise that she was a woman on close inspection, which was why she still couldn't stay at an inn.

The only other thing that had remained was enlisting Tajik's help. Pandora told the stable master she wanted to ride Bellerophon to Edinburgh. He didn't ask why, and she didn't think he would mention her plans to anyone else. Bellerophon could make the journey, but Pandora wanted Tajik's help to make sure her horse would be able to do it and *survive*. Pandora couldn't bear the thought of doing this and losing him. Tajik said he would see to it and that he would tell her more when it was time for her to leave.

Pandora had already packed away most of her things for their return to Wilderland. She had a few gowns out that would be packed as she no longer needed them, but everything else had been put into trunks that would be transported home by wagon. Hers weren't the only things going. All of her family had begun packing to leave, and after Pandora's father finished attending to his business after the end of the Season, the house would be mostly dust-clothed with a minimal staff until the start of Parliament next year. The house wouldn't be completely closed up, as there were occasions when it was necessary for her father or older brothers to come back to town at other times, but the only time the full use of the house was needed was during the Season when the family came *en masse*.

The family traveled by different methods. The duke and the three older boys rode on horseback, while the duchess and the three younger boys went by coach. There was a second coach for the girls, which carried Arachne and Eurydice for the entire trip, but Persephone invariably rode horseback all the way with her brothers. The twins would alternate, riding at times in the coach with their sisters and sometimes riding on horseback.

This time, because the duke and duchess wouldn't be returning at the same time as the rest of the family, Arachne and Eurydice would be traveling in the coach with their younger brothers. Myron and Dorian wouldn't be going until their parents did. Gregory wanted to get back to Glamorgan to attend to his ship docked at Swansea, so he would be going by horseback, but he wouldn't be riding in attendance on his sisters all the way because he would go to Swansea before returning to Wilderland. Pandora and Psyche had already decided they would be able to make the entire journey on horseback, leaving the other coach for their parents when they were ready to go home.

The servants would travel with the baggage. Some rode horseback, particularly Tajik and the other stable hands, who would see to the horses. The lady's maids would travel by coach. Some of the staff had already left for Wilderland to assist with preparation for the family's arrival. There was always a lot of hectic activity involved in arrival and departure for the family; Pandora felt it would be simple for her to slip away before anyone realized she was gone.

They had, of course, decided all of this after Pandora had determined she would be going to Edinburgh, after Pandora had already realized she couldn't return to Wilderland until the plot to kidnap Artois was stopped. She had agreed to the travel plans because she kept hoping Islington and Dorian would find a way to stop it before the twelfth, but it began to look less likely. With only two days left, it was improbable.

Pandora acquired a nice, travel-sized road map that she could put into a saddlebag. It showed the roads and towns along her route, and she had been studying it over the past week to familiarize herself with where she would need to turn from the main road to avoid large towns and still maintain a fairly straight course. Actually, the straighter she kept her path, the easier it would be to avoid the large towns. Unfortunately, it didn't show her any natural obstructions along the way, other than rivers. It wasn't detailed enough to show her every stream, and it showed nothing of the Pennines or Cheviot Hills. She would have to hope the route she planned to take was as simple as it looked on the map. When she went into the map seller's on High Holborn, the clerk thought it odd for a woman to purchase a map, but he didn't question Pandora; a woman's money was just as sound as a man's.

Pandora bought a compass and telescope at one of the shops on Bond Street. The compass was a necessity. If she traveled a course that was just slightly northwest, she would get to Edinburgh. The roads wouldn't keep to that heading, but since she would be on horseback, it would allow her to go across country if need be. The spyglass had been an impulsive purchase. She didn't know why she would need it, but it seemed like a good idea at the time.

Nearly every day, she asked Dorian if he and Islington were any nearer to catching the conspirators. Dorian was always noncommittal, and he soon became impatient with Pandora constantly asking. She also asked if they had sent a letter to Artois to warn him. Her brother flatly said no, and they had no intention of doing so; they would apprise him once he reached London. It frustrated her that they couldn't see the logic of warning him *now*. She tried to convince Dorian the conspirators wouldn't wait until he left London for Edinburgh and would take him before he ever reached the City, but she couldn't tell him why she felt that way without exposing herself and Islington. She suspected he didn't let Islington know what she thought…again.

Tonight was to be her mother's final ball of the Season. Pandora asked her mother if she could see the invitation list. The duchess thought it to be an impertinent question, but she gave the list to Pandora to examine. With some trepidation, she saw that the Marchioness of Morecambe had been invited. Pandora wouldn't mind seeing Georgiana again, but she would be perfectly happy to never see Georgiana's husband—ever. Her mother had invited her usual circle of friends: the Sheernesses, the Stranraers, the Lundeys, the Earl of Lochardale, the Marchioness of Ewes, and so on. All told, it didn't look like her mother had invited nearly as many as she had to attend Pandora and Psyche's come-out ball, but there would still be well over one hundred people present—Islington, Selena, and their mother among them. Pandora hoped some of them would send their regrets. It was, after all, only two days from the end of the Season. Pandora hoped some of them would have already left town, but as the day drew closer, and her mother received responses, it appeared most everyone who had been invited would be attending.

Pandora didn't know why she was dreading the ball. It couldn't be nearly as bad as some of the other social debacles she had endured, and if worse came to worst, she could always escape to her bedroom. Other than the people, social events were tolerable; of course, she couldn't have one without the other. The reason Pandora wasn't looking forward to it was that it was a distraction she didn't need at the moment.

Her grace would be serving food and drink the same as she had for the come-out ball. A sit-down dinner for more than one hundred would be a nightmare to arrange. If the ball were at Wilderland, it wouldn't be a problem, but there wasn't enough room in town to accommodate it.

Pandora wasn't especially looking forward to seeing Islington, and yet when she thought about it, her heart would flutter excitedly. She hadn't seen him since the day on Drury, and she had come to accept he had done what was necessary. She still couldn't quite forgive him for not warning her, but she had forgiven him the rest. She wasn't sure what there was between them. She thought at times that he cared for her, but then there were times when she felt as if he was using her. That was why she wasn't sure she wanted to see him again: she couldn't bear to continue being treated that way.

She had no idea what would happen between them in two days when the Season ended. She would see Selena again; if things continued as they seemed to be heading between her friend and Dorian, she would be seeing a great deal more of Selena. Pandora was unsure whether she would see Islington again. The uncertainty made her anxious; she had never expected she would feel for him the way she did, and the thought of not seeing him at least occasionally troubled her in ways she hadn't thought possible.

Pandora had left out a very light and airy gown for the ball. It was made of several layers of mull in blue, green, and red, all shot through with gold. The low-cut, fitted bodice was made of all three colors combined, which made it appear to be a solid color of emerald green. The skirt had tiers where the different colors ended, which created a very fluttery effect due to the lightness of the material. The sleeves were actually split oversleeves made of the three colors with small puffs of white mull underneath that came to just above midway on her upper arm. The edge of the bodice, undersleeve, and bottom layer of the skirt were all embroidered with gold tinsel in a narrow pattern of tight, intertwining vines. The dressmaker near Pandora's home had outdone herself on creating the dress. It had to be the most beautiful gown Pandora had ever seen.

Maiyin did Pandora's hair in a style similar to the one she had used for the Sheernesses' ball, but rather than several braids around the central knot, she made one braid near the crown of Pandora's head and created the knot around that. After she had the hair pinned in place, she then twined the braid around it, securing it with pins and two ornate gold combs from China. Her face was framed by the natural ringlets around the edges that were too short to be swept up into the coiffure. It was perfect.

Pandora wore short, crocheted gloves with the gown. Being short-sleeved, it was expected for her to wear elbow-length ones, but with only two days of the Season left, Pandora was ready to thumb her nose one more time. She was even tempted to wear no gloves at all, but her mother wouldn't be happy. At least she was wearing gloves. She wore a simple gold cross on a chain around her neck and small garnet drops in her ears. She wanted to avoid wearing anything that detracted from the elegance of the dress.

After she gave herself a once-over in the floor length mirror, she grabbed her fan—an exotic Oriental one that had been presented to her with the gold combs as a birthday gift from Maiyin and Keung last year; then she went to the door of Psyche's bedroom. Her sister was, as usual, still getting ready, but she was almost done.

"You know, one would think from how early you get up from bed that you wouldn't always be going this slowly," said Pandora with a grin.

"Why do you think I get up so early?" returned Psyche with her own grin.

Psyche had chosen to wear a dress made of soft rose silk with an overskirt in matching tulle. The edges of the gown were embroidered with a deeper pink thread and gold tinsel. The sleeves were short and puffed but were slashed with an undersleeve of a silk that matched the deeper pink thread of the embroidery. It was very pretty and suited Psyche perfectly. She wore matching slippers and also chose just a simple gold cross and small pearls for her jewelry. Chrissoula had styled her hair into a loose knot that she had woven through with a string of pearls. Unlike Pandora, however, she wore elbow-length gloves.

"You're wearing that perfume again," said Psyche, leaning close to her sister to inhale.

"Oh, don't start that again," groaned Pandora.

"I can't help it; it just smells so good," she sighed.

"Come on, Psy, I'm not a flower, and you're not a bumblebee," chuckled Pandora, linking her arm through that of her sister. "Would you like me to see if Maiyin can make you a perfume of your very own?"

"Could you?" asked Psyche excitedly.

"I think it can be arranged," said Pandora dryly with a nod of her head and an amused smile over her sister's enthusiasm.

"You know, I don't think we pay our dressmaker enough," said Psyche as they left her room to go down the front stairs.

"I don't think Janet feels underpaid," said Pandora. "*How* much work do we bring her? I sincerely doubt she has to worry if she never has another customer besides our family."

"I suppose," said Psyche. "She does such fabulous work, though."

"Too right," agreed Pandora.

The two of them were running late, as usual, but they happened to catch their mother and father near the bottom of the stairs rather than at the door. The duke and duchess watched them descend with proud smiles and hugged and kissed each of them in turn as they reached the bottom.

"I believe this is your last ball," said the duchess. "Did it turn out to be as ghastly as you had thought it would be?" she asked them.

"It was tolerable," said Psyche dully.

"I'm still alive," said Pandora noncommittally.

Neither twin seemed enthusiastic, and their parents chuckled.

"Well, now it's done. I can tell you're thinking you won't want to do it again, but you can reconsider," said the duchess with a smile.

"Mamà, I don't mean to sound impudent, but can't they have a Season without all the *people?*" asked Pandora sourly.

Her parents laughed outright.

"Not bloody likely," said her father with a chuckle.

"Xan!" gasped the duchess, swatting at his arm with her fan for talking like that in front of the girls. "You two go on to the ball room," she said as she handed them their dance cards. "I think we've had about twenty arrive so far. Arachne and your brothers are already there. Now that you've had a whole season to become acquainted, I don't think you will need an escort, will you?"

"No, Mamà," said the twins in unison. They looked at each other and grinned.

Their parents watched them walk away with pleased smiles. Despite the girls' dislike of having to participate in a London season, both had managed to comport themselves well. They had done as their parents asked, and the duke and duchess were satisfied they had done their best for the girls. The duchess wouldn't be upset if neither of them wanted to return to London for another season; she herself hadn't been overly fond of it when she was a young girl either, which was one of the reasons she had been so happy her father had received a diplomatic position that required her to live in Venice, allowing them to return to her birthplace...and his. It had taken eleven children and twenty-five years of marriage to a wonderful man for her grace to develop an appreciation for the Season. She suspected it would take the same for her daughters.

Pandora and Psyche walked down the hall to the ball room linked arm-in-arm, talking and teasing with each other as they went...at a fairly slow pace. Neither was very concerned about reaching the room; their siblings were there to act as hosts. They couldn't hear music playing, but the musicians in the box would soon begin the first tune. Unfortunately, the hall was not nearly so long as they would have liked, and they eventually arrived at the double doors of the room. Tannaz opened them as Psyche and Pandora approached, and the two girls glided in, still holding onto each other.

They paused for a moment after they entered, taking a quick perusal of the room to see which twenty guests had already arrived. It was easy enough to spot Lord Georgie and Sir James Klein. Both were always good company, usually the first to arrive, and seemed to travel together. The Earls and Countesses of Lundey, Stranraer, and Sheerness were there, which was no surprise, as they were all very close friends of the duke and duchess. Also present were the Baron de Barneville and two of his younger siblings, the fraternal twins Alex and Amalie. Mrs. Ellsworth and Ms. Mahone had arrived, but there was no sign of Gareth. Viscount Drake had come, accompanied by his sister, Penny, but his fiancée, Lilly, wasn't there. After she had sent her regrets for the duchess's dinner party, she hadn't returned to town. Also present was Luke McPike, a friend of Myron's who was in town from Glasgow. Pandora wasn't sure how her brother had met the man, but he was handsome and polite...if aloof. The Earl of Lochardale was there already, as was the Marchioness of Ewes and her son, the Marquess of Ewes, who was home on a brief leave from his post as an attaché for Wellington.

Then, to Pandora's surprise, she saw Georgiana was there, unaccompanied by her husband. She was engaged in conversation with Myron. Pandora was curious if the Earl of Hendon planned to attend. She could only hope he would not.

"I suppose we should go talk to people, shouldn't we?" asked Psyche.

"Yes, I suppose we must," said Pandora just as unenthusiastically.

Pandora first walked over to Dorian, who was talking with Lord Georgie and Sir James. After chatting for a moment, all three signed their names onto her dance card, Dorian several times. That wasn't her intention when she went to speak with them. She wasn't upset, though; by now she was resigned to it. She would see what they had selected in a moment; there were other people she needed to greet.

Pandora was steadily trying to make her way over to Georgiana, but there were several people she had to stop to talk with before she could reach where the young woman still stood talking with Myron not far from the doors leading onto the terrace. Pandora idly wondered what the two of them were talking about. Their voices were soft, so the conversation wouldn't carry above the other chatter, but by their expressions it appeared to be something serious. The two of them seemed to be well acquainted.

At one point, Pandora was talking with both Psyche and Lord Barneville. He was still unhappy with the events of the last ball where the twins were present, and he was trying to engage Psyche in an argument about anything and everything to make up for it. Pandora nervously wondered if it would have been better if she *had* told Psyche what she'd done to make him so angry. It was irrelevant now, though, because Psyche was holding her own. To Pandora, it was a bit like watching a ball being tossed back and forth—never-ending and not very exciting.

"You will not say another word about my cuneiform tablets, Lord Barneville. They are *mine* to do with as I will," said Psyche firmly, a thin white line beginning to form around her lips from clenching her teeth to avoid saying what she really wanted to the arrogant clod.

Those had to be the rocks he had insulted when talking to Pandora.

"But they need to be taken to the Museum to be studied, to be deciphered," he argued back.

Psyche looked at him coldly. "They *are* being studied and deciphered, Lord Barneville."

He clenched his jaw. "I meant by people who know what they're doing," he sneered.

Pandora bit her tongue to keep from inciting an argument of her own. He had just said the wrong thing to Psyche.

"How could I resist such honeyed words," said Psyche sweetly, but she had an angry glint in her eyes. He was close to being pummeled to death.

"I shall take my leave of such pleasant company," interjected Pandora mildly. "I look forward to our waltz later, Lord Barneville."

"As do I, Lady Pandora," he said with a smile, brushing her knuckles.

"I must, however, say one thing: you would stand a better chance of convincing her with marauding bandits," she said with a charming smile.

Both Psyche and Lord Barneville looked at her with shock, their jaws slack in amazement at her audacity, but for entirely different reasons. Pandora gave them a brief, slight curtsy and moved on to the corner where she was finally able to get to Georgiana and Myron.

"Lord Neath, it's very unkind of you to monopolize Lady Morecambe's company this way," she said pleasantly when she reached them.

Myron tilted his head sideways in puzzlement, unaccustomed to his sister addressing him by his title. Pandora had at least remembered the formalities; she wasn't sure how familiar he was with the marchioness.

"I was just catching up with Georgiana on things since last Season. This is the first chance we've had to talk," said Myron casually.

Oh, so it's that *familiar.* Pandora looked at Georgiana, seeing her cheeks were a flushed with embarrassment. Pandora gave her a quick once-over and was relieved that she didn't see any noticeable bruises.

"My sister is right, though; I've taken up entirely too much of your time," said Myron to Georgiana with a warm smile. He took her hand and kissed her knuckles. He didn't immediately release his hold.

"Thank you, Myron, for everything," said Georgiana softly.

The two girls watched him walk over to Gregory where he was talking with Luke McPike, but Myron would occasionally glance in their direction.

"I say, Georgiana, but I think my brother is quite taken with you," said Pandora speculatively.

Georgiana blushed. "Yes, I suppose he is," she admitted.

After a moment's thought, Pandora's eyes grew wide in surprise and instant recognition.

"He wanted to marry you last Season, didn't he?" she gasped. "*You* were the girl he was so upset over, aren't you?"

Georgiana's face saddened. "Yes, again," she said softly.

Pandora remembered last August that Myron had been upset his offer of marriage wasn't accepted by a girl. Pandora hadn't been involved in the Season and wasn't familiar with the names, so she hadn't remembered them; it had taken him awhile to calm down and cheer up. In the end, he consoled himself by thinking he was too young to be married anyhow.

"Why did you not accept his offer?" asked Pandora stiffly. She was upset the girl didn't seem to think her brother acceptable.

"Oh, I would have, and I *wanted* to," said Georgiana wistfully. "Unfortunately, by the time he asked, my father and Hendon had already come to an agreement, and our betrothal was announced." She shrugged defeatedly. "Once it was done, my father wouldn't change his mind. It was as if he thought he was honor-bound to proceed."

Pandora clenched her jaw angrily as she thought about Maiyin's comment on grain in the market and that it was her father's pride that had caused Georgiana so much misery. Pandora rubbed her arm comfortingly.

"Is there no chance you could divorce?" she asked hopefully.

Georgiana laughed. "Not likely," she said bitterly. "When the words 'until death do you part' were spoken, they were never more true."

"I am so sorry," said Pandora softly.

"Oh, no matter," said Georgiana, waving a hand through the air with a pretended calmness. "Did you have something you wanted to talk with me about?" she asked brightly.

"Yes, actually, I did," said Pandora unsurely. Georgiana looked at her expectantly. "I noticed Lord Hendon is not here; will he be coming?"

Georgiana smiled blissfully. "No, he has quit the Season early."

"Oh, my," said Pandora nervously.

"Whatever is wrong?" asked Georgiana with concern, noting the way Pandora paled.

"I'm fine," said Pandora with a reassuring smile. "It was just a bit of a surprise he would have already gone. Do you know if he's left town?"

Georgiana's forehead furrowed thoughtfully. "I'm not sure. He does not appear to have taken anything with him, but he's not at the house and hasn't been for the past two or three days."

It was Pandora's turn to grow thoughtful. If he were going to Edinburgh, or some point between there and London, he wouldn't have gone empty-handed. She wondered if he was still in town, possibly staying in company with Castleton to finalize their plans. In the end, it didn't alter the fact that she needed to get to Scotland as quickly as possible. She was convinced more than ever that they weren't going to wait. She was, however, relieved he wouldn't be attending her mother's ball.

"I suppose we can hope he never comes back," said Pandora finally with a chuckle. Georgiana was able to laugh as well.

"I could only be so lucky," she sighed. Her face grew serious after a moment. "I hope I didn't cause you any trouble," she said solemnly.

Pandora looked at her perplexedly. "In what way could you have caused me trouble?" she asked dismissively.

"The night at Almack's, when we met, my husband caught me coming out of the powder room." Her face grew dispirited. "He made me tell him everything we talked about," she said softly.

Pandora put a hand to her throat in dismay. It made sense to her then, and she felt like more of an idiot than she had ever felt in her life. The whole thing had been a ploy. Just as she had confirmed who his victim was by information from Georgiana, Hendon had been able to confirm that Pandora knew of his plan. He wouldn't have needed to stand outside the residence for hours to find out if anyone was about; a tip to the right servant or just a casual glance as he went by for a walk would have been sufficient. All of the watching had been done intentionally to lure her away from home and dispose of her. Stupidly, she had fallen for it. Pandora couldn't believe she had been so foolish.

She did not, however, blame Georgiana. She looked at the way Georgiana cowered away from her, waiting for some type of physical reprisal. Pandora surprised her by reaching over to quickly give her a hug, patting her back soothingly. She released her and took her hands.

"Georgiana, you need never feel guilty about anything that man makes you do. You have to survive anyway you can, and I understand that," said Pandora with a gentle smile.

Georgiana smiled back. "Thank you."

While they had been talking, the musicians had started playing a quadrille. Pandora took a quick glance at her card and saw it had not been chosen by anyone. As a matter of fact, the first song on her card was the minuet. Either her mother had handed out the wrong dance cards or the musicians were only waiting until the duke and duchess entered to formally commence the ball.

Pandora scanned the room and saw several more people had arrived. Among them were Selena and Lady Bardsey. Her friend waved briefly when she saw Pandora glance in her direction. Islington wasn't in sight. Pandora pretended it didn't concern her, but it did. She looked at Georgiana.

"I see more people I need to talk to," she said with an apologetic smile. "Will you write me occasionally to let me know how you are doing until I see you next Season?" she asked hopefully.

"I'll try," said Georgiana, returning her smile. "Hendon...he...," she trailed off.

"I understand."

Pandora made her way to where Selena was standing with her mother.

"Hallo, Selena," she said, taking her friend's hands. "I'm so glad you could make it. It's nice to see you again, Lady Bardsey."

"And you," said Lady Bardsey with a warm smile. "I'm sorry I was unable to attend your mother's dinner party."

Pandora waved a hand in the air dismissively.

"Perfectly understandable," she said. "Will Lord Islington be attending this evening?" she asked as nonchalantly as possible.

"He said he was," said Selena. She shrugged. "He probably just wanted to stop by the club first."

Pandora wouldn't enquire further on his whereabouts while his mother was there. She was already looking at Pandora speculatively, as if Pandora's interest in her son was more than casual. It was, but it wasn't something Pandora wanted to be questioned on, not by his mother or anyone else.

She continued to talk with them. Although the duke and duchess hadn't entered the room, some of the guests had already begun dancing to the music being played. They had yet to play the minuet, however, and would not until Pandora's parents came in. They had just finished a country dance and were beginning a waltz when Myron walked over to her.

"Excuse me, Lady Selena and Lady Bardsey, but I wish to dance with my sister," he said with a charming smile.

Pandora tilted her head thoughtfully, but she allowed him to lead her onto the floor after she said her goodbyes to the women. His expression was troubled as they began to dance, and Pandora could see he was getting ready to ask her something.

"How do you know Georgiana?" he asked bluntly. Pandora blinked.

"I met her at Almack's about a fortnight past." He nodded.

"Have you met her husband?"

"Yes, I have, and he's a *terrible* man! Thank God he's going to leave her alone at least for a month."

Myron looked at her sharply. "How do you know he's going to be gone that long? Even Georgiana didn't know that," he said suspiciously.

Pandora paled as she realized what she had said.

"Pandora, what do you know?"

Pandora wasn't sure she wanted to tell him what she knew because it would also come out what had happened to his friend.

"Pandora, tell me what you know," demanded Myron, and Pandora gave him a worried look.

"Myron, do you remember when I said there were two men planning to kidnap someone from Edinburgh?"

"Yes, that was a lovely cock-and-bull story."

"Myron, it was no story. Hendon and a man named Castleton intend to kidnap and murder the comte d'Artois."

Myron looked at her in disbelief. "You cannot be serious!" he said exasperatedly and just a little angrily. Pandora shook her head.

"I am deadly serious," said Pandora earnestly. "Dorian and Lord Islington will verify it. We have no *physical* proof they're planning this, but the circumstantial evidence is convincing. Dorian and Islington are trying to find Castleton and hopefully put a stop to it, but Hendon is not only evil, he's also very smart. He's already killed one man and gotten away with it." She wouldn't tell him what had almost happened to her.

Myron still looked at her doubtfully, but she seemed sincere. She had also said their brother and Islington would back it for her so it could be likely.

"Who has he already killed?" asked Myron indulgently.

Pandora didn't want to say, but at Myron's stony look, she decided she might as well confess as much of it as she could.

"The Marquess of Tarlborough," she said softly, and she couldn't look him in the eye.

"Pandora, that's not funny," said Myron angrily.

"I know it isn't," she snapped back. "How could you possibly think I would invent something like this for fun?"

"Hendon killed Bertram Batts?" he asked tightly.

"*Ah-hah-hah*! My *hand*!" gasped Pandora as her brother tightened his grip on her hand painfully, unconscious of what he was doing.

Myron quickly loosened his hold once he was aware, and Pandora wiggled her fingers to return sensation to them. She looked at her brother's face and saw an emotion there she would never have thought to see: rage. In all her life, she could never recall seeing him look that way. It worried her, and it also frightened her. She hoped there might be something she could do to defuse the situation.

"At first, the marquess was an accomplice to their plan, Myron, but he *did* try to get out of it. He threatened to go to the authorities with what he knew so they killed him. That it was Papá's building just happened to be an unfortunate coincidence."

Myron clenched his jaw and nodded, giving her a tight smile. He wouldn't look at her again, and Pandora could see what she told him did nothing to dilute his anger. He was thinking about something very seriously, and it made Pandora anxious. She hoped he wouldn't do something foolish. Given time, his reason would return, and he wouldn't be contemplating what she feared he was. Pandora almost wished she hadn't told him, but he deserved to know the truth. Now that he knew, any lingering doubt he may have had about their father's responsibility could be laid to rest. Still, he was now faced with the knowledge that his friend had considered committing a criminal act for financial gain.

When the dance ended Myron kissed her gently on the temple.

"Thank you for telling me, Pandora," he said softly before he walked away from her.

She worriedly watched after him for a moment from where she stood before walking to the edge of the floor. Her mother and father had finally entered the room, and the musicians began the tune for the minuet that officially began the event. Pandora glanced at her card and saw it had not been claimed, and neither had the next, a cotillion. The third dance would be a quadrille, and it had Lord Georgie's name on. Pandora sighed with relief. She was going to the refreshment tables in the gallery for a glass of punch.

After she reached the room, she went to the table with the punch bowls and asked Jens, the footman in attendance, to pour her a glass of the champagne punch. He gave it to her with a pleasant smile, and Pandora went to sit in one of the chairs along the side of the room, sipping thoughtfully.

She was still deeply chagrined by Hendon's ability to trick her. He would have needed to find someone on her family's staff who worked in the stables to learn her riding tendencies. She didn't believe whoever told him had done it out of spite; their servants were all very loyal. Considering Hendon had appeared the next morning, he had probably gotten the information from Jim outside Almack's. She had no doubt of his respect and devotion.

Hendon would have easily known their driver because of her family's crest on the door of the coach. It could have been as simple as Hendon leading the coachman to believe he was enamored of her and wished to "chance" upon her in the park. It would have been credible. Then all it had taken was for her to see him in the vicinity of Artois's house, and she was hooked, as he knew she would be. For all she knew, Castleton might not even be in London anymore; he could be at a point between the city and Edinburgh lying in wait for the count. In any event, Hendon had managed to manipulate her with a frightening ease.

She soon finished her glass of punch and went for another. The minuet was almost over; then there would be the cotillion before she would have to find Lord Georgie. There were a few other people in the gallery, but most were in the ballroom; the ball had just begun, so none of them had managed to work up an appetite or become thirsty yet. Pandora wasn't thirsty, either; she needed the punch to steady her nerves. By the time she finished the second glass, she was able to breathe a little easier.

She then looked at her dance card. She was particularly curious which dances Dorian had chosen. She wasn't exactly sure how many he had marked, but it was more than three. To her dismay and aggravation, she saw he had only chosen a country dance for himself; for the other *three*, he had penciled in *Vis. Islington.* According to Dorian, she and Islington were going to dance two waltzes and a cotillion.

Pandora wasn't pleased Dorian had taken it upon himself to play matchmaker for the two of them. She was tempted to scribble through them, but she decided to leave it be. Islington had, as yet, not arrived. To her relief, most of the lines were blank, even if most of them were lumped together, giving her several dances in succession with none at the end of the evening. She no longer felt like dancing and was looking forward to the last dance claimed on her card so she would be able to leave.

Pandora was working on her third glass of punch when she was approached by Lady Bardsey. The cotillion had begun, and there were more people coming into the room for refreshment because of the dancing before the ball's official beginning. Pandora stood from her chair when it appeared Lady Bardsey did not intend to sit.

"Will you walk with me?" she asked Pandora after greeting her.

Pandora looked at her with bewilderment for a moment.

"Of course," she said amiably.

The older woman linked her arm through Pandora's at the elbow and led her through one of the side doors of the gallery, taking her into one of the hallways along either edge of the ballroom. The doors into the ballroom were open, but there weren't any people in the hall. The doors into the other rooms that lined the hall were closed—rooms like her father's study, the library, and the family's private sitting room. Pandora waited for the marchioness to begin the conversation because she was sure the woman hadn't asked her to walk simply for the exercise. She hadn't long to wait.

"Lady Pandora, I will be frank: what are your intentions toward my son?" she asked with a pleasant tone.

Pandora blinked in surprise.

"I beg your pardon?" she asked, completely nonplussed.

"My son has asked for your hand, has he not?"

Pandora was astounded he would have mentioned that to his mother. She could only hope he hadn't provided her with details of the circumstances that prompted it.

"Well, yes, he has asked me to marry him, but I cannot," she answered calmly.

The marchioness stopped walking and turned to face Pandora, her expression pleasant but stern.

"If you *cannot* marry my son, as you have stated it, then I would beg you to stop tormenting him," she said firmly.

"What...? I...? Torment *him*?" gasped Pandora, incoherently speechless.

The marchioness resumed walking with her, seemingly unaware of the way Pandora's mouth worked soundlessly; Pandora was so dumbfounded she could not find the words.

"From everything my son and your brother have told me, you are a wonderful girl. You must be in order for my son to care for you as he does. I think I would be pleased to have you as a daughter, but *I* cannot allow you to continue leading him on. Do you understand?"

Pandora was still mute with disbelief. She couldn't breathe. She thought she was going to faint. What had Islington been telling her?

"I—I...," stuttered Pandora. "Yes, Lady Bardsey," she finally got out. It was all she could think of saying to make the woman leave off.

Lady Bardsey patted the hand of the arm she had linked through hers before releasing it.

"Good, I'm glad we understand one another," she said with a smile.

Pandora watched her go back into the ballroom with a stunned expression. She managed to walk back to the gallery and get another glass of punch before sinking bonelessly into a chair. She drained the cup just as the cotillion ended. She managed to regain enough of her senses by then to realize she needed to find Lord Georgie. Luckily, he was already in the refreshment room and approached her just as she stood to go in search of him.

Pandora made her way through the quadrille without much thought to the steps. She was able to give Lord Georgie sensible answers if he asked a question when the movements of the dance brought them together, but she was feeling dulled from all the shocks she had received over the past hour-and-a-half. She was also tipsy from all the drinking she had done within the same period. Granted, it had only been champagne punch, but she had four glasses.

Pandora was tempted to beg off the rest of the ball and retreat to her room, but she wasn't quite ready to give in yet. She consoled herself by reasoning there couldn't possibly be anything more upsetting that could happen. If she went outside for some air, it would help clear her head and put her back in the right frame of mind.

Unfortunately, when the quadrille ended, Sir James arrived to claim her for a country dance. Pandora danced—again—without much concentration, which was a good thing because she couldn't get out of her mind what Lady Bardsey had said.

How could the woman think Pandora was tormenting Islington? It was so ludicrous it bordered on pathetic. It would be more logical if his mother had said *he* was tormenting *Pandora*. Islington said he would speak to her father, but it wasn't an offer of marriage; it was an act of pride. At no time beyond that had he said he still intended to speak to her father, and to Pandora's knowledge, he had never followed through on it. Her father would have told her if he had.

Why would Islington tell Lady Bardsey? No one knew of that day in the gazebo; Pandora thought that would be the end of it. Maiyin was aware something had happened, but she wasn't going to force Pandora to marry anyone, and she was certainly not going to tell anyone. Pandora could only speculate about what Islington had told his mother, and since he wasn't there to provide a reckoning of it, Pandora was left to stew in outrage.

After the country dance, Alex Nichols, Lord Barneville's younger brother, was there to take her for a galop. Pandora was feeling put out. She should have marked through some of the dances on her card to allow herself a free moment in between. Apparently, unlike at her come-out ball, the duchess had not left a few songs off to naturally provide these intermissions. Pandora hadn't expected that. If her mother had left some of the songs off, she had made the time between them much too long.

Pandora only had time to catch her breath at the end of the galop, a hand to her chest as she tried to slow her racing heart, when Lord Barneville approached her with a grim expression. She looked at him with trepidation, sure she was going to collapse from exhaustion.

"Shall we, Lady Pandora?" he asked, holding his hand out to her.

Reluctantly, she took it and let him lead her onto the floor for their waltz. *At least it will be slower*. The music began, and they started the graceful, gliding steps of the dance.

Lord Barneville didn't speak to her at first, but his forehead was wrinkled in thought as they danced. Eventually, he looked down at her. She smiled up at him amiably.

"Lady Pandora, about your comment from earlier," he said slowly.

"Yes, Lord Barneville?" she asked pleasantly.

"I find it peculiar you would say such a thing," he said. "I asked your sister, and she swears she didn't tell you what happened on the terrace."

"Which terrace?" she asked with pretended confusion.

His forehead wrinkled uncertainly. "The terrace at my father's home."

"Oh, *that* terrace. You see, I wasn't sure; *a lot* of houses in London have terraces," she stated flippantly.

"Indeed," he replied reservedly. He looked askance at her for a moment then shook his head as if to dismiss a thought from his mind. "Your sister may be many things, but I've never noted her to be dishonest. If she didn't tell you what happened, why did you make that comment?"

"What happened?" queried Pandora blankly.

"There was a…oh, blast it all! Never *mind*," he stated with a hint of frustration. Pandora tried to hide the amused twitching of her mouth as she heard him continue to mutter under his breath for some time.

The dance ended, and Barneville escorted her to the edge of the floor, where Lord Drake was waiting for her to join him in a minuet. Pandora gave up trying to leave. Sitting with her punch glass, it hadn't seemed there would be so many dances together. Lord Drake eventually escorted her back to the edge of the floor, and she was taken back out for a Scotch reel by Luke McPike. Then the time came for her country dance with Dorian.

She would have been livid with him for putting her down for *three* dances with Islington, but she was exhausted. The only thing she had to cheer herself was that other than those three dances, this was the last, and since she hadn't seen Islington arrive, this appeared to truly be her *last* dance. She didn't intend to dance another for the rest of the evening. She had danced seven consecutive dances, and that was plenty, even as much as she liked the activity itself. She was also relieved the befuddlement she had begun to feel from the four glasses of punch had lessened. She let Dorian lead her onto the floor and gave him a brief smile as they started.

During the first figure, they weren't able to converse, but they soon joined together for the second, giving Pandora a chance to voice her displeasure.

"I happened to look at my dance card earlier, Brother Dorian," she said with a smile. "It's funny how Lord Islington managed to put his name on for three dances when he hasn't even deigned to make an appearance."

"Yes, it was particularly odd how that happened," said Dorian with a smile of his own.

"That is rude on so many levels," chuckled Pandora at his unrepentant demeanor.

"The card looked a little bare; I thought I needed to add something."

"Dorian, how could you?" gasped Pandora with a chiding smile.

She couldn't be upset with him for long, especially since the worry was irrelevant now that it seemed Islington wasn't coming. Her brother was bursting with happiness, and Pandora suspected the reason. When they came back together, she couldn't wait to ask.

"Dorian, did you ask Selena a question?"

"And just what question would that be?"

"Ooh! Don't tease me like that!" she pleaded. "Did you ask her? Did she say yes?" she asked as they moved away from each other.

Dorian came back within talking range. "Yes and yes," he said with a pleased smile.

Pandora shrieked with delight and barely managed to avoid shaking her hands in the air excitedly. Other people on the floor and near its edge turned to look at her, and Pandora's cheeks flushed pink at their stares. She was so happy. They were perfect for each other.

"You spoke to Islington?" she asked.

"Yes, finally, today," said Dorian calmly.

"And what did he say?" asked Pandora curiously.

"He gave us his permission and his best wishes."

"Wonderful," sighed Pandora with a smile. She had expected Islington wouldn't raise any objections. If he had, she would have made him change his mind. "I need to have a word with Selena, though. I talked to her earlier this evening, and she didn't even mention it!"

"She might have done, if Myron hadn't swept you off like that."

"Yes, well, he needed to talk to me. Has he talked to you since then?"

"No, as a matter of fact, I haven't seen him since."

Pandora's expression turned worried. Dorian saw it and was concerned.

"Pandora, what did you tell him?"

"I…he…I told him about Bertram Batts," she said breathlessly.

Dorian's face paled and his expression became grim. He immediately stopped dancing to guide her forcefully by the arm through one of the open sets of doors onto the terrace.

"You did *what?*" he ground out angrily.

"He wanted to know! I tried not to tell him, but he wanted to know how I knew so much about Hendon and his whereabouts. I couldn't *lie* to him!" she said defensively.

"*Couldn't* you have? You do such a bang up job of it when it suits you!" he shouted.

Pandora flinched as if struck, and her eyes stung with tears. He was right, and she couldn't help feeling that if anything happened to Myron, it would entirely be her fault. She looked away from Dorian and nodded her head slowly; there wasn't anything she could say, and she knew it.

Dorian looked at her angrily for a moment longer before he muttered an oath and stalked away from her back into the ballroom.

Pandora stood for a moment at the balustrade in numb humiliation. She hadn't thought anything worse could happen. Now it seemed things would *only* get worse. She wiped at one of her cheeks with the back of a gloved hand and walked down the steps into the garden. She went down the path to the gazebo, the one place where she was usually able to sort her feelings.

Once there, she sat on one of the cushions and curled her knees up to her chest, rocking back and forth as silent, unnoticed tears dampened her cheeks. Her thoughts were a muddled maze of guilt, fear, anger, and uncertainty. Pandora couldn't sort them out, and it frustrated her. Hendon had managed to dupe her, it seemed almost effortlessly. She had possibly led Myron into a dangerous clash with the same man, when she could have diverted it by simply telling a lie. Lady Bardsey thought she was vexing her son when all Pandora wanted was for him to love her. Now she had angered Dorian by actually telling the truth. More than ever, she felt unable to do anything right, and the self-doubt that washed over her angered her because she had always been so sure her reasoning was sound.

She was starting to think it was for the best that she was going to Edinburgh. She felt as if she needed to have time away from everything and everyone. Granted, she would be in uncertain danger, but she would be *away.* Her family would be angry when they discovered she had gone, but by then she would be *gone.* For the moment, Pandora was feeling an overwhelming need to be free, as if she were being pressed in on by a weight that only seemed to grow heavier.

Before tonight, she had felt confident her plan would work, that she would be able to warn Artois and save him. She still wanted to believe that. She couldn't bring herself to believe she was *incapable* of being *capable.* She felt she had prepared as best she could for the journey. She had no idea what she was going to say to Artois to convince him, but she would have a week's worth of traveling to think of something.

Pandora removed her gloves and rested her cheek on her knees. She would spend a few more minutes in the gazebo, and then she would go to her room to get ready for bed. She didn't feel it was necessary to let her parents know. If Dorian told them about Myron, she didn't want to see their worried expressions. They would be too busy with their guests to notice her absence anyhow. Pandora was wrung out, and the best way to avoid any further unpleasantness was to not come in contact with anyone else that night…except Maiyin.

Her head jerked up in surprise when she heard the gate to the mews open and close. She wasn't concerned about it, though. It wouldn't be a guest coming from there; they would enter the house from the front door, but it might be one of the stable hands or other servants going to the house for something. She had some comfort in knowing it wouldn't be Hendon or Castleton. At least, she didn't *think* it could be one of them. Whoever it was wouldn't come to the gazebo; he would continue up the path to the back of the house. She would wait until he went inside before she went to her room. It startled her when the person *did* come into the gazebo.

"I thought I might find you here," said Islington sardonically, standing in the doorway, casually resting his shoulder against the frame and blocking her exit.

Pandora put her feet on the floor in front of her and straightened out her skirt primly. She quickly wiped the remaining moisture from her cheeks and looked at him neutrally. She had hoped to avoid seeing anyone else, especially Islington, but she couldn't ignore the way her heart fluttered with excitement when she heard his voice. This might be the last time she would ever see him.

"Good evening, Lord Islington," she said evenly.

"Is it? I hadn't noticed," he said somewhat derisively.

He straightened up and walked further into the building. Pandora tilted her head sideways and looked at him uncertainly.

"Indeed," she said slowly.

"You know, *my* sister is going to marry *your* brother," he stated with a flourish.

"Yes, I know," said Pandora calmly.

"Of *course* you do," he sneered.

"Is there something troubling you, Lord Islington?" she asked stiffly.

He seemed to be in a foul mood, and she wasn't sure she was willing to deal with it, last time or not.

"Now, why would anything possibly be *troubling* me?" he asked jeeringly as he came to sit beside her on the cushion. "My sister is getting married to my best mate, and there are only two more days left of Parliament. *Why* would I be troubled?"

It was then that Pandora noted the slur to his speech and the somewhat wavering way he sat down. The smell of alcohol was unmistakable. He was moderately inebriated. That he was drunk, by itself, didn't overly concern Pandora. What concerned her was what might have prompted him to become that way. He didn't seem the type to let it happen, but then she really couldn't be sure. It had something to do with Dorian marrying Selena, that much she could tell. She turned to look at him.

"Dorian said you'd given them your blessing and your best wishes, yet you don't seem happy about it. Am I wrong?" she asked critically.

"No, I suppose you're not," he stated dully. "To know *my* friend went behind *my* back to court *my* sister…a most unfair thing," he said self-pityingly.

"Dorian did not go behind your back!" stated Pandora angrily. "Everyone who saw them together knew what was happening, except you! He would have talked to you about it ages ago if he'd realized he could."

"Why didn't he then?"

"There were one or two reasons, not the least of which being that he thought you would react just the way you are!"

"I did give my blessing and my best wishes, as you put it," he defended.

"Yet here you are, so soused you could cure herring with your breath!" spat Pandora furiously. She stood up and moved away.

He looked at her calmly. "That *would* explain seeing two of everything," he stated drolly. "So, what were his other reasons for not asking me?"

"Never you mind," she bit out. That was an argument she didn't want to begin; she was too tired. "Please, tell me you didn't plan to go to my mother's ball in your condition."

He shrugged. "Well, I had thought to," he said evenly.

"Then you're even drunker than I thought! How could you think to appear in public as you are?" Pandora gasped in alarm as a thought occurred to her. "What about your mother and Selena? Do you realize how *embarrassed* they would be if you were to go inside like this?"

"Hmm, I suppose you're right," he said reasonably. "You still have to tell me Dorian's other reasons," he said firmly, and he leveled a serious gaze at her that almost seemed sober.

"No, I don't think I do," said Pandora coldly. "There is no reason I should have to provide you justification for Dorian marrying Selena. There's no way you can object to him, and Selena would never forgive you if you did." She started to leave, but Islington called out to her.

"Pandora, please, wait," he said in such a plaintive tone she stopped in the doorway and turned to look at him expectantly. "Can't you sit with me for a time?"

Pandora started to refuse, but there was enough light filtering in that she could see the almost *lost* expression he wore. This had to do with something more than Dorian's alleged deviousness. She was beginning to suspect he was driven to intoxication by something other than anger. She slowly walked back to the bench and sat down beside him.

"They do love each other, don't they?" Islington asked softly after a time.

Pandora looked at him in surprise. It was a question she hadn't expected.

"Of course they do," she said plainly. "Could you not tell?"

He nodded. "I thought they must; Selena wouldn't marry for anything else."

"Nor should she," affirmed Pandora.

"They'll have children," he stated factually.

Pandora gave him a sideways look of puzzlement. "Well, one would hope so," she agreed slowly.

He turned to look at her earnestly. "*Must* one?"

Then Pandora realized what was troubling him: Louise. Pandora could see the way his sister's death had bothered him when they were talking about the painting, and Louise had died in childbirth. He wasn't angry with Dorian or Selena; he was afraid the thing that had taken his older sister would claim Selena as well. She was the only sibling he had now, and he was terrified he would lose her, whether he wanted to admit it or not. Pandora took one of his hands in both of hers and gave it a comforting squeeze.

"It will be all right," she said gently.

"How do you know?" he asked searchingly.

"Because they love each other, and for it to be any other way would be unthinkable," she said simply.

He leaned toward her then and kissed her softly. Pandora accepted it and returned it tentatively, raising a hand to the side of his face to caress his cheek. He eventually ended the kiss and rested his forehead against hers. After a moment, he raised his head and looked at her reflectively.

"You've been crying," he stated.

"What?" she said confusedly. She wiped at her cheeks and couldn't feel any moisture there. How could he know?

"You've been crying again," he repeated. "I can tell because it makes everything about your face puffy, including your lips."

Pandora put her hands back to her cheeks and then felt her lips. She couldn't feel any difference. She knew it made her eyes puffy, but she hadn't realized the rest of her face became that way as well.

"Yes, I have," she admitted.

"Why?" he asked calmly.

She shrugged noncommittally. "It's been a very bad night."

Islington raised an eyebrow inquiringly.

"I realized Hendon had intended to lure me into God-knows-what from the moment I saw him on South Audley. I told Myron the truth about what happened to his friend, and now he's angry enough he might do something foolish. Dorian is angry with me because I told Myron the truth instead of lying. And your mother thinks I'm a brazen hussy," she prattled, listing the items on her fingers. "That about sums it up."

"My *mother?*"

Pandora was perturbed the last part was apparently the *only* part that had registered with him.

"Well, yes, thanks to you, she now thinks I am tormenting you because I won't marry you."

"What do you mean, *thanks to me?*" he asked stonily.

"You told her you asked me to marry you," stated Pandora accusingly.

"No, I didn't," he denied.

"Then how did she know? She asked me about it as a statement of fact," argued Pandora.

"I didn't tell her. I haven't told anyone," he maintained firmly.

Pandora looked at him doubtfully. There was no way she could have known about it...unless Islington told her.

"But perhaps we should reconsider it," he said calmly.

"*What?*" she gasped disbelievingly.

"Well, there has been so much that has happened, it would be for the best if we did marry," he stated logically.

"*For the best?*" she said incredulously.

"I think we could make a go of it," he said positively.

He didn't notice the way her chest had begun heaving emotionally. She was filled with anger, disbelief, and dejection to find his stance on the matter hadn't changed in all the time that had passed and after everything that had happened since he had first offered it. He still couldn't see why she would object to it, even after they had talked about Dorian and Selena.

She had, for a time, considered accepting the offer just so she could be with him. She had reasoned that perhaps after a time he would come to love her or at least have some affection for her. In the end, though, she knew she couldn't; he hurt her too much as it was, and she was afraid marrying Islington when he didn't love her would be more misery than she could bear.

"You arrogant fool," she said softly with a sad smile.

She stood up then and left the gazebo without looking back. She couldn't do it anymore. She felt her stomach knotting, and her eyes began to tear again, even as she tried to make them stop. She put a hand over her mouth and soon began running up the path to the rear entrance, carefully avoiding the still-open doors to the ballroom where she could hear carefree laughter and conversations above the music. She went in the door that led her directly to the back stairs and took them as quickly as she could. She opened the door to her bedroom and closed it behind her, leaning against it with her back and closing her eyes as she tried to keep herself from bursting into sobs.

Maiyin looked up in surprise from calmly re-sewing some trim on one of Pandora's dresses when she made her agitated entrance. Her forehead wrinkled with concern at the young woman's distress.

"Missy Pandora, what is wrong?" she said soothingly, setting aside her sewing.

She started to rise from the chair when Pandora ran to her and fell to her knees at Maiyin's feet, burying her face in the older woman's lap. Maiyin hadn't seen her do that since she was a child, and she placed her hands on Pandora's back and rubbed it consolingly as Pandora's shoulders shook with the sobs she had fought to control.

It was only moments before the door to the room flew open and Islington stood there with an angry expression. Pandora and Maiyin both looked up in surprise.

"How dare you come here?" gasped Pandora, rising to her feet.

Islington stalked toward her, grabbed her upper arms, and gave her a shake.

"How dare *you* walk away from me?" he asked angrily. "Are you too busy thinking about yourself, Pandora, or would it kill you to consider someone else for a change?" he bit out, giving her another shake.

Maiyin grabbed one of his arms near the wrist. She applied pressure at just the right point between tendons, bone, and sinew, and Islington's hand uncontrollably sprang open. Maiyin then used a similar method on his hand and twisted his arm behind him, seemingly with no effort. Once one arm was restrained, he quickly let go with the other. Anytime he tried to move, it put his arm in excruciating pain, and at one point, Islington gasped at the agony. It was a peculiar sight to see a small-framed woman, just barely five feet tall, have a man over six feet tall at her mercy.

"Maiyin, please, don't hurt him," said Pandora quickly, a hand to her throat in dismay.

"You sure, Missy Pandora? It is rude for man this big to pick on woman," said Maiyin softly, applying pressure to Islington's arm.

"Yes, I'm sure," said Pandora quickly. "He's drunk…among other things. If you can just quietly escort him down the back stairs to the stable. Have Tajik and Jim see him home safely. Jim knows where he lives."

She turned to look at Islington and saw the tight expression of pain and disbelief on his face. He seemed to be quite sober now. She rubbed her upper arms where he had grabbed her, then distractedly massaged the place behind her ear. She was too emotionally exhausted to be angry at him; all she had left was sadness.

"I can't see you again," she said finally, shaking her head.

"Pandora, don't—" he started, Maiyin applied pressure to his arm, and he cut off with a gasp.

"I can't," Pandora whispered, and she put a shaking hand to her lips as she watched Maiyin lead him away.

Chapter Fifteen

Maiyin continued to hold Islington by his arm behind his back as she guided him down the stairs in front of her. Thankfully for Islington, there was no one there to see it. Pandora was right: he was no longer drunk, and he was beginning to realize with self-disgust what he had done.

"How are you doing that?" he gasped when Maiyin adjusted her grip, and he felt the joint at his elbow bend to the point he thought it might break.

"I could tell you, but then I'd have to kill you," said Maiyin, only marginally joking, and she changed her grip again.

"This is so unnecessary; I'll leave of my own accord," he said reasonably.

"Missy Pandora say to escort you to the stables. I am *escorting*," said Maiyin with a tight smile.

She led him out of the house and down the stairs to the garden path. The jostling that came with it made Islington decide he had to get her to let him go. She had his favored arm, and he felt like it was going to snap at any moment.

"See here, Maiyin, was it? I'll let you *escort* me. Will you, please, just let go of my arm before you break it?"

Maiyin looked at him suspiciously but let go. "Try anything foolish, you *wish* I just broke your arm," she said, wagging her finger at him threateningly.

"Yes, madam," he said with a slight bow, massaging his arm.

She raised her hand in the direction of the gate to the mews and tilted her head, indicating he should keep walking. Maiyin gave him sidelong glances, making sure he didn't try to go back to the house. He was the man who had been causing Pandora so much anguish. Maiyin looked at him still rubbing his arm and shook her head scornfully after rolling her eyes.

"I want to apologize for my behavior," said Islington calmly.

Maiyin snorted derisively. "Sure. Men sorry *after* doing something when it so much easier to just not do it in first place. I am not the one you should be apologizing to."

"I know," said Islington softly.

"She has been through more this year—the last four *months*—than most go through their entire life…more than anyone should *have* to go through. It is like *lingchi*."

"Pardon?" he asked confusedly.

"In China, there is method of execution where the condemned is killed by removing bits of his body…one piece at time. Sometimes, the executioner is merciful and stabs him through heart after only one or two cuts. Sometimes, the condemned is lucky and has opium to take him away from his agony. Sometimes, he has to suffer until he dies from the pain. Some of your countrymen call it 'death by a thousand cuts'."

They stopped walking as he turned to look at her palely.

"That's beastly!" said Islington in shock.

Maiyin nodded. "Yes, it is. Missy Pandora not have pieces missing on the outside, but—"Maiyin touched a finger to his chest above his heart—"on the inside, she has lost things she can never get back. Does *she* have a merciful executioner, or will she suffer until she dies from the pain?"

"Wait. You think that I…did she tell you…my *God*!" he said in stunned disbelief.

"She not tell me anything!" said Maiyin, her eyes hardening. "I only go by what I see, and what I see not looking good for *you*!"

She started him toward gate again with a shove of her fingers to his arm.

Islington walked with her in stupefied silence. He hadn't realized how things must appear to someone else. Because of her position, Maiyin knew about things other people wouldn't, things like Pandora's pregnancy and miscarriage, bumps and bruises, and a multitude of other things that when looked at all together were not favorable. When he tried to look at them from the same perspective, he had to agree he had been beastly, and it was easy for Islington to understand why Pandora didn't want to see him again.

Maiyin opened the gate and made sure he went where he was supposed to. She directed him to the master's quarters, which were still lit by a few lights, as Tajik and several hands were still up to ensure guests' carriages and drivers were sent to the front when needed. When they walked in, they found Tajik and two or three other men—including Jim—sitting down to a meal of lamb stew and crusty bread. Tajik placed his napkin on the table and stood when Maiyin entered with Islington.

Islington looked at the man with curiosity and some trepidation. The Arab stood close to six-and-a-half feet tall, and he was muscular in proportion to his size. He wore an elaborately embroidered blue kufi, a skullcap-like head covering, over shortly-trimmed black hair and had a well-trimmed mustache and beard. He had on a white, flowing cotton tunic and loose-fitting trousers of the same material. He was looking at Islington with displeasure for disturbing his meal, but he smiled affectionately at Maiyin when his gaze turned to her.

"Lady Maiyin," he said, taking her hand.

"Good evening, Tajik," she said, smiling back. She looked back at Islington and signaled him to come closer with her hand. "Missy Pandora request I escort this gentleman here and ask that you and Jim see him returned safely home."

"Cor, did she now?" said Jim as he rose from the table, looking disagreeably at Islington.

Jim and Tajik were of comparable size, and Islington felt a little uncomfortable as they crossed their arms over their chests and looked at him with slight hostility. That Pandora had to request he be returned home made it obvious that Islington had done her ill in some fashion, which instantly earned their dislike.

"I wouldn't want to take you gentlemen away from your supper," said Islington calmly. "If you could just get my horse, I'll be on my way."

"Oh, no, it'll be no trouble," said Jim with a dour smile, looking at him assessingly. "If Lady Pandora asked us to do it, we'd be 'appy to."

"Yes, it would be our pleasure," said Tajik, eyeing him with a slight sneer of disdain, as if Islington were as inconsequential as a gnat, and Tajik would have no qualms about swatting him like one.

Islington shrugged resignedly because the men were going to take their duty seriously, and it would be futile for him to try convincing them it was unnecessary. They left the room to saddle the horses, Jim with a piece of his bread in his mouth as he walked by, looking at Islington as if he would be pleased for Islington to try to leave. Islington, however, knew that would be a drunken thing to do, and he wasn't drunk anymore.

The other men in the room resumed their eating, but they would occasionally eye him distrustfully as they did. Apparently, the servants were very loyal, particularly to Pandora. Maiyin also looked at him with contempt, and he couldn't help feeling chastened by their antipathy.

"I never meant to hurt her," he said softly to Maiyin, and he found he couldn't look her in the eye.

Maiyin scoffed disbelievingly, but he seemed sincerely contrite. She was not ready to pardon the way he had treated Pandora, and Maiyin knew *she* wasn't the one he needed to ask for forgiveness. She had watched Pandora throughout the season go from being carefree and happy to worried and sad; Maiyin knew he was in no small way responsible for it. The man in Edinburgh was a part of it, too, but Maiyin suspected Islington was also involved with that.

While he made her unhappy at times, Pandora cared for him a lot, and Maiyin understood that it wouldn't have happened if there weren't *something* redeemable about the man. For the moment, Pandora wasn't willing to let him try to prove it. Maiyin would follow Pandora's wishes on the matter, but she hoped to impart something to him that would make him see he couldn't continue to trample on the girl without paying a price.

"Missy Pandora *very* special," she finally said, "even in family as exceptional as hers. You hurt her again, and there will be *no place* you can hide that I won't find you. Do you understand?" she said sternly.

Islington nodded his head. "I understand," he replied solemnly.

He didn't doubt, after the way she had managed to control him almost effortlessly with the grip she held on his arm, that she could put pay to her words, regardless of the cost to herself. She had a deeper relationship with Pandora than just mistress and servant, and Maiyin would protect Pandora with her life if necessary. Despite her obvious disfavor for him, Islington couldn't help feeling respect and appreciation for Maiyin because of it.

It wasn't long before Jim and Tajik returned. Both still looked at him with dislike, but they were—as they had been before they left—polite. Islington wondered what they would do if Pandora hadn't told them to return him home *safely*. He didn't consider himself incapable in a fight, but he wouldn't be able to take both of them. He didn't feel like trying, and they wouldn't harm him because Pandora had asked them not to.

Tajik didn't speak, but he gestured with his hand that Islington should exit the office. Before Islington did, he turned to look at Maiyin. She looked back at him stonily.

"Goodbye, Lord Islington," she said evenly.

"Goodbye, Maiyin"

Islington started to say something else, but there was nothing further that could be said. He followed Tajik and Jim outside.

After Maiyin watched him leave the office and heard the sound of the horses, she left the office as well and went back to the house. She walked up the back stairs quickly once she got there, impatient to get back to Pandora; she felt she had been away too long. She could hear the sound of music from the ball, but it wouldn't be long before guests began to leave.

Maiyin opened the door to Pandora's room and found her asleep in one of the chairs by the window, still in her ball gown and her hair still up. She had curled her bare feet beneath her and rested her head on her arms on one of the armrests. Even in sleep, her forehead was creased with worry. Maiyin walked over to her and gently shook her shoulder. She awoke with a start and sat up, blinking her eyes owlishly as she tried to focus.

"Is it done?" Pandora asked softly.

"Yes, Tajik and Jim are seeing him home as we speak," said Maiyin. "But you no worry about him now. It is time for bed."

Maiyin went to the dresser and removed one of the few remaining shifts in the drawer. She laid it out on the bed then helped Pandora undress. After Pandora had on her shift, she went to the dressing table for Maiyin to take down her hair. She put a hand over her mouth as she yawned tiredly and watched Maiyin work. She looked at the clock on its stand and saw it was nearing two. No wonder she was tired.

"I think I'll want to leave early on Friday," said Pandora.

Maiyin looked up at Pandora in the mirror. "You still planning to go to Edinburgh?"

"Yes, there's no reason for me not to go," said Pandora practically. "What happened tonight doesn't change anything."

"How early?" asked Maiyin a little charily.

"I think six will be early enough. I want to put as much distance between me and London as possible before everyone realizes I'm gone."

Maiyin nodded. "All right, Missy Pandora, but you better make sure you go to sleep early Thursday."

Pandora provided Maiyin with her own nod. She had one more thing she would need to do before she left: tell Psyche. Pandora had at first thought it would be better not to, but her twin would never forgive her if Pandora didn't let her know. Pandora had been through so much in the past four months that she had kept secret; she felt she *had* to let Psyche know this. Pandora only hoped her sister wouldn't think this was something she had to let their parents know about right away. Pandora was actually hoping she would be able to enlist Psyche's help in disguising her absence. She wouldn't expect her twin to keep up the pretense for long, just long enough to help Pandora be well on her way.

Once Pandora was far enough away from London, there were so many paths to Edinburgh that the chances of someone catching up to her and forcing her to come back would be slim. Granted, she would be taking as straight a course as she could, natural obstacles notwithstanding, but forks in the road did occur. For someone to track her down beyond a certain distance would be difficult. She didn't intend to go through any of the large towns, and she had tried to find a route that would avoid many of the small ones, too; if her family enquired whether anyone had seen her, the likelihood of finding someone who had would be minimal. Now, more than ever, Pandora felt she *had* to do this, and she had tried to take every precaution to make sure no one would be able to stop her.

She would wait until tomorrow to tell Psyche of her plans. Psyche would be shocked to find out Pandora was leaving so soon, but telling her sister at all was already a risk. She could only imagine how Psyche was going to react. She only hoped her twin wouldn't stop her.

Maiyin soon finished taking down Pandora's hair and braiding it. After it was done, Pandora turned to look at her maid solemnly.

"Thank you for earlier," said Pandora softly.

Maiyin shrugged. "You should have let me break his arm."

"Oh, no! He wouldn't have hurt me. At least, I don't think he would have. He was angry because he asked me to marry him again, and I said no...again."

"What you mean *again*? He already ask you to marry him?"

"Well, somewhat," said Pandora with a furrow in her brow. "But it wasn't because he cared about me. At least, he didn't make it seem so."

"Hunh," said Maiyin speculatively, shaking her head.

"What?" asked Pandora, seeing her reaction.

"I don't know what to make of it. He ask you to marry him, you say no. He ask you to marry him again, you still say no. He either glutton for punishment, or he stupid."

"I suppose so," said Pandora, not really seeing the point.

"Oh, well," said Maiyin dismissively with a shrug. "There's no need to worry about it anymore."

"No," said Pandora dully.

She stood up and gave Maiyin a hug. The older woman gathered up the sewing she had discarded earlier and placed it into her sitting room before leaving. Pandora washed her face and climbed into bed, yawning tiredly. Within seconds, she was sound asleep.

The next morning, Pandora and Psyche went for their usual ride in the park. They weren't as concerned about the *ton* coming out, even at their usual time. Most everyone was getting ready to leave for the country and hunting season. Their family wasn't concerned about hunting, although they did participate occasionally, but they were usually just happy to return home to resume their usual pursuits they had to set aside for the Season.

Once the two girls reached the lake, they dismounted and walked down the path, leading their horses by the reins. Pandora thought this would be as good a time as any to let Psyche know about Edinburgh. Pandora was nervous about what her reaction would be. Pandora finally decided the simplest way to do it would be to just get it over with and hope for the best.

"Psyche, I'm about to tell you something, and you have to promise me you will not overreact," she said seriously.

"All right," said Psyche slowly, looking at her curiously.

"On Friday, I'm leaving for Edinburgh to warn the comte d'Artois that he is in danger," she said quickly.

"You *what?*" shrieked Psyche. "Wait, you're having me on, right?" she asked with a half-smile over what she thought was an attempted joke…and not a terribly clever one at that.

"No, I'm not," said Pandora, and after Psyche saw her expression, she could see she wasn't.

"Exactly what kind of danger is he in?"

"He is the man Hendon and Castleton are planning to kidnap and murder. I was able to discover it several weeks ago, but there's no proof of either him being the intended victim or that *they* are the conspirators. Without proof, there's no way to detain the criminals responsible, so I need to take the victim out of the equation."

"Why do *you* have to go?" demanded Psyche.

"Because no one else will. I tried getting Dorian and Islington to take care of it, but they don't seem to realize—no matter how hard I've tried to convince them—that Hendon and Castleton aren't going to wait until Artois is returning from London. I tried getting Papà to send him a letter, as well as Dorian, but Papà still thinks I'm funning, and Dorian thinks he will be able to inform Artois once he arrives here. If I *don't* go warn him, he's going to die."

"Do Mamà and Papà know?"

"No, they wouldn't let me go if they knew, and I *have* to go."

"Well, I'm going with you then," said Psyche determinedly.

"No, Psy, you can't go with me."

"Why not?" she asked crossly.

"Because I need you to stay here and provide me with time to get as far away as I can before they realize I'm gone. I'll leave a note explaining everything; you can give it to them when the time is right. You know about it; Maiyin knows about it. I've tried to plan for any eventuality, so that I can be safe, but I have to be able to leave."

"You are going *completely* alone?" asked Psyche, her eyes wide with dismay. Pandora nodded. "You can't go alone!"

"Psyche, I'll be fine. I'm not a helpless female any more than you are! I'll be taking a gun," she said in an attempt to mollify her sister's concerns.

"A *gun*? Pan, you can't hit *anything* with a gun!" said Psyche with alarm.

"I can so!" huffed Pandora. "I'll have a bow with me, too."

"Well, granted, you're better with a bow," began Psyche, relenting, "but still...."

"Psy, I will be careful. It will be fine. The worst part of it will be sleeping outside, believe me."

Psyche's forehead wrinkled with concern. She thought she should immediately return home and tell their parents. This had to be the most foolhardy thing her twin had ever imagined. She felt very apprehensive about the whole thing, and the thought that something might happen to her twin made her stomach knot into a tight ball.

"Pandora, there's got to be another way to do this," she said vexedly.

"I wish there was, but there isn't. I'm not looking forward to sleeping outside, going without a hot bath, and having to ride on a saddle for over a week from nearly one end of Britain to the other, but this man needs my help. I cannot, with a good conscience, let this crime happen...not when I can stop it," she said earnestly.

"I should tell Mamà and Papà as soon as we get home," threatened Psyche.

"Psyche, no! Please, don't tell them. Please, please, *please,* help me do this," begged Pandora desperately.

"We've never been away from each other," said Psyche in a wavering voice, her eyes shining with tears.

"Oh, don't cry," said Pandora, and she started to become teary as well. "Our faces will become all puffy, and then what will happen?" she teased with an encouraging smile. They both laughed a little. "I'll be all right."

"Do you promise?" asked Psyche solemnly.

"I promise I will be back safe and sound before you know it."

Psyche heaved a big sigh and looked at Pandora tentatively.

"Oh, very well," she said, finally agreeing. "What is it, exactly, that you want me to do? You know I'm no good at pretending to be you."

"I don't think we'll need to take it that far, because—you're right—your dramatic ability is lacking." Psyche looked affronted, which Pandora chose to ignore. "If you can just do things to let everyone *think* I'm still at home for as long as possible. For example, at breakfast, if they want to know why I'm not at the table, tell them I've gone to visit Selena. If they come to my room, tell them I've gone out to the gazebo."

"But that's lying!" said Psyche in a scandalized tone.

"Yes, it is, but you may not ever have to worry about actually telling a lie. If they haven't discovered I really am *not* at home by nightfall, then give them the letter. If they have it found out before then, it will be sitting on the desk in my room."

"I think I can do this, but I hope I don't regret it," said Psyche with misgiving.

"You won't be the one to get in trouble when the truth is found out. Believe me. Once they realize what I've done, any part you had in it will be completely forgotten."

"Too right," agreed Psyche with a grin. "You know this means none of us will be able to return to Wilderland until you get back."

"Yes, I know, and I'm sorry for that, but hopefully it will only be delayed for two weeks, three at the outside."

"Well, I guess another two or three weeks isn't going to *kill* me," conceded Psyche with a smile, bumping her shoulder against Pandora's companionably.

They soon mounted their horses and went home. Psyche was not comfortable with her sister going so far away alone to save a man who may not need it or appreciate it, but she trusted Pandora's judgment…most of the time. Psyche could understand why Pandora felt it was necessary. If she were in the same situation, she couldn't say she wouldn't do the same.

The part that caused her the most anxiety was her twin being alone, going to a place they had never been. They had never been to Scotland; they had never even been to the northern part of England. Going between Glamorgan and London was the extent of their travels, for the most part. Their parents, however, had been all over the world, and their father went overseas quite regularly even now. The duchess occasionally went with him, if he were going somewhere she really liked. Gregory was often traveling to other places with his ship. Dorian and Myron had both toured Europe, but the girls had never been anywhere…except Lundy Island. Psyche trusted that Pandora was capable of fending for herself, but there was still the niggling concern that something would go terribly wrong.

Pandora made sure she had everything ready Thursday night. She finished packing things that would go to Wilderland, and she gathered the final things she thought she would need for her trip to Edinburgh, except for the gun and her father's seal. She would get those in the morning just before she left. She asked Maiyin if everything was in her bag that she would need, and the older woman smiled and said Pandora was going to be pleased with what she had for her. Pandora hoped so.

Pandora had to talk to Psyche because her sister was behaving nervously, and it was somewhat suspicious. Pandora waited for her to tell their parents everything, but Psyche kept her promise not to say a word. Pandora only hoped Psyche would be able to follow through all the way until tomorrow; she had to have the time to get away. When she talked to Psyche, she needed to be reassured that Pandora would be careful. The only thing Pandora was able to tell her was that she would be as careful as she could be. Pandora assured her the two criminals would not be on their way to Edinburgh as well, but that was an empty assurance because Pandora couldn't be certain of it herself.

She had trouble falling asleep because of anticipation and nervousness, as well as the time being much earlier than she was accustomed to, but Maiyin gave her some tea that helped her to relax and go to sleep. The older woman stayed with her until she did. Then she left the room and went to her own bed to be sure Pandora was awake on time in the morning.

Pandora was awakened on Friday morning by Maiyin's gentle shaking of her shoulder. Her eyes opened and closed blearily for a moment in the dim light of the lamp Maiyin had lit. Then she sat upright when she remembered why she was being roused at that hour. She stood up and went to the wash basin, where she splashed some water on her face to clear her head of sleep. Even though she had gone to bed early, she was not as well-rested as she would have liked. Her sleep had been disturbed by dreams she couldn't quite recall in her waking moments, but the feeling they left behind was one of unease.

Maiyin had her usual tea and toast ready, and Pandora ate quickly as she sat in a chair by the window. She became maudlin when she thought this would be the last time for a while that she would have this treat. Every morning, for as long as Maiyin had been with her, the maid had always brought her hot raspberry tea with honey and lemon and toast with butter and lime curd. They would be items that Maiyin could not put into her bag, and Pandora was going to miss having them.

It was still dark outside, and a glance at the clock told her it was only a little after five. It was even too early for Psyche. Pandora had given her a hug and a kiss before they went to bed, and Psyche had wished her luck and a quick journey. They had both cried a little, but Pandora had assured her it would only be two or three weeks. At least, she hoped it would be. If all went well, then she was certain it would. Psyche promised she would do her best to give Pandora the start she needed.

After Pandora finished her first piece of toast and a cup of tea, she began to dress. Instead of going to the closet for her riding habit, she went to her now-empty dresser where she had put one of the sets of clothes she had borrowed from Persephone. She removed her shift and put on a pair of her stockings and a chemise Maiyin had shortened to a length just below her buttocks. Then she pulled on the soft chamois breeches. They fit snugly but weren't tight, and as Pandora moved, they loosened only slightly. It was odd to be wearing them, but it felt strangely liberating. She could see why her sister enjoyed wearing men's clothing.

Pandora pulled on the simple linen shirt and tied it before tucking it into the top of her breeches. She then took one of Islington's cravats out of the drawer, and after putting it to her nose to breathe in the faint scent of him that lingered, she put it around her neck and tied it into a simple mail coach configuration she had learned from Persephone. She put on the plain burgundy waistcoat Persephone had given her but left it unbuttoned for the time being. She went to the closet and pulled out the boots to put them on. Luckily, the sisters wore the same size shoes, and this was a pair of boots Persephone had worn and broke in well. After Pandora was dressed this far, she turned to look at Maiyin, who was watching with her arms folded in front of her, her hands tucked inside her sleeves.

"Well, what do you think?" asked Pandora, her head tilted sideways.

"You never pass for man in that," said Maiyin flatly, shaking her head.

She led Pandora to the full-length mirror for her to look at herself. Maiyin was right. Her hips were too full, her waist too small, and the open waistcoat only accentuated her breasts. Pandora admired the way she looked, though, and again appreciated Persephone's liking for men's clothing. It was very comfortable, except for the cravat. She turned to look at Maiyin.

"I'm not done yet. I still have to button the waistcoat and put on the riding coat. I think that will hide a lot."

"Hunh," said Maiyin doubtfully, her forehead wrinkled. "Let's get your hair put up first."

Pandora went to sit down at the dressing table.

"We don't need to make it anything too complicated; just something to get it onto the top of my head so the hat will fit. And remember, I'll have to do this on my own for a while, so let's keep the pins to a minimum. I don't want to keep track of them," said Pandora with a grin.

"You let me worry about that," said Maiyin, turning her in the seat.

She unbraided Pandora's hair and brushed through it quickly. Once that was done, she swept it on top of Pandora's head and twisted and wound it into a simple, tight knot. Given the length of it, it was surprisingly small. Maiyin secured it in place with only three pins. Pandora tried the hat on and found it fit comfortably, and she didn't think she would have to worry about it falling off. The only thing she lacked was whiskers on the sides of her face, and it wasn't likely that she could acquire any.

She took the hat off and set it on the dressing table for the time being and stood to button her waistcoat. Once she buttoned it, it did much to flatten her breasts, and she suspected Persephone had purposely had it made that way. It would still be obvious she was a woman on close inspection, but after she put on the riding coat, it was passable.

"Much better," said Maiyin with a pleased smile.

She picked up the hat from the table and put it on Pandora's head, the brim lower in the front because her features were much too fine to pass for those of even the most effeminate male. Pandora examined herself in the mirror again and had to agree with Maiyin that she looked much more man-like. From a distance, no one would suspect she wasn't one.

After she had the rest of her toast and another cup of tea, it was time to leave. She was up early, even for her family, but that wouldn't be the case much longer. The only one who *might* be rising would be Psyche, but their younger brothers had a tendency to be up with the sun as well.

Pandora went to the closet for the valise she had there that contained her other men's clothing and some of her own clothing to wear when she met the count. She would have to appear respectable, or his servants would never allow her through the door. She also had a few other things, such as soap for bathing (if she ever got the chance), her depilatory cream (which she suspected she wouldn't get to use), and other toiletry items she felt she couldn't be without. She had also put in her spyglass, compass, map, and a folding pocketknife, which she would move to a saddlebag once she got to the stables.

Pandora made sure she had placed the letter to her family on the writing desk in the corner of her room. She had written it on Wednesday night, and it hadn't been easy to find the words. The wastebasket nearby was full of sheets of paper she had started on only to toss away. In the end, she decided brevity would be for the best because if she went into too much detail or explanation it would fall to melodrama and cause her family more concern than they would already feeling. It wasn't extremely long, but it told them everything she felt they needed to know. She only hoped it explained it well enough. Regardless of what she had written, her family would be unhappy Pandora had done this—and worried, and she wouldn't be surprised, and fully expected, they would come looking for her.

"I have to get a few things from my father's study before I leave. I'll meet you at the stables?" she enquired of Maiyin.

"Yes, that will be fine. I have to get the bags from my room," she said with a nod, putting her hands back into the sleeves of her shirt.

They left Pandora's room, Maiyin going to the back stairs to the servants' quarters, Pandora going to the front stairs to go to her father's study. The house was dark, but Pandora was familiar with its layout and didn't have any trouble finding her way. She was glad the house was dark; it was a sign that none of her family or the servants were up yet. She didn't want anyone to wonder why she was going to her father's study, and she definitely didn't want anyone to see her dressed as she was except for the people involved.

She went down the hall near the ballroom and opened the door on well-oiled, silent hinges. She thought about lighting a candle, but she knew exactly what she needed to get, and she would be able to recognize it by feel alone. The first thing she did was go to her father's desk and open one of the side drawers. His seal was in a small wooden box there. She removed the entire box and put it in her valise. Just taking the seal would have been lighter and less bulky, but she didn't want it to get damaged somehow.

She then went to the cabinet where her father kept the guns. She pulled two small metal picks from her bag and placed them into the lock. After a few turns, it popped open. She first found on the shelf at the top of the cabinet the small box of paper loading cartridges for the gun she was taking. They already had the ball and powder for loading and priming packaged together, which would save her from needing a powder flask *and* a box of balls. She grabbed a package of spare flints as well. She didn't think she would need one, but accidents could happen.

She then knelt and looked on the shelf at the bottom where her father kept the pistols. She was looking for the one her father had first let her use when she was fifteen. It was one of a pair of double-barreled Manton's, and rather large, but it was the one she was best at shooting. She took out several of the wooden pistol boxes, feeling for the right set, remembering the handles were plain compared to the rest they owned, the barrels octagonal rather than round; however, she was yet to find it. She could take one of the Lacy pocket pistols, which were much smaller and would be lighter to carry, but she didn't like the trigger very much, and her aim with them wasn't great.

While she was feeling around on the shelf, she discovered a knife she had forgotten about. She pulled it out of its storage box and examined it, flipping it back and forth between her hands in its sheath, contemplating whether or not she should take it with her. It was a long hunting knife with an intricately carved handle made of ivory and gold with a pommel in the shape of a horse's head. The interesting feature, which made her wonder if she should take it, was that it also had a small pistol built into it. It was fairly old, but her father and brothers always took good care of their guns, and Pandora was sure it was in perfect working order. She put it in her bag then quickly stood up and grabbed the powder flask she had thought she wouldn't need and a box of the smaller balls from the top shelf. She lifted her bag from the floor and was a bit concerned about its weight.

After feeling around a little longer, she was able to find the box she was looking for. The gun was a little over a foot long, and the grip was slightly roughened to enable a firm hold, which for Pandora would be necessary because the recoil from it was jarring to her. She slipped the gun into her bag. She started to close it again when she remembered to grab a simple dirk from the shelf. Now that she felt armed to the teeth, there was nothing else she needed from the cabinet. She closed the doors and locked them. Her father wouldn't find out what she had done until after he discovered she was gone.

She lifted her bag from the floor and started to leave the room, but the slight amount of light from the approaching dawn through the window made her look in the direction of her father's sideboard where he kept his liquor. She shook her head and started to leave the room and then shook it again and went to the table. She looked over the bottles collected there trying to decide which one would be likely. She had a general idea of what she was looking for, but she expected any one of them would do. She then selected an almost full bottle that had some dark amber-colored liquor. She walked closer to the window and leaned near to read what was embossed on the side of it.

"Bowmore, hmm?" she said out loud. *Must be whisky.*

Pandora added the tightly corked bottle to her bag. She didn't know why she would need it, but she remembered the way it had relaxed her when Islington had given her some from his flask. She could also remember the way it had warmed her, and while that sensation had been illusory, if she got wet and chilled, it would be nice to at least not *care*. She lifted her bag up and down in her hand a few times trying to gauge its weight. It felt like it weighed about twenty-five pounds. She hoped that wasn't too heavy.

After giving the room a once-over, she left and closed the door. Instead of returning to the front hall, she turned to the right and went down the hall to the door that would lead her to the terrace and into the garden. She walked down the stairs to the garden path and hurried her step, seeing the way the air around her was beginning to brighten. She was still not quite able to distinguish the true colors of things, but that time was fast approaching. She went to the gate to the mews and opened it. Maiyin, Keung, Tajik, and Psyche all stood waiting for her. She hadn't expected to see her sister there, but Pandora was glad. Psyche looked at Pandora in speechless shock when she saw her.

"Oh, my, Pandora, I cannot believe you are wearing that!" she gasped.

"Why? You should try it. Persephone has it right…seriously. These are much more comfortable than a riding habit. I can't very well go alone looking like a *girl* anyhow," she said with a grin.

"Missy Pandora, what took you so long?" asked Maiyin concernedly as she took the bag Pandora held in her hands.

"I had trouble finding my gun."

"Which one are you taking?" asked Psyche curiously.

"One of the Manton double-barrels."

Psyche nodded approvingly. "At least you can hit something with it, even with your aim," she joked.

"You sure you going to need gun?" asked Maiyin worriedly.

"No, I don't think I'm going to need it, but if I do and don't have one…," said Pandora, letting Maiyin finish the rest for herself.

"Yes, you take gun," said Maiyin, nodding her head.

She started to give the bag to Tajik to fasten to the amassed items tied to Bellerophon's saddle, but Pandora stopped her.

"Wait, I want to move a few things to one of the front saddlebags," she said, walking over to pop open the valise. She fished through it until she found the map, compass, and spyglass and removed them. She put the pocketknife into her coat pocket, and then she closed it back. "There, that should do it," she said with a nod.

Keung took the items from her and handed them to Tajik to place in the left side bag.

"Missy Pandora, what you doing with that bottle of whisky?" asked Maiyin curiously when she happened to see it in the open bag.

"I have no idea," said Pandora mildly. "I just thought it couldn't hurt to have it." Maiyin nodded in agreement.

"You took some of Papá's whisky?" gasped Psyche in a scandalized tone. "You're not going to drink it, are you?"

"I'm not planning to, but again, if I need it and don't have it...."

Psyche's brow furrowed. "Can't see why you'd need a bottle of whisky," she muttered, but she didn't voice any more objections.

"Missy Pandora, come see what we have for you," said Maiyin proudly, motioning toward the saddlebags at the back of Bellerophon's saddle.

Pandora took a good look at her horse for the first time since entering the yard. He was extremely weighted down. She wondered how she would fit into the saddle. There was a small set of saddlebags at the front, a larger set at the back. There was a large piece of rolled up canvas balanced and tied over the top of the set at the back. Her valise was balanced and cinched on there as well. At the front of the saddle, in addition to the saddlebags, were two large bags of what looked like *grain*. Also attached near the front was a holster that held her favorite recurved bow and some arrows. Bellerophon was standing calmly under the load, but Pandora had yet to mount.

Maiyin walked up to Bellerophon's side, and he turned to look at her balefully, as if daring her to tie on anything else. Pandora walked up to him and brushed his nose with her knuckles before planting a kiss there.

"We're going on a trip; would you like that, pretty fella?" she asked. He nickered softly and shook his head up and down.

"This bag has food—things like bread, cheese, cured ham for today, and some fruits and vegetables that will travel well. You should know, I don't think I was able to pack enough food to feed you whole time, but you should be able to find things here and there along the way to make up the difference."

Pandora silently agreed that was true; she knew enough about identifying plants and berries that she wouldn't be likely to eat something poisonous. She just knew she wouldn't be able to actually *hunt* and *kill* anything to eat. She would miss not having meat, but the thought of preparing it herself made her stomach churn. Maiyin moved to the smaller saddlebag at the front on the same side and placed her hand on it.

"This bag has sewing kit, fishing kit, and more apples and vegetables."

"Sewing and fishing?" asked Pandora perplexedly. "When will I have time to do either?"

Maiyin turned to look at her. "Like you say, you may not need them, but better you have them than not."

Pandora shrugged negligibly and followed Maiyin around to the other side, patting Bellerophon on the neck as she went. Maiyin signaled to Keung, and he came with them.

"I let Keung tell you about this one since he packed it," said Maiyin.

Pandora looked at him with an encouraging smile as he nervously moved near. Her horse towered over both Maiyin and Keung, and he gingerly came close to touch the saddlebag.

"This bag has medicine kit," he said softly. "It has herbs and other things in case you not feel well. I put labels on all the bottles that will tell you what they are, what they are for, and how to prepare them. I also gave you jerked meat, nuts, raisins, and…uh…a bottle of plum wine."

"Bless you, Keung," said Pandora with a grateful smile.

Keung returned the smile and bobbed his head, happy she was pleased.

Pandora saw the long length of rope coiled and tied to that side of the saddle. It would be handy for tying to Bellerophon as a lead at night. She didn't expect he would wander off, as he had never been prone to, but she couldn't be sure how he would behave away from home. Maiyin drew her attention to the final, rear saddlebag.

"This bag has more food for you. I put in small pan in case you need to cook something, pot for you to make tea, one tea cup, tea leaves, and more—"

"Apples," finished Pandora with a cheeky grin.

By the end of this trip, she wouldn't care if she saw another apple, but it seemed Maiyin and Keung had provided her with a wide enough variety of things the monotony wouldn't strain her too far. Maiyin pursed her lips to hide her own smile regarding the rather large quantity of apples she had supplied. Finally, Maiyin touched the rolled up canvas.

"This is going to be house for you. It is tent that is waterproof, so you not get wet if it rains, and you not get wet when dew falls in the morning. I also have blankets rolled inside, so if it rains while you are riding, blankets will not get wet. If you're able to find cave or somewhere else to sleep, then you will not need the tent."

"How do I set it up?" asked Pandora in bewilderment. She had never put together a tent before.

"It very easy. Shaped like *triangle*. You smart girl; you will figure it out," said Maiyin with a grin. "Stakes and tie ropes are also inside with blankets. Just be sure to set it up between two trees."

Pandora looked at the canvas with some trepidation. She trusted Maiyin's judgment, but she wasn't sure she could set up a tent. It couldn't be any more complicated than some of her mechanical projects in the solarium, but those were things she had designed herself. Could a small tent be that complicated? Still, if it came down to a choice of either getting wet or learning how to do it, she would figure something out…or hope she could find a *cave*. That didn't seem likely.

There was a canteen attached to the saddle, and she was grateful someone had thought to supply one for her. It would be easy enough to find fresh water to refill it, and it would save her from needing to stop every time she got thirsty. She was eyeing the large bags tied to the front and was curious why neither Maiyin nor Keung had explained them. Then it was time for Tajik to provide her with that information.

"Lady Pandora," he started in his soft, melodious voice, "these bags you have been eyeing with concern are going to be what rests between Bellerophon walking all the way and being able to do *more*." Pandora blinked. "Lady Maiyin and Keung have seen to providing food for *you*; these are food for your *horse*."

"Ahh," said Pandora comprehendingly, nodding her head.

"These bags are waterproof, and they contain a mixture of several grains, some salt, and molasses, just like what he gets here in the stable two or three times a day. This bag—"he put his hand on the left-side bag—"has a scoop and a feedbag inside it. Give him four full scoops a day, not all at once, but one scoop at a time."

"How much do those bags weigh?" she asked ponderously.

"A little over five stone," said Tajik matter-of-factly.

Pandora's eyes widened in alarm. "They weigh over half as much as I do!" she gasped. "Can Bellerophon carry all of that *and* me?"

Tajik laughed softly and nodded his head. "He is a big horse, with a nice strong back and good legs. He will have no trouble carrying you and your supplies. If you are concerned, just remember that the further you go, the lighter his load will become."

Pandora still eyed them doubtfully.

"With everything he has on there, though, he is carrying more than two of you. If either of you want to go fast, don't let him slow trot or canter. Let him lope, or let him gallop for short periods. Use his smooth gaits. He's a smart horse, and he'll let you know what suits him." Pandora nodded.

"In addition to the food in the bags, he will need to forage. When you camp, try to find a place he can graze. Also, stop every two hours, and let him rest thirty minutes. Just because he may want to keep going doesn't mean he should. Do not travel more than ten hours a day." He gave her a stern look that said he expected these orders to be followed exactly. "You do these things, and he'll be able to do all you want and more."

"*Shokran jazeelan*," said Pandora with a grateful smile.

"And one more thing." His expression was serious. Pandora looked at him expectantly. "I put several handfuls of sugar lumps in a small sack in the left-side front saddlebag," he said with a wide grin. Pandora giggled.

She looked around herself thoughtfully for a moment and realized there was nothing further to discuss. Maiyin and Keung had seen to her food and health. Tajik had seen to Bellerophon's. The only thing left, it appeared, was to say her goodbyes. She was reluctant to go, now that the moment was upon her, but it had to be done, and it had to be done by her. She looked at Psyche, who had been watching the proceedings curiously, her hands clasped in front of her tightly.

"Psy, don't look so worried. You see everything I have with me; I don't think there is anything that will happen that I am not prepared for," said Pandora with a comforting smile.

"Yes, that does appear to be so," said Psyche softly, walking near to Pandora. She took her sister's hands in hers, and her eyes clouded up with tears. "I'm going to miss you terribly."

Pandora brought Psyche to her in a tight hug, rubbing a hand on her back soothingly as Psyche choked back a sob.

"I won't be gone for long. I'll be back before you know it," she said gently. She kissed her sister's cheek then released her.

"You better be," said Psyche firmly with a watery smile.

Pandora then turned to Maiyin and Keung. She hugged Maiyin then her husband and tried to pretend she didn't see the tears Maiyin was crying. Pandora wished she could take Maiyin with her, but that wouldn't be a good idea. The little woman was strong in many ways, but her days of being able to survive a long journey in the elements were over.

"*Dāngxīn*," said Maiyin.

"I will," said Pandora with a smile. "You've taken good care of my needs, and I'll be fine."

She then turned to look at Tajik, who was calmly resting his hand on Bellerophon's saddle.

"*Assalamu alaikom warahmatu Allahi wa barakatuhu,*" he said with a kind smile.

"*Bismillah,*" said Pandora, returning his smile.

He then cupped his hands for Pandora to use to mount. Once she was seated, she put on her gloves and adjusted her hat. She wasn't looking forward to wearing the gloves, but they would save her hands from the calluses and blisters she would get if she didn't. She looked down at Tajik and the other three, who had come near as well.

"*Shùn fēng,*" said Maiyin and Keung.

"*Xièxie,*" said Pandora.

"Be careful," said Psyche, blowing her a kiss. "I love you."

"I will, and I love you, too. Give my love to everyone else."

"You'll have to find something to stand on to mount," warned Tajik evenly.

"I know." Pandora sighed preparatorily. "I suppose I'm off." She leaned forward to pat Bellerophon on the neck. "*Yala.*"

Bellerophon turned and started at a fast walk toward the exit of the mews. The other four stood watching as she left, just as the sun was starting to brighten the sky. Psyche looked at her watch on a chain around her neck and sighed.

"Five hundred four hours to go," she said softly.

Chapter Sixteen

Pandora let Bellerophon keep to a walk. There was no one on the streets, but she didn't want to go faster until they were further out. She looked at her watch as they left the mews and turned into Berkeley Square. It was 6:30. It wasn't a bad time to start, only thirty minutes later than she had planned. The first difficulty to getting away undetected wouldn't come for another four hours when her family had breakfast. She would be well away by then, and the longer she had before they found out, the further she could go. If it took them long enough to find out, they wouldn't be able to start after her until tomorrow, and it would be harder for them to catch her.

She went down Davies Street to Oxford and turned left. It would have been easier to cut over to Park Lane and then up to Oxford, but taking Park would have brought her very close to Upper Grosvenor and Islington. After her last failed attempt at stealth going in that direction, she couldn't run the risk of it happening again. He wouldn't recognize her, dressed as she was (regardless of his ability to do so when she was in a dress), but Bellerophon was unmistakable, even when loaded like a pack mule. Islington liked to go for an early ride in the park. It *might* be too early for him to be up and about, but it would be her luck that he would be going to the park just as she crossed Upper Grosvenor.

As Pandora neared the corner to Park and Oxford, she glanced at the Tyburn Gate. Her stomach began to turn flip-flops as a realization struck her: she would have to go through turnpikes! She couldn't believe, in all of her planning, that it had never occurred to her. She quickly pulled out her map and unfolded it to the section nearest London. There were no gates. She folded to the next section—nothing. A panic began to overcome her as she realized the map she purchased didn't provide her with that information, and she had never thought she would need it. She had no idea where they would be and in what way she could alter her route to avoid them.

There had been maps available that provided a direct route to several different locations throughout the country, which probably would have listed every toll gate and turnpike along the way as well as inns and other information useful to travelers, but there had been none available for London to Edinburgh. They wouldn't have been much use to her anyhow because she would be going directly but avoiding the major cities. These turn-by-turn maps, as it were, wouldn't be taking that into consideration, so she would still have been left with the possibility of encountering toll gates. She had purchased a map that provided her with the best overall description of the roads available, but because it was so general, there had been no way for the mapmaker to show toll and turnpike information. It did show which roads were turnpikes and mail coach roads, but there was no way it could list where each and every gate would be situated.

There were several gates between her family's home in Glamorgan and London, and it was a time-consuming chore to get their entire retinue passed through. Usually, the gatekeeper kept a tally of what passed, and when the final vehicle or person (usually, the duke) was through, the toll for all would be paid. The keepers along the way were familiar with their family because they went the same way at the beginning and end of every Season, and the Aberdares wouldn't avoid paying what was due. Pandora, however, never had to take care of it personally.

Pandora let Bellerophon continue to walk as she pondered her difficulty. When she reached the corner of Oxford and the Edgeware Road, she pulled on the reins once she turned and looked at the road ahead of her. It was quite some distance away, but she could clearly see a gate across the road. Her eyes grew round in alarm as she looked at it. It was a tall gate, but not impossible to jump; however, she wouldn't risk letting Bellerophon attempt it because of the load he carried. Pandora didn't know what the consequences would be, legally, if she did jump it, but she was sure it wouldn't be good if she were caught. It wasn't that she didn't want to pay the toll, regardless; she didn't want to be discovered in her dissemblance.

Pandora couldn't go back home. It would be ridiculous to give up because of a toll gate so soon after she started. She wasn't sure it would present that much of a problem; if she paid her tax and kept herself unobtrusive, then she felt fairly confident she could get through without much difficulty. If she didn't speak and kept her hat low, then hopefully the keeper wouldn't discover she was female. If she was able to get through the first one successfully, then she felt certain getting through any others could be dealt with as well.

Gathering her courage, Pandora urged Bellerophon to walk on. She kept her eyes on the gate, and as she approached, she gulped nervously. There was a sign posted that provided the toll amounts. She quickly scanned through it until she found the rate for a horse and rider, near the bottom, just above herds of livestock. She would have laughed if she hadn't been so anxious. It was only a penny-and-a-half. That seemed reasonable. She pulled out the small leather pouch for her money (*men* did not use reticules) and retrieved some coins.

The gatehouse door was closed, which probably meant the gatekeeper was still asleep. There was a bell on a pole near the door, somewhat overhanging the road. She looked for something to use for mounting should she dismount to ring it, but there was nothing. Sighing in frustration, she led Bellerophon to it. After leaning over slightly to reach it, she gave two good pulls on the rope, and it sounded jarringly loud in the silent morning air. Bellerophon stepped sideways at the unexpected noise but otherwise remained calm. Pandora waited for an interminable number of minutes and thought about ringing the bell again, but she eventually heard the sound of footsteps approaching the door from inside.

The door was opened by a man who appeared to be in his early fifties. His hair was gray and bedraggled. He had on clothes, but he had yet to tie his cravat, and his waistcoat was open. Pandora had either roused him from bed, and he had quickly dressed before coming to the door, or he was in the process of getting dressed when she rang the bell. Judging from the way he eyed her disgustedly, Pandora was willing to go with the former. Not speaking, she held out the coins for him to take. He looked from her hand with the money to her face, which she tried to keep averted under the brim of her hat. He then looked at the magnificent animal she was riding and the load it carried, also noting the bow and arrows. Muttering under his breath, he went to open the gate.

"Infernal hunters," he grumbled as he walked back. "Just can't wait to kill something." He came back to her horse and looked up at her. "Headed north to do some hunting?" he asked politely in a louder voice.

"Aye," said Pandora after a moment, attempting the deepest voice she could muster.

"That's what I figured," he muttered, reaching up to take her money.

She touched the brim of her hat with the tip of her fingers.

"Thank you," she said, again trying to sound man-like.

Before he had an opportunity to engage her in further conversation, Pandora urged Bellerophon to continue forward, and he started into a fast walk, as impatient to be off as she. After she was past the gate, she sighed with relief and grinned victoriously. She tried not to let herself get too excited because she would still have more to go, but she felt relieved her ruse had worked.

The gatekeeper, Henry Smoot, watched after the rider on the horse, scratching the back of his head confusedly. He had thought it odd the man had only a bow. It would have been more logical for him to have a rifle, but then Henry reasoned it was possible he would have one wherever he was going. It also seemed to him the man had been rather impolite. After rousing him from his bed at that ungodly hour, Henry felt the least the man could have done was offer a bit of conversation. He looked at the money in his hand and realized he was holding two shillings, over twelve times the required toll.

"Well, I'll be buggered," he said with a grin, jingling the coins together in his hand as he went back into the gatehouse.

<<< >>>

Pandora let Bellerophon keep to the fast walk. She was in no hurry to let him go faster. There was plenty of town still to get through before she let him have his head, even if there weren't any people. Her success making it through the tollgate didn't guarantee her journey would be without mishap, although it *was* an auspicious beginning.

Pandora pulled out her watch to glance at it again. It was nearing seven. She had finally left London. She had planned to be out of the city, almost out of Middlesex, but at least she was on her way. It would still be an hour or so before more people began milling about, but she would be further into the countryside—and hopefully past any further gates—before then.

After she passed through Kilburn, she felt confident she could let Bellerophon go faster if it suited him.

"What do you think, fella?" she asked, leaning forward to pat his neck. "Shall we be on our way to Edinburgh? Go as fast as you want."

Without any further gesture from Pandora, Bellerophon quickened his pace to a steady lope, as if he had been waiting for her to let him do it. She adjusted her hat on her head to keep it from blowing off in the wind and smiled happily. He would be able to maintain this pace for quite some time, even with the load he carried, and she felt sure they would soon make up the time they had lost.

They would occasionally pass small clusters of buildings to either side of the road—farms and inns, and there were other roads that turned off of theirs as well. Pandora stayed to the main road for now. She would eventually need to turn off, but it wouldn't be until she was well into Hertfordshire, past St. Albans.

They soon reached Edgeware. With Edgeware came another turnpike. The gate was open, however. Pandora was able to pay the gatekeeper her toll—this time, tuppence—and continued on with a minimum of delay. He didn't seem as interested in conversation as the man at the first gate, but that suited Pandora. He barely even acknowledged her presence after she gave him her money, and he waved her through without concern.

The sun had risen fully by the time they passed through the town, and it was going to be a glorious day. The weather was warm, the sun was bright, and Pandora felt more at ease than she had in a long time. It was odd she should feel that way, considering she was going somewhere she had never been, entirely alone, but she was looking forward to the adventure. She hated that she was going to worry her family, but she felt she had little choice. Once she returned home, her mother and father would never let her leave the house again, but that suited Pandora just fine.

A few miles past Elstree, once they had passed a stretch of woods, Pandora found a stream margined on one side by a field. It looked perfect as a place to stop for her first rest. She dismounted and led Bellerophon to the water's edge for a drink while she unfastened the top of the left-side bag of grain. As promised, she found a feedbag and a large scoop inside. She took out a portion of the grain, which actually smelled appetizing to her as well, and put it into the bag. After replacing the scoop, she refastened it. Once Bellerophon raised his head from drinking, Pandora removed his bridle to allow him to eat comfortably. She was fairly sure he wouldn't try to run off.

"I've got something very tasty for you, fella."

Bellerophon nickered softly as he smelled the molasses, and Pandora grinned as she put the bag over his head to allow him to eat. Psyche was right: he did have a sweet tooth. While he munched away happily at his food, Pandora opened the front saddlebag where Maiyin had put her "kits" and retrieved an apple for herself. She wasn't very hungry, but an apple would do nicely for the time being. She also unfastened her canteen and drank a little from it as she ate. Pandora would have some of the bread and cheese for dinner around noon. She wanted to ration her food because she wasn't looking forward to finding it for herself.

Once Bellerophon finished his grain, which happened rather quickly, Pandora removed the bag and put it back on the saddle then allowed him to graze on the nearby grass. She had glanced at her watch after she finished her apple. He had another fifteen minutes to rest before putting his bridle back on. She didn't expect that she could find a field of grass every time they stopped so she wanted to let him eat as much as he could.

While he ate, she looked at her map to get some idea of where she would need to begin looking for her side road. It would be past St. Albans, but she wanted to make sure she took the right road, which would lead her to the outskirts of Luton just beyond the border of Bedfordshire. From what she could see on the map, they had gone fifteen or sixteen miles, a respectable distance so far, and they would reach St. Albans soon. She didn't intend to go through the city, however, but would pass to the south and west of it through St. Stephens and St. Michaels. Her road would be about seven miles beyond that. Since it would still be turnpike until then, she hoped there would be a sign at the crossroads that would let her know when she reached it.

Another glance at her watch told her it was time to be off. She walked over to Bellerophon where he grazed and checked his legs and hooves.

Everything was perfect, as she knew it would be. There wouldn't be any possibility of problems until they started onto the less well-tended roads.

"Come on, Bell, time to go," she said.

He raised his head to look at her and calmly let her place the bit back in his mouth after he finished his last bite of grass. She took him back to the water's edge for one last drink then led him toward the road by his reins. She didn't have much difficulty finding something to stand on to mount; there was part of a stone wall nearby that worked perfectly. She again let him set their pace, and he resumed his lope without hesitation.

Skirting around St. Albans proved to be simple enough, but Pandora didn't like the hour getting later. There were more people, and there were also flocks of animals being led across the road, herded from field to field, which required Pandora to occasionally wait for them to be led out of the way. Once she got into the rural areas, this was going to be more common. The animals didn't bother her; their owners, however, concerned her because she didn't want to have them realize she wasn't a man. Usually, they were too busy tending their animals to pay her any mind, but she would touch the brim of her hat sociably should they happen to glance in her direction.

She took note of the first mile marker she saw once she passed back onto Watling Street. If she didn't see a road sign that would lead her in the direction of Luton, she would take the nearest one after she had gone the necessary distance. This would be her first pass onto a more isolated road, even though it did appear there were small villages peppered throughout the countryside. Luckily for her, there was a direction marker once she reached her road, and she sighed with relief.

At some point while she was traveling to Luton, she would cross the border into Bedfordshire, but once she crossed into Bedfordshire, she would have to travel across its entire length from south to north. It had felt so much more like she was making progress when she was able to pass through quickly, but it would take her the rest of the day to make it through the county, provided the weather and roads remained good.

She was enjoying the countryside as she went down the road that was little more than a track between fields. There was a gentle, rolling quality to the landscape that at some points would provide her with nice, scenic panoramas. She could see livestock scattered here and there across the land, and she would see a large manor house to go with them occasionally. It made her feel a little homesick because it reminded her of Wilderland. She firmly put the maudlin thoughts from her mind and comforted herself with the reminder that she would be back in three weeks. She just had to think of this as a holiday.

While she rode, she let her mind wander to Artois and what she would say to him when she made it to Edinburgh. The best approach would be to tell him the entire thing. The only part she couldn't tell him was the specific names of the culprits. Slander was a dangerous business, and because there was nothing more than circumstantial proof—and most of that based solely on *her* word—she couldn't accuse Hendon outright of the crime.

Hendon was cruel enough that if the charges were brought against him, and they were proved false—which they probably would be, she could die. It was melodramatic to think of it like that, and her father would never allow it to happen, but the best way to avoid any possibility of it would be to just not say anything. She would tell Artois there was a plot to kidnap and murder him, and that would be it. He could make his own determinations on who it might be and why.

Pandora wasn't sure how far she had gone (or even if she was headed in the right direction for that matter) until she came to a crossroads with a marker. Luton was to the right, Caddington was to the left, and Badger Dell was forward. She didn't want to go right or left.

"Badger Dell, here I come," she mumbled to herself.

It was not long before she came to yet another crossroads with a sign pointing to the right for Luton. She kept going forward. After yet a third occurrence, she would have thought she was going in a circle if it weren't for the other towns designated on the markers being different. She hadn't realized Luton was such a big town. It didn't look as if it warranted *three* different crossroads on the map, but there they were.

After she passed through Leagrave, slowing to a walk, Pandora looked at her watch. Bellerophon would have another hour before it was time to let him rest. He was holding up extremely well and content to keep to his lope between towns. He would slow down if he needed to; she was letting him set their pace and was quite pleased with it.

As they traveled, the direction ahead of them seemed to be hillier than previously, the dips between peaks lower and the grades climbing upward steeper, but she in no way considered what she saw to be mountains. After they passed through a town that didn't seem large as far as the number of buildings and houses but was spread over a wide area, Bellerophon was willing to remain at a walking pace. He was beginning to tire from the ground-covering lope he had maintained. It was just as well he wanted to walk; the hills would tire him even worse if he didn't. They crossed two or three bridges as they traveled, and Pandora thought to stop to let him rest, but it wasn't quite time. She wanted to keep going as long as she could. She was ready to stop as well: she was hungry, and she needed to relieve herself.

When they came to another road leading to the right, Pandora took it because she felt they were going too far to the west. Toddington was in that direction somewhere, and while it wasn't an enormous town, she didn't want to go through it. It was well past the hour when people in the country would be awake; she didn't want to be seen if it could be avoided. When she came to a crossroads that actually had a marker, she sighed with relief when she saw that one way would lead her to Toddington, the other to Harlington.

The road ahead of her looked even more like just a track between fields, but she didn't want to go to either town so she took it. After going down one side of a hill and up to the top of another, they came to what looked like an actual road. She went right. When they came to another bridge crossing a river, Pandora decided to stop. Bellerophon was tired, she was hungry, and she needed to get her bearings before she wound up going in a circle.

By the time Pandora relieved herself and rinsed her hands in the stream, Bellerophon was through eating. Pandora removed the bag back to its place on the saddle then led him the short distance through the trees to the field. She reached into the left-side saddlebag on the back and retrieved the cheese, bread, and ham Maiyin had put there. The loaf of bread was large, and her maid had given her a half-round of cheddar. She had sliced the ham before wrapping it in a layer of waxed paper, and Pandora would have enough for all three meals. After she made sure Bellerophon was eating contentedly, Pandora began to do the same. She would check her canteen and refill it from the stream before they left.

<<< >>>

Psyche approached the dining room with some trepidation. She could hear some of the family already gathered for breakfast. They didn't have a formal requirement that everyone be present at the same time, but because everyone knew when it was served, it usually happened they were all there. Also, since they tended to rise before most people, and it was too early to go calling for most reasons, there was nowhere else they needed to be. She could hear her younger brothers giggling, which meant that at least her mother was already there.

Psyche was expecting her parents to demand an immediate accounting of Pandora's whereabouts. She wasn't sure she could lie to them. She stopped for a moment before she entered and took a deep breath to calm her jangly nerves then entered the room with as much casualness as she could muster. She went to the sideboard and put food onto a plate then went to take her usual seat beside Eurydice.

"Would you care for tea or coffee this morning, Lady Psyche?" asked Jens politely at her elbow not too long after she sat down.

Psyche nearly jumped out of her skin. Her fork clattered against her plate, and she only managed to avoid letting out a squeak of surprise by biting her lip. Luckily, her family was engaged in their own conversations and didn't notice.

"I'll have coffee this morning. Thank you, Jens," she said calmly, giving him a polite smile.

Psyche attempted to eat her food, taking another calming breath before doing so. She couldn't understand how her twin was able to pull pranks with no effort, especially the ones that required her to lie. Psyche could feel her stomach twisting into anxious knots, and she hadn't even needed to say anything yet. Jens brought her coffee, and she smiled again as he placed it in front of her. She added some cream and sugar then took a small sip.

Psyche tried to eat, but her appetite was lacking. She forced herself, however, because her not eating would make her parents ask if she was unwell, and of course she would say she was fine. Then they would wonder what was making her lose her appetite, and Psyche wouldn't be able to resist telling the truth. She had to give Pandora as much time as she could, so she would have to do her best to lie when the time came.

Psyche was able to eat in silence for a while. No one seemed notice Pandora wasn't there. Psyche hoped she could eat and leave the table before anyone thought to ask her. She didn't rush, though, because her family would want to know why she was in such a hurry. She was feeling herself grow tenser by the minute. She picked up her cup for more coffee and saw her hand shaking slightly when she did.

Psyche wanted to strangle Pandora. She couldn't believe her twin had yet again convinced her to go along with one of her plans. This time, though, there was so much more at stake. Psyche just knew she wouldn't be able to keep up the pretense. She was going to tell everything as soon as anyone said a word. Her nerves were just not able to handle the strain. She would break out in hives any minute.

By outward appearances, Psyche was perfectly calm. She ate her food and drank her coffee, and no one noticed anything amiss. Gregory and Persephone finished eating and rose from the table, going out together for one last trip to the docks. The duke also finished and left to visit an associate near Fleet Street. Arachne took Damon out when she finished so they could free his caterpillars, spiders, and grasshoppers in the garden where he had been collecting them all season. Psyche ate and hoped she wouldn't have to say anything. As her family continued to finish and leave, it was looking more possible, and Psyche began to relax. Dorian and Myron weren't at the table. It was just her mother, Eurydice, Cosmo and Christopher. She felt the ball of tension in her stomach begin to unwind, and she was able to begin enjoying her food.

"Psyche, is Pandora not going to eat this morning?" asked the duchess.

Psyche cursed silently to herself because she had *almost* made it.

"No, Mamà," she said calmly. "I believe she said she wanted to visit Selena one last time before we leave town."

Her mother smiled in understanding and nodded her head. "Ah, yes. She probably went with Dorian then. I don't imagine we'll see those two back before evening."

"No, Mamà," Psyche agreed.

"I think she just wanted to see Lord Islington again," said Eurydice with a slight smile.

"Eurydice!" gasped Psyche. "You know that's not allowed."

"Well, maybe not, but why do you think Selena came to visit Pandora so often? Now *she* is going to be our new sister."

The duchess looked at Psyche's astonished expression, and her lips twitched amusedly.

"She does have a point," said Julia mildly after she cleared her throat.

She looked at her two young sons and saw they had completely quit eating their food and had started to throw bits of it at each other when they thought she wasn't looking.

"That will be enough of that, you two," she said sternly. "A gentleman does *not* throw food at the table." She stood after wiping her mouth on her napkin to hide her amusement. "Come along, Cosmo and Topher. We'll check with Nanny Bixley if all your things are ready for the journey home."

They stood and took her hands, leaving the room swinging their arms back and forth gleefully. Psyche could hear her brothers chattering happily as they went.

"You know he's going to marry her," stated Eurydice as she took a sip from her coffee.

"Who is going to marry whom? I *know* Dorian is going to marry Selena; he told everyone at supper last night," said Psyche dryly.

"Not them! Lord Islington is going to marry Dodo," said Eurydice matter-of-factly.

"I think Pan might have something to say about that," said Psyche flatly as she finished her coffee and stood up. "And I don't think it's going to be yes."

《《 》》

Pandora looked at her watch. It was nearing 5:30. She had still not made it through Bedfordshire, but she was coming very close. At least, she was fairly sure she was. She and Bellerophon hadn't been able to go much faster than a walk for most of their journey since they had stopped that morning for breakfast. She wanted to be into Northamptonshire before she stopped for the night, but she was becoming exhausted. Bellerophon was tired too, but he was bearing up well. They had just finished their last stop until they found somewhere to sleep.

They had made it past Bedford without any difficulties, and while she had been able to find a stream, she hadn't been able to find a field. Pandora would have to make sure she found one when they stopped for the night. Bellerophon wouldn't eat much after dark, but he could graze when he woke in the morning before they started out again.

They had needed to pull to the side of the road to allow carriages or mail coaches to pass. Some were people leaving from London to the country after the end of the Season. There hadn't been many, though. Pandora was avoiding most of them because they took the main roads. Most of the roads she had been traveling were only suitable for foot traffic or horses; they weren't wide enough or maintained well enough for a carriage.

She wondered how things were at home. Had Psyche been able to convince her family Pandora was still there? She did at least for a time; otherwise, they would have already come after her and taken her back. After the first three or four hours, Pandora had quit looking over her shoulder. By afternoon, she felt safe they wouldn't be able to find her or stop her. Psyche would give them Pandora's letter, and it would explain everything.

Pandora didn't intend to make the journey home alone. Someone from her family would arrive in Edinburgh to see her escorted safely. She wouldn't be surprised if her father or Dorian was waiting at Holyrood as soon as she crossed through the gate to speak with the count. She wouldn't mind that…provided they allowed her to deliver her message to him first.

She hoped that leaving to warn Artois herself would make her family realize how earnestly she believed he was in danger. Her father had never believed her, and Dorian just couldn't seem to grasp the urgency of the matter. She was surprised Dorian hadn't spoken to their father about it. If he had, then her father wouldn't have doubted her. In any event, they would be to Scotland for her eventually. If they weren't, she had made the trip *there* alone; she could make the trip *back* if necessary.

Psyche paced the floor of her room nervously, looking out the window then back to the clock on its stand. It was nearing 6:30. The sun was starting to sink below the horizon, but it wouldn't be full dark for at least two hours. After her mother's enquiry about Pandora at breakfast, no one else had asked further. For all her family knew, Pandora was still visiting Selena with Dorian, who had not yet returned himself. Psyche tried to go about her usual business, but she was much too anxious. When it was time for dinner, she couldn't eat anything.

At one point, she had broken out in hives. Chrissoula went to find Maiyin, and they gave Psyche something to make them go away. She took a nap for a few hours from whatever was in the tea, but she had resumed pacing and wringing her hands almost as soon as she awoke. Chrissoula lost patience with Psyche and left the room after about an hour, telling Psyche that she would be in the servants' quarters should she be needed because watching her mistress was making her dizzy. Maiyin tried to calm Psyche and offered to make more tea, but Psyche couldn't sleep the time away until she told her family about Pandora because that by itself would be suspicious. She tried reading, but she was unable to focus on the words.

There were still a couple more hours yet of sunlight. If she could delay it a little longer, even only another thirty minutes, they wouldn't be able to look for Pandora until tomorrow. Time never seemed to pass as slowly as it did when one was waiting for something. Watching the clock and the sky didn't make matters any better, but Psyche couldn't stop herself. She was concerned about Pandora and lying to her family only made it worse. She never should have agreed to do it, but she had promised Pandora that she would help.

"Just thirty more minutes," she said to herself, continuing her pacing.

<<< >>>

"You two should come for supper," said Dorian as he sat having tea with Islington and Selena in their family's private sitting room.

"Do you think we should?" asked Selena. "Do you think your mother would mind?"

"I don't see any reason why she should…you're almost family now anyhow," he said with a grin.

Selena smiled back, blushing. "We still haven't set upon a date," she said, looking at him shyly.

"In three weeks will be fine with me," said Dorian, giving her a wink and taking her hand.

"Oh, I couldn't possibly be ready by then," said Selena, giving him a smile and shaking her head. "There's my trousseau, and we have not decided where to go for our honeymoon. We've not even decided where we are going to be married."

"Sweetheart, we can be married wherever you wish. If you want to wear absolutely nothing, I will be happy. If you want to go to Battersea for our honeymoon, that will be a bit odd, I'll admit, but if we are there together, you will hear no complaints from me."

Islington watched them mildly. He had resigned himself to their marrying. He didn't really mind, but at moments like this—when the two of them became sappy—he would rather not be in the room. He couldn't imagine being that mawkishly indulgent, not even with Pandora, but he had yet to have the opportunity to find out. Dorian dearly loved his sister, and Selena felt the same about Dorian. Islington tried not to dwell on the fact that he would, in essence, be losing his sister and tried to focus on the prospect that he would be gaining a brother…this time one who wouldn't be the equivalent of devil spawn.

The three of them had gone to Kensington for a picnic earlier and had just returned from a ride in the Park. Islington and Selena would be returning to Bardsey in Yorkshire on Monday. Their mother had already left that morning because the Aberdares were coming to visit at the end of the fortnight after the duke finished his business, and she wanted to make sure everything was in order. Islington didn't think the manor was in that terrible of a condition, but his mother would make everything perfect. The only reason they had not left with her, Islington tried to tell himself, was because Selena didn't want to be away from Dorian.

"What do you think, Islington? Would you care to come for supper? Mrs. O'Flaherty makes the best food," said Dorian.

"I don't see where there would be any harm in it. I'm sure our own cook would enjoy the evening off," said Islington agreeably.

He made arrangements for a carriage to be brought around and for Dorian's horse to be returned to his home. The three of them arrived at Aberdare House just slightly after seven. Selena was laughing girlishly over something Dorian had said as Tannaz opened the door. He took their things, and Dorian escorted them to the private sitting room. As they were walking past the duke's study, Dorian noticed his father standing at his desk, going through all the drawers.

"Hallo, Dad," he called in the doorway. "I'm back."

The duke looked up from what he was doing, his forehead wrinkled with puzzlement. "Oh, good evening, Dorian," he said distractedly.

"Are you looking for something?" asked Dorian, walking further into the room.

"Yes, actually," said the duke, scratching the back of his head. "My seal has gone missing. I could swear I put it in this drawer," he said as he tapped the empty drawer, "but demmed if I know where it is now."

"Hmm...," said Dorian thoughtfully. "You don't think it might have gotten packed away already, do you?"

"No, I don't think so. It was there last night."

"Well, let me know if you need help hunting for it. Islington and Selena are here for supper."

They ducked their heads in to give the duke a wave and a smile.

"Oh, hallo, Islington and Selena," said Aberdare with a kind smile. His forehead was still wrinkled with concern about his missing seal, and as the three left, he resumed rifling through things in search of it. It was far too large to just be hiding underneath something.

Dorian continued down the hall with his fiancée and her brother. When they reached the sitting room, the duchess was there with Myron and Gregory talking about their day's activities. The duchess looked up from her needlework when she saw them and smiled happily.

"Oh, good, you're back. Hallo, Islington, Selena. I was wondering if you had decided to stay there for supper," she teased.

"No, actually, they've come *here* for supper," said Dorian, grinning sheepishly.

The duchess chuckled, shaking her head, and put her needlework aside into her sewing box. She stood and straightened out her skirt.

"I'll let Mrs. O'Flaherty know we have company. I don't think it will matter to her, but one never knows." She started to leave the room then turned to look back at Dorian. "Has Pandora gone up to her room?"

"Pandora?" asked Dorian confusedly, giving his head a shake. "I really couldn't say."

Her grace's forehead wrinkled concernedly. "Did she not return with you?"

"Mum, I've not seen her all day," said Dorian seriously.

"Gregory, go get your father from his study," ordered the duchess, her eyes rounding in alarm. He rose from his seat to do as he was told. "Myron, have you seen her?"

"No, Mum. I only returned from tending to some business an hour ago," said Myron calmly.

"I thought she had gone with you to see Selena. She said she wanted to visit one last time before she left," said the duchess, looking at Dorian, and she began to wring her hands together nervously.

"I'm sure it was just a misunderstanding, Mum. She probably *is* up in her room," said Dorian confidently, giving her a placating smile. "How did you find out she was going to visit Selena?"

After Julia thought about it for a moment, she snapped her fingers. Then she went to the doorway and leaned out.

"*Psyche!*" she roared.

Dorian looked at his mother in astonishment. Her voice had reverberated off the walls like cannon shot, and there was no way it couldn't have been heard upstairs. He would be surprised if the residents of the neighboring houses hadn't heard it, adjoining walls or not. He could only ever recall seeing her yell rather than send a servant to retrieve someone once before, and that had been when Pandora had dyed Myron's hair green. Her grace came back into the room and began to pace back and forth nervously. Her sons, Islington and Selena were too dumbstruck after her ear-shattering summons to do anything but watch.

Gregory returned with the duke. He exchanged a speculative glance with Myron, who shook his head uncertainly and shrugged.

"Julia dear, whatever is the matter?" asked Aberdare soothingly as he entered. He went to her to put a comforting arm around her shoulders and took one of her hands in his to stop her from wringing them.

"Xan, Pandora did *not* go with Dorian to see Selena. No one's seen her *all* day," said Julia worriedly, her voice choking. "Psyche said she had gone, but she hadn't."

The duke nodded, and after giving her shoulder a pat, he released her and walked to the door as well.

"*Psyche!*" he bellowed. He walked back to Julia and guided her to sit down on the sofa.

Selena flinched at the loud noise. She was amazed how they yelled rather than send a servant. She was growing concerned about where her friend might be. Selena had thought she might come to call on Pandora tomorrow, as Pandora *never* came to visit Selena at her house because of

Islington. Selena understood…somewhat. She had as yet been unable to determine exactly what kind of relationship her brother and her best friend shared, so she was willing to allow Pandora's dislike for visiting Bardsey House. Selena wondered if she should say something about that peculiarity but decided to keep silent unless someone asked her directly. It would only make them all the more worried.

Islington looked at the family and their growing concern and attempted to control his own. Pandora was independent and often did things she shouldn't, but he couldn't believe anything untoward had happened to her. Still, she had used the ploy of going to visit Selena before as an excuse to do something that had been downright dangerous. He only hoped it was not a similar situation this time because he wasn't there to protect her.

Persephone and Eurydice came barreling into the room after hearing their parents yelling for their sister. They were surprised when it had been Psyche's name they called because the younger girls only ever heard them yell like that for Pandora, so the two of them were sure it had to be something extraordinary. They attempted to compose themselves when they saw Islington and Selena and calmly walked over to sit by their mother on the sofa. They each took one of her hands in theirs to pat them consolingly when they saw her anxious expression.

"Mother, what's wrong?" asked Eurydice solemnly.

"Your sister Pandora's gone missing," said Julia.

"Oh, Mum, we don't know she's gone *missing*," said Dorian exasperatedly. "Let's wait until Psyche comes before we jump to any conclusions." He turned to look at the door. "Where is she anyhow?"

They heard footsteps in the hall, but it was only Arachne coming to see what had caused the commotion as well.

"Is something wrong?" she asked calmly as all the eyes in the room turned to look at her with disappointment.

"We're not sure yet," said Myron.

Arachne nodded acceptingly and calmly went to sit in a chair near her mother and sisters.

The family and their guests waited for what seemed an unbelievably long time for Psyche, and Dorian was tempted to yell like his parents, but just as he was preparing to, they heard another set of footsteps in the hall.

When Psyche entered, she seemed calm and composed. Her face was pale, her features drawn with strain, but she wasn't nervous. Islington thought she looked like the condemned, resigned to her sentence to the gallows. His heart turned when she first entered because she looked so much like her twin had the last time he had seen her. Seeing her demeanor, a knot of dread formed in the pit of his stomach. She wouldn't look that way if something weren't seriously wrong.

She didn't speak, but she calmly went to her father and held out her hand with Pandora's letter. The duke started to say something, but when he saw the letter in her hand, he took it from her, his forehead wrinkling. He tore it open and began to read, his eyes widening with shock as he went further down the page. Julia came to his side.

"Xan, what is it?" she asked worriedly.

He finished the first page and silently handed it to her as he began to read the second and final one. As Julia read, a hand flew to her mouth in horror, and her eyes began to tear. She weaved a bit unsteadily, on the verge of fainting, and Dorian helped her sit down. He took the letter from her limp hand and began to read it himself.

"Dearest family, by the time you read this I shall be well on my way to Edinburgh to warn the comte d'Artois that his life is in danger. I had thought this would be unnecessary, but I have found I am left with little choice. I have taken Papa's seal with me to prove the authenticity of my information. I shall protect it to my utmost capability.

"Do not worry about me, although I am sure you will regardless of what I tell you, and remember I love you all very dearly."

The duke finished with the second page, and Dorian took it from him to read as he handed the first page to Islington.

"I am sorry I had to do this, but you have raised me to do what I felt was the correct and honorable thing. This is it. One man has already died because I did not act when I should have. I could not, in good conscience, let this terrible thing happen. I will be as careful as I possibly can, and I hope you will forgive me for this deception.

"Mama and Papa, do not be angry with Psyche for her part in this, as I am sure she has punished herself enough already. Your ever-loving, Pandora."

After all the men finished reading the letter, there was a stunned silence blanketing the room. Selena and all the sisters, except Psyche, waited to hear what it contained.

Psyche stood in front of her father. When she heard her mother yelling for her, she instantly knew they had discovered Pandora was gone. At her mother's call, it felt as if a weight had been lifted from her, and she felt more at peace than she had all day. Now she could be honest and straightforward, which was the way she preferred. Once Psyche heard her mother, she went to Pandora's room for the letter from her desk; she couldn't deny Pandora was no longer at home, and it was nearing full dark. She had completed her task well and given Pandora the lead she had desperately needed.

"When did she leave?" the duke asked her calmly. He would not, however, look at her for the moment.

"At 6:30 this morning," replied Psyche softly.

"Bloody hell!" bit out Dorian in shock.

"Dorian," said the duchess in a weakly reproving tone.

"Where has she gone, Mother?" asked Eurydice.

"Edinburgh," said Julia flatly.

"Oh, my giddy aunt!" squeaked Arachne, her eyes round in surprise.

"Did she go alone?" asked the duke. He held up a hand to stop Psyche from replying and shook his head just as she opened her mouth to do so. "Stupid question. Of course, she did." He rubbed a hand over his face wearily. "What did she have with her…other than my seal?"

"She had food for Bellerophon and herself, a tent, her bow…and a gun," said Psyche hesitantly.

She was trying to remember all the things she had seen that her father might want to know about. She was *not* going to mention the bottle of whisky. The other odds and ends Maiyin and Keung had given Pandora would also be irrelevant.

"A *gun?*" gasped Julia. She put a hand to her throat and started to shake her head. Eurydice patted her shoulder soothingly and looked from her father to Psyche concernedly.

"She went on *horseback?*" said Myron in surprise.

"Well, at least she knows how to use a bow," said Persephone consolingly. It didn't make anyone feel any more at ease, and Gregory looked at her warningly and shook his head.

"She's not going to stay at an inn?" asked Eurydice. She couldn't imagine sleeping outside.

Dorian left the room for a few minutes and soon returned, his expression grave. He had gone to the duke's study to check the gun cabinet. To outward appearances, it seemed untouched, but once he opened it and took a quick survey of what was there, he was able to determine what was missing.

"She took one of the Manton double-barrels," he told his father. "She also took the Linsley and another knife."

"Egad! She's armed for war!" said Persephone in amazement. The gravity of the situation did not register with her. "That explains a lot," she said with a shrug.

"What do you mean?" asked Dorian darkly.

"Oh…well…I'm just saying, it would explain why she borrowed some of my clothes," said Persephone matter-of-factly.

All of her family turned to look at her, their mouths slightly slack in shock, except for Psyche.

"Why would your clothes be any different than hers?" asked Selena confusedly, not understanding the family's astonishment.

"Oh, because they weren't my *girlie* clothes; they were my *clothes,*" said Persephone with a grin, as if what she said explained everything.

"Men's clothes," said Islington flatly. "She left dressed as a man?" he asked Psyche.

"She did," confirmed Psyche with a nod of her head.

"What clothes did you give her?" the duke asked Persephone.

"Oh, I don't know," said Persephone with a shrug of uncertainty and a thoughtful frown. "A hat, some boots, a riding coat, and two changes of clothes, I guess. I thought she wanted to borrow them for the ride home since she would be going on horseback the whole way this time. Much easier to manage in britches."

The duke turned to look at Psyche. His expression had softened, but Psyche knew she was still going to face consequences from this.

"Do you know if she took a map?" he asked her.

Psyche nodded. "Of course. She had a map, compass, and a spyglass."

"We'll have to go after her," stated Myron resignedly.

"Obviously, but which way would she have gone?" asked Dorian. He pulled his watch from its pocket on his waistcoat and looked at it. "She's been gone over fourteen hours now."

"Well, there are four of us; we'll just go in different directions heading north until we find her," said Myron.

The duke shook his head. "As much as it pains me to say it, I *cannot* go. Aside from that, I think I should stay here, in case she comes back."

"I'll go," chirped Persephone excitedly.

"No, you won't!" said Gregory firmly. Persephone sat back on the sofa and folded her arms in front of her, pouting. He looked at his brothers, his expression unhappy. "I'm afraid I can't go either. I *have* to be to Swansea no later than Monday. If I'm not, the ship will not be re-supplied in time to make its delivery to Toronto, and they desperately *need* those supplies."

Islington looked at the duke. "I'd like to offer my assistance," he said calmly after giving Selena's shoulder a gentle squeeze.

There was no way he was going to let them look for Pandora without him. Once he found out where she had gone, he couldn't help feeling in some way responsible for it. She had tried to tell him and Dorian that the count needed to be warned immediately. Now, she felt they had left her little choice but to do it herself. The ball of tension that had formed in his stomach when he first saw Psyche enter the room had settled and wasn't going to dislodge itself until he found Pandora and brought her back safely. However, because he wasn't a member of the family—even though Selena was soon to be—he would need their permission. Luckily for him, it wasn't difficult to convince them.

The duke and duchess looked at him gratefully, especially Julia. After it had been determined they needed to find her daughter, she had been faced with the alarming possibility that none of her sons would be able to attend to it. Then, here was Islington, playing Pandora's knight errant once again. He had, over the Season, come to be almost as one of the family, and the duke and duchess trusted him implicitly.

"That would be an excellent idea," said the duke, seeing the relief on his wife's face.

Arachne had risen from her seat and went to look out the window. Her expression was concerned and disappointed as she turned to look back at everyone in the room.

"It's too dark to leave tonight," she said flatly.

"The hell you say!" said Dorian in surprise.

"Dorian!" said his mother, this time her tone showing more spirit.

He, too, went to the window. Other than the streetlamps, it was completely dark. He didn't want to admit Arachne was right, but he knew she was. Even though the streetlights would guide their way out of the city, once they reached the country, there would be no way to see where they were going. Although he tried to convince himself one or two miles would be better than none, it was really quite impractical.

"She's right," he said finally.

"Then we'll leave first thing in the morning," said Myron determinedly.

"I agree," said Islington. He turned to look at the duchess. "Your grace, with your permission, I'd like Selena to stay here with you until I return."

"Of course," said Julia with a smile. She looked at Selena. "What say you? We're a mad lot, we Savages, but fairly harmless," she teased.

Selena looked relieved at the prospect. She was concerned for her friend, and now both her fiancé and her brother would be traveling alone across the countryside to find her. While Selena knew they were more capable of taking care of themselves than Pandora (or so she thought), it wouldn't make her any less concerned for their safety. She didn't think she could bear to stay in the house alone.

"That would be lovely," she said with a grateful smile.

"We'll send a message to your mother to let her know our plans are going to be indefinitely delayed," said the duchess kindly.

"I'll go speak to Tajik and let him know of our intentions," said Myron, going to the door.

"I have a map in the library that will give us the information we need to figure which way to go. Although, Islington, you being from the North Country, I don't imagine you'll need it beyond a certain point," said Dorian.

"No, I don't expect I will, but we still need to decide what paths we'll take," agreed Islington.

Dorian nodded and left the room for the library next door.

Islington turned to look at the duke. "Your grace, I wonder if I might speak with you privately for a moment," he asked.

The duke looked at him curiously but nodded his head in consent. "Of course. We can go to my study."

The family watched the two of them leave together, Arachne and Psyche exchanging speculative glances. Selena watched them leave confusedly. It could be something to do with Dorian marrying her, but then again, it could be unrelated.

"Oh, I'll go make sure your room is prepared for tomorrow, Selena," said the duchess with a smile, rising to leave the room as well.

Psyche kept her sisters and Selena entertained with more details of what had transpired that morning. Both Arachne and Eurydice sat with astounded expressions. Selena couldn't help feeling a little angry with her brother and Dorian for putting Pandora into that position. Persephone, as irrepressible as ever, couldn't help voicing her sisterly pride at how well turned-out Pandora had been.

Now that they had determined a course of action, the shock of Pandora's running away was still present, but the activity of seeing to her retrieval had reduced the anxiety they had felt on discovering it to a bearable level. Ceaseless worrying would accomplish nothing, and they were all positive she would be found and returned safely.

≪ ≫

Islington calmly followed the duke to his study. Aberdare closed the door and went to sit at his desk after inviting Islington to be seated as well. He looked at the younger man expectantly, curious to know what this was about. It had nothing to do with Dorian's marriage to Selena; he was completely out of that because his son was old enough to make his own decisions, but his grace couldn't be happier with his son's choice of bride.

Islington looked at the duke contemplatively for a moment. He wasn't sure he wanted to do this, but he had reached the point where he felt it needed to be done before something else happened. He had hoped Pandora would concede defeat without this step, but now it might be necessary.

"Your grace," he began then cleared his throat nervously. "Your grace, I realize this may be an awkward time to ask it, but I would like your permission to marry your daughter."

The duke tilted his head sideways thoughtfully. "Which one?"

"Lady Pandora, of course," said Islington calmly.

Aberdare raised his eyebrows dubiously. "Does *she* know you're asking me about this?" he asked evenly.

"Well, no, your grace…not in so many words."

The duke's lips twitched mildly with amusement as he looked down at the items on his desk, which he marginally adjusted with his fingertips to hide his expression until he could compose it into something more serious.

"I see, and these words that you did use when you talked to her about it, did she seem to be agreeable to them?" he finally asked.

"No, she didn't," said Islington flatly.

The duke chuckled and shook his head. "My boy, I would honestly like to give you my permission, I really would, but if she's not willing, then neither am I or her mother. Pandora will let us know when she wants someone to have permission." He smiled kindly. "You seem like an agreeable fellow, so I wish you the best in convincing her. Maybe you should try using *a lot* more words."

"I see," said Islington softly, trying to hide his disappointment.

Pandora thought she had found an excellent spot to set up her tent. Not far beyond Knotting, she found a stream with a grove of trees that would give her plenty of concealment, but there was also a field nearby where Bellerophon could graze. She didn't see any other houses or buildings nearby, even when using her spyglass, so she felt safe to light a fire. Maiyin said the tent needed to be placed between two trees, but she hadn't mentioned how far apart the trees needed to be or if they needed to be a specific size or type of tree.

Luckily, Pandora had stopped when there was plenty of daylight left. She hadn't expected the tent to be so complicated. After she did her best to set it up, she tilted her head sideways to look at it disappointedly. She would know better tomorrow night.

It was a common tent that was held in place by eight stakes along its bottom edge fastened into the ground. To raise the peak, instead of poles or other bracing she wouldn't have been able to carry, there were ropes connected at either end to be fastened over limbs to keep it straight. Unfortunately, Pandora didn't know this before she began to erect it. The center was dipped in the middle and canted slightly to one side.

"Shaped like *triangle,*" she muttered, mocking Maiyin. She looked at Bellerophon. "What do you think, fella?" she asked.

Bellerophon looked at her, smacking his lips and showing his teeth in what passed for his version of a laugh.

"Aye, keep laughing, Bell. I won't give you sugar for a month," Pandora grumbled then shrugged resignedly. "It will at least keep me dry."

Maiyin had provided a small pillow, two thick, woolen blankets, and a thinner, cotton one that used to be a sheet. Pandora folded one of the wool blankets for use as a makeshift mattress. She had at least managed to find a spot between two trees that was fairly free of roots, so the blanket would do for its purpose. It wouldn't be as comfortable as her soft feather mattress at home, but it was better than the hard ground. She had carried all her belongings into the tent after removing them from Bellerophon's back, taking special note of how they had been put on so she wouldn't have trouble reloading them in the morning.

Once she had unloaded everything, she created a makeshift halter using one end of the rope from the saddle and fastened it onto Bellerophon. She unwound the rest of its length and attached it to a tree near the edge of the field where Bellerophon could graze at his leisure but could still, walking in the other direction, reach the stream to drink. He was smart enough not to tangle himself around the trees.

After seeing to her tent and her horse, Pandora gathered up several small branches and leaves to build a fire. This, at least, was one thing she could do without any difficulty. She struck her flint near the leaves, and they caught easily. By blowing on it a little and gradually adding small twigs, it began to burn brightly. She didn't need an inferno, but something suitable for making tea would be grand.

She had never made her own tea before, but she had watched it made a time or two and was able to create something passable. She didn't have any cream, but she pilfered one of Bellerophon's sugar lumps to sweeten it. After drinking water all day, it was divine. She ate the last of the ham Maiyin had given her because it would be spoiled by tomorrow, and she had a small piece of bread. She wasn't really hungry.

Pandora sat for a time after eating, watching the flames dance around hypnotically. She was tired but felt unable to go to sleep. She looked at her watch and saw it was only ten. No wonder. She hadn't gone to bed at ten since she was a child. Still, if she wanted an early start in the morning, she needed to go to sleep. She banked the fire, hoping it would still have a few coals in the morning to make more tea.

She checked on Bellerophon one last time, and then she crawled into the tent. She had long since removed her hat and riding coat, but once she was inside the tent with the flaps closed, she removed her cravat, waistcoat and boots. She unfastened the tie on her shirt, but she didn't want to get completely undressed in case she needed to dress in a hurry. She unwound her hair and braided it loosely, but she had forgotten to bring a ribbon to tie it. It would stay well enough without one. She folded her waistcoat and placed it on top of her already folded riding coat. Having only two changes of clothing, Pandora would have to keep each set as clean and neat as possible. She folded up the cravat into a little square, but rather than placing it with her other garments, she laid it beside her head on the pillow near her face. Within minutes, she was sound asleep.

Chapter Seventeen

Henry Smoot awoke to the sound of a clanging bell yet again. He was sorely tempted to remove the bell from its post and place it where the sun would never rise on the offensive person ringing it. He sat on the edge of the bed and ran a tired hand over his face then looked out the window. It was about the same time as the morning before. Henry felt he was a reasonable man. He was there for the mail coaches. He was there for the prison system, the clergy, and for king and country, but he felt they should *all* let him get a good night's sleep.

He quickly splashed a bit of cold water on his face. Then he put on his clothes, running a hand through his hair as he went to open the door. He blinked when he saw the rider in front of him. He looked from one direction on the street to the other confusedly then back at the rider.

"Come on, man, I haven't all day!" said Islington impatiently.

"Didn't you come through here yesterday?" asked Henry in confusion.

"No, I did not," said Islington tightly.

Henry inspected the man and his horse. No, he was right. This horse was smaller, and it was a mare. And, although the man the previous morning had been untalkative, he had at least been untalkatively *pleasant.* There was also the matter of the bow; the rider today carried a rifle. He also didn't seem to be carrying as much on his saddle. Henry shrugged. He went to the gate and opened it then walked back to stand beside the horse.

"Penny-and-a-half," he said shortly.

Islington tilted his hat back slightly and sat back in his saddle to look at the gatekeeper speculatively.

"Why would you think I crossed through here yesterday?"

Henry shrugged. "Don't know. Just thought I recognized you, is all," he said noncommittally.

"*Did* you see a rider come through here yesterday morning about this time on a black horse? The horse would have been much larger."

"I suppose I could have," said Henry evasively. "Of course, I don't make special note of it. Number of people come passing through here every day…hard to keep track of who comes and goes."

Islington sighed disgustedly and reached into his pocket where he kept a small amount of the money he carried to retrieve a crown, which he handed to the gatekeeper. Islington looked at him expectantly.

"Oh, sure, now you mention it, I did see a rider on a black horse like yours come through here yesterday. Didn't say much other than that he was going up north to do some hunting."

"Indeed," said Islington dryly. He touched the brim of his hat with his finger and gave the man a tight smile. "Good day to you, sir," he said politely. He took off from the gate quickly, setting his horse to a gallop.

Henry watched after him for a moment then flipped the crown satisfactorily in his hand before walking back into the gatehouse. Maybe *he* would go up north to do a bit of hunting.

Islington, Dorian and Myron set off from the Bruton Mews just after six. The duke and duchess, Gregory, and Selena were there to see them away. The brothers promised their parents that they would find Pandora and bring her back. Islington promised Selena he would be careful, and if he was able, he would go by their home in Bardsey and personally let their mother know what had happened if he was still searching for Pandora by the time he reached the vicinity. He didn't *promise* he would, however, because he suspected it would be well out of his way, and if he hadn't found Pandora by then, he would want every minute to look for her. The duchess had already arranged for a messenger to deliver a letter to the marchioness, so it wasn't really necessary.

Tajik told Myron and Dorian they would treat their horses *kindly*. It wasn't a request. He told them they would stop every two hours to let the horses rest for thirty minutes, and they wouldn't travel more than ten hours a day. He also told them they would return with the horses they left on. After much grumbling, the two agreed to his orders because they knew Tajik wouldn't let them leave the stables until they did, and even their father wouldn't convince him otherwise. The Syrian understood this was a critical situation, but his job was to make sure their animals were treated properly. Tajik tried to soften the demands by letting them know he had told Pandora to do the same, so it wasn't giving her an advantage for her brothers to follow them as well. He also said that even though she had the faster horse, theirs weren't carrying as much weight, which would give them an even or better chance.

The duke and duchess wished them all luck, and Aberdare told them that if they hadn't returned to London with Pandora by the end of the fortnight when he had completed his business, then they would travel up to Edinburgh to meet them. The brothers assured their parents it would be unnecessary, but Islington wasn't quite so confident. Pandora had a day's lead, and the longer they waited, the further ahead she got. He had been tempted to leave the night before, and the only things that had stopped him were knowing he had to see to Selena and that he couldn't travel at night...no matter how much he wanted to.

The three had decided what routes they would take and where they would meet in Edinburgh last night after supper. Each had determined what they thought would be the most logical path for her to follow. Their reasoning behind their decisions was sound, and each agreed the other directions stood as much chance of being correct as his own.

Dorian was going to take the Great North Road. It was a fairly direct route and well maintained as turnpike most of the way. Dorian thought it would be logical for her to go that way because she would want to get there as quickly as possible, and good roads would help her do that.

Myron was heading due west for a time before turning straight north at Gloucester. It seemed likely she would want to go that route because it was also fairly direct, and she was familiar with the road for at least part of the way because they took it when they traveled home to Wilderland.

Islington thought she was going to take *the* direct route. He was going to travel from London to Edinburgh in as much of a straight line as possible, regardless of whether or not it was turnpike, field lane or cross country. He knew she would want to avoid large cities because she was a *woman* and also because she was a woman *dressed as a man*. He also knew she was a more than capable rider, and she wouldn't be deterred by field fences, streams, or any other obstacle that might be in her way.

After his encounter with the gatekeeper, Islington was already fairly confident he had managed to pick the correct route. It irked him that he needed to bribe the man for the information, but if it would put him closer to finding Pandora, then a few coins was inconsequential.

Pandora awoke that morning with a crick in her neck. The pillow wasn't big enough. When she set up camp next time, she would use her saddle to supplement the pillow and see if that helped. The blanket had been fine for a mattress, but she might bolster that with some grass or branches as well. Sleeping on the ground made her realize she had been thoroughly spoiled by her family, and it made her appreciate it and miss it all the more.

There were enough coals burning to make another pot of tea, which she let boil while she began packing. She satisfied herself for breakfast with a handful of raisins and an orange. She would eat more later, but she didn't want to start off on an empty stomach. Once she finished her tea and cleaned the pot, it was just nearing 6:30.

Bellerophon was grazing contentedly in the field, as she had expected he would be, and he seemed much refreshed after their night's rest. He trotted up to her happily when she came out of the tent, and she could tell he was eager to be off again. She saddled him and repacked everything, but she waited to put his bridle on until the last minute to give him more time to graze.

They had been traveling for just over an hour, and Bellerophon had resumed his lope of the previous morning. They would be to Finedon soon. Just a few miles beyond that would put them near Kettering and halfway through the county. Pandora hoped to be into Leicestershire before noon. If they were able to keep to the pace they were going, it was likely they could be to Edinburgh in less than the week Pandora anticipated.

Pandora wasn't sure the weather and terrain would cooperate. Although the hills she could see ahead didn't appear to be steep or plentiful, it would mean Bellerophon would have to slow to a walk. She could also see the sky ahead of them gathering clouds ominously. Her blankets were wrapped tightly inside the waterproof tent, and all of her bags were waterproof as well, but she wasn't looking forward to traveling in the rain. If it was still raining when it came time to set up camp, that would present a set of problems she would rather not have to deal with. She would have to see how it went and hope they would still be able to cover a good bit of distance before the weather stopped them or slowed them down.

Islington was making good time. He had asked the gatekeeper at Edgeware if he had seen a rider traveling on a large, black horse. The man had flatly stated no, and paying him more than his required tax wouldn't coax it out of him; he simply didn't know. Islington was already past Elstree and nearly to St. Albans, where he would turn away from the main road.

His horse was doing well, and even though she was the best in his stable, she was no match for Pandora's horse. If Pandora was riding as quickly as she could, he wouldn't be able to catch her until she made it to Edinburgh…unless something happened along the way to slow her down. He tried to put that from his mind because the things he was imagining only made the knot that had formed in his stomach last night grow even tighter. He wanted to believe she was able to take care of herself. He wanted to believe he would find her, and once he did, he was never going to let her out of his sight again.

《《 》》

Pandora and Bellerophon made it past Kettering without any difficulties. They were starting out after their second stop for the morning, and the weather, while cloudy, remained dry. The road they were traveling was a mail coach road, so the surface was good and the trees were trimmed back. They had skirted just around the edge of Kettering, but there had been several people out on their morning's business already.

The road was busy, and they had been obliged to pull to the side several times for coaches to go by. It slowed them down a bit, and they couldn't cover as much distance as Pandora had hoped, but it wouldn't be long before they turned from the main road again to keep their proper direction. While Pandora appreciated the good surface, the longer she stayed on it, the more the chance increased that she would encounter a toll gate or turnpike.

Pandora sorely missed having ham with the meal she ate on their stop. She ate some of the jerked meat Keung had provided, but it was not as satisfying as the ham. If they stopped early enough for the night, she would try her hand at fishing. She would just have to make sure, if she was lucky enough to catch anything, that she closed her eyes when she skewered the fish to cook it. The fishing wasn't going to be a problem because she had gone with her brothers to watch them fish at home several times, but cooking the fish was an entirely different matter for two reasons: she wasn't terribly familiar with cooking…anything, and the thought of killing something—even something as unattractive as a fish—wasn't appealing to her.

It was then that she felt a large drop of water hit the brim of her hat. She looked up at the sky, peculiarly hoping it was a bird flying over. Another drop hit against one of her saddlebags. Then another. Before long, it was as if the bottom had fallen out of the sky and the huge drops fell in torrents. Bellerophon shook his head to clear them from his ears and slowed his pace to a walk. Pandora adjusted her coat to hang better over her legs and closed the collar tighter about her neck. Her hat, at least, had a wide enough brim that the rain wasn't going down the back of her coat. Her clothes underneath were staying dry for the time being, but they needed to find some place to stop until the downpour let up.

It was raining hard enough that it was difficult to see, especially when the wind shifted to blow it directly into Pandora's face. She tried to console herself that it was at least not thundering and lightning when she heard a boom from a thunderclap. They would definitely need to stop as soon as she found a place that would offer some shelter.

≪ ≫

Dorian and Myron were both covering a good amount of distance in their search. They had still not found anyone who remembered seeing a rider on a large black horse, but they were just beginning. Neither was going to give up hope they were going in the right direction yet. The hour was growing later, and it would soon be time to stop for the night. Dorian thought he would at least make it to St. Neots before he would have to find an inn. Myron didn't think he would make it all the way to Gloucester, but he would make it to Stroud. The weather had been fair, if cloudy, so they had been able to keep their horses traveling quickly, even following Tajik's orders. They both intended to start as early as possible in the morning.

<<< >>>

Islington was almost to Finedon. He would stop at an inn there for the night. Jezebel, his mare, was exhausted, and he had to admit he was also tired. For the past hour or two, he had been traveling through heavy rain, and with the gathering darkness, it was becoming difficult to see where he was going. He was looking forward to a hot meal and a beer followed by a bed that would hopefully not be louse-infested.

While he traveled, he was able to find enough people who had seen a rider passing through on a large, black horse to know he was going in the right direction. He was surprised Pandora was keeping to roads, no matter how meager, and less to going cross country. He suspected she was reluctant to do so because she was not familiar with the area and didn't want to risk injuring her horse. He hoped her doing this would help him find her; if she continued to use roads, he would be more likely to find someone who had seen her and keep himself on the right course.

He was amazed she had made it as far as she had. He had fully expected to find her stranded along the road...or worse. He was grudgingly impressed. He had to wonder, though, if she would have the stamina to make it all the way to Edinburgh. He didn't doubt her horse would, but Pandora just appeared to be far too fragile to make it the four hundred miles alone, staying in the elements. The rain that was now pelting him had come from the north, which meant she had gone through it as well. He hoped she had the sense to get out of it before she gave herself a cold...or worse.

Islington idly wondered how her brothers were doing. He didn't think they had realized they were going the wrong way yet, and it would take until sometime tomorrow before they did. They would all meet in Edinburgh at the inn they had agreed upon.

Edinburgh was a large town, and he was sure Pandora would try to find some place close to Holyrood, even if it meant staying in a less than reputable part of the city, but there were several places she could choose. He could only assume she would stay at an inn once she got there, but he hoped he would find her before she ever made it that far.

He hadn't decided what he would do once he found her, though. He couldn't make up his mind if he would make her turn around and go back to

London or escort her the rest of the way to Edinburgh and let her complete what she had set out to do. It would depend on how quickly he was able to find her and her condition when he did.

He soon saw lights near the road ahead and realized he had finally made it to Finedon. He would stay the night and let the keeper know he wanted to leave as early as possible in the morning. Islington hoped he would be able to catch Pandora tomorrow.

Pandora was falling asleep in her saddle. She hadn't been able to find a place to stop for the night, and the rain was still coming down. It wasn't as bad as it had been, but it was enough to keep her miserable. Bellerophon courageously plodded on, but he was done for the day, too. She didn't know where they were because she was reluctant to use her map in the rain, but her compass showed that she was still headed in the right direction. It was nearing half-past seven, and she needed to find some place to stop before they were traveling in full dark.

The rain that had started that morning just after Kettering had come and gone for most of the day. At some points, it had been bad enough she could barely see a hundred feet in front of her. Bellerophon hadn't been able to do more than walk, and the mud created by the rain made that difficult at times. She hadn't found many suitable places for their rests, and he wasn't as full of energy as the day before because he hadn't been able to graze as much. The schedule she had used yesterday had been unusable today because they had needed to make stops for the weather. They hadn't gone over their ten hour limit, but the weather made them weary enough it seemed like it.

Somehow, they had left the road. She thought they were heading for Twyford, but she eventually realized they were following little more than a game trail that dwindled to nonexistence shortly after they were on it. There were a few rock outcrops here and there, and they at one point crossed a beck, but she had yet to see any trees. Pandora didn't know if she would be able to find a place suitable for setting up her tent. She couldn't have a fire because of the rain. She was about to pull out her compass for another reading when they came upon a road.

She stopped Bellerophon in the middle of it as she looked from one direction to the other contemplatively. She retrieved her compass. The road was an almost exact east-west line. She didn't see a mile marker or road sign, but she didn't want to go east. After thinking a few more minutes, she directed Bellerophon to go west. It wouldn't put them any closer to finding a place to stop, but she hoped they would at least find something to give her an idea of where they were.

After going less than a mile, they came to a village just as the rain slackened to a fine mist. Their road went along the northern edge of it, which relieved Pandora. She didn't want to ride directly through. She didn't see a sign to tell her where she was, but if the rain stayed light, she would risk pulling out her map to determine that for herself. She was tired and desperate enough to find a place for Bellerophon to get water that when she came across an inn with a small pond nearby she hesitated only a moment before she led him to it and dismounted.

It was odd with all the rain that it had been so difficult to find water for him to drink. She should have stopped to let him rest at the beck. Pandora didn't want to disobey Tajik's orders, and she was willing to risk discovery to see Bellerophon tended to. The horse appreciated it, and she patted his neck affectionately as he drank.

Pandora bent over to examine his legs and hooves to make sure he hadn't gotten any injuries or picked up any rocks from their detour across the countryside. When she rose in preparation to go around to the other side, she was startled to see a small, towheaded boy standing nearby, looking at Bellerophon with awe. He was only seven or eight years old, with Pandora thinking of how big her younger brothers were. His clothes were homespun but serviceable, and his shoes needed replacing. He seemed harmless, but Pandora would rather not have been seen.

"Wow, sir, you have a really big horse," he said, daring to come a little closer. Pandora saw a healthy smattering of freckles across the bridge of his nose, and he had curious brown eyes.

"Aye," responded Pandora, trying to keep her voice low.

She went around to the other side to inspect while Bellerophon complacently continued to drink. He found a small patch of grass nearby, which he took a few bites from before going back to the water. She hoped she could find a field when they stopped for the night.

"Does he have a name?" asked the boy.

Pandora closed her eyes and began to pray. He was just curious. She couldn't be mean to him, but if she answered him, he would find out she wasn't a man. Brief yes-or-no answers were easy enough, but an actual conversation was impossible. In the end, she knew not answering him would be worse than doing so.

"Bellerophon," she said calmly.

"Hey, wait! You're not—" he began in surprise.

Pandora put a finger to her lips and shook her head. "Please, don't say anything," she pleaded softly. He put his lips together firmly and shook his head, his eyes round in amazement. "Do you have a name?"

"F-freddie, ma'am. My name is Freddie Bunney."

"Freddie, what is this place?"

She removed her gloves to flex her fingers, which had become red and irritated from wearing the wet leather.

"Thorpe Satchville, ma'am."

"Do you know where that is from Twyford?"

"About a mile-and-a-half north, ma'am."

He still seemed to be awestruck by Pandora being a woman. She hoped that would continue. She was relieved to find she hadn't gone too terribly off course and was actually back onto it again.

"Do you know if there's a grove of trees near a stream and a field near here?" Freddie's forehead wrinkled in thought, and then he shook his head negatively. "I need some place to sleep for the night."

"You can stay at me mum's inn," he said helpfully, looking back over his shoulder toward the building.

Pandora shook her head. "As much as I would love to, I cannot. You see, I'm trying to go somewhere far away from here, and to do that, I have to dress like this," said Pandora, pulling at the lapel of her coat. "People don't like to see women dressed like this, so I can't let anyone know that I am one. Do you understand?"

Freddie scratched his head then nodded. His face suddenly brightened.

"I know where you can stay," he said excitedly.

"Where?" she asked hopefully.

"I call it the Frog's Mouth because that's what it looks like," he said casually. "It's a cave."

"How do I get to it?" asked Pandora, sighing with relief.

"I'll have to show you." He looked around at the darkening air. "It's hard to explain where it is, and you'll never find it in the dark."

"All right."

Her stomach rumbled fitfully, and she realized she hadn't eaten anything for several hours, and even that had only been a small piece of cheese and an apple. Freddie heard it as well.

"Are you hungry? I can get you some food," he said helpfully.

Pandora thought about it. She would love some meat...any meat. Still, she could only guess what might happen to the boy if he were caught.

"I would love food, Freddie, but I don't want to get you in trouble."

"Oh, it won't be any trouble," he assured her. "I'll get some food for your horse, too." He looked around. "You wait here." He looked around again. "I'll be back with food then take you to the Frog's Mouth."

He took off at a trot before Pandora could call him back. She hoped she wouldn't get him in trouble. He seemed very sweet, and she didn't want to think she would lead him to do something that would get him hurt. She nervously stood by Bellerophon, rubbing his neck while he moved back to grazing the sparse patch of nearby grass.

It wasn't long before Freddie came scampering back, his arms laden with items, not the least of which was half of a small bale of hay in a net and a small wicker basket. Pandora's eyes widened in alarm as he approached. She caught the scent of roast beef and apple pie, and she thought she was going to start crying.

"Freddie!" she gasped. "Thank you, but this is too much!"

"Is it?" he asked, his forehead wrinkling uncertainly.

"No, but *yes!*" she whispered.

"Come on, I'll show you to the cave," he said preparing to lead the way, still carrying the items.

"I'll tell you what: would you like to ride my horse?"

His eyes grew round in wonder. "*Could* I?" he sighed.

Bellerophon raised his head to look at them.

"Absolutely. I'll let you ride him while I lead. I'll carry the hay; you carry the basket and point the way. How does that sound?"

"Bloody marvelous!" he said with a grin. Pandora chuckled at his enthusiasm.

She had him set the hay down while she lifted him and the basket into the saddle after shoving her gloves into the pocket of her coat. She couldn't bear putting them back on, and they were ruined anyhow; a woman's leather gloves weren't made to withstand a downpour, and she hadn't thought to ask Persephone for a pair that had been treated. Bellerophon nickered at the slight weight of the boy in the saddle, but Pandora was able to shush him.

"Be good, fella. This boy has gotten you some nice, sweet hay," she said soothingly. She then grabbed the hay in the net in her left hand and Bellerophon's reins in the other. "Which way?" she asked expectantly.

Freddie was looking around himself blissfully, but he was able to point to the road ahead.

"Frederick Leftwich Bunney!" Pandora heard a woman's voice call from the door of the inn. Her eyes widened in dismay. "What do you think you're about?"

Freddie turned to look at his mother unconcernedly. "I'm just showing this man to the crossroads, Mama!" he called.

Pandora was hidden from the woman's full view by the mass of Bellerophon's body between them. Freddie's mother rested a hand with a large wooden spoon in it on one of her hips appraisingly.

"All right, then, but hurry back! It'll soon be suppertime!" she called.

"Aye, Mama!" he called back.

Pandora urged Bellerophon to continue. The sky was coming very near to full dark, and she idly wondered what time it was. Instead of leading her to the actual crossroads, Freddie had her turn off the road to the left for them to go across a field that steadily went downhill. Once they were around a large outcropping of stone, she could hear the sound of a small stream. It was then that she saw the cave in the embankment.

He was right: it did look like a frog's mouth gaping open, but it wasn't what Pandora would call a cave. It was more like a deep indentation in the side of the hill where it had been eroded away or mined. It was big enough that Bellerophon could stand under it to get out of the weather. It was also near a spring-fed stream, and fresh grass was in abundance. After traveling all day in the rain, Pandora thought she had found Nirvana.

"Oh, Freddie, this is wonderful," sighed Pandora.

She helped him down, and he pulled her by the hand into the cave.

"I have wood here, so if you want to make a fire, you can," he said proudly. "I come here all the time. This is me fort."

"Freddie, I could kiss you," said Pandora with a grin. He looked at her disconcertedly. "I won't though," she said with a wink. He grinned back with relief.

"You can leave the basket and things here. I'll come back and get them sometime. I expect you'll be gone by morning?" he asked.

"I hope so, if the weather is fair. How do I get back to the road?"

"Go back up around the rocks, heading straight north. The road will be there. Where are you going?"

"As north as north can be—Scotland," said Pandora.

"Wow," sighed Freddie wonderingly. "When you get to the road, turn left and go not too far. There'll be a road to your right; that'll head you toward Kirby Bellars at the Wreake. That's the closest place to cross, unless you go all the way to Sysonby and Melton Mowbray."

"Thank you so much, Freddie," said Pandora, smiling gratefully.

She reached into the pocket of her coat for her moneybag. She pulled out two sovereigns and placed them into his hand. He looked at them, and his eyes widened in surprise.

"That's for all your kindness," said Pandora. "It's also for the food and the place to sleep."

"Aw, ma'am," he said, blushing.

"Can you make it back home safely?" she asked a little worriedly.

"Oh, sure. I come here all the time. I know these hills like the back of me hand, I do," he said with a grin. "I best be getting home before me mum begins to wonder, though."

"Good night, Freddie, and thank you again," said Pandora.

"Aw, it's nothing," he called as he ran back up around the rocks.

Pandora stood watching for a moment after he left then built a fire while she still had enough light. There was an abundant pile of wood beside a ring of stones where he obviously built a fire often. She got the fire going well, and then she unloaded her things from Bellerophon. He would much prefer the grass, but she found a way to hang the net of hay on the wall of the cave where he could reach it, just in case.

She was surprised to find that Freddie had a small ticked mattress near the back wall of the cave. Sleeping on it was going to be heavenly after only the blanket the night before. She thought of using the saddle as a supplement to her pillow, but it was damp, and both it and the saddle blanket could do with some time by the fire. Bellerophon would appreciate the blanket being dry when it came time to put it back on in the morning.

She took off her hat and coat and found a place to hang them near the fire. Her waistcoat and shirt were still relatively dry after being protected under the oilcloth of her riding coat, but she would change into her other set of clothes before leaving in the morning simply because wearing the same clothes two days in a row was enough for her. She would try to wash them when she stopped tomorrow night, provided the weather was good. She took off her boots and set them near the fire as well. They weren't too damaged from the soaking they had received because Persephone had them well-treated to resist moisture, but they might be a little stiffer when they dried. Once Pandora refashioned the halter for Bellerophon, she fastened it under a large boulder to let him have access to the stream, hay, and grass. She still didn't think he would wander off, but she didn't want to find out.

Once she had everything unpacked and started a pot of tea, she lifted the basket of food and opened the lid. Freddie had put in a bowl containing roast beef and boiled vegetables and half of a small, baked apple pie. There was also a small pitcher, which contained cow's milk.

"Oh, Freddie, you're my knight in shining armor," she said blissfully as she began to enjoy the simple but delicious food that was still hot.

After checking on Bellerophon one last time and banking the fire, she lay on the mattress under her blankets and was asleep within minutes.

Dorian awoke the next morning to pouring rain. He did not, however, let it deter him from resuming his search for his sister. He had still not found anyone who had seen her, but he didn't let it stop him. Even if he wasn't going the path she had taken, he could at least be in Edinburgh when she got there. He would make it to Newark or possibly Gainsborough by day's end; that would put him at almost halfway there.

Myron was able to get an early start. The weather was fair, but it was going to rain. He paid it no mind. He hadn't traveled far when he reached Cheltenham and the first report of a rider on a large, black horse. He took off to the northeast toward Stratford, where the farmer had told him he'd seen the rider heading. He made a few enquiries along the way and had it confirmed by other people that they, too, had seen a rider on a black horse going in that direction. He was hopeful he would soon be able to take his sister home.

Islington left Finedon in the rain. It would make it difficult to ask if anyone had seen Pandora because most, including farmers, would find something to occupy themselves that wouldn't need them to be outside. If he weren't on his fool's errand, *he* wouldn't be out in the weather, either.

Jezebel seemed rested after the night, but she wasn't impatient to be off. Considering how hard he was riding her, Islington couldn't blame the mare for being reluctant. If he hadn't managed to catch Pandora before he made it near home in Bardsey, he would go by there and switch mounts. He then dismissed the idea because he would need to keep following Pandora. He only hoped his horse would last.

He was making good time, even with the rain, because he happened upon a mail coach road. He was able to find one or two people out who told him they had seen a rider on a black horse go through the previous afternoon—in the rain—after he passed Kettering. The further he traveled, however, the fewer people he found to ask, and the few he did find hadn't seen her. He wondered if he might have gone off the route she had followed, but it was possible because of the rain that Pandora had gone through without being seen.

Once he crossed the Welland and traveled through Drayton, he was relieved to find someone who remembered seeing a rider on a black horse. It had been in the late afternoon so Islington was pleased to hear he was narrowing his distance behind her. The rain, for the moment, had stopped, and he urged Jezebel to go faster. He would stop with her after a while to let her rest, but he couldn't contain his excitement about finding Pandora. He didn't expect he would catch up with her that day, but he was near enough now that catching her sometime early tomorrow was a real possibility.

Pandora was moderately perturbed. After having the rest of the apple pie and some tea for breakfast, she and Bellerophon had made an excellent start. The weather was overcast but dry, and they had found their way back to the road without any difficulty. They had crossed the Wreake at Kirby Bellars where Freddie had recommended. They had managed to cross the Grantham Canal at its myriad turnings. They had even managed to cross the Trent by ferry without her being detected as a woman, or at least without the ferryman being *concerned* about her being a woman after the nice tip she gave him. Now, they were going to be delayed from making even better progress because of a traveler on the road ahead of them. To make matters worse, over the past hour, it had started to rain again after remaining dry for most of the day. It was hard for Pandora not to feel frustrated.

She had first noticed the rider not long after they crossed the Trent. She wasn't sure if he had come up through Nottingham or a different road, but he was in front of her now. From what she was able to see at a distance, his mount was small, and he wasn't in a hurry. Several times, Pandora needed to pull up on Bellerophon's reins to slow him down to keep the space between them to her liking, which made her horse cranky. She had hoped to be well out of Nottinghamshire and into Yorkshire before she stopped for the night, but at the rate the man ahead of her was traveling—if he didn't turn off soon—she would be lucky to make it just over into Derbyshire.

<<< >>>

Islington had been traveling for a little over an hour after the sighting at Drayton, and he had just passed through Twyford. No one in the village had seen Pandora, but there were several roads through the area she could have taken. If no one had seen her in Kirby Bellars, then he might become concerned. The rain had stopped, but the sky was cloudy, and the air was misty from all the moisture. Once he made it to Kirby on the Wreake, he would stop to let Jezebel rest and have a late dinner.

They passed a stream to the right when Jezebel stumbled. Islington wasn't sure if she lost her footing on the loose gravel or if she was just too tired. She righted herself without falling or throwing him, but her gait was off. Islington swore softly under his breath and had her come to a stop. He dismounted and looked at her hooves. The front two were fine, if worn, but on the back, the shoe on her right hind hoof had gone completely missing.

"Bloody hell," he muttered disbelievingly.

He looked down the road, wondering if he could get her back to Twyford. He didn't want to let her go too far without a shoe because he couldn't afford the risk of laming her. He looked at the road ahead of him. There was another small village up there somewhere, but he wasn't sure if it would be closer than going back. In the end, he decided to take his chances on the road ahead of him.

"Come on, girl," he said resignedly, leading her by the reins.

The village, which turned out to be Thorpe Satchville, was closer than Twyford, but the blacksmith's shop, which he discovered through enquiring with the vicar at the church on the near end of town, was at the far end, attached to the only inn. The doors to the smithy (which he recognized from the large anvil in front of it) were closed. Islington's forehead wrinkled disconcertedly, and he tethered Jezebel nearby and walked to the door of the inn after giving her a soothing pat on the shoulder.

The common room he entered was moderately-sized with a few tables and chairs placed in front of a large fireplace at the far end. To the left was a small bar. Also to the left of the fireplace was a set of narrow stairs leading to the next floor. When he looked at the bar, he saw a woman behind the counter drying glasses and placing them into a cupboard. She looked up expectantly when she heard him come in.

"Good afternoon, sir," she said kindly. "What can I do for you?"

"Where might I find the blacksmith?" he asked politely.

She nodded and lifted the gate on the bar to go to a doorway at the near end of it.

"If you'll just give me a moment," she said as she reached it.

Islington nodded and watched her leave. She soon returned with a man following behind her.

"My name's Maggie Bunney, keeper of the Hare and Hound." She gestured to the man behind her. "This here's my husband, Harold Bunney, the blacksmith."

"Good afternoon, Mr. Bunney," said Islington.

The man had been roused from a nap. Both he and his wife were in their mid-thirties. She was short and plump, with light hair and brown eyes that twinkled with a friendly kindness. Her husband was tall and muscular because of his trade, with dark hair and eyes that were looking at Islington assessingly. Islington hoped that waking the man had not put him into a foul mood.

"Hunh," said Harold noncommittally.

"Mr. Bunney, I was wondering if I could have you replace a shoe on my horse," said Islington politely.

"No, I'm afraid I can't do that...not until tomorrow," said Harold, firmly shaking his head.

"I noticed the doors to the smithy are closed, but I would be willing to pay you well to do this for me today," said Islington patiently.

"Nothin' doin'," said Harold, folding his arms across his chest. "I don't work on Sundays. Sunday is the Lord's day."

Islington clenched his jaw on an angry retort and attempted to control his temper.

"Mr. Bunney, it's important that I continue on my way as quickly as possible. A young woman's life may be at stake," said Islington with as much calm as he could muster.

"Sir, I feel for your situation, but I don't work on Sundays. It's a sin. Now, you're welcome to take a room at the inn for the night, and I assure you it'll be the first thing I do in the morning," said Harold kindly.

Islington looked at him. The man was serious. No amount of money he offered would make Harold Bunney change his mind, and it would only make him angry if Islington tried. He had to respect it, even if he didn't like it. He could try to take Jezebel back to Twyford, but the distance was over a mile, and he could wind up making her lame, which would delay his journey even longer. He looked at his pocket watch. It was nearing four. Pandora would have four more hours of daylight left to travel, if that, but even at a walk, it would add twenty-four miles to whatever lead she had. He disliked the thought he had come so close to finally catching her only to lose ground, but he had little choice.

"Very well," he said defeatedly with a tight smile. "Mistress Bunney, I'd like a room, please," he said as he turned to her.

"Of course," she said with a smile. "If you'll come this way," she said, going back behind the bar. Harold went back to the keeper's private rooms. "If I can get you entered in the register. Name?" she asked as she took out a large ledger and a pen and ink from beneath the counter, looking up at him expectantly.

"Viscount Islington," he said calmly.

Maggie's eyes grew round with alarm.

"Oh, lud," she gasped. "I'm terribly sorry, my lord."

Islington shrugged negligibly. "It's of no consequence," he said calmly, giving her a genuine smile after seeing she was upset for not addressing him properly.

"We don't have an ostler, my lord," she said sheepishly. "Usually, my husband tends to it, but because it's Sunday...."

"I understand."

"My son can see to your horse, my lord."

She lifted the gate again and went to the back rooms. After a moment, Islington heard a muffled yell and realized her son was not inside. Before long, Maggie came back with a small, blond-haired boy in tow. Islington hadn't realized he was so young.

"Freddie will see to your animal, my lord," said Maggie proudly.

Islington looked at the boy dubiously. He wasn't even four feet tall and only seven or eight years old. He was looking at Islington shyly, but his brown eyes were full of curiosity and intelligence.

"Perhaps I should go with him," said Islington. "Jezebel is rather high-strung. I wouldn't want her to hurt him."

Maggie shrugged negligibly. "Suit yourself, my lord," she said with an amused smile. "I'll show you to your room after you come back."

Islington followed the boy out the front door to the yard. Jezebel was standing tiredly, her head drooping. Her shoulders and flanks were lathered from the hard ride he had given her. He untethered her and let Freddie show him the way to the stable. It was large, much larger than Islington would have expected for a village of that size. It was well-kept, and he had to wonder how an inn of this size in a village this small could manage to stay in business.

"This is a big place," said Islington, looking around.

"Yessir," agreed Freddie politely. "It's quiet most of the year, but during hunting season, we get our share of visitors."

"What do they run around here?" asked Islington conversationally.

"Fox mostly," said Freddie. He led Islington to a stall and opened it. "This one'll do, I think."

Islington guided Jezebel into the stall. Freddie left but returned momentarily with a net of hay that he hung from a hook on the wall. He left again and came back with a bucket of water that he used to fill a pale inside the stall as well. He then went to retrieve a stool, which he placed beside the horse. He turned to look at Islington calmly.

"If you'll get your things to take inside, I'll see to getting her rubbed down after I remove her tack and get it cleaned," said Freddie politely.

"Are you sure you can manage it?" asked Islington concernedly. "I *can* see to it myself."

Freddie's eyes grew round, and he shook his head negatively. "Oh, *no, sir*. Me mum said for me to do it. I can manage just fine."

Islington looked at him doubtfully, but then he watched the boy go stand near Jezebel's head. He grabbed the reins and began to speak to her quietly, rubbing her nose as he did so. She then bent her head a little lower, and the boy was able to remove her bridle without any difficulty. Islington's eyebrows shot up in surprise, and he decided Jezebel was in capable hands. He removed his bag and his rifle in its holster from the saddle and left the stable, walking back to the inn.

Maggie was still behind the bar when he entered, but she was dusting bottles this time. She looked up when he came in.

"Are you ready to see your room now, my lord?" she asked, coming from behind the bar.

"Yes, please," he said with a smile.

Maggie led him up the stairs to the second floor. After taking him down the hall to the left, she opened the door to a room at the corner on the back side of the inn not facing the stable. It wasn't large, but it was clean, and the bed looked comfortable. There was a wash basin on a stand and a small fireplace bracketed by armchairs. He walked to the window and looked out; it gave him an excellent view of the surrounding, rolling hills and the road heading north. It would suit.

"We have larger rooms on the first floor, my lord, but I thought you would appreciate it being quieter. We tend to get a rowdy lot through here early in the morning on the way to the hunt and back. This way, you'll be able to sleep."

"Thank you, this will do nicely," said Islington with a smile, setting his bag on the edge of the bed.

"Can I bring you some food? We don't normally serve supper in the common room until eight or so."

"Yes, I would love something to eat."

"I'll bring that up for you shortly then," said Maggie with a smile. "If you need anything else, just ask."

"Thank you," said Islington kindly, giving her a brief smile.

After Maggie left and closed the door, Islington sat on the edge of the bed contemplatively. He wasn't sure how he was going to sit idly until the morning. Every minute put Pandora further away and increased the possibility she could be hurt in some way. He tried to keep from his mind everything that could happen to a young, beautiful woman alone in the countryside because it filled him with a panic that made the blood throb in his ears. He felt as if he had aged ten years since discovering Pandora had left for Edinburgh.

≪ ≫

Dorian's luck ran out as he was nearing Grantham in Lincolnshire. He was making good time, confident he would be to Newark by nightfall, when his gelding threw a shoe. To make matters worse, when the shoe came off, they were traveling over some sharp rock, which tore the frog on that hoof. Dorian managed to get the limping horse to the nearest inn, but it would be several days, if not more than a week, before his horse would be able to continue...either back to London *or* on to Edinburgh.

Dorian was upset he couldn't continue on to Scotland without delay. He remembered Tajik's warning that he would return with the horse he left on...a warning Dorian hadn't needed because he had no intention of leaving his best horse. The inn he found wasn't one he felt he could trust to tend to his horse properly; he wouldn't feel safe leaving him there to mend while he took one of theirs to continue his journey...not that they seemed to have any Dorian felt wouldn't go lame themselves after only a short distance. He felt somewhat remorseful for the injury because he had been pushing Barbaros hard, and the gelding had been bearing it well until he lost the shoe.

Dorian had already determined Pandora hadn't taken the Great North Road sometime around noon when none of his enquiries from the day before or that morning yielded anyone having seen her. No one he talked to even recalled seeing any rider on a black horse...be it a woman or man on either a small or a large one. After that point, he had simply been attempting to reach Edinburgh and be there when she arrived. Now, he had to hope Myron or Islington would have better success finding her.

Myron was also experiencing a setback. After leaving Cheltenham that morning with news that a rider on a large black horse had been seen going to Stratford, he had arrived in that city only to find the rider on the black horse had been a farmer riding an English Black...definitely not his sister on her Trakehner. Myron was disappointed. He had stopped to quickly eat a meal then turned around to go back to Cheltenham, where he would arrive just in time to stay the night and start out again in the morning. Now, he was faced with knowing he had wasted an entire day. He wouldn't tell his family where he was led astray because one of them would not be able to resist saying he had his own Cheltenham tragedy.

He had thought to continue from Stratford to Edinburgh, but he didn't want to risk the possibility someone might have seen Pandora between Cheltenham and where he would return to the road he had left. After losing a day, he wondered if this hadn't been the route she took. He was still not quite ready to give up. He was hoping Dorian or Islington would be able to find her, unaware that Dorian's horse had gone lame. Islington was, at least, following the right path, but he would not be able to continue until the following day.

《《 》》

Pandora was still following the solitary rider. She made her regular stops to rest and eat, but she would only go at a decent pace for a short distance after each one before meeting up with him again and slowing down. She was in a foul mood. It had been raining since afternoon, not heavily, but enough to make her feel soggy. It only stopped within the past hour. She had traveled onto a mail coach road, which required her to move to the side to allow someone's private coach to pass, slowing her further. Fortunately, because it was Sunday, the mail coaches weren't running, but the delay in time caused by the rider in front of her was worse than any that would have been caused by pulling to the side. To be stuck behind this person who wouldn't allow her to set her own pace was the most irksome thing of all.

She had still covered a good distance. Most of it was accomplished before meeting up with the rider, but he was moving steadily, if not quickly. It was odd, though, that he was taking the same route she used, even skirting around the edge of Mansfield rather than going directly through. She at least made it into Derbyshire, but the hour was growing late. For the past thirty minutes or so, she had been looking for a likely spot to stop for the night.

She had just gone through Pleasley when she came to a fork in the road. Pandora hoped the rider would go left, but—of course—he went right, the same direction Pandora needed to go. She cursed under her breath because there was a toll gate looming ahead of her. The rider paid his toll and continued on, but the gatekeeper began to close the gate after he went. Pandora started to panic and urged Bellerophon to go a little faster. The gatekeeper didn't hear her approaching, and thinking quickly, Pandora whistled to get his attention. He looked down the road, and stood with his hand on the gate. She read on the sign well ahead of it that the toll would be tuppence. She fished it out of her bag to have ready. The keeper stood waiting for her as she approached.

"Looks like you just made it," he said jovially. "I was closing it for the night."

She handed him her money and touched a finger to the edge of her hat sociably before continuing on, heaving a sigh of relief. She didn't want to be trapped in Stony Houghton for the night. It seemed a nice enough place, but there was nowhere for her to sleep or for Bellerophon to eat and drink.

Not far beyond the toll gate, she found a fair stretch of woods near a stream and some grass for Bellerophon. She glanced up the road in the distance to where the rider in front of her continued on before she turned off the road. She hoped he kept traveling or turned off somewhere so she wouldn't have to follow him the next day. At least it had quit raining, and when she looked at the sky, there were quite a few stars. She would have dry weather for sleeping, but the wood and leaves were still too wet to start a fire. She hoped she could have one, if only to dry out her things, but it didn't look likely. She would have to make do with jerked meat, raw carrots and some fruit for dessert…quite a change from the previous night's meal.

≪ ≫

Castleton had become aware of someone behind him on the road shortly after traveling through Arnold beyond Nottingham. At first he thought nothing of it, but he began to grow concerned after the rider maintained the same distance behind him on the road regardless of the speed he went. The rider would occasionally disappear, only to reappear not much later. He had tried going back roads and skirting around major cities, thinking the rider would continue ahead to avoid the delay it sometimes caused, but the person had not.

Someone less paranoid might not have thought anything of it, but Castleton was suspicious because of the secrets he kept. That this person had followed him all day through pouring rain, even when he at times went at a snail's pace, seemed to confirm he was following Castleton. When the person whistled to keep the toll gate open, Castleton knew it for a certainty.

Castleton wasn't sure why the man would be following him, but Hendon had warned him that there were people in London aware of their plans. Hendon had also said the people had been dealt with, but Castleton wasn't confident of Hendon's abilities, regardless of how clever he did seem to be at times. Perhaps the person was there to make sure that when the time came to act, he would stop Castleton. That couldn't happen; he had been waiting over half his life for this, and he wouldn't let anything—or anyone—stop him now.

About a mile past the toll gate, he chanced a look back to see the rider was no longer there. His forehead wrinkled concernedly, but then he looked around himself at how dark it was becoming and thought the rider had stopped for the night. Unfortunately, Castleton would have to do the same. He went into the village of Scarcliff to find a room at an inn. He would start early tomorrow and lose the man somehow, or else he would have to take more drastic measures.

≪ ≫

Islington decided to eat his supper in the common room. He wasn't very hungry because of the ample tray of food Maggie had brought him earlier and also because of his uncertainty about Pandora, but it would give him the chance to ask Maggie if she had seen Pandora the day before. If there were any other people from the area eating at the inn, he might ask them, too. Then, perhaps, he would feel like he had at least accomplished something.

He went downstairs and found no one else. He didn't think he was early. He had told Maggie when she brought the tray to his room that he would be eating there. She was at the bar, as usual, but it seemed he would be the only one dining. His forehead wrinkled thoughtfully as he walked over to the bar.

"Can I get you something before supper, my lord?" asked Maggie with a kind smile.

"Whisky, if you have it," he said calmly.

She nodded and pulled out a bottle and a small glass. She poured some for him and placed it on the counter.

"Mistress Bunney, might I ask you a question?" he asked hesitantly.

"At your leisure, my lord," she consented agreeably as she wiped down the shiny hardwood.

"Did you happen to see a rider pass through here on a large black horse recently?"

Her forehead wrinkled in thought then cleared in recollection.

"Yes, now you mention it, I did see a large black horse pass through here yesterday evening long about dark, my lord."

"Did you see what direction they went?" he asked, trying to contain his excitement. He was closer than he thought if it was actually Pandora.

"Well, no, I didn't, my lord, but my son, Freddie, was on the horse when it left."

"Pardon?" asked Islington in surprise.

"Sure! Freddie took 'em to the crossroads," said Maggie jovially.

"Might I have a word with him?" asked Islington hopefully.

"Certainly," said Maggie, going to lift the gate on the bar. She went to the door to her quarters. "Freddie!" she called.

A few minutes later, the young boy came to the doorway.

"Yes, Mama?" he asked.

"The viscount here wants to ask you about that rider with the black horse from yesternight," she said.

Freddie's face became guarded, but he looked at Islington politely.

"Your mother said you were riding the horse, is that right?"

"Yessir, I got to ride him. It was wonderful. He was so big—just like flying!" said Freddie, his expression becoming dreamy for a moment as he remembered the experience.

"If you got to ride him, then you must have spoken to his owner. Am I right?" asked Islington calmly.

Freddie hesitated, his forehead wrinkling. "Yessir," he answered.

Islington knelt down to be closer to Freddie's height.

"How did she seem?" asked Islington earnestly.

"Sir?" asked Freddie uncertainly.

"*She?*" quipped Maggie, her eyebrows shooting up. "My lord, that was a man on that horse. I saw him watering the animal at our pond while he talked to Freddie, I did. 'Tweren't a woman," said Maggie, shaking her head.

"Freddie, did you take them to the crossroads?" ask Islington.

"Yessir," answered Freddie.

"Frederick Leftwich Bunney, tell him the truth!" said Maggie sternly.

"I am, Mama," said Freddie, but he had a guilty expression.

"No, you aren't because your ears are as red as strawberries," said his mother. "Go on, now," she ordered when he didn't seem to be willing.

"No, sir, I didn't take them to the crossroads," said Freddie finally in a small voice.

"Where *did* you take them?" asked Islington. He had to clench his hands at his sides because Islington wanted to grab Freddie and make the boy tell him everything immediately.

"I took them to the Frog's Mouth…me fort," said Freddie.

"Why on earth would you take them there?" asked his mother.

"Because they needed a place to stay out of the rain," said Freddie. "I got them some hay and some food, and I took them to the Frog's Mouth. They were gone this morning."

"And my inn wasn't good enough?" hooted Maggie in an affronted tone. "*And* you gave our food away?"

"She couldn't stay here, though, could she?" asked Islington softly.

Freddie shook his head negatively, his eyes averted. He felt guilty he was telling this man all this after the woman had been so kind to him. He was smart enough to know she was hiding from something, and he was afraid he might be telling her secrets to what she was hiding from.

"Did she seem well?" asked Islington concernedly.

"Yessir, I think so," said Freddie calmly. "She was awful wet and tired, but she didn't seem sickly. She was a mite hungry, though."

Islington closed his eyes in relief. Finally, someone who had actually seen *her*. She was, for the moment, safe.

"It *was* a woman?" gasped Maggie in surprise.

"Do you know which way she went?" asked Islington.

"Why are you looking for her?" asked Freddie defensively, giving Islington a suspicious glare. Freddie decided he had told the man enough until he found out what he was about.

"Frederick Left—" began Maggie. Islington turned to look at her patiently and held up his hand to quiet her then turned to look at her son.

"Freddie, it's very important I find her," said Islington gravely.

"Still not enough," said Freddie stubbornly, shaking his head.

Islington reached into his pocket and blindly pulled out five sovereigns. He pushed them into Freddie's hand and closed it over them. Maggie's jaw dropped in shock. Freddie wasn't moved. Islington could see he had inherited his father's convictions. He gently took the boy by his arms to look him in the eye.

"Freddie, those coins mean nothing to me. All that I have, all that I am, is worthless if something happens to her. Do you understand?" he asked plaintively.

Freddie nodded, and his expression cleared with relief now that he saw the viscount didn't intend to hurt the woman.

"She said she was going to Scotland, so I sent her in the direction of Kirby Bellars," said Freddie finally.

"Thank you, Freddie," said Islington, smiling gratefully.

He rose and went to the bar to finally down the glass of whisky Maggie had poured for him. He felt better than he had for a while, and he was hopeful now that everything would be fine.

Chapter Eighteen

Myron left early from Cheltenham. The weather was horrid—pouring rain and lightning. When he was able to make enquiries, no one had seen Pandora. The roads were slick, but he pushed his horse. By noon, Myron was finally convinced Pandora hadn't taken this route. He had begun to suspect it the day before, but he didn't give up until that afternoon. He would go to Edinburgh to be there when she arrived with Dorian or Islington, and he continued to make his horse go faster. Then his horse slipped and fell.

When Myron regained consciousness, he was in an unfamiliar bed, his lower left leg bound and splinted. When his mount lost its footing, the stallion had fallen on him. He was taken to the vicarage at Lickey End. Fortunately for Myron, it had happened not far from a turnpike, so he hadn't been left unconscious, face-down in the mud, and out in the rain for long. The local doctor assured him the break wasn't serious, and the sprain to the ankle on the same leg from his foot being caught in the stirrup would also heal, but Myron would have to stay in bed with both for a few days. The doctor, Dr. Felton, told him traveling anywhere, even by coach, was out of the question for at least that amount of time. He also told Myron he was lucky the horse didn't do more damage. Myron didn't feel so lucky.

The local blacksmith, who also operated a livery, had come by to tell Myron his horse would be fine. He had checked his legs and hooves, which were sound. Myron still felt like having him shot, but Tajik would shoot *him* once he got back to London. He made arrangements with the blacksmith to have a messenger sent to London to let his family know what had happened.

The vicar, Mr. Stallsworth, and his wife said Myron was welcome to stay for however long it took him to recover. They had never had a member of the nobility stay with them before and considered it to be a distinct privilege. Myron didn't like that this would add to his mother's worries, but there was little he could do about it now.

Islington was continually able to find people who recalled seeing a rider pass through on a black horse. Some mentioned they had seen a rider on a brown one as well, but Islington knew that wasn't Pandora. The riders weren't together, so Islington suspected the other rider was just someone who happened to be traveling the same way.

When he reached the Trent, he found the ferry Pandora had used to cross. She had paid the man a handsome sum above the required toll, so even though he had been suspicious, he hadn't said a word. Islington paid the man even more to obtain that information. He didn't know where she was getting the money, but Islington suspected Pandora brought everything she had ever saved with her.

He couldn't leave Thorpe Satchville until nearly ten. During the time he waited, he had Freddie take him to the Frog's Mouth, but of course, he hadn't found anything that would even indicate Pandora had been there, other than the large hoof prints left behind by Bellerophon.

Harold had re-shod all of Jezebel's hooves, which had caused the delay in Islington's leaving. He warned Islington that he needed to go a little more easily with her, good roads or not; otherwise, she would only throw another shoe. He was attempting to follow the blacksmith's advice, but he was impatient to find Pandora. He couldn't be far behind.

Because Islington was determined to regain as much ground as possible, rather than skirting the cities, he went straight through. He was hesitant at first because he didn't want to risk losing Pandora's trail, but it was a chance he would have to take if he were going to catch her. Fortunately, there weren't many cities large enough to make her reluctant to go through as well, and he was relieved to find she had been sighted all along the way. No one had been able to provide him with a description of how Pandora herself had appeared except Freddie. He was encouraged by what the boy said, but she couldn't possibly make it all the way alone.

The evening was approaching, however, and Islington would soon have to stop for the night. He was desperate to continue, but traveling through the dark wasn't an option; it wasn't as if he could carry a lantern in his hand and gallop. Aside from that, it had been raining periodically throughout the day, making the roads unsafe. Even as he tried to follow Harold's advice about going slower, he had pushed Jezebel to the point she was done. He made it just beyond Mansfield as the dark was complete. He stopped at an inn and tiredly led Jezebel to the stable.

Pandora stopped for the night somewhere past Drighlington. She was just south of Leeds and had made it into the West Riding, but beyond that, she was too frazzled to care. The day when she had traveled as far as Thorpe Satchville through the rain had been bad, but Pandora felt as if this day was even worse. She was exhausted and strained, and it was the closest she had come to bursting into tears since leaving London.

It rained for much of the day, but again it cleared just as she stopped. She eventually passed under the edge of the storm, and the area she travelled through after she crossed hadn't received rain for several hours. She hoped she could have a fire, and she was looking forward to it.

She was still following the rider, and she was frustrated by the slow progress. Even though she had traveled over fifty miles, she would have been able to go at least seventy if it hadn't been for the sluggard in front of her. If he didn't go faster tomorrow, she would take her chances and go around him. She only had a certain amount of supplies to make it to Edinburgh, and she wasn't sure she could get more should they run out.

In addition to her slow progress because of the rider and the rain, toll gates and turnpikes had abounded. She had gone through—not one or two but—*eleven* of the infernal things. None had been more than tuppence apiece, but it wasn't the cost that made her so anxious: it was the risk of being discovered. She hoped there wouldn't be so many tomorrow. Most of those today were at rivers and bridges. The only benefit the rain had brought was that the gatekeepers had been more concerned with taking her toll and getting back inside where it was dry than looking at her too closely.

Pandora had heard gunshots ringing in the distance throughout the day. It was hunting season, but it was almost comical the way it sounded like a small war in the countryside. She was happy they weren't close to the road, but she would be traveling into the Dales before long. Once she did, the gunshots would be closer, especially if she had to leave the road and travel cross country. Bellerophon withstood the noise well, but his ears twitched every time he heard one of the shots. He didn't shy or show any other nervousness, but the sounds were still quite distant. He had never been exposed to the sound of firearms before because Pandora had never taken him out for a hunt. She wasn't sure what his reaction would be if they grew closer. She hoped they wouldn't because she didn't like them any more than Bellerophon.

She did find a place in the woods near a stream and a field not far beyond a town called Tong. The rider had, of course, continued on, but Pandora had the sinking feeling that she would be back behind him again tomorrow. She was slightly curious about his destination. However, she would have to, at some point, go around him.

She was able to set up her tent quickly, and her ability with it had much improved since the first time she had tried. It looked exactly as Maiyin said it would, and Pandora had little fear that it might collapse. She gathered wood to make a fire and hung her coat as close to it as she could to dry it out. She unloaded everything from Bellerophon and tied him where he could graze and drink. Then she went to the stream herself and washed her other change of clothes and placed them near the fire.

She was aching for a bath, but the water was cold. Freezing in the water was almost as unappealing as being dirty. She also didn't want to risk someone coming upon her while she was naked. It wouldn't be likely, considering she was away from any settlements and it was after dark, but she still wasn't willing to take the risk for the sake of a *cold* bath. For a *hot* one, she might have braved it. She satisfied herself with washing her hair and felt much better afterward.

With her "housework" done, she sat down to supper. At dinner, she found that Maiyin had placed several small, thick-skinned sausages into her bags. They were apparently able to keep for some time because the meat was still edible after four days, and it didn't require cooking. Pandora thought she had discovered a hidden treasure. Her bread had long since gone, but she still had some cheese, and—of course—plenty of apples. Keung's nuts and raisins were starting to dwindle, but they would last another day or two. If she ran out of food before she made it to Edinburgh, she would go through a village market for more and hope she wouldn't be discovered, but it would be extremely risky.

She tried roasting an apple for dessert. After the apple pie that Freddie had given her, the raw apples seemed bland. She thought it would be simple enough, but she was wrong. She found a sturdy, small branch to use as a skewer and pierced the apple through its core. She held it over the fire and waited for it to start cooking. Unfortunately, she didn't realize she would have to turn it occasionally. After a few minutes, she removed it from the fire only to find that one side was still quite raw, the other charred and inedible. Shrugging, she tossed it into the bushes and grabbed another. The second one proved to be better after she thought to rotate it, but it was still a little raw in the center. There was always tomorrow night to try again.

She banked her fire and set her teapot away from it after pouring herself one more cup. There was still quite a bit left for her to reheat in the morning. She had a fair amount of tea leaves left, but she would be upset if she ran out. She checked on her clothes near the fire and found they were dry so she folded them and took them into the tent. After checking on Bellerophon one more time to make sure he was settled in and that his rope was secured, Pandora went into her tent. She prayed the next day would at least be dry. She hadn't realized just how much it rained until she had to be in it all the time.

She drifted off to sleep thinking about her family and how much she missed them. She wondered how they were and if they had come looking for her. After four days, she was sure they weren't going to find her, but she found herself wishing they would. She also let her thoughts drift to Islington for a time, and her throat tightened when she realized how much she missed him and wanted him there. Even at his worst, he made her feel safe, and he would probably know how to hunt, too.

≪ ≫

Castleton took note of when the rider turned off. He had decided that afternoon that he would have to do something to stop the stranger from following. After a second day of the man staying the same distance behind him, Castleton had no choice but to think the person was following him, for whatever reason. Why the rider had still not made any move to state his intentions was unclear, but it was becoming a nuisance of which he had long since wearied.

He traveled on to Fulneck, less than half a mile from where the rider had stopped and got a room at the inn. He had his supper and several pints of ale after unpacking, giving the rider plenty of time to go to sleep. Then, when he felt comfortable that he would be undetected, Castleton went on foot back to the woods where the rider had stopped.

It was difficult to locate the camp in the dark. He might have passed it completely if it hadn't been for the remaining red embers from the fire the stranger had made. He looked over the camp, trying to decide what, short of killing him, would make the man stop. Castleton had, for a time, contemplated killing him and being done with it, but he wasn't violent by nature. There was only one person in particular he wanted dead, and this was not he. That man would be dead soon. For now, Castleton wanted only to make sure this person wouldn't pursue him tomorrow and possibly ruin his plans.

He saw the pot beside the fire and lifted it. It still had something in it, and Castleton absently poured it on what was left of the fire. He saw the tent fastened between the two trees and thought to look into it, but then he decided that might be too risky; the man could wake up, and he might have a gun. Castleton also dismissed untying the supports for the tent, knowing that, too, would wake the person.

He then saw the horse tied to a tree and realized the perfect solution to his problem. If the man didn't have a horse to ride, then he wouldn't be able to follow Castleton. The horse wasn't asleep, and he eyed Castleton balefully from where he stood near the tent. Castleton hadn't realized, after only observing from a distance, just how large he was. The stallion's ears were thrown back, and he shifted his feet threateningly. He seemed to be as high-strung as Castleton hoped he would be.

Castleton cautiously moved his way across the camp to where the rope was tied, not taking his eyes from the horse, because the tether was quite long. The horse continued to watch him but didn't come any closer. He

292

quickly untied the knot and threw the rope well away from the tree so it wouldn't become re-anchored somehow. The stallion blew through his nose at the gesture Castleton made when he tossed the rope and began to paw at the ground. The animal looked to Castleton as if he intended to charge any minute, and Castleton decided it was time to leave the campsite before the horse did exactly that. It was almost as if he were *guarding* the place.

After taking one final inspection of the camp to see if there were anything else he might do to delay or stop the rider and finding nothing, Castleton slowly backed his way out of the camp, never taking his eyes from the horse. The animal had started following him, and while Castleton didn't want him to charge, he felt it was so much the better if the horse left the camp; that had been his intention, after all. When he was out to the field at the edge of the woods and found his way to the road, he headed back to Fulneck at a jog. He needed to get some sleep so he would be well-rested for his early start in the morning.

Pandora awoke the next morning feeling rejuvenated. She had managed to gather some leaves and branches to put under her blanket-mattress, and it was a definite improvement. She stretched indolently before sitting up and yawning, blinking her eyes to clear away the final cobwebs of sleep. The sun was starting to rise; the sky was just at that point when the dark was not quite ready to let go. *Excellent time to be waking. Plenty of time for tea and a toothbrush.* After fastening her shirt and waistcoat and placing her hat back on her head and her boots back on her feet, she crawled out of the tent.

The first thing she noticed, disappointedly, was that the fire was out. She thought there would be plenty of coals to restart it to warm her tea. The next thing she noticed was that her pot wasn't where she had placed it. She had put it to the left of the fire; it was now on the far side of it. She looked around cautiously before coming completely out of the tent, but there was no one there. She walked over to the pot and picked it up; it was empty.

Pandora felt an alarm go through her at that point, and the blood began to throb in her ears. She had at least enough tea left for a cup, maybe two. It couldn't have been a matter of Bellerophon shuffling through the camp and accidentally knocking it over because if he had, the pot would be in the fire or on its side near where she had left it, not sitting neatly on the far side of it. Someone had been in her camp!

She heard a rustling in the bushes behind her and turned in fright, only to heave a sigh of relief when Bellerophon came trotting toward her from the direction of the field. He walked up to her and put his head over her shoulder and put his cheek against hers—his version of giving her a hug. Pandora patted his neck affectionately, still eyeing the surrounding brush suspiciously.

"Good morning, fella. I trust you slept well?" she said with a smile.

He blew at her and pranced to the tree where she had tied his rope. It was no longer tied. Pandora felt panicked, but she tried to remain rational. She went over things from the night before. Did she have tea left? Yes, she had; she knew she had…especially after she had needed some of it to wash down the second roasted apple. She had made sure Bellerophon's rope was tied because it was the last thing she did every night before going to bed. Bellerophon hadn't untied it himself—that was Achilles's trick, not his.

At that point, Pandora looked at the soft ground. She couldn't see any footprints because of the leaves on the floor of the woods, but she *knew* someone had been there. Why they would put out her fire and pour out her tea was a mystery. There could have been any number of reasons for untying her horse. One would have been to steal him. That would have been a wasted effort because Bellerophon wouldn't have let them. Another would have been to turn him loose in the hope that he would run off. He had never been prone to at home, and Pandora was happy to see it held true while they traveled. Why someone would want her horse to run away was also a mystery. If it had been a thief, he—or they—wouldn't have stopped at simply creating inconvenience.

Before she did anything else, Pandora went into the tent and took care of something she should have done the first day she was out: she pulled out the Manton and loaded it. She had been hesitant to do so because she knew of all the things that could go wrong: misfires, damp powder that would keep it from firing when needed, and a temptation to use it when it wasn't really necessary. However, after someone had managed to come into the camp and apparently stroll around as if he owned the place, Pandora felt like she *needed* it. After only a moment's hesitation, she loaded the dagger-pistol as well.

She didn't put any powder into their pans because she would be leaving soon. She was afraid the jarring they would get while she rode could set them off or the powder would drift out of the pans. Pandora had no desire to shoot herself or her horse or accidentally shoot anyone else. If the powder sifted out or got damp, they would be useless. She would load them this far, and then before she went to bed, she would load the pans to have them ready. If they were needed in her waking hours, it would be a simple enough matter to put the powder in and fire.

Feeling safer after doing that, and once she stuck the dirk in the top of her boot, Pandora built another fire and made another pot of tea. She needed a cup of tea. A sip of whisky would settle her nerves better, but she couldn't very well travel down the road if she was in her altitudes. It didn't take long to get the tea started, and once it was making, she broke down her camp and packed things away. She put both guns in the left front saddlebag, along with the powder flask, and moved all the apples that remained to the rear bag on that side.

While in the front bag, out of curiosity (now that the apples were out of the way), she examined the sewing and fishing kits Maiyin had made for her. The sewing kit consisted of a small pair of scissors, a thimble, needles, and two spools of thread—one light, one dark. The fishing kit was more interesting. It contained hooks, fishing line, a small net (Pandora assumed to hold the fish she caught), lead sinkers, two bobbers, a filet knife, and a pair of pointy pliers. Pandora assumed those were to remove the hook from the fish's mouth.

After seeing the fishing kit, Pandora decided if the weather held, and she found a likely place, she would try her hand at catching a fish. After halfway successfully baking an apple, she was ready to try something more complicated. The sausages Maiyin had provided were tasty, but Pandora missed variety in her diet. She still had several of the vegetables Maiyin had given her because she wasn't brave enough to try cooking them yet and some, to her, didn't taste good raw…like a potato. A fish would be easier to cook than vegetables…maybe.

Pandora felt calmer after she had a cup of tea. She had some of the nuts and raisins and an orange for breakfast. She made only enough tea for two cups because she didn't want to waste any. She took the pot to the stream once it was empty to rinse it and brought it back to the camp full of water to douse her fire then packed it away.

Once she was done eating and had come back from the stream after brushing her teeth, she loaded everything onto Bellerophon. He was frisky this morning, and Pandora was looking forward to a good ride. The sky was clear, the air was starting to brighten, and it was going to be pleasantly warm and sunny. She was hoping for good weather, fewer toll gates, and no stranger in front of her.

Islington made an early start from Mansfield, determined to catch Pandora. When he made it to the toll gate just past Pleasley, and the man there told Islington the last person he had let through on Sunday night had been a rider on a black horse, Islington was pleased she could be so close. From all of his enquiries, he had been able to figure she was only managing between fifty or sixty miles a day. If he didn't catch her by the end of today, then he would certainly be able to tomorrow. He was so close, he could almost imagine seeing her, and his heart pounded in time with Jezebel's hooves as he urged the mare to go faster.

The extended rest she had at Thorpe Satchville had helped her, and Jezebel strived to give him the pace he wanted. Completely disregarding the cities, Islington would barely slow her to a trot when he reached one. The only time he slowed to a walk was to pass through a toll gate, and while he was stopped for that, he would ask the keeper if he had seen a rider on a black horse. There were enough toll gates he had no need to ask in the cities. Because of the rain the day before, foot traffic through the gates had been light, and there also hadn't been many carriages or coaches, never mind farmers with their flocks. Most of the keepers remembered seeing a rider on a large, black horse. Islington had to again express admiration for her choice of animal; not only was he a good mount, he was also distinctive.

The weather proved to be fair and sunny, although he could see gray clouds looming to the northwest. He wondered if Pandora was under those. It was uncharitable, but he hoped she was. If she were traveling through rain, it would slow her down, making it more likely he would be able to catch her. He desperately wanted to catch her. He would only stop occasionally to let Jezebel rest, but he would at least make sure her legs and hooves were holding up. At one point, he stopped for a meal himself, but he felt he didn't have a minute to lose.

He realized as he came to the crossroads in Staincross, if he went due north, his home was a little over ten miles away. He had no intention of going home. Not now. His mother would soon have her message from the duchess. If it were being delivered by a professional messenger, and Islington suspected it would be, she could possibly have already received it. A messenger wouldn't be required to stop and make enquiries, and he could also change horses, keeping whatever he was riding at a full gallop if necessary. Islington didn't think the duchess would see the message as being that urgent, but even at a regular pace, his mother would have it very soon. Pandora hadn't realized how close she was either, Islington was sure.

He would like her to see his home. She would appreciate the garden, such as it was, considering her penchant for secluded places. The designer had built a maze…and a gazebo by the small lake. There were little grottoes and secret places hidden everywhere. He had enjoyed playing hide-and-seek there when he was a child. The house was a giant, old pile from Tudor times, half-timber and half-stone, but Islington imagined Pandora would be able to bring it some warmth. He tried to put the thought from his mind. He had to find her first; then he had to convince her to marry him.

He started to go directly through Leeds but instead decided to follow the path he thought she might have taken. He was close. He was *so* close. It was getting well into the afternoon, and he wanted to cover as much road as he could before it got too dark to go any further. When he reached Pudsey and someone told him they had seen a rider on a black horse that *morning,* Islington thought his heart was going to explode from the excitement. He was less than a day's ride behind her.

≪ ≫

Pandora was feeling deflated. After recovering from the morning's excitement of finding someone had been in her camp, she had been looking forward to a good day of travel. It hadn't happened, of course. She couldn't be that lucky. The sky, which had started out bright and fine, had steadily grown cloudy and overcast. It never did turn into a full-out rain, but slightly after noon, the air became filled with a soggy mist that coated everything and eventually turned things unpleasantly sodden. The only thing good was the lack of toll gates. She had only gone through two, and she had done so without incident. Because of the mist making visibility less than optimal, she hadn't been able to travel quickly. Then there was the rider.

She had hoped he wouldn't be there. She had *prayed* he would go elsewhere, but after traveling only ten or so miles, she had met up with him again. She had thought to pass him, but the weather made it necessary for her to check her pace in any event. The risk of passing him wasn't worth it when she wouldn't be able to go any faster regardless. He was still slow, and Pandora thought enviously that it must be nice to not need to be anywhere in a timely fashion.

For the past hour or so, she had been following the Nidd through its valley. The road would occasionally pass from one bank to the other, meandering much as the river did. The altitude was steadily rising, and at one point Pandora had to clear the pressure in her ears. Even with the mist, the terrain was beautiful, and Pandora thought she wouldn't mind coming here again under different circumstances. She hoped to make it to Swaledale by nightfall, but the weather made it unlikely. She would have to stop somewhere in Wensleydale around Askrigg.

She couldn't blame the rider, though. The Dales weren't called dales inappropriately. With them came hills, sometimes steep hills that took a bit of effort to climb. She was entering the Pennine Chain, and the grades and slopes would only continue until she passed the Cheviot Hills and was into Scotland. The weather had also cooled considerably, and she was looking forward to a fire. Before, she only had one for making her tea or for light. Tonight, she would need it for warmth.

She also looked forward to stopping because of the hunters. She had heard rifle shots all day, growing closer than those of the previous day. They were still fairly distant, but because of the mist and the remote nature of the area, it was likely they would come closer. Bellerophon had already shied a few times, and Pandora could see that he didn't like them. She didn't either. She could just imagine some yahoo with a rifle mistaking her for some type of game and shooting at her in the mist.

They eventually left the valley and made their way to Middlesmoor, where they began their ascent over the top of a chain before descending into the next valley. The road was nicely packed but not heavily or frequently traveled. It wouldn't take them to the summit but would skirt round its southwestern edge. The road followed a ridge that fell away to one side, and Pandora looked at the surrounding countryside—what of it she was able to see through the mist. She could see clumps of trees here and there, particularly around the small streams that appeared from nowhere, and she was hopeful she could find a decent place to camp.

<<< >>>

Castleton had been waiting for this moment. He didn't want to do it, but after yet another day of the rider following him, he felt he was faced with little choice. His patience for the matter had long since disappeared, but he had needed to wait for the right opportunity. The hunters in the area gave him the idea, and it had to be a fool-proof plan.

He was surprised when the rider reappeared behind him. He had felt certain untethering the horse had taken care of it, which was why he was so confounded when he casually looked over his shoulder to see the rider there just shortly after noon. Untying the horse again would be just as fruitless so he was left with one option: he would have to shoot the man.

He waited until they were out of the river valley because there had been several settlements along the road. A gunshot would have brought someone. If he waited until they reached some remote area, like the side of a mountain, then he could be well away. The rider would be found eventually, but it would be determined some type of terrible hunting accident.

The mist wasn't going to make the job easier, and Castleton didn't have anywhere he could hide and lie in wait. He waited until the mist between them thickened, and he came to a stop. He retrieved his pocket pistol and waited for the mist to clear enough to take a shot. The rider didn't see Castleton; he was looking around himself at the landscape. Castleton fired just as the mist closed in again.

He heard the horse whinny in alarm and watched as the rider went over the side of the hill, coming to rest in the small valley below and remain motionless. It was hard to distinguish because of the distance and the mist, but Castleton could see the red of blood beginning to seep from a wound on the rider's now-bare head. He smiled satisfactorily and put his gun back in his pocket. He headed his horse up the road for the northwest. He thought casually to himself as he did so that now he could retire early and leave late as he had been wont to do before this person began following him.

<<< >>>

Pandora heard the gunshot in the mist and thought about how close it sounded. It was too close for Bellerophon. Her normally easygoing stallion whinnied and reared in surprise. Pandora realized as he did so that he wouldn't be able to maintain his footing on the side of the mountain with the load he carried. As Pandora felt him begin to fall, she had the presence of mind to quickly remove her feet from the stirrups and attempt to dismount in the opposite direction from the one she felt him going.

It was only partially successful. She was able to prevent herself from being crushed by her horse, but she felt herself flying through the air to land well down the side of the hill. She rolled uncontrollably down the steep, rocky slope, and it was all she could do to keep herself from breaking any bones. She bumped her forehead on a large stone and only stopped her descent when her back wedged against a large boulder. She dazedly thought about infernal hunters as she lost consciousness.

Islington was unwillingly forced to stop as he reached Blubberhouses. It was after 8:30, and it was so dark he was barely able to discern the road. He guided Jezebel into the inn yard, and she came to a stop gratefully. After the hard ride he had made that day, Islington was rather exhausted himself.

He was close, though. He had steadily been closing the distance between him and Pandora. The people he asked along the way had been giving him later times for seeing her that day. He was less than thirty miles behind her now. He was going to find her tomorrow, he was sure. He wanted to go farther, but there just wasn't enough light left for him to continue. He would get a room and supper and then retire early so he could leave as soon as possible in the morning.

Pandora woke to the sensation of something warm, soft and wet being rubbed insistently against her face. She felt a throbbing pain in her head and moaned. She opened her eyes and found it was almost dark. The only light was the half-moon and the few stars that managed to wink through the clouds partially covering the sky. She shortly realized the soft, wet thing she felt was Bellerophon's tongue, and he was standing over her, looking down. She groaned disgustedly and lifted a hand to rub the moisture from her cheek. He blew in her face once he saw that she was awake and lifted his head to move away from her, beginning to graze.

She sat up, wincing at the pain in her back from where she had come to rest jarringly against the boulder, and the world began to spin dizzily from the bump on her head. She raised her hand to her forehead and gingerly touched the giant lump there, caked with dried blood. It was matted into her hair and onto her cheek, and she grimaced after thinking about what a sight she must make. She moved her legs and arms and wiggled her ankles and fingers to make sure nothing was broken. She ached from head to foot, and she cracked the bones in her neck to relax a crick. She had been lucky all she had was a few bumps and bruises; she could have been shot.

After sitting for a few more groggy minutes, attempting to make the world settle back into its usual perspective, Pandora looked around herself dazedly for her hat. It had come to rest several yards away, and she slowly crawled over to it on her hands and knees. She wasn't ready to try standing yet. She didn't want to put the hat back on, suspecting it wouldn't fit over the lump anyhow, but she didn't want to lose it either. She thought she was going to be sick, and she sat still taking several deep breaths as she waited for the nausea and dizziness to pass. Bellerophon walked over to her and put his face close to hers. She patted his cheek and rubbed his nose affectionately, and then she remembered he had fallen, too.

She bravely attempted to stand and felt herself weaving as another wave of dizziness overcame her. For the time being, she would move very slowly. She rubbed her hands over Bellerophon's legs and flanks, checking for any injuries. He, too, appeared to be none the worse for wear...thankfully.

"Well, fella, I don't think we'll be going anywhere until daylight," she said to Bellerophon. "I bet you're hungry, huh?"

Pandora looked around herself in the darkness. There was just enough moonlight to see a small grove of trees nearby, and she could hear the sound of a stream not far from where she stood. Pandora had to express a moment of thanks that she hadn't fallen into it. Going into the water might have made her regain consciousness sooner, but then again, she could have frozen to death or drowned. As it was, she suppressed a shiver from the coolness that came with the darkness and decided it was time to set up her tent and build a fire.

She would build the fire first. She only hoped she could find wood dry enough to make one. It hadn't been raining, but it had been misty, and she was concerned it might have made the wood underneath the trees too wet to use. After making sure none of her belongings had come loose when Bellerophon fell, she grabbed his reins and led him to the stand of trees. She found a likely spot and had him come to a stop. Before unpacking her things, after resting her head against his side to wait out another wave of dizziness, she went in search of wood to build a fire. She didn't start setting up her tent until she had a nice roaring blaze and had warmed herself.

Once she had the fire, it was easier to see how to set up her tent, which she accomplished with only a few pauses for light-headedness. She then took off her coat to start drying by the fire, and after warming herself again, she unloaded the saddlebags from Bellerophon and took them into the tent. She removed the saddle and his bridle and took them in. She fashioned his halter from the rope and fastened it to a tree, but she felt comfortable if the knot didn't stay. He had proven several times already that he wouldn't go anywhere without her, and he would follow her wherever she went. Before going out of the tent, she grabbed a few sugar lumps for her horse and her pot to make tea.

Bellerophon was happy to have the sugar, and he gave her a "hug" before she went to the stream to fill her pot. She had no idea what condition the water was in, but it sounded as if it were moving quickly. Pandora didn't think it had anything in it that would harm her. At this point, it was really the furthest thing from her mind. She got the water started for her tea, and then she went to the tent for her valise.

She pulled out the bottle of whisky and turned it in her hands before pulling out the cork. She brought it to her nose to smell and took it away again quickly. Bracing herself, she lifted it to her lips and took a hefty swig. The alcohol burned its way down as it had before, and Pandora could feel the warmth beginning to radiate through her limbs. It calmed her and warmed her but did nothing for the throbbing in her head. She replaced the cork and put it back in her bag.

She went back to the stream and washed the blood from her face and hair as best she could without submerging her head, flinching at the coldness of the water. It helped revive her, but her head still ached, and the dizziness would come and go at will. She suspected, and wouldn't be surprised to be told by a doctor, that she had a concussion. There was little she could do for it except hope it wasn't severe.

After thinking for a moment, she went back into the tent and came out to sit by the fire with the front saddlebags. She opened the one Keung had packed with medical supplies and looked through it, wondering if he had put anything in there that might help her head. If he hadn't put anything in there specifically for it, she hoped to at least find something that would suit. It was a large collection of items, which he had placed into a hinged wooden box.

Pandora lifted out the box and opened the lid. She saw a large roll of thin muslin, cut in a continuous strip about two inches wide. There were also several multi-layered squares of it in various sizes. She assumed those would be for dressing a wound. She also found a bottle of laudanum. Pandora had no idea why Keung might have thought she would need laudanum. She read the label: *For Severe Diarrhea, fifteen drops in one cup of wine.* That would explain why it was a large bottle (and also why he had given her the plum wine), but the laudanum could be used for pain. If she wasn't able to find anything else, that would do.

There were a dozen smaller stoppered bottles in the box, held in place on the inside of the lid with little ties to keep them from jostling around. Some contained liquids, which Pandora was pretty sure were tinctures or oils. Some were the actual herb in powdered form. She looked at the labels. Lavender, juniper, sage, hops. The labels were in Chinese, which took up less space than English, but Pandora was able to read it. She wasn't seeing anything...until she found the chamomile.

In the bottom of the box, besides the bandaging and laudanum, there was a decent-sized jar that contained an ointment. She opened the lid and smelled. It actually smelled quite good. She looked at the label on the lid. *For wounds—cuts, scrapes, bruises, swellings—apply to injury. Perfect. I have all of the above.* She moved her hair out of the way and gingerly applied some to the lump on her forehead. She had yet to see what it looked like, not having a mirror, and she wasn't sure she wanted to. It had stopped bleeding on its own, and she didn't feel any deep wounds, so externally it probably—other than the swelling—wasn't too serious. It started to feel better almost immediately—once the minor stinging from whatever herbs were in the ointment dissipated. She put the lid back on and looked at it, trying to see if Keung had listed what herbs were in it. He had not. It wasn't important, as long as it worked, and it appeared to do that wondrously.

Also in the bottom of the box, she found another stoppered bottle, slightly larger than those containing the other herbs but not quite as large as the bottle of laudanum. Keung had put on the label: *Pandora Headache*. Pandora put the bottle of chamomile back. Whatever was in the headache medicine was going to be much better than chamomile for what her head felt like. The instructions were simple: five drops in one cup of cold water. Just like the ointment, there were no ingredients listed, but if Keung created it specifically to treat her headaches, she had no doubt it would make everything all better. She took her cup to the stream and added the five drops of tincture. The smell wasn't appetizing, but, then again, it *was* medicine. She put the stopper back into the bottle and put it back in the box. She drank the entire concoction without stopping, and she was glad she had once it was done. It tasted foul.

The last few odds and ends she found in the box included a set of tweezers, a small pair of scissors (probably for cutting the bandaging), and some cotton wool. Keung had thought of just about anything she might encounter on her journey…except for a gunshot. Luckily, she hadn't had one of those…yet.

As she prepared her tea and ate one of the sausages Maiyin had given her, Pandora thought about what had happened. How could someone have mistaken her for a game animal? How could they have mistaken *Bellerophon*? She couldn't be sure they had aimed for her, but the sound of the shot had been close. She also had to wonder why, if they had been shooting at her, they didn't come to find out if they had made a kill. Since she was unconscious for several hours, she suspected they *did* come to find out. Once they discovered she was their supposed rabbit (or whatever it was they thought they were aiming at), they were afraid of what might happen to them and fled. She couldn't blame them…well, yes, actually, she could. Luckily, she hadn't been fatally injured, but she couldn't believe they had left her lying there wounded in the cold and damp. It was downright uncivilized.

It wasn't long before Keung's headache medicine began to have an effect. Pandora could feel herself becoming drowsy, far beyond what might be caused by the bump on her head (at least, she hoped that was the case). Her head was starting to feel better, though. She pulled out her watch and saw it was nearing eleven. Well, if it wasn't the tincture that had done it, the hour probably had. It was an hour past when she usually went to sleep. Pandora finished her tea. Then she checked the pot to gauge how much was left. Enough for a cup or two in the morning. She would try to roast an apple for breakfast and have some of the jerked meat. *Oh, tasty,* she thought unenthusiastically.

As Pandora made her way to the tent after banking the fire and checking Bellerophon, she idly wondered how long the effects of the headache medicine would last. She couldn't take more in the morning because if it was going to make her sleepy, she wouldn't be able to ride. She *had* to be able to ride tomorrow. She had lost at least four hours that day, not to mention the time she had lost because of the hills. While she was settling herself under her blankets, snuggling into them up to her nose, she consoled herself with the knowledge that at least the lost time would have hopefully given the rider in front of her a chance to either get a better distance ahead of her...or go somewhere else.

Chapter Nineteen

Islington left Blubberhouses as early as possible. The innkeeper had to rouse the ostler from bed, but Islington insisted he needed to leave *now*. The keeper thought it had something to do with his establishment, but the marquess assured him it was a matter of being pressed for time. Islington had the innkeeper quickly throw together something for him to eat, tipped him well, and left. It was just after seven in the morning.

He was going to catch Pandora *that* day. He had met a farmer in the common room at the inn the previous night who saw a rider on a black horse going north across the Hessian Moor yesterday afternoon. That confirmed for Islington that he was less than a day's ride behind her, and from the direction she was going, she would go through Nidderdale. He hoped (and partially didn't) that it would be late enough once he reached it that he could make enquiries and find where she went from there.

Most of the roads that led into the Dales didn't generally go from one to the other. The only way to continue her northwesterly course would be to cross over the sometimes barely existent paths across the hills. Even those were few and far between. Knowing she was reluctant to go without a trail or a road, he could determine with a fair degree of certainty which way she *would* go, even without anyone having seen her. She would have to choose where she crossed the rivers in the valleys carefully. With all the rain over the previous days, some wouldn't be easily fordable, and bridges were sometimes unavailable.

Jezebel was still tired, but Islington would let her rest once he found Pandora. If he found Pandora, he would let the mare have a whole day to rest before riding her again, he vowed. She was doing her best, and he couldn't risk pushing her harder.

⋘ ⋙

Pandora's head was throbbing. The headache medicine was not permanent. She raised a hand to the spot just right-of-center on her forehead and gingerly touched it with her fingertips. It was still sore, and she could imagine there was an ugly bruise, but the swelling had gone down quite a bit. She would be able to put on her hat. She opened her eyes and was seeing an unusual amount of brightness through the sides of the tent. She sat up quickly in surprise and wished she hadn't. Now, in addition to the throbbing, the spinning was back. She reached over to her waistcoat and took out her watch. It was 7:30.

"Bollocks," she muttered darkly.

Pandora suppressed a shiver as she got up. She put on her waistcoat and buttoned it then put on her boots. That helped dispel the chill somewhat, but the fire and a cup of tea would be more helpful. She ran the brush through her hair and deftly pinned it back into its bun. She carefully put on her hat, wincing as the brim rubbed against her injury when she had it set lowly as she usually did. She placed it a little further back, and that relieved some of the pressure, but she would have to set it back low before she left camp. For now, she wanted to wear it to keep her head warm. Before leaving the tent, she retrieved the medicine kit and put more of the ointment onto the wound.

She came out of the tent and looked around herself. The sun was rising nicely, and it appeared that—as opposed to yesterday—the sun would be shining, even if the air was cool. She restarted her fire from the coals and set her pot of tea to reheat after she put her coat back on. Pandora took a closer look at her surroundings. Her campsite wasn't as well-disguised as she was wont to choose, but considering she had found it in the dark after a nasty fall, she could have done much worse.

Bellerophon was grazing nearby and trotted up to her happily when he realized she had come out of the tent. Pandora rubbed his nose and forehead and patted his neck affectionately, and then she retrieved a few lumps of sugar from the pocket of her coat. She looked him over again in the daylight and saw that her assessment the night before had been good: he was perfect. She did, however, notice that his shoes were showing signs of wear. She hoped they would last to Edinburgh, and then she would have him re-shod before returning to London.

She had a meager breakfast, her skill at roasting an apple improved. She had yet to use the pan Maiyin had given her, and she thought when she stopped for the night she might try it. Her maid had given her, among the apples and oranges, a few potatoes and turnips. Pandora didn't like eating either one raw, and she didn't have any spices or butter, but they would be a nice change. Maybe she would try putting them with a fish. Either that or she could try frying one of the sausages to season them with. She was hesitant to do that, though, because if she burned the sausage and made it inedible, then she wouldn't have as much meat. She liked meat…a lot.

After Pandora finished eating and drinking her second cup of tea, she pulled out the medicine kit. She couldn't take the headache medicine, not until she went to bed, but she needed something for her headache. Her head was throbbing. The initial dizziness from sitting up too quickly had subsided, and the ointment on the wound stopped that from hurting, but the inside of her head felt like it was tightened in a vice. She pulled out the chamomile. It was an oil, and according to the instructions, all she had to do was put three drops on a lump of sugar. She fished one out of her pocket, added the drops, and popped it into her mouth. It was actually not unpleasant. She put the bottle back in the kit, put the kit in the saddlebag, and then packed everything away. She was running late.

Pandora had finished loading everything onto Bellerophon and found a suitable rock (the one her back had lodged against last night) to stand on and mount. She had her foot in the stirrup when she heard a faint rustling sound behind her in the grass.

"Stand and deliver!" demanded a male voice.

Pandora closed her eyes and gave a slight shake of her head at her unbelievable luck. She had forgotten to load the pans on her guns, which were both still sitting half-loaded in her saddlebag. Her mouth formed into a tight smile. She had just about reached the end of her store of good nature and was becoming annoyed with the world.

She took her foot out of the stirrup and turned to look at her would-be accoster. He was not much taller than she with a build only slightly larger. He had a shock of dark brown hair and brown eyes. His chin was receding, and his beaky nose stood out prominently from the rest of his face…except for ears that seemed to stick out almost as far. He was pointing a knife at her from only a few feet away, but he didn't seem to be sure what he was doing. Bellerophon looked at him and performed his version of a laugh.

"You're having me on, right?" asked Pandora dubiously.

"No, I'm not! Stand and deliver!" he demanded, waving the knife.

"Do highwaymen still say that? I don't think that's been used for about a hundred years now," said Pandora tartly.

"Hey, wot's this now? You're not a man!" he said in surprise.

"No, I'm not," said Pandora flatly. "You're not as stupid as you look then, are you?" she said with a grin.

She just couldn't feel threatened. She tried—she honestly did, but he looked much too buffoonish and timid for her to take him seriously. That he only had a knife rather than a gun was also not a stroke in his favor. When compounded by the fact that she stood a foot taller atop the rock, it was all rather funny.

"Then I'll just take me boodle another way," he said with what Pandora supposed he thought was a lecherous, threatening grin.

"Oh, no, I'm afraid not today," said Pandora pleasantly, stepping down from the boulder.

"Oi, I'm the one with the knife here!" he shouted.

"Honestly…. I'm sorry…? What is your name?" she asked calmly.

"Name's Timmons Wallace, best footpad in these here parts," he said proudly.

"Ah, Mr. Wallace, then, let me explain something—"she said as she reached down to retrieve her dirk from the top of her boot—"we both have knives, see?" She flipped it back and forth between her hands agilely, and his eyes widened in surprise. "Have you ever actually *done* this before?"

"Well, sure I have…onct or twice."

"And have you not learned that in order for this to work properly, you need a *gun?"*

"Oh, I don't like guns," said Wallace firmly, shaking his head.

Pandora chortled. "Timmons Wallace, this is not the profession for you. Find yourself a buxom farm girl, raise a herd of children, and live a long and happy life."

She put her knife back into her boot, completely dismissing him as harmless. Perhaps she judged too quickly. He soon had her in a hold that pinioned her arms against her sides and pressed her against him. She almost gagged at the odor of his breath, which smelled as if he had never brushed his teeth in his life. Judging from the way some of them had rotted away, she realized that was probably a correct assessment. She was surprised, but she was definitely not afraid.

"I don't think you should laugh anymore," warned Wallace.

"Now, Mr. Wallace, I thought we were getting on so well, and you had to do a thing like this," said Pandora disappointedly with a slight pout.

"We may both have knives, but you can't get yours," he taunted.

"Whyever would you think I'd need one?" asked Pandora calmly. She briefly reminisced about *marauding bandits.*

The same movements that worked on Lord Barneville stood her in good stead now. She stepped down sharply on the top of one of Wallace's feet, which shocked him enough to loosen his grip. The only difference this time was that she didn't go gently. She hit Wallace in the solar plexus with the heel of her hand, using all of her strength. It didn't do any internal damage, but it definitely knocked the wind out of him.

"Did your mother not tell you that it's not very nice to pick on girls, Mr. Wallace?" she asked mildly.

Pandora watched as he sank to his knees, gasping for air like a fish out of water. He would pass out from the lack of oxygen before too long on his own, but she didn't want to risk him actually dying. She only wanted to teach him a lesson. She placed a well-aimed blow to the back of his head, and he collapsed, unconscious, to the ground. His breathing returned to normal almost immediately.

"If you're the best footpad in the area, then I think I'll be safe," she said with a grin as she looked down at him.

She climbed back on top of the rock and mounted Bellerophon, who had been standing patiently waiting while she conversed with her attacker. She looked back down at Wallace once she was seated. She hoped this would make him have a change of heart regarding his profession. Somehow, though, she doubted it would.

She headed Bellerophon back up the side of the hill to the road they had been traveling the day before. She had been up for about an hour, and it looked like the weather would hold. Her headache was clearing, and she wasn't suffering any drowsiness. She hoped she could leave Yorkshire before the end of the day. If the weather held, and she didn't encounter any other mishaps for the day, she could conceivably be all the way to Northumberland before stopping for the night.

The weather was clear enough she was able to get a good view of the terrain ahead of her. In the valley below was a river, and on the other side of it was the Whernside. She would pass through at the northern end of Little Whernside, in an area not as steep as the mountains themselves. Pandora could just make out the trail, and she hoped she wouldn't have any trouble finding it from the valley below.

The trail she followed led to a point at the river where travelers crossed quite often. The water level was high, and the current was moving quickly. Provided the water wasn't too deep, Bellerophon wouldn't have any trouble crossing. That proved to be the case, and they were to the other side in minutes without much difficulty. The trail picked up on the far bank, and they began their climb through the pass.

When they reached the top of it, Pandora was able to look down into the dale below. There were more villages dotting this valley floor than in the one behind her, but it was still early yet. She would keep her hat low on her head, which she adjusted with a gasp as it rubbed her forehead, but she would move it back once she was through and heading for the next pass. Fields covered the valley, some marked by stone fences. There were sheep scattered everywhere grazing, as well as a few cows.

Wensleydale wasn't far, and once she reached it, she would continue on a flat plain for a while. The dale below was Coverdale, where she had hoped to stop the night before. On looking at it, she realized she wouldn't have been able to find a suitable place to camp. Perhaps it was just as well she had been forced to stop where she did. She would cross the next ridge to the north of Brown Haw. Then she would travel in a more northerly direction to Wensleydale. She wasn't sure how far it would be, but she hoped to be to the other side of the Ure before she took her first break for the morning.

She stayed on her road once she reached the dale, and there was a small bridge that went across the river that saved her from wading through again. That was a good thing, because the water in this river was flowing much faster than the previous one. Once she was to the other side, she found the trail that would take her through the pass to the next dale. She glanced at her watch and saw it was nearing nine. It would be close, but she felt fairly confident she would be across the Ure by 10:30.

Islington had made it to Nidderdale, and he left Middlesmoor to go across Rain Stang. The people he asked in the dale hadn't seen Pandora, but they did remember seeing a rider on a brown horse. It was the same rider Islington had heard report of before, but it was obviously not Pandora. Islington thought it odd this person was traveling in the same direction, but he didn't think it was suspicious. Most people who had seen both riders had said he was in front of her by quite a distance, but it was still peculiar.

Islington was crossing the edge of the hill and glanced down into the slight valley where it declined below the edge of the road. That was when he saw the figure lying near the bottom. He felt anxiety as he realized what it was and led Jezebel off the road toward it. He couldn't make out who it was, but knowing his mission made him fearful who it *might* be, especially knowing she had come this way.

Once Jezebel reached the person lying near a large boulder, Islington stopped and dismounted, rushing up to the body. He could see, with great relief, that it wasn't Pandora. The person was lying face down, but Islington saw short brown hair. Obviously not Pandora. He rolled the man over and looked at him. He was unconscious, not dead, but Islington was unable to find any sign of injury.

He looked to be no more than twenty years old. His clothing was homespun but neat. There was a knife sheathed at his belt, but there didn't appear to be anything else about him. Islington checked him over again for injuries and didn't see any. Although his breath was foul, Islington couldn't smell alcohol. What was he doing lying unconscious in the middle of nowhere?

Islington shook him and tapped his cheeks. The man didn't come to. He went to the nearby stream and scooped up some of the cold water in his hands. He went back to the man and poured it on his face. That made him revive. The man shook his head back and forth a few times, spluttering, then opened his eyes to look up at Islington from where he lay on the ground. When he realized he was being stood over by a strange man, he sat up groggily to give Islington a wary look.

"What are you about?" he asked testily.

"I could ask the same of you," stated Islington calmly. "I am Viscount Islington, and you would be?"

"Name's Timmons Wallace," said Wallace, rubbing the back of his head gingerly. He touched his abdomen, and a puzzled frown formed on his face when he found there was no mark.

"What happened to you, Mr. Wallace?" asked Islington mildly.

"Don't know really," said Wallace dully. "I was walking along, minding me own business, when ruffians set upon me and took everything I had. Next thing I know, you're here trying to drown me."

"I was not trying to drown you," stated Islington firmly.

There was something about the story that didn't ring true. Perhaps it was that Wallace still had a weapon that made Islington have a hard time believing it. If he had been attacked by ruffians, they wouldn't have left him a knife. He would have been lucky if they didn't steal the boots from his feet and the clothes from his back.

"I didn't notice any injuries on you, Mr. Wallace," said Islington evenly. "How did they manage to knock you out?"

"I don't know. They must have hit me on the back of the head with something," said Wallace testily.

Islington looked around himself on the ground for an obvious weapon...a rock, a stick, anything that might have been used. He felt the back of Wallace's head for a wound as he looked around and wasn't even able to detect any swelling. It was then that he noticed the familiar, large hoof-prints on the ground where it was bare of grass. He also saw a large pile of horse manure not far away, and he was beginning to suspect Wallace was trying to give him a pile as well.

"So, you didn't have a horse?" asked Islington calmly, rising from his crouched position to start walking around the area.

"No, my lord, I can't afford a horse," said Wallace, looking at his abdomen again, going so far as to pull his shirt loose from his waistband to look at the area where the woman had hit him. Not a mark.

"I see," said Islington absently as he continued to look around.

He strolled to the edge of the woods, following one set of hoof-prints, and he found the remnants of the campsite. He walked over to the fire and put his hand to some of the charred remains after removing his glove. It was extinguished, but he could feel a little warmth and could tell it hadn't been out long. He could also see a smallish boot print here and there. He looked back to where Wallace still sat on the ground. He looked from the boot print to the size of the boots the man wore. They were not the same. Whoever made this camp, and Islington suspected it was Pandora, it was not Timmons Wallace. He walked back to Wallace.

It was then Islington noticed the dried blood on the ground near the boulder. Trying to fight his anxiety, he went over to the widespread stain on the ground to look at it closer. It wasn't a large amount, and it didn't appear to trail anywhere, but it was dried blood. He couldn't tell with any certainty how long it had been there, but it had to have happened after the weather cleared. Otherwise, the rain and mist would have washed it away. Since Wallace didn't have any wounds, there could only be one other person it had come from.

"So you were alone, Mr. Wallace?" he asked stilly.

"Yes, my lord. Like I said, I was just walking along minding me own business...."

He trailed off when Islington turned to look at him glacially. Wallace started to get up from the ground on his own, but Islington stalked toward him and grabbed him up by the front of his clothes, looking at him balefully.

"Where is she?" asked Islington savagely, giving him a shake.

"I don't know what you're talking about," said Wallace irritably, looking away from Islington with a stubbornly set jaw.

Islington reached down and pulled the man's knife from its sheath at his waist. He placed it under Wallace's chin, keeping a firm grip on his clothes. He gave the younger man a vicious smile.

"I'm only going to ask this one more time: where—is—she?" He poked Wallace under his chin with the knife to stress his point.

"I don't know where she went, and that's the God's truth, it is!" said Wallace quickly.

"But you were here when she was?" demanded Islington.

"Aye, I was here, but she was leaving. Please, don't kill me," Wallace whined.

"What about the blood?" asked Islington coldly.

"I don't know! She had a big thump on her head." He raised his hands from his sides into the air. "I had nowt to do with it, I swear!"

"Why were you unconscious when I found you?" asked Islington, relenting only slightly.

"I don't know; I must've fainted when I found out she was a girl," said Wallace testily. Islington poked him with the knife. "Awright, she hit me!"

"You let a *girl* hit you and knock you out?" said Islington amusedly. He didn't find it any more believable than Wallace saying he fainted, but it wasn't important for him to know how the man came to be unconscious. "Why did she hit you?" he asked, willing to play along.

"She's crazy, she is!" said Wallace. "She must be to be running around dressed like a man!"

"Here's what I think, Mr. Wallace: I think you were trying to waylay her, and she somehow managed to get the better of you. Am I right?" Wallace looked at him angrily, his lips pressed firmly together. "You know, Mr. Wallace, you've just about reached the end of my patience, so I suggest you come clean."

"Yes, yes, yes! I thought I'd get meself some easy boodle, but that bedlamite set upon *me!* It's gettin' so a man can't make a livin' no more," said Wallace testily.

Islington tossed the knife well away from where they stood, deciding he had heard enough from Mr. Wallace. Something had happened to Pandora last night, and now Islington was all the more keen to find her and make sure she was safe. He grimly thought she could in no way be safe as long as she was wandering across the countryside alone. He gave Wallace one more disgusted look, shaking his head, before he placed a solid punch to the man's jaw, putting him back into the unconsciousness in which he was found.

Islington grabbed Jezebel's reins and mounted, leading her back up the hill to the road. He could be no more than an hour's ride behind Pandora now, judging from the temperature of the ashes left behind at her campsite. He was soon to the bottom of the dale and forded the Nidd before beginning the climb to the hill on the far bank. He didn't try to force Jezebel to run, but he kept her to a quick walk as they climbed. He was unaware Pandora had just went below the ridge behind Brown Haw as he reached the top of Whernside.

≪ ≫

Pandora was following a road along the side of a beck through the bottom of the dale, heading north. She wasn't sure exactly where she was, but she felt confident she would be to Askrigg soon. She would make her first stop for the morning, and she was very pleased with the progress she was making. It was helpful, of course, that the weather was good and she wasn't behind the slow rider who had been plaguing her. She wouldn't be to Edinburgh within her seven days, but it wouldn't be far beyond that.

She hoped her forehead was healed by the time she met the count. Although, if he saw the wound, perhaps he would even better appreciate the sincerity of her warning, to know she had risked her life to deliver it. Her headache had been helped by the chamomile. She wasn't sure how long the effect would last, but she hoped it would last for a while. She wanted to save the sugar for her horse...and her tea.

She passed through several small villages as she traveled up the dale, but none appeared to be anything more than clusters of several farms together. The area really was remote when she thought about it but also very beautiful. She liked the way the land rolled and the water that was everywhere. She liked Wilderland better, though. She missed her home, and she looked forward to being done with this so she could go back.

The road eventually crossed the stream, but Pandora soon saw that the land she was traveling over was a strip between two becks that would merge together. She was relieved to see her road went to the left, and there was another bridge to cross over the other stream. When she crossed it, she was alarmed to see the road appeared to go in four different directions. She quickly ruled out the one that went south; she had seen it going down the side of the beck in a direction she didn't want to go. That left three. After a moment's hesitation, she picked the one in the middle. It led her to a bridge over the Ure.

When Pandora reached the bridge, she stopped midway across to look upstream in awe of what she beheld.

"Aysgarth Falls," she sighed wonderingly.

312

She had heard of them, as most everyone had, and she didn't need to look at her map to know that's what they were. They were beautiful. The water was coursing over the high force quickly, and she watched as it changed color from a dark bluish-brown to a creamy, almost golden honey color as it went over a level of stone. She had heard that when the water was low, one could easily walk from one side to the other. Pandora wouldn't want to try that today. The rain in the area had drained into the river, making the falls treacherous. She looked downstream as well, but she was unable to see the rest of the falls. She shrugged. No matter. The upper force was enough. Her sisters would be jealous when she told them she had seen them.

She was about to continue on when she heard the sound of thunderous hooves approaching from behind. It sounded like one horse, and she didn't hear carriage wheels accompanying it. She started to move on, but something made her turn to look at what was approaching. Her breath caught in her throat as the figure on horseback drew nearer. She at first thought her mind was playing tricks, belated effects from the bump on her head, but the closer he came, Pandora could not deny what she was seeing. It was Islington.

He slowed as he came abreast of her on the bridge, coming between her and the western side of it, blocking her view of the falls. His horse being shorter than hers brought them to the same height, and she looked at him speechlessly, her eyes round in surprise. He looked tired, she thought, but he was still as handsome as she had ever seen him. She couldn't believe he was there, that he had managed to find her after hundreds of miles.

"Hallo," she said softly, unable to think of anything clever.

"You hurt your head," he replied, just as inarticulate.

Pandora smiled faintly and touched her fingers to her forehead. "I rolled down a hill," she said sheepishly.

Islington was looking at her wonderingly. He couldn't believe he had finally found her. She was bedraggled from her days on the road in the elements, and she also looked strained and tired. The bump on her forehead looked nasty with the blue-black bruise under it and the bad scrape, but Islington thought he had never seen anything more beautiful. He had thought about what he would say to her when he finally found her, but all the words had floated away the minute he saw her on the bridge.

Pandora started looking around herself uncomfortably as he continued to stare at her intensely. She looked down at his horse and saw the mare was exhausted and heavily lathered. She appeared on the verge of collapsing, her sides heaving tiredly, and Pandora felt disbelief coursing through her.

"What have you done to your horse?" she gasped.

"Pardon?" he asked, confused by her apparent, sudden anger.

"You've ridden the poor thing into the ground!" said Pandora irately.

Islington continued to stare at her, completely nonplussed by the sudden abuse. Pandora felt Bellerophon shuffling around restively beneath her, and she noticed the way he was paying attention to Islington's mare. Her eyes grew round in alarm and surprise, and her anger grew even more.

"You brought a mare in *heat* around my horse?" she bit out quietly.

"I what?" asked Islington perplexedly. He still didn't understand what was provoking her anger.

"My *God!* What were you *thinking?"* she yelled.

"I could ask the same of you!" Islington yelled back, deciding enough was enough. "What were *you* thinking, gallivanting across the countryside alone?"

"I was doing just fine, thank you very much," said Pandora coldly.

"Oh, right, and you only have that grotesque thing on your forehead because you wanted a *souvenir,*" said Islington sarcastically.

Pandora touched the wound self-consciously. She had no idea what it looked like, but judging from Islington's retort, it must be horrid indeed.

"Do you realize how frantic your family is?" asked Islington darkly, glaring at her. "Right now, Myron and Dorian are scouring the country looking for you! Your mother almost fainted dead away when she found out you'd run off!"

"I told them not to worry," said Pandora softly.

"Well, now you can go back home, and I'll see you make it there in one piece," said Islington finally.

"I'm not going home," said Pandora firmly. "Not until I've done what I left for."

"You can't be serious," said Islington with astonishment.

"I am. I'm going that way," said Pandora, pointing at the northern end of the bridge.

"No, you're going that way," said Islington angrily, pointing back the other direction over his shoulder with his thumb.

"No, I'm going to warn Charles-Philippe de Bourbon his life is in danger because *someone* needs to," said Pandora definitely with a stubborn shake of her head. "You're welcome to accompany me, but I am going."

"Pandora, don't make me force you to go home," said Islington determinedly.

"You can go ahead and try, if you think you've got the stones to do it," said Pandora arrogantly. "I've already knocked one man down today; one more isn't going to make much difference."

Islington's eyes rounded in surprise. He couldn't believe Wallace had been telling the truth. What had she done to him?

"Now," said Pandora quietly as she gathered up her reins more firmly in her hand, "I'm going that way," she said as she again pointed toward the far end of the bridge. "You can come with me, but you're *not* going to make me go back until I'm ready to go."

Pandora heard a gunshot. She soothed Bellerophon, and he settled quickly, having recently become accustomed to the sound. It had come from the woods at the northern end of the bridge. She looked in that direction and could see something (or someone, more likely) rustling in the undergrowth. Her natural instincts came into play. Without thinking, she grabbed her bow from its holster and nocked an arrow. She saw a rider on a brown horse coming out of the trees.

"*Son of a bitch!*" she roared angrily.

She released her arrow after only marginally taking aim, making sure she wouldn't hit the horse. It didn't hit exactly where she had intended, but it did strike the rider, planting firmly into his right buttock as he had risen out of the seat for the horse to gallop away.

"Of all the underhanded, despicable, *mean* things to do!" she yelled, replacing her bow agitatedly.

A riderless black horse went across the bridge, heading for the woods. She thought vaguely that the horse looked like Islington's mare. She looked around herself and realized he was no longer there.

"Islington?" she called uselessly, her voice tinged with concern.

She looked upstream and didn't see him there, and then she felt foolish as she realized he wouldn't be going in that direction anyhow. She moved Bellerophon to the other side and looked downstream. She saw a form floating down the river, heading inexorably toward the falls.

"Bloody hell!" groaned Pandora. "*Yala!*" she urged Bellerophon.

Her horse sprinted to the northern end of the bridge, and Pandora turned him into the woods. For some distance, there was a path worn along the riverbank where countless tourists had come to see the falls over the years. Luckily, none were about today. Pandora guided Bellerophon along, ducking to avoid low-hanging tree limbs, looking into the river for sign of Islington. She watched with alarm as he went over the middle force, and she urged her horse to go faster. She watched in panic as his head bobbed under the water.

Looking ahead in the river, she couldn't see the lower force, and she urged Bellerophon to move faster on the path in an attempt to get ahead of where Islington was floating before he reached them. Once she got to a point that seemed well ahead of him, she pulled off her coat, boots, and hat, laying them over the top of the saddle and quickly securing them as best she could. Bellerophon would try to follow her along the shore if what she planned didn't work, and she didn't want to risk them falling off and getting lost. She found a low point along the bank to go into the river and waded out as she waited for Islington to appear.

The riverbed beneath her stockinged feet was slippery, and the current was strong, but Pandora moved as quickly as she could to the center. Within seconds, she saw Islington floating toward her. His head was barely above the water, and he was ineffectually trying to guide himself with one arm. He was heading directly at her. She tried to move out of the way, but the current was too strong for her to move against very quickly. As he bumped into her, Pandora tried to get him by the arms, but all she could manage was to grab the back of his clothing before his weight and the strength of the current made her lose her footing, and she, too, started toward the lower falls.

Pandora tried to fight her rising panic. She was a strong swimmer, but she had never tried to rescue someone who was drowning from a raging river before. The water was freezing, and she could feel her body going rigid in response to the cold. Her jaw clenched just before her teeth started to chatter. She tried to change her position with the greatest effort, so that she was floating ahead of Islington with her body mostly backward to the oncoming falls. They weren't very high, but regardless of that, there would be rocks and other hazards at the bottom of them. She hoped the depth of the water from the rain would protect them from some of it, but there was a very real risk they could be sucked under or hit something. It looked like the best place for them to stay was the middle of the channel, and Pandora tried as hard as she could to keep them there. She tightened her hold on the collar of Islington's coat and tried to keep his head above water. He appeared to be barely conscious and would not be able to help.

Pandora couldn't understand how he had managed to fall into the river to begin with. The only thing she could assume was that he had come unseated by his horse rearing at the gunshot. It still was beyond her, however, that he should be so insensible. The drop from the bridge hadn't been that far. It was possible he could have hit his head on a rock or something when he fell. She didn't want to believe he was so helpless because he couldn't swim. That just did not seem likely.

She knew the falls were coming as she heard the roar of the river grow even louder. She looked to either bank for a place they could get out before reaching them, but it was, for the most part, sheer rock. She tensed and silently began to pray because she just knew they were going to die. She didn't know how she would possibly have the strength to do what she needed to. She would occasionally try putting her feet to the bottom of the river and found that, with some effort, she could touch, and it was really not deep at all. It was the only way she could find to change their course if they started going too far to one bank or the other until she was able to find a way to get them out of it, but the bottom was too slippery, the current too strong, and Islington's weight too much for her to put her feet down and bring them to a complete stop.

She felt a change in the flow of the water as they went over the first fall, almost as if she were floating into mid-air, but then she landed onto the next shelf and a weightiness returned, along with a whacking thump to her backside on a rock that was sticking up beneath the fall. The drop hadn't been very much, only two feet or so, but as Pandora looked ahead of herself in the river, she could see there were still several more to come. There was only a brief respite before they dropped another foot, followed almost immediately by another. The next drop was further, and Pandora almost lost her grip on Islington's coat when they landed another four feet lower still. She cracked her elbow on a rock, and her eyes watered with the pain, but she wouldn't let go of Islington. That fall appeared to be the highest one, and Pandora tried to keep them to the middle of the channel as they went over several more, lower steps.

The small drops continued for several more yards, and the roiling water occasionally pulled Pandora's head underneath. She struggled to get to the surface, pushing against the bottom of the river with her feet, gasping for air when she reached it. It appeared the falls were over and she could soon start looking for a place to get out, but the river decided it wasn't finished yet. Just as it started to bend to the right, there was another fall, and Pandora sucked in her breath between her teeth as she felt her already aching back scrape against a hidden rock.

Pandora's fingers and toes began to go numb in the frigid water, but she was yet to find somewhere they could get out; the banks of the river remained sheer walls of stone, and there was nowhere for her to go. She could feel herself becoming groggy as the coldness began to overtake her, and still she wouldn't let go of Islington. Pandora determined that if she had jumped in to save him, she'd be damned if she'd let go of him.

When she looked to her right, she saw a beck leading into the river, and the force of the current increased at the added water. She momentarily felt the bottom of the river disappear beneath her where the water had eaten away at the rock below, but it soon appeared again, and Pandora heaved a sigh of relief. Ahead of her in the river, there was a footpath from one bank to the other and someone had placed stones across the river for people to cross. They weren't going to help her. There was no way for her to grab one of them because the water covered them. She doubted anyone would be foolish enough to attempt crossing until the water level dropped, and the stones only presented obstacles she would have to avoid or wind up injuring herself or Islington. She picked the point where the stones were farthest apart and tried to make herself and Islington squeeze between them. She got another scrape on her back for her troubles, but they were able to get by. Unfortunately, she was still not able to get to the shore.

They floated on further still, and in her groggy mind, Pandora began to wonder how far they had gone. She didn't know how long the falls were or where the river had taken them. She felt as if they had been floating for hours. After a small stream joined into the river on the left, it made a sharp bend to the right. Once they went around the bend, Pandora saw a beach. The water was still flowing quickly, but she managed to use her feet and guide them closer to that bank. As she moved toward it, the current began to release them. Once she gained a solid footing in the sand and small stones, she put both of her hands on Islington's collar and pulled him up the bank as far as she could, his feet still remaining in the water. Once she felt safe he wouldn't float off, she collapsed nearby exhaustedly, her chest heaving.

She lay on the bank for a time, her cheek lying against the sand. She didn't care that it was coating her from head to toe. She was never so grateful to be on dry land. She hurt everywhere. She was freezing. All she wanted to do was sleep. But, she managed to roll onto her back, wincing at the pain it caused to the scrapes and bruises, and forced herself to sit up. She raised the arm where she had hit her elbow. She wasn't surprised to see a huge tear in her sleeve and that her arm beneath was skinned and bleeding, but not as badly as she had thought it would be. She bit the inside of her lip to keep herself from uttering a curse when bending it made it throb. She couldn't see her back, but she was sure it didn't look much better.

She crawled across the sand to where she had left Islington. His eyes were closed, but he was breathing. That was a relief. She would hate to have gone through all that effort only to have him drown. His lips had a bluish tinge and his skin was ashen. Pandora suspected it came from his time in the cold water. She didn't doubt she looked the same. She shook him by the shoulder, and he moaned, shaking his head.

"Don't do that," he managed to get out through tight lips.

He opened his eyes and turned his head to look at her. His expression was strained, and his eyes were serious. She saw him shiver from the cold and barely managed to suppress one of her own.

"Oh, good, you're awake," said Pandora with relief. "Can't you swim?"

"Yes, I'm an excellent swimmer," said Islington dully.

Pandora heard hooves on the wide beach, and she looked up to see Bellerophon trotting toward her. She stood up and went to him, reaching for her coat on his back before giving him a gratuitous pat on his neck.

"Good boy," she murmured. She reached into her coat for sugar.

She unfastened the tab on her valise and grabbed the bottle of whisky. She walked back to Islington and put her coat over him. He had been in the water longer, and moving around was helping her to warm up...slightly. Islington needed the coat more. She pulled out the cork and took a hefty swig of the whisky. She then roused Islington by shaking his shoulder. He moaned and shook his head again.

"Please, don't do that," he said softly.

Pandora lifted his head, and he opened his eyes in surprise.

"Here. Drink this," she ordered, and she raised the whisky bottle to his lips for him to drink several swallows.

"What are you doing with whisky?" he asked as she put his head down.

Pandora shrugged. "I don't know. I thought it might be handy for something. It has been...a couple times." She looked around as she re-corked the bottle. "Your horse ran off," she stated matter-of-factly.

"Jezebel is high-strung," said Islington on a gasp as he tried to sit up.

"Jezebel? Why am I not surprised you would have a mare in *heat* named Jezebel?" muttered Pandora as she helped him come upright.

Once he was sitting, she readjusted her coat on him and made sure he wasn't going to fall over. Pandora went to Bellerophon, who stood patiently waiting nearby. After putting the whisky back in her valise, she grabbed her boots and put them on over her stockings, which were now completely shredded on the sole. She stuck her dirk back into the top of her boot and took her hat. She gave Bellerophon a few more lumps of sugar and made sure the reins were fastened out of the way.

"Go find the horse, fella," she said enthusiastically.

Bellerophon nickered softly and took off at a trot back into the woods. Pandora watched him go. She could follow him, but she didn't have the energy. It would be best if she waited on the beach. He would know where to find her. She walked back to where Islington still sat, rather waveringly, and flopped down on the sand beside him.

"You just chased off the only horse we had," said Islington, looking into the woods where Bellerophon had gone.

"I didn't chase him off. He's going to find the...ah...Jezebel."

"Your horse fetches?" asked Islington disbelievingly.

"Of course," said Pandora in a tone that indicated she thought everyone's horse should be able to.

"This has got to be the most memorable birthday I've ever had," said Islington slowly.

Pandora looked at him with wide eyes. "Today's your birthday?" she gasped.

"Yes, it is."

His skin was still ashen, and the blue tinge had not yet gone from his lips. Pandora was feeling much better after her whisky, but she would feel even more wonderful with dry clothes. She was utterly surprised it was his birthday. He was right: this was going to be one he would not soon forget.

"Many happy returns!" said Pandora brightly, her smile a little brittle.

"Can you help me to that oak tree over there?" he asked mildly, raising his right arm to point over his left shoulder.

Pandora looked at him curiously. "I suppose I can," she said calmly, going to take his left arm.

"Please, on the right...please," he said, his eyes closed.

Pandora could see his jaw clench. She didn't think he was still that cold, despite his ashen skin and blue-tinged lips. He didn't seem angry. Her forehead wrinkled, but she went to his right side to let him put his arm over her shoulder. She put her left arm around his back and braced her right hand against his side. It took some effort, but he was able to stand. Pandora looked at his face as she led him to the tree.

"You're not drunk, are you?" she asked as they reached the tree, noting the way he seemed to weave on his feet.

"If only," he sighed with a tight smile. "Can you help me take off my coat?" he asked as he took hers off of his shoulders. "Start with the right arm, please."

Pandora shrugged and willingly helped, seeing he wasn't quite altogether yet. She first took off his wet gloves. She then grabbed the wet material of his coat in her fingers, tugging at it several times before it finally came loose. She got the sleeve off his right arm and went to the other side. Islington was looking at her tight-lipped, and his features were still ashen and somewhat drawn. She began to pull at the sleeve, but it was twisted and bound up on his arm. She held his hand in one of hers and grabbed the bottom of the sleeve in her other hand as she attempted to untwist it. She couldn't figure out how it had become so wound up, but she could see why he needed her help to get it off. Pandora felt his grip tighten on hers almost imperceptibly. She chose to ignore it and worked at unwinding his sleeve. She finally got it.

"Aha!" she said victoriously and started tugging at the sleeve again.

Islington started to weave on his feet, and Pandora moved to put a bracing hand against his left side and her shoulder under his right arm to steady him. She looked up at him concernedly. His features were even paler than before, and Pandora thought if he clenched his jaw any tighter, he was going to crack his teeth.

"Do you want to sit down?" she asked with a frown.

Islington shook his head. "No, please, take off my coat."

Pandora looked at him a few minutes more, but she did as he asked. She grabbed the bottom of the sleeve, and after one or two more tugs, she had it free. Pandora looked for something nearby to lay it on and located a rock a few steps away. She laid the coat out flat to start drying in the sunlight, and then she turned to walk back to Islington. She turned just in time because he was again weaving on his feet. She got to him just before he fell, and she put herself under his right arm and put a hand to his left side to steady him.

"Is everything all right?" she asked concernedly.

Islington looked down at her, and his eyes had an almost hazy cast to them. He gave her a soft smile and nodded. Pandora moved away from him when she felt he could again stand on his own. Once she turned to look at him without his coat on, she noticed one of his shoulders, his left shoulder, didn't look right.

"What's wrong with your shoulder?" she gasped in alarm.

"It seems I've dislocated it," he said blandly. "But I'm about to fix it. I've done this before so I know it's just a simple matter...really...of putting it back in its socket."

Pandora watched in horror as he walked closer to the tree and momentarily put a bracing hand against it. She had heard about this. She wasn't sure she wanted to see this. She put a hand over her mouth as she watched him hit his left shoulder against the tree as hard as he could.

Pandora flinched when she heard a loud pop, and her stomach began to churn uncontrollably.

"Oh, I think I'm going to throw up," she said weakly, and she put her other hand to her stomach.

After a moment, the nausea went away, and she removed the hand covering her mouth. Islington had sunk against the side of the tree once he had put his shoulder back in its socket. He sat unmoving, and Pandora walked to him. She started to touch him with her right hand and frowned when she noticed it was covered with something red. She rubbed at it with her other hand, and it came off easily enough, but she wasn't sure what it was. It took her a moment to realize it was blood. She checked her face and the rest of her body to find out where it had come from. Except for the scrape on her elbow, she didn't have any other injuries (other than the ones she couldn't see or reach on her back). She found some of the blood on her face, but that must have come from when she put her hand over her mouth. It was then that she knew it had to be Islington's.

"Islington?" she called softly as she fell to her knees beside him. "Islington, why are you bleeding?" she asked stilly. She could feel her pulse begin to pound in her head, and it was difficult to breathe.

He had his forehead resting against the bark of the tree, and when she asked the question, he weakly turned to look at her.

"Oh, that," he said slowly. "I've been shot."

"Oh, my *God!* Why didn't you tell me?" she gasped.

She started checking him over, looking for the wound. She found the hole in the left side of his waistcoat, and when she touched it, her fingers came away coated with blood. Pandora tried to fight the wave of nausea that came over her. She had to.

"I was coming to that," he said, and Pandora watched as he started to weave again. She reached over to stop him from completely collapsing.

Pandora heard a rustling through the underbrush, and Bellerophon returned with Jezebel, leading her by the reins. He came to where Pandora was sitting on the ground beside Islington and stopped. Pandora stood up and took Jezebel's reins from her stallion, tethering them firmly to a branch so the mare wouldn't run off again.

"Oh, look, the horses are back!" she said brightly. "Now we can find you a doctor."

Islington shook his head negatively. "I can't ride anywhere. Do you even know where we are?"

Pandora began to panic. "No, not really," she said. "We're on the Ure below Aysgarth Falls. That's about it."

She went to sit beside him, her forehead wrinkling worriedly as she looked at him. She now realized the ashen color to his skin had nothing to do with cold. He needed a doctor. She looked around herself, looking for anything that might tell her where they were or for someone who could help them. She started to look back at Islington when something deeper in the woods behind the beach caught her eye. She stood to get a better look.

"Oh, I see a cottage!" she said relievedly. "In the woods just there. We can get you some help there. Can you walk?"

"Maybe…if you help me," said Islington weakly. He was about to faint.

She quickly went to his side and helped him stand. She struggled under his weight, but she was desperate to get him help. She led him toward the cottage that was well-hidden in the midst of the woods. She could just make out the faded, greening whitewash coating the stone walls. It wasn't very big, but the size didn't matter if she was able to find someone to help Islington. As they came nearer, however, Pandora's face went pale with dismay. It was abandoned.

It *was* small, not more than two rooms with a chimney in between. The roof on one end was still intact, but at the other, the thatch and timbers had mostly fallen in from the impact of a large tree limb. There was only one window. To one side, there was a collapsed mass of timber that might have been a barn once upon a time. She could see the remnants of a wooden hand pump near a trough by the barn. There was a place where there had been a kitchen garden, but it was grown over, and the only things left were weeds, perennials, and annuals that had managed to reseed themselves. The area surrounding the house had been cleared of trees somewhat, but weeds choked the small clearing, and vines had started growing up the walls of the cottage. Pandora couldn't tell how long the cottage had been empty, but it was obvious whoever had once lived there was *not* coming back.

"Oh, no, no, no!" moaned Pandora, and she felt her eyes sting with anxious tears as she looked at it.

"Shh," soothed Islington, squeezing her shoulders comfortingly with his arm. "We shall just have to see to it ourselves."

"*We?*" squeaked Pandora in alarm. "I'm not a physician! I don't know anything about medicine. I stand a better chance of fixing that pump!"

"Let's see what we have first, shall we?" said Islington calmly as he continued toward the door of the cottage leaning on her.

Pandora had to shove at the wooden door several times with her foot before the weather-locked thing gave way. It scraped against the flagstone floor and wobbled on its wooden hinges, but it didn't fall off. It opened into the side of the cottage that still had a roof…and the only window. The surrounding trees made the interior gloomy, and Pandora had to wait a moment for her vision to adjust. Everything was covered with dust and cobwebs, but it wasn't completely bare…or uninhabited. Several small creatures scampered once she had the door open.

Pandora saw a good-sized, roughhewn, wooden table in the center of the room with two chairs nearby, both of which were on the verge of collapsing. In a nook by the fireplace, there was a narrow wooden-framed bed with ropes going across it to support the mattress, which was straw-filled and still there. It was at one time separated from the rest of the room by a curtain, which was no longer there.

The fireplace itself was impressively large considering the size of the cottage, taking up almost half the wall. It had a raised hearth with a recess for storing wood. It also had a stone mantel going across above the firebox with a cast iron sconce embedded into the masonry to either end. That they couldn't be easily removed was probably the only reason they were still there. There were two hooks inside the firebox for hanging pots, and from one there was still hanging a large one of cast iron. There was no dividing wall in the middle of it, and Pandora was able to see through to the partial daylight in the other room. The other room was reached through a doorway just inside the main door, but it was unusable.

Pandora guided Islington to the table, and after testing it to make sure it wouldn't fall, she helped him sit on it. She would have put him in one of the chairs, but the legs on both were canted to one side or the other, and they would fall if any type of weight were put on them.

Islington tried to unbutton his waistcoat with one hand, but he wasn't able to. Pandora did it for him and helped him remove it, carefully easing it over his left shoulder. When the burgundy vest was removed, Pandora could see the blood covering the entire left side of his shirt. She could feel her stomach flip-flop nauseously, but she took a deep breath and tried to control it. She removed his cravat, and then she unfastened the cuffs on his shirt. She untied the laces at the neck, but she couldn't remove it over his head without hurting his arm. Judging from its condition, it wasn't repairable so she grabbed the edges of the placket and ripped the front of the fine linen garment to the bottom hem. Islington looked up at her in surprise.

"It's just a shirt," she said calmly as she helped him remove it.

She looked at the wound in his side, and the blood began to thrum in her ears. She went dizzy for a moment, but she closed her eyes to collect herself and opened them again. There was a hole about half an inch in diameter, which had blood steadily trickling from it down to the waistband on his trousers. It looked bad. There were reddish-purple striations on his shoulder where it had been dislocated, and, although he didn't have any scrapes, she could see bruises and welts where he had bumped into several rocks going down the falls.

"Go get the horses," said Islington calmly as he looked down at the gunshot wound himself.

Pandora gave him a worried look. "You're sure?"

Islington nodded. "I'll be fine, but I think I'm going to need the whisky when you come back."

After giving Islington one last look, Pandora hurried from the cottage and ran back down to the beach where she had left their belongings. She grabbed Islington's coat and hers then untethered Jezebel. Bellerophon was calmly standing nearby.

"Come on, fella," she called over her shoulder as she led the mare to the cottage.

Once she reached it, she tied Jezebel near a small patch of grass. She went to Bellerophon and unloaded her bags. She grabbed her valise and the front saddlebags and quickly went back into the cabin. Islington was still where she had left him. He was extremely pale and weaving slowly in place. Pandora went to him and set her bags on the table. She opened the saddlebag with the medicine kit and pulled out the box.

"I have some things that might help," she said hopefully.

Islington peered into the box. He lifted up the bandaging and looked at it before putting it back. He pulled out the tweezers but shook his head cryptically and put those back as well. He pulled out the jar of ointment and frowned at the Chinese characters on its lid.

"What's this?" he asked.

"It's a wound ointment Keung made. It works quite well."

"Keung?" asked Islington blankly.

"Maiyin's husband," supplied Pandora.

Islington nodded. "You can read Chinese?" he asked disbelievingly.

"Well, I *do* have a Chinese maid," defended Pandora. "I do know how to read several others."

Islington looked at her, and she could see the hazy cast in his eyes deepening. She could feel her heart starting to tighten fearfully. He looked back down in the box and lifted out another bottle from the bottom.

"Medicine for my headaches," she stated. "I don't know what's in it, but it works for my head." She rubbed the spot behind her ear as he put it back and pulled out the other bottle. "Laudanum," she said. He set that one to the side out of the box after giving her a surprised look.

He then went through all the small bottles in the lid, and Pandora named them off for him. He didn't remove any of them, but he would occasionally nod when she translated them. After the last one, he closed the lid and set the bottle of laudanum on top of it. He then looked back at her.

"What else is in your bags of tricks?" he asked with a smile.

Pandora thought he was becoming a bit silly from shock and blood loss. She shrugged uncertainly.

"That's it, really...other than the whisky. Maiyin gave me a sewing kit *and* a fishing kit, but I don't see how those can help."

"Let me see them," he requested.

Pandora shrugged and reached into the other saddlebag to pull them out after she removed the guns, spyglass, and her map to reach them. Islington looked at all the things on the table, and his eyebrows rose.

"Persephone was right: you *are* ready for war," he muttered.

"Pardon?" asked Pandora confusedly.

He didn't explain but simply shook his head dismissively. He removed the set of pliers from the fishing kit and started to take out the knife as well, but he left it and closed it back up. He set the pliers on top of the medicine kit and placed the entire sewing kit beside it. He patted them contemplatively for a moment before looking at her.

"Do you have a knife, other than the one in the kit or this one?" he asked as he lifted the dagger-pistol from the table.

Pandora nodded. "I have this," she said as she pulled the dirk from the top of her boot and set it on the table. "And I also have—"she began as she started to dig through her valise, pulling out the bottle of whisky to set on the table then grabbing her folding pocketknife—"this."

Islington took the pocketknife from her and opened it. He tested the edge of the blade near the tip with his thumb and nodded satisfactorily. He set it beside the other things he had collected and placed the bottle of whisky there as well. He then looked up at Pandora seriously.

"Now, this is what you'll need to do," he began.

"*Me?*" squeaked Pandora.

"Yes, *you.* I can't do this myself, and you need to listen to what I tell you now because I won't be able to tell you again," he said gravely.

"I can't do this," said Pandora anxiously, shaking her head. "*Please, don't make me do this,*" she begged.

"Pandora, you *have* to," he said firmly, his expression plaintive.

He gently grabbed the front of her clothes and brought her near to him for a subdued kiss. He rested his forehead against hers once it ended, and Pandora could feel a cold clamminess there.

"Please, do this for me," he whispered, and Pandora could detect a fear and desperation in his tone.

There was an apprehensive knot forming in the pit of her stomach. So many things about this worried her, but losing him worried her more at this point. She finally nodded.

"Thank you," Islington sighed, closing his eyes in relief. "From what I can tell, the bullet hasn't gone through anything vital. I was able to feel it when I checked with my finger—"Pandora fought back her nausea and had to marvel at the clinical tone he was able to use when speaking about a half-inch wide, gaping hole in his *own* body—"but it's lodged between two of my ribs. It cannot stay." Pandora was sure she was turning a bright shade of green. "You need to cut the hole a little bigger with this—"he touched the knife—"and pull out the ball with these." He lifted the set of pliers.

Pandora put a hand over her mouth. She was sure she was going to throw up…or faint.

"Once you have the ball out, make sure you have *all* of it. Then you can sew up the wound. Do you understand?"

"I can't sew," said Pandora weakly.

"It doesn't have to be perfect," said Islington with an amused smile. He put a hand to the side of her face and rubbed her cheek tenderly as she continued to be on the verge of hysteria. "You can do this." She nodded unsurely, and her eyes began to fill with tears. "I'm going to take some of the laudanum because this is going to hurt. I'm also going to be unmanly and *faint* at some point." Pandora gave him the ghost of a smile. "Put some of the ointment on and one of the square bandages once you've sewn it up. You've got plenty of useful medicines if something goes wrong."

Pandora's eyes widened in dismay, and a tear escaped from one of her eyes to roll down her cheek. Islington brought her against him with his good arm, rubbing her back soothingly as she tried to regain her composure. Her shoulders shook for a moment as she wrapped her arms tightly around his neck, and then she came away from him and wiped her cheeks determinedly.

"All right?" he asked softly. She nodded.

Pandora moved her bags from the table and set them on the floor after she replaced the things that wouldn't be needed. She moved her collection of items to one side where she could reach them. She then took her coat, which was fairly dry, and folded it up for him to use as a pillow. She tried to wipe some of the dust from the table, but it was hopeless.

Islington reached for the bottle of laudanum and gave it to Pandora to remove the stopper. She handed it to him, and he looked at the level of its contents thoughtfully for a moment. He raised it to his lips and swallowed a fair amount, much more than Pandora would have expected him to take based on the dosage Keung had listed, but she wasn't going to question it because he *was* a physician, after all. He grimaced at its taste then handed it to Pandora to stopper and set aside.

He grabbed the bottle of whisky and handed it to Pandora to remove the cork from as well. She did so and gave it to him then watched disappointedly as he poured some of it on the wound, sucking in his breath from the stinging that resulted. She realized, of course, that it would be unnecessary for him to take both the laudanum and the whisky for pain, but she thought pouring it onto the wound wasn't going to kill the pain much. He handed it back to her, and she took a swallow from it before she re-corked it and set the now half-empty bottle to the side. He had an amused smile as he lay back on the table, resting his head on Pandora's coat at one end. His legs were bent at the knees, hanging over the other end. He then turned to look at her.

"I need you to help me grab my right shoulder with my left hand, so my arm will be out of the way," he said slowly, his speech already becoming slurred from the effects of the laudanum.

Pandora nodded and gently grabbed his left arm, bending it at the elbow and crossing it over his chest. She watched him grimace in pain as she moved his left shoulder to complete the motion of crossing his arm, but he didn't make a sound. It appeared that, now, the rest was up to her.

Chapter Twenty

Pandora opened the blade on the pocketknife. She looked at the wound and saw that the direction of the trickle of blood had changed with Islington's position. It steadily, if not speedily, began to drip onto the table. She *really* needed more light, but there was nothing to be done for it. She moved the blade toward the wound and gulped nervously. When Islington spoke, she jumped and nearly dropped the knife.

"Try to make the incision in line with the ribs, and don't cut too deeply," he said lowly.

Pandora looked at his face. His eyelids were half-closed from the opium, blood loss, and shock, but he was looking at her. He was very pale, almost pasty, and the bluish tinge to his lips hadn't gone away and only looked worse as his skin faded. The haze in his eyes had combined with the drugs to make the clear, rich blue of his irises cloudy, his pupils not dilated but unfocused, and Pandora's heart lurched. *He's dying*, she thought anxiously, and she took a deep breath to steady herself.

After another moment of looking at Islington, she looked back to the wound. Lying as he was on the table, it was easy to see his ribs. She put the knife against the edge of the wound and drew it across the skin, making a cut the same length as the diameter of the wound. The trickle of blood became a little thicker. She moved to the other side of the wound and made a cut again as long. Islington groaned as she cut, and she looked up worriedly to see him clenching his jaw, his nostrils flaring, his left hand clutching his right shoulder spasmodically. He nodded when she looked at him, but he didn't speak.

Thinking quickly, Pandora reached down and cut the tabs from the top of one of her boots. She put them together and moved up by Islington's head. She stroked his forehead gently and could feel the sweat beaded there.

"Here, bite down on this before you break your teeth," she said softly, putting the leather near his lips.

He nodded and opened his mouth, biting down on the leather. Once he had it positioned firmly, he nodded again.

Pandora moved back to his side and saw the drops of blood starting to form a small puddle on the dark surface of the table. She shook her head, and her brow furrowed critically as she looked at it. She put down the knife and picked up the pliers. With her other hand, she gently spread apart the edges of the wound. She couldn't see the ball. She widened the incision even further, and then she was able to see it lodged between the two ribs, a dark spot against the red of the sinew and muscle covering the bone. Adjusting the fingers she used to hold open the cut so she could maneuver the pliers, she reached in and clamped onto the lead ball.

She tugged at it firmly, but the ball was lodged tightly. She pulled at it again, and Islington cried out in muffled agony as he bit down on the leather. She couldn't look. She couldn't bear to see the pain on his face because she knew if she did she wouldn't be able to continue, and he would almost certainly die. She loosened the pliers on the ball and adjusted the angle she was pulling from and tried again. It still wouldn't budge. She would have to try wiggling it back and forth to pry it loose. She clenched her jaw, blinking back the tears obstructing her vision, and began. Islington yelled again then went still. Pandora looked up in alarm. Just as he said he would do, he had fainted. It made Pandora all the more determined to get the ball free while he was completely unconscious.

She clamped even tighter onto the ball and worked it back and forth. She slowly began to feel it move, and she continued to wiggle it and pull backward until it finally popped free with a scraping, oozing noise that made her retch. She sighed with relief and walked to the doorway, where there was more light to examine it. It was deformed from her attempts to extract it, and most of it was intact, but there was a small piece missing.

"Bloody *hell*!" she hissed.

She walked back to the table and angrily dropped the ball onto it with a thud and a groan of frustration. She opened the wound again, squinting her eyes in the dim light as she tried to examine the edges of the ribs where the ball had been. On the upper one, she saw the sliver of lead stuck into it. She reached back in with the pliers and pinched down. It came out with barely a tussle, and Pandora smiled giddily. She dropped the lead and the pliers onto the table and looked at his ribs. The bullet had formed little cracks in the bone where it had forced them apart, worse on the upper one where the sliver had been, but they didn't appear to be completely broken. Pandora sighed with relief. Now she could sew it up.

She reached for her sewing kit and examined its contents. She pulled out the scissors, the thimble and one of the needles. She decided to use the black thread; it wouldn't show blood as much as the white. She threaded the needle and rather than forming a knot, she would just leave a long enough tail after the first stitch to secure the end under the stitches that would follow. She closed the bottom edge of the wound together and pushed the needle through the skin on both sides using the thimble. It was different from sewing through material, and Pandora felt herself becoming queasy at the sensation. She gulped for a moment and took a few breaths then grabbed the needle with her fingers. It slipped out of them. She rubbed her fingers together to dry them and tried pulling again with the same result. She picked up the pliers and grabbed the end of the needle and pulled. It fed through.

She steadily worked her way across the wound using an overcast stitch, forcing the needle through with the thimble and grabbing it with the pliers, pulling each loop tight enough to close the edges together but not pucker. The most difficult part was closing the uneven margins formed by the bullet hole itself, and the skin was stretched a little tighter there because of it. Once she was to the other end, she fed the needle back under some of the stitches to secure it and cut the end with the scissors. She looked at her handiwork and shrugged. The bleeding had stopped by the time she was finished.

"Well, he did say it didn't have to be perfect," she muttered as she looked at the widely-spaced loops.

She went outside to retrieve her canteen from Bellerophon, giving him a pat. He shied at the smell of blood on her, but he let her scratch his jaw. She walked back inside and poured some of the water on the wound to clean off the blood. The table would need a larger quantity. She opened the medicine kit and got the ointment and one of the squares of muslin she thought would fit over the wound. She daubed some of the ointment onto the stitches, then covered it with the gauze as Islington had instructed. She didn't have any way to secure it, but the ointment was holding it in place for the time being.

She moved to Islington's head and looked at his unconscious features. His face was much more relaxed than she had seen it over the past hour, and she hoped she had done well enough with his injury. She removed the leather from his mouth and put her ear close to his face, listening satisfactorily to the unlabored sound of his breathing. She put an ear to his chest and could hear the steady beat of his heart. It seemed a little slow, but it was regular. She moved back to his head and brushed the hair away from his forehead before placing a gentle kiss on his lips.

Pandora calmly walked outside to the back corner of the cottage, where she vomited the entire contents of her stomach, one hand braced against the edge of the wall for support. When nothing more would come up, the tears started, and she fell to her knees weakly as she cried. If he died, it would be her fault. If she'd never left London, Islington would never have been shot. She recognized the horse and rider that came out of the woods, who had been responsible for shooting him. Islington wouldn't have been shot had he not been on the bridge with her. She had done what he told her and removed the bullet, but she wasn't a doctor. She knew little better than nothing about medicine. She had to pray he would live because she wasn't sure what else she could do.

Pandora stayed there crying for some time, but she eventually regained control of herself. She looked at her watch, which—surprisingly—still worked after their dunk in the river. It was just nearing noon. She was astonished it was still so early. The morning seemed a lifetime ago.

She rose to her feet and went back into the cottage. She checked on Islington, but he hadn't moved, of course. Pandora didn't expect him to move for quite some time. She stood by the table with her hands on her hips as she surveyed their circumstances. She didn't know how long it would be before Islington was well enough to travel. It would not be that day and just as likely not the next either. This cottage would be their home for whatever time it took. Something would have to be done with it because Pandora couldn't see herself staying there *any* length of time with it in the condition it was, even if it did give her a roof over her head that she didn't have to make herself. Since there was no one else present who could attend to it, she would have to see how well she had paid attention to the things her mother had taught her…whether she wanted to or not.

The first thing she did was go to the fireplace and look up the chimney. The stone and mortar seemed to be in good condition, without any cracks or holes. Pandora could see the sky above inside the chimney. She found the handle for the damper, which was open, and tried it. It was in working order. She went to the doorway into the other room and looked at the stone on that side. It was acceptable as well. Now she felt comfortable building a fire.

She removed the cast iron cooking pot from its hook and set the heavy item to one side on the raised hearth. She went back to the other room and grabbed some of the thatch from the fallen roof, deciding it would be perfect tinder. She went out to the barn and grabbed an armful of some of the smaller pieces of wood and took them back into the house. The wood was aged, and it was oak. Perfect firewood. She laid the wood into the nook in the hearth and went back outside to Bellerophon, where she removed her tent and the rear saddlebags. She would come back out and remove the rest of his tack once she had a fire going. Islington needed a fire. She laid some of the wood on top of the thatch in the firebox then struck her flint. It began to glow, and the wood soon caught, adding a little brightness to the room as well as some much-needed warmth. She would look for a way to seal off the back side of it after she took care of other things. For now, it would suit.

She went outside and removed the bags of feed from Bellerophon's back. He hadn't been fed that day, other than what he had grazed that morning. Before taking them into the cottage, she put a scoop into his feedbag and put it on after removing his bridle. He began to eat hungrily, and Pandora felt guilty as it dawned on her that he hadn't been able to graze. He was probably starving. Jezebel had eaten most of the grass in the small patch Pandora had found for her down to the root. Pandora would see what could be done about feeding and watering both of them. There wasn't enough grass in the clearing, and some of the weeds were things they should not or would not eat.

She placed the bags of feed on the floor on the far wall of the room, and then she went back outside to remove the tack from both animals. She cut her length of rope in two to form makeshift halters for both of them. She put on Bellerophon's after she removed his feedbag, which was empty.

She took everything inside the cottage, and then she went to look at the water in the trough…and the pump. The pump would take some work to repair, and she wasn't sure she had the tools and supplies to do it. It would save her from going to the river for water, but she currently had more pressing matters to attend. The trough was still in one piece, and the water looked like it was still potable. She made sure the horses could reach it on their leads, and they would at least have water, if not immediate food.

Once she was back in the cottage, she stepped over to the "open" room and grabbed two small bundles of thatch, which she bound tightly and formed into torches. They wouldn't last very long, would not smell good, and would be inordinately messy, but they would at least provide more light. When she had those lit, she went back outside for a stick that was sturdy and fairly straight. Finding a suitable one, she went back into the cottage to the open side and grabbed more thatch. She also found one of the strings that had been used to weight down the thatch and untangled it from the pile. She bound the thatch around the stick to fashion herself a broom. She had, at least, used one; the servants at Wilderland refused to clean the solarium, so she and Psyche were responsible for doing it themselves.

She first used the broom to go around the corners and as high as she could reach into the exposed rafters to remove the cobwebs and bird's nests there. Once she cleaned the cobwebs off outside, she swept the floor. It was unbelievably dusty, and a large cloud formed as she swept. Pandora sneezed several times, and her eyes were teary. She was eventually able to get it clean enough, and she could even tell what colors most of the stones were by the time she was finished. She had firmly decided, however, that she wouldn't go so far as to mop. She didn't have the time or the energy.

After the floor was swept, she examined the door. It was held into the frame by three wooden hinges, and the hinges themselves were sound, but the pins for two out of the three were broken—the top one and the bottom one. That explained why it was so difficult to open. She went outside and looked around, trying to find sticks that would be suitable replacements. She couldn't find any. She walked over to the barn, and amidst all the wood, she was able to locate one of the doors, which still remained attached to its frame. It, too, had wooden hinges, and the pins were still in place and in working order. With a bit of effort, she was able to work them out and took them back to the cottage. They were the same size.

She looked closer at the door and realized that even with the new hinges, the door would rub…for whatever reason. It would need to be raised a little. There was enough distance between the top of the door and the frame that she wouldn't have to worry about that being a problem, but she would have to find a way to raise it. She needed washers, something that would let her raise the height by a half-inch. She trekked once again to the barn. She carefully stepped through the wood, lifting pieces out of the way and looking under them. She found various things while she looked, even a large tin tub with a hole rusted through the bottom of it. She found a badly rusted saw blade missing its handle, but it gave her an idea. She went back to the barn door where she had removed the pins and sawed off one of the hinge pieces. It was slow-going, but once she had it removed, she took the piece over to a flat rock to use as a table and sawed it in half across its diameter to fashion herself two perfectly acceptable, half-inch thick, wooden washers.

"Perfect," she said with a victorious grin.

She took the pieces back to the door of the cottage and removed the center pin from its hinge. The door was heavy, but she was able to start the pin through the top hinge and her makeshift washer then slide it through the hinge piece in the frame. She did the same with the bottom one, then the middle, and tried the door. It opened and closed much better. It didn't fit tightly in the frame, but it did at least open and close, and the latch worked. She re-opened it for the time being because the cottage still needed airing out. The scent of small animal droppings and age was strong.

She checked Islington. He hadn't moved. She put a hand to his forehead. He seemed cold, but some of his color was returning. Pandora unwound her tent for one of her wool blankets to place over him. She couldn't leave him on the table. It couldn't be comfortable, even if he wasn't awake to notice it.

She looked at the bed in the corner and walked over to it to examine the mattress. It was dusty, and the straw it was stuffed with had long since flattened down. She lifted it and looked at the underside. She didn't see any holes, surprisingly. With a little effort, she maneuvered it out of the cottage into the yard. She unfastened the flap made into it for removing its stuffing and poured it onto the ground. She did see several things that didn't belong in it—bits of string and other items—which made it obvious some type of animal (or, more likely, several) had used it as a residence at some point. Once she had it emptied, she found a place to hang it over a low limb and retrieved her broom. When she came back out, she found Bellerophon and Jezebel eating the straw.

"Oh, you two, I don't think you should be eating that," she said, her face wrinkling disgustedly.

Bellerophon looked up at her and nickered, but he put his head back down to resume eating it nonetheless. She would have to find them some food…soon. There was no telling what had been in that straw, or how long it had been there. Pandora only hoped it hadn't molded.

She beat the dust out of the mattress cover, but now she was left with an empty mattress. She knew there was nothing near the river, so she took a walk a little farther into the woods and found a nice-sized meadow before going far. She smiled happily and went back for the horses.

"This way, you two," she said with a grin. "I have something *much* better for you than straw covered in mouse droppings."

She tied the horses to separate trees, giving them plenty of room to graze without competing for food. She started pulling up handfuls of the grass herself and took it back to the cottage where she had left the mattress. After stuffing it in, she realized it would take a long time to stuff the mattress at this rate so she took it with her back to the meadow. She stayed to her own little corner of the field and shortly had the mattress stuffed. It would eventually flatten out again, once the grass dried out, but she wouldn't need it for very long and would hopefully be gone before it happened.

She lugged the much heavier mattress back to the cottage and took it inside. Before placing it on the frame, she examined and tightened the ropes to make sure they weren't on the verge of rotting away. Satisfied they were still sound, she laid the mattress back onto the frame and adjusted it, fluffing it here and there to soften the more obvious lumps. She put her thin blanket over it for a sheet and her small pillow, and then she felt it was ready to use.

She turned to look at Islington on the table and realized she couldn't get him to the bed unless he helped. She didn't think she could wake him. She added more wood to the fire as she pondered her dilemma. Finally, she decided the only thing she could do was try. He would be much better off in the bed. She went to the table and put her mouth near his ear.

"Islington," she called. No reaction. "Islington," she said a little louder. His forehead wrinkled, but he didn't move. She gently shook his face back and forth by his jaw. "Islington, wake up!" His frown deepened, and he managed to just open his eyes to look at her. His pupils were disconcertingly small. "Come on, sleepyhead Ted. Let's get you into bed," said Pandora with relief as she began to pull on his right arm to raise him to a sitting position.

Her pulling on his arm was the only thing keeping him from flopping back onto the table. He groaned when his left arm moved, and Pandora thought it could do with a sling. She looked around for something likely and settled on his torn and bloodstained shirt. It was ruined. Holding onto his right arm, she reached over to grab the shirt. When she let go of his arm to put on the sling, he started to fall over, and she had to quickly grab his arm again before he landed on the floor. She went behind him and climbed onto the table to keep him upright and free her hands by letting him fall back against her chest. Once she had both her hands free, she gently put the shirt under his arm and bent it at the elbow, and then she tied the sleeves around his neck. It wasn't pretty, but it would do.

She then leapt off the table quickly to take his arm again before he fell. She put his right arm over her shoulders and pushed on his back with her left hand to get him to move. She stumbled when he weakly swayed into her, but she guided him to the bed as he shuffled beside her, mostly unconscious. Rather than letting him go once she got there, she sat down with him on the edge of the bed, so that if he fell it wouldn't be far.

He did fall—sideways—onto his left side, and Pandora sucked in air through her teeth and cringed as she helplessly watched him go tumbling over. She quickly rolled him onto his back and adjusted his arm as carefully as she could. Then she put the piece of muslin back onto his wound. He was completely unconscious again, but at least she had him to the bed. She moved him around a little, and then she lifted his feet from the floor and straightened his legs. She was surprised the bed was long enough; she hadn't thought it would be.

He still had on his boots, and his trousers were still wet. Her clothing had long since dried after all the moving around she had been doing.

"This should be interesting," she muttered sarcastically.

The boots took some work to get off, but she was finally able to pry the wet leather from his feet. The boots were treated with oil and wax, like hers, and they would be wearable again, if stiff, once they were dry. She set them on the hearth near the fire to begin doing that. She started to leave his trousers on but realized she couldn't (or wouldn't). After all the effort she had gone through to literally *make* the bed, she didn't want it getting wet. Aside from that, staying in the wet clothes couldn't be good for him.

She heaved a long-suffering sigh, shaking her head, and unbuttoned the short rows of buttons at the bottom of each leg. Then she unfastened the buttons and ties at the waistband. She tried pulling at the bottom edge of each leg but found they weren't going to come loose without a lot of effort until she started them down from the top and got them past his backside, especially because the position of the bed made it impossible for her to pull directly downward on them. She thought about ripping them as she had done his shirt, or cutting them off with her sewing scissors, but the wool fabric was too strong to tear, and her scissors were too small. Aside from that, she wasn't sure what clothing he had brought with him, and she didn't want to leave him without anything to wear. It was bad enough she had torn his shirt. She would have to remove them.

With a groan and a shake of her head, Pandora reached under him and pulled down the back. Then she worked at the sides. The wet material wanted to bind, but she eventually got the trousers down far enough that they would be easier to remove. She went back to the legs and pulled. Finally, they came off, and she stumbled backwards when they did because of the force she used to accomplish it. Other than being wet, the dark material appeared moderately clean, without any holes or tears, but then Pandora remembered the blood that had trickled down his side. They would have to be washed, if only to take the stiffness out of them the coagulated blood would cause.

She took the blanket from the table and put it over him after pausing for a moment to admire what she saw. He was a beautifully put together man, and that he was injured and vulnerable did nothing to lessen it. She brushed the hair from his forehead and felt it for his temperature. He was a little warmer, and his skin had lost some of its clammy feel. He would rest much more comfortably on the bed. With Islington attended to, Pandora saw to the rest of the things around the cottage that needed to be done. She looked at her watch as she went outside. It was only 2:30; there was plenty of daylight left.

She walked to the back of the cottage to inspect something she had seen on the way back from the meadow: a large rain barrel. After all the recent rain, it was full. There was a small tin dipper hanging from the side of it, attached by a leather thong. She put some of the water into it after knocking out a few leaves and tasted the water. It was drinkable. That would at least give them water to use until she could fix the pump, and the barrel was large enough they wouldn't need any more than what was in it if she couldn't. She found a wooden bucket nearby that was battered around the rim but still seemed to hold water well enough. She filled it from the barrel and carried it into the cottage to wash the table and clean the inside of the window with a piece of Islington's shirt that she cut off with her sewing scissors for a rag.

Once she went out to clean the outside of the window and came back inside, she looked at the two chairs. With a little hammering from a rock, she was able to fit them back together and reseat the nails well enough they weren't going to be in any danger of falling apart if sat on. She wouldn't want to try leaping from one to the other, but they could at least be sat on.

She spent the better part of the remaining afternoon cleaning out the open room and filling up the nook in the fireplace with wood, pausing to eat an apple and a sausage when her stomach threatened to eat itself if she didn't and periodically checking on Islington as he slept. She hauled the timbers and the branches from the large limb that had caused the roof to collapse into the yard. She would break it up for firewood once she was done with the room. She left behind the thatch after using some to make several more torches, which she placed on the hearth.

Once she cleared out most of the debris, she found a shattered wooden crate with earthenware dishes inside. Most were broken beyond use, and Pandora took it outside to put on the heap where she had been tossing all the other unusable things she had discovered, but she was able to find a cup, two small plates, one larger plate, and a bowl. All were badly chipped but still more usable than nothing. She reckoned the dishes had been broken *before* the roof fell in, which was why they had been left behind. She took those to the other room, where she would eventually (hopefully) find a way to wash them…and some clothes.

She did her best sealing off the fireplace in the open room, using mud she mixed up from clay and dirt in the yard for mortar and whatever rocks she could find. It wasn't permanent, but they wouldn't be at the cottage forever. It would make the main room warmer and keep the fire from disturbing the horses. She was going to use the open room for their stall.

When Pandora had it prepared, she went to the meadow for the animals. They were happy and full after spending most of the day there, and she let them go to the trough when they reached the yard. While they drank, she looked around at the weeds. There were a few that would be useful, but one in particular caught her attention: soapwort. Like the name indicated, it made a wonderful lather for washing things. Pandora felt like she had struck gold. After the horses were settled into their stall, a sturdy branch across the doorway to keep them in, she refilled her bucket and gathered some of the soapwort.

After macerating the leaves and roots into the water and retrieving all the pieces out once it was ready, she washed all the dishes she had placed on the hearth, including the cast iron pot and another, smaller kettle she had found in the open room, and then she washed all the clothing. She draped the clothes wherever she could find to dry them, and then she took the bucket outside to empty and refill with clean water for drinking.

When Pandora looked at the sky, she could see the sun was setting. She glanced at her watch; it was nearing eight. She hadn't had a chance to work on the pump or look at the garden. That would have to wait until tomorrow. She was tired, and her back was killing her, but she had accomplished a lot.

She replaced the thatch torches with new ones and tossed the remnants of the second two she had lit onto the fire after she went inside. They were lasting longer than she thought they would. She started water for a pot of tea and sat on the hearth for some time, watching the flames until she started to doze off. Shaking her head to clear it, she stood and went to check on Islington. She would find something to eat and have a cup of tea before going to sleep herself.

She adjusted the blanket over Islington because it seemed he had moved at some point; either that, or she hadn't put it back when she had cut the material from his shirt. His face was flushed, and his brow was creased with pain as he slept. Pandora frowned and put a hand to his forehead. He had a fever. She frantically pulled back the blanket and removed the bandage. It was swollen and red with the beginnings of an infection. She went to her valise for a handkerchief and got the medicine kit from the table.

She set the kit on the edge of the hearth then dipped the handkerchief in the water bucket to put on his forehead. She put more of the ointment on his wound, and her forehead wrinkled concernedly at the way the swelling pulled the stitches extremely tight. She put the square back over it and looked through the herbs. In the end, she decided to try her headache medicine. She didn't know if it had anything in it for fever, but it certainly helped with pain. Aside from that, it was quick. If she didn't see any signs of improvement after she tried it a couple times, then she would go to something else. She put some water into her teacup, and then she added the drops from the bottle.

She carefully sat beside Islington on the bed and tried to wake him. He was even harder to rouse than before, and when he finally opened his eyes to look at her, they were glassy and unfocused, but the pupils had, thankfully, grown larger. His forehead wrinkled with pain and confusion as she gently lifted his head from the pillow. She raised the cup to his lips for him to swallow, and he continued to look at her, not drinking.

"Islington, I need you to drink this," she said firmly.

He finally took some into his mouth, and he grimaced at the taste of it. Pandora found it perfectly understandable why he would. He started to turn his head away, but she wouldn't let him.

"No. Drink all of it," said Pandora, her voice tinged with worry.

He did as she asked, and Pandora released his head back to the pillow. Islington continued to look at her for a time, his expression still one of bemusement, but eventually his eyelids drooped closed. He had looked at her as if he didn't know her. She put her head to his chest and listened. His heartbeat seemed to be fine, but she could hear a worrying rattle in his lungs every time he inhaled. It wasn't severe, but it wasn't normal, and it hadn't been there when she listened earlier. She re-dampened the linen and patted it over his entire face before placing it back on his forehead. His skin was burning hot. She nervously rubbed the spot behind her ear as she watched him for a few minutes.

The sound of the lid rattling on her pot in the fireplace made her jump. She went to the fire to remove it and put in some tea leaves to steep. She wasn't hungry anymore, but she could use a cup of tea. She went to the table and took one of the chairs to the bed to sit on, so she could watch Islington.

After a little while, she poured herself some tea into the chipped earthenware cup, saving the smaller metal one for medicating Islington. She added a lump of sugar and three drops of chamomile because her headache had returned. She was going to take her headache medicine, but now that Islington was running a fever, she didn't want to take something that would make her drowsy or cause her to sleep too deeply.

She sat beside the bed, occasionally re-dampening the handkerchief to wipe his face and forehead. The lines of pain didn't go away, and his fever didn't go down either. She would drip some of the water from the handkerchief into his mouth because his lips were becoming dry from the heat, but she didn't want to give him water in the cup and risk his choking on it. The stitches had stretched so tightly because of the swelling, she was afraid if he coughed they might burst.

Pandora had fallen asleep. She was slumped forward, her head resting on her arms on the side of the bed. The torches had gone out, the fire was only red embers, and it was cold in the cottage. She sat up quickly, wincing at the pain in her back. Her neck wanted to stay permanently turned to the right.

She looked worriedly at Islington. If nothing, he had worsened. The handkerchief was dry, and Pandora soaked it again to put back on his forehead. He was muttering unintelligibly in his sleep, which must have been what woke Pandora, and he would occasionally shake his head from side to side. She realized with some concern that he was delirious.

Pandora put more wood on the fire, but she didn't light more torches. The fire would brighten the room enough. She pulled out her watch to look at by the glow as the fire rekindled. It was just after midnight. She went to her valise for a second handkerchief. She would leave the first one in place and use the second to rub the rest of Islington down.

Before doing that, she needed to re-medicate him. She lifted the blanket to look at his injury. The swelling wasn't any worse, but the reddening from infection was. She put on more ointment and changed the bandage. She dipped some water into the metal cup and added drops from the bottle...plus a few extra for good measure. She sat on the edge of the bed, rather than the chair, to make it easier to lift his head.

She brushed a hand against his cheek and softly called his name. He continued to cast about fitfully. She tried again, and he opened his eyes. Now she saw the pupils were disconcertingly dilated, almost to the point of not being able to see the blue at all. He wasn't seeing her in his delirium. She wasn't concerned about that (his eyes worried her more than the delirium, oddly), provided he would take the medicine. She slowly lifted his head from the pillow and held the cup to his lips.

"Drink up, *àiren*," she said gently, giving him an encouraging smile.

He turned his eyes to look at her, attempting to focus, as he drank. Pandora sighed in relief as he finished, and she suppressed a smile as he shuddered. She set the cup on the edge of the hearth then turned the handkerchief on his forehead for the cool side to be against his skin.

She dipped the second handkerchief in the bucket and gently rubbed it over the rest of his face and chest. She would occasionally re-wet it to keep it cool and leave behind some of the water to evaporate on his skin. She jumped when he spoke in a voice barely above a whisper.

"Pandora, don't hate me."

Pandora looked at him. He was delirious. She could see, even as he was talking to her, in his mind, he was talking to a *different* her, no matter how conscious he seemed. She paused in what she was doing to brush a soothing hand against his cheek. She shook her head and smiled softly.

"I don't hate you," she said gently, and his forlorn expression tore at her heart. She couldn't imagine why it would matter. "I could never."

He lifted her hand to hold it against his face, and he rubbed his cheek against it longingly.

"I do *everything* wrong. I always make things worse for you than if I would just leave you alone. I can't even rescue you properly."

Pandora felt her throat catch emotionally, and tears started in her eyes. She put her other hand to the other side of his face, and she bent down to kiss him tenderly. She rested her forehead against his.

"I don't *want* you to leave me alone, Theo. You don't have to rescue me. All you have to do is love me," she whispered.

"I do," he sighed as his eyes drifted closed.

Pandora sat back and put a hand over her mouth to fight back a sob, her eyes widening in disbelief. It was as if he were saying goodbye. She wasn't sure she could take to heart what he said, but the reason behind it didn't have anything to do with delirium. He thought he was dying. Pandora squared her shoulders and wiped her cheeks determinedly.

"You are *not* going to die, damn you!" she said angrily. "I suffered through freezing water, blood, stitches...a dislocated shoulder! I swept! I washed dishes! I built you a *bloody* bed!" she yelled.

Pandora stood up and began to pace across the room, trying to think of something—anything—she might do to make him well. If she could have managed it by sheer will, it would have happened instantaneously. Unfortunately, her medical knowledge was wanting. She had read anatomy books and a few medical texts, but it was only because she thought she should, and she had forgotten most of it.

She had given him medicine, but that wasn't enough. Perhaps she hadn't given him the right medicine. She went to the medicine kit and looked at the willow. She smelled the bark in the bottle, and she realized it was in her headache medicine. She put the bottle back and began to pace again after she looked over the other bottles and couldn't find anything likely. Unfortunately, Keung hadn't thought to give her anything labeled *infection and delirium.* She thought about the laudanum, but it did nothing for either of those, and her headache medicine would work for pain.

She would occasionally look at Islington as she paced. He had resumed his fidgeting and muttering. There had to be a way to break the fever. Perhaps it hadn't gotten high enough. She wasn't sure about that, though; he seemed red-hot already. She wasn't sure how much higher it could go before it would kill him. He wasn't sweating, though, which surprised her. She thought he would be sweating profusely. He actually seemed dehydrated, but she wasn't sure how she could get more fluids into him. She had been able to rouse him for medicine. She would have to do it for him to drink water.

She sat back on the edge of the bed and dipped some water into the metal cup. She lifted his head from the pillow and called his name. He wouldn't wake up. She put the cup to his mouth and tipped some of the water in. He swallowed it, and Pandora shrugged. As long as he drank it. Her eyebrows rose as she watched him drain the entire cup. She got more and tried again. She let him have water until he wouldn't drink anymore. She didn't know how much she gave him. She lost count after five cups.

After he quit drinking, Pandora adjusted the blanket over him up to his neck. Then she put the other blanket on top of it. She had decided he needed to sweat, that whatever infection was causing the fever needed to be worked out through his pores. Bleeding him was out of the question. Not only did she not know how, she thought he had lost enough blood. Aside from that, she had *seen* enough blood. She would try this. If he didn't start to improve, she wasn't sure what she could do next.

She resumed her pacing, and on one turn, her hair in its bun flopped uncomfortably, pulling at her scalp. She removed the pins and absently unwound it as she paced. She combed through it with her fingers and put it into a braid. It felt much more comfortable, and her scalp felt lighter.

She looked down at herself and realized her clothes were a mess. She had washed Islington's clothes, but she had on the same grimy things she had worn into the river and worked in all day. She paused in her pacing to retrieve her other set of clothes from her valise, knowing the only thing she could do now was wait. She needed something to occupy herself while she did because the inactivity would drive her insane.

She sat in the chair by the table to pull off her boots and clicked her teeth. Persephone wouldn't be happy when she got them back. Pandora hoped the new pair she had bought her sister for her birthday would make up for it because Pandora wasn't sure these would survive the trip to Edinburgh.

Her waistcoat and trousers were dark, so she couldn't tell how much of Islington's blood she had on her, but they were filthy because of all the work she had done. She took them off and laid them on the table. When she had her stockings off, she looked at the soles. Even if she were an accomplished seamstress, there was no way to repair them. They were in tatters. She looked at her feet. There were a few cuts here and there, but none were deep, which would explain why she had still been able to walk.

She unbuttoned her shirt and removed it to examine the torn sleeve. It had some blood on it, but the soapwort might take it out. It was nowhere near as bad as Islington's. The tear was jagged, but she could sew it. It wouldn't be pretty, but it would be covered by her coat. She looked at her elbow. It had a bad scrape, but it was already scabbed over. Putting ointment on it would not make much difference. The throbbing she had felt when she bent it had faded to a tolerable level, and the chamomile she had taken for her headache had also helped.

Once she had off her chemise, she tried to look at her back, but it was physically impossible for her to see the parts she needed to, even as flexible as she was. She rubbed a hand over it, and she could feel in a few places on her lower back where her skin was roughened by scrapes, but she didn't feel anything requiring immediate attention. She put on her clean chemise and added the dirty one to the pile on the table.

Once she had on her clean shirt and chamois breeches, she added more wood to the fire and poured herself another cup of tea. She looked at her watch; it was two. She sat in the chair by the bed and rubbed a tired hand across her forehead, wincing as she touched the bruise there. She had almost forgotten it. She put on some ointment and sighed with relief when it began to feel better.

She put a hand to Islington's forehead as he continued to toss it back and forth on the pillow. It was still too hot and dry. She went to the saddlebags, retrieving the bottle of plum wine from Keung. After filling the tin cup half full of water, she filled it the rest of the way with wine. At this point, Pandora was grasping for anything. She sat on the edge of the bed and lifted his head from the pillow. She put the cup to his mouth, and he drank it as thirstily as he had the plain water. She gave him another two cupfuls, and then she put the bottle away. If he drank the whole bottle, she wouldn't have any to give him later if she needed to. She gave him more plain water until he stopped drinking.

She lifted the blankets away from his side and looked at his wound. She was hopeful. The infection didn't appear to be any worse, and the swelling was still the same. She put on more ointment and compulsively changed the bandage. If she could keep it from getting worse, then hopefully it would start to get better once he had regained some of his strength, but she had to do something about his fever.

He was still not sweating. She felt certain if she could make him sweat, his fever would break. The room was warm, but there was enough fresh air coming through the doorway to the open room it wasn't stuffy. She had given him lots of fluids, and she had put both blankets on top of him, hoping it would make him perspire, but none of it had worked.

She thought about all the weeds she had seen in the yard, trying to remember if any of them would be useful for making him sweat. Her herbal knowledge, medically, was less than so-so. She knew which ones were poisonous, which were edible, which ones—like soapwort—were chemically useful, but medical usage was lacking. Aside from that, it was too dark for her to find anything. She started to pace again. After a few minutes, she came to a full stop to look at Islington in the bed when she realized what would need to be done.

She would have to add *her* body heat. It was the only way she could think to make him hotter without making the room so stuffy she wouldn't be able to breathe. The bed was small, the ropes were old, but she felt like it would hold both of them. It was the last thing she could try, and it *had* to work. She wasn't ready to give in and let him die.

She made more medicine and sat on the bed. It wasn't easy to get him to drink it. He could tell, even in his delirium, that it wasn't water or wine, but she did get him to drink all of it. He didn't have the strength to fight much. He was slipping further away, and Pandora could feel her heart thudding anxiously. She put her ear to his chest to listen. The rattling she had heard in his lungs wasn't any worse, but his heart was beating incredibly fast, almost as if it would burst from his chest. His breathing was almost a pant, except there would be occasions when there was a long pause, as if he had stopped breathing altogether. Pandora brushed a gentle hand across his forehead and stood up.

She removed all the clothes she had just put on except her chemise. She reasoned the more of her skin came into contact with his, the better, but she didn't want this to be completely indecent. Once she was undressed, she carefully crawled over him, going to his right side because she didn't want to hurt his left shoulder or his wound. She settled in on her side, placing her head onto the small pillow beside his, her cheek resting on his shoulder. She then put her arm around his waist and snuggled beside him under the blankets, putting one of her legs over his.

The bed was comfortable, especially after sleeping on nothing but a blanket on the ground for several days, but Pandora was hot. Underneath the two wool blankets, pressed against a body burning hot with fever, it was at least making *her* start to sweat, and she was glad she had removed most of her clothes. She moved her arm to place her hand on his chest, and she could feel his rapid heartbeat beneath her palm. It wasn't long, however, before she sighed with relief as she felt the longed-for perspiration begin to come out. Now all she had to do was wait and see if it would actually work.

Chapter Twenty-One

For a moment, Pandora couldn't remember where she was. Once her mind adjusted to being awake, she realized she was curled up half-naked in bed beside a fully naked man. When she remembered who the man was and what she was doing there, Pandora turned to look at Islington worriedly. He was sleeping soundly. She put a hand to his forehead. The fever was gone. She put her head on his chest and listened to his heart. It sounded steady and strong with the same slow beat from the day before. The rattle in his lungs was gone. She wasn't sure if her actions or the medicine had been the solution, but she was relieved.

She sighed and rolled onto her back. She stretched languidly, putting her arms above her head to touch the wall behind her. Then the scrapes and bruises on her back protested, and she winced. Thankfully, her headache was gone, and when she sat up, there was no residual dizziness.

She felt hot and sticky from dried sweat. After giving Islington an assessing glance, she climbed over him out of the bed and put her clothes back on. It was eight in the morning. She went back to Islington to look at his side. She lifted the bandage and peered at it critically. The redness was fading, and the swelling had gone down. She put on more ointment and replaced the bandage. She thought of mixing more medicine but decided to wait. She didn't want to wake him from the restful sleep he needed.

She stoked the fire and added more wood then made a pot of tea and had an apple. She took the clothes down that she had hung to dry and folded them neatly into a pile, which she placed on top of the mantel. She pulled all the food from her bags and set it on the table to determine just how much was left. Were she alone, it would be enough for two or three days, but it wasn't going to be enough to feed both of them for very long. She would have to find more food, and that meant fishing…unless she could find them something else.

After she finished her tea, she went to the open room to check on the horses. Bellerophon came to the doorway as soon as he saw her. He was happy to see her, and he was also hungry. She went to the bags of grain and put a scoop into the feedbag for him. She put it over his head to eat. While he was eating, she checked on Islington again. By the time she went back to the open room, Bellerophon was done. She then refilled the feedbag for Jezebel. Once the mare was eating happily, Pandora opened the door and went outside to the yard.

She went to look at the hand pump. The spout was cracked, but it didn't go the full length. She found her saw blade from the previous day and trimmed it just above where the crack stopped. It was much shorter, but it would work, considering it had been almost a foot long. It was missing a handle…well, most of a handle. Pandora could see where it had been attached to the rest of the pump with two metal pins, one attaching it to the piston that created the suction to pull the water from the well, the other to attach it to the pump housing for leverage.

There was still a three- or four-inch piece of the old handle left, but it wouldn't be long enough. Pandora went to the barn and looked through the wood there until she found a piece that would be of the right size without much sawing. The blade Pandora had was extremely dull, and it took a long time to do very little cutting. There was no way to attach the new piece of wood to the old handle, so she would have to find a way to remove the little piece.

She went to the cottage for her dirk. Then she found a rock. Her father and brothers (and Persephone) would gasp in horror, but she had to work with what was available. She used the tip of the knife as a punch, pounding on the hilt, and she was able to work the pins out and remove the old piece of handle. She found a large flat rock and sawed down the middle of her piece of wood, close to the center in two rows, their distance apart the same as the diameter of the pins to a length a little more than the distance apart of the two pins on the old piece of handle. Once she had the two rows sawn, she used her dirk and the rock to break out the piece of wood between the two rows. She didn't have anything to drill the two pin holes, so she would use the slit to fit the new handle onto the pins, and then she would use something to pinch the end together to keep it from sliding off. After all that effort, she would then see if the pump actually still worked.

Pandora used one of the strings from the roof to bind it. It wasn't attractive, and it wouldn't be easy, but it would—or should—work. She tried the handle, and she could feel the piston inside the pump moving—a good sign, but there was nothing there. She primed it with some water from the trough and tried again. After a few more pumps, she heard a gurgling sound and water began to flow from the spout into the trough with each pump. Pandora grinned ecstatically and put her hand into the stream to taste it. Cold and perfect.

She went back inside to check on Islington and found him still sleeping, his position unchanged. She removed the second wool blanket and folded it to the end of the bed and added more wood to the fire. She then went to the open room to remove the feedbag from Jezebel. After she put it back with the grain, she haltered the horses and led them to the trough to drink. Once they were done, she led them to the meadow and tethered them to graze.

Pandora came back to the yard and went to the garden to see just what was growing there. Lots of weeds, mostly. She did find some peas, which she picked and placed into her hat after she took it off her head. There weren't a lot of them, but there were enough for a meal. Then she found two very small heads of cabbage. There were several more, but there were only two that were edible. All the others had either been gnawed on or bolted. While it wasn't her favorite vegetable, Pandora could use it with the sausage and potatoes to make a meal or two. The broth would be good for Islington. She used her pocketknife to cut them loose and then took her bounty into the cottage to set on the table.

She was glad she had found the vegetables; she was hoping she could delay fishing for as long as possible. While she was in the garden, she had noticed a few herbs: dill, rosemary, sage, and thyme, and some leaf lettuce and spinach. She didn't know what she could do with any of it, really, but it was good to know it was there.

She checked on Islington again. He had slightly changed position, but he still slept. His temperature remained normal. She adjusted the blanket over him after she lifted his head and fluffed the pillow. She wasn't too concerned that he was sleeping so much. She would try to wake him at some point to give him something to drink or eat, or some medicine, but the rest was good for him.

After checking on Islington, she took the smaller cast iron pot to the table and cut up the two heads of cabbage. Their Irish cook at home would often make them cabbage with potatoes and ham when they were children, so Pandora wasn't unfamiliar with how it was made. She didn't have any spices or salt and pepper—not to mention ham, but the sausage would be enough to make it taste similar. She peeled her three potatoes and put them in after chopping them into cubes, and then she peeled the skin from her two remaining sausages and sliced them into the pot as well.

When she was done, she poured in the remaining water out of the bucket and took her "experiment" to the fireplace. The pot no longer had its handle, but there was a shelf in the fireplace that was wide enough to hold it and keep it out of the fire. She suspected the shelf was originally used for baking, but it would suit her purpose. It was also handy for her teapot. She didn't know how long it would take to cook, but it would be easy to tell when it was finished—hard cabbage...raw; soft cabbage...done.

Pandora took the bucket outside and refilled it from the pump. She expressed a bit of pride that she had gotten it working again. The water tasted better than what was in the barrel, and now there was an unlimited supply. The crofter who lived here must have kept animals of some type because the pump being there at all was unusual. Most people who lived in the country had only the village pump or a well without one, which they retrieved water from with only a bucket. She took the bucket inside and set it near the bed. She filled the tin cup and set it on the chair near Islington, so if he should wake while she was away, he would at least be able to drink.

Pandora went to bust up the wood she had moved out of the open room. The pieces of limb, at least some of them, were easy enough to break up for the fireplace. The timber from the rafters was not quite so, and she used that for a different purpose. She broke up what she could and set the rest to the side, hoping she would find an axe. She doubted she would be so lucky. The closest she had come was an adze that had been spilt down the middle and was useless for almost anything unless she became extremely desperate.

When she had several pieces of wood, she carried them inside and refilled the nook. When it wouldn't hold any more, she stacked it in the open room. Part of the roof was still there, above the adjoining wall, and Pandora put the wood there to protect it from rain. When she had done what she could with the room debris, she started breaking up pieces of the barn.

Pandora didn't know why she felt it was necessary for them to have so much firewood. It wasn't as if they would be there forever, but it was important for her to keep a fire going while Islington mended. The air was always cool, especially at night, and the only reason it didn't bother Pandora during the day was that she was constantly moving. When the fire had died down last night, it had been very cold in the cottage.

As she cleared away the wood from the barn, her attention was drawn again to the tin tub. It would be the perfect size for bathing, if it weren't for the giant, rusted-out hole in the bottom. Pandora would love a hot bath. She had managed to wash her hair once or twice and brushed her teeth a couple times a day, but she hadn't been able to wash the rest of herself or use her depilatory. The closest she had come to a bath was the many times she had traveled through the rain and the dunk in the river yesterday. She felt cruddy. She looked at the tub longingly for a few minutes more, and then she pulled it out of the debris and hauled it close to the cottage. She wasn't sure she could find a way to use it, but perhaps if she kept it in sight, something would come to her.

She continued to break up firewood and carry it into the house for the rest of the morning, periodically checking on Islington and their food. Whenever she walked in, she could smell it cooking, and it smelled wonderful, even if she *didn't* care for cabbage. She would also check on the horses occasionally, leading them back to the cottage to get water from the trough before taking them back to the meadow.

When it was a little after noon, she finally stopped making firewood. There was a stack in the corner of the open room that came to the level of her chest in height and spanned the wall to the far edge of the closed-off fireplace. That would be enough. The cabbage should have cooked long enough, and Pandora was famished. She should also try to wake Islington.

She washed her hands in the rain barrel using a few leaves of soapwort, examining the scrapes and small blisters that had developed while she worked. Then she went inside carrying four items she had found in the barn and cleaned. One was a larger wooden pail that would be better for washing and leave the other for drinking water. Others were a wooden spoon with a divot missing out of its bowl and a tin ladle with a bent handle and dented bowl. She was able to straighten the ladle into a usable shape, and the chunk missing out of the spoon wasn't going to make it any less useful to Pandora.

The last thing she found was a chipped, earthenware chamber pot. Pandora thought about foregoing this item, but it was eventually, regrettably, going to be needed. The regrettable part was that she wouldn't be the one who needed it, and yet she would have to empty it. It was pretty, as far as chamber pots went. It was of a decent size and glazed white with little blue and pink flowers painted around the outside and along the rim. The rim itself had a few chips missing, and care would need to be taken when it was used to avoid getting cut, but the bowl was still in one piece.

Pandora set the large bucket to one side of the fireplace and put the dishes inside it to organize her clutter. She slid the chamber pot under the edge of the bed. It just fit, as she had expected it would. She looked up at Islington when she was done. He was, as always, sleeping, but it did look like he had moved. She checked his forehead: still normal. She looked in the tin cup. It was still full. She shrugged and moved their food on the table to one side, so she would have a place to eat.

She went to the fireplace and used her waistcoat to lift the pot of cabbage from the shelf. She grabbed the ladle and stirred the contents, inhaling the steam that rose from it. She put some onto a plate and took it to the table. She poured herself a cup of tea and took that to the table as well after she dropped in one of Bellerophon's dwindling supply of sugar lumps. She started to eat with her fingers when she remembered that Maiyin had tossed a pair of chopsticks into the bag where she had placed Pandora's cooking items. Pandora shrugged and carefully picked up a piece of the hot cabbage with her fingers and put it into her mouth; who would know? After the first bite, she did get the chopsticks, but it was only because the food was too hot to pick up quickly with her fingers, and she was starving. After eating mostly cold or dried food for a week, it was like manna from heaven...but she did think it could use a little more salt.

Pandora ate every morsel from the plate and lifted it to drink the broth when she was done. She wouldn't go so far as to lick it clean, but Pandora couldn't think of a time when food had tasted so good. She was full and content with a hot meal, and she was again proud that she had been able to accomplish it all by herself.

After Pandora sat at the table and digested her food for a little while, she went to the fireplace and ladled some of the broth into the bowl to begin cooling for Islington. She would see how he managed with that before giving him something solid. If he would wake up to eat, then she would give him more of her headache medicine. It seemed he was out of danger, but she wasn't yet ready to be complacent. She set the bowl on the chair, and then she sat on the edge of the bed.

She checked his wound while she was there, and it looked much better. Most of the redness was gone, as was the swelling. It was no longer puckered, and the stitches were smooth. She hadn't been checking his shoulder, but she looked at that as well. The red and purple striations were still there, and she suspected they were due to the strain on the muscle from whatever had dislocated it. Pandora was curious what had happened. It couldn't have come from him hitting a rock; it almost seemed it had become caught and twisted on something.

She put a hand on his cheek and put her mouth close to his ear.

"Islington," she said softly.

She watched as his eyelashes fluttered on his cheeks, and then his eyes opened to look at her. He inhaled deeply with a start of surprise and blinked his eyes several times, but Pandora was relieved he seemed to be completely lucid, and his pupils looked absolutely normal.

"Pandora?" he said, his voice cracked and dry.

She raised the tin cup to his lips and lifted his head to let him drink all of it thirstily. She refilled it, and he drank half of it before he turned his head away. She put his head back on the pillow and set the cup aside. He was looking around himself confusedly at the bed and the room.

"Where are we?"

"The cottage." Pandora's forehead wrinkled with concern. "Don't you remember?"

"I remember finding a cottage, but this isn't the same place," he said weakly, shaking his head.

"Yes, it is," said Pandora, and she was relieved he wasn't confused in the way she had first thought. "I cleaned it up a bit. That's all."

"*You* cleaned it up?" he asked with surprise.

"Well, I wasn't going to stay here with it in the shape it was," she said calmly. "It was a sty." She compulsively put a hand to his forehead to check his temperature. "I had to do something to keep myself occupied while you were unconscious."

He felt the bed under him, and he could tell it had been cleaned and re-stuffed. He looked around the room again at the straightened chairs, the way the table shined slightly from its remnants of wax after being washed thoroughly. The grime was gone from the window. He didn't see any dust or cobwebs. He could smell food, and the room was warm from a fire. Islington's forehead wrinkled as he looked at her.

"How long have I been unconscious?" he asked disconcertedly.

Pandora pulled out her watch to look at it. "A little over twenty-four hours," she said softly as she put it back.

He saw the scrapes and blisters on her hands, and he grabbed one to look at it. He barely had the strength to move his arm from where it had been laying. He looked up at her questioningly.

"I've been making firewood most of the morning."

"*Making* firewood?" he quipped, not quite believing he heard correctly.

"Well, I cleared out the other room yesterday afternoon when I was done in here, and I hauled all the wood outside so I could use the room as a stall for the horses. Then, this morning after I fixed the pump, I broke up what I could for firewood. After I did all I could with that, I started on the wood from the barn," said Pandora in one of her typically prattling explanations.

"You fixed the pump?" he asked weakly. His head was spinning, and he couldn't really say that it was caused by his injuries.

"Yes," she said airily. "The handle is a bit stubborn, but it will do. Would you like some broth?"

"You did all this by yourself?" he asked softly in amazement.

"Well, yes. I had to do something to occupy myself. I was so worried I couldn't sit still, else I would have gone mad." She again put her hand to his forehead. "Was that a no for the broth?"

"No...I mean, yes, I would like some broth," said Islington, shaking his head as his forehead wrinkled in bemusement.

Pandora lifted his head and put the pillow against the headboard. She carefully helped him to sit up slightly, so she wouldn't have to hold his head while he ate. He felt as weak as a newborn, and his head spun dizzily when she sat him up. She raised the bowl to his lips, and he wanted to raise his hand to steady it, but he found he hadn't the strength to hold it there very long.

"Oh, this is delicious. Where did you get this?" he asked, drinking more of the broth.

"I made it," said Pandora evenly. "It could use salt, but I haven't any."

"You made it?" He didn't know why he was surprised.

"Well, yes. I found some cabbages in the garden, and then I had some potatoes and sausages. Our cook used to make it all the time, so I thought I would try it. I found a kettle that only wanted a handle and some dishes that only had a few chips missing. I'm really surprised at all the things I've found left behind that are actually still quite useful."

After he finished two bowls of the broth, Pandora set it with her plate to wash later. She then refilled the tin cup and added some drops of the headache medicine. She put the cup to his lips.

"Here, drink this."

He drank it...and grimaced as he usually did.

"Pah! That's foul," he shuddered. "What's in that?"

Pandora gave him a cup of water to rinse the taste from his mouth.

"I'm not really sure," said Pandora, her head tilting sideways thoughtfully. "It has willow, but beyond that I couldn't immediately say. Keung made it for my headaches, and it works rather well. I haven't actually *tried* to figure out what's in it because it tastes too nasty to leave in my mouth for long."

She set the cup aside and pulled down the blanket to look at his side. It didn't look any different than it had thirty minutes before. However, this was Islington's first chance to see how she had done. While he was looking at it, Pandora put more ointment on and got a clean bandage, since she had forgotten to when she checked before. She idly wondered how the ointment would work on his shoulder.

"It doesn't look bad at all," said Islington after he saw it.

"Yes, it's looking much better," said Pandora, nodding her head.

She put her hand back to his forehead. Still normal. Islington looked at her, his brow furrowing.

"Pandora, why do you keep doing that?" he asked exasperatedly.

"I just want to make sure you're not running a fever, that's all," she said calmly, looking at him.

"Pandora, did something happen?" he asked stilly.

"Well, you dislocated your shoulder, and you got shot," began Pandora prevaricatingly, absently rubbing the spot behind her ear.

"No. Did something happen while I was unconscious?" He looked at her assessingly, watching a multitude of emotions flit across her face.

"You had a fever and the beginnings of an infection, but it seems to be better now," she said slowly, not meeting his gaze.

"How bad was it?"

When she didn't answer him, or look at him, Islington briefly raised a finger to her chin to *make* her look at him. Her eyes were cloudy with tears, and her expression told him what he needed to know. She must have been terrified, and yet, somehow, she had found a way…more than found a way. He continued to gaze at her wonderingly.

"Yes, well, anyhow," said Pandora softly. "You seem to be on the mend." She looked at her watch, and her eyes widened in alarm. "Goodness! I need to check on the horses. Let's get you settled back in, and I'll go do that. You're probably very tired."

She carefully helped him to lie down and fluffed his pillow before settling his head onto it. Islington realized disconcertedly that she was right. He was barely able to keep his eyes open. He didn't think he had been awake for more than an hour. Still, if the infection and fever had been as bad as she thought, it was easy to understand. She adjusted the blanket to the middle of his chest and started to get up, but Islington managed to weakly grab the material of her shirt and drew her closer.

He started to kiss her softly, and Pandora put a hand to his chest to keep herself from losing her balance and falling over. As the kiss continued and became deeper, Pandora's hand moved across the exposed skin in a caress to the side of his neck. She could feel an ache of longing beginning in the pit of her stomach as he explored her mouth with his tongue, and she moaned softly at the back of her throat as the sensation continued to grow. With as much self-control as she could muster, Pandora ended the kiss and sat back. She smoothed a tender hand across his cheek and gave him a slightly amused smile when she saw his befuddled expression caused by her ending the kiss.

"Sleep now," she whispered, brushing a gentle hand down his face to make him close his eyes.

Despite desperately wanting to stay awake, Islington drifted back to sleep after only a few minutes. Pandora sat and watched him until she was sure he slept. Then she refilled his cup and placed it on the chair by the bed.

She added more wood to the fire and lit two of the torches, and then she went to get the horses for some water. They both seemed to be doing well from their lazy time in the meadow. Jezebel was doing much better than when Pandora had seen her yesterday morning. Islington must have been driving the mare very hard. And Pandora didn't know why he called Jezebel high-strung; Pandora found her to be very gentle and easygoing, if easily spooked. Bellerophon enjoyed the equine company, but Pandora suspected part of that was due to the mare's being in heat. There would be a new foal in Islington's stable next year. It was something Pandora didn't have the time or energy to prevent.

Pandora led the horses back to the meadow when they were done. It still had plenty of grass. When she came back to the cottage, she mucked out the stall. It wasn't too bad, but Pandora had to be creative to find something to use as a shovel and rake. She wound up using some pieces of wood from the barn.

She checked on Islington, and she managed to restrain herself from putting a hand to his forehead. He seemed to be sleeping well, and he had turned his head slightly to nestle it into the pillow. His hair had fallen loosely onto his forehead, and Pandora felt her heart flutter achingly as she looked at him. Even though she knew he had been delirious last night, she couldn't forget what he said. She wouldn't hold him to it, and she wouldn't mention it, but he had sounded so earnest and sincere. She put a hand to her flushed cheek and turned away. She still had things to do.

Pandora washed the few dishes from their meal and checked the contents of the cabbage pot. There was still plenty for them to eat for supper, and there would probably be enough for at least dinner the next day. She would worry about finding more then. She still had two turnips and a few carrots, as well as half a dozen apples from the things Maiyin had given her. She had some raisins and nuts left, but the jerked meat was gone.

She washed her clothes after she sewed the tear in the sleeve of her shirt. She was able to get the little bit of blood out with some moderate scrubbing. The soapwort had done an excellent job.

When Pandora had washed the dishes and the clothes, she decided to use her depilatory. Now that they had a theoretically unlimited supply of water, and they wouldn't be going anywhere any time soon, she didn't see why she couldn't indulge herself with this one, small thing. While she was retrieving the jar from her valise, she looked at the tent lying nearby, and her forehead wrinkled as she began to think. She looked at the tin tub outside as she went past it to the pump, and her forehead wrinkled even further.

She removed her boots, breeches and stockings by the pump, placing her pants and stockings over the handle. She opened the lid on her depilatory and jerked her head back at the strong smell. As long as she had been using it, she had never become accustomed to the odor.

She and her sisters had been introduced to the concept of removing body hair by their mother, who had been to several Muslim countries where hair removal on both women *and* men was customary. Pandora couldn't imagine not removing what she did. She just felt so much cleaner when she removed the hair from her legs and armpits, and it was always a sensual experience when she got into her bed with freshly-laundered sheets after just doing her legs. Her mother and Arachne preferred to use sugaring, but Pandora found that too painful. She had concocted the depilatory cream she used in the solarium, and while the smell was noxious, it worked quickly and painlessly.

After she smoothed on the cream, she only had to leave it for a few minutes before she rinsed it off. She didn't let any of it go into the trough to contaminate the water for the horses because some of the ingredients were poisonous. The water was cold, and so was the air, so Pandora fanned at her legs with her hands to get them dry enough to put on her stockings, breeches, and boots. She had forgotten to bring her towel outside.

Once she was done with her legs, she took off her shirt and chemise and applied it to her armpits, carefully keeping the hair on her head well out of the way. She looked comical standing with her arms raised away from her sides bent at the elbow while the cream worked. She soon rinsed it off and felt much better as she put her clothes back on. She rinsed the ground around the trough to dilute the smell because it would disturb the horses.

As she walked back to the cottage, she looked again at the tub, pulling at her lip thoughtfully as she went. A plan had formed in her head for taking a bath. She looked at her watch and saw it was nearing five. She would have to start it soon, or it would be too late.

After she placed the jar in her valise, she turned to look at Islington and saw him watching her sleepily. She went to the bed and sat beside him. She had to clench her hand at her side to keep from checking his temperature. She thought it a sign of improvement that he woke without her needing to rouse him.

"Hallo, sleepyhead," said Pandora with a smile. "Are you thirsty?"

He nodded, and Pandora lifted the cup from the chair and raised his head from the pillow to help him drink. When she did, it gave her an unobtrusive way to make sure his fever was truly gone. After he finished the water, Pandora pulled down the blanket to look at his wound. She nodded approvingly as she examined it and put the bandage back. It was going to mend nicely, all things considered.

"So, what have you been doing with your time?" he asked as he looked to the window and saw the sun was setting.

"Hmm," said Pandora thoughtfully. "Not a lot. I washed dishes and clothes after I checked on the horses and mucked their stall. I did my legs, and then I've been trying to come up with a way for a hot bath, which I think I've just about sorted out."

"Did your legs?" he asked confusedly.

"Oh, yes. I just couldn't stand it anymore."

"Couldn't stand what?" he asked, still not understanding.

"The hair. I couldn't stand the hair," said Pandora slowly.

"You do realize courtesans do that?" he said mildly.

Pandora blinked in surprise. "Do they really? I learned it from my mother, but she's most definitely not a courtesan."

"I should say not," agreed Islington with a slight grin. "So how do you intend to have a hot bath?" he asked distractedly.

The thought of seeing her bare, smooth legs was tantalizing, and that she would innocently do something courtesan-like and remove her leg hair was something he found amusing and endearing.

"I found an enormous tin tub, but it has a hole in the bottom. Then I thought if I could find something to line it with, so it would hold water again. Obviously, something not waterproof wouldn't work, but then I realized I have a tent that would work wonderfully well. So, after we have supper, I'm going to have a bath. It's going to take that long to heat up enough water, I think." She looked at Islington. "Are you hungry?"

He chuckled at her seeming impatience to wash, but it made his side hurt, and he grimaced. Pandora frowned, but he shook his head.

"Don't you think the heat is going to remove whatever makes your tent waterproof?"

Her brow furrowed thoughtfully, but then she shook her head.

"Oh, no, I don't think so. It will make it more flexible and soften it until it cools, but gutta percha doesn't wash off, really."

"Gutta percha?" he asked, frowning.

"Yes. It's a juice from a tree my mother brought back from Asia that's in her greenhouse. It's wonderful for all sorts of things, especially water resistance. The Malayans and whatnot are really fond of it."

"Is it like India rubber?"

"Much better." Pandora grinned. "It doesn't get brittle like rubber."

Islington continued to frown. "How do you know?"

"I play with it every so often, just to see what I can do with it."

Islington looked at her in surprise. Chemistry was apparently a hobby for her. He knew she was intelligent and resourceful, but he was beginning to see he didn't know the half of it. He tried to sit up on his own but found he was still not quite strong enough, although he felt stronger than he had earlier. His ribs and shoulder pained him terribly. Pandora helped him, and once he was situated, wincing slightly as he adjusted his shoulder, he looked down to actually examine his sling.

"Is that my shirt?" he asked.

"Yes…what's left of it. I've used bits and pieces for other things, but I thought it would suit nicely for a sling. I hope you have another."

"I do," he said calmly as he continued to look at it.

He reached behind his neck to unfasten it and winced again as the weight of his arm pulled against his shoulder once it was loose. He rested his arm onto his stomach, and that relieved it somewhat, and anything was an improvement over the way it had felt yesterday before he put it back in its socket. He pulled the shirt away and looked at it. Other than the arms and the part they attached to, there was very little of the garment left.

"It was very difficult to put that on, you should know," said Pandora shortly.

"And an excellent job you did, too," said Islington with a grin as he looked at her unhappy expression. "I'd just like it off for a while."

"Would you like something to eat?" she asked again after a moment.

"Yes, please."

He watched her get up and followed her with his eyes as far as he could, admiring the way the chamois hugged the curve of her buttocks. The breeches were a fetching look for her. She soon returned, carefully carrying the battered bowl full of warm broth. She sat on the edge of the bed and held it for him. He was able to lift his arm and help hold the bowl much better than he had earlier.

"After you get done, I'll see about putting some ointment on your shoulder. I think it will help with the pain and stiffness," she said calmly as she held the bowl to his mouth. "But I don't think you need to leave it out of the sling very long."

He looked at her concerned expression. She still wasn't convinced he was getting better. She was expecting him to take a turn for the worse any moment. Islington felt guilty he had caused her so much worry.

"Of course," he said agreeably.

Once he finished eating, Pandora got the jar of ointment after she put the bowl on the hearth. She sat beside him on the bed and opened the lid to put a small amount on her fingers. She gently touched his shoulder and rubbed it in, trying not to hurt him. He turned his head to watch, and he inhaled the scent of what she was putting on. He could also feel it starting to work, cooling, numbing and loosening, and his shoulder began to feel better immediately. He looked up at her curiously.

"I don't suppose you know what's in *that*, do you?"

Pandora lifted the jar to her nose and smelled, her forehead wrinkling thoughtfully as she did so.

"Hmm. Wintergreen, definitely." She smelled again. "Oil of roses, probably. Maybe some feverfew and marsh mallow, but other than that, I couldn't say," she said with a shrug as she resumed rubbing it onto his shoulder. "How did you do this, by the way?"

"I tried to hold onto the edge of the bridge. Then, when I lost my grip, my coat sleeve got caught on something and twisted around."

Pandora sucked in air through her teeth and grimaced, imagining how painful it must have been. He was lucky his arm wasn't broken. How long must he have hung there before he fell? Probably about as long as it had taken her to shoot her arrow and foolishly look upstream for him, she thought guiltily.

"Well, the man who shot you is going to have something to think about for a while," said Pandora consolingly as she finished rubbing on the last bit of ointment on her fingers. She set the jar aside after putting on the lid.

"Why would you think that?" asked Islington, his forehead wrinkling perplexedly.

"Because I shot him in his bum with an arrow, that's why," said Pandora firmly.

Islington's eyebrows shot up. "You didn't?"

Pandora nodded. "I did," she said calmly. "I was aiming for something else, but at least I didn't shoot his horse."

Islington's shoulders started to shake, and then he started to laugh, putting a hand to his side.

"Ow," he groaned, still chuckling. "Thank you, m'dear."

"Anytime," said Pandora distractedly, watching his hilarity with some concern. "Let's get you back in your sling. Mayhap this time I won't have such a hard time getting you to stay put while I put it on."

"What do you mean?"

"Only that you weigh a ton, and you are very floppy while you're unconscious," she grumbled.

Pandora chose to ignore his shoulders shaking as he laughed silently. She looked at the shirt, trying to decide if she could make it less unsightly. She retrieved her sewing kit, ignoring the blood that had stained into the leather, and got the scissors. She trimmed more from the body, getting rid of the last remnants of blood, and she also pared off the collar.

She tied the laces, and then she fit the body of it under his forearm, near the elbow, with the front facing inward. Then she realized she wouldn't be able to quite reach around him from where she was sitting to fasten the sling the way she wanted. Intent on her task, she maneuvered herself so that she was straddling his lap on the bed. She flipped one arm of the garment over the front of him to his right shoulder, and then she leaned him forward, so his face rested against her breasts while she fed the other sleeve around the back and tied the two together. Once she was done, she rested Islington against the pillow and looked at her handiwork satisfactorily. Then she looked up to see Islington's flushed features. Pandora's eyes widened in alarm, and she felt his forehead.

"Are you all right?" she asked worriedly. "I didn't hurt you, did I?"

"No, I'm fine," said Islington constrainedly, trying with great difficulty to ignore the erotic sensations of her pelvis rubbing against his...and the way it had felt to have his face buried in her breasts.

"Are you sure? You're looking flushed," said Pandora, her brow furrowed concernedly. She put her ear to his chest; his heart was beating just the least bit faster.

"I'm fine. Just have mercy on a weak man, and, please, get off me," he said stilly, closing his eyes and breathing through his nose.

Pandora quickly scrabbled off his lap and sat on the bed, her expression still worried. After a few minutes, he opened his eyes to look at her, taking her hand to kiss her palm and give her a soothing smile.

"I'm fine," he said softly. "Truly."

She looked at him assessingly, but her features started to relax as she saw his face return to a normal color. She dipped some water into his cup and gave it to him. He was able to hold it and drink by himself. After he finished, she refilled it and set it on the chair within reach.

"Do you need more medicine right now?" Islington's face formed into a moue of distaste, and he shook his head. "Then if there's nothing else you need right now, I want to get the horses and bring in the tub and get the water started."

"Well, there's something I need to do, but...," Islington trailed off uncomfortably.

"I think I've got just the thing under the edge of the bed, if you can manage it," said Pandora discreetly. "Honestly, I'd rather not have to help, but...."

"No, no. I *think* I can manage," said Islington quickly. He was mostly sitting up; he could go a little further on his own, but he was becoming tired.

"Very good," said Pandora relievedly. "I should caution that it's not in the best condition, so you'll have to be careful." Her forehead wrinkled concernedly for a moment. "You *are* sure, aren't you?"

"Yes. Go get the horses," said Islington with an exasperated smile.

Pandora looked at him one more time then went to get the animals. It was already nearing six. It was a short walk to the pump, so it wouldn't be too terrible to do it in the dark, but she would just as soon not. Besides, she was yearning for a bath. And, now that Islington had mentioned it, she needed to relieve herself, too.

She did that first, and then she went to get the horses. She hoped she had given Islington enough time to tend to things. She kept her eyes averted from the corner when she led in the horses, just in case, and took them to the open room. She removed their halters and laid the rope on top of the wood pile after giving both animals a lump of sugar. After she fastened the limb across the doorway, she went to check on Islington…and found him sprawled on the floor, naked and unconscious.

"*Islington!*" she gasped, rushing over to kneel beside him.

She gently rolled him onto his back. His head shook back and forth as he began to come around. He must have fainted, and Pandora was anxiously checking to make sure he hadn't injured himself worse. She thought of the edge of the hearth and looked at his head. No injuries. Then she thought about the chamber pot and looked for it—no longer under the edge of the bed and still in one (well, no worse) piece. She checked his shoulder to make sure it wasn't dislocated again, and it seemed fine. The bandage had come loose from his stitches, but they were still intact. His head was still lolling as he tried to wake up, but he was, at least, waking up. Pandora grabbed his right arm and put a hand behind his neck and managed to pull him to a sitting position on the floor.

"Islington?" she said loudly.

His eyes finally fluttered open, and he looked around himself confusedly when he realized he was sitting naked on the floor with Pandora looking at him anxiously.

"What happened?"

"I could ask the same of you," said Pandora flatly. "You fainted. Come on, let's get you back in bed," she said with a long-suffering sigh.

With some effort, they were able to get him into bed, and once he was there, Pandora covered him with the blanket to his waist. She couldn't find the bandage, so she got another from the medicine kit and put it over the stitches. Then she pulled the blanket up further. She checked his temperature, and then she put her ear to his chest and listened to his heart. It seemed fine. She looked at him consideringly.

"Did you at least get to tend to things?" she asked calmly.

"Yes," said Islington, and Pandora couldn't believe it when he blushed.

"You tried to stand all the way up, didn't you?" said Pandora critically as she came to the realization.

"Well, I thought I was doing fine," defended Islington.

Pandora shook her head and tchicked, like a mother scolding her child. She handed him the water, which he dutifully drank. He had a smudge of dirt on one cheek, and Pandora reached over to wipe it off.

"You could have hurt yourself," said Pandora disappointedly. "You should have asked for my help."

"I'm sorry. I thought I would try on my own," he said softly. "Where are my clothes, by the way?"

"On the mantel," said Pandora shortly, as if she were daring him to try to stand up again.

She stood up and walked outside. She stalked around the yard for a few minutes with her hands on her hips, kicking at small limbs laying around and muttering, as she tried to calm her temper. She couldn't blame him, really. She would have tried, too. But when she thought of how close she had come to losing him and how much better he was today.... To think his pride could have ruined it made her angry. She eventually stopped pacing and took a few calming breaths. In the end, she knew the worst *hadn't* happened, and he seemed sincerely apologetic.

She grabbed the tin tub and half-carried, half-pulled it inside. Once she had it situated where she wanted it, she went to the corner and sat on the edge of the bed. She kissed Islington soundly and sat back from him.

"Don't do that again. You scared me," she said softly.

"I won't," he managed to get out, dazed by her passionate kiss.

Pandora stood up and went to get the tent. She unrolled it on the floor to determine the best way to put it in. She finally decided on one of the sidewalls. She laid it over the top of the tub with one side up, and then she pushed on it until it lined the tub nicely.

She retrieved the chamber pot and emptied and rinsed it outside. She brought it back in and put it under the edge of the bed, ready for its next use. She removed the dishes from the bigger bucket and took it outside to the pump to fill. She carried it back in and set it on the hearth. Then she put the large cast iron pot on its hook, which would conveniently swing about for her to fill the pot and push it back into the firebox. She did so with the first bucket, and then she went to get more. The pot would hold three buckets. She would need to heat the pot three or four times to have enough water for a bath, she calculated.

She put more wood on the fire, put the cabbage on to reheat and started water for a pot of tea, and then she took the bucket for drinking water outside and refilled it. Once she came back in from doing that, she replaced the torches, folded her clothes, and put them back with her things. She seemed finished, but then she snapped her fingers as a thought came to her, and she went back outside. She came back in momentarily, carrying several handfuls of soapwort.

"Pandora, would you, please, come sit with me? You are making me tired just watching you," said Islington, his expression amused.

Pandora placed the soapwort on the table, away from their food, then went to sit on the bed beside Islington. The chair had become a table. She looked at him expectantly.

"Do you ever sit still?"

Her face grew thoughtful for a moment, and then she shook her head.

"Not really, no," she said honestly.

"Not even when you're at home?" he asked disbelievingly.

"Well, sometimes, when I'm working out an equation or something."

"What kind of equation?"

"Calculus, usually. I've got one right now that I've been working on for months." She shook her head. "I don't know how many notebooks I've filled with it so far."

She heard the lid on the teapot start to rattle, and she got up to remove it from the fire. She didn't get the piece of linen placed on it just right, though, and she burned her thumb.

"Darn it!" she squeaked, putting her singed digit in her mouth then taking it out to shake it and examine before putting it back in.

She removed the lid and put in the tea leaves from her dwindling supply. Thinking better of trying to remove the cabbage with the linen, she used her waistcoat as she had earlier. She checked her tub water, and then she went to sit on the bed for a few minutes.

"What happened?" asked Islington, his lips twitching at her oath.

"Oh, I burned my thumb," said Pandora as she took it out of her mouth to look at it.

"Let me see it," said Islington, taking her hand in his.

There was an area on the edge of her thumb, near the tip by her nail, that had been burned white. It would be another blister to add to her collection. Islington brought her thumb to his mouth and kissed it gently. He then released it, and Pandora looked at him silently, her eyes round in surprise.

"Better?" he asked. Pandora nodded.

"I have to start filling the tub," she said softly as she got up.

She carefully pulled the kettle out of the fireplace and dipped in the bucket to pour into the tub. She watched happily as the steam began to rise, and she got another. She couldn't get all the water out of the kettle, but she got most of it. She went outside to refill the bucket and pour it into the kettle, and then she put the kettle back into the firebox to start heating again. It was going quicker than she thought it would, and she was anticipating a nice soak. Once she was done, she went to sit on the bed again.

"I take it things are going well?" asked Islington with a grin as he watched her look at the steam rising from the tub with longing.

"Most definitely," said Pandora with a nod. "Supper is reheated, if you'd like some. Do you want broth or something solid?"

"I would like something solid now," said Islington after thinking about it. Other than the fainting spell earlier, he was feeling much better, if still not quite strong enough.

Pandora nodded and went to ladle some of the food onto plates for them. She would see if he was able to manage on his own before she got hers. She could already see steam starting on her second kettle of water. The remaining water from the first time and the hot cast iron were helping it heat quicker. She was giddy as she thought about her bath. She carried the plate to Islington and sat on the edge of the bed again.

"There are no utensils," she told him calmly. "However, I am willing to consider it socially acceptable for cabbage to be a finger food…unless you know how to use chopsticks."

"No, I don't even know what they are," he said calmly.

"They're quite clever, really."

She left the plate heating up his stomach where she placed it and came back momentarily carrying two equally-sized, ivory sticks. She positioned them in her fingers and snapped the ends together before reaching onto the plate for a piece of food. She lifted it to his mouth, and he opened it for her to put in the sausage. She held the sticks out to him.

"Would you like to try?"

"I suppose. It doesn't look that complicated," said Islington with an agreeable shrug.

She helped him position them in his right hand, the top stick held with his thumb, index, and middle finger, the bottom one wedged underneath and held steady by his ring finger. He moved the chopsticks to the plate and tried to pick up a piece of potato, only to have it fall onto the plate. He tried again and almost had it to his mouth, but it fell.

"I think I'll eat with my fingers," he muttered, giving Pandora the chopsticks. "I don't know how you can pick anything up with those. If *my* left arm were working properly, I might stand a better chance," he said petulantly.

Pandora shrugged, her lips twitching amusedly. "Suit yourself."

She went to get her own plate and sat back down. She ate all her food without dropping anything using the chopsticks. She was done much quicker than Islington. She tipped the plate to her mouth to drain the broth from it and pulled it back down to find him looking at her. She grinned amusedly.

"Very tasty," she said with a wink.

She put her plate on the edge of the hearth with the bowl. The second kettle of water for her bath was ready, so she pulled it out of the fireplace and poured it into the tub. She looked at how full it was, and then she bent down to feel the temperature. It was still extremely hot. She would need to add at least one bucket of cold water to make it tolerable, but she would need another kettle-full of hot water for good measure. She took the bucket out to the pump and refilled the kettle then pushed it back into the fireplace for what she hoped would be the last time. She was impatient to wash.

She went to sit on the bed beside Islington. He was still not done eating. He was having a difficult time picking up the soft, slippery pieces of cabbage with his fingers. Pandora went back to the fireplace and retrieved the chopsticks from where she had put them on her plate to be washed then went back to the bed. She easily picked up a piece of cabbage with them and lifted it to his mouth.

"I am able to feed myself," he said irritably, but he ate the cabbage.

"Yes, but you'll be hungry again by the time you're through at this rate," said Pandora with a soft, teasing smile. "Besides, my bath will be ready soon, and I want to make sure you're tended to before I take it."

"Hunh."

Pandora helped him finish eating, but he drank the broth on his own. She took the plate and chopsticks to the hearth and came back. She started to mix more medicine, but he put a hand on hers to stop her.

"I don't need that anymore," he said. "Do you have anything else? I think it makes me sleepy."

Pandora shrugged. "Your fever does seem to be gone. I don't think you have any serious infection, as long as we keep using the ointment. What about pain?"

"There is that," said Islington, adjusting his shoulder gingerly.

"Well, what do you think? You're the physician," she said calmly.

"I don't remember what you have. Some things are foggy from yesterday."

"I don't doubt that," said Pandora understandingly. "There's the laudanum."

Islington shook his head negatively. "I don't want laudanum."

Her face brightened as it came to her. "I have something that will work, at least somewhat, and it doesn't taste nearly as vile as the headache medicine."

She retrieved a sugar lump from the bag on the table, and then she added some drops of the chamomile oil. She took it back to the bed and handed it to Islington.

"Try that. Medicine and dessert rolled into one," she grinned.

He put it in his mouth and started to suck on it, letting the sugar dissolve. He agreed the flavor was much more palatable.

"A definite improvement," he said with a smile. "Chamomile?"

Pandora nodded and went to check her water. It was ready. She filled the tub until it was just under the depth she wanted and gauged the temperature. She went to the pump and got another bucket of cold water and poured it in. She checked the temperature again. It was perfect for her, which some people would think was scaldingly hot. She went to the pump for another bucket of water to top off the kettle and put it back over the fire to begin heating again…for Islington.

"Huzzah! My bath is ready," she said, clapping her hands with glee.

She added more wood to the fire and changed the torches before she got in because she wasn't planning to get out for a while…maybe not until the water got cold. She went to her bags for her change of clothes, her towel she had forgotten when she had treated her legs, her flannel, and her soap. She took them over by the tub and used the other chair as a table to set them on close by. Islington had turned his head over his shoulder and was watching her dubiously.

"I think you may have a slight problem."

"What's that?" asked Pandora, her forehead wrinkling.

"I can see you," he said flatly.

"I'll expect you to be the perfect gentleman and not turn your head all the way 'round like an owl, like you're doing now," said Pandora calmly. "If you don't lean over and crane your neck, you can't see me, which is why I put the tub where I did. Please, I really *want* a bath," she pleaded.

Islington started to object, but he could see she was pining for a bath. She was right: he couldn't see the tub unless he leaned over slightly and looked around the edge of the fireplace, and it wasn't easy for him to do because of his shoulder and side. She had placed it fairly close to the fireplace longways, leaving just enough space between the tub and the hearth to walk through. It would be tempting to peek, but it was the least he could do for her after all she had done for him.

"Very well. I promise I won't look," he said, grinning at her ecstatic smile. Islington straightened himself up in the bed.

Pandora quickly took off her clothes and got in the tub before he changed his mind. She sank down in the hot water as far as she could and sighed blissfully. She could feel her skin becoming red from the heat, and the same heat began to relax the aches out of her back. She floated her hands around under the surface of the water then splashed some onto her face. She thought her raspberry tea and toast with lime curd would be the things from home she missed the most, but it was actually a hot bath.

"Is the chamomile working?" she asked conversationally after a time as she poured soap onto her cloth to lather up and wash her legs.

"I'm not sure yet. I think it will take…a…few…," Islington trailed off, his eyes focused on the far wall of the cottage in disbelief.

"I'm sorry?" called Pandora, finishing one leg and starting the other.

"I think it will take a few more minutes to tell," said Islington quickly after clearing his throat, still looking at the wall.

What Pandora didn't know, but Islington found to his distraction, was that her placing the tub in front of the fire caused a shadow to appear on the far wall. While he wasn't actually looking at *her,* and therefore not breaking his promise, he could clearly see her lifting her legs in the air to wash them, wiggling her toes as she worked the soap between them before putting them back down. He gulped nervously and could feel a film of perspiration starting on his upper lip.

"I found it worked well for my head after I bumped it," said Pandora as she got up on her knees to wash her arms and torso, completely oblivious.

"I'm sure it will do fine," said Islington breathlessly as he received a perfect profile view of her breasts and the top of her buttocks on the wall.

"Oh, I agree," said Pandora definitely. "Keung used to be an apothecary in China, and a monk before that, before he came to work for us," she said as she began to unbraid her hair to wash it.

"Really?" said Islington distractedly.

He was trying to fight his reaction, but he didn't have the strength. He had an erection that was starting to throb as he watched her bathe. He had a moment's respite when she put her head under the water to wet her hair and disappeared from view, but only a moment. Islington tried not to look at the wall, but he was mesmerized. He closed his eyes and took deep, calming breaths, but his body seemed to have a mind of its own. The scent of her perfumed soap floating through the air kept even closing his eyes from being something to help him regain control.

"Oh, yes. He's one of our gardeners now, but he's also lots of other things...a somewhat unofficial family physician among them. He and Maiyin taught everyone in our family *wǔshù* and *t'ai chi ch'uan*, too, which are very handy."

"Mm-hmm," said Islington vaguely, not really listening and unable to say more because Pandora had come out of the water to wash her hair.

"You would get on well with each other," said Pandora decisively.

"Indeed."

"Oh, yes. He's very medically knowledgeable," averred Pandora as she continued to work the lather through her hair, combing her fingers through it to work out some of the tangles before rinsing it.

She ducked her head under the water and tried to rinse the soap out as gently as she could to avoid creating tangles. She had brought her comb and brush, obviously, but she would rather not use the comb. Once she came back up, she kept her body under the water as far as she could. It was still pleasantly hot, and she relished her time there because she didn't know when she would get another bath.

"How did you bump your head, by the way?" asked Islington calmly, and he sighed with relief as she kept her body under the water and off the back wall.

"Well, when it happened, I thought it was a hunter who had fired his gun too close. It spooked Bellerophon, and he reared and started to fall, so I had to jump off before he fell on me. Then I tumbled down the hill."

"You don't think it was a hunter now?" asked Islington thoughtfully.

"Not after yesterday. I think it was the man I had been following for several days. He shot you."

"You're sure?" asked Islington stilly.

"Oh, yes. I recognized his back and the scrawny brown thing he was riding. I don't know why he was perturbed enough to shoot me...or you. I never got close enough to him to speak to him or anything."

"No telling," said Islington, his brow furrowing thoughtfully.

Pandora stood up from the water and grabbed her towel to dry off. Once she got each of her feet dried, she placed them on the floor to get dressed. She wrapped her towel around her hair to wick away as much of the water as she could before drying and brushing it.

Islington was watching her shadow again, but he maintained his composure. He had, at least, managed to get his aroused member to return to a semi-relaxed state so it wasn't as painful, and it wasn't easy to do that until she put on her clothes. He had closed his eyes and started to breathe through his nose, trying not to think about it. If that hadn't worked, his next course of action would have been to poke himself in the ribs.

Islington heard the sound of something splashing into the water followed by the door being opened. He could hear her footsteps as she came back in and more splashing. His forehead wrinkled, and he opened his eyes as he tried to figure out what she was doing. The third time, he chanced turning to look around the corner of the hearth to see what she was up to. He watched Pandora dip the bucket into the tub and empty it outside. She was out for a few minutes longer and returned carrying the bucket still full of water.

"Pandora, what are you doing?" he asked curiously.

"I'm getting the tub ready for you," she said matter-of-factly.

"I don't need a bath," said Islington quickly.

"Yes, you do," said Pandora calmly. "I don't know if you've had one since you left London, but it would do you some good."

"I don't need a bath," he repeated. "Besides, I don't think I could make it over there."

"I'll help you," said Pandora, giving him a cheery smile as she pulled the kettle from over the fire. After she poured in the bucket of cold water, she dipped into the kettle to retrieve a bucket of hot water and added that. She looked at Islington. "Do you like extremely hot, just hot, or tepid?"

"I am *not* taking a bath," said Islington finally, shaking his head.

"Why do you not want a bath?" asked Pandora cajolingly. "I feel so much better now I've had one. My back was *killing* me."

"What was wrong with your back?" he asked, his brow wrinkling.

"What wasn't?" hooted Pandora. "I whacked it into a boulder when I fell down the hill. Then the falls yesterday really banged it up."

"Let me see it," he said firmly.

Pandora thought about it for a moment then shrugged and came to sit on the edge of the bed, turning her back to him. She pulled her freshly-braided, still-damp hair out of the way, and he pulled her shirt and chemise loose from her waistband and lifted the material to look at her back. Pandora held it for him once he had lifted it by reaching her hands over her shoulders.

"I'm not sure what it looks like, as I am not able to bend like that. Does it look awful?"

Islington's face paled. She looked as if she had been beaten. Large, purple bruises started at the top between her shoulder blades, going all the way down her spine to the small of her back. Just above her waistband, there was a wide scrape that had scabbed over, going nearly from one side of her back to the other. Just above that, there was a large bruise of almost the same size as the scrape with small areas in it that were a darker reddish-purple, and he could clearly see where her back had impacted into the uneven surface of the boulder at the bottom of the hill where he had found her blood the previous morning. Islington smoothed a gentle hand over the skin and swallowed an emotional lump as he thought about the pain she had endured that caused every mark.

"No," he finally said softly as he pulled her clothes loose from her grip to put them back into place. "I don't think it looks bad at all."

She turned to look at him. "I thought not," she said with a smile. "Now, let's see to your bath."

Islington set his chin stubbornly and shook his head. "I told you, I'm *not* taking a bath."

"It's true I cannot get you into the tub without your help, not any more than you can get into it without mine, but you'll be washed one way or the other," said Pandora firmly.

"And what do you mean by that?" he asked stiltedly.

Pandora got up and went to fill the bucket with water from the tub and came to set it on the floor beside the bed, flannel in hand.

"Only that if you will not sit in the tub, then I will wash you where you *do* sit. It is simply that if you are in the tub, then I can flip and fluff the mattress and remake the bed while you soak for a little while." Pandora arched her eyebrow questioningly and wagged the cloth at him. "So which will it be?"

Islington considered his options. It wasn't that he didn't want a bath, because he did, but there was a certain part of his anatomy that hadn't been behaving itself recently. She was determined to have him cleaned, with or without his cooperation, and the rest of his anatomy was in no condition to fend her off. He decided he stood a better chance in the tub.

"I'll get in the tub," he said finally.

Pandora grinned victoriously. "Most excellent." She stood up and poured the bucket of water back into the tub. She looked back at Islington. "So, what temperature do you prefer?"

"Hot, please," he said charily.

Pandora ran her hand through the water to gauge its temperature. It was a little cooler than she preferred, but she liked to take an extremely hot bath. She was fairly sure she hadn't filled it too full, although a little water on the floor wouldn't do it any harm; it would make an improvement. She went back to the bed with the towel in her hand.

"Do you need to, um, do anything before you get in?"

Islington flushed a bright red, but she was right. He nodded.

"All right, then," said Pandora. She put the towel on the back of the chair and grabbed the bucket for their drinking water. "I'll go refill this while you do that, and then we'll get you in the tub." She started to turn away but turned back. "Please, don't try to stand up without me," she said softly.

"I wouldn't dream of it," said Islington with a grin.

Pandora turned and left the cottage with the bucket.

Chapter Twenty-Two

Pandora returned with the drinking water. Islington was sitting on the edge of the bed with his feet on the floor. He was unsteady but not in danger of falling. He had the blanket over his waist, but Pandora didn't want the wool near the tub, which was why she had the towel.

"Not unconscious on the floor. That's a good sign," said Pandora with a grin as she set down the bucket.

She grabbed the towel and put it over her right shoulder, and then she went to stand in front of Islington.

"Are you ready?"

"Not really," said Islington dryly, "but do I have a choice?"

Pandora grinned cheekily. "No."

She bent down and removed the bandage covering his stitches. She would put on another and more ointment after he washed. She would remove his sling once she had him into the tub; he could rest his arm on the edge for support. The most difficult part would be getting him in the tub with his dignity intact.

"Put your right hand on my left shoulder," she said as she stood slightly bent at the waist. Islington did as she asked, frowning. "Now, slowly stand up. If you get dizzy and start to fall, I'll try to make sure you fall on top of me so you won't get hurt."

"So *I* won't get hurt?" he hooted, his eyebrows shooting up.

"It will be fine," said Pandora with an encouraging smile.

"What about the blanket?" he asked worriedly.

"I promise I won't peek. We'll wrap this around you—"she lifted the towel slightly from her shoulder—"once we get you standing up."

Islington was unsure about this entire idea. He kept his eyes on hers and slowly rose from the bed. He could feel himself weaving and saw a few white spots at the edge of his vision, but he held onto Pandora's shoulder while she put bracing hands at his waist until things settled back into their proper perspective. He nodded his head once he felt steady.

Pandora removed the towel from her shoulder and brought it around his waist. True to her word, she didn't look as she did it, and she wrapped it and fastened it securely at one of his hips. He looked down at the job she had done and tilted his head acceptingly. It was no less respectable than attire she'd seen him in before, and he *knew* she hadn't kept her eyes closed when she undressed him and put him into bed, not to mention when he had fainted earlier.

"Now, we'll walk to the tub. Put your right arm over my shoulders."

He did as she asked and leaned on her as they went the short distance to the tub. He felt occasional beginnings of dizziness, but having her to lean on made it easier for him to wait the episodes out. Had he been trying by himself (as he had done earlier), he would have already fainted. When they reached the tub, he looked at the water and saw a slight opacity to it from when she had bathed. There was steam rising from the top of the water, and Islington was looking forward to this.

"You need to be careful when you step in. The gutta percha didn't dissolve, but it's slippery. Once we get you standing in the tub, we'll take off the towel, and then I'll help you sit down and remove your sling."

Islington nodded. He kept his arm over her shoulders and carefully stepped over the edge with one foot then the other. The coating on the tent was slick, almost oily, but he maintained his balance. The water was a little hotter than he was accustomed to, but it would begin to cool before long. Pandora moved around the side of the tub, still keeping his arm resting on her shoulders. She tugged at the towel, and it easily came loose. She tossed it onto the back of the nearby chair while she continued to hold him steady.

"I'll start to bend down with you until you can reach the edge of the tub; then you can settle yourself in."

"All right," agreed Islington.

This was going much better than he expected. He was able to sit down in the tub with only one minor problem when his foot slipped a little on the tent. He sucked in air through his teeth as the hot water covered the wound in his side, but it felt excellent to the rest of his body. Pandora had him put his left elbow onto the edge of the tub, and she removed his sling. He was now officially bathing. She took the towel from the back of the chair and placed it near the fire to dry.

"There," said Pandora with a grin. "That wasn't too bad, was it?"

"No, it wasn't," agreed Islington, giving her a relieved smile.

"I'll leave you to your own devices for a bit while I tend to other things. Then I'll help you wash and get you out."

"I don't need help washing," said Islington flatly.

"Now, now," soothed Pandora, shaking her head. "Let's not go through this again. It will be fine."

Islington looked at her a moment longer but settled himself further into the tub. He eventually lifted his left arm from the edge and rested it onto his waist to submerge his shoulder. The heat felt marvelous on the pulled muscles, and he could feel them beginning to relax.

Pandora took the chamber pot out to empty and rinse. She hoped she wouldn't need to do it many more times. After she came in and put it back under the edge of the bed, she removed the covers and pillow. The mattress was a little settled, but it wasn't in danger of becoming completely flattened yet. She pulled it off and checked the ropes, and then she fluffed up the grass inside the mattress before putting it back on the frame reversed from the way it was. She nodded satisfactorily and remade the bed. Now she was done with that, she could help Islington wash.

She retrieved the soapwort from the table then took the now-empty washing bucket and turned it over to use as a stool. She placed it on the floor at the end of the tub by Islington's head and pulled the chair closer to set down the plants. Islington looked at them with his eyebrow raised.

"Soapwort. You'll see," she replied to his unspoken question. "It's either this, or you get to smell like oranges and ginger."

"Thank you," said Islington appreciatively, his lips twitching.

"You'll need to sit up a little for this. I'm sure the water must be doing wonders for your shoulder. We'll put on more ointment after you get out, and that will help, too."

"It did help earlier," he agreed as he straightened himself up and repositioned his left arm back onto the edge.

Pandora dipped her flannel into the tub and macerated some of the leaves into it until she had a nice lather. After she picked the leaves off the cloth, she began to wash Islington, first starting with his right arm. She had him lean forward a bit as she washed his back, then dipped the washcloth back into the water and took more leaves to make more lather to continue her task. She eyed her supply of leaves closely, but she would have enough.

Islington had his eyes closed as she washed, enjoying the feel of her hands and the cloth as she smoothed it across his skin. She was very gentle and thorough as she worked, and the soft kneading action she used along his shoulders and neck eased knots of tension he hadn't even realized were there. She was very careful with his left arm and shoulder, and any discomfort he felt was kept to a bearable level.

He was amazed she was able to produce soap from the leaves, but at one point he looked at his arm to see the residue left behind. There was not really any scent, but it did clean. He would occasionally feel her hands leave his body as she made more lather, but then they would return to continue in their ministrations.

He felt her rest a hand on his right shoulder for balance as she leaned forward to begin washing his chest over his left. Her head was very close to his as she worked, and when Islington slightly turned his face toward her, he could inhale the soft, exotic orange and ginger scent of her soap. He knew her perfume smelled the same. It was a smell so perfect for her that he couldn't imagine her any other way. He opened his eyes to look at her and saw her keeping her gaze focused on the wall of the cottage. His lips twitched amusedly when she, at least, was trying to do this honorably…if a woman washing a man she wasn't married to could be considered in any way *honorable.*

Pandora realized he was looking at her, and she turned toward him. She saw his amused expression and calmly smiled back before returning her eyes to the wall, continuing to rub the cloth across his chest.

"I promised you I wouldn't peek," she said mildly.

"So you did," he returned softly, closing his eyes.

She carefully washed the area on his ribs where he was injured, but it was difficult to do without looking. She then moved down the side of the tub to wash his left leg and foot then to the other side to wash the right. There wasn't much more that she would feel comfortable washing beyond that, but he would be able to manage on his own. She looked at Islington's face and saw his eyes were closed. He didn't appear to be sleeping or distressed, though.

"We need to wash your hair," she said calmly.

Islington opened his eyes with surprise to look at her. She had taken her chipped earthenware cup from the hearth and filled it with water to wet his hair. She poured water over his head then set the cup aside to work some of the soapwort with her palms. She came back to her seat near his head and started to move her fingers through his hair. She gently massaged his scalp with her nails and fingertips, and Islington groaned at how good it felt.

"Where did you learn to do that?" he sighed relaxedly.

"Maiyin," said Pandora amusedly.

She continued to work her fingers through his hair, using her soap-slicked fingers to massage his earlobes, neck, and face as well. When he was relaxed enough that she could feel his head start to loll on his neck, she decided he'd had enough.

"Time to rinse," she said with a chuckle, grabbing the cup.

Once she had his hair rinsed, she worked more leaves into the flannel. She reached over his shoulder to hand it to him.

"I'm sure you have other things that need washing, but I'm *not* doing it for you. I'll even go outside for a few minutes. I'll help you get out, dry off, and back to the bed when I come back in," she said calmly.

"Thank you, Pandora," he said lowly, looking at her intently and holding onto her hand briefly as he took the cloth from her.

Pandora blushed and ducked her head. "You're welcome," she said softly before standing and leaving the cottage.

Pandora went outside and put her quickly cooling hands against her warm cheeks. She didn't know what she had been thinking when she said she would bathe him. Yes, she did. She had been thinking how much she wanted to touch him. It honestly hadn't started out that way, but she had become excited by it nonetheless. It hadn't been easy not to look. Her hands remembered every line of his body, and she had felt her heart start to thump against her ribs as her hands had moved over him. She was surprised he hadn't noticed.

She stood for a few minutes more, taking a few calming breaths, and then she went to relieve herself. She washed her hands in the rain barrel and went back around to the door. After taking a composing breath with her hand on the handle, she opened the door and walked into the cottage. Islington was sitting calmly in the tub, waiting for her.

She put the dried and heated towel over her right shoulder and moved the chair back to the table. She went to the edge of the tub and knelt for him to put his right arm over her shoulder. They got him to his feet, but he had to remain still for a few minutes as a wave of dizziness swept over him. He felt nauseous for a moment, but then his vision cleared, and he was able to stand relatively well with her help. She quickly dried off the upper half of his body then had him put his right foot out of the tub onto the floor, where she bent down to dry it and his leg while he put a bracing hand to her shoulder. Once she stood up, she had him take out his left foot and repeated.

"Can you bend down a little?" she asked.

When he did, she reached up and rubbed the towel vigorously against his head to dry his hair. When she removed it, he was tousled, but it was an attractive look. Pandora chortled amusedly. She wrapped the towel around his waist and fastened it again, and they walked to the bed. She had noticed while she was helping him to the tub that he walked much better than the last two times she had needed to move him from one place to another, and there was even more improvement on the way back to the bed. He was getting stronger, but he was still not strong enough, and there was no question of him being able to ride until his shoulder was a little better. She helped him onto the bed in a semi-reclining position, with his back resting against the headboard, and put the blanket over him. Once he was covered by that, he removed the towel and handed it to her.

"And you thought it couldn't be done," she said with a teasing grin.

"I stand corrected…well, *sit* corrected," he said, grinning back with a chuckle.

Pandora looked at her watch. She was a little alarmed when she saw it was 10:30. She still needed to drain the tub and move it so she would have a place to sleep, and she still had not finished tending to Islington. She made sure he had water in his cup and retrieved his sling from the table where she had placed it. She got the jar of ointment and a clean bandage and went to sit beside him on the edge of the bed.

His wound was a little red from the time in the water, but it would be fine. She put on the ointment and placed the bandage over it while he looked on. Once she was done with that, she put some ointment into both of her hands and bent forward to gently massage it into his shoulder.

"Better?" she asked, looking at his face.

"Much," he said with a smile.

"Is the chamomile working? Do you need more...something different?"

"I feel fine," he said, looking at her calmly.

She put on his sling, except this time she brought both ends up the front of his chest to tie around his neck and found it was much easier to do that way.

"Does that feel all right, or should I tie it the way I had it before?" she questioned, looking at his face for any sign of discomfort.

"I feel fine," he repeated. "Everything is wonderful," he grinned.

Pandora got up and put more wood on the fire. She would have to move more over from the open room tomorrow, but there was enough for the night and to rekindle in the morning. The torches had guttered out, but she wouldn't light more because it was bedtime. She lifted the wash bucket and dunked it into the tub to begin draining it enough to move out of the way. She didn't have time to drain it completely, but she could empty it enough to at least get it from in front of the fireplace for the night. She would finish in the morning.

"Pandora, do you *have* to drain that tonight?" asked Islington exasperatedly, amazed at her seemingly endless supply of energy.

"I do if I want a place to sleep," she said mildly, hauling another bucketful to the door and pouring it out.

"Are you planning to sleep in it?" he asked perplexedly. He knew she liked her tub, but it wouldn't be comfortable for sleeping.

"No, I need to empty it enough so I can move it," she said as she grabbed another bucketful. "I'm going to sleep on the floor in front of the fireplace, where it's sitting right now."

She tried moving the tub and found it wouldn't budge.

"*Dà pàng yùgāng!*" she muttered frustratedly, retrieving more water.

"*What* did you say?" asked Islington as she came back.

"What?" asked Pandora perplexedly, filling up the bucket again.

"Before...in Chinese?"

"Oh, nothing," said Pandora dismissively as she emptied the bucket.

"It sounded naughty," he said with a grin.

Pandora looked at him and started to giggle as she filled the bucket. "No, it was nothing like *that* at all," she said, still chuckling and shaking her head as she went to empty the bucket.

"What did you say?"

"I just said 'big, fat tub'. That's all."

She again tried to move the tub, and it still wouldn't move.

"Before you wear yourself out doing that, why don't you just sleep here?" he asked casually, seeing how winded she was from lugging the bucket to the door. He didn't think her back could take sleeping on a hard surface; no matter what he had told her, it wasn't fine.

"And where would you sleep? You need the bed more than I do," she said amusedly, placing a hand on her hip.

"We could share it," he said calmly, not looking at her.

Pandora dropped the bucket into the tub in surprise.

"It's not big, but it's better than the floor," he continued.

"You're serious?" she asked disbelievingly, slowly bending to remove the bucket before it became too waterlogged to lift.

"I am," he said calmly.

"But…," Pandora trailed off.

"It's not like you have anything to worry about," said Islington self-deprecatingly. She was unconvinced. "I will do my best to behave."

Pandora's brow furrowed. She had already slept there the night before. And he was right: it would be infinitely more comfortable than sleeping on the floor. She really wasn't looking forward to that. However, he was conscious now, and last night she had only done it to break his fever. She rubbed the spot behind her ear as she continued to think, but she wasn't going to turn down the offer, no matter how wrong it was. She set the bucket on the hearth and went to close the door.

"All right," she said softly after she came back.

"It will be fine," it was his turn to say, seeing she was still concerned.

Pandora sat in the chair at the table and removed her boots. She started to unbutton her shirt and looked over to see Islington watching.

"Don't peek!" she said in alarm. "Close your eyes or something," she said nervously.

Islington did as she asked with a slight smile at her anxiety. After she made sure he wasn't looking, Pandora removed all her clothes except her chemise. She forgot how short it was. She had a shift, but it was in her valise on the other side of the room, and the fire didn't give her enough light to search for it. Aside from that, even though the cottage was warm, it felt cooler without her clothes. She scurried across the floor to the bed. She carefully climbed over Islington and got under the blanket. She lay on her side, facing the wall, her back turned to Islington.

"Pandora, can you help me with the pillow, please?" he asked calmly, his lips twitching in amusement at her behavior.

She rolled over to look at him and sat up. The blanket fell away when she did it, but she didn't notice. She had to get on her knees, and it wasn't as easy from this side as the other, but she helped him settle onto his back in the bed. She took the pillow and fluffed it, and then he lifted his head for her to place it underneath.

"How's that?" she asked, a little winded from the effort it had taken.

Islington looked at her for the first time since she got in the bed and felt his mouth go dry. He hadn't been aware her chemise was as that short. It didn't even come to the middle of her thigh. He watched in the firelight the way her breasts rose and fell through the thin material covering them, and the erection he had been fighting with raged back again. He noticed her looking at him expectantly.

"That's fine," he said breathlessly, closing his eyes to block out the vision in front of him.

Islington began to think this might not have been the best idea after all. He felt Pandora shift around beside him as she lay back down and pulled the blanket over herself. Islington thought he might try to move over a little in the bed to put more space between them, and he winced and gasped as it jarred his shoulder. Pandora rolled over to look at him concernedly, and her breasts pressed against his right arm as she did so. He kept his eyes closed and started to breathe in and out deeply through his nose, trying to fight the urges burning through him.

"Are you all right?"

He calmly lifted his right arm and folded it over his stomach in an effort to move it away from temptation.

"I'm fine," he said softly through stiff lips, keeping his eyes closed.

Pandora looked at him for a few minutes uncertainly, but then she shrugged and rolled back over to close her eyes tiredly. While she had her eyes open, her energy appeared to be limitless, but once she was in bed, everything shut off quickly. She shifted slightly as she started to nod off and snuggled up under the covers, almost asleep.

"Bloody hell!" gasped Islington in a strangled voice.

Pandora rolled over again, blinking sleepily. "What's wrong?" she asked in alarm.

Islington was fighting a losing battle. He thought he stood a chance once she rolled over to face the wall again, but then she pressed her bare bottom against his thigh. Only, it wasn't enough for her to just rest it there—she started to *wiggle* it. It was too much. He was throbbingly erect. As long as she was in the bed with him, there was only one way to relieve it, and he could *not* make her sleep on the floor. He had only said he would do his best to behave, and he had been trying. He was about to find out just how much better he was feeling with what he hoped would be a pleasurable test.

Pandora continued to look at him sleepily, propped up on one elbow to look down at him. He was troubled by something. He was flushed and seemed to be in pain, but every time she asked, he insisted he was fine. She hadn't seen anything to indicate he wasn't telling the truth; his injuries were healing, and he had no signs of his fever or infection returning. She couldn't help him if he wouldn't tell her what was wrong. Islington finally opened his eyes to look at her with an apologetic expression, and then Pandora knew what was bothering him.

"You promised," she said softly, looking away from him.

"I'm sorry," he said quietly. He raised a finger to her chin and turned her face to make her look at him. "I said I would do my best, and I have tried. You have *no* idea how hard I've tried."

Pandora looked intently at his face. She could see the conflicting emotions in his expression. There was desire but also guilt. There was a strain to his features that made it obvious he had been struggling. She believed him. She could see from the look on his face that he felt he had no choice, and she couldn't deny she wanted him as well. She knew in the back of her mind that she had accepted this could happen, had wanted this to happen, before she ever got into the bed with him. Pandora put a gentle hand to his cheek and bent forward to kiss him softly.

Islington at first lay still as she kissed him, but as she deepened the kiss, parting his lips with her tongue, her hand slowly trailing down his neck to his chest where she could feel his heart pounding against his ribs, he quivered and groaned deep in his throat with longing. He hungrily began to kiss her back, and she was startled by his almost frantic need for her. He worked his right arm beneath Pandora to pull her closer, and she adjusted her position so that her right hand balanced on the pillow on the other side of his head, her breasts pressed against his chest.

She felt his hand smooth up the back of her left thigh before it came to rest on her bottom. He lightly trailed his fingers across the delicate flesh there, and she moaned at the sensation. He pulled up at the bottom of her chemise impatiently, trying to remove it. Pandora sat up to pull the garment over her head and laid it aside, straddling his legs just above the knees.

He looked at her hungrily and tried to touch one of her breasts with his hand, but they were just out of his reach. Pandora smiled wantonly as she continued to stay just beyond his grasp, looking at his almost desperate expression, but she eventually bent forward to put a hand under his neck and helped him to a sitting position. Pandora sighed silkily and wrapped her arms around his head as he took a nipple into his mouth.

She moved herself closer to him, and she gasped when she rubbed against his erection. It felt unbelievably hard. She started to reach for it, but Islington raised his hand from where he had been smoothing it down the bare softness of her leg to stop her.

"Don't," he sighed. "Not yet."

Pandora put a hand to either side of his face and kissed him passionately, rubbing herself against him achingly. She cried out against his lips when she felt him move his hand to start teasing her. She quivered at his touch, and her limbs began to go liquid as he stroked her expertly.

"No fair, *àiren*," she moaned.

As he touched her, he drew one of her breasts into his mouth, placing teasing bites against her nipple as his tongue flicked against its crest, and Pandora could feel that familiar knot growing in her stomach. She clutched her hands convulsively in his hair as he continued to tease her, and she was astonished by how it felt as if he were everywhere, even when he only had the use of one arm.

"Theo," she whimpered.

"I'm just giving you what you want," he whispered back.

Islington watched with gratification as Pandora orgasmed, finding unbelievable beauty in the arch of her back and the small, wondering smile that spread over her features as the sensations worked their way through her body. She relaxed against him momentarily, and brought her mouth to his for an appreciative kiss. She rested her forehead against his for a few minutes as her breathing returned to normal.

Pandora moved her lips back to his for more teasing kisses, and she moved a hand down his chest to rub her palm against one of his nipples. She felt it harden at the caress, and she felt the way he reacted to it in the intensity of his kiss. She tweaked it slightly between her thumb and forefinger and heard him groan pleasurably. She smiled slightly against his lips, finding yet another piece of ammunition.

"My turn," she whispered, giving him a teasing smile.

She smoothed her hand against his chest and put the other behind his neck to guide him back to the pillow. She sat across his thighs, bending forward to continue kissing him. She trailed her lips across his jaw to one of his ears to nibble at the lobe, and Pandora felt him tense and suck in his breath. He reached up his hand to touch her breast, and Pandora felt a renewed tension building as he kneaded it with his palm, drawing the tip between his knuckles. She slowly trailed her lips down his neck to his chest, and licked his nipple softly before raising it teasingly between the tip of her tongue and her teeth. She felt him arch his back toward her, and she smiled happily at his reaction.

"Pandora," he gasped, putting his hand to the side of her neck to bring her mouth back to his for a ravenous kiss that made her moan with its intensity.

She could feel his erection between them, and Pandora rose up and took it in her hand. She was astonished by how hard it felt, much harder than she remembered, but there was still that silken texture that fascinated her. She felt Islington tense at the contact, and Pandora positioned herself above him. She slowly settled down onto the shaft, and she gave a smile of pleasure and sighed as she felt herself become filled by him. She bent forward to kiss him, and Islington gently trailed his fingers across her back before grasping her bottom in an effort to raise her.

Pandora nipped at his bottom lip and raised herself ever so slightly before settling back down to gyrate her pelvis against his, shuddering at the sensations it produced. Islington groaned deep in his throat and opened his eyes to look at her, his expression almost tortured.

"Clever Pandora," he sighed, reaching up a finger to trail across her chin.

She gripped one of her hands onto the edge of the headboard and began to move up and down, her pace steadily increasing as she felt herself moving toward another orgasm. She looked down at Islington's face and saw him watching her, his expression one of exquisite concentration as he tried to wait for her. She began to move faster still, and in her excitement, her knee came up to firmly plant into his side against the cracked ribs and stitches.

Pandora watched, almost as if time were moving slower than usual, as a look of complete surprise and agony came over Islington's face, which had suddenly gone white, followed by a strangled gasp before his eyes closed, and he went still with unconsciousness.

A hand flew to her mouth in horror and mortification, and Pandora felt tears of worry sting her eyes as she hurriedly checked his heart and his breathing. Both were faster than normal, which was only to be expected, and they both seemed to be slowing down but in no danger of stopping. She lifted the bandage from his side and looked at his wound, her face tense as she expected to see the worst. The stitches were still intact. There was a little blood on the bandage, but it seemed that other than the intense pain she had caused him, there was no lasting damage. She leaned down and kissed his lips gently, brushing a hand across his cheek.

"Oh, Theo, I am *so* sorry," she whispered contritely.

She climbed off him and nestled into his right side, resting her head into the crook of his shoulder and putting his arm around her before pulling up the blanket to cover them both. She put her hand onto his chest and felt the steady and much slower beat of his heart. She kissed the skin beneath her cheek and closed her eyes. *At least I didn't kill him.* Pandora knew one thing for certain: he was *not* going to be happy when he woke up in the morning.

Pandora awoke the next morning feeling very relaxed. Her eyes slowly opened as the sun was rising, but it was still fairly dark in the cottage. The sky was overcast, and it looked like they would have some rain, but Pandora didn't care. She smoothed her hand languidly over the soft, warm skin beneath her palm, feeling the heartbeat there. She was still snuggled into Islington's side, and his arm was still around her the way she had placed it. She felt cozy and warm, even though she was sure the fire was nothing but embers. She looked up at Islington's face and saw he still slept, his features relaxed and peaceful.

She moved her hand further down his body, feeling the ridges of taut muscle beneath the velvet of his skin. It could almost be marble, but stone could never be so warm in the shade. She worked her hand even lower, letting her fingers play across the indentation of his navel and the soft hair that started growing there. Her eyes widened in surprise when her hand brushed against something unexpected. She looked up at Islington's face to find him still sleeping. She lifted the blanket to look at what she had touched. He was aroused. She was sure he hadn't been after he lost consciousness last night. It was extraordinary.

She moved her hand back down his body to grasp his erection gently. It wasn't as hard as it had been the night before, but it was definitely stiff in her hand. She had to wonder what he was dreaming about that would cause such a reaction, or even if he was dreaming at all. She released it and softly played her fingers across its surface, still marveling at how soft the skin felt. After another look at Islington's sleeping features, she lifted the blanket again. There was something she just had to know, and since he was sleeping, Pandora didn't see where there would be any harm in finding out.

She carefully changed her position and moved her body further down in the bed. It was hot with her head under the blanket, but her curiosity was driving her at the moment. Once she was far enough down, she took his erection in her hand again, and then she moved her head toward it and softly ran her tongue along its surface. It did feel just as smooth. There was a slight saltiness to it, but she didn't find it unpleasant, and she wasn't sure that it didn't come from her.

After Pandora's original curiosity was satisfied, she began to wonder what kind of reaction she could get from Islington. She was partially urged by a desire to make up for what had happened the night before, but her curiosity was probably her greatest impetus. He liked it when she took him in her hand. What else did he like? She softly began to move her hand up and down the shaft, ever-fascinated by the texture, while she contemplated what she should try. It began to grow even harder in her hand, and she felt him shift in his sleep. She needed to see his face. She slowly pulled the blanket lower with her free hand until her head was uncovered. It was easier to breathe, and now she could watch Islington.

His head had turned a little on the pillow and his lips had parted, but he seemed to still be sleeping. She ran her tongue along the edge of the tip, just where it met the shaft, and then she took the tip completely into her mouth as she continued to stroke him with her hand. She moved her tongue around its circumference, and then she removed her hand to run her tongue along the shaft again before repeating her previous action. Islington groaned in his sleep, and his eyes flew open in surprise, just as she took him as deep into her mouth as she could, massaging her tongue along the underside of the shaft.

"Oh, my God!" he groaned, his expression one of pleasure and disbelief. "Pandora, what are you *doing*?"

She looked at him, removing her mouth as she continued to stroke him with her hand.

"Apologizing," she said after a few minutes, a wanton smile playing at her lips when she saw his reaction. He liked it…a lot.

"Apology accepted," he sighed, reaching down to grab her by the shoulder and pull her upward.

He brought her mouth to his for a hungry kiss, and Pandora pressed against his right side, rubbing one of her legs against his sensuously. One of her breasts was near his left hand in the sling, and he carefully reached out to knead its fullness, playing his thumb against the nipple until it puckered tautly.

"Help me sit up," he whispered, and Pandora did as he asked, placing a hand under his neck and straddling him as she had the night before.

He used his right hand to draw her closer, bringing his erection to rest between her legs. Pandora felt it rub against her teasingly, and she sighed longingly. She rose up on her knees until she found the right spot and lowered herself onto him with a sigh. He put his mouth to one of her breasts, and Pandora arched toward him with a moan.

Pandora carefully began to move up and down, but there was less chance of kneeing his ribs with him sitting up, as had been Islington's objective, and her pace began to increase with her need. She looked down at his face and saw a tender passion and pleasure as she rose and fell onto him, her hand braced against his right shoulder. She bent down to kiss him just as she felt the first waves of her orgasm begin to wash over her, and she cried out against his mouth at the intensity of it. She continued to move for Islington's sake, and she moved her mouth to his ear to tease the lobe with her teeth and tongue.

Pandora heard him moan and felt him begin to shudder against her as he reached his climax, and she held onto him as the exquisite sensations shook him and left him weak. He rested his sweat-soaked face against her breasts, and Pandora helped him to lie back down before she nestled into his side, lifting her face to place tiny kisses along his jaw.

"How are you feeling?" she finally asked, propping her head on one of her hands to look down at him, casually tracing a finger over his chest.

"Outstanding," said Islington heartily with a grin.

"You lecherous profligate," said Pandora softly with a teasing smile. "Behave."

Islington's face became calm as he thought about it. "Despite activities that shall go unmentioned—"he grinned again—"I'm feeling better."

He was feeling stronger, and the drowsiness from the day before was gone. He suspected, however, that it had been due as much to his injuries and complications as from the medicine Pandora had given him. His shoulder still hurt when he moved it too much or the wrong way, and that would last for some time. His side was tender; certain movements made it difficult for him to breathe, and he tried not to laugh if he could help it (which Pandora sometimes made it impossible for him not to do), but he could feel a slight itchiness around the stitches that let him know it had already started to heal. His ribs would take much longer to improve, but the wound itself was doing well.

"You're sure?" she asked uncertainly.

"You have done a marvelous job, doctor," he said with a fond smile, and Pandora blushed at the praise.

Pandora looked out the window, and while the grayness to the sky had not improved and only appeared to be worse, the sun behind it made it obvious the hour had grown later. As much as she was enjoying herself, there were things to do. She bent down and started to place tiny nibbles along Islington's neck up to his ear, and she heard his sharp intake of breath. She moved her mouth to his and kissed him thoroughly, smoothing a hand across his chest to tease one of his nipples before she sat up and climbed out of bed to stand on the floor.

"I need to see to the horses," she said quickly as she slid on her chemise and went across the floor to put on the rest of her clothes.

"But...," began Islington as he carefully raised himself to a sitting position, disappointed she wasn't going to continue what she had started.

She finished putting on her boots, grabbed two apples from the table, and tossed some wood on the fire. She filled up the teapot with water and put it on to boil. Then she went back to the bed and sat. She leaned forward to kiss Islington again and sat back. She handed him an apple.

"That's breakfast, sad to say," she grinned. "I shouldn't be gone more than fifteen or twenty minutes, and I'll make tea when I get back." She gave him another quick peck and stood up to go to the open room.

Islington sat in a somewhat bemused state. He could hear her talking to the horses in the other room, and then he heard her open the door and lead each of them out, closing the door behind her. He turned to look around the edge of the fireplace, and then he turned back to face the wall in front of him, his brow furrowed thoughtfully.

"Brazen hussy," he said unhappily, taking a bite from the apple.

Pandora was gone longer than she said she would be, and Islington grew worried as twenty, then thirty minutes, and then an hour passed. He could hear the water boiling away in the teapot, the rattle of the lid quieting down to be replaced by a hissing noise. He was about to try getting out of bed to go look for her when he heard the door open. He looked around the edge of the fireplace to see Pandora closing it behind her. Her shirt was bunched up in one hand as she carried something bundled inside it.

"Where have you been?" he asked severely.

Pandora looked at him and blinked, surprised by his harsh tone. She slowly walked over to the table and removed the items from her shirt. She put down several apples and pears and turned to face him.

"I was foraging," she said calmly.

"I was worried something had happened to you," said Islington, his forehead wrinkled with irritation.

Pandora went to sit beside him on the edge of the bed, and she reached out to smooth a hand against his cheek.

"I'm sorry. I just happened to find some trees. We *need* food. I didn't think it would take so long to get them."

Islington's features relaxed.

"Your water is boiling away," he said softly.

"Bollocks!" cried Pandora, jumping up from the bed.

She grabbed the piece of linen she used as a towel and pulled the pot from the shelf in the fireplace. When she lifted the lid, there was only about an inch of water left, not enough to make tea. She dipped the pot back into the bucket to refill, and it hissed as the metal cooled in the water. She put the lid back on and put it back on the shelf. She also put the leftover cabbage and potatoes on to reheat as well. There would be enough for dinner, but she would have to find something else for supper.

After she got the food started, she moved wood from the open room and stacked it into the nook by the fireplace. She drained the tub of most of its water and pulled it to the doorway and tipped it to remove the rest. She pulled the tent out and found a place to hang it to dry. The gutta percha made it somewhat resistant to mildew, but she didn't want to put it away wet either. She examined the tent and made sure that heating it hadn't damaged the coating. It was fine, as she was sure it would be. She got water in the bucket and some soapwort and washed up their few dishes and took it outside to empty once she was finished.

She came back into the cottage and removed the teapot from the fire as the lid began to rattle and added some leaves to begin steeping. There wouldn't be many more pots of tea, Pandora thought sadly. She moved the leaves around in the tin to measure. There might be enough for three or four more pots, but that would be it.

She sat on the edge of the hearth as she waited for the tea to be ready and looked at the food on the table. Lots of fruit and some vegetables, but no meat. Pandora missed meat...real meat. She would dearly love some ham, roast chicken or beef, leg of mutton, stuffed pheasant with currant jelly, fried breaded oysters. She shook her head to clear away the visions because it only made her homesick. She would have to fish.

She poured herself a cup of tea then leaned over to look at Islington.

"Would you like some tea?" she asked.

"Yes, please."

He gave her a considering look. She seemed preoccupied.

"I can't offer you any milk. I have a few sugar lumps, but you might have to fight Bellerophon for them," said Pandora with a grin as she took his cup from the chair and poured some tea into it.

"I think he would win at this point," said Islington, grinning back with a chuckle. "I prefer it without anything, thank you."

She came around to hand his cup to him, holding her own in her hand, and sat on the edge of the bed. A thought occurred to her, and she went to the medicine kit for the bottle of chamomile. He hadn't said he was in pain, but his face was a little strained. She got a lump from the pocket of her coat and placed some drops onto it and handed it to him.

"Bellerophon will understand," she said as he looked about to protest.

They sat drinking their tea in silence for a time, and Pandora's features were pensive as she would occasionally look out the window. She heard sporadic thunder, and she needed to get the horses.

"Exactly how bad is our food problem?" Islington finally asked her.

Pandora looked at him in surprise then glanced to the table.

"We've lots of fruit, and I can get more. We have two turnips, three carrots, some peas, and there is spinach and leaf lettuce in the garden."

"Sounds tasty," said Islington with a grin.

"I'm going to muck out the other room and get the horses before they're frightened by the weather and run off, and then we'll have some dinner. After I do that, I'll try to fish."

"You've never fished?" asked Islington in surprise.

"I understand the concept from watching my brothers, and I have my fishing kit," she said calmly.

"What do you intend to use for bait? I don't think a fish will be enticed by a slice of apple," said Islington, his lips twitching amusedly.

"Bait?" asked Pandora blankly.

Islington chuckled, and he grimaced as it made his side hurt. He shook his head.

"You can't use a plain hook. It's what's on it that catches the fish."

"I don't have bait," said Pandora, her brow furrowing disconcertedly.

"You can look for some worms or crickets, I suppose."

"But...," began Pandora, and she shuddered.

"Don't tell me you're squeamish about it," said Islington disbelievingly.

"Why would you think I wouldn't be?"

"I don't know. You managed to cut and sew me up well enough."

"That was different; I had to," said Pandora softly as she looked at him. She sighed resignedly and shrugged. "I suppose I'll have to do this as well. Would you like more tea?"

"No, thank you. I would like some water, though."

Pandora filled his cup, and Islington saw that her forehead was wrinkled as she thought about the unappealing task of finding bait. He put his hand on hers as she placed the cup on the chair.

"You don't have to do this," he said calmly.

She nodded her head. "No, I do." She started to leave for the other room but turned back. "Do I need to empty the...ah...," she trailed off as she pointed under the bed.

"No, not yet."

Pandora nodded and briefly smiled and went to take care of things. She looked up at the sky through the open roof of the other room as she cleaned. It was a steel gray color, and although she hadn't seen any lightning, she could hear the sound of thunder rolling distantly and knew a bad storm was approaching. It would complicate things because she had depended on taking the horses to the meadow to graze. Now she would have to use the grain Tajik had given her for Bellerophon to feed both animals, and the supply was dwindling. It would last them the day, possibly tomorrow if the rain persisted, but not beyond that. If she had some hay, that would help, but it wasn't likely.

She led the horses to the cottage and put them into the room. Bellerophon didn't seem bothered by the thunder, but Jezebel flared her nostrils and became wild-eyed every time it rumbled. The mostly-open roof wasn't going to keep them dry, but at least they would be enclosed and somewhat sheltered. When they were settled in, Pandora put the limb across the doorway and went back to the other room.

Just as she walked in, she saw lightning flash and heard the closest sound of thunder yet. She went to the bed, and Islington looked up from gazing out the window himself as she sat down.

"I hope you're not still planning to go fishing."

"Not in that, no," said Pandora. She looked up at the thatched roof above them. "I guess we'll get to see how well this roof was made."

"Very soon, yes," agreed Islington.

"Are you hungry?"

"I could eat."

Pandora got their plates and dished out the last of the cabbage and potatoes. There was some broth left in the kettle, but she would use that to cook the carrots and turnips. There was still some seasoning left in it from the sausage, and she might add a few of the herbs from the garden to make up the difference. It would still need salt, and she had no idea whether it would be more than edible, but it would be food, and that was something in short supply. She grabbed her chopsticks and carried the plates to the bed. She gave Islington his plate and saw that he was able to hold it balanced with his left hand.

"You can use your left arm!" she said in surprise.

"It's not using my *arm* that's the problem. It's my shoulder that hurts," said Islington as he began to eat.

Pandora's forehead wrinkled thoughtfully while she ate. She pondered what she could do to help him use his arm without making it worse for his shoulder. She would sometimes tilt her head sideways and look at his shoulder, tapping the chopsticks against her teeth meditatively. Islington would look at her curiously when she did it, and she would resume eating, her expression still one of contemplation.

It began to rain while they were eating, and Pandora would occasionally hear a drop hiss as it fell down the chimney to land on the fire. She had to light the torches because it became very dark once the storm arrived, and the light from the fire was no longer enough. Fortunately, the part of the roof that was intact still seemed to shed water, and they were able to at least stay warm and dry. Pandora got up to check on the horses once the rain began. They were able to move into a corner of the room that still retained a portion of the roof. Jezebel was skittish, but she would be safe from injuring herself inside.

"So, how are you going to occupy yourself now it's raining?" asked Islington after they finished eating while Pandora was putting their dishes near the bucket for washing.

She went to the medicine kit and retrieved the ointment, a new bandage for his side, and the long, wound-up strip of muslin.

"I'm going to play doctor," she said with a grin as she sat down.

She pulled off her boots after she set down the items she held in her hands because she didn't want to get the bed dirty.

"I see," said Islington with an amused smile.

She put ointment and the new bandage on his side after she took a closer look at his stitches. They seemed to be doing well, the blow she gave to his side notwithstanding. She reached up to untie his sling, and Islington sighed and closed his eyes as her breasts brushed against his chest. Pandora thought it was from the pain of her removing his sling. She put ointment onto her hands and gently worked it into his shoulder. She could feel knots in the muscle below her fingers, but she didn't want to actually *massage* it because she was afraid it might do more damage. However, when she did apply a little more pressure, he seemed to like it.

"More?" she asked, an eyebrow shooting up in surprise. He nodded.

She put the lid back on the ointment and set it aside, and then she put her hands back onto his shoulder and moved her fingers over the muscle, gently kneading and smoothing. She could feel the knots starting to ease as the muscle loosened. Islington would occasionally grimace while she worked, but whenever she began to stop, he would reach over to put his hand over hers and make her continue. She worked the muscles from his neck all the way down to his biceps, and there was a lot of improvement in the way it felt beneath her fingers once she was finished.

"Now, you said you can use your arm but not your shoulder, so I think I've come up with something to make it easier for you to do that," she said calmly, as she started to unwind the long strip of muslin, her forehead slightly wrinkled.

Islington watched interestedly as she wound the muslin around his biceps, just above the elbow, after leaving a strip loose that she measured out a little wider than his chest. When she had wound it several times, she tied the tail around it in a loop. She measured out the distance from his right shoulder and back again twice before measuring across his chest, and then she tore the strip of muslin. She wound the muslin around him in the same pattern she had measured, bringing the second chest-measured piece across his back after she straddled him to reach behind him and grab it. Pandora tied the pieces together on his right side and looked at her work. The only problem was that his arm covered the wound in his side, but that would help keep the bandage in place.

"Try that," she said softly as she leaned back a little further, absently massaging one of her temples to try to clear away white spots at the edge of her vision as the migraine she had been fighting grew worse.

Islington was able to move the lower half of his arm well with a minimal amount of pain. The bandage kept him from lifting or moving his shoulder by the piece tied across his chest, while the one tied over his right shoulder took some of the pressure away from the weight of his arm pulling down on it without the sling under his forearm. Between the ointment, the massaging, and the new bandage, it was feeling much better. He looked up at Pandora in admiration.

"Bloody brilliant!" he said with a grin.

Pandora smiled back reflexively, still massaging her temple. She couldn't have a headache...not now, but it had started earlier in the day, and now there was no way to stop it. She had hoped it would go away, but she knew from past experience it seldom did. Her peripheral vision was slowly disappearing, and the white spots that had only been around the edges were starting to float in front of her eyes until she wasn't able to focus anymore. The dull ache was starting in the left side of her skull, and the dizziness, and it was only going to get worse. Islington noticed her distant expression, and the small lines that wrinkled her forehead.

"What's wrong?" he asked concernedly as he looked at her.

Pandora smiled dismissively and shook her head. "It's just a headache," she said calmly, but it was worsening quickly.

"A headache or a *migraine*?" he asked as he took her wrist in his hand to feel her pulse. He didn't need her to tell him; he could feel the way it fluttered as the pain started to take over. "Take some of your medicine," he said firmly.

"But I can't," she said anxiously. "It will make me sleepy."

"There's not anything you need to do. Take your medicine," he repeated gently, reaching up to brush a hand across her cheek.

Pandora was about to refuse again, but she knew he was right. She unsteadily rose from the bed and concentrated all of her effort to reach the medicine kit on the table. She reached her hand into the bottom and took out the bottle. Islington watched nervously as she weaved around, instinctively putting a hand in front of her to feel for obstacles as if she'd gone blind. She made it back to the hearth and the bed and filled the tin cup with water. She sat on the edge of the bed and removed the stopper from the bottle, but she couldn't quite seem to coordinate her hand to put the drops into the cup. Islington took it away.

"How much?" he asked quickly, worriedly watching the way she swayed back and forth.

Her forehead wrinkled as she tried to focus beyond the building pain in her head.

"Um, five drops," she said disjointedly.

He added them to the cup and handed it to her, and then he watched to make sure she drank all of it. She shuddered distastefully as she finished it and set the cup on the chair. She put a balancing hand on the bed beside her as the dizziness made the room tilt.

Islington took her by the arm and helped her to situate herself on the bed between his thighs, her back resting against his chest with her head on his right shoulder. She whimpered slightly as the pain increased, and she waited for the medicine to start working. Islington kissed her soothingly on the top of her head and reached up his hands to gently rub her temples. He could feel a film of perspiration on her skin, and he reached around to unbutton her waistcoat and shirt, pulling it and her chemise loose from her waistband, trying to make her more comfortable. Her body was drawn tight from the pain, but as the medicine began to work, he could feel her slowly relax. Whatever Keung had put in it made her drift off to sleep, and Islington sighed with relief as he put a hand to the pulse at her throat and felt that it was steady and untroubled.

He hadn't realized she got migraines. He couldn't understand why Keung would have made a medicine just for her headaches or why it was so strong until now. He put his arms around her waist and rested his cheek against the top of her head. She always seemed so determined and independent; then something like this would remind him that she was no less fragile than anyone else, including himself.

Islington lay for a time watching the storm through the window, enjoying holding her against him without all the frenetic distractions it usually included, but the sound of the rain eventually made him drift off to sleep as well.

Pandora woke slowly. The pain in her head had dropped to a tolerable level, and when she opened her eyes, she was able to focus on objects without any disturbing spots or blurring. She snuggled into Islington's body, enjoying the way his arms were placed protectively around her waist. She could tell from the steady rise and fall of his chest that he was sleeping...if the gentle, occasional snore he made hadn't already informed her. She slowly shifted around, but Islington's eyes fluttered open when he felt her moving, and he looked down at her.

"How's your head?" he asked sleepily, smoothing a hand down her back.

"Better," she said honestly. It wasn't *much* better, or *all* better, but it was better than it was, and she at least felt functional again.

She looked out the window. The storm was over, for the most part. There was no more thunder and lightning, and the rain had calmed to a slight drizzle, the sky gray with the remnants. The fire was burning low, and the torches were out. The horses hadn't been fed or watered for several hours. Pandora started to get out of bed, but Islington held onto her.

"Stay still for a little while longer," he said gently.

She turned to look at him. "There are things to do," she said softly.

"There are *always* things to do," he said, slowly rubbing her back.

Pandora turned around and leaned forward to kiss him. She put her hand against his cheek and could feel the roughness to his skin from needing a shave. She mentally added that to her list of things to do. She relaxed against him, enjoying the feel of both his hands reaching down to cup her bottom then working their way up beneath the back of her clothing. She was very tempted to stay where she was, but she couldn't. Pandora sat up and looked down at him.

"There are *really* things to do," she said, putting a hand to his chest, "and I *have* to do them."

Islington tightened his jaw and looked away, raising his hands up and away from her. Pandora looked at him and started to say something, but instead she moved to the edge of the bed and pulled on her boots. She buttoned her shirt and tucked it back in all around then buttoned her waistcoat and stood up. She threw more wood on the fire and lit more torches. After she lit the second one, near the nook, she looked down at the bed and saw Islington with his arms folded across his chest, his expression morose.

"There are no servants here, *àiren,* and unless you can figure out a way to make food magically appear from the air, we are going to starve if *I* can't find some," she said quietly.

She refilled his cup with water and placed it on the chair before putting on her coat and hat, placing her fishing kit into the pocket, and going to the open room for the horses. She angrily wiped the tears off her cheeks and haltered the horses to lead them out to the trough. It was lightly misting, but it wouldn't bother the horses; the grass would taste just the same, and there was no longer thunder and lightning to frighten them. She led them to the meadow and returned to the yard.

She shivered slightly in the mist and pulled the collar of her coat closer around her neck as she tried to decide what to use for bait. She looked at her watch. It was after six. It was too wet for crickets. She went to the fertile, loose soil of the garden and turned over a few rocks here and there. Plenty of worms. She looked through the pile of refuse that had been collecting and retrieved an old leather boot she had thrown there. The lace was missing, and it had started to come unsewn, but it would suit. She went to the garden, and after swallowing distastefully a few times, she picked up several of the worms and tossed them into the boot. She hoped she wouldn't have to go through all of them before catching a fish.

Once she had enough worms, she took the boot with her through the woods and down to the beach. When she looked back, it was difficult to see the cottage, but she could just make out the light glowing from its single window. She hoped she could catch a fish before it became too dark, or she might have trouble finding her way back. She found a rock to sit on and pulled her fishing kit out of her pocket. She threaded the line through one of her hooks and attached a sinker, and then a little further up the line, she placed the bobber. She thought about finding a makeshift pole, but the bobber would be sufficient.

Then the moment arrived that she was dreading. It was hopeless to think the worm would go on the hook and stay there if all she did was ask politely. She reached into the boot, ignoring the slimy sensation from all the worms wiggling and grabbed one. She held the hook in one hand and the worm in the other for a few minutes, and then as her face wrinkled into a moue of disgust, she put the worm on the hook. She retched a couple times and let go after she made sure it wasn't going to come loose. She moved to the river's edge and tossed her line in close to the middle of the channel.

She kept a firm grip on it, wrapping it once around her hand, because the river hadn't receded any over the days since she saw it last and was, if anything, worse after the most recent rain. She stood on the riverbank, impatiently waiting for something to tug on the line. She shifted from one foot to the other, wondering how long it would take. She put her free hand in her pocket to warm it because she no longer had her gloves.

About that time, she felt a sharper pull on her line than what was caused by the current. She grinned excitedly as she began to haul the line toward the shore. She wasn't sure what she caught, but it was fighting. She would let a little bit of line unwind from her hand before winding it back on again, pulling as hard as she could. She almost had it to the shore when she felt the oddest sensation. Whatever was on there was now *crawling* up the line toward her instead of fighting to get loose. She tried not to panic and continued to pull the line in, hoping she was imagining things. But then she saw it starting to *slither* past the bobber.

She squeaked in fright and nearly dropped the line and ran, but she was curious to know what it was, because it was most definitely *not* a salmon or a trout. It was a little over a foot long and solid black. She thought it was an eel, but it wasn't like any she had ever seen. It didn't seem to have a head or a mouth really, but she could see the hook attached to it. After watching for a few more minutes, she decided she had seen enough and reached into her coat for her pocketknife. She found a nearby rock and pulled as much of the line toward her as she could before the thing reached her. She cut the line and sighed with relief when she watched it disappear back into the river.

She walked over to the rock where she had placed her boot and fishing kit to re-do her line. She only hoped this time she wouldn't catch another one of those *things*. It had looked vile. She retched again as she put the worm on the hook and walked with some trepidation back to the edge of the river to throw in her line.

She had only to wait a few minutes when something once again began to tug at her line. It felt even stronger than the thing. She pulled and fought with it for the better part of thirty minutes before she was able to get it to shore. It was at least a fish, but it was a lot smaller than she had thought it would be. It didn't weigh any more than two pounds.

Pandora watched as it continued to flop around on the sand and gravel, trying to get back to the water. She kept her hand on the line and walked back to the rock for her kit to retrieve her pliers and put them in her pocket. She nervously stepped closer to the fish, but every time she tried to grab it with her hand to remove the hook, it would flip away from her. She looked down at her hand and saw the slime coating it. She felt queasy. She gulped a few times and grabbed a rock that filled the palm of her hand and squatted by the fish. Once it stopped flopping for a few seconds, she hit it in the head with the rock, and it quit moving completely. She unwound the fishing line from her hand and pulled her pliers out of her pocket. She removed the hook from the fish's mouth and looked at it where it lay on the shore for a few minutes.

She stood up and took a few deep breaths then walked back to her kit to retrieve the net bag folded up inside it. She scooped the fish into it and took it to the river to run through the water to rinse off the sand. She cleaned her pliers and put away her things into the kit, and then she headed back to the cottage.

Once she got back to the yard, she released the worms she hadn't used back into the garden and tossed the boot back on the refuse pile. She found a place where she could clean the fish and dispose of the parts that wouldn't be used, and then she threw up once she was done. When she was done doing that, she weakly went to the pump and cleaned the taste out of her mouth, and Pandora knew she never wanted to go fishing again.

Chapter Twenty-Three

Pandora carried the cut-up fish into the cottage on a small piece of wood from the barn. She had other intentions for her pans, so she would use the piece of wet oak set on the shelf in the fireplace to cook it. She wasn't sure it would work, but she was using what she had available. She set it on the table for the time being and removed her fishing kit from her pocket to set there as well. She didn't look at the corner where Islington was when she came in. She just set down her items and quietly left again to retrieve the horses. It was after eight, and it was hard to see.

The horses were happy for their short time in the meadow, and she let them stop at the trough before she took them inside. She unhaltered them, wound up the rope to put away, and then she went back outside to the overgrown garden. She took off her hat to use as a bowl and cut off some of the dill and rosemary. She picked some of the lettuce and spinach and put those in as well. She started to turn back for the house when she noticed something she had previously mistaken for grass. She pulled at one of the bunches and found tiny pearl onions. She didn't know how she had missed those before. She went back to the cottage, stopping by the pump to rinse the dirt from the onions, and carried all of it in to set on the table.

She removed her coat and laid it on the nearby chair. She leaned her hands on the table and looked at what she had. Supper would be interesting, at least. She would save the peas and onions for tomorrow, but tonight's meal would use most everything they had, except for—of course—apples. What she would serve tomorrow besides peas, onions, apples, and pears was a mystery, but she would *not* go fishing…ever again.

She went to the fireplace for the kettle of leftover broth and peeled and cut the carrots and turnips into it. She added a little more water, some of the onions, and some of the rosemary, and she put it on the shelf in the fireplace to cook. She got the pan from her saddlebag and cut up some apples and pears and added the raisins. She poured her remaining nuts onto the table and chopped them into small pieces then got the bottle of plum wine. She poured some of the wine over the fruit, sprinkled the nuts on top, and put that into the fireplace to cook as well. She used her knife to cut thin slits in the fish and stuffed a few sprigs of dill into each piece and took it to the fireplace. She would keep a close eye on it so the wood wouldn't dry out and catch fire, but the fish shouldn't take long to cook.

She took the bucket for drinking water to the pump and refilled it and brought it back then did the same with the washing bucket to take care of the dishes after they ate. She went back to the table and picked up the bottle of plum wine, but instead of putting it back in her bag, Pandora tipped the bottle up and drank what was left without stopping.

"Pandora, what are you doing?" asked Islington in disbelief.

He had been waiting for her to talk to him. He had seen her return with the fish and had noted her pallor. He had watched as she prepared their supper and tended to other things. He supposed he deserved her silence after the way he had behaved before she left; he realized not long after she had gone that it was uncalled for. But to see her pick up the bottle of wine like that was completely unexpected.

Pandora ignored him. Once she was done, she calmly set the empty bottle on the table and daintily wiped her upper lip with her little finger and cleaned it off in her mouth. Then she looked in his direction.

"Yes?" she asked calmly, arching her eyebrow.

"Why did you do that?" he asked, trying to ignore how erotic he found her actions when she was finished.

"Plum wine doesn't keep very long once it's been uncorked. I didn't want it to go to waste," she said dryly. "I would have offered to share, but you've already had some."

The wine didn't have a high alcohol content, but Pandora had nothing in her stomach. It immediately began to have an effect, and the tension she had been feeling after fishing began to soften. It helped the residual pain she had been feeling from her headache, and it also made her able to look at Islington without being so disappointed.

She went to the fireplace and checked the fish. The wood was holding up nicely. She had placed it far enough away from the fire that the fish would be done before the wood dried out. She hoped Islington liked it; she wasn't having any. She looked up from checking the food and saw Islington leaning around the fireplace.

"Are you feeling all right?" he asked her concernedly.

"Peachy," she said with a cheeky grin.

"I should think so after drinking a bottle of wine," said Islington dryly, holding back a smile. He had the impression she was tipsy.

"It wasn't a *full* bottle of wine. It wasn't even *half* full," she defended.

"Are you sure you should be around a fire?"

Pandora came over to stand in front of him, one hand on her hip, the other holding the knife she had been using to turn the fish.

"And what's *that* supposed to mean?" she asked tartly.

Islington looked at her. "Absolutely nothing."

"Hunh," scoffed Pandora with a shrug.

She looked down and noticed the chamber pot was not where she had placed it. She would take care of that *after* supper; doing it now would completely destroy her already nearly nonexistent appetite.

She went back to the fireplace to tend to dinner. The fish was by far the fastest thing to cook. It wasn't long before she could flake it with her knife. She looked for something to remove it from the fire, but she unbuttoned her waistcoat and removed it to use. She reached in and pulled out the piece of wood and set it on the hearth. The vegetables were almost done and so was her fruit creation. She had no idea how either would taste, but she thought she would be able to eat enough of them to make up for not having any fish.

"Would you like some salad?" she asked Islington.

"Yes, please," he said politely, not wanting a repeat of the knife stance.

He was astonished when she walked over to the table, tossed the greens in her hat, and brought it to him.

"Here you go. Eat what you want, and I'll finish the rest," she said calmly. "Provided, of course, there's more than just the hat left."

Islington looked from her to the hat. "Are you sure you're not drunk?"

"No, I am *not* drunk!" said Pandora testily. "I'm sorry, but the Spode doesn't travel well," she said blithely.

Islington took the hat from her, trying not to laugh. He began to eat the "salad" with his fingers. Eating it from the hat didn't do anything to the flavor one way or the other, so he shrugged and ate about half of it, leaving behind most of the spinach. He could hear Pandora moving around plates and pots, and he looked around the corner as she removed the pan containing the fruit. The smell drifted over to him, and it seemed familiar. She said he had some of the wine, which is what he assumed he smelled, but he certainly didn't remember it.

"What is that?" he asked interestedly.

Pandora looked at him. "I have absolutely no idea what to call it. It's not a pandowdy or a pie. I'll just call it dessert." She grinned.

Islington looked at her. She *said* she wasn't drunk, but she was acting just the least bit strange...almost euphoric. He wondered if it might have anything to do with her migraine.

"How's your head?" he asked mildly.

"Fine," she said calmly as she began to put food on their plates.

Actually, he was surprised to see her put fish and vegetables onto the plate she had been using for him and ladled some of the vegetables and broth into the bowl. He assumed that was what she intended to eat, and his forehead wrinkled perplexedly.

"Are you not having fish?"

"No," she drew out, shaking her head.

She held her chopsticks with her teeth and carried the dishes to the bed. She set her bowl on the chair and then took her hat away from him and handed him his plate. She sat on the edge of the bed and began to eat calmly. Islington looked down at his plate.

"Why are you not having fish?" he asked curiously.

It smelled more than edible. He carefully flaked a piece off and put it in his mouth. It *was* more than edible. He didn't think he'd ever had smoked trout that tasted as good. He looked at her expectantly.

"I'd rather not talk about it," she said softly, eating her spinach.

"It tastes very good."

"Marvelous. I'm glad it turned out," said Pandora, pointedly ignoring the fish on his plate and continuing to eat her greens. "You don't like spinach, I see," she said mildly as she flipped the leaves over in her hat.

"Not especially, no."

Pandora shrugged and continued to eat from her hat. The vegetables weren't as good as the cabbage. They weren't intolerable, but they were plain, even with the onions and rosemary. They could desperately do with some salt. It would have been worse without the leftover broth. Pandora ate it regardless because she didn't know when she would be able to eat anything more than fruit again. She saw Islington was having the same difficulty. Fortunately (or unfortunately, depending on perspective), there weren't any vegetables left except for the peas and onions.

"Would you like more fish?"

"Oh, yes," said Islington with a smile. "You really should try some."

"I'm sorry, but I *cannot* eat that fish," said Pandora shortly as she took his plate from him.

"Is it that you don't eat fish or this particular fish?"

"Just this particular fish," said Pandora as she came back and handed him his plate. Then, her forehead wrinkled thoughtfully. "Actually, not any fish now."

"That bad?" he asked gently.

"Could we, please, not talk about it?" she asked tightly, giving him an aggravated look. "It's hard enough keeping my food down already."

Islington's eyebrow shot up at her tone. He ate all the fish on his plate with relish. He was surprised by how few bones there were. Trout were usually rather bony. Then he looked at Pandora.

"You didn't try to pull *all* the bones out, did you?" he asked in disbelief.

"No, I didn't. There were too many, and it was too dark. Besides, after I...when I...ah, bloody hell!" she groaned, and she got up from the bed and ran to the door with her hand over her mouth.

Islington watched her go with dismay. Now he felt guilty. She had asked him not to talk about it and said it was bothering her, and he had persisted. He couldn't understand how he always managed to make things worse for her. He usually considered himself to be quite capable and effective, but she always left him feeling inadequate. He wanted to think his finding her was better for her, but all he had done so far had seemed to make it more difficult.

After a few minutes, Pandora came back. Her face was pale, and her forehead was creased tiredly.

"Pandora—" began Islington.

Pandora held up her hand. "Shh. Don't talk to me," she said softly.

She went to the bed and took his plate, and then she put some of the dessert onto it and brought it back after she had scraped the few bones into the fire. She went to her bag for her toothbrush and tooth powder and went outside. She soon returned and put her things away, and then she went to the bed, retrieved the chamber pot, and went back out. She came back with it and put it under the bed, also carrying soapwort to wash the dishes. She looked at Islington and noticed he hadn't eaten the dessert.

"You better eat that," she said flatly, giving him a stern look.

Islington did as he was told. It wasn't difficult. Whatever it was she had made was delicious. He had never had anything like it. Considering who she was, he was amazed she was able to cook, seemingly with no effort. The only thing she had fed him that had been less than wonderful was the vegetables she had made that night, and even those had been edible. They would have been fine if she had some salt. He soon finished and leaned around the edge of the fireplace to look at her.

"I'm done," he said calmly.

"Would you like more?" she asked as she came to get his plate.

"No, thank you. I'm full. You should eat some," he said softly.

"I'm not hungry," she said firmly as she took the plate to the bucket and washed it.

She poured what was left of the tea and took a small sip. The torches were guttering, and she checked her watch. It was nearing eleven. That would be at least one of the reasons she was tired. She had hoped to shave Islington, but she would save that for tomorrow…after she went looking for food. She added more wood to the fire and finished her tea.

"Do you need more chamomile?" she asked Islington as she came around to sit on the bed beside him, yawning tiredly.

"No, I'm fine for now. Are you coming to bed?"

"Yes."

He watched with interest as she removed all her clothes except her chemise without any hesitation. After last night and that morning, for her to make him not look would be ridiculous and a show of false modesty at best. She seemed to realize that. She climbed over him and settled herself under the blanket.

"Do you need help lying down, or are you comfortable that way?"

"I think it helps to sleep like this," he said, looking at her questioningly. "I can lie down on my own now, if I need to."

She was distant, and he couldn't blame her. He appreciated that Pandora had made sure he was cared for despite how upset he had made her. She turned on her side away from him facing the wall, her arm folded under her head for a pillow. Islington looked down at her. He had made her unhappy…again. He reached over and gently ran his hand down her back. He felt her stiffen, and she rolled over to look at him.

"You *cannot* be serious!" she said in disbelief.

"I just want to hold you," he said calmly, and Pandora felt ashamed at his hurt expression.

Pandora looked at him for a few long minutes, but she rolled over and curled into him, placing her head on his chest and putting one of her arms across his waist. Islington put his arms around her and sighed peacefully, closing his eyes, rubbing a soothing hand on her back. She didn't stiffen again, and he soon felt her relax onto him even more as she drifted off to sleep. He enjoyed having her pressed against him, inhaling the scent of her, and he was soon able to go to sleep as well.

Pandora awoke to a gnawing hunger. She lifted her head slightly and was about to get up to pull the cord for Maiyin to bring her tea and toast when she remembered she wasn't at home. She opened her eyes slowly and blinked, looking around herself at the cottage. She'd had a nightmare about some long, black, slithery thing with sharp, pointy fangs chasing her through endless water, but her night had been, for the most part, dreamless.

Islington had moved down onto his back and changed position during the night. She felt her head nestled beneath his chin. He was holding her hand in his left on his chest, and his right hand had come to rest just at the top of her buttocks. Pandora could tell from his occasional soft snores that he was sound asleep. He had said he just wanted to hold her, and that is all he had done. She liked being held by him; it gave her a feeling of contentment to wake up wrapped possessively in his arms every morning.

Then Pandora's mind turned to the reason they were at the cottage, why both of them were so far away from the things that were familiar to them. She did some mental calculations, and she realized with some anxiety that she had only nine days to reach Edinburgh and warn the count before he left for London. Despite everything that had happened, Pandora had to warn him. If she didn't, it would all be for nothing.

She hadn't stated her intentions to Islington, had pointedly *not* mentioned them to him. He had been determined to make her go back to London when they were on the bridge before he got shot, and she hadn't forgotten that. She couldn't leave him here, especially because he was injured without anyone to take care of him if she left, but she could feel an even greater urgency for him to get better.

She began to wonder about that. How much longer would it be before he could travel? He seemed to be healing extremely fast. He hadn't tried to get out of bed again, but he managed when she helped him take a bath. He also did well with other activities, although she had done most of the work. How much longer would it be before could ride? Despite what he had said, Jezebel was gentle, and she wouldn't be difficult to control as long as he didn't try to ride her the way he had been. If he went with Pandora to Edinburgh, she would make sure he didn't. But she didn't see him willingly letting her go. It was pointless to mention it until he was well enough to stay or go on his own.

She turned her eyes to look out the window at the sky. It was gray, but it was still early yet. She couldn't tell whether it was going to be sunny, and for the moment, she didn't care. She still felt sleepy, but she was also hungry. Her appetite had returned, and that was what woke her. She wasn't ready to get out of bed, though. As long as she stayed there, she didn't have to worry about anything. She felt safe where she was. It was a false sense of security, but she was willing to pretend. As long as she stayed there snuggled against Islington, there was no cleaning, no tending to the animals, and no need to find food.

Pandora didn't know what she was going to do. They couldn't live on apples and pears...well, they could, but she would much rather not. She was heartily tired of apples. She couldn't fish again; she would rather starve. Hunting for rabbits or birds was also out of the question. It had been distressing enough with the fish. Aside from that, her skill with a gun wasn't good enough, and it would be difficult to do with her bow. She needed to find something else for Islington. He would never get well on a diet of apples and pears...not even one supplemented by leaf lettuce and spinach. For now, though, she didn't have to think about it.

She snuggled closer to Islington and closed her eyes. She felt his hand move soothingly on her back, and Pandora looked up at his face. He was awake, somewhat, looking down at her sleepily. She had been so deep in thought that she hadn't heard the change in his breathing. He was tousled and rough from needing a shave, but he looked so unguarded, it made Pandora's heart flutter.

"Good morning," he said softly, bringing her hand to his lips for a kiss and trying to ignore the stiffness in his shoulder.

"Good morning," replied Pandora breathlessly. "You're not sitting up anymore."

"You had a bad dream," he said by way of explanation, rubbing his hand on her back again.

Pandora's eyes rounded in surprise. She hadn't realized she might have been flailing around or something when she had her nightmare. It *had* been vivid and frightening. The thing was chasing her because she caught the fish. She tried to swim away from it, and telling it that she needed food didn't make it stop. Thankfully, she couldn't remember how it ended. She rose up on her elbow and looked down at him.

"I'm sorry you had to move. I hope I didn't bother you too much."

Islington ran a finger down her cheek. "No bother," he said absently, moving his finger down the side of her neck to trace her collarbone.

Pandora leaned forward to kiss him, simply because he looked so utterly kissable, and his intent gaze made her stomach turn somersaults. The roughness of the stubble on his chin caused an interesting sensation, and she reached up her hand to his cheek to feel it against her palm. He moved a hand to cup her bottom and slid her further on top of him, and her head came up in surprise when she felt his arousal.

"Do you always wake up like that?" she asked in amazement.

"Like what?" he asked confusedly.

Pandora reached down to trace her fingers along his erection, and she watched the way he breathed in sharply. Islington grinned wickedly and ran his fingers in circles over the skin of her bottom.

"Always," he said silkily.

"Oh, my," said Pandora with a blink as she thought about it. "Are all men like that?"

Islington found it somewhat disturbing she might be thinking about other men, especially considering how curious she was. He didn't want to think she might be tempted to find out.

"Mostly, yes," he said flatly.

"Extraordinary!" said Pandora, her eyes round with wonder.

She leaned forward to kiss him again, smoothing a hand down his chest to one of his nipples, and Islington soon forgot about his concern as she continued to explore with her fingertips and mouth. She was quickly becoming skilled at finding the things that excited him, and she had even discovered a few he hadn't realized existed.

She rose up at one point on her knees to take off her chemise, and Islington noticed her hair was steadily working loose from her braid. Once she came close enough, he reached behind her and worked it loose the rest of the way, and he felt goose bumps as it fanned across his skin like feathers. She sat back up to look at him, and Islington felt his heart tighten as he thought he had never seen anything more beautiful. She swept it away from her face with one of her hands and grinned at him.

"You might regret doing that," she said as she straddled his lap and bent forward to kiss him. "It gets everywhere."

"I've never seen you with your hair down," said Islington, reaching up to touch the spiraled tendrils with his fingers before he moved his hands down to cup her breasts.

Islington surprised her when he managed to roll over and place her beneath him, balancing some of his weight off of her onto his right arm, bent at the elbow near her head.

"You're getting better," she said softly, smoothing her hands down his back to gently run her fingernails across his buttocks and rub one of her legs against his.

"We'll see," he said with a smile as he slowly pushed into her, enjoying the way her breath caught as he filled her completely.

He stayed still inside her, bending down to kiss her and bring up his left hand between them to cup her breast and tease the nipple between his fingers. She moved her hips against his impatiently, and he smiled against her lips as he kissed her, raising himself up to thrust into her solidly. She moaned and gently bit his bottom lip in playful retaliation.

He steadily began to move in and out of her, taking his time to conserve energy and reduce the risk of injuring himself. He shouldn't have done it this way, but he *needed* to feel her beneath him. He could feel the way she raised her hips to meet his as she moved nearer to her climax becoming less coordinated and driven more by instinct than thought, and her breath came out in gasps and sighs of inarticulate pleasure. Her eyes were closed in abandon as an expression of ecstatic wonder lit up her features, and she cried out his name disjointedly and began to shudder as she orgasmed. Islington felt the intensity of it, and he reached his own shortly after. He sucked in his breath between his teeth as the pleasure of his climax was tempered by a stabbing pain through his side, and he lowered his head to tenderly kiss her neck, trying with difficulty to breathe through the sharp twinge in his ribs.

Pandora cradled his head against her breasts, smoothing a hand across his sweat-dampened hair and back. She could hear the slight hitch at the end of every breath he took, and she knew without much effort that he had overestimated how well he was. She stifled a yawn with one of her hands and rearranged the blankets over them. She could feel the prickly sensation of the stubble on his face against her breasts, and she decided he definitely needed a shave just as she drifted back to a satiated sleep, her hunger temporarily forgotten.

Pandora didn't know how long she slept, but when she opened her eyes, Islington was propped up on his elbow looking down at her, running his fingers through her hair in fascination. He was no longer lying on top of her, and he was able to breathe normally again. She smiled sleepily when he saw that she was awake and reached up to rub her hand across his jaw. The stubble tickled against her palm and made a rasping noise when she did it, and she chuckled amusedly.

"I don't suppose you have a razor?" she asked, stretching languidly.

"I do," he said absently, running his fingers down the side of her neck to the edge of one breast before resting his hand on her stomach. "It would be hard for me to use without a mirror, though, and with my right hand."

"I can do it for you," she offered breathlessly as his hand came back up to begin teasing one of her nipples.

His hand stopped at her suggestion and he looked at her dubiously, one of his eyebrows raised.

"Have I done something to make you angry?" he teased.

"No," she almost purred as he resumed his touching. "I know how to use a razor. It's how I used to do my legs before I made my depilatory."

"And you still have legs?" he continued.

"Ooh," she groaned. "I assure you my legs are perfectly fine," she said aggravatedly.

"Oh, I agree," he said with a lecherous smile as he bent down to kiss her thoroughly.

"You're just trying to distract me," she said breathlessly after he raised his head.

He shrugged. "Perhaps," he said with a grin. "Perhaps not."

Pandora looked at him poutily and fluttered her eyelashes playfully. He looked askance at her. He could do with a shave, and she seemed insistent he let her do it, but he had just recovered from blood loss; he wasn't sure his body could survive it again so soon.

"All right, I'll risk it," he said finally. Pandora grinned victoriously. "But, I would like to die with some dignity—out of bed in some clothes."

"We can arrange that," said Pandora agreeably as she engaged in some teasing of her own, running a hand down the outside of his thigh under the blanket before casually running it back up the inside to brush across his semi-erect member and up his chest. "I don't suppose you know what time it is."

"Morning…sometime, I think," he said slowly, waiting to see what she was going to do.

Pandora sighed longingly. It would be nice to make love again, but there were things to do.

"You have things to do, don't you?" said Islington calmly.

"Always," sighed Pandora resignedly.

She sat up and looked for her chemise. Once she found it, she pulled it over her head and pulled her hair free. She would re-braid it after she brushed it. She leaned forward to kiss Islington and got out of bed.

It was cold in the cottage. There were barely any embers left, and Pandora leaned forward to blow on them to start the wood burning after she added more. She pulled her head back quickly as her hair brushed through the ashes. She shook it and reached for the nearby chopsticks, twisting her hair around them and using them to pin it up securely on the back of her head out of the way. She leaned forward again to blow on the coals, and the wood finally caught and began to burn.

She looked at the remnants of their supper from the night before. There was a little trout left, which she was sure Islington would eat, and also most of the dessert. She filled the teapot with water and put it on to boil. There were only enough leaves left for two more pots, at most. She would miss it when it was gone; her day just did not seem right if she didn't have at least one cup of tea.

Once she had that tended to, she put her clothes on and braided her hair. She took down Islington's clothes from the mantel and carried them to him. It was only his socks, trousers, and his waistcoat with the hole in it. She set them on the edge of the bed.

"Can you bring me my bag?" he asked as he looked at the clothes.

Pandora shrugged agreeably and went to get it from where she had placed it with the rest of their luggage on the far side of the cottage. She set that on the edge of the bed as well. She watched as Islington pulled out another shirt, and her brow furrowed thoughtfully.

"We'll have to undo your shoulder," she said as she watched him sit up and move to the edge of the bed.

She needed to take the horses to the meadow, but she didn't want to leave until she was sure he was able to get dressed. She looked at her watch and was surprised to see it was nearing eleven. She watched as he pulled the trousers onto his legs after he put on the socks, and then he stood to pull them up the rest of the way. He must have risen too quickly because he started to weave in place. Pandora moved forward and reached out steadying hands. She looked at him concernedly.

"Are you sure you want to do this?" she asked, watching as his eyes slowly refocused.

"Any longer in that bed, I'm just being lazy," he said with a smile.

Pandora fastened the waistband, but she didn't do the buttons at the bottom. She would only do those if he was well enough to put his boots on. Pandora didn't think he was. He was fine when he was lying or sitting down, but he still became dizzy if he stood up for too long.

"Sit back down, and I'll undo your shoulder to put your shirt on," she said, and she watched assessingly as he did, weaving again momentarily.

She carefully unwound the muslin, rolling it up so that she would be able to put it back on once his shirt was on. Before she put on the shirt, she got the ointment and put more on his side and shoulder. She helped him into the shirt and tied it for him.

"Your waistcoat, too?" she asked, holding it in her hands.

"Yes," he said, resting his left forearm on his lap to relieve some of the pressure of it hanging on his shoulder.

Pandora helped him put it on and buttoned it. Once it was on, she rewrapped his shoulder. It looked strange, but it pained him less when it was on. Unfortunately, his waistcoat buttoned in the wrong direction, or he could have used it to rest his hand inside of like a sling to relieve the weight even further. The bandage fit tighter over the clothing, which braced it even better, but he was either resting it on his lap or holding it in his right hand to keep it from hanging after a while.

"Now, for my cravat," he said, looking at the piece of fabric.

"We don't need to worry about that, not until I shave you. Besides, it's not as if anyone is going to see you—except me, and I don't care."

Islington shrugged agreeably. "What about my boots?"

"If you can make it to the chair by the table without me helping you, then we'll put on your boots," said Pandora, calmly folding her arms.

Islington looked at her; then he looked at the table. It was a short distance. He shouldn't have any problem doing that. He had been doing rather strenuous activities in bed; *walking* shouldn't be a problem. He stood up again, and he started to weave. Pandora began to reach out a steadying hand but restrained herself when he straightened out again. Islington started for the table, but after taking only one or two steps, he began to weave;, and Pandora had to get to his side and take his arm before he fell. She helped him to the chair.

"No boots," she said firmly.

The lid on the teapot began to rattle, and Pandora removed it to make tea. While she was at the fireplace, she put what was left of the trout onto a plate for Islington and added some of the fruit. When she went to the table, she noticed he continued to hold his forearm with his right hand and shook her head. She retrieved his sling from where it was draped over the back of the chair by the bed and put it on.

"You can't eat if you have to hold your arm," she said calmly as he looked about to protest.

She poured him a cup of tea and one for herself after she pushed the water left in the large kettle back over the fire to begin heating and took the cups to the table. She cleared off the chair by the bed and took it to the table to sit down. After a few minutes, she reached into the bag of sugar lumps and pulled one out to put some chamomile on for him. Islington looked at it for a minute as if he weren't going to take it, but she continued to hold it until he did.

"Did you think you would be completely fine?" she asked him gently after a few minutes when she noticed his frown. "You could have *died.*"

Pandora watched as a nerve ticked in his jaw. She knew why he wasn't happy. He thought the fainting and dizziness were unmanly. Pandora didn't think of it that way. He was doing remarkably well, all things considered. She had no expectations of him being completely capable, and the things he *was* able to do were more than adequate for her. When he still sat silently eating, Pandora grabbed a pear from the table for herself and two of the apples for the horses and stood. She bent down and kissed the side of his neck and rubbed his back soothingly.

"I'm taking the horses to the meadow. I'll shave you when I come back," she said quietly.

Pandora took her time with the horses. Islington needed some time alone. He didn't like depending on her, even if he appreciated the job she had done. He was a man, and it was only natural. He thought it should be reversed, that she should depend on him. Now that he was getting better and out of bed, he thought he should be able to immediately resume his role in the natural order of things, and it chafed him to find out he couldn't. She didn't expect him to, but it was what he expected of himself. Although there were occasions when he could be unreasonable, Pandora believed he would realize that on his own eventually.

She tethered the horses to their trees and walked a little further into the woods on the other side of the meadow. She had found the fruit trees the previous day by going a different route back to the cottage; she was hopeful she might find more food going another way. The thought of eating nothing but fruit for the remainder of whatever time they were at the cottage didn't appeal to Pandora, and she wished she would have been able to tolerate fishing, but she couldn't.

She wished it had been her who was shot. It should have been. The man who did it had been in front of her and taken issue with *her*, not Islington. If she had been the one shot, it would be easier for Islington to find food. They couldn't be far from a town or village. Even Aysgarth couldn't be more than a mile or so upstream. Because she was a woman, Pandora couldn't stroll into town and buy things, and that made it complicated. Until recently, she thought she had been doing well.

She hadn't walked more than a quarter of a mile when she could see the trees clearing ahead of her. She walked toward it and found herself on the edge of a huge vegetable garden. Beyond it, she could see a small house and barn. She could tell by the size that it wasn't someone's kitchen plot; the owner obviously grew the vegetables to take to market to sell. It was mostly maize, but there were cabbages, peas, and turnips, and what might also be potatoes. Pandora began to salivate.

She quickly ducked behind a tree when she saw someone working in the field. She chanced a peek around the edge of her hiding place and saw the farmer tending to the rows, weeding and occasionally pinching off buds and beginning vegetables that were damaged or stunted. It wouldn't be much longer before he would harvest the produce to sell.

Pandora looked everything over closely, judging the distance from the edge of the woods to the first rows of the garden. She had walked in a fairly straight line from the meadow to the field. She had walked often enough to the meadow that she wouldn't have any trouble finding her way there, even in the dark. After one last, longing look at the vegetables, she turned and went back into the woods, a plan forming in her mind. Pandora walked back to the meadow, taking note of any unusual trees or other objects in the landscape along her route. She checked on the horses and returned to the cottage.

Islington was still sitting at the table when she got there, but she hadn't thought he would try to move. After fainting and completely collapsing on the floor, he did have some sense of self-preservation. He looked up when she came in, and his expression had, if not completely improved, at least changed to one of boredom.

"Let's get you shaved," she said with a grin as she pulled the kettle from over the fire.

"I can hardly wait," said Islington unenthusiastically.

Pandora got his bag from the bed and took it to him. She could have dug through it to find things herself, but she didn't feel comfortable going through it, not any more than she would feel comfortable having him go through her valise; she would rather have him get his things. He removed his razor, a strop, a brush and a cup with soap caked into the bottom of it, and a small bottle of some brownish liquid. He looked down at the things on the table, and then he looked up at Pandora.

"Are you sure you can do this?" he asked nervously.

Pandora bent down to kiss his cheek as she grabbed his plate from the table to put on the hearth to wash. She was smiling amusedly as she came back. She casually lifted the bottle of brown liquid and opened it to smell a hint of sandalwood and realized it was his shaving lotion. She could perfectly understand why he was anxious.

"It will be fine," she said calmly.

He stood up while she turned the chair around then sat back down. After she dipped the brush in the hot water, she turned it upside down beside the cup and went to get her towel and flannel. She went to put some of the hot water from the kettle into the washing bucket. She dipped the flannel into the bucket and placed it over his face after she had drained some of the excess water and let it cool slightly. She laughed amusedly when he stuck out his tongue to make it pooch out.

"Are you planning to melt it off?" he asked through the cloth.

"You'll see."

She worked the soap with the brush and lifted it to his face after she removed the cloth, applying it to his face and neck, working it into a wonderfully thick lather, playfully swirling it into interesting patterns.

"You do realize you're not instilling any confidence by doing that?"

"Shush," said Pandora with a giggle.

She opened the razor and passed it up and down on the strop for what Islington thought was an eternity, but she soon stopped to look at him. She tilted her head sideways as she thought about which side she would start on. Once she made up her mind, she had him lean his head back slightly and began. She would make a pass with the grain, rinse the blade then draw it across against the grain. Her hand moved skillfully, and her forehead was wrinkled with concentration as she worked. Once she was done with his face, she had him tilt his head back further and shaved his neck. Islington tried not to swallow until she was done. She wiped the little remaining lather from his face then tilted his head one way and the other to examine her handiwork.

"Don't move."

She went outside with the cloth and came back to put it on his face, freezing cold from the pump. She left it there for a few minutes and removed it, and then she patted his face dry with the towel and smoothed on some of the lotion.

"How's that?" she asked as she began to clean things up.

Islington reached up and ran a hand across his face and grinned.

"My valet doesn't even do that well," he said admirably, reaching out to wrap an arm around her waist and pull her close.

Pandora bent down to kiss him, putting a hand to his cheek, and she found the scent of his freshly-shaved skin intoxicating. She raised her head with a teasing grin.

"I bet you don't do *that* to your valet."

"Oh, no, Tompkins is much too stuffy for that," said Islington, moving his hand down to grab her bottom. "I do occasionally pinch his cheek, though," he teased.

"I'm sure you do," said Pandora with a grin, smoothing her hands across his cheeks to his neck then gently resting her hands on his shoulders. Her expression turned serious. "I may have found more food for us."

"Do tell," said Islington mildly as he continued to smooth his hand over her bottom. "Are you going to fish again?"

"No," said Pandora firmly, and she shuddered at the thought of it. "I found some vegetables, but I won't be able to get them until tonight."

Islington's hand stopped moving, and he looked at her inquiringly. "Why would that be?"

"Because the farmer they belong to would probably see me taking them if I did it in broad daylight," said Pandora softly.

"No," said Islington flatly, shaking his head.

"It's a market garden. I wouldn't be taking food from his table. I would never do that," said Pandora earnestly.

"No," said Islington again.

"I'm not going to take much, only a cabbage or two and perhaps some potatoes. We need more than just apples and pears. I'm sick to death of apples, and you'll never get well eating that."

"I'm getting well enough without you stealing, Pandora," he said sharply.

"I will leave him some money!" said Pandora exasperatedly. "I would even leave a note, except I don't happen to have a paper and pen handy to do it, and there wouldn't be any guarantee he could read it."

Islington looked askance at her. He wished more than ever that he was better. He felt guilty Pandora had been reduced to midnight raids on a farmer's garden to provide for them. He should be taking care of *her*. If they had one more day, two at the most, he could find a village and get all the food they needed. She continued to look at him pleadingly.

"You will leave him money?" he asked searchingly.

Pandora bent down and kissed him. "I *promise* I will pay the man," she said solemnly.

Islington continued to look at her worriedly. He didn't like this at all. He was sure in one more day he would be able to walk on his own without the dizziness, or at least little enough of it that she wouldn't be so concerned about him falling on his face. He understood why she couldn't find a village to buy food. Even if there weren't people there to gossip about it in London, a woman walking around in men's clothes just wasn't something any level of society considered appropriate. If she were going to get them food, and for now she was the only one who could, unless she could find something growing wild to sustain them, getting it from someone's garden was her only option.

He understood why she didn't want to fish anymore. He didn't know exactly what her nightmare had been about, but she had muttered enough for him to realize she had been traumatized by whatever had happened while she was fishing. Even if she did go fishing again, she wouldn't eat it, so that would still leave her without food.

"You promise me you'll be careful," he said firmly.

"I will be careful," said Pandora softly, sitting down to straddle his lap and kiss him, moving along his jawline to his ear.

"All right," he sighed, moving his hand up her side to cup her breast.

"I'm done with all my work for now."

"Then I suppose we'll have to find something to keep you occupied," grinned Islington, working at the buttons on her waistcoat.

Pandora left the cottage and quietly closed the door. Islington was on his way to sleep. He was worried, but he was also exhausted. His freedom from the bed had been short-lived, but he hadn't been idle once he returned to it. Other than when she had occasionally gone to check on and water the horses or tend to some other small chore like adding wood to the fire, they had spent most of the day making love. Pandora really didn't have anything else to do; the cottage was as sufficient as it could be, and now she was just waiting for him to get better. She did realize, however, that their activities were not helping matters.

After she got the horses and settled them in for the night, their dinner of peas and onions with more leaf lettuce and spinach followed by apples and pears helped to further convince him that she needed to go to the farmer's garden. Cabbage and potatoes wasn't fancy, but it was better than what they were eating, even if they only needed to eat it for one or two more days.

It was dark outside. The moon was barely a sliver in the sky, and the sun had been down for hours. Pandora didn't leave the cottage until after midnight because she wanted to make sure the farmer was in bed asleep before she went to "shop" in his garden. She had several coins in one of her pockets, and she would leave them somewhere he was likely to find them once she got what she needed. The money she left would be more than enough to cover the cost. She carried the net bag from her fishing kit in the other pocket to carry the vegetables once she got them. Luckily, the sky was clear and bright with stars, so Pandora could see where she was going without too much difficulty. A full moon would have made it much easier, but that wouldn't happen for several weeks.

Pandora tightened the collar of her coat around her neck and adjusted her hat. The air was cold, and she wanted to get this done so she could get back to the cottage and snuggle beside Islington. She made it to the meadow after tripping over only one root on the way and proceeded through the tall grass to the other side of it. This part of her journey would be unfamiliar, and she tried to find the landmarks she had taken note of during the daylight.

She made it to the edge of the field and looked at the garden. It was much easier to see without the trees overhead, and she stood for a moment as she contemplated where she should start. She went to the nearest row, wading through the knee-high grass and knelt down to examine what was there. Turnips. She felt around at the base of the leaves, trying to find one of a decent size. When she found one, she pulled on it and shook the dirt from the root. It was about the size of her fist. She pulled the net bag out of her pocket and put it in. One would be enough for now; perhaps she would come back for more. She *really* wanted a cabbage.

She carefully picked her way over the row of turnips and moved down a little to the cabbages. She had bent down and pulled the knife out of her pocket to cut a head loose when she heard the sound of a dog barking close at hand, followed by the sound of it running through the garden toward her. Pandora quickly put the knife away and ran for the woods. She hadn't realized the farmer had a dog. She ran blindly, and she could hear the dog closing in behind her. After his initial barks, he could do no more than growl as he put his energy into running after her.

Pandora began to panic, and she found a tree with low enough limbs that she could grab them and climb. She scrambled into the boughs just as the dog got close. He stood below the tree looking up at her, barking vociferously, trying to jump up the trunk to get her. Pandora put her feet up on the branch and slid her bottom along to where it joined the trunk.

He wasn't very large, but he was big enough that he frightened Pandora. Actually, most any dog frightened Pandora. Her family didn't have dogs, not as pets, and she wasn't familiar with them. She only knew dogs carried rabies sometimes, and she didn't want that. She didn't think this particular dog had the disease, but he would bite her if she got out of the tree and that was enough to make her stay exactly where she was for the time being.

"Shoo!" she hissed, waving her free hand at him.

That only made the dog bark louder and seem more determined to get up the tree. Pandora looked around herself for a way to escape. There was another tree nearby. She wondered if she could jump over to it and then get down and run away. She shoved the turnip in the bag into her pocket and worked her way around the tree she was on, moving onto the branch that overlapped the other tree. She could feel the bough starting to sag as she moved her weight further out, but she had to jump a fair distance onto the other tree, or she would land on the ground, and the dog would have her. Pandora took a steadying breath and leaped.

She made it to the other tree without falling to the ground, but she scraped her right cheek along the bark on the trunk, and she felt it cut her palm as she grabbed onto it to keep herself from falling. The risk and the injuries, however, were useless. She looked down to see the dog sitting at the bottom of the new tree, looking up at her and barking.

"*Go home!*" she hissed impatiently. He did not, of course.

The tree Pandora found herself in was at least slightly more comfortable than the one she had started in. The trunk split into three, and she was able to sit in the crotch and balance her back against one of the offshoots. She tried to examine her hand in the darkness. The bark had torn open some of the blisters on her palm, and one had a little blood trickling out of it. She reached up her fingers to her cheek and brushed away the bark from the scrape there. Both injuries stung terribly.

Maybe if she had something to throw at the dog to scare him off. She looked around herself, but of course there was nothing. Other than the coins, knife, and turnip, she didn't have anything in her pockets, either. At this point, getting away from the dog was more important than a turnip. She didn't like the thought of living another day on apples and pears, but at least she didn't have to worry about getting gnawed on by a dog to get them. She fished the bag out of her pocket and pulled out the turnip. She pulled off the leaves and the pointy tip of the root.

She looked down at the dog. He continued to bark, but he had slowed down, now only barking occasionally. She repositioned herself and took aim. The turnip came close, but it missed by a foot. When it landed, the rocky ground it hit made it shatter into little chunks. Now, not only did she still have the dog barking at her at the bottom of the tree, but she also no longer had a turnip to at least justify her foray.

She groaned frustratedly and leaned back into the tree. The dog quit barking for a moment and turned his head sideways as he looked up at her. He was a cute dog, in a doggy kind of way. His hair was long and dark, but it was too dark for Pandora to tell if it was solid or different shades. His ears were floppy, but they would prick up to stand comically straight when he listened. He would occasionally wag his tail as he sat, but Pandora didn't let it fool her into thinking he was harmless. A dog barking that loudly couldn't possibly just want to play fetch.

Pandora shifted a little to sit more comfortably, and her movement made the dog start barking again. She heaved a long-suffering sigh and relaxed her head against the trunk and closed her eyes. She put her hands inside her coat to warm them. She would have to wait until he grew tired of sitting at the bottom of the tree and went home before she would be able to get down and leave. She didn't know how long that would be, but eventually he would grow hungry. She hoped Islington had truly gone to sleep. If he were sitting up waiting for her to come back, he would be frantic by the time she returned.

Pandora started to nod off. She tried to keep herself awake so she could get down as soon as the dog was gone, but she was exhausted. She would begin to feel her chin drop down to her chest, and she would snap it back up again and blink her eyes several times to keep them open. The dog had lain down and rested his head on his paws, but as soon as she made any large movements, he would raise his head to start barking again. Pandora didn't know what time it was because she hadn't brought her watch, not that she would have been able to see it in the dark, and she didn't know how long she had been gone. Eventually, she drifted off, too tired and too cold to fight it anymore.

Pandora awoke with a start, and she felt momentary panic as she nearly fell out of the tree. Then she remembered where she was. The sky was growing lighter, and she realized with dismay that she had been in the tree all night. She looked down at the ground. The dog was still there, and when she woke up and flailed about, he sat up and stretched, issuing a single bark after he yawned. In the gathering light, she could see his coat was mostly black with dark brown patches here and there.

Pandora was pondering her predicament, wondering what she could do to get rid of him, when the dog tilted his head sideways and pricked up his ears, listening to a sound Pandora couldn't hear. After barking at her one last time, he turned and trotted back toward his home. Pandora sighed with relief. She waited a few minutes to make sure he had truly gone, and then she climbed out of the tree to the ground.

Her legs were wobbly, and she was stiff from sleeping in the tree in the cold. She turned her neck a few times to pop the joints and relax the crick out of it. After looking around to get her bearings, she turned in the direction of the meadow and the cottage. She trudged along slowly. Her sleep had been fitful and uncomfortable. She was exhausted, cold, and hungry, and she was disappointed she had nothing to show for it.

She opened the door to the cottage when she reached it and, to her surprise, caught Islington mid-pace. He had somehow managed to put on his clothes (minus his cravat), including his boots, and bound his shoulder. He turned toward the door, and the look of anxiety on his face turned to relief when he saw her.

"You're up walking," said Pandora dumbly.

"Where have you been?" he said sharply.

"I was getting vegetables," said Pandora tiredly. "Well, I got a turnip," she clarified lamely.

"Where is it?" asked Islington as he looked at her empty hands.

"I threw it at the dog," said Pandora sadly as she walked inside.

"What dog?" asked Islington, his forehead wrinkling, and he began to get an image in his mind.

"The dog that chased me up the tree," said Pandora woefully. She could feel self-pitying tears starting and tried to blink them back.

She walked over to the hearth and sat down after she removed her coat and hat, looking at the damage done to her palm in the light. Her head jerked up when she heard Islington begin to laugh heartily. Her forehead wrinkled and her mouth tightened angrily when he found her misfortune so amusing. He was holding his hand against his side, and he was hurting, but he continued to laugh helplessly.

"Just keep laughing," said Pandora darkly. "I hope you bust your stitches open; you know I don't sew well."

He laughed even harder, and she watched as he had to sit down in the chair or fall over. Then she realized had she not been the one it had happened to, she would find it funny herself. She started to laugh a little as well, and seeing the way it made Islington laugh so hard despite the pain it caused him, made her begin to laugh even more. She reached up to her cheek where she had scraped it and placed her hand against it because the laughter stretched the skin and made it hurt. Islington eventually calmed down and wiped the tears away from his eyes and looked at her. He slowly got up from the chair and walked over to sit beside her on the hearth.

She looked exhausted. He reached up his hand to brush it across the scrape on her cheek, and she winced slightly. She had a few twigs and leaves in her hair, and he slowly pulled those out. He looked at her hand lying in her lap and saw the torn skin on her palm. He lifted it to his mouth and kissed it gently.

"Are you all right?" he asked softly.

"Nothing fatal," she said calmly, putting up her hand to cover a yawn. "He was a cute dog," she said thoughtfully.

Islington smiled amusedly, hugging her to him. He closed his eyes and sighed with relief that nothing had happened to her.

"You didn't wait for me all night, did you?" asked Pandora, raising her head to look at him.

"I would like to say yes, but I only woke up an hour ago and found you hadn't come back." Pandora fought another yawn. Islington looked at her. "You need to get some sleep," he said matter-of-factly.

"Oh, yes, please," sighed Pandora agreeably.

She reached down to pull off her boots and grimaced at the pressure on her palm, but she managed to get them off without too much difficulty. She stood up and took off her clothes and raised her arms above her head in a stretch to work the kinks out of her back. Islington pulled her close and nuzzled her stomach affectionately. He stood up and walked with her over to the bed, helping her get under the covers and sitting on the edge of it. He reached for the jar of ointment and put some onto her cheek and hand.

"Better?" he asked.

"Mm-hmm," said Pandora as her eyes started to droop closed.

Islington leaned forward and kissed her softly on the lips, and Pandora was soon sound asleep. He sat watching her for a long time, his brow furrowed thoughtfully. He had been extremely worried when he woke up and Pandora wasn't there. It had taken him some effort, but he had managed to dress himself. He had taken some of the chamomile and some of the whisky, and now he felt somewhat better. And while he had occasional dizziness as he paced, he was able to stand for quite some time without problems. He had almost made up his mind to go looking for her when she walked in the door. He brushed the hair from her forehead and bent down to kiss her temple where the bruise from her tumble down the hill was starting to fade. He sighed and stood up. It was his turn to take care of her now...as it should be.

Pandora slowly, reluctantly, began to awaken. She was having a wonderful dream. She was sitting at the breakfast table with her family, enjoying a cup of coffee and a plate of bacon and eggs with toast. Psyche was laughing over a joke she had made, and the rest of her family was chattering as they enjoyed their meal. She tried to make herself go back to sleep, but her body decided she had rested long enough, and her stomach growled at her for emphasis. She opened her eyes and blinked them a few times, snuggling under the blanket drowsily.

She propped herself up on her elbows and inhaled. She smelled food...real food. She threw off the blanket and sat up. Then she rubbed her eyes to make sure she wasn't still dreaming. There was a loaf of bread and cheese on the table. There was a lidded, brown earthenware bottle she suspected contained milk, and there were strawberries! There was a large wicker basket, but she couldn't see what was in it. The food cooking was ham, and her mouth started to water. That was what had prompted her dream. She looked around the edge of the fireplace to the hearth and saw Islington sitting there, intently turning over a piece of ham with the knife in his hand. Pandora quietly got out of bed and snuck up behind him. She bent down and put her arms around his neck to whisper in his ear.

"You've been busy."

Islington started in surprise and nearly dropped the knife he was holding into the fire. He turned to look at her.

"I couldn't bear the thought of having you chased up any more trees by dogs," he said with a smile.

"My knight errant returns," chuckled Pandora, kissing his cheek.

She straightened and went to the table, reaching into the small basket of strawberries to pop one into her mouth. She moaned blissfully at the flavor and closed her eyes as she savored it. She perused the items inside the large basket and saw a small, cloth-wrapped ham he had cut the pieces from that he was cooking, a few eggs, tomatoes, a small cabbage, and some potatoes. A burlap sack contained more sugar. There were also a few small jars, and when she opened them, she found they contained salt, pepper, and more tea. She turned to look at Islington.

"You found a village?" she asked softly as she picked up another strawberry.

"Yes, Redmire is less than a mile from here," said Islington casually as he removed the pan from the fire.

He added the pieces of ham to the plates where he already had scrambled eggs and cut-up slices of tomato. Pandora was impressed. He had managed to cook. Pandora never would have thought a *man* would be able to cook. It was somewhat expected of women, and she managed, but she was surprised he would be capable of doing so. What he made wasn't complicated, but he hadn't burned it, which was easy enough to do even with the simple things.

"You were able to walk a *mile?*" asked Pandora in surprise.

"A little bit more than that, actually, when you consider I had to walk back," he said as he rose from the hearth and took the plates to the table.

She could see his left arm shake slightly from even the marginal weight of the plate in his hand, but she was impressed he was able to carry it. He had on the shoulder wrap, and the sling was around his neck, but he didn't have his arm in it. Pandora's forehead wrinkled as she sat down. She heard the lid on the teapot begin to rattle and turned to look over her shoulder, and then she looked at Islington.

"I'm afraid I don't know how to make tea," said Islington, grinning sheepishly, "but I thought you might like some."

Pandora got up to remove the pot and added some leaves to begin steeping. While she was up, she put on her clothes. The chair was a bit uncomfortable on her bare bottom. She came back to the table, carrying the pot and their cups. She looked to the edge of her plate and was surprised when she saw utensils—a real fork and knife—sitting there. They weren't fancy, and they didn't even match, but they were real. She sat slowly, and the furrows in her forehead deepened even further.

"Where did you learn to cook?" she asked as she began to eat.

"I'm afraid ham and eggs is the extent of it," said Islington with a grin. "We had to supplement our meals up at school somehow."

She ate quietly, and she enjoyed the food immensely. She had to try very hard not to wolf it down and to savor it because she was so hungry. Her mind kept going over one fact again and again: he had walked over a mile. He was well enough for them to leave. That knowledge caused her mixed emotions. She was overjoyed he was better, and that it had happened so quickly amazed her. Yet she was also sad because their time together was going to come to an end.

She felt they had grown closer over the past few days, not just physically, but emotionally as well. They hadn't argued once the whole time they had been at the cottage, and she recalled her mother's words about their getting on well when they didn't bicker about who was in charge. Pandora knew as soon as she broached the subject of leaving, it was going to end. She knew Islington well enough to realize that.

His activities for the day also caused her a bit of confusion. She had thought she was doing well taking care of them, and in less than a day he had made her feel her capabilities were wanting. He hadn't done it purposely, but it made her feel like what she had done wasn't good enough. Still, she was relieved that finding food for them was one less concern she had to carry. It still left other things, though, like tending to the animals.

When that thought occurred to her, her eyes rounded in alarm and she pulled out her watch. It was after noon.

"Oh, no!" she cried, starting and rising from the table.

"What's wrong?" asked Islington, his forehead wrinkling when he saw her panic.

"The horses haven't been taken to the meadow!" she said, running to grab her boots and pull them on quickly.

When she got to the open room, she set aside the limb across the doorway and stepped in. Bellerophon nickered softly and walked up to her. Pandora felt tears sting her eyes when she thought how hungry and thirsty they must be. She grabbed the ropes and haltered them then led them outside to the trough. Both animals bent their heads and began to drink immediately, and Pandora rubbed her hands across their backs, talking to them soothingly as she stood between them. After they had drunk their fill, she led them to the meadow and tethered them. Once she saw they were settled in, she walked back to the cottage, and Islington was waiting for her in the doorway. He had put his arm in the sling, and he was leaning with his right shoulder against the frame.

"I'm sorry. I didn't even think about them," he said quietly.

Pandora shrugged. She hadn't expected him to; taking care of the horses was her responsibility. She looked up at the sky. It was sunny and cloudless; they would be able to stay in the meadow and eat to their hearts' content for the rest of the day.

"They'll be fine for tomorrow," said Pandora calmly.

She walked past him in the doorway and went into the open room to muck it out for what she hoped would be the last time. Islington followed Pandora and looked at her with his brow furrowed.

"What about tomorrow?" he asked.

"Well, to continue on to Edinburgh, of course," she said evenly.

Chapter Twenty-Four

Islington looked at her in astonishment. He couldn't believe he heard her correctly. The tone she used was so matter-of-fact and calm, as if it were a foregone conclusion that she would be going. That she would mention it at all was unexpected; he thought she had entirely forgotten about it. For her to mention it now, immediately after he was able to move, made it seem she had simply been biding her time.

"You cannot mean it," he said stilly.

Pandora walked past him out of the room to dispose of the manure, her features barely covering the distaste she had for the chore. She took it out to the yard where she had been piling it and came back. She had expected him to react this way, so she wasn't angry…yet.

"I do mean it," she said calmly as she worked. "You're well enough to take care of yourself now. If you can walk a mile, riding a horse shouldn't be a problem. You don't need help getting dressed or getting food, so what is the point of delaying?"

She walked past him with more manure, and Islington stood with his arms folded across his chest, disbelief still etched into his features. He followed after her into the yard.

"Are you mad I went? Is that what this is about?" he asked tightly.

Pandora tipped the manure onto the pile and turned to face him. Her expression was calm, but she was growing impatient. It was true his ease in finding food compared with her difficulty had left her feeling deficient, but it hadn't made her angry. That was something a man would do.

"I'm not mad. For the first time in days, I had food that I didn't have to cook or find for myself, and it was *good* food," she said soothingly. "Going to Edinburgh has nothing to do with you going to Redmire, other than that you were able to walk there let me know you don't need me to take care of you anymore."

She walked past him back to the open room to scoop up what was left of the manure and came back out with it.

"Would you rather I was still too ill to get out of bed?"

Pandora looked at him disappointedly. "How could you even think to ask me such a question?" she said sadly.

"Why would you think I'm well enough for us to go anywhere?"

Pandora looked at him incredulously. "You're having me on, right?"

She went to the rain barrel and washed her hands with some of the soapwort then dried them by wiping them on her waistcoat.

"Why would you think I'd let you go to Edinburgh?" he asked, deciding she had a point about the question of his wellness being foolish.

"Why would you think you could stop me?" asked Pandora a bit sharply, his anger starting to affect her. "And why would you think I would need you to go with me or to have your permission?"

Islington tightened his jaw with a scowl. Pandora sighed in aggravation and shook her head, walking past him back into the cottage. The open room was clean enough for the horses now. She grabbed some of the wood there and took it into the main room to put in the nook by the fireplace. She tossed a few pieces onto the fire then went back to the open room to get more. She thought filling the nook would give them enough wood for the night. After that, it wouldn't matter.

"How could you think of still going to Edinburgh after everything that's happened?" he asked quietly after he entered the cottage himself.

Pandora finished stacking her fourth and final load of wood into the nook and dusted off her hands, turning to face him.

"If I don't go, what purpose will it have served?" she asked simply.

"What about your family? They're worried sick," he said tightly.

Pandora's face colored guiltily, but she raised her chin and looked at him firmly.

"I know they're worried about me, and not a day—not an hour—goes by that I don't think about them and miss them, but they understand why I'm doing this," she said softly, her eyes sparkling with tears.

"Do they? I certainly don't," said Islington angrily.

"An innocent man's life is in danger. He isn't just going to die; he's going to be murdered! Do you not understand *that?*" she shouted angrily. "No, I don't know him. No, he's never done anything for me. No, he's not even from my country. But he *is* a human being! Maybe you can stand idly by and let it happen, but I can't, not when I can stop it."

She groaned and raised her hands in the air in defeat, walking back outside. She needed to make firewood, even if she didn't *need* to make firewood. Why was it so difficult for him to understand that she had to go to Edinburgh? She didn't have the patience or the energy to explain it to him. She was angry, and she was frustrated and hurt, and if she didn't find a way to let it out, she was going to explode…or have a migraine.

Pandora walked over to the remnants of the barn and found a piece of wood. She took it to the rafter beams she had stacked on top of one another in two rows and laid it across them. She did some exercises to loosen up then took a few deep breaths, bringing her hand to the board a few times. Then she hit it with her hand, releasing a loud yell to focus herself, just as Keung had taught her. The board snapped in two. She picked up the longer of the two pieces and placed it across the beams and repeated the action. She could feel the tension start to work its way out of her, but it was going to take several more boards. She went back to the barn and found another.

She went through two of them, but she was still frustrated. She went to the barn and grabbed another piece, but instead of laying it across the beams, she stood it on end by a nearby tree, using a strong low-hanging limb and a large rock on the ground to wedge it against so there was nothing behind it. She kicked it with her foot, and the board broke.

"What are you doing?" asked Islington behind her.

Pandora pivoted around, her foot still raised on her outstretched leg. When she brought it around, she just missed hitting Islington in the nose. She slowly straightened and put her foot on the ground, looking at him coldly. If he persisted in arguing, there wouldn't be enough boards left from the barn to take care of it. Pandora didn't speak to him; she just went for another board and laid it across the beams. She focused herself and broke the board. Islington rushed up to her and spun her around, taking her hand in his to examine it worriedly.

"Are you *insane?*" he shouted as he turned her hand over in his, expecting to see broken bones.

Other than a slight redness from the impact, there wasn't a mark. Islington looked at her in astonishment. Pandora jerked her hand out of his and retrieved the longer piece of board and placed it over the beams.

"Please, go away, Islington," she said shortly. She brought her hand down and broke the board.

She started to walk back to the barn for another piece of wood, and Islington grabbed her by the wrist to stop her. She looked down to his hand on her arm and then looked up at his face. Her mouth was tight with anger. He was looking at her with disbelief and concern.

"Would you stop doing that?"

"Let go of my arm, and go away, Theo," she said stilly. "I am angry, and I am trying to calm down as quickly as I can, but if you do not leave me alone, I *will hurt you*," she bit out slowly.

"I am *not* going to let you keep doing this!" he said angrily. "You're going to injure yourself."

Pandora looked at him sadly and impatiently and lifted her free hand to his right arm. She used the same grip Maiyin had used to make him release Pandora on that night that seemed a lifetime ago. He winced and let go of her arm. Pandora turned him loose as soon as he released her.

"You don't understand," she said softly with a fixed smile. "I'll be fine. I need to be alone. Please, just go away," she said defeatedly, waving a hand through the air as she walked off.

She went to the barn for another piece of wood and placed it over the beams. Islington moved into her way so she couldn't break it. She looked at him angrily for a minute as she felt her eyes beginning to sting, and she shook her head incredulously and turned away.

She wiped at the tears on her cheeks frustratedly and walked through the woods to the meadow. It wasn't time for the horses to have more water so she would stay with them until it was. At least they didn't try to argue with her, and they were much easier to understand than Islington. Both animals looked up and nickered at her in greeting when she reached the meadow, and they trotted up to her happily.

Pandora fished out a few sugar lumps she had perpetually in the pocket of her waistcoat and gave them to the horses. She petted them, scrubbing their foreheads and under their cheeks. They went back to grazing after they realized she had no more sugar for them, and Pandora let them go.

She went to an area of the meadow that had been grazed short and took off her waistcoat and boots. If Islington wouldn't let her break boards to release her frustration, then she would have to do the only other thing that worked. She preferred breaking boards because it was quicker. This would, however, save her from getting splinters in her hands.

She took several deep breaths and began the practice exercises of the *wǔshù* Keung had taught her. She hadn't done them since leaving London, and she had forgotten how soothing they were. They helped her focus her mind and let go of things that were bothering her, and she desperately needed that at the moment.

Islington quietly followed Pandora after she left the yard. He was concerned she might do something else to hurt herself, although he truly hadn't seen any damage to her hand. The things she had done in the past twenty minutes were enough to make him realize she was more than she seemed. He didn't think she was inhuman, but she was no ordinary woman in more ways than he could have possibly imagined.

When he reached the edge of the meadow, he stayed to the shadows and leaned against a nearby tree to rest. He hadn't told Pandora how *long* it had taken him to walk to Redmire. He had been concerned about making it back. The dizziness was mostly gone, but he would still become weak and short-winded. Bellerophon looked at him, chewing casually on some grass, but after he decided Islington was harmless, he bent his head again.

Islington watched as Pandora began the fluid movements across the grass. At first he thought she was dancing, but he began to realize she was performing exercises unlike anything he had ever seen. He watched as she did things that required a lot of dexterity, physical control, and strength, things women shouldn't know how to do. He soon realized they weren't just exercises, but practice for some form of martial art.

He remembered the way she had grabbed his wrist, exactly the way Maiyin had. She hadn't thought twice about it; she hadn't even really looked. He tried to remember the conversation she had with him the night she had her bath. There were many things Keung and Maiyin had taught her and her family. This had to be one of them. He realized with some amazement that she was more capable of defending herself than he was. He boxed, fenced, and rowed to keep himself fit, and yet he knew without much doubt she could incapacitate him if she had to.

I will hurt you, she had said; he realized she hadn't been bluffing. It also made him think back to the night of her come-out ball when she had flipped him onto his back in the gazebo. He had thought it was a matter of luck, not skill. All the other times when she should have hurt him and hadn't (like in the alley and in the coach afterward), it was because she hadn't wanted to…not because she couldn't.

He now understood why she had been able to escape from Timmons Wallace. Granted, he hadn't been very long on intelligence, but a typical woman alone would have been no match for him. Pandora had flicked him off like a flea. And the guns! Her family had taught her how to use them, but she didn't need them, unless she was trying to defend herself against someone else who had one. If her attacker were close enough, her reflexes were fast enough she would be able to disarm him whether she had a gun or not. Her family's concern on finding she had taken firearms wasn't caused by her having them, but that she was going somewhere she thought she might need them.

Why would you think I would need *you to go with me?* Why indeed? She had told him several times she wasn't a typical female. He had been friends with Dorian long enough to know even *he* was atypical. Islington didn't know why he should be surprised to find the same thing followed for every member of his family. After everything he had discovered over the past few days, he knew the only thing that made her incapable of going to Edinburgh alone without the slightest difficulty was that she had to disguise herself as a man to do it. On close inspection, there was no concealment good enough to hide that she was, at least outwardly, every inch a woman.

He *could* understand why she felt she needed to warn Artois. Islington didn't want to see an innocent man murdered any more than she did, and he didn't think she was exaggerating the gravity of the problem. It was simply that sentiments and decisions of that sort weren't normal for a woman, but it was because they usually weren't placed into a situation where that kind of choice would need to be made by them. Most wouldn't know what to do if they *were* placed in that kind of situation.

Islington admitted with some chagrin that she had tried to leave it to him and Dorian, even when she hadn't wanted to, but it hadn't been dealt with to her satisfaction. Knowing more about her now, he couldn't argue with her logic; it would be as bad as him telling another man that he was a simpleton. Pandora was no simpleton, and the things that normally motivated a woman didn't always apply to her.

Islington watched a few minutes more, his brow furrowing. When he realized his concern for her harming herself was unnecessary, and even a little foolish, he turned and left for the cottage.

≪ ≫

Pandora returned to the cottage after she had taken the horses back to the meadow from the trough. They seemed none the worse for wear after their delayed start to eating. She felt very guilty they had needed to wait, especially Jezebel because she was probably eating for two. Pandora wasn't looking forward to mentioning *that* to Islington.

Pandora's time in the meadow had relaxed her a great deal. She was resigned. She wasn't going to argue with Islington about it anymore. She was going to state it as firmly as she could. He had three choices: go with her, go his own way, or stay at the cottage. Regardless of which he chose, Pandora was leaving for Edinburgh tomorrow.

If Islington didn't go with her, it would be hard to leave him, but she had no expectations. She doubted she would ever stop loving him, and the time at the cottage had only deepened it, but she couldn't make him love her, and she couldn't stay with him if he didn't.

When Pandora opened the door, she found Islington standing in front of the fire, thoughtfully looking down at the flames, a pipe in his hand. She inhaled the scent of the tobacco, and it reminded her of many times before in London when she had been near him and caught the faintest hint of it. It was a smell she would forever associate with him. He started to extinguish it when she came in, and Pandora held up her hand.

"Don't put it out," she said, shaking her head. "It doesn't bother me."

"You're sure?" he asked, noting her calmness. Pandora nodded.

She went to the table for her cup and poured some tea. She came near him by the fire, and she could smell he had also been into the whisky, but that didn't bother her either…as long as there was some left. He didn't seem to be intoxicated, so she was sure there was.

"I don't want to start another row, but I've been thinking," he said softly.

Pandora looked at him levelly. "Yes?" she said calmly, taking a sip from her cold tea.

"You would be more comfortable sleeping at inns on the way to Edinburgh," he said slowly.

418

"Not easily accomplished, sadly," said Pandora with a wry smile.

"Not if you're going alone," agreed Islington mildly.

Pandora raised an eyebrow inquiringly, taking another sip from her tea. It seemed he had at least become adjusted to the fact she would be going, which was a step in the right direction. Before he spoke again, she went back to the table for the teapot and put it near the fire to reheat. She looked at him expectantly when she was finished.

"So?" she asked leadingly.

"I've decided to go with you, if only to give you a roof over your head at night and food to eat that you don't have to fight a dog for."

Pandora walked closer to him and put a hand to his cheek and kissed him briefly.

"You are a dear, kind man. I don't care what everyone else says about you," she teased with a fond smile.

"Hunh," said Islington, and he put his pipe to his lips to draw on it a few times.

"Thank you," she said softly. Pandora's expression turned serious. "What made you change your mind?" she asked gently.

"I saw you...in the meadow," he said evenly. Pandora raised an eyebrow. "I thought you were going to hurt yourself." He smiled self-deprecatingly. "Silly, I know now. How'd you do that...with the wrist?" he asked with grudging fascination.

Pandora giggled. "It's quite simple, really." She took the pipe out of his hand and set it on the mantel because she didn't want him to drop it and break the meerschaum. "You just put your fingers like so—"she said, putting her fingers on his wrist—"and add a little pressure." She didn't press too hard, but Islington got the idea. "You probably better understand what's under there that makes it work." She giggled at his amazed expression. "Persephone is much better at it than I am. She knows one that can render a man *unconscious* just with her fingertip in the right spot, and Psyche can break *bricks!* Of course, Keung is *dà shī*, the great master."

"And Keung taught you that?" Pandora nodded. "Your parents *let* him teach you that?"

"Of course," said Pandora calmly. "What parents wouldn't want their daughter to know how to protect herself? And there is so much more to it than that. You learn discipline, self-reliance, confidence, and how to break boards," she said with a wink.

"Mm-hmm. I can think of several who wouldn't...but then again, I can think of several who probably wish now that they did."

"Too right," said Pandora with a grin.

"How did you get away from Timmons Wallace?"

Pandora blinked in surprise. "How did you know about him?"

"I found him at the bottom of the hill Wednesday morning. After I woke him up and got him to tell the truth, he said you knocked him out."

"Well, I did but only so he could breathe again." Islington raised an eyebrow. "I stepped on his toes, and then I hit him in his solar plexus to knock the wind out of him. I felt a little sorry for him because he was only confused and not terribly dangerous, so I hit him on the back of his head to knock him out and let him breathe again before he suffocated."

"He didn't have a mark on him."

"No, I suppose not." She pulled out her watch. "I expect I need to start supper. Cabbage and ham?" she enquired with a lopsided smile.

"I'm very fond of your cabbage and ham," said Islington, pulling her close to nuzzle her throat.

Pandora lifted a hand to the back of his head as his lips trailed up her neck to her mouth, and she almost dropped her cup weakly as she felt the heat beginning to curl through her stomach. Oh, how she loved this man. He finally ended the kiss and raised his head to look at her, a slow smile of amusement forming as he saw her reaction.

"Cold cabbage isn't very appealing, you realize," she finally said with a slow smile. "And if you keep doing that, that is what we will have."

He let her go with a tender smile and reached for his pipe. Pandora retrieved the small kettle and took it to the table to begin cutting up the vegetables, a small smile staying on her lips for quite some time.

They woke around seven. The sky looked like it would stay clear and sunny, but because they would be traveling, there was no guarantee it would hold once they started moving. Pandora had packed most of their things last night after supper, and she had seen to the rest, including rolling the blankets from the bed back into the tent, while Islington cooked the remaining ham and eggs with tomatoes for breakfast.

The only food that had to be packed was what remained of the bread and cheese Islington had purchased in Redmire. Pandora firmly decided against getting more pears or apples. She didn't care if she ever saw another of either. She had to redistribute things in her saddlebags to even out the weight, but everything had grown lighter after their time at the cottage. Once Islington was done cooking, Pandora quickly washed the frying pan and packed it as well.

She had divided the remaining grain for the horses between the two bags, but they were less than half full. That would have worried Pandora if Islington weren't going with her, but they could stop for more should they need to with him there. She refilled her canteen with water from the pump. Then she sat down with Islington at the table to eat after she took the horses to the meadow one last time.

"So, you found Redmire, but how do we get to an actual road from here?"

"I think if we go north, there's a turnpike road fairly close," said Islington after he thought about it for a moment.

Pandora got her map from her saddlebag and looked at it while she ate. Islington leaned over to look at it. After he saw it, he was even more surprised she had managed to get as far as she did.

"That's your map?" he asked dubiously.

"Yes." She saw his face. "What's wrong with my map?"

"Oh, that's rubbish," he said flatly. "Smith's is so much better."

He went to his bag and pulled out his own maps. Pandora looked at them. His maps were much better than hers. There were three parts, but they didn't take up any more space than her inadequate *one*. Islington's showed tollgates and turnpikes. His was also prettier.

"Where did you get this?"

"The Strand," said Islington calmly while he resumed eating his breakfast. "Of course, it is about seven years old."

Pandora waved a hand dismissively as she continued to look. "Mine is less than a year old, and this one is much more detailed."

She took a sip from her tea and continued to look. She agreed there should be a road just to the north of where they were. Now that Islington was traveling with her, turnpikes and tollgates wouldn't be as much of a complication, but she still wouldn't make a special effort to use that type of road. She would stay with her plan to continue in as much of a straight line as possible. After a time, she folded the map closed and finished eating.

After they were through, Pandora insisted on rinsing off the dishes and stacking them neatly. Islington thought it was a waste of time, but Pandora found she was going to miss the little cottage. She had grown attached to it, and she hoped that if some other poor traveler were to happen upon it at a time of need, he wouldn't have to go through as much effort to make it usable as she had. When that was done, she went to get the horses and began saddling them.

She saddled Bellerophon first. He stood calmly while she packed all the bags and the tent back on, making sure the weight was evenly distributed; although, Pandora figured he wasn't carrying even half as much as he had been. It would make things easier for him.

Islington stood in the doorway and watched, leaning against the frame for support, while she began to saddle Jezebel. The mare stood calmly while Pandora put on her blanket but skittered a little when Pandora put on the saddle. Pandora frowned and took it off. She flipped it over and looked at the tree. She ran her hand along the surface and found a place where a piece of leather had worked loose and become dried and sharp after getting wet. When she determined it wasn't essential, she pulled her pocketknife out of her coat and cut off the piece of leather.

"Are you dismantling my saddle?" asked Islington mildly.

"No, just making it more comfortable for Jezebel to breathe without something poking her in the ribs." She turned to look at him with a grin. "You can understand that."

When she placed the saddle back on, Jezebel let her do so. The mare turned to look at Pandora and shook her head up and down. Pandora giggled. She reached for the girth and began to gently tighten it down.

"You'll have to make sure it's on extra tight," said Islington. "Jezebel has a tendency to blow out and make it loose."

"She'll be fine," said Pandora calmly as she inspected the tightness of the cinch. She pulled on it just a little bit more then stood and patted Jezebel's neck appreciatively.

"I don't think it's tight enough," said Islington doubtfully.

"It *is* tight enough," said Pandora exasperatedly as she got the bridle. "Trust me. It's not going anywhere."

Jezebel placidly let Pandora put on her bridle, and Pandora gave her a sugar lump once she was done.

"Good girl," said Pandora soothingly, brushing her nose.

She tied down Islington's bag to the rear of the saddle and attached the holster with his rifle. When the horses were saddled and bridled, Pandora checked their hooves and legs one last time to make sure they were ready. Bellerophon's shoes were a little thin, but they would get to Edinburgh, especially since she wouldn't be going quickly. Jezebel's were showing wear, but they were fairly new shoes.

She walked past Islington back into the cottage to take a look around to make sure they hadn't forgotten anything. The table was cleared. There were no bags beside the far wall. The dishes were neatly stacked on the hearth, and the fire was out. Everything was done. She looked at Islington.

"Are you ready to go?"

"Let's go to Edinburgh," he said gamely, slapping his thigh with his gloves and straightening up to walk into the yard.

Pandora closed the door, and then she grabbed Bellerophon's reins to lead him to where she had re-stacked the rafter beams to use as a mounting block. Once she was up, she turned to look at Islington.

"That should be stable enough to hold you while you mount, and you'll want to go from the right," she said helpfully.

"I don't need a mounting block," he said dismissively. "I haven't needed a mounting block since before my horse was taller than I."

"You need to use the wood to mount," said Pandora slowly. "You'll hurt yourself if you don't."

Islington looked at her peevishly. "I don't need it," he said flatly.

Pandora shrugged and tilted her head sideways as she watched him try to mount. He pulled himself into the saddle using his right hand, mounting from the left. Jezebel sidled a little at his unusual technique. He came very close to falling off, and Pandora could see from his strained expression that he had hurt his side, even if he hadn't hurt his shoulder. Once he was seated, she looked at him with a grin.

"Feel better now?" she asked smartly.

"Oh, that's funny," said Islington tightly.

"*Yala,*" she blithely said to Bellerophon, turning him in the direction of the meadow and northward.

By the time they made their second stop for the day, Islington had resigned himself to *needing* something to mount. After Pandora had warned him before they left the cottage, she hadn't said anything again because it would only make him more determined to prove he could do without it. He would not, however, mount from the right. Pandora wasn't going to press the issue; she was happy he wasn't being too stubborn for his own good and had started to use something to mount at least.

Even though they had a late start, they were making good time. The horses were well-rested and full of energy, and they stayed to a fast walk. The weather was mild and sunny, if a bit windy at times. Other than the problems he caused for himself when mounting and dismounting, Islington was doing fair, but when it was time to stop for the horses, she didn't have to argue with him about it. When they made their second stop, she gave him some chamomile, and she also made him have some of the whisky. She wondered if another day at the cottage would have been such a bad thing.

When Islington discovered Pandora liked Yorkshire and that she had never been there, he began to make a special effort to point out things he thought she might find interesting. Once they crossed into Durham, when they passed through Barnard Castle, he pointed out the ruins for her once they reached the Tees. She was glad he had, because she probably wouldn't have noticed if he had not, and they were beautiful.

"This is going to sound like a silly question, but how do you know about all of these things? Is it a pastime?" she finally asked after he pointed out another feature of the landscape.

"No, it's not a pastime, just something I've learned. Actually, I'm more familiar with the West Riding, around Leeds," he said casually.

"Really?" asked Pandora with surprise. "Why is that?"

"That's where my home is," said Islington evenly.

Pandora blinked. "Oh! I never realized! I always thought the name came from the island. You don't talk like you're from Yorkshire," she said, looking at him suspiciously, as if she thought he was teasing her.

Islington grinned and shook his head. "No, but then I wouldn't have survived very long at St. John's if I did."

Pandora smiled back. "No, I suppose not."

Islington tilted his hat back on his head to scratch his scalp where it was becoming hot and sweaty from the sun.

"Instead of just stopping by a stream and a field next time, I want to stop at an inn for a proper dinner, if that is agreeable?"

"Oh, yes," sighed Pandora. "A chair with a nice, fat cushion would be lovely. It's been so long since I've ridden, my arse is killing me."

She blushed when she realized what she said. Islington looked at her in surprise for a moment, and then he began to laugh uncontrollably, letting go of the reins to place a hand to his side.

"Ow...oh...that hurts!" he said, still laughing and gasping for breath.

"I'm sorry," said Pandora, her forehead wrinkled concernedly.

Islington finally managed to regain his composure, and he put his hand up to wipe the corners of his eyes. He reached over to grab her reins and pull Bellerophon to a halt. He started to pull Pandora toward him for a kiss, but at that moment a coach came into view, heading toward them on the road. He realized how odd it would look to passersby if he did kiss her, dressed as she was. Islington decided he would have to wait until they were alone...if he could.

It was nearing complete darkness when they finally stopped for the night. They had been looking for a place for some time, but the area they were traveling through was sparsely populated. When they would find a town, it wouldn't have an inn. Pandora was glad when they found one; Islington was tired and in pain, though he tried to hide it. They crossed the South Tyne into Haltwhistle and found a small inn called the Spotted Cow. Pandora would have laughed, except she was too tired.

"Are we in Scotland yet?" she grumbled as they rode into the yard.

"Tomorrow," said Islington mildly.

"I want a bath."

Islington looked at her. "Do you really need one?"

"No, but I *want* one," said Pandora. Her forehead wrinkled. "Well, actually, I think I *need* one."

"We'll see what we can do," said Islington with a half-smile.

He dismounted with some difficulty, and Pandora grew concerned she might need to catch him before he fell. She thought again that they should have stayed at the cottage one more day. They had ridden over sixty miles. It was too much for Islington, and Pandora felt guilty she had been so impatient. They took the horses to the stable and were met by the ostler. As they had decided Pandora would pretend to be his *man* while they traveled, she gathered their belongings. Islington started for the inn, but Pandora tugged at his sleeve to get his attention and tilted her head at the ostler.

"Oh, right," he said softly as he remembered and turned back. "Give them all they want to eat and drink, and be careful with them because they're very temperamental."

The ostler touched his forehead and led them to the stable. Pandora watched anxiously. Bellerophon had never been tended to by anyone other than her family's servants. She hoped he would be all right.

"Come along, George," called Islington over his shoulder as he continued on to the inn. Pandora turned to look at him and tilted her head in puzzlement. *George?*

She hefted the bags in her hands and hurried to catch up with him. They walked into the small common room, which had a few people sitting at the tables near the fire. It was dark, and Pandora had a hard time seeing whether or not it was clean. She really was so tired, she didn't care. Momentarily, a short, rotund, balding gentleman wearing a white apron came to greet them.

"Good evening, gentlemen," he said with a smile. "Welcome to the Spotted Cow. I'm William Hobart, the proprietor."

"Mr. Hobart, I am Viscount Islington. I'd like a room, please."

"Oh, yessir, my lord. Come right this way," he said, leading them through a doorway into an alcove with stairs leading upward and a small counter. He walked behind it and pulled out his ledger with a pen. "Now, Viscount Islington, was it?" he asked pleasantly.

"That is correct," said Islington mildly.

"And who might this other gentleman be?" asked Mr. Hobart.

"That will be my valet, George Brazen," said Islington.

Pandora glared at him from under the brim of her hat. They hadn't discussed what her name would be, but that was certainly not what she would have chosen. *Brazen* indeed! Islington looked over his shoulder at her, and he could just make out the way her eyes were burning with indignation. His lips twitched amusedly as he turned back to Mr. Hobart.

"Will you be wanting separate rooms? We can house your valet in the servants' quarters if you like."

Pandora gave Islington a hard look. He wouldn't dare.

"No, Mr. Hobart, that's unnecessary. I require my man to be with me to tend to my needs as they arise." Pandora heaved a sigh of relief, and she tried to ignore the double entendre of his words. "If you can just have a cot brought in for him, that will suit." Pandora bit the inside of her lip to keep herself from yelling in outrage. She was going to strangle him. "Also, I'd like a supper tray brought up. Whatever you have will suffice, with a pitcher of beer and a bottle of claret, if you have it."

"Very good, my lord," said Mr. Hobart, making notations. "Will there be anything else?"

Islington was getting ready to say no, and Pandora knocked him in the back of the leg with the bag she held. He turned slightly to look at her, and she signaled him with her eyes and tilted her head. His shoulders started to shake with silent laughter, and he cleared his throat as he turned back to Mr. Hobart.

"Would it be possible to have a tub brought up?"

"A tub, my lord?" asked Mr. Hobart blankly.

"Yes, Mr. Hobart, for bathing," said Islington dryly.

"I'm sorry, my lord, but we haven't any."

"Hmm, pity." Pandora could detect the undertone of amusement in his voice, even if the innkeeper couldn't. "Well, then, that will be all. When the supper tray is brought up, make sure to bring enough wood for the night as well. My man will attend to it. I'll expect a breakfast tray in the morning at nine sharp. I don't want to be disturbed until then," said Islington firmly.

"Very good, my lord," said Mr. Hobart, making more scribbles. He came from behind the counter. "If you'll wait a moment, I'll get the staff to preparing your tray, and then I'll show you to your room."

"Excellent," said Islington curtly.

When Hobart left, Islington turned around to look at Pandora. He could see she didn't enjoy his amusement at her expense. Her eyes were shooting green sparks, and her mouth had tightened as she fought to keep herself from yelling at him. It made him find the whole thing only more amusing, and he put a hand to his side as even the silent laughter made it hurt. Mr. Hobart momentarily returned before Pandora had a chance to rail at him.

"If you'll come this way, my lord," said Mr. Hobart, waving his arm in the direction of the stairs.

He led them to a door on the first floor. It was already open as a maid had immediately gone in to get it ready. She had placed a small cot in one corner near the fireplace and started a fire burning. There was a night table to either side of the large, four-poster bed, and the oil lamps on both were lit. She was just turning down the covers when Mr. Hobart escorted them in. She curtsied slightly as they entered and quickly left the room.

Pandora looked around. It was very spacious. There were two wing chairs, one to either side, near the fireplace with a low table situated between them. The bed was large with a feather mattress, and Pandora looked at it longingly from the doorway. If Islington so much as asked her to sleep on the cot, she would have to knock him out. She was sleeping in that bed, and violence would ensue if he tried to stop her. There was a stand with a wash basin and mirror on the wall opposite the fireplace, and Pandora sadly reckoned she would have to make do with just washing her face and brushing her teeth.

"Your supper tray and your wood should be brought up before too long, my lord," said Mr. Hobart. "Will you want them to come get the tray tonight?"

"No, Mr. Hobart. They can get it when they bring the breakfast tray in the morning," said Islington evenly. "I've been traveling a very long way, and I do not want to be disturbed."

"Of course, my lord," said Mr. Hobart with a smile. "If you'll be needing anything else, just let me know," he said as he left the room.

The innkeeper had no more than closed the door before Pandora rounded on Islington.

"*Brazen?*" she hissed as she threw her hat on the bed. "Tend to your *needs* as they *arise?*" she bit out, pulling off her coat to add to her hat. "You…are…the most…," she gasped, so outraged she could scarcely speak.

"You might want to put that back on until they bring the food," said Islington, trying not to laugh. He was enjoying the way her indignation brought out the color in her cheeks and made her eyes flash; it was a very becoming look.

Pandora grumbled under her breath and put her things back on, glaring at him the whole time. She had no sooner shoved her hat back onto her head when there was a knock at the door.

"Come," called Islington.

The door opened and a line of servants entered. Two girls had the tray and the beer and wine, which they set on the small table in front of the fire. Then two boys came in carrying armloads of firewood, which they stacked neatly by the hearth. They started to leave, and Islington was going to let them, but Pandora quickly grabbed his sleeve, reaching into her pocket to retrieve some coins for him to give them. After he distributed them, all four bowed and curtsied with large smiles and left the room, closing the door behind them.

"That is their job, you know," said Islington mildly as he slowly tried to work off his coat.

"Yes, but people still like to know what they're doing is appreciated," said Pandora levelly, removing her own coat and hat and tossing them back onto the bed.

He was still having trouble with his coat, and Pandora went to help him. She tossed it onto the bed where she had placed her own with his hat. Then she reached up and unfastened his cravat and folded it up neatly. When she realized she still had on hers, she untied it and folded it, too. Once it was off, she felt like she could breathe again, and she still couldn't understand why men insisted on wearing one. She took off her waistcoat and added it to the pile. She caught Islington looking at her with mild amusement.

"What?" she asked blankly.

"Oh, I was just waiting to see how much more you were going to take off," he said with a smile.

"That's it...for now," said Pandora evenly.

Her irritation with him for having fun at her expense had slackened. It was harmless, and she realized there was no point to holding onto it. *Someone* had to invent a name for her, and while it wasn't what she would have chosen, it was as good as any other. She took all their baggage and set it on the cot. It was a convenient place for it, and she was not going to be sleeping there. She was sure Islington had never intended for her to do so.

She looked at the covered dishes on the tray and went to sit in one of the chairs, folding her legs beneath her. She lifted the lid on one dish and found asparagus, and she picked up a spear and began to munch happily while she lifted another lid. Roast beef with new potatoes. She peeled off a piece of the meat and ate that while she lifted another lid. When she saw a whole trout with tomato aspic, its dead eye looking up at her, Pandora put the lid back on and tried not to retch. She lifted the lid from a tureen of cucumber soup and another held pumpkin custard. It all smelled wonderful, and what she had sampled was delicious.

Islington eventually came over to sit in the opposite chair, easing himself into it. He poured some beer and drained the whole glass, and then he got another. Pandora glanced at his face. He was trying not to look pained. She went to the saddlebags, pulling out the medicine kit and a lump of sugar. She put some chamomile on it and took it to Islington.

"Don't argue. Just take it," she said gently as he started to protest.

She sat back down and ladled some of the soup into a bowl for herself. It was fabulous. She couldn't quite decide, however, if it only tasted that way because of her recent diet. At that point, she didn't care. She looked up from eating and saw that Islington was not. He continued to sip from his beer. His brow was creased with exhaustion and pain still, but he needed to eat something.

"Would you like me to ladle some soup for you?"

"No," said Islington flatly.

"It's very good," she said coaxingly.

"I just want to drink my beer," said Islington, lifting the glass.

Pandora shrugged and continued to eat. His short demeanor could be caused by pain and tiredness, but he seemed preoccupied. She removed the cork from the claret and poured some into a glass. She found it to be oaky, but other than that, it was quite good. She ate until she couldn't eat anymore, and she sat back in the chair and stretched and yawned with satisfaction. Islington hadn't touched a bite. She tilted her head sideways and looked at him concernedly.

"Are you all right?"

"Peachy," said Islington distantly, giving her a tight smile.

Pandora looked at him uncertainly. She fought another yawn and looked at the bed. It was much too tempting to resist. She shifted around and pulled off her boots, setting them on the floor by the chair. After she wiggled her toes in her stockings for a few minutes, she stood.

"I'm going to bed," she said quietly. Islington didn't answer her. "Do you want me to take care of your shoulder? Put some ointment on?"

"No," said Islington laconically, staring into the fire.

Pandora continued to frown, but she was tired. She went to the side of his chair and leaned down to kiss him on the cheek. He tilted his head away from her, and Pandora straightened up in surprise, a lump forming in her throat. She nodded once awkwardly, not knowing what else to do, and turned for the bed. She gathered up their things and took them to the cot, trying to fight back the hurt tears his unwarranted disdain had caused.

She got undressed and went to the wash basin to rinse her face and brush her teeth. Once she had braided her hair, she climbed into the bed. She turned off the lamp on the side she had chosen and dimmed the one on the other side, and then she pulled the covers up and curled on her side, her back turned to Islington. She blinked several times to stop her tears and closed her eyes with a tired sigh. The bed was soft and comfortable, and despite her unease, she finally drifted off to sleep.

Pandora was awakened by Islington roughly turning her over onto her back. She blinked at him sleepily in the dark and had only a moment to realize he was naked in the bed before he began to kiss her hungrily, pinning one of his legs over hers and smoothing a hand up her side to begin massaging her breast harshly through her chemise. Her sleep-fogged brain was trying to comprehend what was happening as she tried to push him away, but she wasn't awake enough to get it accomplished.

She could smell alcohol, and she realized he had been into the claret in addition to the beer he had been drinking when she went to bed. As her mind began to adjust itself, she began to think he *might* be drunk, but she couldn't understand why he was doing what he was. His behavior the whole night had been a mystery. She tried to think of anything she might have done to make him angry and nothing came to mind. She continued to push at him, and he grabbed both of her wrists tightly and pinned them together above her head as he moved on top of her. Pandora finally managed to free her mouth and turn her head away, and she tried to fight a rising panic at his actions.

"No...Theo...don't," she gasped out, and she could feel tears of humiliation starting in her eyes as he forced her legs apart and thrust into her. "Ow...no...you can't," she sobbed.

She redoubled her efforts to make him stop as she felt him begin to move in and out of her, until Pandora felt she was left with only one choice. She brought up her knee and planted it into his side as hard as she could with the little leverage she had.

Islington stilled on top of her and began to gasp as his hold loosened on her wrists. Still crying softly, Pandora weakly brought her hands down between them and pushed at his chest to make him roll off of her. Now that he couldn't breathe, Pandora was able to succeed.

She scooted away from him off the bed onto the floor and moved to the cot in the corner, her eyes never leaving Islington where he still struggled for air on the bed. She began feeling around for things while continuing to watch him, and her hand brushed over the open medicine kit. Her forehead wrinkled in confusion, but that wasn't what she was looking for. She found the front saddlebags and reached into the one containing her guns. She pulled out the Manton and the powder flask and perched on the edge of the cot. She removed the tamper and made sure the ball, powder, and wadding were still tightly packed into the barrels. Then, she put powder in the pans and set it to half-cocked.

She continued to warily watch him on the bed, and his breathing somewhat returned to normal. He didn't appear to be in any condition to move yet, however. She wasn't sure she would actually be able to shoot him, but she couldn't allow him to do that again. She moved toward the hearth with the gun still pointed at him on the bed and added more wood to the fire, which was nothing but embers. Once it kindled and began to brighten the room, she could see he hadn't rewrapped his shoulder once he had gotten undressed. The furrows in her forehead deepened further.

She sidled back to the open medicine kit on the cot and picked it up. She carried it with her to one of the armchairs and sat down to look through its contents. One of the small bottles in the lid had been removed and was sitting in the bottom. Pandora felt a knot in her stomach and turned it to the light of the fire to read the label, and then she turned to look at Islington on the bed.

"Oh, no, Theo, what have you done?" she gasped in dismay.

She looked at the dosage on the bottle of mugwort, and her heart began to beat against her ribs anxiously. *One drop to one cup of water. Take one ounce no more often than every four hours for lethargy. Discontinue use if hallucinations occur.* Pandora could only assume he thought it was the chamomile, which meant he had taken far over the recommended dosage. She checked the beer pitcher and the claret bottle. Both were empty.

Pandora uncocked the gun and set it on the edge of the table and ran a shaking hand over her face. Then she put the bottle of mugwort back into its place in the lid and closed the medicine kit to put it back in the saddlebag. She charily moved toward the bed and climbed onto it to Islington's side. His eyes were closed, and Pandora watched as he shook spasmodically in his unconsciousness. She cautiously put a hand to his cheek. He wasn't feverish, but he was tremoring and clammy from the effects of the mugwort. She wasn't going to try waking him because she wasn't sure if whatever made him attack her might not still be at work.

Pandora wasn't sure how long the effects of the mugwort would last or even if it was fatal. It explained some part of his actions, but not all of them; he hadn't taken the mugwort until after she went to bed. She idly wondered what time it was and crawled off the bed to get her watch from her waistcoat. It wasn't even midnight. She brought the watch back to the bed with her and set it on the night table. She sat close to the headboard and curled her knees up to her chest, wrapping her arms around them, as she watched Islington continue to twitch periodically as he slept. All she could do was watch and wait to see what happened.

Islington jolted awake. He blinked and rubbed a hand over his brow disjointedly. The first thing he noticed after he got past the pounding pain in his skull was that he was in bed. The next thing he noticed was that his shoulder wasn't bandaged and that it and his side were throbbing. He looked around himself in the darkened room and saw Pandora curled up far away from him near the headboard, watching him warily.

"Pandora, what are you doing over there?" he asked confusedly.

"How are you feeling?" she asked, still eyeing him cautiously and ignoring his question.

"Terrible," he croaked. "What happened?"

"You took mugwort instead of chamomile," she said flatly, still not moving.

"Bloody hell," he muttered, rubbing his hand over his face. That would explain the nightmares.

"Why didn't you wake me to get it for you?" she asked acutely.

"Because I already felt like I was imposing on you too much after what you said; I didn't want to wake you," he said shortly, rubbing his temples with his fingertips.

"What did I say?" asked Pandora confusedly.

She wasn't aware of saying anything out of the way to him. She had calmed down regarding his alias and other comments for her long before she had the chance to say anything to him about it, and it wouldn't have had anything to do with whether or not she thought he was making an imposition of some type. She had done nothing all night but try to be helpful, and he had refused every offer.

"That people like to know what they're doing is appreciated. I thought you were subtly trying to tell me I was being an ungrateful wretch, and I was," he said wryly.

"I didn't mean to make it sound that way. I've never done anything for you with the expectation you should be grateful or appreciative. That's not why I did it," said Pandora softly, now understanding his behavior from before she went to bed.

"I am grateful, though," said Islington gently, reaching his hand over to touch her foot, the only part of her he could reach.

His forehead wrinkled perplexedly when she flinched at the contact, but she didn't pull away. The skin on her wrists where she had her hands clasped around her knees looked dark—bruised, but the dim light in the room made it hard to tell. He turned to look at the fire to make sure it wasn't going out to account for the shadows. When he saw it wasn't, he began to turn back toward her. He almost completed the motion when the light from the fire glinting off the gun on the table caught his attention. He turned to face Pandora, his frown deepening worriedly.

"What happened?" he asked her stilly.

"Nothing," said Pandora shortly, looking away from him.

Islington raised himself up on the bed to look at her. "Would you quit being so damn *noble*?" he bit out impatiently. Pandora flinched at his tone. "Quit hiding things from me like I'm some kind of *womanish* weakling! Why are your wrists bruised, and why is that bloody gun out?" he asked exasperatedly.

"You...tried...to rape...me," she choked out between heaving gasps, and she began to cry helplessly after she said it, her body shaking with sobs.

She wasn't going to tell him because he was going to feel guilty about it. He hadn't known what he was doing; she had realized it was because of the medicine once she found out he had taken it. It had hurt her and upset her when it happened, but she didn't hold him fully responsible for it. Given time, she would have dealt with her feelings about it, and he wouldn't have been any the wiser, but when he snapped at her like that, as if being noble was an insult and seeming to imply she thought him less than a man because she wouldn't tell him, she had been left with little choice other than to tell him the truth.

Islington swallowed an emotional lump in his throat as his features went ashen with regret and mortification. It was inexcusable, and he knew it. Even if it had happened under the influence of too much alcohol and an overdose of the wrong medicine, it wouldn't have happened if the intention to do it hadn't already been growing somewhere in the back of his mind. Whether what he had intended to do and what had actually happened were the same thing was irrelevant.

After a few minutes, Islington reached out to pull Pandora toward him. She resisted at first, angrily trying to push his hand away, but she eventually let him bring her close to cradle her head against his chest and hold her comfortingly. He turned on his right side and lay down with her spoon fashion and carefully pulled the blankets over them, using his left arm with a wince. Pandora eventually cried herself to exhaustion and went to sleep.

Islington wasn't so lucky. He was awake for quite some time berating himself for hurting her yet again. When he finally did manage to go to sleep, his dreams were vividly unpleasant.

Chapter Twenty-Five

Pandora woke up slowly. Her eyes were stuck closed. She wrinkled her forehead confusedly, and then she remembered she had cried for some time before she fell asleep. She finally forced them open, and she imagined her whole face was puffy. The room was still dark, and the fire had died down but wasn't quite out. She looked out the window. The sun wasn't even rising yet, and she idly wondered about the time.

Islington slept pressed close behind her. His right arm was under her neck beneath the edge of the pillow, and his left arm was curled around her waist. His face was nestled into the curve at the base of her neck. She could tell because his breath moved the hair every time he exhaled. She thought, of all the ways she had woken up being held by him, this was her favorite so far. She shifted slightly, and she could feel his usual morning arousal pressing against her bottom. Oh, yes, she liked this position.

"Shh, go back to sleep," whispered Islington sleepily, smoothing his hand across her stomach. "It's barely five yet."

"I thought you were sleeping," she said softly.

"I was but not too well. Mugwort does that," he said, yawning tiredly. "Go back to sleep."

Pandora closed her eyes and tried to do as he asked, snuggling closer to him. She heard his sharp intake of breath, and she smiled because she knew why. Her eyes opened, and her forehead wrinkled thoughtfully.

"It wasn't your fault," she said quietly, twining her fingers with his.

His fingers tightened around hers, and he nuzzled the back of her neck.

"Yes, it was," he sighed ruefully.

"But you took the wrong medicine. If you hadn't, it wouldn't have happened," said Pandora calmly.

"Yes, but if I hadn't drank too much, I wouldn't have taken the wrong medicine," said Islington tightly.

"You couldn't read Chinese before you got drunk; it wouldn't have made any difference," persisted Pandora.

"Chamomile and mugwort don't taste the same. I would have known that, " he said shortly.

"Fine. It was your fault," said Pandora flatly.

She had absolved him of any blame. She had let him know that, but if he wanted to wear a hair shirt for it, she couldn't stop it. The more she thought about it, the more she began to suspect he hadn't even been *awake* when he did it. It had all happened so fast, she hadn't thought to check. But Islington was the one who would have to come to terms with it; she already had.

"Go to sleep," he sighed tiredly, tightening his hold on her and placing a kiss on her neck.

"I can't sleep," she said fussily, shifting again.

"Pandora…," he whispered, his tone one of disbelief and amusement.

"I can't help it. It's right *there*," she grumbled.

Islington chuckled. "You're a wanton," he said teasingly, bringing his hand up her side to cup her breast.

"And you like it," she said breathlessly as he began to gently tease her nipple through the fabric of her chemise and nibble at her earlobe.

"Mm-hmm," agreed Islington wholeheartedly.

He curled his right arm around to bring her mouth to his for a kiss, and his left hand moved down to begin teasing her button. Pandora moaned against his lips, and she rubbed against him longingly. Islington could feel that she was already wet and waiting for him, and he groaned ardently as he played his tongue against hers.

After only a minor amount of shifting, he was inside her, and he felt her release that same inarticulate sigh of pleasure against his lips as he filled her that he found so erotic. He continued to tease her as he began to glide in and out of her slowly, and Pandora arched against him feverishly from the exquisite pleasure of both sensations combined. Islington trailed his lips across her jaw to the side of her neck, and Pandora raised her hand to grab the back of his head weakly as she felt him biting on it passionately just where it joined her shoulder.

"Oh, Theo!" she gasped disjointedly as she felt herself drawing very near to her climax. Her hand clutched in his hair spasmodically as she felt everything become disconnected and gossamer.

"I love…the way you say my name," he sighed, delighting in the way she quivered uncontrollably as she orgasmed, the breath catching in her throat almost as if she were in pain. After only a few moments, he moaned fervently, burying his face in her hair as he joined her.

Once his breathing had somewhat returned to normal, he placed a gentle kiss at the corner of her mouth and twined their fingers together, keeping her wrapped tightly against him. He smiled tenderly as he felt her drift off to a satiated sleep just as he did the same.

The next time Islington awoke, Pandora was no longer in the bed. He looked around the room worriedly until he saw her sitting in one of the chairs by the fire, dressed and putting on her second boot. When she saw him looking at her, she stood up and scampered onto the bed with a grin.

"Wake up, sleepyhead," she said as she snuggled against him and kissed him enthusiastically. "They'll be bringing breakfast any minute."

"Is it that late already?" he asked groggily. He rubbed a hand over his face and sat up, grimacing at the pain it caused in his shoulder.

"Come on!" said Pandora impatiently, pushing him toward the edge of the bed. "You don't want to make the maids blush, do you?" she teased.

"All right, all right," he grumbled, swinging his legs over the side of the bed to stand up.

He walked to the chair by the fire where Pandora had neatly folded and stacked his clothes. He knew she had to have done it, because he wouldn't have; even if he could remember taking them off at all, he wasn't prone to folding and neatness. She had put the supper dishes on the tray for the servants to clear away. The gun was nowhere in sight. Their baggage was neatly stacked on the cot, but he could see she had removed everything and mussed the covers to make it look like it had been slept in before doing so.

"How long have you been awake?" he asked, grimacing as he reached down to pull up his trousers.

"About an hour," she said casually as she knelt at his feet to fasten the buttons at the bottom of his legs.

After she was done, she stood up and put her hands on his shoulders to have him sit in the chair. She went to the saddlebags and retrieved the jar of ointment. She put some onto her hands and massaged it into his shoulder, and Islington closed his eyes and sighed with relief as the stiffness he felt there began to loosen. It would be a long time before that went away. Pandora continued to work the knots out of the muscles, and Islington wrapped an appreciative hug around her legs as she did. Pandora smiled affectionately.

Once she was done with his shoulder, she had him rest his left elbow onto the arm of the chair to look at his side. He looked down at it as well. There was some bruising that wasn't there before, and he put his right fingers to it to examine it curiously.

"How...?" he said confusedly. "That shouldn't be there."

"I'm sorry. I did that last night," said Pandora softly. He looked up at her in surprise. "I had to get you off me somehow," she said calmly.

Islington nodded. He couldn't see her wrists because of the sleeves of her shirt, but they had looked bruised last night, even in the dimness of the firelight. He understood why she did it. He looked back to his side.

"Those stitches need to come out," he mused. They were loose, and the edges of the wound had sealed together. He looked up at Pandora. "Can you remove them?"

"I can try, if you tell me how," she said nervously. It didn't look as bad as it used to...either that, or she had just grown accustomed to it.

"Get the scissors and the tweezers," he said calmly. She did as he asked. "Now, carefully cut the stitches with the scissors, and once you have them cut, you can pull the strands out with the tweezers."

Pandora did as he asked, and Islington looked on. He would occasionally feel an itching sensation as she pulled the thread out, and it would feel itchier as the wound healed. Having the ointment on it eased that somewhat. The edges didn't begin to open, and he felt certain they wouldn't. Contrary to what Pandora thought, she had done an excellent job with the stitches, and while there would be a scar, it wouldn't be as ghastly as some Islington had seen.

Pandora was able to get through the stitch removal without retching or becoming queasy, and she sighed with relief when she was done. She put the scissors and tweezers away and got a clean bandage from the medicine kit. She put on some ointment and then the bandage. As she put the ointment away, while she still had the kit open, she put some chamomile on a sugar lump and took it to Islington. He eyed it warily.

"It's chamomile, I promise," said Pandora with a grin. She held it near his mouth, and he let her put it in.

They had gotten on his shirt and his waistcoat and were just beginning to fasten his bandage when there was knocking at the door, signaling their breakfast tray had arrived. Pandora made sure she had on her hat and kept her back to the door.

"Don't forget to tip them this time," she said quietly with a grin as she continued to wrap.

"I wouldn't dream of it," Islington grinned back. "Come," he called.

The door opened, and two maids entered. One maid took away the supper tray while the other set down the one for breakfast. Pandora smelled bacon, and her mouth began to water hungrily. She finished tying the bandage under Islington's arm, and he stood up, reaching into the pocket of his waistcoat.

"One moment," he called as the maids almost left the room. He smiled and put a couple coins into each of their hands, and both young girls curtsied and blushed and closed the door behind them.

"*You* are a ladykiller," teased Pandora with a grin as she began to remove lids from the dishes.

"Pardon?" asked Islington confusedly as he went to sit down and pour himself a cup of coffee.

"You had those young misses wrapped around your little finger," said Pandora casually with a twinkle in her eye as she began to nibble on a piece of bacon, curling her feet beneath her in the chair and hanging her hat from the back of it. "It must be the dimples."

Islington choked on the swallow of coffee he was taking at that moment, and Pandora giggled as she watched his face color red.

"Dorian was right: you are an incorrigible chit," said Islington after he quit coughing and was able to breathe again.

Pandora's face saddened when she thought about her brother. "I miss him," she said softly.

"I'm sure he's waiting in Edinburgh right now," soothed Islington.

"I hope so," sighed Pandora as she resumed eating her bacon.

"Why are we going this way again?" asked Pandora as Islington led the way beside a narrow burn.

"Because there's something I want you to see," he said secretively.

"Yes, you said that," said Pandora in vexation.

When they left the inn, Pandora thought they would resume their journey on the same road, but Islington had insisted they go this way. They were traveling through fields and crossing between stone-walled pastures on little more than a cow path. The scenery was pretty, and it wasn't out of their way, so Pandora was willing to indulge him. At one point, they crossed over a major road, but Islington kept to the burn, and Pandora's curiosity continued to build the further they went. Eventually they crested the top of a hill, and Pandora pulled Bellerophon to a stop, her eyes wide in wonder.

"Oh, my!" she gasped, and her throat tightened emotionally as tears stung her eyes. "Psyche would *love* to see this."

She was looking at Hadrian's Wall. It was impressively intact where they were, and when she looked in either direction, it seemed to go on forever. Psyche would have appreciated it more, but even Pandora couldn't help but be moved by it when she thought of the engineering skill and the time it must have taken to construct it. Pandora looked at Islington and smiled.

"Thank you, Theo," she said affectionately.

"You're welcome," he returned. He looked around, and seeing no one, he leaned close to kiss her warmly. "We can follow it that way for a while," he said, pointing to the east. "We have to go that way to get to the nearest road anyhow."

"All right," said Pandora agreeably.

At one point Islington had her stop while he made sure his rifle was loaded. She didn't know how he planned to shoot it because of his shoulder and his side, but his wariness made her anxious. She kept the flap on the left front saddlebag unfastened, and the Manton rested there, fully loaded after the night before. She checked her bow and made sure the string was sound. And, although she was capable of defending herself adequately, having Islington there made her feel safer.

They didn't talk very often as they traveled through the remote landscape, but Islington told her they would be in Scotland soon. He assured her once they were across the border and out of the hills they would find more people and a better road. Pandora believed him; he had traveled more than she had, and so she trusted his judgment.

They skirted around the edge of the Border Forest to the northeast for some time. Pandora wanted to go straight through, but Islington dissuaded her for several reasons, the two most important being that there were no roads and the possibility of being waylaid by criminals. He had given her others, but she hadn't needed them; those two were enough.

Once they crossed the Rede not far beyond Hillhead, Pandora was relieved when they came to a coaching road. To verify it, they needed to move to the side of the road quickly as a mail coach went speeding past on its way north. Pandora was so happy to be back to civilization she felt giddy. Islington saw her relief and smiled.

"Byrness should be not too far, I think. There will be a place we can stop for dinner," said Islington once they were able to continue.

"By not too far, do you mean a mile or five miles?" asked Pandora, adjusting her bottom in the saddle. It was time for them to stop.

"Well, I can't say *exactly* how far it is, but it should be very close," said Islington amusedly when he saw her shifting around.

Pandora looked at her watch. It would be a little beyond time, but a nice cushioned chair and grain for the horses would be grand.

"All right," she said agreeably. "But the horses need to stop soon, especially Jezebel."

Islington looked at her in puzzlement. "And just what are you trying to imply by that?"

Pandora's eyes rounded in dismay. "Nothing about *you*, honestly," she assured. "It's just she's in foal and shouldn't be pushed too hard."

"Whyever would you think my mare is in foal?" quizzed Islington with a wry grin.

"Because you brought a mare in heat around my perfectly capable stallion," said Pandora slowly. "I made no effort to keep them apart because I had other things to tend to. They've had plenty of opportunity to go at it like bunnies, so why would I *not* think she's in foal?" asked Pandora logically. Her forehead furrowed. "You probably don't remember I mentioned that at Aysgarth, do you?"

"No, I don't," said Islington flatly, his features frozen.

"Well, she's certainly not in heat anymore," called Pandora airily over her shoulder, as Islington had slowed his pace somewhat.

He watched after Pandora, and his forehead began to wrinkle with misgiving. He could think of two people who had been given plenty of opportunity to *go at it like bunnies,* as she had so eloquently put it. He urged Jezebel on and came up beside Pandora, looking at her speculatively.

"I think you'll be happy with the outcome," said Pandora blithely.

"Pardon?" he asked confusedly.

"Well, Bell *is* an outstanding horse. I think whatever he gets is going to be just lovely," said Pandora with a happy smile.

"Hmm," said Islington in a preoccupied tone.

Pandora looked at him. "Are you all right? You seem a little pale," she said, her forehead wrinkling as she checked him over.

"I'm fine."

"Hmm," said Pandora ponderingly as she continued to look at him. "I think we'll need to give you more chamomile and whisky when we stop." She shifted in the saddle and winced. "I think *I'll* have some whisky, too."

Byrness proved to be less than a mile up the road, and they found an inn without much difficulty. Islington did have whisky…and a couple pints. Pandora also made sure he had some chamomile. She didn't have any whisky after all, but she did have a beer. It was dark and rich, almost like drinking a loaf of bread, and she found it very tasty. It went well with the hearty lamb and lentil pottage they were served. They didn't dawdle over their meal, and they left within an hour. Islington looked much better after their stop, and Pandora was relieved to see the color return to his face. She thought he might still be pained, though, because he was rather quiet.

Pandora was glad they didn't stay long. They hadn't left Haltwhistle until ten. That was late. She was used to leaving with the sun. Now that she was riding with Islington, she was getting up later and stopping earlier. She wasn't too concerned; they would be to Edinburgh in a day or two at the most, and that would give her plenty of time to warn Artois. Besides, it was well worth the delay to sleep in a soft bed and be with Islington.

Islington had been looking at the occasional road signs as they passed them, and when they came to the top of a high hill after traveling for about an hour, he had her come to a stop. He looked around himself, his forehead wrinkled thoughtfully. Pandora looked around as well. The view was spectacular. She might not be traveling quickly, but she was enjoying it far more. He had shown her a lot of things she might have otherwise overlooked. She tilted her head sideways in inquiry as she looked at him.

He pointed down the hill. "That's Scotland," he said with a smile.

"Truly?" she asked happily. Islington nodded. "Wonderful!"

She looked around herself again. She couldn't see any difference between the landscape on one side of the hill and the other, but to know that Scotland was ahead of her just made it look so much better. It seemed to be leveling out somewhat, although still rolling, and they were leaving the Cheviot Hills.

"Will we make it to Edinburgh tonight?" she asked as they continued to look at the view.

"I sincerely doubt that," said Islington with an amused chuckle. "We will definitely be there tomorrow before dark."

"Marvelous!" sighed Pandora. "I just want to get this over with so I can go home."

She signaled Bellerophon to continue on, and Islington looked after her for a few minutes from the top of the hill. The concern that had been growing before dinner had not gone away, and after she made the comment about going home, it only grew in a different direction. He was still not sure if she just wasn't thinking or if she just didn't care. Either way, something would have to be done, and she wasn't going to like it. Islington urged Jezebel down the hill to catch up with Pandora.

"Can we at least find a place to stay where I can have a bath this time?" she asked when he finally caught up to her.

"We'll see what we can do," said Islington mildly.

"Yes, you said that last night, and I was bathless," frowned Pandora.

"I'm sorry, but most people don't view bathing as favorably as you do," said Islington, his lips twitching in amusement.

"Well, it is easier if one doesn't have to lug buckets full of water to get it done. We wouldn't do it quite as often at home if that weren't the case."

"You don't?" asked Islington, in surprise.

"No. We have bathing rooms, and the water is piped in through a system from the kitchen where the water heater is."

"You're having me on," said Islington, shaking his head.

"Oh, no!" averred Pandora. "My father, Psyche, and I drew up the plans and had it put in...." Pandora's forehead wrinkled as she did some calculations. "Hmm, six or seven years ago, I guess. We have it both at Wilderland and on Bruton Street. The servants love it, especially since several are from countries where bathing is much more commonplace."

"Yes, I imagine they would appreciate the reduction in work," said Islington. He did some calculations of his own and realized she had done that when she was only a child.

"Well, not only that, but they have their own bathing rooms," said Pandora. She shrugged. "In any event, can we please find somewhere to stay that at least knows what a *tub* is?"

"We'll see what we can do," he repeated. "Can't you wait until we get to Edinburgh? It would be more likely to find one there."

Pandora grew thoughtful. "Well, I suppose I can wait until tomorrow, but I don't want to see the count smelling like a farm laborer."

"You have *never* smelled like a farm laborer," chortled Islington.

"Now you're just trying to flatter me," said Pandora with a frown. "Fine. I'll wait until tomorrow."

They stopped for the night in Earlston at the White Swan. It was a larger inn than the Spotted Cow, and they would have been able to provide Pandora a bath, but she had told Islington she would wait until they got to Edinburgh. As Earlston was a market town on the main coaching road, there had been several places to choose from for their stay, but Islington let Pandora decide. She liked the name.

They took their meal in the common room, as Islington seemed to be much better, and there weren't many people to be suspicious about Pandora. The keeper had their bags taken up to their room, and they enjoyed a meal of ham and parsnips, chicken pudding and shepherd's pie.

Pandora had two glasses of the wonderful dark brown beer, and she started to nod off as she waited for Islington to finish. They were seated fairly close to the fire, and the combination of the good food, beer, and heat was making Pandora very drowsy. Islington watched with amusement as her head jerked upright after her chin drifted down to her chest. He finished eating and set his napkin aside after wiping his mouth.

"I think you're ready for bed," said Islington with a smile.

"Oh, yes, please," sighed Pandora with a yawn.

The innkeeper had a maid show them to their room, and Pandora disrobed as soon as the door closed. The room was smaller than the one at the Spotted Cow, but it was more than adequate. It was either that the room was smaller, or perhaps it was that the bed was larger. It was one of the old-fashioned four-posters with the curtains hanging around the sides. Pandora didn't care, as long as it was soft and comfortable.

Islington watched as she took down her hair, retrieving the brush from her valise to run through it before putting it into a braid. She went to check over their things, mussing the covers on the cot before placing the baggage onto it, and then she went to the wash basin to splash water on her face and brush her teeth. He thought, as she moved from one place to the next, that she was like a butterfly flitting about, never staying still for long.

Eventually, she thought everything had been addressed to her satisfaction, and she was ready for bed. She looked at Islington to see he had only removed his coat and hat. She frowned slightly, and then she went to their bags to retrieve some chamomile for him.

"Are you coming to bed?" she asked as she handed it to him.

"In a moment; I'm not tired," he said as he put the sugar in his mouth.

"I could help with that," said Pandora with a licentious grin.

Islington smiled amusedly and ran a finger across her cheek to her chin, pulling her face close for a kiss. He released her and shook his head.

"You go on to bed. I'll be there after a while," he said softly.

"You're sure?" she asked uncertainly.

Islington kissed her forehead. "Go to sleep," he said, giving her an affectionate swat on her bottom.

Pandora giggled. "All right," she said, running to the bed to flip onto it. "Oh, this is lovely," she sighed as she got under the covers. "Good night, Islington."

"Good night, Pandora," he said amusedly, sitting in a chair by the fire.

He sat watching the flames for some time, his features thoughtful. Pandora was completely oblivious to the position in which they had placed themselves. There were so many other things she was concerned about, their situation wasn't something that occurred to her. He could see that now. He couldn't be so fortunate. When he had offered his assistance to her family, he never imagined the things that had happened would have. He should have known it wouldn't be as simple as he had thought it would be. If he were honest with himself, he would admit he hadn't *really* thought it would be simple.

He had thought once he found Pandora and made her go back to London that he would be able to convince her to marry him. Now there wasn't any choice for her in the matter: she would *have* to marry him. Even her family, as liberal-minded and understanding as they were, would see that. No one knew what the two of them had been doing, but if what he suspected were true, whether or not anyone knew would be irrelevant.

She wouldn't willingly marry him, and Islington wasn't sure even her family could convince her. He didn't know what she found so distasteful about it. True, he had been heavy-handed with her at times, not taking her opinion on matters into consideration and simply doing what he felt he should at the time. But they got on extremely well together, and he loved her more than anything. She didn't find him completely objectionable, but he had already asked her to marry him twice, and he had met with refusal both times. Speaking to Aberdare hadn't gotten him anywhere either. Of course, he had refrained from mentioning to her father *why* he wanted to marry Pandora. Perhaps he should have been less discreet.

As Islington sat watching the fire, occasionally stirring it around and adding more wood, he finally came to a decision for his peace of mind. It would be underhanded and cruel, but he felt he was left with little choice. He wasn't sure he could fool Pandora, but he was willing to try. It was for her own good, and perhaps, given time, she would forgive him.

"You git! Why are you still in your clothes?" giggled Pandora, sitting up on the bed beside him and waking him from a sound sleep.

Islington opened his eyes and blinked groggily. He had eventually gone to bed, but he had left on everything but his boots and cravat and slept on top of the covers, well away from Pandora. It was probably useless to be taking such precautions now, but just on the chance it wasn't yet, until he could proceed with his plan, it was for the best.

He turned his head on the pillow to look at her. She was still in her chemise and sitting up on her knees, her hands on her hips, looking at him with amused incredulity. He rubbed a hand over his face and across his chin to keep himself from reaching over to pull her close. He needed a shave…again, he thought tiredly.

"Well?" asked Pandora expectantly, not changing her stance.

"I was too tired to take them off," said Islington softly, taking a deep breath and grimacing at the pain it caused in his side.

Pandora smiled and bent down to kiss him. "Poor *àiren,*" she said soothingly, rubbing his cheek. She lifted her head further back. "You need a shave," she chortled.

"Yes, I was just thinking that myself," said Islington, slowly sitting up on the bed. "I'll go to a barber when we get to Edinburgh."

"That would be a good idea. I would offer, but I don't do as well shaving with just cold water, and you wouldn't want to use my depilatory on your face; it smells vile."

Islington picked up his pocket watch from where he had placed it on the night table. It was 7:30. He hadn't gone to bed until after midnight. His shoulder throbbed and his side ached from sleeping flat on his back. He sighed tiredly and stood up. He went to the wash basin and splashed water on his face, and it revived him somewhat. Pandora came to him and handed him her brush. After looking in the mirror, he had to agree with her silent opinion that he could use it.

After the maid brought in their breakfast tray, and they finished their meal, it was after 8:30. The horses were saddled and waiting for them, and Pandora loaded their belongings. Once Islington was safely mounted, she mounted Bellerophon, and they set off.

Pandora would occasionally look at Islington while they traveled, and she thought he seemed preoccupied. She had offered to put more ointment on his shoulder before they left the inn, but he had said he would be fine and wanted to leave for Edinburgh. She made sure he had taken his chamomile, and because he was so aloof, she had even asked if he wanted laudanum. He had flatly refused it. He didn't seem angry or in extreme pain, and he did speak, but he was more subdued than usual; his smile wasn't as frequent or nearly as relaxed as she was wont to see.

Pandora was enjoying the scenery. She especially liked the mounds of rock that appeared from nowhere. Islington explained they were remains of old volcanoes. Pandora found that intriguing, considering there weren't any volcanoes in the British Isles.

The horses were well-rested from the slow pace they kept, and being well cared for at the inns where they stopped also helped. Islington had even made the comment Jezebel seemed a different horse. Pandora laughed and assured him she wasn't. She told him the mare's only problem had been that he wasn't paying attention to her limitations, and when she acted unruly it was because she was tired of him not doing so.

They stopped for lunch in Fala. It was beautiful country, and Islington continued to provide Pandora with information about things she might find interesting. She did notice, though, that when he looked at her, he would frown somewhat. It soon got to the point she became self-conscious and decided to ask if she had something stuck between her teeth from dinner.

"Islington, is there something bothering you?" she finally asked.

"Perhaps," he said mildly.

"Out with it," said Pandora flatly.

"I was just wondering if you brought other clothes," he said calmly.

"Well, yes, I have the dark trousers and waistcoat," said Pandora slowly.

"No, that's not what I meant. Did you bring *women's* clothes?"

"Yes, I did. Why were you wondering?" asked Pandora with a frown.

"Would a riding habit be among these other clothes?"

"Ye-es," said Pandora, her frown deepening. "Why do you ask?"

"Oh, don't look at me like that," said Islington with an amused smile.

"Like what?" asked Pandora perplexedly.

"You're looking at me like you think I'm up to something."

"It never crossed my mind," said Pandora, and she attempted to compose her features into something less accusatory. "Why do you want to know if I have a riding habit?"

"I was just thinking it would be a good idea for you to change into it before we get to Edinburgh, that's all," he said casually.

"Why?" asked Pandora with a blink.

"It's going to seem odd if you go into a room with everyone thinking you're a man, and then you come back out dressed as a woman," said Islington practically. "The attitude for that sort of thing in Scotland is no different than it is in England."

Pandora did think about it. He was right. She hadn't brought her habit with the intention of wearing it before she reached Edinburgh. She had intended to wear it home. It would be scandalous for her to appear as a man one minute and a woman the next, but she hadn't thought about it until that moment. Of course, she hadn't intended to stay at an inn once she reached Edinburgh; she thought she would go directly to Holyrood, see the count and see to the rest afterward. Having Islington along changed things.

"You're absolutely right," agreed Pandora, her frown relaxing even further. "How far are we from Edinburgh?"

"Less than fifteen miles, I should think," said Islington after he did some mental figuring. "We'll see a mile post at some point that will tell us for sure, but it's not any further than that."

"Then I'll change shortly before we get there," said Pandora agreeably with a grin. "I'll miss riding in my britches. Now I know why Persephone likes wearing them so much," she said with a chuckle. She looked over to see that Islington was still frowning somewhat. "Now what?" she asked with some exasperation.

"I'm going to say something, and I want you to hear me through before you lose your temper," he said levelly, giving her a serious look.

"Well, I suppose it depends on what it is," said Pandora archly. Islington looked at her chidingly. "I will listen," she said with a smile.

"When we get to the inn in Edinburgh, you won't be disguised as a man anymore," began Islington. Pandora raised an eyebrow and gave him a half-smile. "The only way we'll get lodging without causing some type of scandal is if you pretend to be my wife," finished Islington plainly.

"*What?*" shrieked Pandora, her eyes rounding in disbelief.

"I said *pretend.*" His tone was patient, but there was a tightening to his jaw at her disdain. "It would only be until your family arrived."

"Well, why not brother and sister?" she said in a panicked tone.

"Because the innkeeper where we'll be staying knows me…and Selena," he said flatly.

"Then we'll just stay at another inn," said Pandora stubbornly.

"No, we will not," said Islington firmly. "Aside from that, we cannot. This inn is where your brothers and I agreed to meet once we arrived in Edinburgh. Given the size of the city and the number of inns, we did that to save ourselves trouble and effort. It's one of the better inns in the Old Town and close to Holyrood. We're *not* staying somewhere else."

"But…," said Pandora, trailing off because she couldn't think of any further argument against it.

"Would *pretending* to be my wife for a few days be so awful?" asked Islington tightly.

Pandora looked at him consideringly. She had hurt his feelings. She didn't know why it would be so difficult to pretend to be his wife. She had been *behaving* like his wife for the past several days. It would only be a ruse to save themselves a lot of bother, and once it was over, no one would be the wiser. It wasn't as if someone from London would be there to gossip about it. Her family would understand why she did it and would probably advise her to do it if any of them had been there. Her brow furrowed as she continued to think.

It would only be for a few days, surely. The fortnight that her father needed for business in London was almost over; he would be to Edinburgh in less than a week, she was sure. Dorian and Myron could possibly—should probably—already be there, if they hadn't encountered any problems while they were looking for her. If they were there, then the whole farce would be unnecessary. The only person who would know about it would be the innkeeper. She wouldn't tell Artois they were "married." It would be irrelevant in any case.

"All right," she said finally. "I'll pretend to be your wife."

"It will be fine," said Islington with a soft smile, and the frown on his features finally went away.

Pandora became as preoccupied as Islington once they decided she would pose as his wife. It made her nervous to do it, but he was right. It would be harmless, but she couldn't escape the feeling something would go terribly wrong. It seemed such a simple plan, it couldn't actually *be* that simple…things like that never were for her.

Her thoughts on actually marrying him hadn't changed. He had been charming and attentive since they had met on the bridge at Aysgarth, but he had yet to say anything to indicate his feelings went any deeper than lust…other than his delirium-induced confession, which she couldn't take seriously. She was enjoying their time together, far more than she should, and she had grown accustomed to him being there, but she had never let herself forget that he viewed the proposals he had made to her as nothing more than a contract. She would not do that.

Once they went over a low hill and began their descent onto a rolling plain, Pandora saw a giant hill looming in the hazy distance. It was another of the giant remnants of a volcano. The closer they got, she could see several lower hills with a swirling haze at the base of them. They were going directly toward it, and Pandora was excited about seeing it at close hand. There were hills and mountains near her home in Wales but not any that looked like this.

"What is that?" she asked Islington, pointing at the hill.

"Arthur's Seat," said Islington, smiling at her amazement.

"Do we have to go over it?"

Islington chuckled and shook his head. "No," he drew out. "That's Edinburgh."

"Wow."

Islington pointed to one of the lower hills. "That's Tower Hill, where Edinburgh Castle is. Holyrood is on the plain behind Arthur's Seat. You can't see it, but Calton Hill is hiding behind it as well." He pointed at a range of hills to the left of Edinburgh. "Those are the Pentland Hills." He pointed in an easterly direction. "Over that way is the Firth of Forth."

"Oh, my," said Pandora in wonder.

Islington looked at her. "You should change now," he said softly.

Pandora's features clouded. "All right," she said in a subdued tone.

They came to a dense glade and went into it for a distance from the road. Pandora stopped Bellerophon and dismounted. She untied her valise and took it with her a little further into the woods. She pulled out a full-length chemise and her burgundy habit and redingote. It was wrinkled, but she didn't have time to air it. She thought her body heat would flatten most of them. She quickly changed into the habit and put her other clothes into the valise. She took down her hair from its knot and put it into a braid and put her hat back on. She hadn't brought another, and she also hadn't brought a set of her own boots. There hadn't been room for either in her bag. It was much emptier now, even with her man's riding coat. She walked back into the clearing. Islington looked at her when she did and smiled admiringly.

"Just lovely," he said softly.

Pandora's face scrunched up disagreeably. "You wear it then," she said tartly as she adjusted the constricting bodice over her breasts.

Islington chuckled amusedly as she tied her valise onto the saddle. He saw Pandora looking around herself.

"What are you looking for?"

"Something to stand on to mount," she said calmly. "This silly dress gets in my way."

She found a rock that looked likely and stood on it. She would still have to ride astride, and she adjusted her skirts to disguise it. It wasn't very comfortable, and she couldn't believe she had been doing it for so long. She had a sour expression once she was seated and arranged. Islington led Jezebel closer and pulled Pandora toward him for a kiss.

"It will be fine," he said softly, running a finger down her cheek.

Pandora nodded with a slight smile and turned Bellerophon for the road. Islington kept saying it would be fine, but Pandora couldn't escape the feeling it wouldn't be. She didn't know *why* she felt that way, but nothing ever went as she intended. Sometimes that was better, but usually not.

The closer they got to Edinburgh, the more fascinated she became. She could begin to make out the shapes of buildings and houses, and the nearer they got the easier it was for her to see the shapes of the buildings at the top of Tower Hill. She could see buildings in the city that towered over the others, some as tall as ten or eleven stories. Everything was so close together, Pandora had the feeling Arachne would not enjoy Edinburgh. Pandora, however, thought it was impressive.

As they rounded Arthur's Seat, the edge was a hill that sloped upward for a distance only to become almost sheer cliffs. At the summit on the back side was a steep downward grade. Islington explained the high hill they were going past was actually Arthur's Seat; the cliffs she was admiring were the Salisbury Crags. She imagined the view of the city from there would be breathtaking. Soon, however, the view of the hill was obscured by the close buildings as they entered the city. The streets were teeming with people. The sights, sounds, and smells almost overwhelmed Pandora after being away from everything that accompanied a large town for such a long time.

"What street is this?" asked Pandora, pulling up beside Islington.

"It's called the Pleasance," said Islington with a smile.

Pandora grinned. "Seriously?"

"A long time ago, it was called Goodenough."

Pandora giggled. "I suppose pleasance should be considered an improvement over good enough."

"Indeed," agreed Islington with a chuckle.

Islington turned into a low archway in the side of a building, and Pandora followed him into a large cobbled courtyard. The ground floor all the way around was comprised of stables and coach bays. There were piles of hay and manure from the mucking of the stalls, and there was a flurry of activity wherever Pandora turned. Everything was tidy and organized pandemonium. The walls were made of stone in varying shades of brown from the lightest beige to almost black. Most of the windows facing the courtyard were small, but they were plentiful. Some even had flowerboxes blooming with pansies, geraniums, and violets. Despite being completely enclosed the sides being four stories or more, the courtyard was well-lit by the sun because of its size. Pandora thought it was just lovely.

"Welcome to the Black Bull," said Islington calmly.

"Charming," sighed Pandora happily.

Islington guided them to a stop near a large set of stairs leading up to the first floor on the back side of the wing with the archway. A boy of about eleven or twelve years quickly came to take their reins.

"Do ye need 'elp wi' ye walises?" asked the boy as they dismounted.

"Yes, please," said Islington, placing his left arm back into its sling and adjusting his riding coat over his shoulder.

The boy whistled sharply and was shortly joined by another dark-haired lad of about the same age. Pandora unfastened the baggage from the saddles to give to him. She could have carried their luggage herself, but she realized she was a *woman* now, and women of society didn't carry their own luggage. It was going to be something of an adjustment for her to make. As she saw him struggling under the weight and amount of everything, she was tempted to help, but the first boy whistled again, and a third boy came to assist. Once they had everything, they ran up the wide stairs and through the doorway. Islington took her left arm and linked it through his right.

"Shall we?" he asked with a slight smile.

"Might as well," said Pandora. Before they started up the stairs, she turned to look back at the boy with their horses. "The stallion is very fond of sweet feed, if you have it, and he also needs to be re-shod. The mare is in foal, so she's liable to be a bit cranky."

The boy touched the edge of his cap. "Dinna hae a care, ma'am," he said with a grin.

Pandora turned to look back up the stairs and sighed preparatorily. Islington saw her anxious expression, and he reached over with his left hand to pat hers soothingly.

"It's just pretend," he said softly as they walked up the stairs.

"I know," she sighed agreeably.

The doorway led them into a space that wasn't quite a common room but was much grander than a simple alcove. There was a large oak counter that gleamed brightly in the lamplight and smelled as if it had been freshly polished with lemon oil. There was an area near a large fireplace furnished with two large couches and armchairs with a low table between them to one end. Behind the counter was a doorway, and to the side of it on the wall were small slots with numbers beneath them. Several doorways led off the room, and there was a set of stairs leading up to the next floor and a set to the ground floor. Pandora didn't think it qualified as a common room or tavern because she didn't see any taps, bottles, or glasses, but it was too spacious to be called a clerk's office.

The two boys were standing patiently near the counter, where an older, well-built man stood looking toward the door as they entered. He had a thick thatch of steel gray hair that curled in every direction as if it had a mind of its own, with whiskers that went down the sides of his face to almost join beneath his chin. He had twinkling blue eyes and a ruddy complexion that spoke of an amiable nature. When he saw them, his already friendly expression turned to one of surprise and happiness as he recognized Islington.

"Och! Well now, an tain't raffan Islington!" he said with a huge smile, coming from behind the counter.

"Good evening, Mr. Lee," said Islington with a pleasant smile.

He unlinked his arm from Pandora's to shake the innkeeper's hand heartily. Pandora watched interestedly. Islington had said the innkeeper knew him. She was curious to know *why* he knew him. Mr. Lee looked Islington up and down, his forehead wrinkling when he saw the sling.

"Och! An' what's 'appened till ye now?" he asked. "Ye han't bin studyin' on yoursel', hae ye?"

Islington chuckled and shook his head. "No, we had a bit of trouble with a highwayman in Yorkshire on the way here," he said casually.

"Och! Ye didna tak a coach?" asked Mr. Lee in surprise.

"No, she wanted to enjoy the air because she's never been to Edinburgh before," said Islington with a smile as he turned to look at Pandora. She gave him a hard look under her lashes. Mr. Lee chuckled amusedly. He turned to look at Pandora.

"An' wha is this now? It's nae Leddy Selena," said Mr. Lee.

"This is my wife, Pandora, Marchioness of Bardsey."

Mr. Lee looked at her wonderingly, giving her the same appraising once-over he had given Islington, noting the fading scrape on her cheek and bruise on her forehead and suspecting they came from the same event that had wounded Islington. He looked back at the younger man.

"An' a bonnie lass she is, an whin clours," he said happily. "Mrs. Lee!" he called loudly.

Momentarily, there was the sound of feet hurrying up the stairs from the ground floor. A woman of roughly the same age as Mr. Lee came to the top of them, her face expectant. Her hair was still a gingery red, and a smattering of freckles covered her face. She had friendly dark brown eyes and bow-shaped lips with small lines at the corners of all to indicate she smiled often. She had a white work apron on over her simple cotton dress, neither of which did anything to hide her ample bosom. When she saw Islington, she shrieked happily and raised her hands in the air with excitement. She bustled up to him to put a hand on either side of his face and kissed him.

"Islington, ma heart!" she said affectionately. "Whar hae ye bin?"

"Gettin' married 'twould appear," said Mr. Lee with a chuckle.

Mrs. Lee turned to look at Pandora, and she placed a fluttery, elated hand to her breast.

"Bless me," she sighed emotionally. She turned back to Islington. "How lang will ye bide till?"

"A week, possibly more. We're here to attend to some business, but I'm not sure how long it will take," said Islington mildly.

"Then let's see till gettin' ye sorted," said Mrs. Lee with a smile. "I'll show ye till ye room mysel'." She turned to Mr. Lee. "Mr. Lee, Mr. Padgorny is in fer his usual."

"I'll see till it," said Mr. Lee with a nod. "We need till get thir gentles registered first," he said.

"Oh, aye," agreed Mrs. Lee. "Haimish, Sean, take their bags till the Montrose," she said to the two boys, who had been standing patiently awaiting instructions. She excused herself for a moment and went back down the stairs to the ground floor then returned after a few minutes.

Mr. Lee took out the ledger and set it on the counter. He turned it toward them and placed the pen and inkpot beside it. Islington took his arm out of the sling and signed it *Theodore Marshall, Marquess of Bardsey.* He then stepped to the side and gestured toward the book for Pandora. She looked at the way he had signed it, thinking it somewhat peculiar, but she assumed it was because they were in Edinburgh or perhaps his familiarity with the proprietors. She took the pen and signed it *Pandora, Marchioness of Bardsey.* Once they were done, Mr. Lee blotted the ledger, closed it, and put it back under the counter.

"Let's get ye till ye rooms," said Mrs. Lee with a pleasant smile. "This way," she called blithely over her shoulder as she led the way.

Islington put his arm back in the sling and linked his right arm back through Pandora's as they followed her through one of the doorways off the office to the side of the fireplace. She led them down a long hallway that turned down the left wing of the inn to a stairwell and began climbing up, chattering with Islington all the while and asking after his family. When they reached the top landing, three floors later, Pandora realized they were just beneath the roof in the attic. There was only one door. Mrs. Lee reached for a ring of keys in a pocket on her apron and fitted one into the lock on the door. She turned to look at them.

"Now, I ken this is a long way up, an' it's definitely nae whar ye stayed afore, but I trow the leddy will like it," she said with a smile and opened the door for them to enter.

Pandora was impressed. The ceilings were high and vaulted from their position beneath the roof. The beams of the roof were exposed, but between them the ceiling had been covered with lath and plaster. There was a bank of shuttered windows at either end of the room, and the shutters and curtains had been opened to let in the fading sunlight. A fire had been freshly built in the large fireplace, and an ample supply of firewood was neatly stacked beside it. There was a couch and two side chairs placed in front of it. There were rugs on the floor over the dark, polished wood that smelled of the same lemon oil as the clerk's counter. There was a large wardrobe and a chiffonier for their clothing as well as a dressing table and a stand with a wash basin. Near the wash basin was a beautiful Chinese screen in the corner. Pandora suspected the chamber pot was behind it. There was a writing desk to one side of the fireplace and to the other was a sideboard with a tray on top, which held glasses and several types of alcohol.

As pleased as Pandora had been with the bed at the White Swan, the one in this room was…monumental. Pandora didn't think she had ever seen a bed as big. Even her parents' bed was not this big. It was a four-poster lined with brocaded, burgundy velvet curtains on a platform raised about a foot above the rest of the floor. The blankets were turned down, and a coverlet of the same velvet as the curtains was spread over it. The mattress looked thick and soft with feathers, and Pandora was sure it was going to be comfortable.

She turned to look at Mrs. Lee with a pleased smile. "This is wonderful," she said softly.

"Gude, I'm glad ye like it," said Mrs. Lee with a smile. "Now, I'll leave ye till get settled in, bat Mr. Lee an' I will be expectin' ye to join us to bruik a drappie in the tavern when ye're dane."

"Oh, Mrs. Lee, if it's not too much of an imposition, would it be possible to have a bath brought up?" asked Pandora hopefully.

"No imposition at all," said Mrs. Lee with a twinkle. "We'll hae tha' arranged for ye while ye tak your ease in the tavern."

"Thank you," said Pandora with a relieved smile.

Mrs. Lee nodded and left the room, closing the door behind her. Pandora walked to the nearest bank of windows, facing the courtyard, and looked down. She could see all the activity still occurring below her, but the sounds were muffled by the distance. She would have to make sure Bellerophon had been re-shod in the morning. There really wasn't any rush, and she was sure it would be taken care of.

When she looked above the roof of the opposite wing, she had an unobstructed view of Edinburgh Castle on top of its hill, starkly outlined as the sun began to set for the day. She could just make out the light of lamps and torches being lit for the night, and they would steadily grow brighter as the sky darkened, limning the walls with shadows. Beneath it were the impressively tall buildings on Parliament Square that glowed dimly with lamplight. Then she walked to the other bank of windows to look out.

"Oh, my," she sighed in wonder, putting a hand to her chest.

Because the land sloped away from the inn, and because there weren't many buildings in front of it, the roofs nearby were lower. Pandora was amazed by the view of the rooftops stretching out before her when she looked slightly to the left. What really impressed Pandora was the view of Arthur's Seat and Salisbury Crags. When she looked beyond it to the horizon, there was the dark blue-green of the Firth of Forth. It was breathtaking.

Islington came behind her and wrapped his arms around her waist, resting his chin on her shoulder as he looked also. She put her arms over his and sighed contentedly.

"Just lovely," she said with a smile as she continued to gaze. "I'm sure it will look even more so at sunrise."

"I agree," said Islington as he turned to place a kiss on her neck near her ear. "I didn't have a view like this the last time I was here."

Pandora turned in his arms and put hers around his neck to bring his lips to hers for a kiss. She could feel that familiar knot in her stomach as he began to tease his tongue against hers sensually while his hands traveled down to cup her buttocks, but Pandora had questions. She put a hand to his cheek and pulled her head away.

"The Lees seem to be very familiar with you," she said calmly.

"As well they should. I lived here for almost two years," said Islington agreeably, casually smoothing his hand over her back.

"Why?" asked Pandora curiously.

"After I finished at Cambridge, I came here to study. I had thought to take more permanent lodgings, but the Lees were friendly, and the inn is close to all the places I needed to go for my studies, so I stayed."

"They seem to know a lot about your family," said Pandora mildly.

Islington released her after placing a gentle kiss on her forehead and went to get his bag. Pandora looked after him for a moment with a puzzled frown when it seemed he didn't intend to reply. She looked back over her shoulder at the view one more time, and then she went to get her own bag from where the boys had placed everything just inside the door.

She didn't have much to unpack. She took out her one, white muslin morning dress she had brought and laid it out on the bed to remove the wrinkles because she was going to change into it before they went to the tavern. She also laid out a green velvet spencer and the matching brimless bonnet. She really wished she had an iron.

She had brought a simple, dark blue, sleeveless pelisse to wear over her morning dress to change the appearance of it, but other than her habit, she had brought no other outer clothing. She took the pelisse to the wardrobe to hang, but luckily the cashmere didn't wrinkle. She took her remaining clothes—another chemise, a shift, a dressing gown and another pair of stockings—to the chiffonier and placed them in a drawer. She got her serviceable pair of black kid slippers and crocheted, wrist-length gloves out of the bag and put them on the bed also.

After she had her clothing put away, she took her bag to the dressing table and set out her toiletry items, and then she put the bag and the remaining items in it at the bottom of the wardrobe. Once she was done, she turned to see Islington looking at her in puzzlement.

"Yes?" she asked calmly.

"Did you not bring any other clothes?" he asked her uncertainly.

"Now, haven't we been through this?" she asked with a teasing smile. Islington didn't seem to be amused. "The only other clothes I brought are Persephone's," she said flatly. "Why?"

"You don't have enough. We'll have to go shopping tomorrow."

Pandora chuckled and shook her head. "I don't think I've *ever* heard a man tell a woman she doesn't have enough clothes. That's funny. Why do I need more clothes?" she asked with a smile, shrugging diffidently.

"Because, even though this is Edinburgh, you have an appearance to uphold as a marchioness. One dress isn't going to be sufficient," said Islington tightly.

Pandora blinked in surprise at his tone and slightly shook her head. She removed her redingote and took it to hang in the wardrobe. Then she turned to look at him and calmly folded her arms over her chest. Her expression was chilled.

"*Nǐ xiǎng fān yīqǐ qù ma?* I am *not* a marchioness," she said firmly. "If I brought enough clothes for the daughter of a duke, *that* is sufficient."

She set her jaw and removed her habit. Once she had it off, she placed it in the wardrobe. She calmly walked over to the bed to put on her *one* dress that Islington seemed to find so unacceptable. She reached behind her and fastened the buttons then adjusted the bodice. She smoothed out the skirt and put on her slippers. She was pointedly ignoring Islington because he had insulted her.

Islington watched her get dressed, ignoring the feelings he had when she was in nothing but her chemise, and then he watched her go sit at the dressing table and calmly begin to unbraid her hair and brush it. He took a deep, steadying breath and walked behind Pandora to look at her in the mirror as she styled her hair into something more feminine than the knot she had been wearing it in over the last several days. She looked up at his reflection in the mirror.

"I know you're not a marchioness," he said evenly. "But do you really want to wear the same dress every day? We don't know how long this is going to take. If it's a question of being able to afford it, I'll buy them for you," he said neutrally.

She turned to look at him directly. "I can buy my own clothes, thank you," she said stiltedly, but her features softened. "I must admit, though, that I *have* grown tired of constantly wearing the same thing." Islington's expression grew relieved when she relented and turned back to styling her hair. "Two or three more dresses wouldn't be such a bad thing, and I do need to find another pair of riding gloves," she said with a half-smile as she twined around more locks into her coiffure.

"Thank you," said Islington with a smile, bending to place a kiss on her shoulder where it was exposed by the neck of her gown.

"As for how long this will take, it will surely not be more than a week," said Pandora certainly.

"How can you be so sure?" asked Islington, his eyebrow raised quizzically.

Pandora finished her hair and turned to look at him, her expression serious.

"Because Artois will be leaving for London then."

Chapter Twenty-Six

"I like the Lees," said Pandora unsteadily as they made their way back to their room several hours later.

"Mm-hmm," said Islington amusedly as he guided her upward. "Is it them or their *tap* that you found so charming?"

Pandora giggled. "Well, their *tap* was quite appealing as well, I'll admit, but they're very nice, honest, practical people," she said as she raised a hand to the railing. She glanced over at Islington, her expression sober. "We shouldn't be lying to them."

Islington's step slowed as he looked at her. It hadn't occurred to him that she might begin to have misgivings about that. He chose his words carefully.

"I think, for the time being, that we should leave things as they are," he said evenly. "Let's wait and see how things go when we send our message to Artois tomorrow, or better yet, until your family gets here. We've already told the Lees we're married, and even as nice as they are, it will not go over well when they find out we aren't."

Pandora looked at him for a moment. "All right," she said agreeably.

They had gone to the tavern for supper and some pints with the Lees. Pandora enjoyed talking with them. They were very funny, and they didn't hesitate to regale Pandora with stories of Islington from when he was there for school. Pandora never would have suspected Islington capable of doing things like *borrowing* cows or going swimming in the firth in October on a dare. He just seemed too serious to do that.

It was nearing eleven when they bade their goodbyes, and Pandora was moderately tipsy from having three or four pints and a *wee* dram or two of whisky. She didn't consider herself to be completely drunk, however; she could still walk without weaving and carry on an intelligent conversation.

They made it to the door of their room, and Islington opened it for Pandora to enter in front of him. The curtains had been drawn, and the lamps were lit low, and there was a very nice-sized copper tub sitting in the room full of steaming hot water.

"Bloody marvelous," sighed Pandora when she saw it.

After walking to the side of it and seeing that there was a table placed nearby with towels and flannels, she took off her hat and spencer on her way to the wardrobe. She hung them up and then took off her slippers and tossed them into the bottom. She reached behind her and unfastened the buttons on her dress and took that off to hang up as well. She started pulling the pins and combs out of her hair on the way to the dressing table and laid them there, and then she retrieved her bottle of soap.

Islington watched amusedly as she went from one place to the next, her gaze never leaving the tub for long and completely ignoring him. He didn't mind; he enjoyed watching her become steadily more disrobed. He took off his hat and placed it on the sideboard beside Pandora's and removed his frock coat and began to undo his cravat.

After Pandora placed her bottle of soap on the table by the tub, she bent down to remove her hose. She took them to the chiffonier and placed them in the drawer she was using, and then she pulled off her chemise and added that after she folded it. She retrieved her shift and dressing gown and took those to the bed. Then she was ready for her long-awaited bath.

She sank into the tub and sighed blissfully, closing her eyes with a huge smile. She settled herself into it up to her neck and leaned her head against the back while the tendrils of heat curled around her limbs soothingly. After soaking for a few minutes, she submerged her head and left it there until she could no longer hold her breath and brought it back out again, smoothing her hair back from her face with a relaxed sigh.

Islington had lit his pipe and gotten a glass of whisky and was sitting in one of the chairs near the fireplace watching her with a fond smile. The tub was situated near the fire to prevent a chill, and Pandora sat in it so that she was facing him and the room. When she smelled his pipe, Pandora opened her eyes to look at him with a slow smile.

"This is a very big tub," she said softly, slowly moving her arms back and forth beneath the water.

"Yes, it is," he said, taking a sip of his whisky to hide a knowing smile.

"I bet it would hold two people," said Pandora with an impudent grin.

"Mm-hmm," agreed Islington lazily as he watched her reach for her soap and a flannel, admiring the way her breasts gleamed from the water as she rose out of it.

"It looks like Mrs. Lee had soap sent up that doesn't smell like oranges and ginger," she said as she began to wash her legs. She dipped them back into the water and began to wash her arms and breasts. "The water would feel good on your shoulder."

Islington finished his whisky as he watched her wash. Her expression was seductive and inviting, and he knew he could do with a bath; he wasn't sure how much washing would actually happen if he got in with her. She dipped her head under the water to re-wet her hair and washed it. Islington could smell her soap on the air, and he was sorely tempted. He took a few draws from his pipe, watching as she rinsed her hair and brought her head back up to relax against the edge of the tub.

"This water won't stay hot forever," she said with a teasing smile.

Islington chuckled and shook his head. "All right, you win."

He stood up and put the ashes from his pipe into the fireplace. He unwrapped the bandage from around his shoulder and carefully rolled it up, setting it on the mantel. Pandora watched languidly as he took off his waistcoat and shirt and draped them over the back of the chair then sat to remove his boots. He pulled off his socks and unfastened the buttons on the legs and waistband of his trousers and stood up to pull them off.

Pandora's breath caught in her throat when she admired his magnificent form as he slowly walked toward the tub to look down at her. He bent at the waist and placed a hand at the back of the tub, a sensual smile playing about his lips as he leaned down to kiss her hungrily. When he raised his head, Pandora's eyes opened slowly, and she licked her lips softly as if savoring the taste of him. She arched her eyebrow suggestively and gave a sidelong glance to the water in the tub.

Islington smiled and stepped in, sitting with his back at the opposite end. He clenched his jaw when the hot water washed over the healing wound on his side, but he began to relax as his body adjusted to the temperature. He looked at Pandora in surprise when he felt her slowly working her foot up his stomach to his chest and on to his right shoulder. She smiled amusedly as she used it to push him further into the water.

"It won't actually do your shoulder any good unless it's *under* the water," she said with a chuckle when she saw his expression.

Pandora was able to raise herself a little further up in the water to give him more room and still keep all of her body except for her head beneath it. The water in the tub had risen close to the edge, but it wasn't in danger of overflowing, provided there weren't any big movements to create waves. She smiled happily as he closed his eyes, and the frown of discomfort that was constantly on his face in recent days began to ease.

The chamomile wasn't enough—even when supplemented by whisky, it wasn't. The ointment helped, but she could tell his shoulder constantly pained him, even more than his side. The marks on his skin were starting to fade to an odd yellowish-green, but—just like with his ribs—the damage internally had been more severe than what appeared on the surface. Pandora's forehead wrinkled thoughtfully as she looked at him, and when Islington opened his eyes to look at her, he saw her concerned expression.

"What's wrong?" he asked softly.

"I don't think the chamomile is working well enough. We should give you some of the laudanum and—"

"No," cut in Islington sharply, shaking his head firmly and setting his lips in a tight line.

Pandora's frown deepened further at his adamant tone and the way he had cut her off before she even had a chance to finish her thoughts.

"The chamomile will be fine. I don't *need* the laudanum," he said evenly when he saw the look on her face, not meeting her eyes.

"If you will hurt less, isn't that be better?" asked Pandora confusedly.

"Sometimes, pain is better," said Islington stilly, giving her a look that silently asked her to leave it alone.

Pandora continued to look at him with a frown as she reached for the soap provided by Mrs. Lee and another flannel. She lifted one of his legs out of the water and propped his foot onto her shoulder to wash it, and then she put it back into the water and did the other.

"Turn around here, so we can get the rest of you," she said softly, her expression distracted.

She placed her back further against the side of the tub to raise herself out of it more as Islington turned around to lean back against her. She washed his arms and front, and then she had him sit forward for a bit while she washed his back and his shoulders. Once she was done with that, she helped him dunk his head under the water to wash his hair, and she gave him the soothing scalp massage again and was gratified to see he provided the same blissful response. Once she was done and his hair was rinsed, she wrapped her arms around him and placed a tender kiss on his temple.

"The water's getting cold," said Pandora absently, resting her cheek on the side of his head.

"Yes," agreed Islington calmly.

She smoothed a hand over his chest then moved her hands to his back to gently push on it for him to lean forward.

"I think I'll get out before I wrinkle into a prune," she said quietly.

Pandora stood and grabbed a large towel and wrapped it around herself, then stepped out of the tub. Islington helplessly watched after her as she walked to the edge of the bed to dry off and put on her shift and dressing gown before going to the dressing table to brush her hair.

She was unhappy, and Islington felt several conflicting emotions. She was only trying to help, but she didn't understand. He wasn't sure he was prepared to explain it to her. He sighed tiredly and stood to take a towel to wrap around his waist. He stepped out of the tub and grabbed a smaller towel to dry his hair.

Pandora had finished braiding her hair and gone to the sideboard to pour herself a glass of Moselle. She was sitting on the sofa in front of the fire, her legs curled up beneath her, the base of the wineglass balanced on her thigh. She had her elbow resting on the arm of the sofa with her cheek resting on her hand as she watched the flames dance around on the logs. The jar of ointment was sitting on the small, round stand to the end of the sofa near her elbow.

When Islington came to sit down beside her, she quietly set down her wineglass and picked up the jar.

She put some ointment onto her hands and went onto her knees to work it into his shoulder. Every time she did it, she could feel the way the muscles beneath the skin were knotted and taut, and every time, when she was finished, they would be much smoother and relaxed. She supposed it would stay that way until the muscles *remembered* how they were meant to behave on their own. Pandora wasn't sure how long that would take, or even if they would. He would always grimace and wince when she did it, but she could tell he felt better when she was through. The effects never lasted. Once she was done, she gently ran her fingers down his shoulder and resumed her previous position, picking up her glass.

"I want laudanum," said Islington quietly. Pandora turned her gaze in his direction in surprise. "I will *always* want laudanum…which is why I can't have it."

Pandora's forehead wrinkled as she shook her head. "I don't understand."

Islington picked up his whisky glass and poured himself another drink. He came back to the sofa and sat down, his expression unreadable.

"I was still young and foolish when I came here after Cambridge," he said as he looked at the fire, rolling the glass in his hands. He briefly looked at Pandora with a half-smile. "The Lees didn't tell you even half the things I got into. I met a girl while I was here, we got engaged, and there were things I did to make it work. It didn't. That was the first thing."

Pandora could only assume he was talking about Jessica Wainwright. She wasn't going to tell him she knew about it because she was sure he would only find it disconcerting to hear about it *at all* right now.

"I tried to tell myself it didn't matter, that it had worked out for the best." He shrugged negligibly. "It did, but I didn't really believe it at the time. Not long after that, I hurt myself badly in a prank similar to those mentioned by the Lees at dinner. The attending physician prescribed laudanum for the pain. That was the second thing.

"I *knew* the dangers of taking it too long." He shook his head and smiled self-deprecatingly. "But it's so seductive. If you're in pain—any kind of pain—it might still hurt, but you simply don't *care*. There's this euphoria and disassociation that you have, and it just makes *everything* go away. And for a time, it makes you see things so clearly—so *precisely*—you can't imagine how you were able to think before. The only problem is, by the time you don't *need* it anymore, you *want* it. Your body craves it like the air you need to breathe and the food you need to eat."

He took a large swallow from his whisky and took a deep breath as he stared into the glass. Pandora could feel her heart pounding uneasily the more he said. His expression when he described the effects of the drug had been so intense, Pandora could see it still held an attraction for him. She took a calming sip from her wine as he began to speak again.

"By the time my father came to visit at the beginning of my second term, I was hooked. My studies were suffering, and I was associating with people similar to my older brother, which I had sworn to myself I would never do. I hadn't taken up gambling or anything criminal yet, but it was only a question of time because of the company I kept." He took another swallow from his whisky. "I will never forget the look of disappointment on my father's face when he realized he had a laudanum freak for his son and heir," he said tightly. "That was the third thing."

Pandora felt tears sting her eyes, and her hand went to her throat in dismay. She didn't want to hear anymore, but he wasn't finished.

"I was so gone, I couldn't even attend his funeral when his heart failed him six months later." He rubbed a hand over his face and shook his head.

"I took an overdose shortly after that. I'm not sure now whether it was accidental or not. Mrs. Lee found me and decided enough was enough. After she made sure I wasn't going to die, she went through my room and found every drop of the stuff and got rid of it. Then she locked the door."

He went back to the table and refilled his glass, and Pandora could hear the bottle clinking against the side of it as his hand shook. He stood there for a minute with his back to her and rested his hands on top of the table.

"You don't have to tell me anymore," said Pandora softly.

He lifted his glass and turned to look at her.

"No, I do. You *need* to understand," he said earnestly.

Pandora nodded reluctantly, and he came to sit beside her on the sofa.

"The withdrawal was not pleasant. It started within hours, and it lasted for *days.* I was so sick, I wished I *had* died. Eventually, I got better. Mrs. Lee sent for my mother and sister in the meantime and told them everything. My father hadn't. She saved my life, and it's something I can never repay her for.

"I hadn't touched laudanum in over four years until that day at Aysgarth. I was hesitant to use it at first, but I thought: maybe the addiction would be gone, maybe four years would be long enough. I was wrong." He sucked in air through his teeth and shook his head. "When I held that bottle in my hand, I just couldn't resist. I took more than I needed to because I *wanted* it, and it nearly killed me.

"You thought I took more than I should have, didn't you? You could tell," said Islington knowingly. Pandora nodded her head and looked away from him, attempting to blink away the tears in her eyes. "Not everything you saw and what I put you through was because I had been shot. It was because of my addiction and how much I *still* couldn't resist it. So you see, I will *always* want laudanum, but I can't have it," he finished bleakly.

Pandora choked back a sob and put a hand over her mouth. She took a deep breath and wiped her hands over her cheeks after a minute. Then she moved toward Islington on the sofa and straddled his lap to gently pull his head to her breast, softly running a comforting hand over his hair. She bent to place a kiss at his hairline, and Islington wrapped his arms around her waist and hugged her tightly with relief and adoration. He had been afraid she would detest him once she found out. He should have realized he needn't have worried.

"So, laudanum is right out," she said calmly after clearing her throat, rubbing a soothing hand over his back. "We'll just have to see what else we can find because the chamomile isn't working well enough, and I can't bear to see you suffering anymore. If Keung were here, he would know exactly what to do."

Islington lifted his head to kiss her, and Pandora trailed her hand over his shoulder to the side of his neck. She returned his kiss ardently, and he slowly worked a hand up her side to cup her breast, teasing the nipple through the fabric until she moaned against his lips. Pandora broke the kiss gradually and stood up, holding her hand out to him.

"Take me to bed, husband," she said with a teasing, gentle smile.

Islington looked at her with an odd expression, and Pandora wondered if she had gone too far. He finished the whisky in his glass and set it on the table. Then he stood to take her hand with a soft smile.

"Absolutely, my wife," he said, placing a tender kiss on her lips.

Pandora took off her dressing gown and shift when she reached the edge of the bed and crawled onto it. It was as soft and snug as she had imagined it would be. When she reached the middle of it, she stood up on her knees and turned to look at Islington over her shoulder with a soft smile as he removed his towel and climbed on after her.

He reached for her and pulled her close to begin kissing her passionately, and Pandora twined her arms around his neck and moaned softly as she felt his erection pressed firmly against her stomach. He ran his hands down her back to cup her bottom before softly trailing his fingers over the flesh to her thighs, and Pandora arched against him longingly as his tongue continued to explore her mouth erotically.

He carefully guided her onto her back on the softness of the bed, and he left off the exploration of her mouth to trail his lips down her neck to the tip of one breast where he teased the nipple with his teeth and tongue until Pandora gasped and clutched her fingers into his hair weakly as she felt the swarm of butterflies in her stomach began to swirl ever faster.

She tried to pull his mouth back to hers for a kiss, but Islington traced the edge of her breast with his tongue, along the edge of her ribs to her navel, and Pandora quivered with anticipation when she realized where he was going. He gently ran his fingers up the inside of one thigh as he traced his lips over her hip to the skin his fingers had just touched, and then his mouth moved to the juncture of her thighs. Pandora's fingers clutched convulsively in his hair, and she gasped inarticulately at the explosion of sensations she felt as he began to tease her with his mouth and tongue.

Islington put a steadying hand to her hip as she writhed against him, and her fingers moved to grip the bedcovers mindlessly as her breath came out in choked, whispery sighs. She raised her head to look down at him, her features a mixture of ecstasy and astonishment.

"My God, Theo! How are you *doing* that?" she gasped in awe. It was just not humanly possible to produce the sensations she felt.

She cried out incoherently as she climaxed, and she could feel herself shuddering uncontrollably as her back arched off the bed like a charge of electricity was spiraling through her body.

She was panting for air, and she felt weak as he slowly trailed his lips up her body to her mouth for a hungry kiss. She could feel his erection pressed against her, and she moved her hands down to his hips and wrapped her legs around his thighs as she brushed against him restlessly. Islington lifted his head to look down at her with a knowing smile.

"I want you inside me," she sighed longingly, her features frantic.

Islington filled her slowly, watching with a mixture of tenderness and desire as she smiled softly in wonder and sighed. He brushed a tendril of hair from her cheek that had escaped from her braid and bent to kiss her reverently as he began to move inside her. Pandora raised her hips to meet him, her eyes closed as she surrendered herself to the sensations she felt.

"*Àiren,*" she sighed gently, reaching up to softly trace his features with her fingertips, loving the expression of pleasure and intense concentration on his face as the pace of his thrusting steadily began to quicken.

She felt herself beginning to climax, and she brought his mouth to hers for a feverish kiss as she did so, and it became all the more intense as she felt him begin to shudder as he reached his came with her. He rested his forehead against hers as he tried to regain his breath, smoothing a hand down her cheek to her neck where he could feel her pulse pounding in her throat and the air coming out of her in gasps.

He eventually moved off of her onto his back and pulled her close to his side. Pandora stayed there for a moment before she reached down and pull the blankets over them. She placed a gentle kiss on his lips then snuggled back against him and laid her head on his chest, her hand going to his side near his hip. The sound of his heart soon lulled her into a contented sleep.

Islington lay awake for some time after she drifted off, staring at the canopy as his thoughts swirled chaotically. He felt as if he were drowning in a sea of confusion, and the cause of it—and his salvation from it—was cuddled beside him sleeping, oblivious to the turmoil she had wrought. Eventually, though, he knew he wasn't going to arrive at any logical solutions to the things bothering him, and he smoothed his hand down Pandora's back to rest it at the top of her buttocks and placed a gentle kiss on the crown of her head.

"I love you, Pandora," he whispered softly as he closed his eyes and slipped into a troubled sleep.

"How long will take him to answer?" asked Pandora anxiously as they walked down the sidewalk, her arm casually linked through Islington's.

Islington chuckled. "I don't know. We only sent the message twenty minutes ago. He may not even be awake yet." He shrugged. "We may know something by the time we return to the inn."

They had awakened early enough to watch the sun rise over Arthur's Seat, and Pandora had sighed and clapped her hands gleefully as the first rays shot out behind it like a crown. They had watched as the sun burned the mist away, and the firth became visible, like a mirror of blue-green glass, dotted here and there with ships as they sailed in and out from Leith. Then they had gone back to bed to make love, and Pandora somehow discovered that Islington was especially ticklish when she nibbled at his hip bones.

They had eventually gotten out of bed again, and Pandora decided to do her legs while the water in the tub was still there. She helped Islington dress, and she opened the windows because she didn't think he would want to stay while she did it otherwise. She had only opened the jar and put the cream onto her legs when Islington excused himself from the room, saying he was going to find a barber. Pandora wasn't insulted. The smell was intensely chemical and made the eyes water. By the time he returned cleanly shaven, Pandora was finished, and the smell had dissipated almost to the point of being unnoticeable. Islington was relieved.

He had made arrangements to have a breakfast tray brought up, and they ate their meal while the maids came in to drain the tub and take it away. Pandora had Islington give them a nice tip for their efforts; five floors was a long way to haul the buckets of water it had taken to fill the tub, and it couldn't have been easy to carry the copper tub itself up or back down. They replenished the firewood and changed the sheets while they were there, and Pandora had to admire the efficiency of the Lees' staff.

Once they finished eating, Islington sat down to write a message for Artois, requesting to meet with him. Pandora wanted to write the letter herself, but Islington managed to convince her that his seal (which he had brought) would be fine and that a letter from one gentleman to another might be better received. She balked, but she couldn't argue with the logic of it. She paced back and forth behind him, offering suggestions, and Islington chuckled at one point and reminded her that he did know how to write. After Islington made arrangements to have it delivered, they chatted with the Lees in the tavern for a time before leaving to shop.

Now they were walking down St. Mary's Wynd, looking into the windows of the few shops there on their way to High Street. When they came to one particular storefront, Pandora made Islington go in. It was an apothecary. They walked up to the counter and were met by a little man with thick spectacles pinched on the end of his nose.

"Can I help you?" he asked pleasantly.

"We need something for pain relief," said Pandora evenly.

"Hmm," said the man. He reached behind him and set a bottle of laudanum on the counter.

"No, that won't suit," said Pandora, shaking her head curtly.

"Hmm," said the man again, frowning as he put the bottle back on the shelf. "Chamomile?"

"Not strong enough," said Pandora calmly. Her forehead wrinkled. "Do you have anything that will relax muscles systemically rather than externally?"

The man shook his head after a moment. "Just laudanum."

"No, thank you all the same," said Pandora dully and left the shop with Islington.

"Pandora, chamomile will be fine," he said, patting her hand soothingly where it rested on his arm. "Now that we're not riding across the country, I'm feeling much better. We'll just keep using the chamomile and the ointment."

"Did my headache medicine help?" she asked as she looked up at him.

"Ye-es, it helped, but it also made me so sleepy I couldn't function." He gave her a serious look. "At the time, that was probably for the best."

"Well, perhaps I can figure out what's in it that makes you sleepy, and we can make something similar without it."

"You can do that?" he asked in surprise.

"I can try," she said calmly. "Some of it I can determine by smell, but I'll probably have to take a nap to figure out the rest," she said with a grin.

"If you're sure," he said uncertainly.

"We have to find something," said Pandora determinedly as they continued to walk. "Keung would get you sorted out immediately, but he's not here. When I'm at home, I don't have to take that medicine for my headaches. Keung just does *zhēnjiŭ*. He has *gong fu* in *zhēnjiŭ*."

"Are you going to explain what that is?" chortled Islington.

"*Zhēnjiŭ* is this skill Keung has where he sticks tiny needles into your skin at certain points on your body to make a different part feel better. It's extraordinary, but it works wonderfully well, even on my migraines."

"It sounds painful," said Islington with a grimace.

"Oh, no!" disagreed Pandora, shaking her head. "It doesn't hurt at all. The best part is there's no nasty medicine to swallow, and you remain perfectly lucid." She grinned. "You might look odd, though, depending on where he has to stick the needles and how many he has to use."

They started to pass another store, and Pandora halted to look in the window. Then she looked at Islington. It was a men's clothing store, as evidenced by the pre-made coats, trousers, and other items displayed in the large glass front.

"We're going in here," she said calmly.

"This is a men's store," said Islington disconcertedly.

"Yes, it is, Mr. You-have-an-appearance-to-uphold," she said with a grin. "If I have to buy new clothes, so do you."

"But I don't need clothes," said Islington stubbornly.

"You have a shirt, two pairs of britches, a riding coat, a frock coat, and two waistcoats—one of which, need I remind you, has a bullet hole in it," said

Pandora with a teasing smile as she moved behind him to push on his back. "You have fewer clothes than I do, so…quit…complaining…and *go*," she grunted as she continued to push him toward the doorway.

Islington chuckled and suddenly started walking to the door, and Pandora had to quickly grab his arm to keep herself from stumbling. She giggled as she looked up at him, and they entered the store to look at what was available.

Pandora would move from one rack to another with Islington at her side. She would pull an item down and hold it up to him before she would either shake her head or smile happily and drape it over her arm. A few times, she held something up to herself and draped it over the other arm. Now that she had been introduced to wearing men's clothes, she wanted to buy some of her own and replace the ones she had borrowed from Persephone. Islington would look at her and shake his head with an indulgent smile, but she did look fetching in pants. There were several other people in the store also shopping, but Pandora and Islington both ignored any odd stares they received when it was apparent that some of the items were intended for her. When she thought they had a large enough wardrobe to befit a marquess on holiday, they went to the back of the store to take care of their purchases.

They were waiting for the clerk to sort through everything after taking a few quick measurements for minor alterations and making arrangements to have it delivered to the Black Bull when a woman's voice calling from the other side of the store caught their attention.

"Islington? Is that really you?"

Pandora turned to look at the woman with polite curiosity, and she winced as she felt Islington's grip on her hand go from relaxed ease to painful tightness as he also turned to look at her.

She was stunningly beautiful. She was somewhere in her twenties, but where—exactly—was difficult for Pandora to pin down. She was shorter than Pandora with a voluptuous figure, accentuated by a light pink muslin walking dress she wore. Her skin was a pale ivory that was complimented by raven hair and deep, blue-violet eyes. Her face was heart-shaped and flawless with bow-shaped lips, a small chin, and rosy cheeks. Pandora didn't know her, but it was obvious from the way he stiffened beside her that Islington did.

"It *is* you!" said the woman, smiling hugely, moving toward Islington and completely ignoring Pandora to kiss him familiarly on both cheeks.

"Hello, Miss Wainwright," said Islington cordially with a slight bow. "But you're something else now, aren't you?" he enquired mildly.

"I'm Countess von Weilheim now," she said proudly. "I'm here with my husband visiting family. He's just in the back with the tailor at the moment seeing to some alterations. You really *must* be introduced," she almost purred.

Pandora felt her jaw set angrily when she realized who the woman was and now understood completely why it felt as if Islington intended to twist off her fingers. Jessica turned her gaze to Pandora then, and her expression was less than complimentary as she looked the taller girl up and down. Pandora bristled at the insulting look, but she remained casually poised and held out her hand with a charming smile.

"Hallo, we've not been introduced. I am Pandora, Marchioness of Bardsey...his wife," she said calmly.

Jessica's eyes rounded in surprise. She looked at Islington. "You're married now?"

"So it would seem," drawled Islington with a slight smile.

"That's wonderful," said Jessica weakly, her features frozen. "And you've inherited?"

"Yes, Countess...everything," said Islington evenly.

"Lovely," said Jessica dully, her features pale. "Congratulations."

Islington turned back to attending to business with the clerk, and Jessica looked at Pandora, her features cold and envious. Pandora saw a man coming from a doorway near the back of the store to move behind Jessica and put an arm around her waist possessively.

"All right, strudel, all done," he said.

Pandora casually looked him over. He was in his late thirties, somewhat paunchy, and not much taller than Pandora. He had receding, grayish-brown hair that he had pomaded and swirled until it almost stood on end. His complexion was a splotchy red, his eyes were a muddy brown, and he had a receding chin to match his hairline. Another thing Pandora noticed was that he smelled distinctly of sauerkraut and sausage. Pandora thought Jessica had definitely gotten the short end of the bargain. He appraised Pandora when he noticed her, and his sexual appreciation was unmistakable.

"Who is this, strudel?" he asked Jessica.

"Wilhelm, this is Pandora, Marchioness of Bardsey," said Jessica slowly, and Pandora could tell it galled her to say it.

He took Pandora's hand in his to place a sloppy kiss on her knuckles. Even through the crocheted glove, Pandora could feel the moisture, and she fought the urge to wipe it off.

"I am Count Wilhelm von Weilheim," he said ingratiatingly.

"Charmed," said Pandora with an amiable smile.

Islington turned back after he finished with the clerk.

"Wilhelm, this is Theodore Marshall, the Marquess of Bardsey," said Jessica, and Pandora fought back a giggle of glee as she watched the girl turn from ivory to a shade of green.

"Pleasure," said Islington mildly as he reached out his hand to shake the count's. He turned to Pandora. "We're done here," he said casually.

"Very well. It was nice to meet you," said Pandora to Jessica.

"The same to you," said Jessica weakly.

Pandora and Islington started to leave the store, but as they reached the door, Pandora momentarily squeezed his arm and thoughtfully walked back to lean close to Jessica and speak to her in a soft, confidential voice that was still clear enough for everyone else to hear without much effort.

"Countess, let me just say: I didn't marry him for his title *or* his money, in case you're wondering. I married him because he's hung like a stallion, and there's this thing he can do with his mouth that is to *die* for," she said with a charming smile. Jessica's jaw dropped in shock.

Pandora turned to return to Islington's side but paused a few feet away to turn back to Jessica and hold her hands up in front of her, her eyes wide in amazement and nodding her head.

She went to link her arm through Islington's. His face had turned a bright shade of red and his nostrils were flaring as they went onto the sidewalk to continue up the street. He didn't speak as they walked, and Pandora began to grow worried she might have gone too far.

"I'm sorry; I probably shouldn't have done that," she said softly.

Islington began to shake, and then he began to laugh so hard they had to pause for a minute for him to put a hand to his side while he caught his breath. Pandora looked at him concernedly, but her features began to relax as he straightened up to link his arm back through hers. He lifted her hand to his lips to kiss her knuckles adoringly.

"Thank you. That was brilliant," he said with an affectionate smile.

"Not a problem," said Pandora calmly. "She deserved it. Lady Ramsey was right: she's awful."

Islington looked down at her in surprise. "You know who she was?"

"I do," said Pandora softly with a nod. "Lady Ramsey and Lucy Cranston told me this ridiculous story about you and Jessica Wainwright when I went to see them about Hendon. Selena sorted it out for me later. Those two women have absolutely no sense of propriety."

Islington chuckled. "You should talk!" he hooted.

"That was a bit improper, wasn't it?" asked Pandora with a blush.

"Yes, it was," said Islington with a smile as he turned onto High Street with her, "but greatly appreciated."

"I didn't embarrass you too much, did I?"

"Not too terribly," said Islington mildly. They came to a store with women's clothes. "What do you think?" he asked as they stopped.

Pandora looked at it. They didn't have anything pre-made displayed in the window, and it would be useless to choose something from fashion plates; by the time the items were prepared, she would already be leaving Edinburgh. She was willing to look.

"We'll see," she said agreeably, walking in with him.

A pleasant older woman bustled up to them as they entered and gave them a friendly smile.

"Gude mornin'," she said.

"Good morning," said Pandora with a smile.

"I'm Mrs. Glenn. What can I do for ye?"

"I need to buy a few dresses, but I can't wait for them to be made. Would you happen to have anything?" asked Pandora hopefully.

The woman looked Pandora up and down. She took her by the hand to move her a little away from Islington and walked around her in a circle appraisingly, her forehead wrinkled thoughtfully. Her features cleared and her eyes brightened as she came to stand in front of Pandora.

"Funny ye sud spier tha'," said Mrs. Glenn. "I had a lass come in, oh, three months back, I s'pose, an' ordered a trousseau till be sent till India, of a' places. Then, just yesterday, she sent word tha' it wadna be needed na mair. Now, I'd understand an ye're nae interested—some lasses ken it's wanchancy till wear anither's trousseau, bat she was just about your size."

Pandora didn't think her luck could get any worse. "May I see what you have, please?" she asked with a smile.

"O' course," said Mrs. Glenn with a chuckle.

She went to a curtained-off room at the back of the store and returned a few minutes later with several boxes loaded into her arms and followed by an assistant carrying even more. When the assistant set down her boxes, Pandora saw with some surprise that she was Hindi.

"Oh, this is my assistant, Amrita," said Mrs. Glenn, noting Pandora's interested expression.

"*Namaste,*" said Pandora with a smile.

"*Namaste,*" returned Amrita with a shy smile.

"Ah, ye've bin till India then?" asked Mrs. Glenn with a pleased smile.

"No, just Wales," said Pandora with a grin.

Mrs. Glenn directed Pandora and Islington to a settee near where she and Amrita had placed the boxes and opened them. Everything was just lovely. Whoever the girl had been, her taste was excellent, and the colors were exactly what Pandora would have chosen had she requested the dresses herself.

Mrs. Glenn had been correct when she said an *entire* trousseau. There were morning dresses, walking dresses, ball gowns, riding habits, coach dresses, and all the accessories to go with them, including hats, shawls, slippers, parasols, reticules, and gloves. There were coats and spencers, cloaks and pelisses and muffs. Then there were dressing gowns, sleeping shifts, chemises, and stockings. There were also stays and corsets, but Pandora did not, and would not, wear them. The embroidery and lace were exquisite, and she wasn't able to decide which items she wanted. She looked at Mrs. Glenn.

"I can't make up my mind, but I don't think I need all of it. They look to be the right size, but might I try one on first to make sure they fit?"

"Certainly," said Mrs. Glenn with a smile. "If ye'll come this way," she said, directing Pandora to the curtained room.

Pandora turned to look at Islington. "I'll be right back," she said as she stood, taking a walking dress, coat, and matching pair of slippers.

"Take your time," smiled Islington, relaxing back onto the settee.

Pandora followed Mrs. Glenn into the small room and removed her pelisse and morning dress. Mrs. Glenn looked at her in surprise.

"Why, ye're nae wearin' a corset or stays, dearie," she said with wonder.

"Ooh, no," said Pandora mildly. "Wouldn't dream of it. That would be like telling a man to wear a codpiece with his kilt."

Mrs. Glenn looked at her in surprise at the statement, and then she began to laugh with hilarity and shook her head.

"Whist now!" she chortled as she helped Pandora pull the new dress over her head.

Mrs. Glenn fastened the back and came around the front to look at the fit. The length was fine, but the bodice would need to be altered to a tighter fit. Pandora tried on the slippers. They were a little loose, but they wouldn't be in any danger of falling off or rubbing blisters. The coat fit perfectly. Pandora smoothed her hands over the dress and took a look at it in the full-length mirror. She turned to look at Mrs. Glenn.

"How long would it take to make the alterations?"

"Hae ye decided which dresses ye want?"

"All of them, please. They're all so lovely. I can't decide, and who knows when you'll get someone else in not bothered by superstitions and the right size for them," said Pandora with a grin.

Mrs. Glenn thought for a moment. "The only thin's tha' wad need takin' in wad be the gowns, I expect, an' those nae by much. Amrita is a quick hand wi' a needle. By the end o' the day?"

"Perfect," said Pandora with a smile.

"Now, will ye be payin' for this, or your husband?"

"Oh, he's not my husband," said Pandora calmly.

"In tha' case, I hae one other thin' till show ye," said Mrs. Glenn with a twinkle.

She went to a shelf and pulled down another box. She set it on a nearby table and lifted the lid and folded back the tissue. Pandora peered into the box and sighed. It was intended to be a wedding dress, made of a pale cream-colored silk. The sleeves were short and puffed, and the bodice was covered in exquisitely complicated embroidery. The skirt was sewn from a striped silk, made that way from heavier and thinner weaves through the material. The bottom edge was trimmed in a wide, embroidered lace with small, darker cream-colored silk roses along the top where it met the bottom of the skirt. It was breathtaking.

"Oh, Mrs. Glenn, this is lovely," sighed Pandora.

"Wad ye be interested?"

Pandora thought about it. Islington had asked her to marry him twice, and both times she had refused because he had presented it as a business arrangement. She loved him more than anything in the world, but she couldn't say what his feelings were for her. She thought they had at least become *friends*...friends who enjoyed having sex with each other. She didn't think she could marry anyone else, but he hadn't asked a third time, and unless he asked for the right reasons, she would still refuse, even as hard as it would be. She reached out to gently touch the delicate material then looked at Mrs. Glenn.

"I'll take it," said Pandora softly. "One never knows when one may need a wedding dress," she said with a slight smile.

Mrs. Glenn smiled and nodded happily. "Let's get ye out o' this one, an' we'se hae them a' made up just right for ye."

Once Pandora was down to her chemise, Mrs. Glenn brought out a tape to measure her chest, and then Pandora put back on her morning dress and pelisse. They agreed on the price for the dresses and other items (minus the corsets and stays) and the cost of the alterations. Pandora gave Mrs. Glenn the money from her purse, which grew decidedly lighter after the transaction, and the address where they would need to be delivered.

"Och, Mrs. Lee is a friend o' mine!"

"She's a remarkable woman," said Pandora with a smile.

"I've been meanin' to stop by to see her. Mayhap I'll see ye agin," said Mrs. Glenn as she went to pull the curtain aside for Pandora to go back to the front room.

"That would be lovely," said Pandora with a smile. Islington stood when they came in. He had been dozing. She turned to look at Mrs. Glenn. "Thank you for everything, Mrs. Glenn."

"Ye're welcome," said Mrs. Glenn with a smile.

"Are you done?" asked Islington with some surprise, looking at the dresses still lying out.

"Yes, shall we go?" asked Pandora, taking his arm. Islington nodded, and they walked out. He paused with her after the door closed.

"Do you want to look somewhere else?"

"No, I'm done. If I don't have enough dresses now, I never will," said Pandora with a sigh.

Islington frowned. "But you didn't buy any."

"I bought all of them," said Pandora calmly. "Can we go back to the inn now? I'm hungry."

They turned on the sidewalk to return to St. Mary's Wynd.

"Why didn't you let me pay for them?" asked Islington quietly as they walked.

Pandora looked up at him. His face was troubled.

"I told you I could buy my own clothes, and I did."

"How much was it?"

Pandora looked at him in surprise. "Oh, I'm not going to tell you that," she said evenly.

He looked down at her and stopped on the sidewalk.

"Pandora, how could you have bought *all* that with pin money?"

"Well, I didn't buy the corsets," said Pandora prevaricatingly.

"Pandora...," he sighed exasperatedly.

"Why does it matter?" she asked him as she resumed walking. "If I have the money to pay for them, then is it not up to me to do that?" He wasn't appeased, and Pandora heaved a long-suffering sigh. "My Grandfather Sanders had but one child. When he died, everything was divided among her and his grandchildren living at the time—including his granddaughters—of which I am one. None of his estate was entailed, so it was a fairly sizable amount. It is entrusted, and I receive a monthly allowance from the interest."

"How much?"

Pandora looked at him and shook her head. "I don't know why I am telling you *any* of this," she said calmly. "It really is none of your affair."

"I don't want to think you spent all your money buying dresses when you could have let me pay for them," said Islington moderately.

Pandora laughed and reached over to pat his arm soothingly. "I didn't spend *all* my money, and I'll have more come the first. Besides, it's not your responsibility to buy them; it's mine."

They almost passed a store, and Pandora stopped to look.

"Hmm…I'm going to need one of those," she said thoughtfully.

"One of what?" asked Islington, looking in the window as well.

"A trunk for all those clothes. They won't fit in my valise and saddlebags, and they'll have to be loaded onto the coach somehow."

"What coach?" asked Islington perplexedly.

"Papà's coach, of course," said Pandora, shaking her head over what she thought was a foolish question.

They went into the store, and Pandora found what she thought would be a trunk of suitable size and configuration, but Islington insisted on buying it for her. Pandora thought he was just being silly, but he wouldn't take no for an answer. He reluctantly bought a smaller one for himself also.

"I wonder why Dorian and Myron aren't here yet," said Pandora worriedly as they left the store, resuming their walk back to the inn. "They surely should have been by now. I was surprised they hadn't already been here for days."

"It is curious," agreed Islington, concerned about it himself.

"Dorian, at least, should have been here a week ago, considering he took the Great North Road."

"Why didn't you?"

Pandora looked at him. "There would have been too many coaches and too many towns. Besides, I thought the most direct route would be quickest. It would have been, had circumstances been different." She grimaced. "There would have been far too many toll gates as well." Islington smiled. "Myron should have been here quite some time ago. I hope nothing terrible has happened," said Pandora, and her features became anxious when she thought that some harm might have come to her brothers because of her actions.

Islington reached over to pat her arm. "I'm sure they're fine," he said softly. "They'll arrive at any time." But his features were worried as well.

When they returned to the inn, there was a response waiting for them from Holyrood. Pandora wanted to open it at the desk, but Islington made her wait until they were in their room. He broke the seal on the single sheet and read through it quietly, his brow furrowing. He handed it to Pandora.

"I am sorry you have traveled such a great distance, but *Monsieur le Comte* is not receiving visitors at this time," muttered Pandora aloud as she read it. "Signed Armand de Chateauville, Secretary to His Royal Highness, et cetera." She looked up at Islington, her forehead wrinkled as well. "We'll just send him another note," she said determinedly.

Islington looked at her doubtfully. "Do you think that will work?"

Pandora sighed frustratedly. "No, but what else can we do? If he refuses again, then I shall camp on his doorstep until he does see us. I have a tent, and I'm not afraid to use it." Her forehead wrinkled even further as she went to the writing desk. "One has to wonder if he was even given the message," she muttered as she picked up the pen and a piece of paper.

"What are you thinking?" asked Islington as he came behind her to watch her write.

He saw that she was writing it in French, which he had not done, her handwriting neat and feminine.

"I'm thinking if he has a secretary seeing to his correspondence, if said secretary has been instructed to decline all visitors, then Monsieur de Chateauville will do just that. As soon as he sees the word *meet,* the answer will automatically be no, especially if the request is in English. I'm sure you worded what you wrote sufficiently to convey this was an urgent matter, and had Artois seen it, he would have let us come for a chat."

"But you don't think he did?" asked Islington speculatively.

Pandora put down the pen and blotted her message before standing to look at him.

"Absolutely not," she said calmly.

She went to the wardrobe for her father's seal from her valise. Then, she went to the dressing table for her bottle of perfume and brought both back to the writing desk. She folded her note and sealed it then took the stopper from her perfume and dabbed a little onto the note. Islington inhaled deeply and had to fight the urge to grab Pandora and ravish her.

"What are you doing?" he asked with a frown.

"I'm trying to seduce the count," she said with a grin as she stood up.

"*What*?" he roared angrily.

"Oh, shh!" said Pandora with a giggle, placing a hand to his cheek and giving him a kiss. "Charles-Philippe de Bourbon was quite the ladykiller when he was younger. He's *very* Catholic these days, but something like that doesn't ever completely go away. He is a man, after all. If he should be within sniffing distance of this, I don't think he's going to let Monsieur de Chateauville snub whoever sent it without at least reading it himself first."

"So the perfume is a decoy?" asked Islington, his features relaxing.

"Exactly, *áiren*," said Pandora with a patent smile. "One would think you were jealous," she teased with a speculative arch to her eyebrow.

Islington colored brightly because for a moment he had been *intensely* jealous. The thought of her attempting to attract another man also terrified him. He wouldn't be able to bear it if she were with someone else, but she was far too independent to tolerate possessiveness.

"I've no need to be jealous," he said evenly. "You can do as you will."

Pandora's smile became slightly brittle at his words. That had not been what she wanted to hear. She reached up to rub the spot behind her ear and picked up her perfume to take it back to the dressing table. A knock at the door made her jump and nearly drop it.

"Come," called Islington.

One of the maids opened the door and entered. "Beggin' yer lordship's pardon, bat there're several packages tha' hae been delivered for ye an' her leddyship," she said with a curtsy.

She moved slightly to the side of the doorway to let in Sean and Haimish and the other young stable boy carrying large stacks of boxes.

"Oh, just set them to the side there," said Pandora quickly. She could see they were tired from carrying them up the stairs. She looked at Islington. "Those will have to be from the men's store. Mrs. Glenn said the others would be ready by the end of the day. I'm sure Amrita is an excellent seamstress, but there were *a lot* of dresses to alter."

"I'd say you're right," agreed Islington as he went for a whisky.

Pandora found her purse and retrieved some coins for each of them. She handed them out with a smile, and they all returned her smile happily with bows and a curtsy before leaving the room.

"Oh, darn!" said Pandora after they left.

"What's wrong?" asked Islington.

"I forgot to give the message to one of the boys to take to Holyrood."

Islington finished his whisky and went to the table to pick it up. "I'll take care of it." He gave her a teasing grin. "You can open all the boxes."

"How's your shoulder?" It was early for whisky.

"It's a little stiff but tolerable," said Islington honestly.

Pandora nodded. "I'll see what I can do on deciphering my headache medicine after I get through with the boxes." Her stomach rumbled. "Actually, I think I'd rather have some food first."

"I'll have Mrs. Lee send up a tray, or would you rather go for a picnic on Calton Hill?"

"I'm hungry, but a picnic sounds lovely," said Pandora with a smile.

"All right. I'll arrange to have this delivered to Artois and see to getting a buggy and a basket."

"Thank you," said Pandora happily, going to the boxes as he closed the door behind him.

By the time they returned from their picnic, the rest of their purchases had arrived from the stores, but there was no response from Artois. It was nearing six in the evening, and Pandora hoped it meant he was at least *thinking* about meeting them. She would like an answer by that night, but she was sure they would have one tomorrow.

Calton Hill had been wonderful. Islington had pointed out several things in the city and surrounding area, including Holyrood. It was beautiful, and the top of the hill afforded them a wonderful view. They had managed to find a spot that was secluded, and once they finished eating, Islington had taken a short nap, resting his head in Pandora's lap. She had let him because if he was sleeping, then he wasn't being bothered by his shoulder and ribs.

Once they returned to the courtyard, Pandora went to see Bellerophon and Jezebel. They were placed in stalls beside each other, and both had whinnied loudly when she whistled at the head of the row. They had plenty of food and water, and their stalls were clean. Her stallion had been re-shod as she had requested, and the farrier had done an excellent job. She made sure to give both of the animals several sugar lumps before she left.

When she and Islington reached their room, Pandora finished unpacking the boxes from the men's clothing shop that she hadn't gotten to before their picnic. She put the clothes from the store that she had purchased for herself and Persephone into her trunk because she wouldn't need them while she was in Edinburgh. She put the box containing the wedding dress from Mrs. Glenn's into her trunk unopened. She didn't want Islington to know she had bought it; it would provoke too many questions she wasn't prepared to answer, especially after his comment about her being free to do as she willed. She packed away most of the other things she had bought, keeping out only three or four of the dresses and some of the other items because she wouldn't need them all for what she hoped would be her brief stay.

"I'm ready to work on the headache medicine now," she said as she closed the lid to her trunk.

"Are you sure you want to do that?" asked Islington uncertainly.

"Of course," said Pandora calmly, giving him a wink.

She went to the wardrobe for the medicine kit and took the box to the writing desk and opened it. Before she began, she got some chamomile for Islington. He had not taken any since that morning, and he had been steadily sipping a glass of whisky since they returned from their picnic. He took it without complaint, and Pandora went back to the desk. She rubbed the sides of her nose preparatorily and removed the bottle of headache medicine. She removed the stopper, put it near her nose, and inhaled.

She grimaced at the odor. It didn't smell any better than it tasted. She picked up the pen and a piece of paper and wrote down willow, which she already knew it contained. She smelled again then picked out one of the smaller bottles from the lid to remove the stopper and inhale. She shook her head and removed another to repeat the process. She lifted the pen and wrote down the herb on her list. She continued to smell and write for the better part of an hour. In the end, she had to put a drop of the medicine onto her tongue. She grimaced and cleared her throat, but she lifted the pen and wrote down the final two herbs with her eyes watering. She blotted the page and took it to Islington.

"This should be it," she said, still trying to get the taste of the medicine out of her mouth.

She rubbed her throat and went to the sideboard for a glass of Moselle. She now understood why Keung had her dilute it in a cup of water. It was too harsh to take otherwise, but she would have needed to taste more if it had been weaker. This way, she could stay awake. She sat on the sofa beside Islington as he looked at the list.

"Well? Does it look likely?" she asked as he continued to look at it.

After a minute he looked at her. "You're sure it has all of these?"

"Oh, yes," said Pandora with a nod, still rubbing at her throat. She took another sip from her wine.

"And you were able to discover that by smelling it and tasting it?"

"It's a bit like an equation or a puzzle, really. You determine what one part is and exclude it, and then you move on to the next piece until they're all accounted for." She cleared her throat and took another sip. "Trust me, they're all accounted for."

"But these aren't all in the kit. How do you know what they are?"

"Theo, they are all in there," said Pandora, smiling with a bit of exasperation. "Now, which one—or *ones*—make you sleepy?"

Islington looked back at the list. "These three," said Islington, pointing to them. "But you probably want to leave in the valerian."

"Really? Are you sure? That has got to be the most vile smelling...." Islington looked at her with an arched eyebrow. "All right," she said with a shrug. She took back the list. "We can go to the apothecary tomorrow to get the herbs we don't already have and an empty bottle. He's closed by now."

Islington pulled out his watch to look at it and nodded. It was after eight. He looked at Pandora and saw the way she continued rub her tongue against the roof of her mouth as she tried to remove the aftertaste of the medicine. He set down his glass and pulled her toward him for a kiss, thoroughly exploring her mouth with his tongue. He drew his head back, and Pandora slowly opened her eyes.

"What was that for?" she asked weakly.

"I'm helping," said Islington with a grin.

Pandora smiled and straddled his lap, wrapping her arms around his neck.

"Then *help* me, please," she said with an indecent smile as she bent down to resume kissing him.

Pandora's head came up in surprise when there was a knock on the door. She sighed wistfully as she looked down at Islington and climbed off his lap to straighten her skirt. Islington chuckled and stood up, looking at the door.

"Come," he called, still chuckling as he walked toward it.

The door opened and a maid entered, carrying a letter. Islington took it from her and gave her a coin. He looked at the seal on the flap and held it up in the air as he carried it to Pandora on the couch. It was addressed to her. She took it from him and broke the seal to open it and unfolded the page, her lips moving silently as she began to read, and a slow smile began to spread across her features.

"It's from Artois directly, *not* Chateauville," she said with a grin as she handed it to Islington to read.

"*Mademoiselle, I was most intrigued by your message just read. I would be honored to receive you and your escort, the Marquess of Bardsey, at Holyroodhouse on tomorrow, 27 August, at five in the evening. Until that time, Charles-Philippe.*"

Islington set down the letter and pulled Pandora back onto his lap. He nuzzled her neck then looked up at her with a soft smile.

"I *love* your perfume," he said appreciatively.

"Yes," said Pandora as she began to untie his cravat. "Now, you were supposed to be *helping* me," she said with a smile.

Chapter Twenty-Seven

Pandora was giddy with excitement over meeting Artois. She didn't know why. The things that would have excited another girl didn't even register for her. By all accounts, he was attractive, but he was older than her father, and he was *not* Islington. He was royalty, but he was expatriated *French* royalty, and Pandora's pulse hadn't even fluttered when she was presented to the Prince Regent during the Season. There was nothing to tempt her.

The only thing to account for it was her knowledge that meeting him would complete something she had been laboring over for five months. Pandora did realize the sensation was similar to what she felt when she finished an equation or experiment she had been working on for a long time, and that was what it had to be. It was a feeling of accomplishment, that she was able to make a mark in some fashion on the fabric of things.

Islington tried not to let her enthusiasm worry him. He didn't want to believe it was due to some infatuation she may have developed for Artois. She had told him the perfume on the letter had only been a ploy to get the Frenchman to read it, and it had worked. If she hadn't done it, Chateauville would have refused her request without the count ever reading it. Her demeanor made him uneasy, though, and he couldn't dismiss his concern that something was not right.

They had gone to the apothecary after breakfast, once Islington returned from going to the barber for a shave, and purchased the herbs to make his new medicine. The man had been surprised to see them return, but he had been able to give them what they needed, including the bottle.

When they got back to their room, Pandora had carefully measured out the different tinctures and oils into the bottle, and after shaking it well to mix them, she had made a cup for Islington to try. It worked much better than just the chamomile, and it didn't make him as sleepy as the headache medicine. The taste, however, was just as unpleasant. Islington wasn't going to complain; anything that saved him from being mildly inebriated to keep the pain at bay was a blessing.

"We didn't put ointment on your shoulder this morning," said Pandora reflectively after she had placed the medicine kit back in the wardrobe and left Islington's medicine on the sideboard.

"No, we didn't," agreed Islington.

"Let's take care of that then," said Pandora, getting the jar.

She watched as Islington untied the bandage, and she helped him remove it and roll it up. Then she helped him take off his waistcoat and shirt. Islington looked up at her with a grin from where he sat on the sofa and put his right arm around her knees to pull her close.

"I think you just want an excuse to get my shirt off," he teased, nuzzling her stomach.

Pandora lovingly ruffled her fingers through his hair and sighed with a soft smile. "Yes, it is hard to resist," she mused. She tugged at his hair playfully and sat beside him on the sofa. "Can you move it at all?" she asked, setting the jar aside temporarily and putting both hands on his shoulder to feel the knots of bunched muscle beneath the skin.

"Some. It's easier to move once the ointment is on. The ligaments still need to heal, though. Otherwise, if I move it too much, the joint will go out of socket again." He carefully raised his arm from his side, and it began to shake after he lifted it a short distance. "That's as far is it goes for now."

Pandora got the ointment and applied a small amount to the healing wound on his side, and then she put some on her hands to work into his shoulder, carefully smoothing out the usual knots and tautness. Once she was done, he could lift it a little farther before the shaking started again.

"I'll have to start using it more, whether it hurts or not, else the muscle will become too weak, and it will make it all the more difficult for me to use again," said Islington as she helped him put his shirt back on and tie it.

Pandora looked at him pensively. "Will it ever be the same again?"

"No," said Islington evenly, "I don't think so." He shook his head and gave her a dismissive smile. "I'm happy I still have it."

Pandora nodded and tucked in his shirt and helped him with his waistcoat. "Maybe Keung can help you. He knows a lot about the human body." Islington looked at her with an arched eyebrow. "He *did* make my headache medicine…and the ointment," she defended.

"You have a point," he conceded as he tilted his head sideways in consideration with a smile.

"The only question is *how* we'll get him to see you," said Pandora with a thoughtful frown. "I suppose when Mamà and Papà go to see your mother after all this, they can take Keung with them to look you over."

"Perhaps."

Pandora saw his troubled expression. "Try to be open-minded," she said, running a hand down his cheek. "He's very unassuming, but he's a genius."

Islington pulled her close and kissed her warmly. Pandora moaned softly against his lips and wound her arms around his neck as his hand moved up her side to splay across her ribs just below her breast. After a time, Islington raised his head to look at her.

"We have a few hours before we go to meet Artois," he said suggestively.

Pandora moved a hand to his face to trace her fingers across his jaw to his chin then up to his lips. Her expression was tender but reserved. She kissed him briefly but not indifferently and picked up the bandage.

"Can we go to Arthur's Seat for a picnic?" she asked calmly as she began to reapply it.

For a moment, Islington was nonplussed. She had just refused him. He had none-too-subtly invited her to spend the time until their appointment making love, and she had no-less-slyly rebuffed him. Pandora had *teased* him before, but she had never outright *denied* him. It put him at something of a loss. When coupled with her unusual demeanor he had already observed, it made Islington all the more troubled that something was wrong. She wasn't angry, but she had distanced herself from him.

Islington wouldn't ask her why. Part of him wasn't sure he wanted to know the answer. Aside from that, it smacked too much of him trying to force himself on her, and he felt he had already done too much of that. It could be something as uncomplicated as Pandora not being interested at the moment. He wanted to believe that was the cause of it, although she had never been *un*interested before. It worried him too much to think it might be something else, and yet, in the back of his mind, the seed of it had already taken root. He looked at her with an agreeable smile as she continued to look at him questioningly.

"I don't see why not," he said softly, his gaze thoughtful.

"Excellent!" said Pandora with a happy grin as she finished tying the bandage. "I imagine the view from there is spectacular."

"It is indeed," he affirmed, reaching over to trace a finger down her nose before tweaking the end of it gently.

Pandora giggled. "The horses would like to go for a ride."

"Yes, probably so, but my shoulder would appreciate a buggy," said Islington as he put the sling back around his neck and rested his arm into it.

Pandora clicked her teeth with a mildly disappointed shake of her head. "You are right," she said calmly.

Islington stood and looked down at her, his expression contemplative. "I'll go see Mrs. Lee about getting a cart and a basket…again," he said with a brief chuckle.

Pandora stood up and gave him a soft kiss. "I'll wait here," she said with a smile.

She watched him leave and sighed gustily after the door closed, rubbing the spot behind her ear. She would eventually have to tell him, she supposed, but it wasn't something she felt comfortable mentioning. She didn't know why it was so difficult. He would understand. At least, she hoped he would. It had been hard for her to refuse, but it was a wise decision. Pandora sighed again and went to the wardrobe to retrieve some items from her valise.

"In a few days it will be done," she said to herself consolingly.

"Does he have run of the whole palace?" asked Pandora as they were riding down the South Back of Canongate for the second time that day with the horse and buggy.

Islington looked at her and smiled, shaking his head. "No, he doesn't. The Duke of Hamilton actually has bigger apartments. The Earls of Breadalbane and Haddington have apartments, too, and I think the Duke of Argyll does also. A lot of people stay at Holyrood, so many that when Artois came, they had no choice but to place him in the royal apartments."

"My goodness!" said Pandora with a blink. "You wouldn't think it would hold that many people just from looking at it."

Islington chuckled and bumped his knee against hers companionably while he used his hands to drive. "Some of the rooms are rather small."

The Black Bull was close to the palace, and it wouldn't have been hard for them to walk the distance, but Pandora and Islington weren't sure how long their business would take, and some of the areas between the two weren't safe after dark.

When they pulled into the courtyard, Pandora gazed at the front of the palace in the late afternoon sunlight. From a distance, the stone appeared to be gray, but on closer inspection, it was made of the same stone as the Black Bull, in the varying shades of brown. She looked up at the imposing crest over the doorway, bracketed by Doric columns and surmounted by an impressive clock tower. As she craned her neck to look up at all of it, Pandora realized it was much larger than it seemed.

They weren't sitting long when a stable hand came to take the head of their horse. Islington stepped down and went around to Pandora's side of the buggy to help her down. She continued to look up at the front of the building, admiring the stonework.

Islington was looking at *her* admiringly. The outfit she had chosen suited her, and it wasn't what he thought she would select. The gown was a royal blue muslin walking dress that had been ruffled and frilled at the neckline to almost resemble a cravat and a man's shirt. Over that she wore a black, green and blue plaid coat that had been edged with black fur. Her slippers were traditional, laced-up gillies, and she wore a black velvet, brimless bonnet with feathers dyed in colors to match the plaid. She looked lovely. He kissed her hand before tucking it into the crook of his arm, and he opened the door for them to enter.

"Shouldn't we have knocked?" asked Pandora curiously.

"No, we'll do that when we get to his apartments, if we need to."

"Oh, my," said Pandora when she looked at her surroundings.

She hadn't expected the courtyard to be so large. She knew it was there from their picnics, but—again—it was bigger on closer inspection. There were women and men, as well as a few children and dogs, going about in the quadrangle and strolling along the piazza. She didn't recognize anyone, but that was for the best. If she knew them, Islington would know them, and the pair's presence together at Holyrood could cause gossip if word of it reached London. They stood for a moment in the piazza while Islington thought.

"Where is his apartment?"

"I'm trying to decide," said Islington mildly with a patient smile. "I came to see Mary's apartment when I was in school. It's in that tower above the Duke of Hamilton's," he said, pointing to the left.

The matter was soon decided for them when a gentleman walked toward them with a suspicious gaze. He was about Islington's age or perhaps slightly older. He was fairly tall and barrel-chested with a thatch of dark auburn hair and bright blue eyes. Pandora could perfectly picture him striding across the Highlands in a kilt, but he was dressed in a riding coat and beaver, and while he appeared to be friendly, Pandora suspected he was charged with making sure that people who weren't supposed to enter the palace did not, by whatever means necessary.

"Can I help ye gentles?" he asked.

"We're here to see the comte d'Artois," said Islington.

"Is he expectin' ye?"

"Yes, he is."

The man relaxed a little and smiled. "My name's Haimish Padgorny, one of the constables here, an' ye wad be?"

"I am Theodore Marshall, the Marquess of Bardsey."

Pandora looked at him curiously. He didn't usually mention his marquessate. He had been using it quite a bit more since their arrival in Scotland—first, on the register at the inn and now to this gentleman. She didn't know what it was about Edinburgh that made him feel it was necessary, but she found it rather odd.

"Your Lordship," said Mr. Padgorny, shaking Islington's hand. He looked at Pandora, and his features softened even further.

"I am Lady Pandora Savage," she said with an amiable smile.

"Your Leddyship," he said with a gentle smile. "The plaid suits ye, an I may say without seeming too forward."

"Thank you, Mr. Padgorny," said Pandora, blushing a little at the compliment from the stranger.

Mr. Padgorny looked back to Islington. "An ye'll come this way, I'll escort ye till the comte's lodgings," he said, directing them with his hand toward the right.

Islington's lips had tightened at the constable's attentions to Pandora. He thought Padgorny's comment had been forward, and he had felt a stab of jealousy when Pandora's cheeks had pinkened.

The two of them followed Mr. Padgorny to a doorway at the far end of the piazza that led them into an impressive stairwell. Pandora looked up at the ceiling and admired the ornate plasterwork, but she preferred the spiraling front stairs of her family's house in London or the grand staircase at Wilderland. Those were both much better-suited to sliding down the banister. When they reached the top of the stairs, there was a sentry standing at the top of them.

He didn't have a rifle or sword, but there was a bulge beneath his coat at his right hip, which Pandora suspected was a pistol. He had been standing in a slightly relaxed pose before, but he straightened when he saw them. He nodded to Mr. Padgorny when he recognized him.

"Monsieur Padgorny," he said neutrally.

"Mr. Almont," said Mr. Padgorny. "Thir fine people are here ta see Monsieur."

Almont looked at Pandora and Islington suspiciously. Pandora was curious why everyone seemed to regard them so distrustfully. She supposed, considering the count's origins and the state of affairs in Europe at the moment, a healthy amount of caution was warranted.

"*Bonjour,*" said Almont finally.

"*Bonjour,*" replied Islington and Pandora calmly.

"If you will wait 'ere for a moment, I will 'ave someone see to you," he said with a very thick accent.

"Very good," said Mr. Padgorny.

Pandora watched as the young Frenchman opened a door to the right and closed it behind him. She walked to the balustrade and rested her hand on it to look down the stairwell to the floor below. She examined the railing and decided it was indeed not well-suited to sliding. She looked up at the paintings and tapestries, but she couldn't determine what the subjects were. Perhaps if she had longer, she might. She inhaled deeply with her eyes closed, and she detected the scent of old things.

Islington watched her, his lips twitching with amusement as he thought of what could possibly be going through her mind. He had discovered her senses were finely honed. He never would have imagined she could discover the recipe for her headache medicine by smell and taste alone, but she had. He had also found that once she had a smell or taste imprinted on her memory, she didn't forget it. He was sure when she described her visit to the palace, the way it smelled would be part of what she included.

Almont returned accompanied by another man. He was dressed more formally, with an impeccable black frock coat and knee breeches with white hose and black, silver-buckled shoes. He was older, Pandora suspected in his mid-forties, with gray hair and shrewd, dark brown eyes. His expression when he saw Pandora and Islington was polite, but she had the impression their visit was an imposition. She was just beginning to believe he was Monsieur de Chateauville when he proved her wrong on introducing himself.

"*Bonjour*, I am Monsieur Dravet, secretary to *Monsieur, le comte*," he said mildly. "If you will come this way, he is expecting you."

Pandora turned to look at the constable. "Thank you for your assistance, Mr. Padgorny," she said with a smile.

He took her hand to place a gallant kiss on her knuckles. "You are most welcome, leddy," he said with a charming smile. He looked at Islington and nodded curtly before going down the stairs to the piazza.

Pandora followed Monsieur Dravet, her arm linked through Islington's. The man walked with his back arrow straight as he led them through the first room, containing a set of spiral stairs, into a larger room that was sparsely furnished with rich mahogany furniture with tapestried cushions. The dark paneling had been polished until it gleamed, and a fire was burning on the grate, but because of the position of the room, it was quite gloomy. Monsieur Dravet turned to look at them.

"If you will wait here, I will inform Monsieur that you have arrived," he said formally.

"Monsieur Dravet, just a moment, please," said Pandora as he started to turn. He looked back at her enquiringly. "We received a message from a Monsieur de Chateauville, stating *he* was Monsieur's secretary; were we misinformed?"

"*Oui*, mademoiselle. Monsieur de Chateauville is *my* secretary," said Monsieur Dravet, his features relaxing as she spoke to him in perfect French. He bowed slightly and went through the door to the next room.

"That was odd," mused Pandora with a frown after Dravet closed the door.

"I imagine Artois has a lot of business that requires addressing. If Chateauville is an under-secretary, perhaps his duties involve responding to miscellaneous correspondence," said Islington mildly. He looked down at her with an admiring smile. "That was nicely done, by the way."

"What?" asked Pandora blankly.

"He seemed a bit stodgy at first."

"Wouldn't you be? Imagine if you were living in a country where everyone else spoke a different language and people of your religion were treated as inferior, relying on the grace and favor of the government to provide the food you eat and the roof over your head. And then, to make it even worse, you couldn't go home," said Pandora softly. "I just thought he might appreciate it if at least *one* of those things wasn't a problem."

Islington inclined his head. "Absolutely, but I'm afraid most of my French falls to the indecent variety," he grinned.

Pandora chuckled. "You should let me do most of the talking then."

Dravet came to the door momentarily and motioned for them to enter. When they walked into the room, it was an office of some type. There was an enormous mahogany desk with ornate carving along the edge and in the center panel at the front, framed by fluted pilasters at the corners. There were two chairs placed in front of the desk with ebonized wood and red damask cushioning that was slightly faded and worn. Pandora suspected they were very old. There was a sideboard with a tray of several different wines. Near the fireplace was a settee and two chairs with a low table. On the wall between two windows was a small writing desk with the top closed that Pandora suspected was Monsieur Dravet's usual seat.

The man behind the desk rose at their entrance, and Pandora received her first look at the comte d'Artois. Statements of his being an attractive man were not unfounded. He was shorter than she thought he would be, taller than herself but not taller than Islington. He was trim and still had an athletic frame at fifty-six years. His hair was gray and cut short, the natural waviness of it, like Islington's, completing a style many men of fashion strove for with pomades and ironing tongs. His dark eyes were kindly, but there was a weariness in his gaze that his twenty-four years in exile and the loss of his great *amore* had etched permanently. His features were well-formed, with a high forehead, a strong chin, and full lips bracketed by lines that indicated he (at least used to) smiled often. Yes, Pandora did think he was attractive, but he wasn't Islington.

Pandora performed her most graceful curtsy as he came around the desk, and she felt Islington bowing deeply at the waist beside her. She knew that had to be causing him no small amount of pain because of his ribs. After what she thought was a respectable amount of time, she rose to an upright position and looked at him calmly.

"Monsieur," she said obeisantly.

He reached out to take her hand and placed a kiss on her knuckles. "Mademoiselle Savage, *enchanté,*" he said with a warm smile. He looked at Islington. "And you would be Lord Bardsey," he stated in English, reaching out to shake Islington's hand.

"Monsieur," said Islington evenly.

Once the greetings were accomplished, Artois looked at Dravet and gave a slight nod. The other man left through a door beyond the desk and closed it behind him. Artois directed Pandora and Islington to the furniture in front of the fireplace with a graceful wave of his hand, and they took a seat on the settee while Artois went to the more ornate of the two chairs.

"I have sent for tea; it will arrive momentarily. You will join me," said Artois. It wasn't a request. He looked at Pandora speculatively. "I must say, mademoiselle, your message piqued my curiosity. I am happy to see at least part of it has been well-satisfied," he said with a charming smile.

"*Merci,* Monsieur," said Pandora lightly, and she could feel herself blushing to the roots of her hair, which made the count chuckle amusedly.

"You must forgive my teasing," he said with an amiable smile. "Life these days is of little entertainment, except for my whist. Your father is the Duke of Aberdare, *non?*"

"Yes, that's true," said Pandora calmly, slowly feeling the pinkness fade from her cheeks.

Artois nodded. "I have had the opportunity to meet him a few times while in London. He is a very astute Englishman," said Artois warmly.

"Well, actually, he's Welsh, but that's neither here nor there," said Pandora, and she could feel the pink returning. Artois chuckled again. "Thank you, Monsieur," she said lamely.

He rested his elbow on the arm of the chair and balanced his face in the arch of his thumb and forefinger. "So, what is it you wish to impart to me that is of such vital importance to the safety of my person? I believe those were your words, were they not?"

"I apologize if that sounded extreme, Monsieur, but we had already been refused an opportunity to see you once; I wanted to make sure I stressed the urgency of the matter," said Pandora gravely.

"I see," said Artois, his expression still one of lazy indulgence.

"Monsieur, I will come directly to the heart of the matter. We—that is Lord Bardsey, my brother—the Viscount Glamorgan, and myself have strong reason to believe there will be an attempt on your life very soon," said Pandora seriously.

Artois's expression remained pleasant, but there was a slight, wary hardening in his eyes.

"Mademoiselle, since my time in exile, I have become insignificant. Not even the supporters of a possible restoration of the greatness that was France in times past bother to concern themselves with me anymore. Why would causing my death be of interest to anyone?"

"I don't know, Monsieur," said Pandora quietly.

A man entered carrying a tray with tea service. He brought it to the low table and set it down, having to bend very low from his great height. Pandora looked at him, and she felt as if she had seen him somewhere before. She didn't know *where*, but there was something vaguely familiar about him that tickled the edge of her memory. She watched as he remained bent over with his back to her, pouring tea into the three cups on the tray. Once done, he straightened to hand one of those to Artois after placing in one lump of sugar. He briefly bent to whisper something in the count's ear, to which Artois gave a slight nod in response. Without a word to either Pandora or Islington, or even an acknowledgement of their presence other than pouring their tea, he left the way he came.

Pandora's forehead was wrinkled with confusion as she absently reached down to hand Islington his preferred plain cup of tea before stirring a lump of sugar into her own and picking it up to take a sip.

She couldn't get over the man who had brought the tea. He had been very tall and thin. His clothes, while not threadbare, weren't as fine as those of either Artois or Monsieur Dravet. She hadn't been able to see his face to know whether or not she recognized him. In profile, she had seen that he had deep set eyes, possibly of a dark color, a prominent nose and thin lips. His hair was dark and straight with an almost greasy limpness. She had been able to see enough to know that, by appearance, he was a stranger, and yet he was achingly familiar in a way that was making the hair rise on the back of her neck forebodingly.

"Forgive me, Monsieur, but who was that gentleman?" asked Pandora pensively.

"Monsieur de Chateauville," said Artois calmly. "Why do you ask?"

Pandora's frown increased. "I see. I feel like I have met him before," said Pandora thoughtfully.

Islington looked at Pandora, and a frown of his own formed. He was feeling a bit useless sitting there as she and Artois talked and was almost on the pointing of dozing off, but her statement called him to attention. He hadn't recognized the man, as Chateauville or otherwise. He didn't know why the man seemed familiar to Pandora, but considering how frightening her memory and intellect could be at times, it would come to her, and that she was concerned about it could not be good.

"Oh?" said Artois with an arched eyebrow. "I find that to be most unlikely, mademoiselle," he said dismissively, shaking his head. "In any event, you think someone is planning to murder me, and yet you do not know why. I believe that is the point we had reached."

"It is true, Monsieur. I don't know why these individuals wish to kill you, but they plan to hold you for ransom before they do. Once they have received the payment of whatever it is, you will be disposed of."

Artois laughed outright. "Mademoiselle, look around you!" he said amusedly, waving his arm at their surroundings. "It is absurd someone would want to hold me for ransom. I have barely tuppence to rub together. All you see was provided by your own countrymen. It does not belong to me. I think you are mistaken," he said with a dismissive shake of his head.

"I wish I were, Monsieur," said Pandora gravely. "On the first of September, you will leave for London," she said calmly. Artois's amusement died, and the wary expression returned. "You don't want anyone to know you're going, so you won't be traveling with many of your suite. You'll only be staying a fortnight before you return here. I don't know what your business is, but apparently it is quite secretive."

"How did you discover this?" asked Artois in a shocked tone.

"I heard two of the conspirators talking about it. Unfortunately, I don't think you'll ever make it to London," said Pandora firmly.

"Who are these conspirators?" demanded Artois.

"There were three that I know of. One is dead because he tried to pull out, so I'll not mention his name. Of the other two, one is a British peer, and the last is, as of yet, undetermined except by name."

"And we believe that the name is not real," provided Islington.

Pandora looked at him in surprise. She had doubted that Castleton was his real name, but she had not found anything to prove otherwise. Islington, however, had made inquiries of his own, of which he had not seen fit to provide her the results, so he had at least been able to determine one thing she had not.

"Who are they?" demanded Artois again.

"Monsieur, I'll not give you the name of the peer. Although I know he is guilty, there's no proof. The second man is named Castleton. If we could find him, then we would have a witness to convict the other."

"And you have no description of this man, Castleton?"

"Not exactly," said Pandora. Artois arched his eyebrow. "I can tell you that he is tall and...."

Pandora's words trailed off and died on her lips, and her eyes grew round in surprise and alarm because then she knew...everything. There were so many little bits and pieces it had taken that one point of focus to make them crystallize into a larger, clearer image. She didn't think she was wrong, but she would ask a few questions just to be sure.

"Monsieur, you may consider this impertinent, but how long has Monsieur de Chateauville been in your employ?" she asked stilly.

Artois appeared taken aback by the question that seemed to come from a tangent, but he was not insulted. "He's been back in my service for almost five months now," he replied with a puzzled frown.

"*Back* in your service?"

"I do mis-state things," said Artois mildly. "It wasn't Armand but his parents, Sophie and Henri, who were in my employ before the exile."

"Indeed?"

"Yes. They were urged to leave but would not. They did, however, send Armand here for safety with the belief they would eventually come to get him and take him home once the danger had passed, but they perished in the Terror," said Artois sadly. "It was a regrettable loss. Armand came to me and asked for a position, and he was employed."

"I see," said Pandora quietly, and the motive became clear. "Monsieur, if you could possibly indulge my curiosity for just a bit more?" He nodded agreeably. "Was Monsieur de Chateauville here about two weeks ago?"

Islington and Artois looked at her in surprise, but for different reasons. As Pandora continued her questioning, Islington was able to see where her logic was taking her, and he was agreeing with it. However, knowing whether or not Chateauville had been in Edinburgh at the fortnight was puzzling. Artois was surprised because the young mademoiselle was providing him with details and asking questions that were almost presentient in their nature. When he answered her queries, she didn't seem surprised by the responses. He had at first invited the English to visit as a diversion, but thus far Lady Pandora's warning in her message had not proven to be mere amusement.

"As a matter of fact, mademoiselle, Monsieur de Chateauville only just returned from a visit to London in preparation for my own journey four days ago," said Artois quietly. "Now, indulge *my* curiosity. Why do you have this interest in young Armand?"

"Monsieur, I very strongly suspect that Castleton and Monsieur de Chateauville are one and the same," said Pandora earnestly.

"You are mistaken, *assurément,*" said Artois firmly.

"Monsieur, I don't think I am," said Pandora softly. "If you Anglicize his name, Castleton is a close approximation of Chateauville. He is tall, thin, and stooped, just like Castleton. He also, forgive me if this sounds silly, *smells* like Castleton. I've not heard Monsieur de Chateauville speak, but I would recognize his voice. He has only just returned from London and has only been in your employee for five months, which is about the time I first heard of this plan. What would make it easier for a murderer to commit his crime than to insinuate himself into the life of his victim?"

"But why would Armand wish to kill me? I had nothing but the greatest respect for his parents. Though I could scarce afford it, I could not deny him a position in my household out of respect for their memory when he asked it of me. Again, mademoiselle, you must be mistaken."

"There is one further proof, Monsieur, if my recognition of him by voice is not sufficient," said Pandora calmly.

"Yes, mademoiselle?" asked Artois doubtfully.

"I realize this may be improper, but if you could but ask him to sit."

Islington looked at her in astonishment, as did Artois. Islington knew why she would want the man to sit, but how she had managed to determine Chateauville was their assailant from the bridge at Aysgarth mystified him. That would explain why she wanted to know where he was two weeks ago.

"Might I ask why?" asked Artois with an amused smile.

"I had the distinct annoyance of following behind a man for several days on my journey here from London. This individual, I now realize, snuck into my camp one night and untied my horse, among other things, in an effort to delay me. When that didn't prove successful, this same person shot at me but—fortunately for me—didn't succeed in hitting me or my horse. The next day, he shot at me again, which is why you see Lord Bardsey in this condition, because the man shot him instead."

Islington looked at Pandora. She had never mentioned the man had gone into her camp.

"At the time, I wondered what I could have possibly done to make this man so angry he felt the need to shoot me. I now realize a man such as Castleton—or Chateauville—aware someone was alert to his intent, would have felt a person following behind him day after day—regardless of speed, terrain, or weather—could only be interested in foiling his plans. I *was*—and still am—seeking that end, but at the time my only interest was concealing that I was a woman disguised as a man."

"You *what?*" asked Artois in astonishment.

"Monsieur, I did what I felt was necessary to warn you. At this point, it's unimportant," said Pandora shortly. "The crux of all I am telling you is this: when the man shot Islington—I mean, Lord Bardsey—I shot *him.*"

Artois looked at her with even further amazement. "How can you be sure you hit him, and why would it be necessary for him to sit?"

"I know I hit him, Monsieur, because I shot him with an arrow, and I saw it in his backside as he rode away. *That* is why I would like him to sit."

Artois looked at her in stunned silence, and then he began to chuckle. His chuckle soon turned to uproarious laughter. Pandora looked at Islington, who inclined his head silently and brushed his hand against hers soothingly where it rested on the settee. After a moment, Artois calmed and looked at her with a fond smile.

"Mademoiselle, you are truly a treasure beyond worth," said Artois. Pandora blinked. "Very well, we shall do as you request." He stood and went to retrieve a bell from his desk, and Pandora and Islington stood also. "I do not believe any of this is possible, but you seem far too sincere for me to dismiss it lightly."

Artois rang the bell, and Monsieur Dravet momentarily entered the room. Artois spoke to him quietly, and Pandora looked at Islington.

"You're sure?" he asked.

"Believe me. I rode behind that man for three days through rain and all else, and then on the fourth day, he shot you. I'm not likely to forget what his back and profile look like," said Pandora softly. "Even if he isn't Castleton, but I'm sure he is, that he shot you is enough."

Islington took her hand in his to brush a kiss across her knuckles and squeeze it comfortingly. Dravet left to attend to the count's request. Artois came back to Pandora and Islington and looked at them speculatively.

"Now we shall see what we shall see," said Artois with a smile. He thoughtfully scratched at his temple for a moment and looked at Pandora. "So, tell me, mademoiselle, am I correct in understanding that you came here from London *alone*?"

"For the most part," said Pandora calmly. "I had made it to Yorkshire before Lord Bardsey found me at the request of my parents."

"Your parents do not know you are here?" asked Artois with some concern.

"Oh, no, they know I'm here, but they didn't know I was going until I had already left."

"You are quite brave, mademoiselle, and determined, it would seem," said Artois with some amusement.

"As I said, Monsieur, I only did what I felt was necessary," said Pandora softly.

Chateauville entered the room, and Pandora received her first real look at him. He was tall and thin with limbs that almost seemed spidery in their length. His face was long and gaunt in a fashion that came from leading a difficult life, his dark eyes set deep into his skull, which made his hawkish nose seem all the more prominent. His black hair hung in lifeless hanks that it seemed no amount of grooming could tame. Pandora wasn't able to determine his age. He could have been anywhere from thirty to fifty, but the apparent hardness of his life made him look old before his time. He glanced at Pandora and Islington with a wary, calculating expression before walking further into the room.

"You wished to see me, Monsieur?" he asked calmly.

That was all the proof Pandora needed. He *was* Castleton. She would have to let him sit to convince Artois. She reached over to take Islington's hand and gripped it tightly as her heart began to thud against her ribs anxiously.

"*Oui,* Armand. These two people are under the impression they have seen you before. You will sit with us so we can discuss where and how that might have happened," said Artois firmly, but his expression was pleasant. He said it as a command rather than a request.

Chateauville turned to look at Pandora and Islington again, his gaze far more scrutinizing. He looked them both up and down, and when he took in Islington's arm resting in its sling, Pandora could see realization dawning on his features. He looked back at Pandora, and she saw a surprise mingle with the knowledge. *He knows. He's not going to sit down.* Chateauville directed his gaze back to Artois with a slight smile and inclined his head, as if in acquiescence.

Pandora released a startled gasp when her hand was wrenched free from Islington's as Chateauville seized her. Before she had time to react, he had pinioned her in front of him with her arms to her sides, her back to his front, and Pandora jerked her head back skittishly when she felt the blade of a knife touch the side of her throat. He moved with her toward the wall with windows, just in front of the secretary's writing desk. Islington and Artois were both aghast at this unexpected turn of events.

Pandora struggled against Chateauville's hold on her, but he was stronger than he appeared, and the length of his arms made it easy for him to keep a firm grip. She was barely able to move her arms above the elbows. When she strained her eyes to look down without moving her neck, she wasn't able to see what kind of knife he was holding to her throat, but it was definitely sharp. She would eventually get loose, but whether she would have the time to figure out how to do it without having him cut her throat *before* he cut her throat was another matter entirely.

"*Traître ingrat!*" roared Artois.

Pandora flinched as she felt Chateauville press the knife tighter against her throat at the count's words. She could feel a sting and a slight tickling sensation along her neck as the blade broke the skin and blood started to trickle from it. It didn't feel as if it were more than a nick to Pandora, but she watched as Islington's face paled at the sight of it.

She gave him a slight smile to try to calm his worry, and she lifted her hands briefly from her sides and made a motion to let him know she was all right. He tilted his head sideways to let her know he understood, but his uneasy expression did not change. She watched as he clenched and unclenched his hand at his side helplessly.

"*Ungrateful?*" spat Chateauville at Artois. "What have you done to deserve my gratitude?"

"I took you under my roof! I entrusted you with my care!" said Artois angrily.

Pandora surreptitiously brought her hands closer together in front of her and looked down with her eyes to let Islington know she wanted to know about the knife. Once she had her hands the correct distance apart, he inclined his head slightly to let her know she had reached the length of the blade. Then, to her dismay, she watched as he made the shape of a gun with his left hand where it rested in his sling. Her eyes rounded in alarm when she realized Chateauville had a dagger-pistol, probably much like the one she had. That made her predicament all the more dangerous.

"And a fool you were to have done it!" hissed Chateauville.

Both doors to the room flew open, and Padgorny and Almont entered with their pistols drawn. Artois must have told Dravet to get them after he had sent in Chateauville, just in case. Pandora closed her eyes and took several deep breaths to smother the anxiety she felt. Now, more than ever, she would have to keep her wits about her. Having the two men there was going to make it even more difficult to escape from Chateauville without further injury.

"Come closer, and she will die," said Chateauville coldly. He moved the knife at Pandora's neck, and she felt another sting and trickle begin.

"Gentlemen, could you please not upset this man any further?" she said in as calm a tone as she could muster. "Monsieur de Chateauville, I think I understand why you are doing this, but could you, please, explain it to everyone else?"

"*Monsieur le comte d'Artois* killed my family!" shouted Chateauville angrily.

"I did *not* kill them. They were seized by the Committee and sent to the guillotine. You know that," said Artois imperiously.

Pandora wanted them to keep talking in at least a semi-civilized manner to buy some time. Eventually, the constable and the guard were going to take it upon themselves to try to shoot Chateauville. If they did, she would die with him. It was a simple fact. But Pandora wasn't ready to die yet. Her brain was working furiously as she tried to find a way to disarm him and free herself because Pandora was the only one in a position to do it without causing her further harm.

"*Non! You* killed them! You could have made them leave, but you did not! You and your family, the nobility and the monarchy, with your greed, and your lust, and your *pompous* intransigence for not listening to your people! I lost everything I had because of *you* and your kind!"

"You are not the only one who lost everything!" roared Artois. "How selfish of you to think that way!"

"And yet here you sit, in a *palace*, surrounded by opulence and bosom companions!" spat Chateauville. "For twenty-four years, I *struggled*! First, from a foundling home, to a workhouse, then to whatever menial job I could find just to buy bread to eat! But then one day, as I strolled along Oxford Street, the solution to my suffering came to me as I looked in a window. It was such a beautiful necklace, and it would do much to relieve my discomfort, but I realized I could have so much more if I had the right currency to buy it."

He was talking about the necklace in the jeweler's window. Pandora was seriously beginning to believe the thing was cursed.

"I don't know what you are talking about," dismissed Artois coldly. "I have no necklace. I have no money. *Certainement,* you must know by now that all you see here is not mine. I did not kill your family. They were told to leave, repeatedly, but they would not listen. I *implored* them to come with me when I left, but they stayed for *Madame* and for the *Dauphin.* I am sorry you lost your family, but I *did* lose mine, too," said Artois wearily.

Pandora had been steadily trying to move Chateauville's grip on her left arm to just a little higher. Between pressing at the bottom of his arm where he held her and surreptitiously swinging hers back and forth, she had been able to give herself a little more freedom without letting Chateauville realize she had done it. She tried it, and found that she now had the movement to touch his right forearm with her left hand, but she would have to make sure her aim was exact because she would only be able to use her thumb. Chateauville's attention was elsewhere, and he thought he held a helpless woman. Both were in her favor.

Pandora looked at each of the men in the room. Padgorny and Almont watched the drama before them uncertainly, their attention focused on Chateauville. Artois also continued to look at the man, his expression a mixture of disdain and sympathy. The only one who was *not* looking at the Frenchman was Islington. He had concern only for her. She looked at him with a soft smile and made a motion with her hand to indicate what she intended to do. His brow furrowed apprehensively, but he trusted her. After a moment's hesitation, he gave a slight nod of understanding.

Almont and Padgorny looked at each other, and both started to move toward Chateauville just as Pandora intended to take action, forcing her to wait and rethink her plan. Chateauville let go of her arms to raise his hand to her forehead and tilt her head back to further expose her neck. He put the knife closer to her throat for yet a third time.

"I warned you! Do not come any closer!" yelled Chateauville.

"Why would you hurt an innocent woman?" asked Islington quickly.

"*Innocent?*" spat Chateauville. "This English bitch shot me!" he roared.

Pandora reached up to grab Chateauville's wrist, applying pressure to make him drop the weapon. The pistol discharged when it hit the floor, and Pandora felt a breeze between her legs as a cloud of smoke began to rise from where it landed at her feet. She didn't release her grip on Chateauville, but continued to apply steady pressure. She ducked slightly to release his hold on her forehead without much effort. She twisted his captured arm behind him, and as she did so, he tried to turn away from her, toward the secretary's desk, bent over slightly at the waist. Pandora placed a hand to the back of his neck and pushed forcefully, making Chateauville hit his face into the closed cover on the desk, which splintered at the impact. Only then, as he started to collapse dazedly to the floor, did Pandora feel safe enough to let him go.

She looked down at him disgustedly. "I am not an *English* bitch," she muttered to herself. "I'm a *Welsh* bitch."

"*Mon dieu!*" said Artois in astonishment.

Islington rushed to her and hugged Pandora to him tightly with relief, placing a solemn kiss on her forehead. He moved her away from where Chateauville lay on the floor and reached into his pocket for a folded handkerchief to put on her neck.

"Are you all right?"

Pandora nodded and sighed softly. "Yes, I think so." Islington kissed her forehead again. "I think it went well."

Almont and Padgorny rushed to take Chateauville into custody. The Scotsman looked up at her in admiration as he knelt down beside the criminal and placed the discharged weapon into the top of his boot.

"Ne'er be in me, Leddy Pandora, bat I do nae think I'll be e'er wantin' ta make ye tetchy," he said with a chuckle. He looked over Chateauville as he lolled mostly senseless on the floor. "Wad ye look at tha'? He's shot himsel' in the foot. That's gonna make it a hard walk ta the tollbooth."

"That would explain the breeze I felt under my dress," said Pandora mildly as she let Islington continue to hold her close.

He rubbed his hand on her back soothingly, and she rested her head against his chest relievedly as she watched the two men try to revive Chateauville enough to take him to jail. She was feeling the beginnings of a migraine, but she was sure they would be back to the inn before it became too painful, and then she would take some of her medicine.

"Mademoiselle Savage, I am eternally in your debt," said Artois formally.

Pandora raised her head from Islington's chest and turned to look at Artois. He was shaken by the entire turn of events, but he looked at her with great admiration and respect.

"A thank you will be sufficient," said Pandora with a slight smile.

Artois warmly took her hand in both of his and kissed her knuckles. He gave her a slight bow and released it. "Thank you, most sincerely, mademoiselle. A prince could not wish for a better defender than you."

"You're quite welcome," said Pandora, blushing profusely at the compliment. Her eyes settled on the sideboard. "I don't suppose you have any whisky on your table over there?" she asked wistfully.

"No, mademoiselle, but I do have some very nice Calvados. Will that suit?" asked Artois, his lips twitching amusedly.

"Oh, yes," she sighed gratefully. He started to get it for her, but Pandora put a hand to his arm. "Oh, no, Monsieur, I can get it myself," she said with a smile.

Pandora walked to the table and looked over the bottles until she found the brandy. She opened one of the doors on the front of the cabinet and found a glass without much difficulty. As she began to pour, Almont and Padgorny had managed to raise Chateauville from the floor and began to escort him from the room, going for the door beyond Artois's desk. She had just taken a soothing swallow from the glass when she caught an unexpected movement from the corner of her eye.

Pandora briefly realized Chateauville had struggled against his captors and managed to get free and take Almont's gun. In the next instant, she watched in horror as he placed the gun into his mouth and pulled the trigger before the two men could stop him. She saw and felt a pink spray as the crown of his head completely disintegrated, and then she watched as his lifeless body collapsed to the floor, twitching from residual nerve impulses from his no longer existing brain.

Pandora calmly looked down at herself and realized she was completely covered in Chateauville's blood and bits of brain matter and bone. She could feel herself moving automatically as she turned to look at Islington and Artois, a ringing noise in her ears as her vision began to go out of focus.

"Oh, darn," she said dazedly, "he's completely ruined my favorite new dress." Then she collapsed to the floor in a dead faint.

Dorian arrived at the Black Bull just after 8:30. He was glad he had made it. The trip from Grantham had been long and tedious, made so because he didn't want to push his horse too hard so soon after he had mended. It had taken more than a week, but the hoof had finally become sound enough to travel again. It would need a little more time to completely heal. Dorian hadn't let the animal go at more than a walk.

He reached back to untie his valise before he dismounted, and a boy was already there to take his horse. Dorian casually flipped him a coin as he went for the stairs to the office, walking up tiredly. He could hear the sounds of laughter and merriment drifting up a stairwell from the tavern, and he would go there once he was settled into his room. After looking around briefly when the door closed behind him, he saw a woman behind the counter, looking at him expectantly.

"Gude e'enin' till ye, sir," she said with a friendly smile as he walked to the desk and dropped his bag on the floor at his feet. "I'm Mrs. Lee. Will ye be needin' a room?"

"Good evening, and yes, I will," said Dorian tiredly.

"What will ye ware?" she asked with a smile.

"Pardon?" asked Dorian confusedly.

"Will ye hae strae or feathers?" asked Mrs. Lee in an attempt to clarify.

"Um, feathers," said Dorian uncertainly. Mrs. Lee nodded.

"Did ye stable a naig?" she asked as she bent to retrieve the ledger.

Dorian's forehead continued to wrinkle. He knew she was speaking English, and perhaps if he weren't so tired he would understand her better, but at the moment he was bumfuzzled.

"Yes, I believe so," he said slowly. Mrs. Lee nodded again.

"How lang will ye bide till?" she asked as she opened the ledger to the current page and set down the pen and inkpot.

"I'm sorry?"

"How many days will ye bide?" she asked slowly, her lips twitching amusedly.

"I'm not sure," said Dorian firmly. He looked at her. "Can you tell me if either the Earl of Neath or Viscount Islington are staying here?"

Mrs. Lee's forehead wrinkled. "I can say the earl is nae here, bat the Marquess of Bardsey arrived on Wednesday," she said calmly.

Dorian looked at her in surprise. Islington didn't normally use his marquessate, but this woman seemed to know exactly who he was. Dorian picked up the pen and signed his name in the ledger. Mrs. Lee turned it toward her and blotted it, reading his name.

"Thank ye, Lord Glamorgan," she said with a smile. "An ye wad wait here, I sall find a maid till get ye sorted."

"Mrs. Lee, just a moment, please," said Dorian, holding up his hand, bravely willing to go on. She looked at him enquiringly. "Is Islington here right now?"

"Why na, my lord. He's down at Holyroodhouse wi' Leddy Bardsey," she said with a shake of her head.

Dorian shook his head confusedly. "His *mother* is here?"

Mrs. Lee shook her head and chuckled. "O' course nae, my lord. Ye're a bonnie chiel, bat ye're a bit in the bees."

"I beg your pardon?" said Dorian in an affronted tone. "Do you know if Lady Pandora Savage is here?"

"Na, my lord," said Mrs. Lee. "Leddy Bardsey is down at Holyroodhouse wi' Islington."

"Yes, you said that, but the only Lady Bardsey I know is his mother," said Dorian patiently.

"An' I tauld ye she is nae here."

"Yes, I remember," said Dorian, rubbing a tired hand over his face. "Do you mind if I have a look at your ledger, please?"

"Suit yoursel'," said Mrs. Lee with a pleasant smile as she turned the ledger back toward him. He was a braw callant, and if he knew Islington, she saw no harm in having a bit of sport with him.

Dorian looked at the page he had just signed, but there was nothing familiar. He turned to the previous page and started at the bottom. When he was about to the middle, his eyes grew wide in shock.

"Bloody hell!" he gasped.

"Och, mind how ye go, now!" said Mrs. Lee in a mild tone.

Chapter Twenty-Eight

Pandora woke up lying on the settee in the count's office. Thankfully, her coat and hat had been removed, and the blood had been washed from her skin. She wasn't out long, but during that time, the count sent for his physician, despite Islington telling him that he was one himself and could take care of her. Artois told him only a fool was a physician for his family; Islington didn't correct him. There hadn't been anything wrong, of course; she had just fainted from the shock of what she had been covered in.

Chateauville's body had been removed, and the servants had been in to clean up the mess his suicide had left behind. Pandora was grateful she didn't have to see it again. She would have been sick if she had. She tried to feel some sympathy for the man, but she couldn't bring herself to do it. His life had been difficult, but it had been no different for any of the other *émigrés*, and kidnapping and murder were never the answer.

Pandora felt her migraine was still coming when she woke up. With the danger to Artois ended, she rushed Islington to take her back to the inn. She would need to take medicine as soon as they got there if she wanted to avoid the worst pain. She wasn't having the visual disturbances yet, but it wouldn't be long. Artois let them go with the promise they would return the next night for supper. Pandora assured him they would.

Now they were riding in their buggy back up the South Back to the inn, Pandora snuggled close to Islington with her arm under his coat. Without her own coat, the air was very cool and the thin muslin of her dress did nothing to keep it out. She intended to take some medicine, and then, provided she could stay awake, she would have Mrs. Lee bring her a bath. The blood may have been washed off, but she wasn't going to feel completely clean until she had soaked in the hottest water she could stand.

"What's going to happen to Hendon?" she asked Islington softly.

He looked down at her, his brow furrowed thoughtfully. "Nothing," he said finally.

"There is *nothing* that can be done to him for his part in all this?" asked Pandora in dismay.

"There's no *proof* he had a part. He probably goaded Chateauville into this plan of action, and the man was so insane Hendon didn't have to push too hard. In all likelihood, Chateauville was the one who killed Tarlborough, but we're likely never to know for sure. Something might have happened to you that day on Drury, but it didn't. Beating his wife is despicable, but it is—unfortunately—not illegal. If Chateauville hadn't killed himself, we would have had a firsthand witness of proven guilt to implicate Hendon but not now."

"Do you think Hendon will still try to go after Artois?"

Islington thought about it for a moment. "No, I don't. He needed Chateauville to do all the dirty work, and it's too risky an enterprise for Hendon to do it alone when there is so little to be gained from it. He's more likely to try poisoning or some other underhanded method if he's acting alone. I wouldn't be surprised to learn he did the whole thing as a lark."

"*That* man is the one who is *insane*," said Pandora heartily with a shudder. She rubbed a hand across her forehead. "I'll be glad when we get back to the inn. I need to take some of my medicine."

Islington looked down at her concernedly. "How bad is it?"

"Not too bad yet. I've got a little time," said Pandora, squeezing his waist assuringly.

"How is your neck?"

Pandora put a hand up to the three cuts. They had stopped bleeding, but they were tender. None of them had been deep enough to require stitches. This whole adventure had left her battered and bruised, but she hoped those marks would be the last. She didn't think they would leave bad scars, and Keung's ointment would make them feel better.

"It's fine," she said, resting her head on his shoulder and closing her eyes.

"I was terrified," said Islington softly. "I felt so damned *helpless.*"

Pandora rubbed a comforting hand on his back under his coat. "There wasn't anything you could have done, Theo. I was the only one who could save me," she said softly.

"But if you hadn't been able to, if you were any other woman, he could have killed you, and…," he trailed off, and Pandora felt him shake slightly as he thought about it.

"Shh," said Pandora soothingly. "I am *not* any other woman. You know that," she said with a slight chuckle as they turned into the courtyard of the inn. "Lucky for all of us, Chateauville didn't."

Islington helped her down from the buggy after Haimish came to take the horse's head, and he reached into the small baggage compartment on the back to remove a burlap sack that held Pandora's coat and hat. He didn't know if Mrs. Lee would be able to clean them, but he knew from past experience that she was quite skilled at removing stains. The damage to the clothes was quite extensive, though. Pandora linked her arm through his, and they walked up the stairs into the office.

As soon as Mrs. Lee saw them, she raised the gate on the counter to rush toward them.

"Och, mercy!" she said when she reached them, embracing both of them in an emotional hug. "I just heard what happened! Mr. Padgorny was in fer 'is usual an' tauld it a'. It pert near stopped ma heart frae beatin', it did." She looked at Pandora. "Och, ye poor lamb!" she said, placing her hands to Pandora's cheeks. "We'll be gettin' ye sorted straight away wi' a bath an' a drappie, till be sure!"

Pandora's head began to spin from the flutter and flurry that was Mrs. Lee. What she really wanted was to take some of her medicine, and Mrs. Lee would see to everything else. Pandora appreciated the woman's kindness. She nodded and gave the older woman a soft smile.

"I almost forgot, Islington. There's a man asked after ye," said Mrs. Lee, tilting her head toward the small sitting area in front of the fireplace.

Pandora and Islington looked over to see her brother sitting there, his feet propped on the low table, his chin resting on his chest in a sound sleep.

"*Dorian!*" squealed Pandora, moving toward him with a huge smile.

Dorian woke up when he heard her voice and stood up from the couch. Pandora flung herself at him for a tight hug, and Dorian hugged her back.

"I'm so happy to see you!" said Pandora elatedly. "When Islington and I got here, and you weren't here, I was so worried. What took you so long?"

"Barbaros tore a frog, and I had to wait for it to heal."

Dorian put Pandora away from him to arm's length to get a look at her. He saw the nearly faded bruise on her forehead and the scrape on her cheek, and then he saw the fresh cuts on her neck. She was pale, and her features were strained. His brow furrowed concernedly.

"What's happened to you?" he asked stilly.

Pandora waved a dismissive hand through the air before raising it to rub the spot behind her ear. Dorian looked at Islington still standing beside Mrs. Lee, and his lips tightened into an angry line.

"Come sit with me," said Dorian firmly. "I need to talk to you."

"Don't you want to speak to Islington?" asked Pandora curiously.

"No!" he bit out succinctly. "He needs to stay right where he is."

Pandora blinked and her forehead wrinkled concernedly at Dorian's harsh tone. She went to sit with him on the sofa and looked at him expectantly. Dorian took both her hands in his and looked at her gravely.

"When I arrived here, I discovered the Marquess and *Marchioness* of Bardsey are staying here," he said softly.

Pandora shook her head and smiled negligibly. "It was just pretend, Dorian. The Lees know Islington too well for me to pose as Selena, and it would have caused a scandal for me to arrive here as a single woman and stay alone so I posed as his wife."

"Pandora, this is Scotland," said Dorian gravely.

"Yes, I know that," said Pandora, her head tilting sideways confusedly.

"Please, tell me you've not gone to bed with him," said Dorian earnestly. Pandora's face colored, and Dorian closed his eyes and shook his head. "Did he force you?"

"Dorian, you of all people should know that *no one* forces me to do anything," said Pandora softly.

"Who knows about this?" he asked, his expression still grim.

"The Lees, obviously." Her forehead wrinkled as she tried to think who else would know. "The Count and Countess von Weilheim."

"Who?" asked Dorian blankly.

"The former Jessica Wainwright and her husband, visiting from Germany." Pandora was confused, but Dorian shook his head again. It was worse than he thought. "What does it matter?"

"Pandora, this is *Scotland,*" said Dorian again soberly.

"Yes, you said that," said Pandora vexedly. "I know where I am. I may be on the verge of a full-blown migraine, but I do still have my wits about me. Again, what does it matter?"

"Pandora, you're married," said Dorian patiently.

"No, I'm *not,*" denied Pandora with a long-suffering sigh. "I told you, it was just *pretend.*"

Dorian gripped her hands tighter and shook his head. "No, Dodo. Scotland is more different from England than you could possibly imagine. When you signed your name on that ledger as *Pandora, Marchioness of Bardsey,* that is who you became."

"*What?*" she shrieked, on the verge of utter panic, her eyes growing wide in alarm and disbelief.

Dorian nodded his head with a sympathetic expression as he watched her eyes begin to glitter with unshed tears. She inhaled deeply through her nose and squared her shoulders, giving a slight nod of her head.

"Thank you for telling me, Dorian," she said quietly, withdrawing her hands from his after giving them a squeeze.

Dorian stood as she did, and she calmly walked toward Islington where he still stood with Mrs. Lee. Pandora looked at him silently for a moment before she raised her left fist to land a punch firmly against his jaw. He staggered at the blow and dazedly raised a hand to his face, but his expression didn't really show much surprise.

"Och, mercy!" gasped Mrs. Lee, her eyes wide in astonishment.

"If I were a man, I would demand satisfaction," said Pandora coldly.

She turned and walked away from him, examining her knuckles and shaking her hand tenderly as she sucked in air through her teeth. She nodded briefly to Dorian, who watched her depart with a shocked expression, and went through the doorway by the fireplace that would lead her to her room. She *really* needed to take her medicine.

After Pandora was gone, Dorian walked over to Islington, who continued to rub his jaw gingerly, and looked at him irately.

"If it weren't for our years of friendship, I would do it for her without hesitation," said Dorian coldly. "You had better have a good accounting of yourself, or I may change my mind."

Islington nodded stoically and looked at Mrs. Lee. He handed her the bag. "These are her coat and hat. I don't know if you can do anything with them, but she would be overjoyed if you could. I'll warn you, they're very gory. I don't want you to be shocked when you see them."

Mrs. Lee nodded and rubbed his shoulder comfortingly. "I'll see what I can do, love," she said softly.

"Also, she has a migraine. If you can make sure she takes her medicine and that she's comfortable…," he trailed off.

"Whist now," said Mrs. Lee with a warm smile. "Dinna trouble yoursel'." She gave Dorian a hard look before she left.

Dorian folded his arms and arched an eyebrow as he looked at Islington.

"Do you mind if we sit down?" asked Islington tiredly as he massaged his shoulder. He needed to take some of his own medicine.

"Fine," said Dorian stiffly.

They went to sit on one of the sofas by the fire, and Islington looked at Dorian for a moment as he tried to compose his thoughts.

"You ruined my sister, man," said Dorian flatly before he could speak.

"I know," said Islington calmly. "I asked her to marry me twice, and she refused both times. Your father wouldn't make her."

"And so you *tricked* her into marrying you by signing her name the way she did?" asked Dorian coldly. "Did you ever think perhaps she had a *reason* for not wanting to marry you?"

"She *needed* to marry me," said Islington. Dorian looked at him unmovingly. "She's already miscarried one baby, and she's probably carrying another right now. What would you have had me do under the circumstances?" asked Islington plainly.

"You shouldn't have put a hand on her to start!" bit out Dorian angrily.

Islington groaned torturedly and rubbed a hand over his face. "I *know* that," he said softly. "I tried not to, but she just…she's so…," he said frustratedly and shook his head defeatedly. "I can't let her go."

Dorian looked at his friend shrewdly. He could, in a way, understand that the man had felt he was doing the honorable thing. He could also see that, whatever else, Islington cared a great deal for his sister. He and Selena had hoped the two of them would marry, but Dorian had never anticipated this would be the path taken. He didn't like that Islington had deceived Pandora. Dorian knew she was angry and distressed, and it was beyond him to provide her any consolation.

"Well," he said finally, "now you have her…'til death do you part. *That*, by the by, probably won't be so very long when Dad finds out."

Islington looked at Dorian uncertainly and saw that his friend's expression was serious.

"I should go talk to her," said Islington dimly.

"I don't think that would be such a great idea; at least, not right now," said Dorian lightly. "She was mad enough to *punch* you. That's not a good sign. Why don't you tell me why you have your arm in a sling and why Pandora looks like she's been beaten, brother?"

≪ ≫

Pandora went straight for the medicine kit as soon as she entered the room and got her medicine to make a dose. After she swallowed it, she went to the sideboard and poured herself a glass of whisky, which she tipped and drained completely before setting it down. She put some ointment on her neck, and that, at least, began to feel better. She started to pace from one end of the room to the other, twisting her hands anxiously in front of her as she thought about what she was going to do.

What *could* she do? She could get it annulled. He had lied to her. He tricked her. She had *not* consented. That was a valid reason for an annulment. But she had signed her name, and it had definitely been consummated. If she went that route, it would cause a scandal for her family. She didn't want that. She could go away. She could go to Canada or America…anywhere. The language didn't even need to be English. She had always wanted to see China. But if she went away, she would most likely never see her family again, and she wished for that even less than causing a scandal.

She was drowsy from her medicine and the whisky, but she couldn't stop pacing. She rubbed the spot behind her ear as her thoughts swarmed. A soft knock at the door made her jump and look at it warily.

"Who is it?" she asked breathlessly.

"It's Mrs. Lee, dear. May I come in?" she called.

Pandora sighed with relief and went to open the door, glad it wasn't Islington. She wasn't ready to see him. Mrs. Lee entered carrying a tray with food and a pot of tea. Pandora didn't think she could eat, but she stood out of the way for Mrs. Lee to bring it in and set it on the table beside the fireplace. She turned to look at Pandora and saw that she was almost hysterical.

"Come till the ingleside now an' hae yoursel' some vivers," said Mrs. Lee soothingly.

"Oh, Mrs. Lee, I don't think I can eat anything, but I could do with a cup of tea," said Pandora softly.

"Whist now, Leddy Bardsey."

"Oh, *please,* don't call me that," begged Pandora anxiously. "Pandora will suffice."

She went to sit on the couch while Mrs. Lee poured her a cup of tea.

"Do ye take cream an' sugar?"

"Just a lump of sugar, please," said Pandora, still twisting her hands in her lap.

"There now," said Mrs. Lee as she handed the cup to Pandora. She added a few more logs to the fire and poked them around to get it burning brightly. She wiped her hands on her apron and turned to look at Pandora. "I was asked till make sure ye took your medicine."

"Yes, I did," said Pandora dully.

It was making her dozy, and it was definitely helping her headache, but she was too wound up to sleep, which is what she wished she could do…just to forget about everything for a while.

"They'll be bringin' yer bath in a trice," said Mrs. Lee with a smile.

She lifted the napkin from the tray, and the stew with dumplings, breaded fried oysters, veal rice pie, asparagus and sliced tomatoes looked delicious. It had been a while since Pandora had anything to eat, and part of the tension she felt in her stomach was caused by its emptiness.

"Well, I suppose I could try to eat," said Pandora hesitantly, picking up one of the fried oysters with her fingers.

"An ye dinna mind my sayin', ye've a nice nieve," said Mrs. Lee with an amused smile.

Pandora lifted her hand and looked at her knuckles. They were a little red, but the skin was still in one piece.

"He'll hae a clour frae tha'," said Mrs. Lee softly.

"No more than he deserves," said Pandora darkly as she ate an asparagus spear.

"An' wha is th' Viscount Glamorgan?"

"My brother and Selena's fiancé," said Pandora as she ate another oyster.

"Aha, I thought th' eyes looked familiar," said Mrs. Lee with a smile.

"You didn't ask me why I punched him," said Pandora curiously.

"I *ken* why," said Mrs. Lee softly. Pandora looked at her in surprise. Mrs. Lee sighed gustily and shook her head. "I tried till warn 'im. I tauld 'im he needed till tell ye straight afore someone else did." She shrugged. "He only thought he was doin' th' right thin'."

"Hunh," said Pandora noncommittally as she began to eat the veal and rice pie.

There was a knock on the door, and Pandora started to get up, but Mrs. Lee raised a staying hand.

"Eat now. I'll see till tha'," she said with a smile.

It was the maids bringing her bath. Pandora continued to eat as they set up the tub. She discovered while they did that there was a panel on the wall that opened to reveal a dumbwaiter. Pandora was relieved to see the girls didn't have to haul the buckets up five flights of stairs, and Pandora never would have guessed the device was there. The joinery in the wall disguised it well. Considering this was probably one of the nicer rooms (if not the nicest) in the inn, the likelihood that someone staying in it would want a bath made the elevator a necessity rather than a convenience. By the time they were done, Pandora was full, but she hadn't nearly eaten everything Mrs. Lee had brought her. Mrs. Lee retrieved the tray from the table and placed it in the dumbwaiter to go back to the kitchen.

"Well, there ye gang," said Mrs. Lee. "Are ye feelin' better?"

"I am full now. My headache is tolerable. I'm about to have a relaxing bath before I go to bed. The rest will just take a little more time," said Pandora softly. Mrs. Lee patted her shoulder soothingly and left the room.

Pandora took a long soak. By the time she got out, her skin was pink from the heat and the scrubbing she had done to remove the invisible traces of Chateauville from her body. She felt better, at least physically, but her brain continued to buzz incessantly at her predicament. After she brushed her teeth and tended to the rest of her toilette, she went to the sideboard and poured herself a glass of Moselle. The clock on the mantel struck eleven as she sat on the sofa and curled her legs beneath her.

Her head was better. She had managed to take the medicine before the pain and accompanying nausea had become unbearable. The stress she had felt at the time kept her from going to sleep, but she was tired regardless. She yawned and finished her glass of wine before she added more logs to the fire. She was turning off lamps on her way to bed when there was a knock on the door. The only lamps still lit were the two by the bed. She made sure her dressing gown was tied and hesitantly walked closer to the door.

"Who is it?" she called warily.

"It's Islington."

"Go away!" said Pandora firmly, and she was glad there was a door between them because as soon as she heard his voice, she could feel the sting of tears beginning.

"I'm not going anywhere until I talk to you," he said just as firmly.

"I have nothing to say to you!" said Pandora coldly.

There was a brief moment of silence. "Pandora, please, let me in," said Islington softly.

Pandora looked at the door, and she wiped at the tears on her cheeks frustratedly because she didn't want him to have the power to still make her cry. She didn't want to see him, she tried to tell herself, but she *knew* she was going to open the door, as if it were something beyond her control. She took a deep breath and turned the knob. She held the door open, but she didn't look at Islington. Once he walked past her into the room, she closed it behind him and folded her arms in front of her protectively.

Islington walked to the sideboard and poured a glass of whisky. He added some drops of his pain medicine and downed the glass, gasping and grimacing at the foul concoction. It didn't taste any better that way than when it was mixed with water…it probably tasted worse, but the alcohol would ease the pain until the medicine took effect. He rubbed a tired hand over his face and turned to look at Pandora.

She was standing with her arms folded in front of her, looking at him distrustfully. Under the circumstances, he couldn't blame her. She was dressed for bed, the marks on her neck showing up starkly on her skin.

"How's your head?" he asked concernedly.

"Fine," said Pandora shortly.

"How's your neck?"

"Fine," said Pandora again in the same tone. "Is that all you wanted to know?" she asked tartly.

"No, it isn't," said Islington tiredly, and he went to sit in one of the chairs by the fireplace.

Pandora went behind the couch and rested her hands on the back of it.

"Then say what you came to say and leave," said Pandora angrily. "I'm tired, and I want to go to bed."

"Fair enough," said Islington shortly. "I'm not going to apologize for what I did. One day, while you may not thank me, you'll appreciate it."

"I'll *appreciate* it?" she hissed. "You arrogant, insufferable, loutish *bastard*!" she yelled. "Why would I ever appreciate you *deceiving* me into marrying you? You've used me and duped me before, but I've always been free to walk away from it. Now, I can't...you won't...and I can't...!" she said brokenly, putting a hand over her mouth to choke back a sob. She took a deep breath and pointed her finger at the door. "Get out!"

"I'm not done yet," said Islington firmly.

"Yes, you are," said Pandora tightly. "Get out before I *throw* you out!"

"No, you're not," said Islington determinedly. "I'm not leaving until I've finished what I came to say."

Pandora gripped the back of the couch tightly and glared at him, her chest heaving emotionally. She could hear a ringing in her ears as her heart beat anxiously in her chest. She was close to sobbing uncontrollably, and she didn't want him to see it. She thought he had said enough. What more could he say to her to make her feel any more miserable?

"I had already asked you to marry me twice, and both times you refused. I even spoke to your father before I left London. I didn't tell him *why* I wanted to marry you, and he refused. I made the decision to do this after we left Aysgarth because you *needed* to marry me to give our child a name."

"*What* child?" asked Pandora stilly, her forehead etched with confusion.

"The one you're carrying," said Islington flatly.

"*What*?" gasped Pandora disbelievingly, her face going pale.

"When you so expressively stated that our horses had been *going at it like bunnies*—I believe it was, it called to mind our own activities. You reached the conclusion that Jezebel was pregnant, and what else could I believe about you? I knew that asking you again would be pointless, so I did what I had to do to make sure my child would not be born a bastard."

Pandora was breaking out in a cold sweat. The ringing in her ears rose to a pitch so loud she could scarcely hear herself think. She thought there was nothing further he could do to make her feel worse, but he surprised her. She thought she was going to be sick.

"You condemned us both to a life of misery because you think I am *pregnant*?" she said breathlessly.

"That's a bit harsh, but yes," said Islington evenly.

"I'm not pregnant," she said faintly.

"Don't act like it's such a shock," said Islington harshly. "You know how these things work."

"No, you *don't* understand," said Pandora, shaking her head and taking a deep breath to calm herself before she collapsed. "I'm *not* pregnant," she said more firmly.

Islington looked at her critically. "How can you be so sure?" he asked suspiciously.

"I am *sure* because this morning while you were out getting your shave, I was getting my courses," said Pandora numbly, and she leaned on the couch to keep herself from falling down. "Oh, hell, I'm going to throw up," she said weakly, and she hurried to the chamber pot behind the screen in the corner and vomited until nothing more would come out.

After she was through, Pandora dazedly ran a hand across her forehead. She went to the nearby wash basin to splash water on her face and rinsed her mouth then dried her face on the towel. She came back to the couch and went to sit on the end farthest from Islington. She was emotionally drained. She was physically tired. And she really wanted Islington to leave because she wanted to cry. She weakly clasped her hands in her lap and looked at him.

"Now that you know your reason for doing this is unfounded, we can get it annulled," she said dully.

"Oh, no," said Islington, shaking his head. "The marriage will stand."

"*What*?" gasped Pandora disbelievingly.

"You could do worse for a husband," said Islington evenly, not meeting her eyes. "I have enough money to see you want for nothing. Being a marchioness is a bit of a step up from being the daughter of a duke. We get on well together. It's time for me to produce an heir. Once you've provided me with one, should you find someone who interests you, and you can carry on your affair *discreetly*, I'll not say a word."

Pandora put a hand over her mouth as the air caught in her throat, and she tried to silence the choking sobs that made her shoulders shake uncontrollably. She shook her head as she looked at him, her tear-streaked eyes begging him to stop.

"Go away, you *horrible* man!" she sobbed.

"*Horrible*?" said Islington tormentedly. "What do you *want* from me? Please, tell me, because trying to figure it for myself is exhausting!" He looked at her with anguished eyes. "I don't have anything else I can give you," he said brokenly. "You've had my heart and my soul from the first moment I saw you. The only thing I had left was my name and everything that went with it." He raised his hands from his lap defeatedly. "Just, please, tell me what you want. I'll try to get it for you, whatever it is, as long as it isn't your freedom, because I love you too damn much to live without you."

Pandora had calmed remarkably as he spoke. She wiped at her cheeks with her sleeve and stood up to go to Islington where he sat with a hand covering his eyes as his elbow rested on the arm of the chair. She gently reached out to brush a hand through his hair. His head jerked up in surprise at the caress, and Pandora bent forward to kiss him tenderly, her hand smoothing across his cheek. She carefully climbed onto the chair with him and straddled his lap. She finally ended the kiss and looked down at him with a fond smile.

"Thank you, Theo," she said softly, brushing a hand across his jaw to his lips. "That was the only thing I ever wanted."

"That was it?" asked Islington doubtfully.

Pandora nodded and placed a kiss on his forehead. "I never wanted anything else but for you to love me, *àiren*. I told you that once, but you wouldn't remember…you were delirious at the time."

"We could have been married all this time if I had just told you I loved you?" She nodded. "Could you not tell?" asked Islington disbelievingly.

"Well, I thought you did, but then every time you would talk about marriage, you made it sound like a business arrangement." Pandora's face wrinkled up distastefully.

"I guess I could have saved myself a lot of time and effort if I had just started with the simplest thing," said Islington softly. "Most women want things like money, status, protection…the freedom to take a lover."

"I don't need money. I don't give a fig about status. I can protect myself. You are the only lover I need, *àiren*."

"What does that word mean?" asked Islington curiously.

Pandora smiled amusedly. "It depends on what part of China you're in." Islington pursed his lips, and she bent down to briefly kiss him again. "But when I say it, it means sweetheart."

Islington tilted his head sideways in thought. "I like *àiren* better."

"Me, too," said Pandora with a grin. She put a hand to his cheek and rested her forehead against his. "I love you, Theo," she said softly.

Islington smiled and kissed her. "I like the sound of that; say it again."

"I love you, Theo," said Pandora with a smile.

"I love you, Pandora," he replied back, running his hand down to tickle her bottom.

Pandora giggled. "So, we're really married?"

"Oh, yes, most definitely," said Islington with a wicked grin. "Mr. Lee even sometimes stands in as the minister at the local Methodist church."

"I don't know how you managed to sneak the whole thing past me," said Pandora with a pout. "I'm usually fairly swift on the uptake."

Islington smiled as he nuzzled her neck. "Luckily, you weren't this time."

Pandora sighed wistfully. "I guess that makes one of the dresses I bought at Mrs. Glenn's unnecessary."

"And just what did you buy?" asked Islington as he kissed and nuzzled.

"A wedding dress," said Pandora softly. Islington looked up at her in surprise. "Well, you had asked me twice. I was hoping the third time would be the charm."

"Maybe you can wear it for me some time," said Islington as he untied her dressing gown to bury his face in the cleft of her breasts. He looked up at her. "Are you really having your courses?"

Pandora sighed wistfully and nodded. "I'm afraid so."

"Well, I guess that would explain why...oh, never mind," said Islington, shaking his head.

"What?" asked Pandora with an arched eyebrow.

"This afternoon before our picnic. You were acting peculiar all morning, and then when you turned me down...I thought it was because you were interested in Artois."

Pandora chortled amusedly. "Never in a million years!" she sighed. "I was excited because this entire business was about to be over. It was difficult for me to decline, it really was, and I wasn't sure how to tell you. I eventually would have. As for Artois, he *is* a handsome man, but he's also older than my father, and he's not you."

Islington smiled happily and smoothed his hands over her bottom and up to her waist. He frowned and moved them back down again. He looked up at Pandora questioningly.

"I don't use one of *those,*" said Pandora, understanding his silent question. "I use a...um...." She made a few hand motions to get her point across.

Islington smiled amusedly. "You know, courtesans use those?"

"Do they really?" said Pandora in surprise. "Because I learned it from my mother, and she's—"

"Most definitely not a courtesan. I know," said Islington with a chuckle. His face grew serious. "And you weren't pregnant?"

Pandora put a hand to his cheek and shook her head negatively. "No, Theo," she said softly. "Not this time. Everything is quite normal."

"I felt so guilty about that," he said gently. "You shouldn't have needed to go through that."

"Shh," said Pandora, putting a hand to his lips. "There was nothing you or I could have done. If Maiyin hadn't told me, I never would have known I was pregnant or that I had miscarried. She thinks my body just wasn't strong enough for it at the time." Pandora kissed him tenderly and smiled. "I don't think that's a problem now. Like Maiyin said: there will be others."

Islington leered wolfishly. "Lots of others."

Pandora tilted her head sideways and smiled amusedly. "I do come from *very* fertile stock."

Islington's face grew contemplative. "When your parents get here, could you please not tell them I tricked you? I'd like to stay married to you for several more years, but Dorian seems to think that won't happen when your father finds out."

Pandora put a hand to his cheek and smiled amusedly. "It will be fine."

"You know, you never did explain to me why it took Dorian so long to ask for permission to marry Selena," said Islington as he casually smoothed his hands down her ribs to her hips.

Pandora chuckled. "Now, it's amusing. It was then, too." Islington raised an eyebrow. "They thought they couldn't get married because you and I had an *understanding,* and they thought there was something unlawful about their getting married if we did or intended to." Pandora smoothed a hand over his shoulder and gave him a teasing smile. "I made sure I set Selena straight on that, but she got the impression we had one in the first instance because you sent her to Ramsey's to find out if there were any rumors about us and because you would get angry whenever she would try to tease you about me."

Islington blushed and smiled sheepishly. "I was hoping there would be some damaging rumor about us because I was determined to have you marry me one way or another. I thought if there were *anything*, then you would have to do it whether you wanted to or not. As for the teasing, I was just so frustrated you wouldn't accept my offer that every time Selena would mention your name, it was like sticking pins under my thumbnails."

Pandora chuckled. "Maiyin once told me that she thought you were a glutton for punishment."

"Well, it just never occurred to me to tell you the real reason I wanted to marry you. Would you have believed me?"

Pandora kissed him tenderly and smoothed a hand down his cheek. "Yes, I would have."

"Oh, if your bruises and cuts haven't healed by the time Maiyin sees you, please, make sure she knows I didn't do it." Pandora raised an eyebrow enquiringly. "That little woman scares me."

Pandora giggled. "She's harmless."

"Harmless?" he hooted. "I thought she was going to break my arm!"

"You'll see. Once you get to know her, you'll love her as much as I do," said Pandora with a smile.

"I suppose she *will* have to come with you," said Islington mildly.

"If you want me, you have to take her and Keung. One won't go anywhere without the other, and I won't go without Maiyin."

"We could do with another gardener," said Islington, reaching up to kiss Pandora.

"So, I find it very hard to believe you loved me from the first moment you saw me," teased Pandora.

"No one calls me a big oaf quite so endearingly as you," said Islington with a chuckle.

"I have another question," said Pandora, running her fingers through the hair at the back of his head. He raised an eyebrow. "How did your mother know you had asked me to marry you?"

Islington grinned amusedly. "I asked her about that. That was one of my mother's winkling expeditions. She didn't really *know* I had asked you to marry me, and if you hadn't admitted to it, she never would have been any the wiser. Needless to say, I wasn't very happy when I found out. I had to explain to her how elusive you were being and that she had probably scared you away for good." He chuckled. "She was mortified."

Pandora giggled. "I did nearly have a fit of vapors when she accused *me* of tormenting *you*."

He yawned tiredly. "Can we go to bed now, wife?"

Pandora bent down to kiss him before climbing off his lap and holding out her hand with a happy smile.

"Take me to bed, husband."

The duke and duchess arrived in Edinburgh the following Tuesday. Needless to say, they were surprised at the turn of events, but when they saw how happy Pandora was with her new husband, they were overjoyed. The duke's only response was to take Islington aside and give his hand a congratulatory shake with the comment his new son-in-law must have used a lot more of the *right* words. Dorian remained mum on the actual occurrence of events, and Pandora wasn't going to tell her parents the truth of it either.

The duchess determined there *would* be an official wedding, if only for propriety's sake. The duke left not long after his arrival (with his seal safely returned) to begin the proceedings for the reading of the banns in both Bardsey and the Savages' home parish, Glyncorrwg, in Wales. Islington provided his grace a letter closed with his own seal to give to his parish vicar to make it possible. He also gave the duke a letter for his mother, who by that point was probably frantic about her children.

Selena had insisted on coming to Edinburgh with the duke and duchess. When Myron had returned to London with his leg broken, the young woman would not be happy until she saw both her brother and fiancé were still in one piece. Pandora was upset that Myron had been injured, but she was relieved to hear he was mending well when her parents left. It took some restraint to prevent Dorian and Selena from doing the same thing Pandora and Islington had done, but the duchess firmly decided one merk marriage for the year was enough.

Mrs. Lee wasn't able to repair Pandora's clothes, but she was able to have Mrs. Glenn remake the outfit. As Islington had said, Pandora was overjoyed to have it. Selena liked Mrs. Glenn and Amrita's work so much she ordered her own wedding dress and trousseau from the woman while in Edinburgh, much to her brother's chagrin. He finally found out how much Pandora had paid for her own.

The comte d'Artois left for London on the first of September and arrived at his destination without mishap. Pandora never felt she knew him well enough to ask him what his business was, but she was glad he made it safely. She was more than a little surprised when, not long after her wedding, she received a package containing a single, yellow, Peruzzi-cut diamond on a gold chain. There was a card with only the brief message: *Congratulations. With warmest regards, Charles-Philippe.* Pandora wasn't sure she wanted to wear it. She knew where the diamond had to have originated. She never thought of herself as superstitious, but there was so much misery associated with the original necklace for her, Pandora simply put the stone in her jewel box and forgot about it.

Islington's prediction that nothing would be done to Hendon proved correct. As a matter of fact, not long after word spread of Chateauville's demise—and it had traveled alarmingly fast to Pandora's mind—the Earl of Hendon took a trip to the continent to stay with his sister, the Countess von Stockerau, in Austria for an indefinite period of time. There wasn't anything that could have *legally* been done, but Hendon had, at least in one respect, saved Myron from himself. Once his leg healed, Pandora's brother had been determined to challenge the earl to a duel. Thankfully, that appointment was postponed, much to the relief of his family.

In other respects, however, the earl's absence sent Myron down another dangerous path: he began an affair with Hendon's wife, Georgiana. They were very discreet, and the only people who knew were Pandora and Islington. His sister tried to discourage Myron, but she was all too aware from personal experience that love would sometimes lead one to do things that weren't very wise. She was just afraid what might happen should Hendon find out.

Learning her twin had married was a bittersweet moment for Psyche. She was happy her sister had found someone who loved her, but it saddened her that her cohort would no longer be with her. She brightened marginally when Pandora told Psyche she could visit at Marshcliff in Bardsey whenever she liked. She cheered even more when she discovered there were ancient ruins of some type in the vicinity. What made her even happier was when Pandora told her that Islington and their parents had given their consent to let Psyche come with the newlyweds on their honeymoon...until she learned they were only going to Edinburgh. Pandora thought she would wait until they were in Scotland before telling her twin they were going to Bermuda as well.

Pandora finally convinced Psyche they had tied for their bet on cravats. Pandora told Islington about the wager he had wondered about so long ago, and he was unable to do anything more than shake his head and laugh when he learned the truth. Pandora still had the two cravats he had given her, folded up neatly and stored in a small chest where she kept her most treasured mementoes. Psyche was surprised to learn she had the contested earrings in her possession the entire time.

Maiyin and Keung were ecstatic Pandora had married Islington, if only because he had finally made an honest woman of her. Their parting from the employ of the duke and duchess was sad, but to stay without Pandora would have been worse. Keung was able to help Islington with his shoulder, and the first thing he did was make the marquess completely do away with the sling. Keung also began to tame the grounds around Marshcliff, which was—as the name implied—built on the edge of a cliff. Traditional English gardening didn't work with much of the landscape, so Keung looked to his homeland for solutions. The new Dowager Marchioness of Bardsey was overjoyed with the result.

Bellerophon settled well into his new surroundings. He was happy just about anywhere as long as Pandora was there, regardless. Jezebel was expected to foal around July of the following year, and Pandora was looking forward to seeing the result. She and Islington had a wager on whether or not the foal would be sheer black (Pandora's bet) or some other color (Islington's). Pandora had already decided, regardless of whether the foal was male or female, she was going to name it Aysgarth Falls.

As for Pandora and Islington, they were married (again) in a double ceremony with Dorian and Selena at the ancient parish church in Bardsey near the end of September. Pandora discovered, much to her amusement, that his middle name was Adonis. He found it no less amusing that one of hers was Aphrodite. She much preferred Theo. He had started calling her Pan, just as Psyche did; he never thought Dodo suited her.

As a wedding present, Pandora gave Islington the book by John Pringle that she had purchased for him at Beacham and Bagley. He thought it was amusing, and he didn't have the heart to tell her that he already had a copy. He would make sure the other copy *disappeared* before she realized it. As for what Islington gave her, it took him a lot of thought. Pandora was surprised when she opened the large box containing her gift and found an adorable, black and tan Collie puppy. She thought it looked remarkably like the dog that had chased her up the tree...only much smaller. She named him Bo—Chinese for turnip.

Dorian and Selena left for their honeymoon in Venice shortly after the wedding, while Pandora and Islington left with Bo, Psyche, Maiyin, and Keung in tow for Edinburgh before sailing to Bermuda. Maiyin came because Pandora would need her maid. Keung wouldn't let Maiyin go anywhere that far away without him. Psyche, while she would have preferred Egypt and Greece, decided Bermuda *was* at least out of the country when she found out they would be going there.

Pandora discovered somewhere between Edinburgh and Hamilton that she was pregnant. She waited to tell Islington until they were on dry land because she was sure he would demand the ship be turned around for England, and Pandora *really* wanted to see Bermuda. As it was, he decided they only needed to stay a month rather than two, after it had taken them more than a month to get there. Pandora wasn't completely sure when it happened, but Maiyin was able to tell her with a fair degree of certainty that she would give birth in July…just like Jezebel.

Author's Afterword

Charles-Philippe de Bourbon, comte d'Artois, became Charles X of France in 1824. He was the only French Bourbon monarch of the 19th Century to have an actual coronation ceremony (the only other coronations, at all, were those of Napoleon in 1804 and Napoleon III in 1853).

During my research on the count, I saw conflicting dates on where he resided at certain points during his exile in Great Britain, which lasted from 1795 to 1814. The two locations most often provided were the Palace of Holyroodhouse in Edinburgh and 72 South Audley Street in London. One source speculated that he spent part of this time in the United States, but I find that unlikely.

Most sources state the time he spent at Holyrood was due to the sanctuary it provided from his creditors, and it is true that the furniture for his sojourn in the Royal Apartments there was purchased by the British government. He paid the rent for the house on South Audley, but the funds for it came from a £500 monthly stipend he received, again, from the British government. There were many unsubstantiated rumors that he left France with a fair-sized portion of the royal crown jewels, but I find it highly unlikely a man who had access to that kind of wealth would have required sanctuary from creditors or depended on the grace and favor of the Government.

The comte d'Artois was always considered a handsome man for his time and not too shabby even for ours. During his youth, he was known for his many affairs, but the one that lasted the longest and had the most effect on his life was the relationship he had with Louise de Polastron. When she died of consumption in 1804, her heart was removed, and no one is quite sure where it went. I would tend to believe (romantic that I am) that Artois kept it, possibly to have buried with him when his own time came. After her death, he became devoutly religious, even taking a vow of chastity.

He remained throughout his life always regarded as charming and affable, but he also believed in the absolute power of a king over his realm. One well-known quote has him stating he would rather be a wood cutter than a king after the English fashion.

Although the comte d'Artois's role in this novel was brief, because he was an actual, living, breathing individual, I tried to do my best to portray him in a manner that seemed plausible. I hope I succeeded.

With that said, on to other things. Those familiar with novels set in the Regency era have probably been reading this one shaking their heads and rolling their eyes throughout, if they even made it all the way to the end without throwing it down in disgust. Let me just say that the Savages are *not* a typical family of the era, but there is nothing I had them doing that was not beyond the realm of possibility for the time.

When I created these characters, one of my thoughts was: "What would happen if you had a family of polymaths with access to the funds and other resources to do whatever they wanted?" This novel, and the following novels in the series, is my attempt to answer that question. I realize this may not be everyone's cuppa, but I don't think you would have picked up this book if you were expecting the typical boy-meets-girl by candlelight shenanigans.

I will also say that I chose the Regency era for a reason, and you are *not* going to find people inventing automobiles, airplanes, or computers. I want to reiterate they do things that were not *normal* for the time, but not *impossible* for the time. I'm writing historical fiction here, not fantasy or sci-fi.

I did my best to research things for this novel, especially the unusual things. I have folders and bookmarks in my browser for anything from plumbing to horses to phases of the moon and days of the year for 1813. I kid you not. If you don't believe me, check it out for yourself. Aha! Didn't notice that, did you? Meteorological data would have been sweet, but if you're that nit-picky, you have entirely too much time on your hands, and if I can't at least make up something, it's not any fun.

When I knew I was going to write this afterword, I had originally planned to explain every unusual thing that happens in this book and provide justification for it. Then the list of things grew to a point that my afterword would have grown into another book by itself. If you question something I have happening or have someone doing, do the research like I did, and don't just take Wikipedia's word for it, either, because I definitely didn't. It's a great resource, but it's a starting point.

Now that I've said all that, I also want to say that this *is* a work of fiction. Part of the fun of being a writer of fiction is *getting to make things up.* I tried to stick to historical details as closely as possible, but if the data was lacking or if the detail was fictional anyway, I just let my id do what it wanted to. So, if you're wondering if the Spotted Cow really had a room with a four-poster bed, I couldn't say, but there *was* a Spotted Cow.

I began writing this book many years ago, and then I put it down and didn't touch it again for a very long time. During the interim, the internet became a thing, and it opened up a whole new world of possibilities that made me decide this book could be so much more than I had originally intended. The date you see below my name at the bottom of this afterword was when I finally finished the first draft, more than a decade after I wrote the first sentence. I hope you enjoyed reading this book as much as I enjoyed writing it. If you didn't, well, there's always the next one. If you did, woohoo; there's always the next one.

Emyll O'Bryan
October 31, 2007

About the Author

Emyll O'Bryan lives in a small, gray box on the edge of nowhere with an onion and two cats. She would say the middle of nowhere, but she knows someone who lives there. It's close but not quite within rock-throwing distance. She had dreams of becoming a member of a big-hair 80s band in her teens; started on an anthropology degree with ambitions of becoming an archeologist in her twenties; and decided in her thirties that she should just stick with what she knew: telling stories. She enjoys history (although anything after 1865 is current events to her), languages (both real and imaginary), cooking (mostly Italian and Greek), watching movies (a *good* sci-fi horror adventure), singing in the shower (it provides its own special auto-tune), and sleeping (*lots* of sleeping). Not necessarily in that order. She also finds it very peculiar to be referring to herself in the third person as she writes this but feels it would be bucking the system and just the least bit vain to do otherwise.

www.ingramcontent.com/pod-product-compliance
Lightning Source LLC
Chambersburg PA
CBHW051934020726
47501CB00001B/113